Brain Wave

Unbeknown to its inhabitants, the solar system has for millions of years been caught in a force field that has had the effect of suppressing intelligence. When in the course of normal galactic movement the solar system breaks free of the force field that has held it in its sway for so long, gone are the inhibiting effects and a remarkable change begins to sweep across the Earth. Now, the entire world is turned upside-down as humanity deals with the sometimes surprising, sometimes chilling after-effects of this watershed event.

The Boat of a Million Years

Early in human history, certain individuals were born who live on, unaging, undying, through the centuries and millennia. This tale follows them through over 2,000 years of history to contemporary times and beyond – to the promise of utopia and the challenge of the stars.

The Guardians of Time

Time patrolmen guard the past. No matter how good or evil an event, it must be held inviolate. The slightest slip, and Time would become Chaos, and all that has ever been or will ever be will tumble into darkness. When the Birth of Civilisation is endangered by the malign counter-emperor Varagan, the patrol must be on its mettle …

Also by Poul Anderson

Poul Anderson
SF GATEWAY OMNIBUS

BRAIN WAVE
THE BOAT OF A MILLION YEARS
THE GUARDIANS OF TIME

GOLLANCZ
LONDON

First published in Great Britain in 2013 by
Gollancz
An imprint of the Orion Publishing Group
Orion House, 5 Upper St Martin's Lane,
London WC2H 9EA

An Hachette UK Company

A CIP catalogue record for this book is
available from the British Library

ISBN 978 0 575 10693 2

1 3 5 7 9 10 8 6 4 2

Typeset by Jouve (UK), Milton Keynes

Printed and bound by CPI Group (UK) Ltd, Croydon, CR0 4YY

The Orion Publishing Group's policy is to use papers
that are natural, renewable and recyclable products and
made from wood grown in sustainable forests. The logging
and manufacturing processes are expected to conform to
the environmental regulations of the country of origin.

www.orionbooks.co.uk
www.gollancz.co.uk

CONTENTS

ENTER THE SF GATEWAY . . .

Towards the end of 2011, in conjunction with the celebration of fifty years of coherent, continuous science fiction and fantasy publishing, Gollancz launched the SF Gateway.

Over a decade after launching the landmark SF Masterworks series, we realised that the realities of commercial publishing are such that even the Masterworks could only ever scratch the surface of an author's career. Vast troves of classic SF and fantasy were almost certainly destined never again to see print. Until very recently, this meant that anyone interested in reading any of those books would have been confined to scouring second-hand bookshops. The advent of digital publishing changed that paradigm for ever.

Embracing the future even as we honour the past, Gollancz launched the SF Gateway with a view to utilising the technology that now exists to make available, for the first time, the entire backlists of an incredibly wide range of classic and modern SF and fantasy authors. Our plan, at its simplest, was – and still is! – to use this technology to build on the success of the SF and Fantasy Masterworks series and to go even further.

The SF Gateway was designed to be the new home of classic science fiction and fantasy – the most comprehensive electronic library of classic SFF titles ever assembled. The programme has been extremely well received and we've been very happy with the results. So happy, in fact, that we've decided to complete the circle and return a selection of our titles to print, in these omnibus editions.

We hope you enjoy this selection. And we hope that you'll want to explore more of the classic SF and fantasy we have available. These are wonderful books you're holding in your hand, but you'll find much, much more ... through the SF Gateway.

www.sfgateway.com

INTRODUCTION

from The Encyclopedia of Science Fiction

Poul Anderson (1926–2001) was a US author, born in Pennsylvania of Scandinavian parents; he lived in Denmark briefly before the outbreak of World War Two. In 1948 he gained a degree in physics from the University of Minnesota. His knowledge of Scandinavian languages and literature and his scientific literacy fed each other fruitfully through a long and successful career, during which he gained the SFWA Grand Master Award for lifetime achievement in 1978, though in fact he remained prolific and popular for the rest of his life; he was inducted into the Science Fiction Hall Of Fame in 2000. He was Greg Bear's father-in-law. He was perhaps unique among the top rank of American sf writers, with the possible exception of Fritz Leiber, in that his fantasy work – he wrote a large number of fantasy tales – is also of considerable significance.

Anderson's first years as a writer were spent in Minnesota, where after World War Two he joined the Minneapolis Fantasy Society (later the MFS) and associated with such writers as Clifford D. Simak and Gordon R. Dickson, both of whom shared with him an attachment to semi-rural (often wooded) settings peopled by solid, canny stock (frequently, in Anderson's case, of Scandinavian descent) whose politics and social views often register as conservative, especially among readers from the urban East and the UK, although perhaps this cultural style could more fruitfully be regarded as a form of romantic Libertarian individualism most comfortably adhered to far from the large cities of the world, where it tends to register in terms of denial.

Although he became his generation's most prolific sf writer of any consistent quality, Anderson began quite slowly, starting to publish sf with 'Tomorrow's Children' with F. N. Waldrop, for *Astounding* in 1947, and releasing only a few further stories in the 1940s. But in 1950 the flood began – there were seven stories in that year alone – and he never seriously slackened his rate of production over the next half century; a selection of eloquent early tales is assembled as *Alight in the Void* (1991). In 1950 he also released his first novel, a Ruined Earth tale for the Young Adult market, *Vault of the Ages* (1952), whose young protagonist defies the superstitious anti-science Taboos of his culture, which he saves from worse barbarians through his discovery of pre-Fall science.

By 1953 Anderson had become a significant figure in the field: in addition to nineteen stories, he published magazine versions of three novels, *Brain Wave*, *Three Hearts and Three Lions* and *War of Two Worlds*. The trio neatly prefigures the shape of his work for half a century: the Hard SF, in which an unceasing interest in the implications of science and technology infuses plots of at times considerable emotional intensity; the succession of fantasies, most of them eventide and nostalgic; and the entertainments, most of them Space Opera, which he produced with a seemingly relaxed competence, and with love. The last of these examples is, for instance, one of Anderson's many well told if occasionally not sufficiently demanding entertainments, in this case a tale sprucely displaying a betrayed Earth, Alien overlords and plucky humans; the other two are successful, mature novels, each in its separate genre. In *Three Hearts and Three Lions*, a Parallel World fantasy, an Earthman is translated from the middle of World War Two into Faerie, where he fights the forces of Chaos in a tale whose humour is laced with a conspicuous sexual unease that (along with its religious politics) marks it as a Christian Fantasy. *Brain Wave*, perhaps his most famous single novel, remains very nearly his finest (see below).

After this bravura season, Anderson began to formulate and write the numerous stories and novels making up the complex Technic History series, in reality two separate sequences. The first of these centres on Nicholas van Rijn, a rambunctiously dominant merchant prince of the Polesotechnic League, an interstellar club of traders which dominates a *laissez-faire* galaxy of scattered planets. Anderson has been widely criticized for the conservative implications it is possible (though with some effort) to draw from these stories, whose philosophical implications he modestly curtails, and whose clear recipes for the building of an interstellar corporatism he does not follow. The second sequence properly begins about 300 years later, after the first flowering of a post-Van Rijn Terran Empire which, increasingly decadent and corrupt, is under constant threat from other empires. Most of the second sequence features Dominic Flandry, a Terran agent who – sophisticated, pessimistic and tough – gradually becomes a figure of stature as Anderson fills in and expands his story, the first instalment of which had been composed as early as 1951. A somewhat smaller sequence, the Psychotechnic League stories, similarly told but unconnected, traces the gradual movement of Man into the solar system and eventually the galaxy itself.

The early Time Patrol stories are contained in *Guardians of Time* (1960) and *Time Patrolman* (1983), both assembled as *Annals of the Time Patrol* (1984); subsequently, early and later material was rearranged as *The Shield of Time* (coll of linked stories 1990) and *The Time Patrol* (coll 1991), the latter of which conveniently resorts long stories from the first volumes along with a new novel, "Star of the Sea"; plus *The Year of the Ransom* (1988) and other new material. The History of Rustum sequence, mainly concerned with the establishing on *laissez-faire* lines of a human colony on a planet in the Epsilon Eridani system, includes *Orbit Unlimited* (1961) and *New America* (1982). With Gordon R. Dickson, Anderson wrote the Hoka series about furry, teddybear-like aliens who cannot understand nonliteral language (i.e., metaphors, fictions) and so take everything as truth, with results intended (usually successfully) as comic, beginning with *Earthman's Burden* (1957).

Over and above the career awards listed above, he was repeatedly honoured by the sf community, serving as Science Fiction Writers Of America President for 1972–1973, and receiving seven Hugos and three Nebula Awards for sf in shorter forms. Remarkably, and unjustly, none of his novels won any sf award of any stature until the late, elegiac, concise *Genesis* (2000) was given a John W. Campbell Memorial Award in 2001.

Though Anderson was a very prolific story writer, this plentitude should not lead to the assumption that he was a hasty one, which he was not. Indeed, it might be argued that his short stories and novelettes constitute, with a few exceptions, his very finest work. Those stories honoured by awards are good examples of his skill, but out of the hundreds of tales that gained no awards many are superb, especially perhaps those from the 1960s, a single but representative example being 'Kyrie', in which several unlikely ingredients – Lunar convents, a repressed protagonist, Telepathy, a Black Hole and an energy-based Alien – generate in a very few pages an ending which surprises but is inevitable, and of almost excruciating poignancy. There are many more.

Out of the welter of remaining book titles, four singletons and Anderson's final ambitious series can be mentioned as outstanding. *The High Crusade* (1960) is a delightful wish-fulfilment conception: an alien Spaceship lands in medieval Europe where it is taken over by quick-thinking Baron Roger and his feudal colleagues who, when the ship transports them to the stars, soon trick, cajole, outfight and outbreed all the spacefaring races they can find, and found their own empire on feudal lines. It is Anderson's most purely uninhibited long tale. *Tau Zero* (1970) is less successful as fiction, though its speculations on Cosmology are fascinating, and the hypothesis it embodies is strikingly well conceived. A spaceship from Earth, intended to fly near the speed of light so that humans can reach the stars without dying of old age (as a consequence of the time-dilation of Special Relativity described by the Lorentz-Fitzgerald equations), uncontrollably continues to accelerate at a constant one gravity after reaching its intended terminal velocity, so that the disparity between ship-time and external time becomes ever greater: aeons hurtle by outside, until eventually the universe contracts to form a monobloc. After a new Big Bang the ship begins to slow gradually and the crew plans to settle a new planet in the universe that has succeeded our own. The felt scope of the narrative is convincingly sustained throughout, though the characters tend to the soap-operatic. In *The Avatar* (1978) a solitary figure

typical of Anderson's later work searches the galaxy for an Alien race sufficiently sophisticated to provide him with the means to confound a dratted
non-libertarian Earth government. *The Boat of a Million Years* (1989) is
perhaps his last fully successful singleton (see below).

Anderson's last major enterprise was the Guthrie Family sequence –
comprising *Harvest of Stars* (1993), *The Stars Are Also Fire* (1994), *Harvest the
Fire* (1995) and *The Fleet of Stars* (1997) – which puts on display both his continued grasp of current dreams of Technology fixes for our planetary woes,
and also an oddly resentful sense of disenchantment not untypical of writers
at the end of the last century. These drives govern a tale in which Earth – after
centuries of savage environmental exploitation (Anderson, typical of his
generation, explicitly blames environmentalists for this) – is no longer capable of sustaining humanity's quest for new adventures, and for a new home.
The escape from the dying planet is sustained and exhilarating. Through the
four volumes, the scale and complexity expands inexorably; there is no quick
way to represent the final effect, except perhaps to suggest that Anderson had
decided here to tell every kind of story he was capable of – fantasy, Hard SF
and entertainment routines intermix constantly – as a summary and *summa*
of his long career. On the evidence of this sequence, it is clear that for half a
century he knew what he was doing. And he gave it all to us.

Brain Wave, the first of the three titles presented here, makes hay with an
hallucinatingly attractive premise: for millions of years the part of the galaxy that contains our solar system has been moving slowly through a vast
forcefield whose effect has been to inhibit 'certain electromagnetic and
electrochemical processes', and thus slow down certain neuronic functions.
When Earth escapes the inhibiting field, synapse-speed immediately
increases, causing a rise in Intelligence. The heart lifts. After the tale has
traced various absorbing consequences of this transformation, a transfigured
humanity leaves for the stars, leaving behind former mental defectives and
bright animals to inherit the planet.

The second title here is *The Boat of a Million Years* (1989), an ambitious
saga which follows the long lives of a group of Immortals, whose interactions
with each other over the past centuries are touchingly (if wryly) conveyed.
Their growing disaffection with the recent course of Earth history again
points up a sense of disenchantment noticeable in Anderson's later work, but
also gives a strong sense that, under the romance and the politics, a great
long agenda is unfolding, as in one of the great future histories of Olaf Staple-
don: endure; evolve; discover the universe.

The final work here is *The Guardians of Time*, which collects the first five
tales of Anderson's Time Patrol series. The Time Patrol itself has been established by humanity's remote descendants to keep secure the main timeline of

world history; travelling through time and alternate realities, the officers of the Patrol make universe-changing decisions as a matter of course. The action is impeccably accomplished. These stories are Anderson at play. They make us want a few hundred more.

For a more detailed version of the above, see Poul Anderson's author entry in *The Encyclopedia of Science Fiction*: http://sf-encyclopedia.com/entry/anderson_poul

Some terms above are capitalised when they would not normally be so rendered; this indicates that the terms represent discrete entries in *The Encyclopedia of Science Fiction*.

BRAIN WAVE

To *Karen,* of course

CHAPTER ONE

The trap had closed at sundown. In the last red light, the rabbit had battered himself against its walls until fear and numbness ached home and he crouched shaken by the flutterings of his own heart. Otherwise there was no motion in him as night and the stars came. But when the moon rose, its light was caught icily in his great eyes, and he looked through shadows to the forest.

His vision was not made to focus closely, but after a while it fell on the entrance to the trap. It had snapped down on him when he entered, and then there had been only the flat bruising beat of himself against the wood. Now slowly, straining through the white unreal haze of moon light, he recalled a memory of the gate falling, and he squeaked ever so faintly with terror. For the gate was there now, solid and sullen against the breathing forest, and yet it *had* been up and *had* come thunking down, and this now – then double-ness was something the rabbit had never known before.

The moon rose higher, swinging through a sky full of stars. An owl hooted, and the rabbit froze into movelessness as its wings ghosted overhead. There was fear and bewilderment and a new kind of pain in the owl's voice, too. Presently it was gone, and only the many little murmurs and smells of night were around him. And he sat for a long time looking at the gate and remembering how it had fallen.

The moon began to fall too, into a paling western heaven.

Perhaps the rabbit wept a little, in his own way. A dawn which was as yet only a mist in the dark limned the bars of the trap against grey trees. And there was a crossbar low on the gate.

Slowly, very slowly, the rabbit inched across until he was at the entrance. He shrank from the thing which had clamped him in. It smelled of man. Then he nosed it, feeling dew cold and wet on his muzzle. It did not stir. But it had fallen down.

The rabbit crouched, bracing his shoulders against the crossbar. He strained then, heaving upward, and the wood shivered. The rabbit's breath came fast and sharp, whistling between his teeth, and he tried again. The gate moved upward in its grooves, and the rabbit bolted free.

For an instant he poised wildly. The sinking moon was a blind dazzle in his eyes. The gate smacked back into place, and he turned and fled.

*

Archie Brock had been out late grubbing stumps in the north forty. Mr Rossman wanted them all pulled by Wednesday so he could get the ploughing started in his new field, and promised Brock extra pay if he would see to it. So Brock took some dinner out with him and worked till it got too dark to see. Then he started walking the three miles home, because they didn't let him use the jeep or a truck.

He was tired without thinking of it, aching a little and wishing he had a nice tall beer. But mostly he didn't think at all, just picked them up and laid them down, and the road slid away behind him. There were dark woods on either side, throwing long shadows across the moon-whitened dust, and he heard the noise of crickets chirring and once there was an owl. Have to take a gun and get that owl before he swiped some chickens. Mr Rossman didn't mind if Brock hunted.

It was funny the way he kept thinking things tonight. Usually he just went along, especially when he was as tired as now, but – maybe it was the moon – he kept remembering bits of things, and words sort of formed themselves in his head like someone was talking. He thought about his bed and how nice it would have been to drive home from work; only of course he got sort of mixed up when driving, and there'd been a couple of smashups. Funny he should have done that, because all at once it didn't seem so hard: just a few signals to learn, and you kept your eyes open, and that was all.

The sound of his feet was hollow on the road. He breathed deeply, drawing a cool night into his lungs, and looked upward, away from the moon. The stars were sure big and bright tonight.

Another memory come back to him, somebody had said the stars were like the sun only further away. It hadn't made much sense then. But maybe it was so, like a light was a small thing till you got up close and then maybe it was very big. Only if the stars were as big as the sun, they'd have to be awful far away.

He stopped dead, feeling a sudden cold run through him. Jesus God! How far up the stars were!

The earth seemed to fall away underfoot, he was hanging on to a tiny rock that spun crazily through an everlasting darkness, and the great stars burned and roared around him, so far up that he whimpered with knowing it.

He began to run.

The boy rose early, even if it was summer and no school and breakfast wouldn't be for a while yet. The street and the town outside his windows looked very clean and bright in the young sunshine. A single truck clattered down the road and a man in blue denim walked towards the creamery carrying a lunch pail, otherwise it was as if he had the whole world to himself. His father was already off to work, and Mom liked to go back to bed for an hour after fixing his breakfast, and Sis was still asleep, so the boy was all alone in the house.

His friend was coming over and they'd go fishing, but first he wanted to get some more done on his model plane. He washed as thoroughly as you could ask a ten-year-old to, snatched a roll from the pantry, and went back to his room and the littered table there. The plane was going to be a real beauty, a Shooting Star with a CO_2 cartridge to make a jet. Only somehow, this morning it didn't look as good as it had last night. He wished he could make a real jet motor for it.

He sighed, pushing the work away, and took a sheet of paper. He'd always liked to doodle around with numbers, and one of the teachers had taught him a little about algebra. Some of the fellows had called him teacher's pet for that, till he licked them, but it was real interesting, not just like learning multiplication tables. Here you made the numbers and letters do something. The teacher said that if he really wanted to build spaceships when he grew up, he'd have to learn lots of maths.

He started drawing some graphs. The different kinds of equations made different pictures. It was fun to see how x=ky+c made a straight line while $x^2+y^2=c$ was always a circle. Only how if you changed one of the x's, made it equal 3 instead of 2? What would happen to the y in the meantime? He'd never thought of that before!

He grasped the pencil tightly, his tongue sticking out of the corner of his mouth. You had to kind of sneak up on the x and the y, change one of them just a weeny little bit, and then –

He was well on the way to inventing differential calculus when his mother called him down to breakfast.

CHAPTER TWO

Peter Corinth came out of the shower, still singing vigorously, to find Sheila busy frying bacon and eggs. He ruffled her soft brown hair up, kissing her on the neck, and she turned to smile at him.

'She looks like an angel and cooks like an angel,' he said.

'Why, Pete,' she answered, 'you never –'

'Never could find words,' he agreed. 'But it's gospel truth, me love.' He bent over the pan, inhaling the crisp odour with a contented sigh. 'I have a hunch this is one of those days when everything will go right,' he said. 'A bit of

Hubris for which the gods will doubtless visit a *Nemesis* on me. *Ate*: Gertie, the slut, will burn out a tube. But you'll amend it all.'

'*Hubris, Nemesis, Ate*.' A tiny frown creased her broad clear forehead. 'You've used those words before, Pete. What do they mean?'

He blinked at her. Two years after marriage, he was still far gone in love with his wife, and as she stood there his heart turned over within him. She was kind and merry and beautiful and she could cook – but she was nothing of an intellectual, and when his friends came over she sat quietly back, taking no part in the conversation. 'What do you care?' he asked.

'I was just wondering,' she said.

He went into the bedroom and began dressing, leaving the door open so he could explain the basis of Greek tragedy. It was much too bright a morning to dwell on so sombre a theme, but she listened closely, with an occasional question. When he came out, she smiled and went over to him.

'You dear clumsy physicist,' she said. 'You're the only man I ever knew who could put on a suit straight from the cleaners and make it look like you'd been fixing a car in it.' She adjusted his tie and pulled down the rumpled coat. He ran a hand through his black hair, immediately reducing it to unkemptness, and followed her to the kitchenette table. A whiff of steam from the coffeepot fogged his horn-rimmed glasses, and he took them off and polished them on his necktie. His lean, broken-nosed face looked different without them – younger, perhaps, only the thirty-three years which was his actual age.

'It came to me just when I woke up,' he said as he buttered his toast. 'I must have a well-trained subconscious after all.'

'You mean the solution to your problem?' asked Sheila.

He nodded, too absorbed to consider what her query meant. She usually just let him run on, saying 'yes' and 'no' in the right places but not really listening. To her, his work was altogether mysterious. He had sometimes thought she lived in a child's world, with nothing very well known but all of it bright and strange.

'I've been trying to build a phase analyzer for intermolecular resonance bonds in crystal structure,' he said. 'Well, no matter. The thing is, I've been plugging along for the past few weeks, trying to design a circuit which would do what I wanted, and was baffled. Then I woke up just this morning with an idea that might work. Let's see –' His eyes looked beyond her and he ate without tasting. Sheila laughed, very softly.

'I may be late tonight,' he said at the door. 'If this new idea of mine pans out, I may not want to break off work till – Lord knows when. I'll call you.'

'Okay, honey. Good hunting.'

When he was gone, Sheila stood for a moment smiling after him. Pete was a – well, she was just lucky, that was all. She'd never really appreciated how lucky, but this morning seemed different, somehow. Everything stood out sharp and clear, as if she were up in the Western mountains her husband loved so well.

She hummed to herself as she washed the dishes and straightened up the apartment. Memory slid through her, the small-town Pennsylvania girlhood, the business college, her coming to New York four years ago to take a clerical job at the office of a family acquaintance. Dear God, but she had been unsuited for that kind of life! One party and boyfriend after another, everybody fast-talking, jerky-moving, carefully hard-boiled and knowing, the expensive and market-wise crowd where she always had to be on her guard – All right, she'd married Pete on the rebound, after Bill walked out calling her a stupid – never mind. But she'd always liked the shy, quiet man, and she had been on the rebound from a whole concept of living.

So I'm stodgy now, she told herself, *and glad of it, too.*

An ordinary housewifely existence, nothing more spectacular than a few friends in for beer and talk, going to church now and then while Pete, the agnostic, slept late; vacation trips in New England or the Rocky Mountains; plans of having a kid soon – who wanted more? Her friends before had always been ready for a good laugh at the shibboleth-ridden boredom which was bourgeois existence: but when you got right down to it, they had only traded one routine and one set of catchwords for another, and seemed to have lost something of reality into the bargain.

Sheila shook her head, puzzled. It wasn't like her to go daydreaming this way. Her thoughts even sounded different, somehow.

She finished the housework and looked about her. Normally she relaxed for a while before lunch with one of the pocket mysteries which were her prime vice; afterwards there was some shopping to do, maybe a stroll in the park, maybe a visit to or from some woman friend, and then supper to fix and Pete to expect. But today –

She picked up the detective story she had planned to read. For a moment the bright cover rested between uncertain fingers, and she almost sat down with it. Then, shaking her head, she laid it back and went over to the crowded bookshelf, took out Pete's worn copy of *Lord Jim*, and returned to the armchair. Mid-afternoon came before she realized that she had forgotten all about lunch.

Corinth met Felix Mandelbaum in the elevator going down. They were that rare combination, neighbours in a New York apartment building who had become close friends. Sheila, with her small-town background, had insisted on getting to know everyone on their own floor at least, and Corinth had been glad of it in the case of the Mandelbaums. Sarah was a plump, quiet, retiring *Hausfrau* sort, pleasant but not colourful; her husband was a horse of quite another shade.

Felix Mandelbaum had been born fifty years ago in the noise and dirt and sweatshops of the lower East Side, and life had been kicking him around ever since; but he kicked back, with a huge enjoyment. He'd been everything from itinerant fruit picker to skilled machinist and O.S.S. operative overseas, during the war – where his talent for languages and people must have come in handy. His career as a labour organizer ran parallel, from the old Wobblies to the comparative respectability of his present job: officially executive secretary of a local union, actually a roving trouble shooter with considerable voice in national councils. Not that he had been a radical since his twenties; he said he'd seen radicalism from the inside, and that was enough for any sane man. Indeed, he claimed to be one of the last true conservatives – only, to conserve, you had to prune and graft and adjust. He was self-educated, but widely read, with more capacity for life than anyone else of Corinth's circle except possibly Nat Lewis. Fun to know.

'Hello,' said the physicist. 'You're late today.'

'Not exactly.' Mandelbaum's voice was a harsh New York tone, fast and clipped. He was a small, wiry, grey-haired man, with a gnarled beaky face and intense dark eyes. 'I woke up with an idea. A reorganization plan. Amazing nobody's thought of it yet. It'd halve the paper work. So I've been outlining a chart.'

Corinth shook his head dolefully. 'By now, Felix, you should know that Americans are too fond of paper work to give up one sheet,' he said.

'You haven't seen Europeans,' grunted Mandelbaum.

'You know,' said Corinth, 'it's funny you should've had your idea just today. (Remind me to get the details from you later, it sounds interesting.) I woke up with the solution to a problem that's been bedevilling me for the past month.'

'Hm?' Mandelbaum pounced on the fact, you could almost see him turning it over in his hands, sniffing it, and laying it aside. 'Odd.' It was a dismissal.

The elevator stopped and they parted company. Corinth took the subway as usual. He was currently between cars; in this town, it just didn't pay to own one. He noticed vaguely that the train was quieter than ordinarily. People were less hurried and unmannerly, they seemed thoughtful. He glanced at the newspapers, wondering with a gulp if *it* had started, but there was nothing really sensational – except maybe for that local bit about a dog, kept overnight in a basement, which had somehow opened the deep freeze, dragged out the meat to thaw, and been found happily gorged. Otherwise: fighting here and there throughout the world, a strike, a Communist demonstration in Rome, four killed in an auto crash – words, as if rotary presses squeezed the blood for everything that went through them.

Emerging in lower Manhattan, he walked three blocks to the Rossman Institute, limping a trifle. The same accident which had broken his nose years ago had injured his right knee and kept him out of military service; though being yanked directly from his youthful college graduation into the Manhattan Project might have had something to do with that.

He winced at the trailing memory. Hiroshima and Nagasaki still lay heavily on his conscience. He had quit immediately after the war, and it was not only to resume his studies or to escape the red tape and probing and petty intrigue of government research for the underpaid sanity of academic life; it had been a flight from guilt. So had his later activities, he supposed – the Atomic Scientists, the United World Federalists, the Progressive Party. When he thought how those had withered away or been betrayed, and recalled the brave clichés which had stood like a shield between him and the Soviet snarl – there for any to see who had eyes – he wondered how sane the professors were after all.

Only, was his present retreat into pure research and political passivity – voting a discouraged Democratic ticket and doing nothing else – any more balanced? Nathan Lewis, frankly labelling himself a reactionary, was a local Republican committeeman, an utter and cheerful pessimist who still tried to salvage something; and Felix Mandelbaum, no less realistic than his chess and bull-session opponent Lewis, had more hope and energy, even looked forward to the ultimate creation of a genuine American Labour Party. Between them, Corinth felt rather pallid.

And I'm younger than either one!

He sighed. What was the matter with him? Thoughts kept boiling up out of nowhere, forgotten things, linking themselves into new chains that rattled in his skull. And just when he had the answer to his problem, too.

That reflection drove all others out. Again, it was unusual: ordinarily he was slow to change any train of thought He stepped forward with a renewed briskness.

The Rossman Institute was a bulk of stone and glass, filling half a block and looking almost shiny among its older neighbours. It was known as a scientist's heaven. Able men from all places and all disciplines were drawn there, less by the good pay than by the chance to do unhampered research of their own choosing, with first-rate equipment and none of the projectitis which was strangling pure science in government, in industry, and in too many universities. It had the inevitable politicking and backbiting, but in lesser degree than the average college; it was the Institute for Advanced Study – less abstruse and more energetic, perhaps, and certainly much more room. Lewis had once cited it to Mandelbaum as proof of the cultural necessity for a privileged class. 'D'you think any government would ever endow such a thing and then, what's more, have the sense to leave it to itself?'

'Brookhaven does all right,' Mandelbaum had said, but for him it was a feeble answer.

Corinth nodded to the girl at the news stand in the lobby, hailed a couple of acquaintances, and fumed at the slowness of the elevator. 'Seventh,' he said automatically when it arrived.

'I should know that, Dr Corinth,' grinned the operator. 'You've been here – let's see – almost six years now, isn't it?'

The physicist blinked. The attendant had always been part of the machinery to him; they had exchanged the usual pleasantries, but it hadn't meant a thing. Suddenly Corinth saw him as a human being, a living and unique organism, part of an enormous impersonal web which ultimately became the entire universe, and yet bearing his own heart within him. *Now why*, he asked himself amazedly, *should I think that?*

'You know, sir,' said the attendant, 'I been wondering. I woke up this morning and wondered what I was doing this for and if I really wanted more out of it than just my job and my pension and –' He paused awkwardly as they stopped to let off a third-floor passenger. 'I envy you. You're going somewhere.'

The elevator reached the seventh floor. 'You could – well, you could take a night course if you wanted,' said Corinth.

'I think maybe I will, sir. If you'd be so kind as to recommend – Well, later. I got to go now.' The doors slid smoothly across the cage, and Corinth went down hard marble ways to his laboratory.

He had a permanent staff of two, Johansson and Grunewald, intense young men who probably dreamed of having labs of their own someday. They were already there when he entered and took off his coat.

'Good morning … 'Morning … 'Morning.'

'I've been thinking, Pete,' said Grunewald suddenly, as the chief went over to his desk. 'I've got an idea for a circuit that may work –'

'*Et tu Brute*,' murmured Corinth. He sat down on a stool, doubling his long legs under him. 'Let's have it.'

Grunewald's gimmick seemed remarkably parallel to his own. Johansson, usually silent and competent and no more, chimed in eagerly as thoughts occurred to him. Corinth took over leadership in the discussion, and within half an hour they were covering paper with the esoteric symbols of electronics.

Rossman might not have been entirely disinterested in establishing the Institute, though a man with his bank account could afford altruism. Pure research helped industry. He had made his fortune in light metals, all the way from raw ores to finished products, with cross connections to a dozen other businesses; officially semi-retired, he kept his fine thin hands on the strings. Even bacteriology could turn out to be useful – not very long ago, work had been done on bacterial extraction of oil from shales – and Corinth's study of crystal bonds could mean a great deal to metallurgy. Grunewald fairly gloated over the prospect of what success would do to their professional reputations. Before noon, they had set up a series of partial differential equations which would go to the computer at their regular scheduled time to use it, and were drawing up elements of the circuit they wanted.

The phone rang. It was Lewis, suggesting lunch together. 'I'm on a hot trail today,' said Corinth. 'I thought maybe I'd just have some sandwiches sent up.'

'Well, either I am too, or else I'm up you know what creek with no paddle,' said Lewis. 'I'm not sure which, and it might help me straighten out my ideas if I could bounce them off you.'

'Oh, all right. Commissary do?'

'If you merely want to fill your belly, I suppose so.' Lewis went in for three-hour lunches complete with wine and violins, a habit he had picked up during his years in pre-Anschluss Vienna. 'One o'clock suit you? The peasantry will have gorged by then.'

'Okay.' Corinth hung up and lost himself again in the cool ecstasy of his work. It was one-thirty before he noticed the time, and he hurried off swearing.

Lewis was just seating himself at a table when Corinth brought his tray over. 'I figured from your way of talk you'd be late,' he said. 'What'd you get? The usual cafeteria menu, I suppose: mice drowned in skim milk, fillet of sea urchin, baked chef's special, baked chef – well, no matter.' He sipped his coffee and winced.

He didn't look delicate: a short square man of forty-eight, getting a little plump and bald, sharp eyes behind thick, rimless glasses. He was, indeed, a hearty soul at table or saloon. But eight years in Europe did change tastes, and he insisted that his post-war visits had been purely gastronomical.

'What you need,' said Corinth with the smugness of a convert, 'is to get married.'

'I used to think so, when I began leaving my libertine days behind. But, well, never mind. Too late now.' Lewis attacked a minute steak, which he always pronounced as if the adjective were synonymous with 'tiny,' and scowled through a mouthful. 'I'm more interested in the histological aspect of biology just now.'

'You said you were having trouble –'

'That's mostly with my assistants. Everybody seems jumpy today, and young Roberts is coming up with even wilder ideas than usual. But it's my work. I've told you, haven't I? I'm studying nerve cells – neurones. Trying to keep them alive in different artificial media, and seeing how their electrical properties vary with conditions. I have them in excised sections of tissue – Lindbergh-Carrel technique, with modifications. It was coming along pretty good – and then today, when we ran a routine check, the results came out different. So I tested them all – Every one is changed!'

'Hm?' Corinth raised his eyebrows and chewed quietly for a minute. 'Something wrong with your apparatus?'

'Not that I can find. Nothing different – except the cells themselves.

A small but significant shift.' Lewis' tones came faster, with a hint of rising excitement. 'You know how a neurone works? Like a digital computer. It's stimulated by a – a stimulus, fires a signal, and is thereafter inactive for a short time. The next neurone in the nerve gets the signal, fires, and is also briefly inactivated. Well, it turns out that everything is screwy today. The inactivation time is a good many microseconds less, the – well, let's just say the whole system reacts significantly faster than normally. And the signals are also more intense.'

Corinth digested the information briefly, then, slowly: 'Looks like you may have stumbled onto something big.'

'Well, where's the cause? The medium, the apparatus, it's all the same as yesterday, I tell you. I'm going nuts trying to find out if I've got a potential Nobel Prize or just sloppy technique!'

Very slowly, as if his mind were shying away from a dimly seen realization, Corinth said: 'It's odd this should have happened today.'

'Hm?' Lewis glanced sharply up, and Corinth related his own encounters.

'Very odd,' agreed the biologist. 'And no big thunderstorms lately – ozone stimulates the mind – but my cultures are sealed in glass anyway –' Something flashed in his eyes.

Corinth looked around. 'Hullo, there's Helga. Wonder what made her so late? Hi, there!' He stood up, waving across the room, and Helga Arnulfsen bore her tray over to their table and sat down.

She was a tall, rangy, handsome woman, her long blonde hair drawn tightly around the poised head, but something in her manner – an impersonal energy, an aloofness, perhaps only the unfeminine crispness of speech and dress – made her less attractive than she could have been. She'd changed since the old days, right after the war, thought Corinth. He'd been taking his doctorate at Minnesota, where she was studying journalism, and they'd had fun together; though he'd been too much and too hopelessly in love with his work and another girl to think seriously about her. Afterwards they had corresponded, and he had gotten her a secretarial post at the Institute, two years before. She was chief administrative assistant now, and did a good job of it.

'Whew! What a day!' She ran a strong slim hand across her hair, sleeking it down, and smiled wearily at them. 'Everybody and his Uncle Oscar is having trouble, and all of them are wishing it on me. Gertie threw a tantrum –'

'Huh?' Corinth regarded her in some dismay. He'd been counting on the big computer to solve his equations that day. 'What's wrong?'

'Only God and Gertie know, and neither one is telling. Allanbee ran a routine test this morning, and it came out wrong. Not much, but enough to throw off anybody that needed precise answers. He's been digging into her ever since, trying to find the trouble, so far without luck. And I have to reschedule everybody!'

'Very strange,' murmured Lewis.

'Then different instruments, especially in the physics and chemistry sections, are a little crazy. Murchison's polarimeter has an error of – oh, something horrible like one tenth of one per cent, I don't know.'

'Izzat so?' Lewis leaned forward, thrusting his jaw out above the dishes. 'Maybe it's not my neurones but my instruments that're off whack – No, can't be. Not that much. It must be something in the cells themselves – but how can I measure that if the gadgets are all awry?' He broke into vigorous German profanity, though his eyes remained alight.

'Lots of boys have come up with brave new projects all at once, too,' went on Helga. 'They want immediate use of things like the big centrifuge, and blow their tops when I tell them to wait their turn.'

'All today, eh?' Corinth pushed his dessert aside and took out a cigarette. '"Curiouser and curiouser," said Alice.' His eyes widened, and the hand that struck a match shook ever so faintly. 'Nat, I wonder –'

'A general phenomenon?' Lewis nodded, holding excitement in check with an effort. 'Could be, could be. We'd certainly better find out.'

'What're you talking about?' asked Helga.

'Things.' Corinth explained while she finished eating. Lewis sat quietly back, blowing cigar fumes and withdrawn into himself.

'Hm.' Helga tapped the table with a long, unpainted fingernail. 'Sounds – interesting. Are all nerve cells, including those in our own brains, suddenly being speeded up?'

'It's more basic than that,' said Corinth. 'Something may have happened to – what? Electrochemical phenomena? How should I know? Let's not go off the deep end till we've investigated this.'

'Yeah. I'll leave it to you.' Helga took out a cigarette for herself and inhaled deeply. 'I can think of a few obvious things to check up on – but it's your child.' She turned again to smile at Corinth, the gentle smile she saved for a very few. 'Apropos, how's Sheila?'

'Oh, fine, fine. How's yourself?'

'I'm okay.' There was a listlessness in her answer.

'You must come over to our place sometime for dinner.' It was a small strain to carry on polite conversation, when his mind was yelling to be at this new problem. 'We haven't seen you in quite a while. Bring the new boyfriend if you want, whoever he is.'

'Jim? Oh, him. I gave him the sack last week. But I'll come over, sure.' She got up. 'Back to the oars, mates. See you.'

Corinth regarded her as she strode towards the cashier's desk. Almost in spite of himself – his thoughts were shooting off in all directions today – he murmured: 'I wonder why she can't keep a man. She's good-looking and intelligent enough.'

'She doesn't want to,' said Lewis shortly.

'No, I suppose not. She's turned cold since I knew her in Minneapolis. Why?' Lewis shrugged.

'I think you know,' said Corinth. 'You've always understood women better than you had any right to. And she likes you better than anyone else around here, I think.'

'We both go for music,' said Lewis. It was his opinion that none had been written since 1900. 'And we both know how to keep our mouths shut.'

'Okay, okay,' laughed Corinth. He got up. 'I'm for the lab again. Hate to scrap the phase analyzer, but this new business –' Pausing: 'Look, let's get hold of the others and divide up the labour, huh? Everybody check something. It won't take long then.'

Lewis nodded curtly and followed him out.

By evening the results were in. As Corinth looked at the figures, his interest lost way to a coldness rising within him. He felt suddenly how small and helpless a thing he was.

Electromagnetic phenomena were changed.

It wasn't much, but the very fact that the supposedly eternal constants of nature had shifted was enough to crash a hundred philosophies into dust. The subtlety of the problem held something elemental. How do you remeasure the basic factors when your measuring devices have themselves changed?

Well, there were ways. There are no absolutes in this universe, everything exists in relation to everything else, and it was the fact that certain data had altered relatively to others which was significant.

Corinth had been working on the determination of electrical constants. For the metals they were the same, or nearly the same, as before, but the resistivity and permittivity of insulators had changed measurably – that had become slightly better conductors.

Except in the precision apparatus, such as Gertie the computer, the change in electromagnetic characteristics was not enough to make any noticeable difference. But the most complex and delicately balanced mechanism known to man is the living cell; and the neurone is the most highly evolved and specialized of all cells – particularly that variety of neurones found in the human cerebral cortex. And here the change was felt. The minute electrical impulses which represented neural functioning – sense awareness, motor reaction, thought itself – were flowing more rapidly, more intensely.

And the change might just have begun.

Helga shivered. 'I need a drink,' she said. 'Bad.'

'I know a bar,' said Lewis. 'I'll join you in one before coming back to work some more. How about you, Pete?'

'I'm going home,' said the physicist. 'Have fun.' His words were flat.

He walked out, hardly aware of the darkened lobby and the late hour. To the others, this was still something bright and new and wonderful; but he couldn't keep from thinking that perhaps, in one huge careless swipe, the universe was about to snuff out all the race of man. What would the effect be on a living body –?

Well, they'd done about all they could for now. They'd checked as much as possible. Helga had gotten in touch with the Bureau of Standards in Washington and notified them. She gathered, from what the man there said, that a few other laboratories, spotted throughout the country, had also reported anomalies. *Tomorrow*, thought Corinth, *they'll really start hearing about it.*

Outside – the scene was still New York at evening – hardly changed, perhaps just a little quieter than it should be. He bought a newspaper at the corner and glanced at it as he stood there. Was he wrong, or had a subtle difference crept in, a more literate phrasing, something individual that broke through the copyreader's barriers because the copyreader himself had changed without knowing it? But there was not mention of the great cause, that was too big and too new yet, nor had the old story altered – war, unrest, suspicion, fear and hate and greed, a sick world crumbling.

He was suddenly aware that he had read through the *Times'* crowded front page in about ten minutes. He shoved the newspaper into a pocket and hastened towards the subway.

CHAPTER THREE

There was trouble everywhere. An indignant yell in the morning brought Archie Brock running to the chicken house, where Stan Wilmer had set down a bucket of feed to shake his fist at the world.

'Look a' that!' he cried. 'Just look!'

Brock craned his neck through the door and whistled. The place was a mess. A couple of bloody-feathered corpses were sprawled on the straw, a few other hens cackled nervously on the roosts, and that was all. The rest were gone.

'Looks like foxes got in when somebody left the door open,' said Brock.

'Yeah.' Wilmer swallowed in his rage in a noisy gulp. 'Some stinking son of a –'

Brock remembered that Wilmer was in charge of the hen house, but decided not to mention it. The other man recalled himself and paused, scowling.

'I don't know,' he said slowly. 'I checked the place last night as usual, before going to bed, and I'll swear the door was closed and hooked like it always is. Five years I been here and never had any trouble.'

'So maybe somebody opened the door later on, after dark, huh?'

'Yeah. A chicken thief. Though it's funny the dogs didn't bark – I never heard of any human being coming here without them yapping.' Wilmer shrugged bitterly. 'Well, anyway, somebody did open the door.'

'And then later on foxes got in.' Brock turned one of the dead hens over with his toe. 'And maybe had to run for it when one of the dogs came sniffling around, and left these.'

'And most of the birds wandered out into the woods. It'll take a week to catch 'em – all that live. Oh, Judas!' Wilmer stormed out of the chicken house, forgetting to close the door. Brock did it for him, vaguely surprised that he had remembered to do so.

He sighed and resumed his morning chores. The animals all seemed fidgety today. And damn if his own head didn't feel funny. He remembered his own panic of two nights before, and the odd way he'd been thinking ever since. Maybe there was some kind of fever going around.

Well – he'd ask somebody about it later. There was work to do today, ploughing in the north forty that had just been cleared. All the tractors were busy cultivating, so he'd have to take a team of horses.

That was all right. Brock liked animals, he had always understood them and got along with them better than with people. Not that the people had been mean to him, anyway for a long while now. The kids used to tease him, back when he was a kid too, and then later there'd been some trouble with cars, and a couple of girls had got scared also and he'd been beaten up by the brother of one of them. But that was years back. Mr Rossman had told him carefully what he could do and could not do, kind of taken him over, and things had been all right since then. Now he could walk into the tavern when he was in town and have a beer like anybody else, and the men said hello.

He stood for a minute, wondering why he should be thinking about this when he knew it so well, and why it should hurt him the way it did. *I'm all right*, he thought. *I'm not so smart, maybe, but I'm strong. Mr Rossman says he ain't got a better farm hand nor me.*

He shrugged and entered the barn to get out the horses. He was a young man, of medium height but heavy-set and muscular, with coarse strong features and a round, crew-cut, red-haired head. His blue denim clothes were shabby but clean; Mrs Bergen, the wife of the general superintendent in whose cottage he had a room, looked after such details for him.

The barn was big and gloomy, full of the strong rich smells of hay and horses. The brawny Percherons stamped and snorted, restless as he harnessed them. Funny – they were always so calm before. 'So, so, steady, boy. Steady, Tom. Whoa, there, Jerry, easy.' They quieted a little and he led them out and hitched them to a post while he went into the shed after the plough.

His dog Joe came frisking around him, a tall Irish setter whose coat was like gold and copper in the sun. Joe was really Mr Rossman's, of course, but Brock had taken care of him since he was a pup and it was always Brock whom he followed and loved. 'Down, boy, down. What the hell's got into yuh, anyway? Take it easy, will yuh?'

The estate lay green around him, the farm buildings on one side, the cottages of the help screened off by trees on another, the many acres of woods behind. There was a lot of lawn and orchard and garden between this farming part and the big white house of the owner, a house which had been mostly emptied since Mr Rossman's daughters had married and his wife had died. He was there now, though, spending a few weeks here in upper New York State with his flowers. Brock wondered why a millionaire like Mr Rossman wanted to putter around growing roses, even if he was getting old.

The shed door creaked open and Brock went in and took the big plough and wheeled it out, grunting a little with the effort. Not many men could drag it out themselves, he thought with a flicker of pride. He chuckled as he saw how the horses stamped at the sight. Horses were lazy beasts, they'd never work if they could get out of it.

He shoved the plough around behind them, carried the tongue forwards, and hitched it on. With a deft motion, he twirled the reins loose from the post, took his seat, and shook the lines across the broad rumps. 'Giddap!'

They just stood, moving their feet.

'Giddap there, I say!'

Tom began backing. 'Whoa! Whoa!' Brock took the loose end of the reins and snapped it with whistling force. Tom grunted and put one huge hoof on the tongue. It broke across.

For a long moment, Brock sat there, finding no words. Then he shook his red head. 'It's a ac-ci-dent,' he said aloud. The morning seemed very quiet all of a sudden. 'It's a ac-ci-dent.'

There was a spare tongue in the shed. He fetched it and some tools, and began doggedly removing the broken one.

'Hi, there! Stop! Stop, I say!'

Brock looked up. The squealing and grunting were like a blow. He saw a black streak go by, and then another and another – The pigs were loose!

'Joe!' he yelled, even then wondering a little at how quickly he reacted. 'Go get 'em, Joe! Round 'em up, boy!'

The dog was off like burnished lightning. He got ahead of the lead sow and snapped at her. She grunted, turning aside, and he darted after the next. Stan Wilmer came running from the direction of the pen. His face was white.

Brock ran to intercept another pig, turning it, but a fourth one slipped aside and was lost in the woods. It took several confused minutes to chase the majority back into the pen; a number were gone.

Wilmer stood gasping. His voice was raw. 'I saw it,' he groaned. 'Oh, my God, I saw it. It ain't possible.'

Brock blew out his cheeks and wiped his face.

'You hear me?' Wilmer grasped his arm. 'I saw it, I tell you, I saw it with my own eyes. Those pigs opened the gate themselves.'

'Naw!' Brock felt his mouth falling open.

'I tell you, I saw it! One of 'em stood up on her hind legs and nosed the latch up. She did it all by herself. And the others were crowding right behind her. Oh, no, no, no!'

Joe came out of the woods, driving a pig before him with sardonic barks. She seemed to give up after a minute and trotted quietly towards the pen. Wilmer turned like a machine and opened the gate again and let her go in.

'Good boy!' Brock patted the silken head that nuzzled against him. 'Smart dog!'

'Too God damned smart.' Wilmer narrowed his eyes. 'Did a dog ever make like that before?'

'Sure,' said Brock uncertainly.

Joe got off his haunches and went back into the woods.

'I'll bet he's going after another pig.' There was a kind of horror in Wilmer's voice.

'Sure. He's a smart dog, he is.'

'I'm going to see Bill Bergen about this.' Wilmer turned on his heel. Brock looked after him, shrugged heavy shoulders, and went back to his own task. By the time he finished it, Joe had rounded up two more pigs and brought them back, and was mounting guard at the gate of the pen.

'Good fellow,' said Brock. 'I'll see yuh get a bone for this.' He hitched Tom and Jerry, who had been standing at their ease. 'All right, yuh bums, let's go. Giddap!'

Slowly, the horses backed. 'Hey!' screamed Brock.

This time they didn't stop with the tongue. Very carefully, they walked onto the plough itself and bent its iron frame with their weight and broke off the coulter. Brock felt his throat dry.

'No,' he mumbled.

Wilmer nearly had a fit when he learned about the horses. Bergen only stood there, whistling tunelessly. 'I don't know.' He scratched his sandy head. 'Tell you what. We'll call off all work having to do with animals, except feeding and milking, of course. Padlock every gate and have somebody check all our fence lines. I'll see the old man about this.'

'Me, I'm gonna carry a gun,' said Wilmer.

'Well, it might not be a bad idea,' said Bergen.

Archie Brock was assigned to look at one section, a four-mile line enclosing the woods. He took Joe, who gambolled merrily in his wake, and went off glad to be alone for a change.

How still the forest was! Sunlight slanted down through green unstirring leaves, throwing a dapple on the warm brown shadows. The sky was utterly blue overhead, no clouds, no wind. His feet scrunched dully on an occasional clod or stone, he brushed against a twig and it scratched very faintly along his clothes, otherwise the land was altogether silent. The birds seemed to have quieted down all at once, no squirrels were in sight, even the sheep had withdrawn into the inner woods. He thought uneasily that somehow the whole green world had a waiting feel to it.

Like before a storm, maybe?

He could see how people would be scared if the animals started getting smarter. If they were really smart, would they keep on letting humans lock them up and work them and castrate them and kill and skin and eat them? Suppose Tom and Jerry, now – but they were so gentle!

And – wait – weren't the people getting smarter too? It seemed like in the last couple of days they'd been talking more, and it wasn't all about the weather and the neighbours either, it was about things like who was going to win the next election and why a rear-engine drive was better in a car. They'd always talked like that now and then, sure, but not so much, and they hadn't had so much to say, either. Even Mrs Bergen, he seen her reading a magazine, and all she ever did before in her spare time was watch TV.

I'm getting smarter too!

The knowledge was like a thunderclap. He stood there for a long while, not moving, and Joe came up and sniffed his hand in a puzzled way.

I'm getting smarter.

Sure – it had to be. The way he'd been wondering lately, and remembering things, and speaking out when he'd never said anything much before – what else could it be? All the world was getting smarter.

I can read, he told himself. *Not very good, but they did teach me the al-phabet, and I can read a comic book. Maybe I can read a real book now.*

Books had the answers to what he was suddenly wondering about, things like the sun and moon and stars, why there was winter and summer, why they had wars and Presidents and who lived on the other side of the world and –

He shook his head, unable to grasp the wilderness that rose up inside him and spread till it covered creation further than he could see. He'd never wondered before. Things just happened and were forgotten again. But – he looked at his hands, marvelling. *Who am I? What am I doing here?*

There was a boiling in him. He leaned his head against the cool trunk of a tree, listening to the blood roar in his ears. Please, God, let it be real. *Please make me like other people.*

After a while he fought it down and went on, checking the fence as he had been told.

In the evening, after chores, he put on a clean suit and went up to the big house. Mr Rossman was sitting on the porch, smoking a pipe and turning the pages of a book over in his thin fingers, not really seeing it. Brock paused timidly, cap in hand, till the owner looked up and spied him.

'Oh, hello, Archie,' he said in his soft voice. 'How are you tonight?'

'I'm all right, thank you.' Brock twisted the cap between his stumpy hands and shifted from one foot to another. 'Please, can I see you for a minute?'

'Why, of course. Come on in.' Mr Rossman laid his book aside and sat smoking while Brock opened the screen door and walked over to him. 'Here, take a chair.'

'That's all right, thanks. I –' Brock ran his tongue across dry lips. 'I'd just like to ask you 'bout something.'

'Ask away, Archie,' Mr Rossman leaned back. He was a tall spare man, his face thinly carved, proud under its kindness of the moment, his hair white. Brock's parents had been tenants of his, and when it became plain that their son would never amount to anything, he had taken charge of the boy. 'Everything okay?'

'Well, it's about, uh, about this change here.'

'Eh?' Rossman's gaze sharpened. 'What change?'

'You know. The animals getting smart and uppity.'

'Oh, yes. That.' Rossman blew a cloud of smoke. 'Tell me, Archie, have you noticed any change in yourself?'

'Yes, I, uh, well, I think maybe I have.'

Rossman nodded. 'You wouldn't have come here if you hadn't changed.'

'What's happening, Mr Rossman? What's gone wrong?'

'I don't know, Archie. Nobody knows.' The old man looked out into a gathering blue twilight. 'Are you so sure it's wrong, though? Maybe something is finally going right.'

'You don't know –'

'No. Nobody knows.' Rossman's pale blue-veined hand slapped the newspaper on the table beside him. 'There are hints here. The knowledge is creeping out. I'm sure much more is known, but the government has suppressed the information for fear of a panic.' He grinned with a certain viciousness. 'As if a world-wide phenomenon could be kept secret! But they'll hang on to their stupidity to the very end in Washington.'

'But, Mr Rossman –' Brock lifted his hands and let them fall again. 'What can we do?'

'Wait. Wait and see. I'm going to the city soon, to find out for myself – those pet brains of mine at the Institute should –'

'You're leaving?'

Rossman shook his head, smiling. 'Poor Archie. There's a horror in being helpless, isn't there? I sometimes think that's why men fear death – not because of oblivion, but because it's foredoomed, there's nothing they can do to stop it. Even fatalism is a refuge from that, in a way – But I digress, don't I?'

He sat smoking for a long while. The summer dusk chirred and murmured around them. 'Yes,' he said at last, 'I feel it in myself too. And it's not altogether pleasant. Not just the nervousness and the nightmares – that's merely physiological, I suppose – but the thoughts. I've always imagined myself as a quick, capable, logical thinker. Now something is coming to life within me that I don't understand at all. Sometimes my whole life seems to have been a petty and meaningless scramble. And yet I thought I'd served my family and my country well.' He smiled once more. 'I do hope I'll see the end of this, though. It should be interesting!'

Tears stung Brock's eyes. 'What can I do?'

'Do? Live. Live from day to day. What else can a man do?' Rossman got up and put his hand on Brock's shoulder. 'But keep on thinking. Keep your thinking close to the ground, where it belongs. Don't ever trade your liberty for another man's offer to do your thinking and make your mistakes for you. I had to play the feudal lord with you, Archie, but it may be that that's no longer necessary.'

Brock didn't understand most of it. But it seemed Mr Rossman was telling him to be cheerful, that this wasn't such a bad thing after all. 'I thought maybe I could borrow some books,' he said humbly. 'I'd like to see if I can read them now.'

'Why, of course, Archie. Come on into the library. I'll see if I can find something suitable for you to begin on –'

CHAPTER FOUR

Selections from the New York *Times*, June 23:

PRESIDENT DENIES DANGER IN BRAIN SPEEDUP

'Keep Cool, Stay on Job,' Advises White House – No Harm To Humans in Change

**U. S. Scientists Working On Problem – Expect Answer Soon
FALLING STOCK MARKET WORRIES WALL STREET**

Declining Sales Bring Down Stock Market and Prices

**U. S. in Danger of Recession, Says Economist
CHINESE TROOPS MUTINY**

**Communist Government Declares Emergency
NEW RELIGION FOUNDED IN LOS ANGELES**

**Sawyer Proclaims Self 'The Third Ba'al' – Thousands
Attend Mass Meeting
FESSENDEN CALLS FOR WORLD GOVERNMENT**

**Iowa Isolationist Reverses Stand in Senate Speech
JOHNSON SAYS WORLD GOVERNMENT
IMPRACTICAL AT PRESENT TIME**

Oregon Senator Reverses Former Stand

REBELLION IN UPSTATE HOME FOR FEEBLE-MINDED

RIOT IN ALABAMA

Conference.

Everybody was working late, and it was ten o'clock before the meeting which Corinth had invited to his place was ready. Sheila had insisted on putting out her usual buffet of sandwiches and coffee; afterward she sat in a corner, talking quietly with Sarah Mandelbaum. Their eyes strayed occasionally to their husbands, who were playing chess, and there was a creeping fear in the gaze.

Corinth was playing better than he had ever done before. Usually he and Mandelbaum were pretty evenly matched, the physicist's slow careful strategy offsetting the unionist's nerve-racking bravura. But tonight the younger man was too distracted. He made schemes that would have delighted Capablanca, but Mandelbaum saw through them and slashed barbarically past his defences. Corinth sighed at last and leaned back.

'I resign,' he said. 'It'd be mate in, uh, seven moves.'

'Not so.' Mandelbaum pointed a gnarled finger at king's bishop. 'If you moved him over here, and then –'

'Oh, yes, you're right. No matter. I'm just not in the mood. What's keeping Nat?'

'He'll be along. Take it easy.' Mandelbaum removed himself to an armchair and began stuffing a big-bowled pipe.

'I don't see how you can sit there like that when –'

'When a world's falling to pieces around my ears? Look, Pete, it's been falling apart as long as I can remember. So far, in this particular episode, no guns have come out.'

'They may do so yet.' Corinth got up and stood looking out the window, hands crossed behind his back and shoulders slumped. The restless glimmer of city light etched him against darkness. 'Don't you see, Felix, this new factor – if we survive it at all – changes the whole basis of human life? Our society was built by and for one sort of man. Now man himself is becoming something else.'

'I doubt it.' The noise of a match, struck against Mandelbaum's shoe, was startlingly loud. 'We're still the same old animal.'

'What was your I.Q. before the change?'

'I don't know.'

'Never took a test?'

'Oh, sure, they made me take one now and then, to get this or that job, but I never asked for the result. What's I.Q. except the score on an I.Q. test?'

'It's more than that. It measures the ability to handle data, grasp and create abstractions –'

'*If* you're a Caucasian of West European-American cultural background. That's who the test was designed for, Pete. A Kalahari bushman would laugh if he knew it omitted water-finding ability. That's more important to him than the ability to juggle numbers. Me, I don't underrate the logic and visualization aspect of personality, but I don't have your touching faith in it, either. There's more to a man than that, and a garage mechanic may be a better survivor type than a mathematician.'

'Survivor – under what conditions?'

'Any conditions. Adaptability, toughness, quickness – those are the things that count most.'

'I think kindness means a lot,' said Sheila timidly.

'It's a luxury, I'm afraid, though of course it's such luxuries that make us human,' said Mandelbaum. 'Kindness to whom? Sometimes you just have to cut loose and get violent. Some wars are necessary.'

'They wouldn't be, if people had more intelligence,' said Corinth. 'We needn't have fought World War II if Hitler had been stopped when he entered the Rhineland. One division could have bowled him over. But the politicians were too stupid to foresee –'

'No,' said Mandelbaum. 'It's just that there were reasons why it wasn't – convenient, shall we say? – to call up that division. And ninety-nine per cent of the human race, no matter how smart they are, will do the convenient thing instead of the wise thing, and kid themselves into thinking they can somehow escape the consequences. We're just built that way. And then, the world is so full of old hate and superstition, and so many people are nice and tolerant and practical about it, that it's a wonder hell hasn't boiled over more often throughout history.' Bitterness edged his voice. 'Maybe the practical people, the ones who adapt, are right after all. Maybe the most moral thing really is to put "myself, my wife, and my little Hassan with the bandy legs" first. Like one of my sons has done. He's in Chicago now. Changed his name and had his nose bobbed. He's not ashamed of his parents, no, but he's saved himself and his family a lot of trouble and humiliation. And I honestly don't know whether to admire him for tough-minded adaptability, or call him a spineless whelp.'

'We're getting rather far from the point,' said Corinth, embarrassed. 'What we want to do tonight is try and estimate what we, the whole world, are in for.' He shook his head. 'My I.Q. has gone from its former 160 to about 200 in a week. I'm thinking things that never occurred to me before. My former professional problems are becoming ridiculously easy. Only, everything else is confused. My mind keeps wandering off into the most fantastic trains of thought, some of them pretty wild and morbid. I'm nervous as a kitten, jump at shadows, afraid for no good reason at all. Now and then I get flashes where everything seems grotesque – like in a nightmare.'

'You're not adjusted to your new brain yet, that's all,' said Sarah.

'I feel the same sort of things Pete does,' said Sheila. Her voice was thin and scared. 'It isn't worth it.'

The other woman shrugged, spreading her hands. 'Me, I think it's kind of fun.'

'Matter of basic personality – which has not changed,' said Mandelbaum. 'Sarah's always been a pretty down-to-earth sort. You just don't take your new mind seriously, Liebchen. To you, the power of abstract thought is a toy. It's got little to do with the serious matters of housework.' He puffed, meshing his face into wrinkles as he squinted through the smoke. 'And me, I get crazy spells like you do, Pete, but I don't let it bother me. It's only physiological, and I haven't time for such fumblydiddles. Not the way things are now. Everybody in the union seems to have come up with some crank notion of how we ought to run things. A guy in the electrical workers has a notion that the electricians ought to go on strike and take over the whole government! Somebody even fired a shot gun at me the other day.'

'Huh?' They stared at him.

Mandelbaum shrugged. 'He was a lousy shot. But some people are turning crank, and some are turning mean, and most are just plain scared. Those like me who're trying to ride out the storm and keep things as nearly normal as possible, are bound to make enemies. People think a lot more today, but they aren't thinking straight.'

'Sure,' said Corinth. 'The average man –' He started as the doorbell rang. 'That must be them now,' he said. 'Come in.'

Helga Arnulfsen entered, her slim height briefly concealing Nathan Lewis' bulk. She looked as cool and smooth and hard as before, but there were shadows under her eyes. 'Hullo,' she said tonelessly.

'No fun, huh?' asked Sheila with sympathy.

Helga grimaced. 'Nightmares.'

'Me too.' A shudder ran along Sheila's small form.

'How about the psych man you were going to bring, Nat?' asked Corinth.

'He refused at the last minute,' said Lewis. 'Had some kind of idea for a new intelligence test. And his partner was too busy putting rats through mazes. Never mind, we don't really need them.' Alone of them all, he seemed without worry and foreboding, too busy reaching for the sudden new horizon to consider his own troubles. He wandered over to the buffet and picked up a sandwich and bit into it. 'Mmmmm – *delikat*. Sheila, why don't you ditch this long drink of water and marry me?'

'Trade him for a long drink of beer?' she smiled tremulously.

'*Touché!* You've changed too, haven't you? But really you ought to have done better by me. A long drink of Scotch, at the very least.'

'After all,' said Corinth gloomily, 'it's not as if we were here for any special purpose. I just thought a general discussion would clarify the matter in all our minds and maybe give us some ideas.'

Lewis settled himself at the table. 'I see the government has finally admitted something is going on,' he said, nodding at the newspaper which lay beside him. 'They had to do it, I suppose, but the admission won't help the panics any. People are afraid, they don't know what to expect, and – well, coming over here, I saw a man run screaming down the street yelling that the end of the world had come. There was a monster-sized revival in Central Park. Three drunks were brawling outside a bar, and not a cop in sight to stop them. I heard fire sirens – big blaze somewhere out Queens way.'

Helga lit a cigarette, sucking in her cheeks and half closing her eyes. 'John Rossman's in Washington now,' she said. After a moment she added to the Mandelbaums: 'He came to the Institute a few days back, asked our bright boys to investigate this business but keep their findings confidential, and flew to the capital. With his pull, he'll get the whole story for us if anyone can.'

'I don't think there is much of a story yet, to tell the truth,' said Mandelbaum. 'Just little things like we've all been experiencing, all over the world. They add up to a big upheaval, yes, but there's no overall picture.'

'Just you wait,' said Lewis cheerfully. He took another sandwich and a cup of coffee. 'I predict that within about one week, things are going to start going to hell in a hand-basket.'

'The fact is –' Corinth got out of the chair into which he had flopped and began pacing the room. 'The fact is, that the change isn't over. It's still going on. As far as our best instruments can tell – though they're not too exact, what with our instruments being affected themselves – the change is even accelerating.'

'Within the limits of error, I think I see a more or less hyperbolic advance,' said Lewis. 'We've just begun, brethren. The way we're going, we'll all have I.Q.'s in the neighbourhood of 400 within another week.'

They sat for a long while, not speaking. Corinth stood with his fists clenched, hanging loose at his sides, and Sheila gave a little wordless cry and ran over to him and hung on his arm. Mandelbaum blew clouds of smoke, scowling as he digested the information; one hand stole out to caress Sarah's, and she squeezed it gratefully. Lewis grinned around his sandwich and went on eating. Helga sat without motion, the long clean curves of her face gone utterly expressionless. The city banged faintly below them, around them.

'What's going to happen?' breathed Sheila at last. She trembled so they could see it. 'What's going to happen to us?'

'Christ alone knows,' said Lewis, not without gentleness.

'Will it go on building up forever?' asked Sarah.

'Nope,' said Lewis. 'Can't. It's a matter of neurone chains increasing their speed of reaction, and the intensity of the signals they carry. The physical structure of the cell can take only so much. If they're stimulated too far – insanity, followed by idiocy, followed by death.'

'How high can we go?' asked Mandelbaum practically.

'Can't say. The mechanism of the change – and of the nerve cell itself – just isn't known well enough. Anyway, the I.Q. concept is only valid within a limited range; to speak on an I.Q. of 400 really doesn't make sense, intelligence on that level may not be intelligence at all as we know it now, but something else.'

Corinth had been too busy with his own work of physical measurements to realize how much Lewis' department knew and theorized. The appalling knowledge was only beginning to grow in him.

'Forget the final results,' said Helga sharply. 'There's nothing we can do about that. What's important right now is: how do we keep organized civilization going? How do we eat?'

Corinth nodded, mastering the surge of his panic. 'Sheer social inertia has carried us along so far,' he agreed. 'Most people continue in their daily rounds because there's nothing else available. But when things really start changing –'

'The janitor and the elevator man at the Institute quit yesterday,' said Helga. 'Said the work was too monotonous. What happens when all the janitors and garbage men and ditchdiggers and assembly-line workers decide to quit?'

'They won't all do it,' said Mandelbaum. He knocked out his pipe and went over to get some coffee. 'Some will be afraid, some will have the sense to see we've got to keep going, some – well, there's no simple answer to this. I agree we're for a rough period of transition at the very least – people throwing up their jobs, people getting scared, people going crazy in one way or another. What we need is a local interim organization to see us through the next few months. I think the labour unions could be a nucleus – I'm working on that, and when I've got the boys talked and bullied into line, I'm going to approach City Hall with an offer to help.'

After a silence, Helga glanced over at Lewis. 'You still haven't any idea as to the cause of it all?'

'Oh, yes,' said the biologist. 'Any number of ideas, and no way of choosing between them. We'll just have to study and think some more, that's all.'

'It's a physical phenomenon embracing at least the whole Solar System,' declared Corinth. 'The observatories have established that much through spectroscopic studies. It may be that the sun, in its orbit around the centre of the galaxy, has entered some kind of force-field. But on theoretical grounds – dammit, I won't scrap general relativity till I have to! – on theoretical grounds, I'm inclined to think it's more likely a matter of our having *left* a force-field which slows down light and otherwise affects electromagnetic and electrochemical processes.'

'In other words,' said Mandelbaum slowly, 'we're actually entering a normal state of affairs? All our past has been spent under abnormal conditions?'

'Maybe. Only, of course, those conditions are normal for us. We've evolved under them. We may be like deep-sea fish, which explode when they're brought up to ordinary pressures.'

'Heh! Pleasant thought!'

'I don't think I'm afraid to die,' said Sheila in a small voice, 'but being changed like this –'

'Keep a tight rein on yourself,' said Lewis sharply. 'I suspect this unbalance is going to drive a lot of people actually insane. Don't be one of them.'

He knocked the ash off his cigar. 'We have found out some things at the lab,' he went on in a dispassionate tone. 'As Pete says, it's a physical thing, either a force-field or the lack of one, affecting electronic interactions. The effect is actually rather small, quantitatively. Ordinary chemical reactions go on pretty much as before, in fact I don't think any significant change in the speed of inorganic reactions has been detected. But the more complex and delicate a structure is, the more it feels that slight effect.

'You must have noticed that you're more energetic lately. We've tested basal metabolism rates, and they have increased, not much but some. Your motor reactions are faster too, though you may not have noticed that because your subjective time sense is also speeded up. In other words, not much change in muscular, glandular, vascular, and the other purely somatic functions, just enough to make you feel nervous; and you'll adjust to that pretty quick, if nothing else happens.

'On the other hand, the most highly organized cells – neurones, and above all the neurones of the cerebral cortex – are very much affected. Perception speeds are way up; they measured that over in psych. You've noticed, I'm sure, how much faster you read. Reaction time to all stimuli is less.'

'I heard that from Jones,' nodded Helga coolly, 'and checked up on traffic accident statistics for the past week. Definitely lower. If people react faster, naturally they're better drivers.'

'Uh-huh,' said Lewis. 'Till they start getting tired of poking along at sixty miles an hour and drive at a hundred. Then you may not have any more crack-ups, but those you do have – wham!'

'But if people are smarter,' began Sheila, 'they'll know enough to –'

'Sorry, no.' Mandelbaum shook his head. 'Basic personality does not change, right? And intelligent people have always done some pretty stupid or evil things from time to time, just like everybody else. A man might be a brilliant scientist, let's say, but that doesn't stop him from neglecting his health or from driving recklessly or patronizing spiritualists or –'

'Or voting Democrats,' nodded Lewis, grinning. 'That's correct, Felix. Eventually, no doubt, increased intelligence would affect the total personality, but right now you're not removing anyone's weaknesses, ignorances, prejudices, blind spots, or ambitions; you're just giving him more power, of energy and intelligence, to indulge them – which is one reason why civilization is cracking up.'

His voice became dry and didactic: 'Getting back to where we were, the most highly organized tissue in the world is, of course, the human cerebrum, the grey matter or seat of consciousness if you like. It feels the stimulus – or lack of inhibition, if Pete's theory is right – more than anything else on Earth. Its functioning increases out of all proportion to the rest of the organism. Maybe you don't know how complex a structure the human brain is. Believe me, it makes the sidereal universe look like a child's building set. There are many times more possible interneuronic connections than there are atoms in the entire cosmos – the factor is something like ten to the power of several million. It's not surprising that a slight change in electrochemistry – too slight to make any important difference to the body – will change the whole nature of the mind. Look what a little dope or alcohol will do, and then remember that this new factor works on the very basis of the cell's existence.

The really interesting question is whether so finely balanced a function can survive such a change at all.'

There was no fear in his tones, and the eyes behind their heavy lenses held a flash of impersonal excitement. To him this was sheer wonder; Corinth imagined him dying and taking clinical notes on himself as life faded.

'Well,' said the physicist greyly, 'we'll know pretty soon.'

'How can you just sit there and talk about it that way?' cried Sheila. Horror shook her voice.

'My dear girl,' said Helga, 'do you imagine we can, at this stage, do anything else?'

CHAPTER FIVE

Selections from *The New York Times*, June 30:

CHANGE DECELERATING

Decline Noted, Effects Apparently Irreversible

Rhayader Theory May Hold Explanation
UNIFIED FIELD THEORY ANNOUNCED

Rhayader Announces Extension of Einstein Theories – Interstellar Travel a Theoretical Possibility
FEDERAL GOVERNMENT MAY RESIGN FUNCTIONS

President Asks Local Authorities to Exercise Discretion

N. Y. Labour Authority Under Mandelbaum Pledges Co-operation
REVOLUTION REPORTED IN SOVIETIZED COUNTRIES

News Blackout Declared – Organized Insurrection Spreading

Revolutionaries May Have Developed New Weapons and Military Concepts
WORLD ECONOMIC CRISIS WORSENING
Food Riots in Paris, Dublin, Rome, Hong Kong

Shipping Approaches Complete Standstill as Thousands of Workers Quit
THIRD BA'AL CULT REVOLTS IN LOS ANGELES

National Guard Demoralized Fanatics Seize Key Points – Street
Fighting Continues –

N. Y. City Hall Warns of Local Activities of Cultists
TIGER KILLS ATTENDANT, ESCAPES FROM BRONX ZOO

Police Issue Warning, Organize Hunt

Authorities Consider Shooting All Formidable Specimens
FRESH RIOTING FEARED IN HARLEM

Police Chief: 'Yesterday's Affair Only a Beginning' – Mounting Panic Seems
Impossible to Halt
PSYCHIATRIST SAYS MAN CHANGED 'BEYOND COMPREHENSION'

Kearnes of Bellevue: 'Unpredictable Results of Neural Speed-up
Make Old Data and Methods of Control Invalid – Impossible
Even to Guess Ultimate Outcome'

They had no issue the following day; there was no newsprint to be had.

Brock thought it was strange to be left in charge of the estate. But a lot of funny things had been happening lately.

First Mr Rossman had gone. Then, the very next day, Stan Wilmer had been attacked by the pigs when he went in to feed them. They charged him, grunting and squealing, stamping him down under their heavy bodies, and several had to be shot before they left him. Most had rushed the fence then, hitting it together and breaking through and disappearing into the woods. Wilmer was pretty badly hurt and had to be taken to the hospital; he swore he'd never come back. Two of the hands had quit the same day.

Brock was in too much of a daze, too full of the change within himself, to care. He didn't have much to do, anyway, now that all work except the most essential was suspended. He looked after the animals, careful to treat them well and to wear a gun at his hip, and had little trouble. Joe was always beside him. The rest of the time he sat around reading, or just with his chin in his hand to think.

Bill Bergen called him in a couple of days after the pig episode. The overseer didn't seem to have changed much, not outwardly. He was still tall and sandy and slow-spoken, with the same toothpick worried between his lips, the same squinted pale eyes. But he spoke even more slowly and cautiously than he had done before to Brock – or did it only seem that way?

'Well, Archie,' he said, 'Smith just quit.'

Brock shifted from one foot to another, looking at the floor.

'Said he wanted to go to college. I couldn't talk him out of it.' Bergen's voice held a faintly amused contempt. 'The idiot. There won't be any more colleges in another month. That leaves just you and my wife and Voss and me.'

'Kind of short-handed,' mumbled Brock, feeling he ought to say something.

'One man can do the bare essentials if he must,' said Bergen. 'Lucky it's summer. The horses and cows can stay out of doors, which saves barn cleaning.'

'How about the crops?'

'Not much to do there yet. To hell with them, anyway.'

Brock stared upward. In all his years on the place, Bergen had been the steadiest and hardest worker they had.

'You've gotten smart like the rest of us, haven't you, Archie?' asked Bergen. 'I daresay you're about up to normal now – pre-change normal, I mean. And it isn't over. You'll get brighter yet.'

Brock's face grew hot.

'Sorry. I didn't mean anything personal. You're a good man' He sat for a moment fiddling with the papers on his desk. Then: 'Archie, you're in charge here now.'

'Huh?'

'I'm leaving too.'

'But, Bill – you can't –'

'Can and will, Archie.' Bergen stood up. 'You know my wife always wanted to travel, and I have some things to think out. Never mind what they are, it's something I've puzzled over for many years and now I believe I see an answer. We're taking our car and heading west.'

'But – but – Mr Rossman – he's de-pen-ding on you, Bill –'

'I'm afraid that there are more important things in life than Mr Rossman's country retreat,' said Bergen evenly. 'You can handle the place all right, even if Voss leaves too.'

Fright and bewilderment lashed into scorn: 'Scared of the animals, huh?'

'Why, no, Archie. Always remember that you're still brighter than they are, and what's more important, you have hands. A gun will stop anything.' Bergen walked over to the window and looked out. It was a bright windy day with sunlight torn in the restless branches of trees. 'As a matter of fact,' he went on in the same gentle, remote one, 'a farm is safer than any other place I can think of. If the production and distribution systems break down, as they may, you'll still have something to eat. But my wife and I aren't getting any younger. I've been a steady, sober, conscientious man all my life. Now I wonder what all the fuss and the lost years were about.'

He turned his back. 'Good-by, Archie.' It was a command.

Brock went out into the yard, shaking his head and muttering to himself. Joe whined uneasily and nuzzled his palm. He ruffled the golden fur and sat down on a bench and put his head in his hands.

The trouble is, he thought, *that while the animals and I got smarter, so did everybody else. God in Heaven – what sort of things are going on inside Bill Bergen's skull?*

It was a terrifying concept. The speed and scope and sharpness of his own mind were suddenly cruel. He dared not think what a normal human might be like by now.

Only it was hard to realize. Bergen hadn't become a god. His eyes didn't blaze, his voice was not vibrant and resolute, he didn't start building great engines that flamed and roared. He was still a tall stoop-shouldered man with a weary face, a patient drawl, nothing else. The trees were still green, a bird chattered behind a rosebush, a fly rested cobalt-blue on the arm of the bench.

Brock remembered, vaguely, sermons from the few times he had been in church. The end of the world – was the sky going to open up, would the angels pour down the vials of wrath on a shaking land, and would God appear to judge the sons of man? He listened for the noise of great galloping hoofs, but there was only the wind in the trees.

That was the worst of it. The sky didn't care. The Earth went on turning through an endlessness of dark and silence, and what happened in the thin scum seething over its crust didn't matter.

Nobody cared. It wasn't important.

Brock looked at his scuffed shoes and then at the strong hairy hands between his knees. They seemed impossibly alien, the hands of a stranger. *Sweet Jesus,* he thought, *is this really happening to me?*

He grabbed Joe by the ruffed neck and held him close. Suddenly he had a wild need for a woman, someone to hold him and talk to him and block out the loneliness of the sky.

He got up, sweat cold on his body, and walked over to the Bergens' cottage. It was his now, he supposed.

Voss was a young fellow, a kid from town who wasn't very bright and hadn't been able to find any other employment. He looked moodily up from a book as the other man entered the small living room.

'Well,' said Brock, 'Bill just quit.'

'I know. What're we gonna do?' Voss was scared and weak and willing to surrender leadership. Bergen must have foreseen that. The sense of responsibility was strengthening.

'We'll be all right if we stay here,' said Brock. 'Just wait it out, keep going, that's all.'

'The animals –'

'You got a gun, don't you? Anyway, they'll know when they're well off. Just be careful, always lock the gates behind you, treat 'em good –'

'I'm not gonna wait on any damn animals,' said Voss sullenly.

'That you are, though.' Brock went over to the icebox and took out two cans of beer and opened them.

'Look here, I'm smarter than you are, and –'

'And I'm stronger'n you. If you don't like it, you can quit. I'm staying.' Brock gave Voss one can and tilted the other to his mouth.

'Look,' he said after a moment, 'I know those animals. They're mostly habit. They'll stick around because they don't know any better and because we feed 'em and because – uh – respect for man has been drilled into 'em. There ain't no bears or wolves in the woods, nothing that can give us trouble except maybe the pigs. Me, I'd be more scared to be in a city.'

'How come?' Despite himself, Voss was overmastered. He laid down the book and took up his beer. Brock glanced at the title: *Night of Passion*, in a two-bit edition. Voss might have gained a better mind, but that didn't change him otherwise. He just didn't want to think.

'The people,' said Brock. 'Christ knows what they'll do.' He went over to the radio and turned it on and presently got a newscast. It didn't mean much to him; mostly it was about the new brain power, but the words were strung together in a way that didn't make a lot of sense. The voice sounded frightened, though.

After lunch, Brock decided to take a scout through the wood and see if he couldn't locate the pigs and find out what they were up to. They worried him more than he would admit. Pigs had always been smarter than most people knew. They might also get to thinking about the stores of feed kept on a farm watched by only two men.

Voss wasn't even asked to come; he'd have refused, and in any event it was wise to keep one man on guard at home. Brock and Joe went over the fence and into the six hundred acres of forest alone.

It was green and shadowy and full of rustling in there. Brock went quietly, a rifle under one arm, parting the underbrush before him with habitual ease. He saw no squirrels, though they were ordinarily plentiful. Well – they must have thought it out, the way crows had done long ago, and seen that a man with a gun was something to stay away from. He wondered how many eyes were watching him, and what was going on behind the eyes. Joe stuck close to his heels, not bounding on all sides as he normally did.

An overlooked branch slapped viciously at the man's face. He stood for an instant of creeping fear. Were the trees thinking too, now? Was the whole world going to rise in revolt?

No – After a moment he got control of himself and went stolidly on along the sheep trail. To be changed by this – whatever-it-was – a thing had to be able to think in the first place. Trees had no brains. He seemed to recall hearing once that insects didn't either, and made a note to check up on this. Good thing that Mr Rossman had a big library.

And a good thing, Brook realized, that he himself was steady. He had never gotten too excited about anything, and was taking the new order more calmly than seemed possible. One step at a time, that was it. Just go along from day to day, doing as much as he could to stay alive.

The thicket parted before him and a pig looked out. It was an old black boar, a big mean-looking creature which stood immovably in his path. The snouted face was a mask, but Brock had never seen anything so cold as its eyes. Joe bristled, growling, and Brock lifted the rifle. They stood that way for a long time, not moving. Then the boar grunted – it seemed contemptuous – and turned and slipped into the shadows. Brock realized that his body was wet.

He forced himself to go on for a couple of hours, ranging the wood but seeing little. When he came back, he was sunk in thought. The animals had changed, all right, but he had no way of telling how much, or what they would do next. Maybe nothing.

'I been thinking,' said Voss when he entered the cottage. 'Maybe we should move in with another farmer. Ralph Martinson needs extra help, now his hired man has quit.'

'I'm staying.'

Voss gave him a cool glance. 'Because you don't want to go back to being a moron, huh?'

Brock winced, but made his answer flat. 'Call it what you like.'

'I'm not going to stay here forever.'

'Nobody asked you to. Come on, it's about time for the milking.'

'Judas, what'll we do with the milk from thirty cows? The creamery truck ain't come around for three days.'

'Mmmmm – yeah – Well, I'll figger out something. Right now, we can't let 'em bust their teats.'

'Can't we just?' muttered Voss, but followed him out to the barn.

Milking thirty cows was a big job, even with a couple of machines to help. Brock decided to dry up most of them, but that would take some time, you had to taper them off gradually. Meanwhile they were restless and hard to control.

He came out and took a pitchfork and began throwing hay over the fence to the sheep, which had flocked in from the woods as usual. Halfway through the job, he was roused by Joe's wild yammer. He turned and saw the farm's enormous Holstein bull approaching.

He's loose! Brock's hand went to the pistol at his belt, then back to his fork. A popgun wasn't much use against such a monster. The bull snorted, pawing the ground and shaking his horn-cropped head.

'Okay, fella.' Brock went slowly towards him, wiping sandy lips with his tongue. The noise of his heart was loud in his ears. 'Okay, easy, back to the pen with yuh.'

Joe snarled, stiff-legged beside his master. The bull lowered his head and charged.

Brock braced himself. The giant before him seemed to fill the sky.

Brock stabbed under the jaw. It was a mistake, he realized wildly, he should have gone for the eyes. The fork ripped out of his hands and he felt a blow which knocked him to the ground. The bull ground his head against Brock's chest, trying to gore with horns that weren't there.

Suddenly he bellowed, a horror of pain in his voice. Joe had come behind him and fastened jaws in the right place. The bull turned, one hoof grating along Brock's ribs. The man got his gun out and fired from the ground. The bull began to run. Brock rolled over, scrambled to his feet, and sprang along-side the great head. He put the pistol behind one ear and fired. The bull stumbled, falling to his knees. Brock emptied the gun into his skull.

After that he collapsed on the body, whirling towards darkness.

He came to as Voss shook him.

'Are yuh hurt, Archie?' The words gibbered meaninglessly in his ears. 'Are you hurt?'

Brock let Voss lead him into the cottage. After a stiff drink he felt better and inspected himself. 'I'm all right,' he muttered. 'Bruises and cuts, no bones broke. I'm okay.'

'That settles it.' Voss was shaking worse than Brock. 'We're leaving here.'

The red head shook. 'No.'

'Are you crazy? Alone here, all the animals running wild, everything gone to hell – are you crazy?'

'I'm staying.'

'I'm not! I got half a mind to make you come along.'

Joe growled. 'Don't,' said Brock. He felt, suddenly, nothing but an immense weariness. 'You go if you want to, but leave me. I'll be all right.'

'Well –'

'I'll herd some of the stock over to Martinson's tomorrow, if he'll take 'em. I can handle the rest myself.'

Voss argued for a while longer, then gave up and took the jeep and drove away. Brock smiled without quite knowing why he did.

He checked the bull's pen. The gate had been broken down by a determined push. Half the power of fences had always lain in the fact that animals didn't know enough to keep shoving at them. Well, now they did, it seemed.

'I'll have to bury that fellow with a bulldozer,' said Brock. It was becoming more and more natural for him to speak aloud to Joe. 'Do it tomorrow. Let's have supper, boy, and then we'll read and play some music. We're alone from here on, I guess.'

CHAPTER SIX

A city was an organism, but Corinth had never appreciated its intricate and precarious equilibrium before. Now, with the balance gone, New York was sliding swiftly towards disruption and death.

Only a few subways were running, an emergency system manned by those devoted enough to stay by a job which had become altogether flat and distasteful. The stations were hollow and dark, filthy with unswept litter, and the shrieking of wheels held a tormented loneliness. Corinth walked to work, along dirty streets whose traffic had fallen to a reckless fragment of the old steady river.

Memory, five days old: *the roads jammed, a steel barricade ten miles long, honking and yelling till the high windows shivered, filling the air with exhaust fumes till men choked – blind panic, a mob fleeing a city they had decided was finished, flying from it at an estimated average speed of five miles an hour. Two cars had locked bumpers and the drivers got out and fought till their faces were bloody masks. Police helicopters had buzzed impotently overhead, like monster flies. It was saddening to know that multiplied intelligence had not quenched such an animal stampede.*

Those who remained – probably three-fourths of the city's dwellers – were still scraping along. Severely rationed gas, water, and electricity were being supplied. Food still trickled in from the country, though you had to take what you could get and pay exorbitantly. But it was like a pot, rumbling and seething and gathering itself to boil over.

Memory, three days old: *the second Harlem riot, when fear of the unknown and rage at ancient injustice had stood up to fight, for no reason except that untrained minds could not control their own new powers. The huge roar of burning tenements, giant red flames flapping against a windy night sky. The restless luminance like blood on a thousand dark faces, a thousand ill-clad bodies that stamped and swayed and struggled in the streets. A knife gleaming high and slaking itself in a human throat. A broken howling under the noise of fire. A scream as some woman went down and was stamped shapeless beneath a hundred running feet. The helicopters tossing and twisting in the storm of superheated air rushing up from the flames. And in the morning, empty streets, a haze of bitter smoke, a dim sobbing behind shuttered windows.*

Yes, still a thin tight-held semblance of order. Only – how long could it endure?

A tattered man with a ragged, new-looking beard was ranting on a street corner. Some dozen people stood around him, listening with a strange intensity. Corinth heard the words loud and harsh in the quiet: '– because we forgot the eternal principles of life, because we let the scientists betray us, because we all followed the eggheads. I tell you, it is life only that matters before the great Oneness in whom all are one and one are all. Behold, I bring you the word of the returned –'

His skin crawled, and he made a swift detour around that corner. Was it a missionary of the Third Ba'al cultists? He didn't know, and didn't feel like stopping to find out. Not a cop in sight to report it to. There was going to be real trouble if the new religion got many followers here in town. It gave him some comfort to see a woman entering the Catholic church nearby.

A taxi rounded a corner on two wheels, sideswiped a parked car, and was gone in a burst of noise. Another automobile crept slowly down the street, the driver tight-faced, his passenger holding a shotgun. Fear. The shops were boarded up on either side; one small grocery remained open, and its proprietor carried a pistol at his belt. In the dingy entrance to an apartment house, an old man sat reading Kant's *Critique* with a strange and frantic hunger which ignored the world around him.

'Mister, I haven't eaten for two days.'

Corinth looked at the shape which had slunk out of an alley. 'Sorry,' he answered. 'I've only got ten bucks on me. Barely enough for a meal at present prices.'

'Christ, I can't find work –'

'Go to City Hall, friend. They'll give you a job and see that you're fed. They need men badly.'

Scorn: 'That outfit? Sweeping streets, hauling garbage, trucking in food – I'd starve first!'

'Starve, then,' spat Corinth, and went on more swiftly.

The weight of the revolver dragging down his coat pocket was cheering. He had little sympathy for that type, after what he had seen.

Though could you expect anything different? You take a typical human, a worker in factory or office, his mind dulled to a collection of verbal reflexes, his future a day-to-day plodding which offered him no more than a chance to fill his belly and be anesthetized by a movie or his television – more and bigger automobiles, more and brighter plastics, onward and upward with the American Way of Life. Even before the change, there had been an inward hollowness in Western civilization, an unconscious realization that there ought to be more in life than one's own ephemeral self – and the ideal had not been forthcoming.

Then suddenly, almost overnight, human intelligence had exploded towards fantastic heights. An entire new cosmos opened before this man, visions, realizations, thought boiling unbidden within him. He saw the miserable inadequacy of his life, the triviality of his work, the narrow and meaningless limits of his beliefs and conventions – and he resigned.

Not everybody left, of course – not even the majority. But enough people did to throw the whole structure of technological civilization out of gear. If no more coal was being mined, then the makers of steel and of machines could not stay by their jobs even if they wanted to. Add to that the disturbances caused by emotions gone awry, and –

A naked woman walked down the street, carrying a market basket. She had set out to think for herself, Corinth imagined, and had decided that clothes in summer were ridiculous, and had taken advantage of the fact that the police had other worries to shed hers. No harm in that per se, but as a symptom it made him shiver. Any society was necessarily founded on certain more or less arbitrary rules and restrictions. Too many people had suddenly realized that the laws were arbitrary, without intrinsic significance, and had proceeded to violate whichever ones they didn't like.

A young man sat on a doorstep, his arms clasped about knees drawn up under his chin, rocking to and fro and whimpering softly. Corinth stopped. 'What's wrong?' he asked.

'Fear.' The eyes were bright and glazed. 'I suddenly realized it. I am alone.'

Corinth's mind leaped ahead to what he was going to say, but he heard out the panic-blurred words: 'All I know, all I am, is here, in my head. Everything exists for me only as I know it. And someday I'm going to die.' A line of spittle ran from one corner of his mouth. 'Someday the great darkness will come, I will not be – nothing will be! You may still exist, for you – though how can I tell that you aren't just a dream of mine? – but for me there will be nothing, nothing, nothing. I will never even have been.' The weak tears dribbled out of his eyes, and Corinth went on.

Insanity – yes, that had a lot to do with the collapse. There must be millions who had not been able to stand that sudden range and sharpness of comprehension. They hadn't been able to handle their new power, and it had driven them mad.

He shuddered in the hot still air.

The Institute was like a haven. When he walked in, a man sat on guard: submachine gun lying beside his chair, chemistry text on his lap. The face that lifted to Corinth's was serene. 'Hullo.'

'Had any trouble, Jim?'

'Not yet. But you can never tell, with all the prowlers and fanatics.'

Corinth nodded, feeling some of the clamminess leave him. There were still rational men who did not go kiting off after suddenly perceived stars, but stuck quietly to the immediate work.

The elevator attendant was a seven-year-old boy, son of a man in the Institute; schools were closed. 'Hi, sir,' he said cheerily. 'I been waiting for you. How on earth did Maxwell work out his equations?'

'Huh?' Corinth's eyes fell on a book lying on the seat. 'Oh, you've been studying radio, have you? Cadogan is pretty stiff to start out on, you should try reading –'

'I seen circuit diagrams, Mr Corinth. I wanna know why they work, only Cadogan here just gives the equations.'

Corinth referred him to a text on vector calculus. 'When you've been through that, come see me again.' He was smiling when he got off on the seventh floor, but his smile faded as he walked down the corridor.

Lewis was in his laboratory, waiting for him. 'Late,' he grunted.

'Sheila,' replied Corinth.

The conversation here was rapidly becoming a new language. When your mind was of quadrupled capability, a single word, a gesture of hand, a flicker of expression, could convey more to one who knew you and your mannerisms than whole paragraphs of grammatical English.

'You're late this morning,' Lewis had meant. 'Have any trouble?'

'I got started late because of Sheila,' Corinth had told him. 'She's not taking this well at all, Nat, frankly, I'm worried about her. Only what can I do? I don't understand human psychology any more, it's changing too much and too fast. Nobody does. We're all becoming strangers to each other – to ourselves – and it's frightening.'

Lewis's heavy body moved forward. 'Come on. Rossman's here and wants a confab with us.'

They went down the corridor, leaving Johansson and Grunewald immersed in their work; measuring the changed constants of nature, recalibrating instruments, performing all the enormous basic labour of science again from the ground up.

Throughout the building the other departments mapped out the altered faces of their own disciplines. Cybernetics, chemistry, biology, above all psychology – men grudged the time for sleep, there was so much to do.

The department heads were gathered around a long table in the main conference room. Rossman sat at its end, tall and thin and white-haired, no movement in his austere features. Helga Arnulfsen was at his right and Felix Mandelbaum at his left. For an instant Corinth wondered what the labour organizer was doing here, then realized that he must be representing the emergency city government.

'Good day, gentlemen.' Rossman went through the forms of Edwardian courtesy with a punctilio that would have been laughable if it were not so obviously a desperate effort to cling to something real and known. 'Please be seated.'

Everyone seemed to be here now for Rossman got directly to business:

'I have just returned from Washington. I have called you together because I feel that an exchange of ideas and information is urgently needed. You will feel better for knowing what I can give you of the overall picture, and I will certainly be happier for what scientific explanation you have found. Together we may be able to plan intelligently.'

'As for the explanation,' said Lewis, 'we've pretty well agreed here at the Institute that Dr Corinth's theory is the right one. This postulates a force-field of partly electromagnetic character, generated by gyromagnetic action within atomic nuclei near the centre of the galaxy. It radiates outward in a cone which, by the time it has reached our section of space, is many light-years across. Its effect has been to inhibit certain electromagnetic and electrochemical processes, among which the functioning of certain types of neurones is prominent. We suppose that the Solar System, in its orbit around galactic centre, entered this force-field many millions of years ago – hardly later than the Cretaceous. Doubtless many species of that time died out. However, life as a whole survived – adapted nervous systems compensated for the inhibiting force by becoming that much more efficient. In short, all life forms today are – or were, immediately before the change – about as intelligent as they would have been anyway.'

'I see,' nodded Rossman. 'And then the sun and its planets moved out of the force-field.'

'Yes. The field must have a rather sharp boundary, as such things go in astronomy, for the change took place within a few days. The fringe of the field – from the region of full intensity to the region of no effect at all – is perhaps only ten million miles wide. We're definitely out of it now; physical constants have remained stable for several days.'

'But our minds haven't,' said Mandelbaum bleakly.

'I know,' cut in Lewis. 'We'll come to that in a minute. The general effect of Earth's coming out of the inhibitor field was, of course, a sudden zooming of intelligence in every life form possessing a brain. Suddenly the damping force to which every living organism was adjusted, was gone.

'Naturally, the lack of that force has produced an enormous unbalance. Nervous systems have tended to run wild, trying to stabilize and function on a new level; that's why everybody felt so jumpy and frightened to begin with. The physical layout of the brain is adapted to one speed – one set of speeds, rather – or neurone signals; now suddenly the speed is increased while the physical structure remains the same. In plain language, it'll take us a while to get used to this.'

40

'Why aren't we dead?' asked Grahovitch, the chemist. 'I should think our hearts and so on would start working like mad.'

'The autonomic nervous system has been relatively little affected,' said Lewis. 'It seems to be a matter of cellular type; there are many different kinds of nerve cells, you know, and apparently only those in the cerebral cortex have reacted much to the change. Even there, the rate of functioning has not really gone up much – the factor is small – but apparently the processes involved in consciousness are so sensitive that it has made an enormous difference to what we call thought.'

'But we will survive?'

'Oh, yes, I'm sure no psychological damage will result – to most people, anyway. Some have gone insane, to be sure, but that's probably more for psychological than histological reasons.'

'And – will we enter another such force-field?' queried Rossman.

'Hardly,' said Corinth. 'On the basis of theory, I'm pretty sure there can only be one such, at most, in any galaxy. With the sun requiring some two hundred million years for its orbit around galactic centre – well, we should have more than half that period before we have to start worrying about getting stupid again.'

'M-hm. I see, gentlemen. Thank you very much.' Rossman leaned forward, clasping his thin fingers before him. 'Now as to what I have been able to find out, I fear it is not much, and that little is bad news. Washington is a madhouse. Many key men have already left their posts; it seems that there are more important things in life than administering Public Law Number Such and such –'

'Well, I'm afraid they're right,' grinned Lewis sardonically.

'No doubt. But let us face it, gentlemen; however little we may like the present system we cannot scrap it overnight.'

'What's the word from overseas?' asked Weller, the mathematician. 'How about Russia?'

'We'd be helpless against an armed attack.' said Rossman, 'but what military intelligence we have left indicates that the Soviet dictatorship is having troubles of its own.'

He sighed. 'First things first, gentlemen. We have no worry about our own breakdown. Washington grows more helpless every day: fewer and fewer people listen to the President's commands and appeals, less and less force is at his disposal. In many areas martial law has already been declared, but any attempt to enforce it would only mean civil war. Reorganization is going to have to be on a local basis. That is essentially the news I bring to you.'

'We've been working on it, here in New York,' said Mandelbaum. He looked tired, burned out by days and nights of unresting effort. 'I've got the unions pretty well into line by now. Arrangements will be made to bring in and distribute food, and we hope to get a volunteer militia to maintain some kind of order.'

He turned to Rossman. 'You're an able organizer. Your other interests, your business and your factories are going down the drain, and here's a job which has to be done. Will you help us?'

'Of course,' nodded the old man. 'And the Institute –'

'Will have to keep going. We've got to understand just what's happened and what we can expect in the near future. We've got to have a thousand things developed immediately if not sooner.'

The talk turned to organizational details. Corinth had little to say. He was too worried about Sheila. Last night she had woken up screaming.

CHAPTER SEVEN

Wato the witch doctor was tracing figures in the dust outside his thatch and muttering to himself. M'Wanzi heard him through the clank of weapons and the thick voices of the drums, as tall warriors passed back and forth. '– the law of similarity, that like causes like, may be expressed in the form ya or not-ya, thus showing that this form of magic obeys the rule of universal causality. But how to fit in the law of contagion –?'

M'Wanzi threw him an amused look as he strode by. Let the old man build his dusty dreams as he wished. The rifle on his shoulder was solid reality and enough for him. And it would be guns and not magic which fulfilled an ancient wish.

Free the black man! Drive the white oppressors back beyond the sea! Since his youth and the days of horror on the plantation, it had been his life. But only now –

Well, he had not been frightened by that which was happening within his soul, as the others were. He had seized this power to think with a swift fierce gladness, and his will had dominated whole tribes driven half-crazy with fear, ready to turn anywhere for the comfort of leadership. Over thousands of miles, from Congo jungle to the veldts of the south, men tormented and enslaved and spat upon had lifted weary faces to a message blown down the wind. Now was the time to strike, before the white man also rallied – the scheme was ready, lying in the soul of M'Wanzi the Elephant, the campaign was planned in a few flashing days, the subtle tongue won over leaders of a hundred conflicting groups, the army was stirring to life, now was the time to be free!

The drums talked around him as he went towards the edge of the jungle. He stepped through a wall of canebrake into the thick hot shadows of the forest. Another shadow moved down, flitted across the earth and waited grotesquely before him. Wise brown eyes regarded him with an inborn sadness.

'Have you gathered the brethren of the forest?' asked M'Wanzi.

'They come soon,' said the ape.

That had been M'Wanzi's great realization. All the rest, the organization, the planned campaign, that was nothing beside this: that if the souls of men had suddenly grown immensely bigger, so also the souls of animals must have grown. His guess had been confirmed by terrified stories of raids on farms made by elephants of demoniac cunning, but when those reports came he was already working out a common language of clicks and grunts with a captured chimpanzee. The apes had never been much less intelligent than man. M'Wanzi suspected. Today he could offer them much in exchange for their help; and were they not Africans too?

'My brother of the forest, go tell your people to make ready.'

'Not all of them wish this thing, brother of the fields. They must be beaten before they wish it. That takes time.'

'Time we have little of. Use the drums as I taught you. Send word throughout the land and let the hosts gather at the appointed places.'

'It shall be as you wish. When next the moon rises full, the children of the forest shall be there, and they shall be armed with knives and blowguns and assagais as you showed me.'

'Brother of the forest, you have gladdened my heart. Go with fortune and carry that word.'

The ape turned and swung lithely up a tree. A stray sunbeam gleamed off the rifle slung at his back.

Corinth sighed, yawned, and got up from his desk, shoving the papers away. He did not say anything aloud, but to his assistants, hunched over some testing apparatus, the meaning was clear: (To hell with it. I'm too tired to think straight any more. Going home.).

Johansson gestured with his hand, conveying as well as if he had spoken: (Think I'll stay here for a while, chief. This gimmick is shaping up nicely.). Grunewald added a curt nod.

Corinth fumbled automatically for a cigarette, but his pocket was empty. Smokes just weren't to be had these days. He hoped the world would get back on an operating basis soon, but it seemed less likely every day. What was happening outside the city? A few radio stations, professional and amateur, were maintaining a tenuous web of communications across western Europe, the Americas, and the Pacific, but the rest of the planet seemed to be swallowed by darkness – an occasional report of violence like lightning in the night, and then nothing.

Mandelbaum had warned him yesterday to be on his guard. Missionaries of the Third Ba'al were definitely known to have entered the city despite all precautions and were making converts right and left. The new religion seemed to be wholly orgiastic, with a murderous hatred for logic and science and rationality of all kinds – you could expect trouble.

Corinth went down hallways that were tunnels of dusk. Electricity must be conserved; only a few power stations were still operating, manned and guarded by volunteers. Elevator service ended at sunset, and he walked down seven flights to ground level. Loneliness oppressed him, and when he saw a light in Helga's office he paused, startled, and then knocked.

'Come in.'

He opened the door. She sat behind a littered desk, writing up some kind of manifest. The symbols she used were strange to him, probably her own invention and more efficient than the conventional ones. She still looked as severely handsome, but there was a deep weariness that paled her eyes.

'Hullo, Pete,' she said. The smile that twitched her mouth was tired, but it had warmth. 'How've you been?'

Corinth spoke two words and made three gestures; she filled in his intention from logic and her knowledge of his old speech habits: (Oh – all right. But you – I thought you'd been co-opted by Felix to help whip his new government into shape.).

(I have,) she implied. (But I feel more at home here, and it's just as good a place to do some of my work. Who've you got on my old job, by the way?)

(Billy Saunders – ten years of age, but a sharp kid. Maybe we should get a moron, though. The physical strain may be too much for a child.)

(I doubt it. There isn't much to do now, really. You boys co-operate pretty smoothly since the change – unlike the rest of the world!)

'I don't know if it's safe for you to come so far from where you live.' Corinth shifted awkwardly on his feet. 'Look, let me take you home.'

'Not necessary.' She spoke with a certain bite in her tones, and Corinth realized dully that she loved him.

And all our feelings have intensified. I never knew before how much of man's emotional life is bound up with his brain, how much more keenly he feels than any other animal.

'Sit down,' she invited, leaning back in her seat. 'Rest for a minute.'

He smiled wearily, lowering himself into a chair. 'Wish we had some beer,' he murmured. (It'd be like the old days.)

'The old days – the lost innocence. We'll always regret them, won't we? We'll always look back on our blindness with a wistful longing that the new generation simply won't understand.' She beat a clenched fist against the desk top, very softly. The light gleamed gold in her hair.

'How's your work coming along?' she asked after a moment. The silence hummed around them.

'Good enough. I've been in touch with Rhayader in England, over the short wave. They're having a tough time, but keeping alive. Some of their biochemists are working on yeasts, getting good results. By the end of the year they hope to be able to feed themselves adequately, if not very palatably as yet – food synthesis plants being built. He gave me some information that just about clinched the theory of the inhibitor field – how it's created. I've got Johansson and Grunewald at work on an apparatus to generate a similar field on a small scale; if they succeed, we'll know that our hypothesis is probably right. Then Nat can use the apparatus to study biological effects in detail. As for me, I'm going into the development of Rhayader's general relativity-cum-quantum mechanics – applying a new variation of communications theory, of all things, to help me out.'

'What's your purpose, other than curiosity?'

'Quite practical, I assure you. We may find a way to generate atomic energy from any material whatsoever, by direct nucleonic disintegration: no more fuel problems. We may even find a way to travel faster than light. The stars – well –'

'New worlds. Or we might return to the inhibitor field, out in space – why not? Go back to being stupid. Maybe we'll be happier that way. No, no, I realize you can't go home again.' Helga opened a drawer and took out a crumpled packet. 'Smoke?'

'Angel! How on earth did you manage that?'

'I have my ways.' She struck a match for him and lit her own cigarette with it. 'Efficient – yeah.'

They smoked in silence for a while, but the knowledge of each other's thoughts was like a pale flickering between them.

'You'd better let me see you home,' said Corinth. 'It's not safe out there. The prophet's mobs –'

'All right,' she said. 'Though I've got a car and you haven't.'

'It's only a few blocks from your place to mine, in a safe district.'

Since it was not possible as yet to patrol the entire sprawling city, the government had concentrated on certain key streets and areas.

Corinth took off his glasses and rubbed his eyes. 'I don't really understand it,' he said. 'Human relationships were never my long suit, and even now I can't quite – Well, why should this sudden upsurge of intelligence throw so many back to the animal stage? Why can't they see –'

'They don't want to.' Helga drew hard on her cigarette. 'Quite apart from those who've gone insane, and they're an important factor, there remains the necessity of not only having something to think with, but something to think about. You've taken millions – hundreds of millions – of people who've never had an original thought in their lives and suddenly thrown their brains into high gear. They start thinking – but what basis have they got? They still retain the old superstitions, prejudices, hates and fears and greeds, and most of their new mental energy goes to elaborate rationalization of these. Then someone like this Third Ba'al comes along and offers an anodyne to frightened and confused people; he tells them it's all right to throw off this terrible burden of thought and forget themselves in an emotional orgy. It won't last, Peter, but the transition is tough.'

'Yeah – hm – I had to get an I.Q. of 500 or so – whatever that means – to appreciate how little brains count for, after all. Nice thought.' Corinth grimaced and stubbed out his cigarette.

Helga shuffled her papers together and put them in a drawer. 'Shall we go?'

'Might as well. It's close to midnight. Sheila'll be worried, I'm afraid.'

They walked out through the deserted lobby, past the guards and into the street. A solitary lamp cast a dull puddle of luminance on Helga's car. She took the wheel and they purred quietly down an avenue of night.

'I wish –' Her voice out of darkness was thin. 'I wish I were out of this. Off in the mountains somewhere.'

He nodded, suddenly sick with his own need for open sky and the clean light of stars.

The mob was on them so fast that they had no time to escape. One moment they were driving down an empty way between blind walls, the next instant the ground seemed to vomit men. They came pouring from the side streets, quiet save for a murmur of voices and the shuffling of a thousand feet, and the few lamps gleamed off their eyes and teeth. Helga braked to a squealing halt as the surge went in front of them, cutting them off.

'Kill the scientists!' It hung like a riven cloud for a moment, one quavering scream which became a deep chanting. The living stream flowed around the car, veiled in shadow, and Corinth heard their breathing hot and hoarse in his ears.

Break their bones and burn their homes,
take their wimmin' the sons of sin,
wallow hollow an' open the door,
open an' let the Third Ba'al in!

A sheet of fire ran up behind the tall buildings, something was in flames. The light was like blood on the dripping head which someone lifted on a pole. They must have broken the line of the patrols, thought Corinth wildly, they must have smashed into this guarded region and meant to lay it waste before reinforcements came.

A face dirty and bearded and stinking shoved in through the driver's window. 'Uh woman! He got uh woman here!'

Corinth took the pistol from his coat pocket and fired. Briefly, he was aware of its kick and bark, the stinging of powder grains in his skin. The face hung there for an eternal time, dissolved into blood and smashed bone. Slowly it sagged, and the crowd screamed. The car rocked under their thrusts.

Corinth braced himself, shoving at his own door, jamming it open against the milling press of bodies. Someone clawed at his feet as he scrambled up on the hood. He kicked, feeling his shoe jar against teeth, and stood up. The firelight blazed in his face. He had taken off his glasses, without stopping to think why it was unsafe to be seen wearing them, and the fire and the crowd and the buildings were a shifting blur.

'Now hear me!' he shouted. 'Hear me, people of Ba'al!'

A bullet whanged past him, he felt its hornet buzz, but there was no time to be afraid. 'Hear the word of the Third Ba'al!'

'Let 'im talk!' It was a bawling somewhere out in that flowing, mumbling, unhuman river of shadows. 'Hear his word.'

'Lightning and thunder and rain of bombs!' yelled Corinth. 'Eat, drink, and be merry, for the end of the world is at hand! Can't you hear the planet cracking under your feet? The scientists have fired the big atomic bomb. We're on our way to kill them before the world breaks open like rotten fruit. Are you with us?'

They halted, muttering, shuffling their feet, uncertain of what they had found. Corinth went on, raving, hardly aware of what he was saying. '– kill and loot and steal the women! Break open the bottle shops! Fire, clean fire, let it burn the scientists who fired the big atomic bomb. This way, brothers! I know where they're hiding. Follow me!'

'Kill them!' The cheering grew, huge and obscene between the cliff walls of Manhattan. The head on the pole bobbed insanely, and firelight wavered off its teeth.

'Down there!' Corinth danced on the hood, gesturing towards Brooklyn. 'They're hiding there, people of Ba'al. I saw the big atomic bomb myself, with my own eyes I saw it, and I knew the end of the world was at hand. The Third Ba'al himself sent me to guide you. May his lightnings strike me dead if that ain't the truth!'

Helga blew her horn, an enormous echoing clamour that seemed to drive them into frenzy. Someone began capering, goat-like, and the others joined him, and the mob snakedanced down the street.

Corinth climbed to the ground, shaking uncontrollably. 'Follow 'em,' he gasped. 'They'll get suspicious if we don't follow 'em.'

'Sure thing, Pete.' Helga helped him inside and trailed the throng. Her headlights glared off their backs. Now and then she blew the horn to urge them on.

There was a whirring high in heaven. Corinth's breath whistled between his teeth. 'Let's go,' he mumbled.

Helga nodded, made a U-turn, and shot back down the avenue. Behind them, the mob scattered as police helicopters sprayed them with tear gas.

After a silent while, Helga halted before Corinth's place. 'Here we are,' she said.

'But I was going to see you home,' he said feebly.

'You did. Also you stopped those creatures from doing a lot of harm, to the district as well as us.' The vague light glimmered off her smile, it was shaky and tears lay in her eyes. 'That was wonderful, Pete. I didn't know you could do it.'

'Neither did I,' he said huskily.

'Maybe you missed your calling. More money in revivals, I'm told. Well –' She sat for a moment, then: 'Well, good night.'

'Good night,' he said.

She leaned forward, lips parted as if she were about to say something more. Then she clamped them shut, shook her head. The slamming of the door was loud and empty as she drove off.

Corinth stood looking after the car till it was out of sight. Then he turned slowly and entered his building.

CHAPTER EIGHT

Supplies were running low – food for himself, feed and salt for the animals left to him. There was no electricity, and he didn't like to use fuel in the gasoline lamp he had found. Brock decided that he would have to go to town.

'Stay here, Joe,' he said. 'I ought to be back soon.'

The dog nodded, an uncanny human gesture. He was picking up English fast; Brock had a habit of talking to him and had lately begun a deliberate programme of education. 'Keep an eye on things, Joe,' he said, looking uneasily to the edge of the woods.

He filled the tank of a battered green pickup from the estate's big drums, got in, and went down the driveway. It was a cool, hazy morning, the smell of rain was in the air and the horizon lay blurred. As he rattled down the county road, he thought that the countryside was utterly deserted. What was it – two months – since the change? Maybe there wouldn't be anyone in town at all.

Turning off on the paved state highway, he pushed the accelerator till the motor roared. He wasn't eager to visit normal humanity, and wanted to get it over with. His time alone had been peaceful – plenty of hard work, yes, to keep him busy; but when he wasn't too occupied or tired he was reading and thinking, exploring the possibilities of a mind which by now, he supposed, was that of a high-order genius by pre-change standards. He had settled down phlegmatically to an anchorite's life – there were worse fates – and didn't relish meeting the world again.

He had gone over to Martinson's, the neighbour's, a few days ago, but no one had been there, the place was boarded up and empty. It had given him such an eerie feeling that he hadn't tried anyone else.

A few outlying houses slid past, and then he was over the viaduct and into the town. There was no one in sight, but the houses looked occupied. The shops, though – most of them were closed, blind windows looked at him and he shivered.

He parked outside the A & P supermarket. It didn't look much like a store. The goods were there, but no price tags were shown and the man behind the counter did not have the air of a clerk. He was just sitting there, sitting and – thinking?

Brock went over to him, his feet curiously loud on the floor. 'Uh – excuse me,' he began, very softly.

The man looked up. Recognition flickered in his eyes and a brief smile crossed his face. 'Oh, hello, Archie,' he said, speaking with elaborate slowness. 'How are you?'

'All right, thanks,' Brock looked down at his shoes, unable to meet the quiet eyes. 'I, well, I came to buy some stuff.'

'Oh?' There was a coolness in the tone. 'I'm sorry, but we aren't running things on a money basis any more.'

'Well, I –' Brock squared his shoulders and forced himself to look up. 'Yeah, I can see that, I guess. The national government's broken down, ain't – hasn't it?'

'Not exactly. It has just stopped mattering, that is all.' The man shook his head. 'We had our troubles here at the beginning, but we reorganized on a rational basis. Now things are going pretty smoothly. We still lack items we could get from outside, but we can keep going indefinitely as we are, if necessary.'

'A – socialist economy?'

'Well, Archie,' said the man, 'that's hardly the right label for it, since socialism was still founded on the idea of property. But what does ownership of a thing actually mean? It means only that you may do just what you choose with the thing. By that definition, there was very little complete ownership anywhere in the world. It was more a question of symbolism. A man said to himself, "This is my home, my land," and got a feeling of strength and security; because the "my" was a symbol for that state of being, and he reacted to the symbol. Now – well – we have seen through that bit of self-deception. It served its purpose before, it made for self-respect and emotional balance, but we don't need it anymore. There's no longer any reason for binding oneself to a particular bit of soil when the economic function it served can be carried out more efficiently in other ways. So most of the farmers hereabouts have moved into town, taking over houses which were deserted by those who chose to move away from the neighbourhood altogether.'

'And you work the land in common?'

'Hardly the correct way to phrase it. Some of the mechanically minded have been devising machines to do most of this for us. It's amazing what can be done with a tractor engine and some junk yard scrap if you have the brains to put it together in the right way.

'We've found our level, for the time being at least. Those who didn't like it have gone, for the most part, and the rest are busy evolving new social reforms to match our new personalities. It's a pretty well-balanced setup here.'

'But what do you do?'

'I'm afraid,' said the man gently, 'that I couldn't explain it to you.'

Brock looked away again. 'Well,' he said finally, his voice oddly husky, 'I'm all alone on the Rossman place and running short on supplies. Also I'm gonna need help with the harvest and so on. How about it?'

'If you wish to enter our society, I'm sure a place can be found.'

'No – I just want –'

'I would strongly advise you to throw in with us, Archie. You'll need the backing of a community. It isn't safe out there any more. There was a circus near here, about the time of the change, and the wild animals escaped and several of them are still running loose.'

Brock felt a coldness within himself. 'That must have been – exciting,' he said slowly.

'It was.' The man smiled thinly. 'We didn't know at first, you see; we had too much of our own to worry about, and it didn't occur to us till too late that the animals were changing too. One of them must have nosed open his own cage and let out the others to cover his escape. There was a tiger hanging around town for weeks, it took a couple of children and we never did hunt it down – it just was gone one day. Where? What about the elephants and – No, you aren't safe alone, Archie.' He paused. 'And then there's the sheer physical labour. You'd better take a place in our community.'

'Place, hell!' There was a sudden anger in him, bleak and bitter. 'All I want is a little help. You can take a share of the crop to pay for it. Wouldn't be any trouble to you if you have these fancy new machines.'

'You can ask the others,' said the man. 'I'm not really in charge. The final decision would rest with the Council and the Societist. But I'm afraid it would be all or nothing for you, Archie. We won't bother you if you don't want us to, but you can't expect us to give you charity either. That's another outmoded symbol. If you want to fit yourself into the total economy – it's not tyrannical by any means, it's freer than any other the world has ever seen – we'll make a function for you.'

'In short,' said Brock thickly, 'I can be a domestic animal and do what chores I'm given, or a wild one and ignored. For *my* sake – huh!' He turned on his heel. 'Take it and stick it.'

He was trembling as he walked out and got back into the truck. The worst of it, he thought savagely, the worst of it was that they were right. He couldn't long endure a half-in-half-out pariah status. It had been all right once, being feeble-minded; he didn't know enough then to realize what it meant. Now he did, and the dependent life would break him.

The gears screamed as he started. He'd make out without their help, damn if he wouldn't. If he couldn't be a half-tamed beggar, and wouldn't be a house pet, all right, he'd be a wild animal.

He drove back at a reckless speed. On the way, he noticed a machine out in a hayfield: a big enigmatic thing of flashing arms, doing the whole job with a single bored-looking man to guide it. They'd probably build a robot pilot as soon as they could get the materials. So what? He still had two hands.

Further along, a patch of woods came down to the edge of the road. He thought he glimpsed something in there, a great grey shape which moved quietly back out of sight, but he couldn't be sure.

His calm temperament reasserted itself as he neared the estate, and he settled down to figuring. From the cows he could get milk and butter, maybe cheese. The few hens he had been able to recapture would furnish eggs. An occasional slaughtered sheep – no, wait, why not hunt down some of those damned pigs instead? – would give him meat for quite a while; there was a smokehouse on the place. He could harvest enough hay, grain and corn – Tom and Jerry would just have to work! – to keep going through the winter; if he improvised a quern, he could grind a coarse flour and bake his own bread. There were plenty of clothes, shoes, tools. Salt was his major problem – but there ought to be a lick somewhere within a hundred miles or so, he could try to look up where and make a trip to it – and he'd have to save on gasoline and cut a lot of wood for winter, but he thought he could pull through. One way or another, he would.

The magnitude of the task appalled him. One man! One pair of hands! But it had been done before, the whole human race had come up the hard way. If he took a cut in his standard of living and ate an unbalanced diet for a while, it wouldn't kill him.

And he had a brain which by pre-change measures was something extraordinary. Already, he had put that mind to work: first devising a schedule of operations for the next year or so, and secondarily inventing gadgets to make survival easier. Sure – he could do it.

He squared his shoulders and pushed down the accelerator, anxious to get home and begin.

The noise as he entered the driveway was shattering. He heard the grunts and squeals and breaking of wood, and the truck lurched with his panicky jerk at the wheel. *The pigs!* he thought. *The pigs had been watching and had seen him go –*

And he had forgotten his gun.

He cursed and came roaring up the drive, past the house and into the farmyard. There was havoc. The pigs were like small black and white tanks, chuffing and grunting. The barn door was burst open and they were in the stored feed bags, ripping them open, wallowing in the floury stuff, some of them dragging whole sacks out into the woods. There was a bull too, he must have run wild, he snorted and bellowed as he saw the man, and the cows were bawling around, they had broken down their pasture fence and gone to him. Two dead sheep, trampled and ripped, lay in the yard, the rest must have fled in terror. And Joe –

'Joe,' called Brock. 'Where are yuh, boy?'

It was raining a little, a fine misty downpour which blurred the woods and mingled with the blood on the earth. The old boar looked shiny as iron in the wetness. He lifted his head when the truck came and squealed.

Brock drove straight for him. The truck was his only weapon now. The boar scampered aside and Brock pulled up in front of the barn. At once the pigs closed in, battering at the wheels and sides, grunting their hate of him. The bull lowered his head and pawed the ground.

Joe barked wildly from the top of a brooder house. He was bleeding, it had been a cruel fight, but he had somehow managed to scramble up there and save himself.

Brock backed the truck, swinging it around and driving into the flock. They scattered before him, he couldn't get up enough speed in this narrow place to hit them and they weren't yielding. The bull charged.

There wasn't time to be afraid, but Brock saw death. He swung the truck about, careening across the yard, and the bull met him head on. Brock felt a giant's hand throw him against the windshield.

Ragged darkness parted before his eyes. The bull was staggering, still on his feet, but the truck was dead. The pigs seemed to realize it and swarmed triumphantly to surround the man.

He fumbled, crouched in the cab and lifting the seat. A long-handled wrench was there, comfortingly heavy. 'All right,' he mumbled. 'Come an' get me.'

Something loomed out of the woods and mist. It was grey, enormous, reaching for the sky. The bull lifted his dazed head and snorted. The pigs stopped their battering attack and for a moment there was silence.

A shotgun blast ripped like thunder. The old boar was suddenly galloping in circles, wild with pain. Another explosion sent the bull crazy, turning on his heels and making for the woods.

An elephant, gibbered Brock's mind, *an elephant come to help.*

The big grey shape moved slowly in on the pigs. They milled uneasily, their eyes full of hate and terror. The boar fell to the ground and lay gasping out his life. The elephant curled up its trunk and broke into an oddly graceful run. And the pigs fled.

Brock was still for minutes, shaking too badly to move. When he finally climbed out, the wrench hanging loosely on one hand, the elephant had gone over to the haystack and was calmly stuffing his gullet. And two small hairy shapes squatted on the ground before the man.

Joe barked feebly and limped over to his master. 'Quiet, boy,' mumbled Brock. He stood on strengthless legs and looked into the wizened brown face of the chimpanzee who had the shotgun.

'Okay,' he said at last. The fine cold rain was chilly on his sweating face. 'Okay, you're the boss just now. What do you want?'

The chimpanzee regarded him for a long time. It was a male, he saw, the other was a female, and he remembered reading that the tropical apes couldn't stand a northern climate very well. These must be from that circus which the man in the store had spoken of, he thought, they must have stolen the gun and taken – or made a bargain with? – the elephant. Now –

The chimpanzee shuddered. Then, very slowly, always watching the human, he laid down the gun and went over and tugged at Brock's jacket.

'Do you understand me?' asked the man. He felt too tired to appreciate how fantastic a scene this was. 'You know English?'

There was no answer, except that the ape kept pulling at his clothes, not hard, but with a kind of insistence. After a while, one long-fingered hand pointed from the jacket to himself and his mate.

'Well,' said Brock softly, 'I think I get it. You're afraid and you need human help, only you don't want to go back to sitting in a cage. Is that it?'

No answer. But something in the wild eyes pleaded with him.

'Well,' said Brock, 'you came along in time to do me a good turn, and you ain't killing me now when you could just as easy do it.' He took a deep breath. 'And God knows I could use some help on this place, you two and your elephant might make all the difference. And – and – okay. Sure.'

He took off the jacket and gave it to the chimpanzee. The ape chattered softly and slipped it on. It didn't fit very well, and Brock had to laugh.

Then he straightened his bent shoulders. 'All right. Fine. We'll all be wild animals together. Okay? Come along into the house and get something to eat.'

CHAPTER NINE

Vladimir Ivanovitch Panyushkin stood under the trees, letting the rain drip onto his helmet and run off the shoulders of his coat. It was a good coat, he had taken it off a colonel after the last battle, it shed water like a very duck. The fact that his feet squelched in worn-out boots did not matter.

Vision swept down the hill, past the edge of forest and into the valley, and there the rain cut it off. Nothing stirred that he could see nothing but the steady wash of rain and he could hear nothing except its hollow sound. But the instrument said there was a Red Army unit in the neighbourhood.

He looked at the instrument where it lay cradled in the priest's hands. Its needle was blurred with the rain that runnelled across the glass dial, but he could see it dance. He did not understand the thing – the priest had made it, out of a captured radio – but it had given warning before.

'I would say they are some ten kilometres off, Vladimir Ivanovitch.' The priest's beard waggled when he spoke. It was matted with rain and hung stiffly across his coarse robe. 'They are circling about, not approaching us. Perhaps God is misleading them.'

Panyushkin shrugged. He was a materialist himself. But if the man of God was willing to help him against the Soviet government, he was glad to accept that help. 'And perhaps they have other plans,' he answered. 'I think we had best consult Fyodor Alexandrovitch.'

'It is not good for him to be used so much, my son,' said the priest. 'He is very tired.'

'So are we all, my friend.' Panyushkin's words were toneless. 'But this is a key operation. If we can cut across to Kirovograd, we can isolate the Ukraine from the rest of the country. Then the Ukrainian nationalists can rise with hope of success.'

He whistled softly, a few notes with a large meaning. Music could be made a language. The whole uprising, throughout the Soviet empire, depended in part on secret languages made up overnight.

The Sensitive came out of the dripping brush which concealed Panyushkin's troops. He was small for his fourteen years, and there was a blankness behind his eyes. The priest noted the hectic flush in his cheeks and crossed himself, murmuring a prayer for the boy. It was saddening to use him so hard. But if the godless men were to be overthrown at all, it would have to be soon, and the Sensitives were necessary. They were the untappable, unjammable, undetectable link which tied together angry men from Riga to Vladivostok; the best of them were spies such as no army had ever owned before. But there were still many who stood by the masters, for reasons of loyalty or fear or self-interest, and they had most of the weapons. Therefore a whole new concept of war had to be invented by the rebels.

A people may loathe their government, but endure it because they know those who protest will die. But if all the people can be joined together, to act at once – or, most of them, simply to disobey with a deadly kind of peacefulness – the government can only shoot a few. Cut off from its own strong roots, the land and the folk, a government is vulnerable and less than a million armed men may be sufficient to destroy it.

'There is a Red Star,' said Panyushkin, pointing out into the rain. 'Can you tell what they plan, Fyodor Alexandrovitch?'

The boy sat down on the running, sopping hillside and closed his eyes. Panyushkin watched him somberly. It was hard enough being a link with ten thousand other Sensitives across half a continent. Reaching for unlike minds would strain him close to the limit. But it had to be done.

'There is – they know us.' The boy's voice seemed to come from very far away. 'They – have – instruments. Their metal smells us. They – no, it is death! They send death!' He opened his eyes, sucked in a sharp gasp, and fainted. The priest knelt to take him up and cast Panyushkin a reproachful look.

'Guided missiles!' The leader whirled on his heel. 'So they *do* have detectors like ours now. Good thing we checked, eh, priest? Now let us get away from here before the rockets come!'

He left enough metallic stuff behind to fool the instruments, and led his men along the ridge of hills. While the army was busy firing rockets on his camp, he would be readying an attack on their rear.

With or without the help of the priest's incomprehensible God, he felt quite sure that the attack would succeed.

Felix Mandelbaum had hardly settled into his chair when the annunciator spoke. 'Gantry.' The secretary's tone of voice said that it was important.

Gantry – he didn't know anybody of that name. He sighed and looked out the windows. Morning shadow still lay cool across the streets, but it was going to be a hot day.

There was a tank squatting on its treads down there, guns out to guard the City Hall. The worst of the violence seemed to have passed: the Third Ba'al cult was falling apart rapidly after the prophet's ignominious capture last week, the criminal gangs were being dealt with as the militia grew in size and experience, a measure of calm was returning to the city. But there was no telling what still prowled the outer districts, and there were surely going to be other storms before everything was finally under control.

Mandelbaum sat back in his chair, forcing tensed muscles to relax. He always felt tired these days, under the thin hard-held surface of energy. Too much to do, too little time for sleep. He pushed the buzzer which signalled: Let him in.

Gantry was a tall raw-boned man whose good clothes did not quite fit him. There was an upstate twang in the ill-tempered voice: 'They tell me you're the dictator of the city now.'

'Not exactly,' said Mandelbaum, smiling. 'I'm just a sort of general trouble shooter for the mayor and the council.'

'Yeah. But when there's nothing but trouble, the trouble shooter gets to be boss.' There was a truculence in the swift reply. Mandelbaum didn't try to deny the charges, it was true enough. The mayor had all he could do handling ordinary administrative machinery; Mandelbaum was the flexible man, the coordinator of a thousand quarrelling elements, the maker of basic policy, and the newly created city council rarely failed to vote as he suggested.

'Sit down,' he invited. 'What's your trouble?' His racing mind already knew the answer, but he gained time by making the other spell it out for him.

'I represent the truck farmers of eight counties. I was sent here to ask what your people mean by robbing us.'

'Robbing?' asked Mandelbaum innocently.

'You know as well as I do. When we wouldn't take dollars for our stuff they tried to give us city scrip. And when we wouldn't take that, they said they'd seize our crops.'

'I know,' said Mandelbaum. 'Some of the boys are pretty tactless. I'm sorry.'

Gantry's eyes narrowed. 'Are you ready to say they won't pull guns on us? I hope so, because we got guns of our own.'

'Have you got tanks and planes too?' asked Mandelbaum. He waited an instant for the meaning to sink in, then went on swiftly: 'Look, Mr Gantry, there are six or seven million people left in this city. If we can't assure them a regular food supply, they'll starve. Can your association stand by and let seven million innocent men, women, and children die of hunger while you sit on more food than you can eat? No. You're decent human beings. You couldn't.'

'I don't know,' said Gantry grimly. 'After what that mob did when it came stampeding out of the city last month –'

'Believe me, the city government did everything it could to stop them. We failed in part, the panic was too big, but we did keep the whole city from moving out on you.' Mandelbaum made a bridge of his fingers and said judicially: 'Now if you really were monsters you'd let the rest of them stay here to die. Only they wouldn't. Sooner or later, they'd all swarm out on you, and then everything would go under.'

'Sure. Sure.' Gantry twisted his large red hands together. Somehow, he found himself on the defensive. 'It ain't that we want to make trouble out in the country. It's just – well, we raise food for you, but you ain't paying us. You're just taking it. Your scrip don't mean a thing. What can we buy with it?'

'Nothing, now,' said Mandelbaum candidly. 'But believe me, it's not our fault. The people here want to work. We just haven't got things organized enough yet. Once we do, our scrip will mean things like clothes and machinery for you. If you let us starve, though – where's your market then?'

'All that was said at the association meeting,' replied Gantry. 'The thing is, what guarantee have we got that you'll keep your end of the bargain?'

'Look, Mr Gantry, we do want to co-operate. We want it so much that we're prepared to offer a representative of your people a seat on the city council. Then how can we double-cross you?'

'Hmmm –' Gantry's eyes narrowed shrewdly. 'How many members on the council all told?'

They bargained for a while, and Gantry left with a city offer of four seats which would hold special veto powers on certain matters concerning rural policy. Mandelbaum was sure the farmers would accept it: it looked like a distinct victory for their side.

He grinned to himself. How do you define victory? The veto power wouldn't mean a thing because rural policy was perfectly straightforward anyway. The city, the whole state and nation, would gain by the reunification of so large an area. Perhaps the piled-up debt to the farmers would never be paid – society was changing so rapidly that there might be no more cities in a few years – but that, however lamentable, was a small matter. What counted now was survival.

'North and Morgan,' said the annunciator.

Mandelbaum braced himself. This was going to be tougher. The waterfront boss and the crazy political theorist had their own ambitions, and considerable followings – too large to be put down by force. He stood up politely to greet them.

North was a burly man, his face hard under its layers of fat; Morgan was slighter physically, but his eyes smouldered under the high bald forehead. They glared at each other as they came in, and looked accusingly at Mandelbaum. North growled their mutual question: 'What's the idea bringing us in at the same time? I wanted to see you in private.'

'Sorry,' said Mandelbaum insincerely. 'There must have been a mix-up.

Would you mind both just sitting down for a few minutes, though? Maybe we can work it out together somehow.'

'There is no "somehow" about it,' snapped Morgan. 'I and my followers are getting sick of seeing the obvious principles of Dynapsychism ignored in this government. I warn you, unless you reorganize soon along sensible lines –'

North brushed him aside and turned to Mandelbaum.

'Look here, there're close to a hundred ships layin' idle in the port of New York while th' East Coast and Europe're yellin' for trade. My boys're gettin' fed up with havin' their voice go unheard.'

'We haven't had much word from Europe lately,' said Mandelbaum in apologetic tone. 'And things are too mixed up yet for us even to try coastwise trading. What'd we trade with? Where'd we find fuel for those ships? I'm sorry, but –' His mind went on: *The real trouble is, your racket hasn't got any waterfront to live off now.*

'It all comes from blind stubbornness,' declared Morgan. 'As I have conclusively shown, a social integration along the psychological principles I have discovered would eliminate –'

And your trouble is, you want power, and too many people are still hunting a panacea, a final answer, thought Mandelbaum coldly. *You sound intellectual, so they think you are; a certain class still wants a man on a white horse, but prefers him with a textbook under one arm. You and Lenin!*

'Excuse me,' he said aloud. 'What do you propose to do, Mr North?'

'New York started as a port an' it'll be a port again before long. This time we wanna see that the workers that make the port go, get their fair share in governin' it!'

In other words, you also want to be dictator. Aloud, thoughtfully: 'There may be something in what you both say. But we can't do everything at once, you know. It seems to me, though, like you two gentlemen are thinking along pretty parallel lines. Why don't you get together and present a united front? Then I'd find it a lot easier to put your proposals before the council.'

Morgan's pale cheeks flushed. 'A band of sweaty human machines –'

North's big fists doubled. 'Watch y'r langwidge, sonny boy.'

'No, really,' said Mandelbaum. 'You both want a better integrated government, don't you? It seems to me –'

Hmmm. The same thought lit the two pairs of eyes. It had been shockingly easy to plant it. *Together, perhaps, we could … and then afterward I can get rid of him –*

There was more discussion, but it ended with North and Morgan going out together. Mandelbaum could almost read their contempt for him; hadn't he ever heard of divide and rule?

Briefly, there was sadness in him. So far, people hadn't really changed much. The wild-eyed dreamer simply built higher castles in the clouds; the hard-boiled racketeer had no vocabulary of ideas or concepts to rise above his own language of greed.

It wouldn't last. Within months, there would be no more Norths and no more Morgans. The change in themselves, and in all mankind, would destroy their littleness. But meanwhile, they were dangerous animals and had to be dealt with.

He reached for the phone and called over the web operated for him alone. 'Hullo, Bowers? How're you doing? – Look, I've got the Dynapsychist and the rackets boss together. They'll probably plan a sort of fake Popular Front, with the idea of getting seats on the council and then taking over the whole show by force – palace revolution, *coup d'état*, whatever you call it. – Yeh. Alert our agents in both parties. I'll want complete reports. Then we want to use those agents to egg them on against each other. – Yeah, the alliance is as unstable as any I ever heard of. A little careful pushing, and they'll bury the hatchet all right – in each other. Then when the militia has mopped up what's left of the tong war, we can start our propaganda campaign in favour of common sense. – Sure, it'll take some tricky timing, but we can swing it –'

For a moment, as he laid the phone down, his face sagged with an old grief. He had just condemned some scores of people, most of whom were merely bewildered and misled, to death. But it couldn't be helped. He had the life and freedom of several million human beings to save – the price was not exorbitant.

'Uneasy sits the butt that bears the boss,' he muttered, and looked at his appointment list. There was an hour yet before the representative from Albany arrived. That was going to be a hot one to handle. The city was breaking state and national laws every day – it had to – and the governor was outraged. He wanted to bring the whole state back under his own authority. It wasn't an unreasonable wish, but the times weren't ripe; and when they eventually were, the old forms of government would be no more important than the difference between Homoousian and Homoiousian. But it was going to take a lot of argument to convince the Albany man of that.

Meanwhile, though he had an hour free. He hesitated for a split second between working on the new rationing system and on the plans for extending law and order to outer Jersey. Then he laid both aside in favour of the latest report on the water situation.

CHAPTER TEN

There was a dimness in the laboratory which made the pulsing light at the machine's heart stand out all the brighter, weirdly blue and restless between the coils and the impassive meter faces. Grunewald's face was corpse-coloured as he bent over it.

'Well,' he said unnecessarily, 'that seems to be that.'

He flicked the main switch, and the electric hum whined and the light died. For a moment he stood thoughtfully regarding the anesthetized rat within the coils. Hairlike wires ran from its shaven body to the meters over which Johansson and Lewis stood.

Lewis nodded. 'Neural rate jumps up again.' He touched the dials of the oscilloscope with finicking care. 'And just about on the curve we predicted. You've generated an inhibitor field, all right.' There would be other tests to make, detailed study, but that could be left to assistants. The main problem was solved.

Grunewald reached in with thick, oddly delicate hands and took out the rat and began extracting the probes. 'Poor little guy,' he murmured. 'I wonder if we're doing him a favour.'

Corinth, hunched moodily on a stool, looked up sharply.

'What use is intelligence to him?' pursued Grunewald. 'It just makes him realize the horror of his own position. What use is it to any of us, in fact?'

'Would you go back, yourself?' asked Corinth.

'Yes.' Grunewald's square blond face held a sudden defiance. 'Yes, I would. It's not good to think too much or too clearly.'

'Maybe,' whispered Corinth, 'maybe you've got something there. The new civilization – not merely its technology, but its whole value system, all its dreams and hopes – will have to be built afresh, and that will take many generations. We're savages now, with all the barrenness of the savage's existence. Science isn't the whole of life.'

'No,' said Lewis. 'But scientists – like artists of all kinds, I suppose – have by and large kept their sanity through the change because they had a purpose in life to start with, something outside themselves to which they could give all they had.' His plump face flashed with a tomcat grin. 'Also, Pete, as an old sensualist I'm charmed with all the new possibilities. The art and music I used to swoon over have gone, yes, but I don't appreciate good wine and cuisine the less; in fact, my perception is heightened, there are nuances I never suspected before.'

It had been a strange conversation, one of a few words and many gestures and facial expressions thrown into a simultaneous discussion of technical problems:

'Well,' Johansson had said, 'we've got our inhibitor field. Now it's up to you neurologists to study it in detail and find out just what we can expect to happen to life on Earth.'

'Uh-huh,' said Lewis. 'I'm not working on that just now, though, except as a kibitzer. Bronzini and MacAndrews can handle it. I'm co-opting myself into the psychological department, which is not only more interesting but of more immediate practical importance. I'll handle the neurological-cybernetic aspect of their work.'

'Our old psychology is almost useless,' nodded Corinth. 'We're changing too much to understand our own motivations any more. Why am I spending most of my time here, when maybe I should be home helping Sheila face her adjustment? I just can't help myself, I have to explore this new field, but – To start afresh, on a rational basis, we'll have to know something about the dynamics of man – As for me, I'm off this baby too, now that we've actually succeeded in generating a field. Rossman wants me to work on his spaceship project as soon as he can get it organized.'

'Spaceship – faster-than-light travel, eh?'

'That's right. The principle uses an aspect of wave mechanics which wasn't suspected before the change. We'll generate a psi wave which – Never mind, I'll explain it to you when you've gotten around to learning tensor analysis and matrix algebra. I'm collaborating with some others here in drawing up plans for the thing, while we wait for the men and materials to start building. We should be able to go *anywhere* in the galaxy once we've got the ship.'

The two threads coalesced: 'Running away from ourselves,' said Grunewald. 'Running into space itself to escape.' For a moment the four men were silent, thinking.

Corinth got to his feet. 'I'm going home,' he said harshly.

His mind was a labyrinth of interweaving thought chains as he went down the stairs. Mostly he was thinking of Sheila, but something whispered of Helga too, and there was a flow of diagrams and equations, a vision of chill immensity through which the Earth spun like a bit of dust. An oddly detached part of himself was coolly studying that web of thought, so that he could learn how it worked and train himself to handle his own potentialities.

Language: The men of the Institute, who knew each other, were involuntarily developing a new set of communication symbols, a subtle and powerful thing in which every gesture had meaning and the speeding brain of the listener, without conscious effort, filled in the gaps and grasped the many-levelled meaning. It was almost too efficient, you *gave* your inmost self away. The man of the future would likely go naked in soul as well as in body, and Corinth wasn't sure he liked the prospect.

But then there was Sheila and himself; their mutual understanding made their talk unintelligible to an outsider. And there were a thousand, a million groups throughout the world, creating their own dialects on a basis of past experience which had not been shared with all humanity. Some arbitrary language for the whole world would have to be devised.

Telepathy? There could no longer be any doubt that it existed, in some people at least. Extrasensory perception would have to be investigated when things had quieted down. There was so much to do, and life was so terribly short!

Corinth shivered. Fear of personal extinction was supposed to be an adolescent reaction; but in a sense, all men were adolescents once more, on a new plane – no, children, babies.

Well, no doubt the biologists would within the next few years find some means of lengthening the lifespan, prolonging it for centuries perhaps. But was that ultimately desirable?

He came out on the street and located the automobile Rossman had provided for him. *At least,* he thought wryly as he entered it, *the parking problem has been solved. No more traffic like there once was.*

Eventually, no more New York. Big cities had no real economic justification. He came from a small town, and he had always loved mountains and forests and sea. Still, there was something about this brawling, frenetic, overcrowded, hard, inhuman, magnificent city whose absence would leave an empty spot in the world to come.

It was a hot night. His shirt stuck clammily to him, and the air seemed thick. Overhead, between the darkened buildings and the dead neon signs, heat lightning flickered palely and all the earth yearned for rain. His headlights cut a dull swath through the gummy blackness.

There were more cars abroad than there had been even a week ago. The city was just about tamed now; the gang war between Portmen and Dynapsychists, suppressed two weeks back, seemed to have been the last flare of violence. Rations were still short, but people were being put to work again and they'd all live.

Corinth pulled up in the parking lot behind his apartment and walked around to the front. The power ration authority had lately permitted this building to resume elevator service, which was a mercy. He hadn't enjoyed climbing fifteen flights when electricity was really short.

I *hope* – He was thinking of Sheila, but he left the thought unfinished. She'd been getting thin, poor kid, and she didn't sleep well and sometimes she woke with a dry scream in her throat and groped blindly for him. He wished his work didn't take him away from her. She needed companionship badly. Maybe he could get her some kind of job to fill the hours.

When he came out on his floor, the hall was darkened save for a vague night light, but radiance streamed under his door. Glancing at his watch, he saw that it was later than her usual bedtime. So she couldn't sleep tonight, either.

He tried the door, but it was locked and he rapped. He thought he heard a smothered scream from within, and knocked harder. She opened the door so violently that he almost fell inside.

'Pete, Pete, Pete!' She pressed herself to him with a shudder. With his arms about her, he felt how close the delicate ribs lay to her skin. The lamplight was harsh, filling the room, and oddly lustreless on her hair. When she lifted her face, he saw that it was wet.

'What's the matter?' he asked. He spoke aloud, in the old manner, and his voice was suddenly wavering.

'Nerves.' She drew him inside and closed the door. In a nightgown and bathrobe she looked pathetically young, but there was something ancient in her eyes.

'Hot night to be wearing a robe,' he said, groping for expression.

'I feel cold.' Her lips trembled.

His own mouth fell into a harsh line, and he sat down in an easy chair and pulled her to his lap. She laid her arms about him, hugging him to her, and he felt the shiver in her body.

'This is not good,' he said. 'This is the worst attack you've had yet.'

'I don't know what I'd have done if you'd been much longer about coming,' she said tonelessly.

They began to talk then, in the new interweaving of word and gesture, tone and silence and shared remembering, which was peculiarly theirs.

'I've been thinking too much,' she told him. 'We all think too much these days.' (Help me, my dearest! I am going down in darkness and only you can rescue me.)

'You'll have to get used to it,' he answered dully. (How can I help? My hands reach for you and close on emptiness.)

'You have strength –' she cried. 'Give it to me!' (Nightmares each time I try to sleep. Waking, I see the world and man as a flickering in cold and nothingness, empty out to the edge of forever. I can't endure that vision.)

Weariness, hopelessness: 'I'm not strong,' he said. 'I just keep going somehow. So must you.'

'Hold me close, Pete,' *Father image*, 'hold me close,' she whimpered. Pressing to him as if he were a shield against the blackness outside and the darkness within and the things rising through it: 'Don't ever let me go!'

'Sheila,' he said. (Beloved: wife, mistress, comrade.) 'Sheila, you've got to hang on. All this is just an increased power to think – to visualize, to handle data and the dreams yourself have created. Nothing more.'

'But it is changing *me!*' The horror of death was in her now. She fought it with something like wistfulness: '– and where has our world gone? Where are our hopes and plans and togetherness?'

'We can't bring them back,' he replied. Emptiness, irrevocability: 'We have to make out with what we have now.'

'I know, I know – and I can't!' Tears gleamed along her cheeks. 'Oh, Pete, I'm crying more for you now,' (Maybe I won't even go on loving you.) 'than for me.'

He tried to stay cool. 'Too far a retreat from reality is insanity. If you went mad –' Unthinkableness.

'And it doesn't help you to know –' he said, and wondered if the engineers would ever be able to find the breaking strength of the human spirit. He felt very near to giving way.

CHAPTER ELEVEN

Summer waned as the planet turned towards winter. On a warm evening late in September, Mandelbaum sat by the window with Rossman, exchanging a few low-voiced words. The room was unlit, full of night. Far below them the city of Manhattan glowed with spots of radiance, not the frantic flash and glare of earlier days but the lights of a million homes. Overhead, there was a dull blue wash of luminance across the sky, flickering and glimmering on the edge of visibility. The Empire State Building was crowned with a burning sphere like a small sun come to rest, and the wandering air held a faint tingle of ozone. The two men sat quietly, resting, smoking the tobacco which had again become minutely available, Mandelbaum's pipe and Rossman's cigarette like two ruddy eyes in the twilit room. They were waiting for death.

'Wife,' said Rossman with a note of gentle reproach. It could be rendered as: (I still don't see why you wouldn't tell your wife of this, and be with her tonight. It may be the last night of your lives.)

'Work, city, time,' and the immemorial shrug and the wistful tone: (We both have our work to do, she at the relief centre and I here at the defence hub. We haven't told the city either, you and I and the few others who know. It's best not to do so, eh?) *We couldn't have evacuated them, there would have been no place for them to go and the fact of our attempting it would've been a tip-off to the enemy, an invitation to send the rockets immediately. Either we can save the city or we can't; at the moment, there's nothing anyone can do but wait and see if the defence works.* (I wouldn't worry my Liebchen – she'd worry on my account and the kids' and grandchildren's. No, let it happen, one way or the other. Still I do wish we could be together now, Sarah and I, the whole family –) Mandelbaum tamped his pipe with horny thumb.

(The Brookhaven men think the field will stop the blast and radiation), implied Rossman. *'We've had them working secretly for the past month or more, anticipating an attack. The cities we think will be assailed are guarded now – we hope.* (But it's problematic. I wish we didn't have to do it this way.)

'What other way?' *We knew, from our spies and deductions, that the Soviets have developed their intercontinental atoms rockets, and that they're desperate. Revolution at home, arms and aid being smuggled in to the insurgents from America. They'll make a last-ditch attempt to wipe us out, and we believe the attack is due tonight. But if it fails, they've shot their bolt. It must have taken all their remaining resources to design and build those rockets.* 'Let them exhaust themselves against us, while the rebels take over their country. Dictatorship is done for.'

'But what will replace it?'

'I don't know. When the rockets come, it seems to me they'll be the last gasp of animal man. Didn't you once call the twentieth century the Era of Bad Manners? We were stupid before – incredibly stupid! Now all that's fading away.'

'And leaving – nothing.' Rossman lit a fresh cigarette and stubbed out the old one. The brief red light threw his gaunt, fine-boned face into high relief against darkness.

'Oh, *yes*,' he went on, 'the future is not going to look anything like the past. Presumably there will still be society – or societies – but they won't be the same kind as those we've known before. Maybe they'll be purely abstract, mental things, interchanges and interactions on the symbolic level. Nevertheless, there can be better or worse societies developed out of our new potentialities, and I think the worse ones will grow up.'

'Hm.' Mandelbaum drew hard on his pipe. 'Aside from the fact that we have to start from scratch, and so are bound to make mistakes, why should that necessarily be so? You're a born pessimist, I'm afraid.'

'No doubt I was born into one age, and saw it die in blood and madness. Even before 1914, you could see the world crumbling. That would make a pessimist of anyone. But I think it's true what I say. Because man has, in effect, been thrown back into utter savagery. No, not that either; the savage does have his own systems of life. Man is back on the animal plane.'

Mandelbaum's gesture swept over the huge arrogance of the city. 'Is that animal?'

'Ants and beavers are good engineers.' *Or were. I wonder what the beavers are doing now?* 'Material artifacts don't count for much, really. They're only possible because of a social background of knowledge, tradition, desire – they're symptoms, not causes. And we have had all our background stripped from us.

'Oh, we haven't forgotten anything, no. But it's no longer of value to us, except as a tool for the purely animal business of survival and comfort. Think over your own life. What use do you see in it now? What are all your achievements of the past? Ridiculous!

'Can you read any of the great literature now with pleasure? Do the arts convey anything to you? The civilization of the past, with its science and art and beliefs and meanings, is so inadequate for us now that it might as well not exit. We have no civilization any longer. We have no goals, no dreams, no creative work – nothing!'

'Oh, I don't know about that,' said Mandelbaum with a hint of amusement. 'I've got enough to do – to help out with, at least – for the next several years. We've got to get things started on a worldwide basis, economics, politics, medical care, population control, conservation, it's a staggering job.'

'But after that?' persisted Rossman. 'What will we do then? What will the next generation do, and all generations to come?'

'They'll find something.'

'I wonder. The assignment of building a stable world order is herculean, but you and I realize that for the new humanity it's possible – indeed, only a matter of years. But what then? At best, man may sit back and stagnate in an unchanging smugness. A horribly empty sort of life.'

'Science –'

'Oh, yes, the scientists will have a field day for a while. But most of the physicists I've talked to lately suspect that the potential range of science is not unlimited. They think the variety of discoverable natural laws and phenomena must be finite, all to be summed up in one unified theory – and that we're not far from that theory today. It's not the sort of proposition which can ever be proved with certainty, but it looks probable.'

'And in no case can we all be scientists.'

Mandelbaum looked out into darkness. *How quiet the night is,* he thought. Wrenching his mind from the vision of Sarah and the children: 'Well, how about the arts? We've got to develop a whole new painting, sculpture, music, literature, architecture – and forms that have never been imagined before!'

'If we get the right kind of society.' (Art, throughout history, has had a terrible tendency to decay, or to petrify into sheer imitation of the past. It seems to take some challenge to wake it up again. And again, my friend, we can't all be artists either.)

'No?' (I wonder if every man won't be an artist and a scientist and a philosopher and –)

'You'll still need leaders, and stimulus, and a world symbol.' (That's the basic emptiness in us today: we haven't found a symbol. We have no myth, no dream. "Man is the measure of all things" – well, when the measure is bigger than everything else, what good is it?)

'We're still pretty small potatoes.' Mandelbaum gestured at the window and the bluely glimmering sky. (There's a whole universe out there, waiting for us.)

'I think you have the start of an answer,' said Rossman slowly. (Earth has grown too small, but astronomical space – it may hold the challenge and the dream we need. I don't know. All I know is that we had better find one.)

There was a thin buzz from the telecom unit beside Mandelbaum. He reached over and flipped the switch. There was a sudden feeling of weariness in him. He ought to be tense, jittering with excitement, but he only felt tired and hollow.

The machine clicked a few signals: 'Space station robot reports flight of rockets from Urals. Four are due at New York in about ten minutes.'

'Ten minutes!' Rossman whistled. 'They must have an atomic drive.'

'No doubt.' Mandelbaum dialed for Shield Centre in the Empire State Building. 'Brace your machinery, boys,' he said. 'Ten minutes to go.'

'How many?'

'Four. They must figure on our stopping at least three, so they'll be powerful brutes. Hydrogen-lithium warheads, I imagine.'

'Four, eh? Okay, boss. Wish us luck.'

'Wish *you* luck?' Mandelbaum grinned crookedly.

The city had been told that the project was an experiment in illumination. But when the blueness strengthened to a steady glow, like a roof of light, and the sirens began to hoot, everyone must have guessed the truth. Mandelbaum thought of husbands clutching wives and children to them and wondered what else might be happening. *Prayer? Not likely; if there was to be a religion in the future, it could not be the animism which had sufficed for the blind years. Exaltation in battle? No, that was another discarded myth. Wild panic? Maybe a little of that.*

Rossman had seen at least a good deal of truth, thought Mandelbaum. *There was nothing for man to do now, in the hour of judgment, except to scream with fear or to stoop over those he loved and try to shelter them with his pitiful flesh. No one could honestly feel that he was dying for something worthy. If he shook his fist at heaven, it was not in anger against evil, it was only a reflex*

Emptiness – Yes, he thought, *I suppose we do need new symbols.*

Rossman got up and felt his way through the dusk to a cabinet where he opened a drawer and took out a bottle. 'This is some '42 burgundy I've been saving,' he said. (Will you drink with me?)

'Sure,' said Mandelbaum. He didn't care for wine, but he had to help his friend. Rossman wasn't afraid, he was old and full of days, but there was something lost about him. To go out like a gentleman – well, that was a symbol of sorts.

Rossman poured into crystal goblets and handed one to Mandelbaum with grave courtesy. They clinked glasses and drank. Rossman sat down again, savouring the taste.

'We had burgundy on my wedding day,' he said.

'Ah, well, no need to cry into it,' answered Mandelbaum. 'The screen will hold. It's the same kind of force that holds atomic nuclei together – nothing stronger in the universe.'

'I was toasting animal man,' said Rossman. (You are right, this is his last gasp. But he was in many ways a noble creature.)

'Yeah,' said Mandelbaum. (He invented the most ingenious weapons.)

'Those rockets –' (They do represent something. They are beautiful things, you know, clean and shining, built with utter honesty. It took many patient centuries to reach the point where they could be forged. The fact that they carry death for us is incidental.)

(I don't agree.) Mandelbaum chuckled, a sad little sound in the great quiet around him.

There was a luminous-dialed clock in the room. Its sweep-second hand went in a long lazy circle, once around, twice around, three times around. The Empire State was a pylon of darkness against the dull blue arc of sky. Mandelbaum and Rossman sat drinking, lost in their own thoughts.

There was a glare like lightning all over heaven, the sky was a sudden incandescent bowl. Mandelbaum covered his dazzled eyes, letting the goblet fall shattering to the floor. He felt the radiance on his skin like sunshine, blinking on and off. The city roared with thunder.

– two, three, four.

Afterward there was another stillness, in which the echoes shuddered and boomed between high walls. A wind sighed down the empty streets, and the great buildings shivered slowly back toward rest.

'Good enough,' said Mandelbaum. He didn't feel any particular emotion. The screen had worked, the city lived – all right, he could get on with his job. He dialed City Hall. 'Hello, there, All okay? Look, we got to get busy, check any panic and –'

Out of the corner of one eye he saw Rossman sitting quietly, his unfinished drink on the arm of the chair.

CHAPTER TWELVE

Corinth sighed and pushed the work from him. The murmurs of the evening city drifted faintly up to him through a window left open to the October chill. He shivered a little, but fumbled out a cigarette and sat for a while smoking.

Spaceships, he thought dully. *Out at Brookhaven they're building the first star ship.*

His own end of the project was the calculation of intranuclear stresses under the action of the drive field, a task of some complexity but not of such overreaching importance that the workers couldn't go ahead on the actual construction before he finished. He had been out there just today, watching the hull take shape, and his professional self had found a cool sort of glory in its perfected loveliness. Every organ of the ship, engine and armour and doors and ports and controls, was a piece of precision engineering such as Earth had never seen before. It was good to be a part of such work.

Only –

He swore softly, grinding out the cigarette in an overloaded ashtray and rising to his feet. It was going to be one of his bad nights; he needed Helga.

The Institute hummed around him as he went down the familiar halls. They were working on a twenty-four hour schedule now, a thousand liberated minds spreading towards a horizon which had suddenly exploded beyond imagination. He envied the young technicians. They were the strong and purposeful and balanced, the future belonged to them and they knew it. At thirty-three, he felt exhausted with years.

Helga had come back to resume directorship here: on its new basis, it was a full-time job for a normal adult, and she had the experience and the desire to serve. He thought that she drove herself too hard, and realized with a muted guilt that it was largely his fault. She never left before he did, because sometimes he needed to talk to her. This was going to be one of those times.

He knocked. The crisp voice over the annunciator said, 'Come in,' and he did not miss the eagerness in her voice or the sudden lighting in her eyes as he entered.

'Come have dinner with me, won't you?' he invited. She arched her brows, and he explained hastily: 'Sheila's with Mrs Mandelbaum tonight. She – Sarah – she's good for my wife, she's got a sort of plain woman sense a man can't have. I'm at loose ends –'

'Sure.' Helga began arranging her papers and stacking them away. Her office was always neat and impersonal, a machine could have been its occupant. 'Know a joint?'

'You know I don't get out much these days.'

'Well, let's try Rogers'. A new night club for the new man.' Her smile was a little sour. 'At least they have decent food.'

He stepped into the small adjoining bathroom, trying to adjust his untidy clothes and hair. When he came out, Helga was ready. For an instant he looked at her, perceiving every detail with a flashing completeness undreamed of in the lost years. They could not hide from each other and – she with characteristic honesty, he with a weary and grateful surrender – had quit trying. He needed someone who understood him and was stronger than he, someone to talk to, to draw strength from. He thought that she only gave and he only took, but it was not a relationship he could afford to give up.

She took his arm and they went out into the street. The air was thin and sharp in their lungs, it smelled of autumn and the sea. A few dead leaves swirled across the sidewalk before them, already frost had come.

'Let's walk,' she said, knowing his preference. 'It isn't far.'

He nodded and they went down the long half-empty ways. The night loomed big above the street lamps, the cliffs of Manhattan were mountainously black around them and only a rare automobile or pedestrian went by. Corinth thought that the change in New York epitomized what had happened to the world.

'How's Sheila's work?' asked Helga. Corinth had obtained a job for his wife at the relief centre, in the hope that it would improve her morale. He shrugged, not answering. It was better to lift his face into the wind that streamed thinly between the dark walls, She fell into his silence; when he felt the need for communication, she would be there.

A modest neon glow announced Rogers' Cafe. They turned in at the door, to find a blue twilight which was cool and luminous, as if the very air held a transmuted light. *Good trick*, thought Corinth, *wonder how they do it?* – and in a moment he had reasoned out the new principle of fluorescence on which it must be based. Maybe an engineer had suddenly decided he would prefer to be a restaurateur.

There were tables spaced somewhat farther apart than had been the custom in earlier times. Corinth noted idly that they were arranged in a spiral which, on the average, minimized the steps of waiters from dining room to kitchen and back. But it was a machine which rolled up to them on soft rubber wheels and extended a slate and stylus for them to write their orders on.

The menu listed few meat dishes – there was still a food shortage – but Helga insisted that the soya supreme was delicious and Corinth ordered it for both of them. There would be an aperitif too, of course.

He touched glasses with her over the white cloth. Her eyes were grave on his, waiting. '*Was hael.*'

'*Drinc hael*' she answered. Wistfully: 'I'm afraid our descendants will not understand our ancestors at all. The whole magnificent barbarian heritage will be animal mouthings to them, won't it? When I think of the future I sometimes feel cold.'

'You too,' he murmured, and knew that she let down her reserve only because it made it easier for him to unburden himself.

A small orchestra came out. Corinth recognized three men among them who had been famous musicians before the change. They carried the old instruments, strings and a few woodwinds and one trumpet, but there were some new ones too. Well, until philharmonic associations came back, if they ever did, no doubt serious artists would be glad of a chance to play in a restaurant – at that, they'd have a more appreciative audience than usual in the past.

His eyes went around among the customers. They were ordinary-looking people, horny-handed labourers side by side with thin stoop-shouldered clerks and balding professors. The new nakedness had obliterated old distinctions, everybody was starting from scratch. There was an easy informality of dress, open-necked shirts, slacks and jeans, an occasional flamboyant experiment. Physical externals were counting for less every day.

There was no conductor. The musicians seemed to play extemporaneously, weaving their melodies in and out around a subtle, tacit framework. It was a chill sort of music, ice and green northern seas, a complex, compelling rhythm underlying the sigh of strings. Corinth lost himself for a while, trying to analyze it. Now and then a chord would strike some obscure emotional note within him, and his fingers tightened on the wine glass. A few people danced to it, making up their own figures as they went. He supposed that in the old days this would have been called a jam session, but it was too remote and intellectual for that. Another experiment, he thought. All humanity was experimenting, striking out after paths in a suddenly horizonless world.

He turned back to Helga, surprising her eyes as they rested on him. The blood felt hot in his face, and he tried to talk of safe things. But there was too much understanding between them. They had worked and watched together, and now there was a language of their own, every look and gesture meant something, and the meanings flickered back and forth, interlocking and breaking and meeting again, until it was like talking with one's own self.

'Work?' he asked aloud, and it meant: (How has your task been the last few days?)

'All right,' she said in a flat tone. (We're accomplishing something heroic, I think. The most supremely worthwhile job of all history, perhaps. But somehow I don't care very much –)

'Glad see you tonight,' he said. (I need you. I need someone in the lightless hours.)

(I will always be waiting), said her eyes.

Dangerous subject. Hide from it.

He asked quickly: 'What do you think of the music here? It seems as if they're already on the track of a form suited to ... modern man.'

'Maybe so,' she shrugged. 'But I can still find more in the old masters. They were more human.'

'I wonder if we are still human, Helga.'

'Yes,' she replied. 'We will always remain ourselves. We will still know love and hate, fear and bravery and laughter and grief.'

'But of the same kind?' he mused. 'I wonder.'

'You may be right,' she said. 'It's become too hard to believe what I want to believe. There is that.'

He nodded, she smiled a little: (Yes, we both know it, don't we? That and all the world besides.)

He sighed and clenched his fists briefly: 'Sometimes I wish – No.' *It's Sheila I love.*

(Too late, isn't it, Pete?) said her eyes. (Too late for both of us.)

'Dance?' he invited. (Come to forgetfulness.)

'Of course.' (Oh, gladly, gladly!)

They got up and moved out on the floor. He felt the strength of her as he put his arm around her waist, and it was as if he drew of it. *Mother image?* jeered his mind. No matter. The music was entering him more fully now, he felt its curious beat in his blood. Helga's head was almost level with his, but her face was hidden from him. He was not a good dancer, he let her take the lead, but the pleasure of rhythmic physical movement was sharper for him now than it had been before the change. For a moment he wished he could be a savage and dance his sorrow out before the gods.

No, too late for him. He was a child of civilization – even now; he had been born too old. But what do you do, then, when you see your wife going mad?

Ah, Love, could thou and I with Fate conspire – What a childish thing that was! And yet he had liked it once.

The music ended, and they went back to their table. The hors d'oeuvres had arrived, borne by the machine. Corinth seated Helga and picked moodily at his dish. Presently she looked at him again.

'Sheila?' she asked: (She isn't well these days, is she?)

'No.' (Thank you for asking.) Corinth grimaced. (Her work helps fill the time, but she's not good at it. She broods, and she's begun seeing things, and her dreams at night –)

Oh, my tormented dearest! 'But why?' (You and I, most people, we're adjusted now, we aren't nervous any more; I always thought she was more stable than average.)

'Her subconscious mind ...' (Running wild, and her consciousness can't control it, and worry over the symptoms only makes matters worse ...) 'She just isn't made for such power of mind, she can't handle it.'

Their eyes met: *Something lost, of old innocence, all we once treasured stripped from us, and we stand naked before our own solitude.*

Helga lifted her head: (We have to face it out. Somehow we have to keep going.) *But the loneliness!*

(I'm coming to depend too much on you. Nat and Felix are wrapped up in their own work. Sheila has no strength left, she has been fighting herself too long. There's only you, and it's not good for you.)

(I don't mind.) *It's all I have, now when I can no longer hide from myself.*

Their hands clasped across the table. Then, slowly, Helga withdrew hers and shook her head.

'God!' Corinth's fists doubled. (If we could only learn more about ourselves! If we had a workable psychiatry!)

(Perhaps we will before long. It's being studied.) Soothingly: 'And how is your own task coming?'

'Well enough, I suppose.' (We'll have the stars within our grasp before spring. But what good is it? What use are the stars to us?) Corinth stared at his wine glass. 'I'm a little drunk. I talk too much.'

'No matter, darling.'

He looked at her. 'Why don't you get married, Helga? Find someone for yourself. You can't pull me out of my private hell.'

Her face spoke negation.

'Better leave me out of your life,' he urged in a whisper.

'Would you leave Sheila out of yours?' she asked.

The machine waiter came silently to remove their dishes and set the main course before them. Corinth thought vaguely that he ought to have no appetite. Didn't misery traditionally mean pining away? But the food tasted good. Eating – well, yes, a compensation of sorts, like drinking and daydreaming, work and anything else you cared to name.

(You have to endure) said Helga's eyes. (Whatever comes, you have to live through it, you and your sanity, because that is your heritage of humanness.)

After a while she spoke aloud, three clipped words which held an overwhelming meaning: 'Pete, would you' (like to go out on the star ship?)

'Huh?' He stared at her so foolishly that she had to laugh. In a moment she spoke again, seriously and impersonally:

'It's being planned for two men.' (Mostly robot-run, you know. Nat Lewis talked me into giving him one of the berths, as biologist. The problem of life elsewhere in the universe –)

His voice shook a little: 'I didn't know you could control who went.'

'Not officially.' (In practice, since it's largely an Institute project, I can swing it for any qualified person. Nat wanted me along –) They traded a brief smile. *You could do worse, I could do better too.* 'But of course a physicist is needed.' (You know as much about the project, and have done as much for it, as anyone.)

'But –' He shook his head. 'I'd like to –' (No, there isn't a strong enough word for it. I'd trade my chances of immortality for a berth like that. I used to lie on my back on summer nights, when I was a kid, and look at the moon rising and Mars like a red eye in heaven, and dream.) 'But there's Sheila. Some other time, Helga.'

'It wouldn't be a long trip,' she said. (A couple of weeks' scouting around among the nearer stars, I imagine, to test out the drive and a number of astronomical theories. Nor do I think it's at all risky – would I let you go if I imagined that?) *As it is, I'll watch the sky every night and feel its great cold and clench my fists together.* (It's a chance I think you ought to have, for your own peace of mind. You're a lost soul now, Pete. You need to find something above your own problems, above this whole petty world of ours.) She smiled. 'Maybe you need to find God.'

'But I tell you, Sheila –'

'There's several months yet before the ship leaves.' (Anything can happen in that time. I've kept in touch with the latest psychiatric research too, and there's a promising new line of treatment.) She reached over the table to touch his arm. 'Think it over, Pete.'

'I will,' he said, a little thickly.

Part of him realized that she was holding out that tremendous prospect as an immediate diversion for him, something to break the circle of his worry and gloom. But it didn't matter. It was working anyway. When he came out again on the street with her, he looked up to the sky, saw a few suns dim through its haze, and felt a rush of excitement within him.

The stars! By Heaven, the stars!

CHAPTER THIRTEEN

Snow fell early that year. One morning Brock came out of the house and all the world was white.

He stood for a moment looking over the sweep of land, hills and fields and buried roads, to the steel-coloured dawn horizon. It was as if he had never seen winter before, bare black trees against a sky of windless quiet burdened roofs and frost-glazed windows and a single crow sitting dark and disconsolate on a cold telephone pole. *And indeed*, he thought, I *never have – not really*.

The snowfall had warmed the air but his breath still misted from his nostrils and he felt a tingle in his face. He slapped his hands together, a startlingly loud crack in the stillness, and blew out his cheeks and said aloud: 'Well, Joe, looks like we're settled down for the next half year. White Thanksgiving, and I wouldn't be surprised if we had a white Easter too.'

The dog looked up at him, understanding most of it but with little means of replying. Then instinct got the better of him and he went romping and barking to wake the farm with his clamour.

A small stocky form, so bundled up that only the proportions of arm and leg indicated it was not human, came out of the house, shuddered, and bounded quickly over to stand by the man. 'Cold,' she chattered. 'Cold, cold, cold.'

'It'll get colder, I'm afraid, Mehitabel,' said Brock, and laid a hand on the chimpanzee's fur-capped head. He still feared that the apes would not last out the winter. He had tried to do what he could for them – making clothes, and assigning most of their work in the house or barn where it was warm – but still their lungs were frail.

He hoped desperately that they would live. In spite of their natural flightiness and laziness, they had laboured heroically with him: he could not have readied for winter alone. But more than that, they were friends – someone to talk to, once a pidgin dialect had been worked out between him and them. They didn't have much to say, and their grasshopper minds would not stay on one subject, but they broke the solitude for him. Just to sit watching their antics in the gymnasium he had rigged up for them was to laugh, and laughter had become a rare thing.

Curiously, Mehitabel had taken best to the farmyard chores while her mate, Jimmy, handled cooking and housekeeping. Not that it mattered. They were strong and clever helpers, whatever they did.

He trudged over the yard, his boots leaving a smudge in the virginal whiteness, and opened the barn door. A wave of animal heat struck him as he entered the dimness, and the strong odour was heady. Mehitabel went to get hay and ground corn for the livestock – fifteen cows, two horses, and the vast form of Jumbo the elephant – while Brock gave himself to milking.

What stock was left seemed to have fallen into a placid acceptance of the new order. Brock winced. They trusted him, he seemed to be a kind of informal god, and today he would have to violate their trust. No use putting it off any longer, that would only make it the more difficult.

The door creaked open again and Wuh-Wuh came lumbering in and found a milking stool and joined Brock. He said nothing, and his work went ahead mechanically, but that was not unusual. Brock imagined that Wuh-Wuh was incapable of speech, except the inarticulate stammering and grunts which had earned him his name.

The imbecile had come tracking in one day a few weeks ago, ragged and filthy and starving. He must have escaped from some asylum – a small, knotty hunchback of uncertain age, his sloping head ugly to look on and a vacancy in his eyes. Wuh-Wuh's intelligence had, obviously, gone up like everyone else's, but that didn't change the fact that he was a defective, phys-ically as well as mentally.

He had not been especially welcome. Most of the big tasks of harvest were done by then, and there was enough worry about supplies for winter without adding an extra mouth. 'I kill him, boss,' said Jimmy, reaching for a knife.

'No,' said Brock. 'We can't be that hard.'

'I do it quick and easy,' grinned Jimmy, testing the edge of the blade on one splay thumb. He had a charming jungle simplicity in him.

'No. Not yet, anyway.' Brock smiled wearily. He was always tired, there was always something to do. *We're the lost sheep, and I seem to have been appointed bellwether. We all have to live in a world that don't want us.* After a moment he had added: 'We need a lot of wood cut, too.'

Wuh-Wuh had fitted in tolerably well, he was harmless enough once Jimmy – probably with the help of a stick – had broken him of some undesir-able habits. And the business had made Brock realize with a new force that there must be many of his sort, struggling to live when civilization got too big to concern itself with them. Eventually, he supposed, the morons would have to get together somehow, establish a community and –

Well, why not admit it? He was lonely. Sometimes the depression of his loneliness was almost suicidally great. There were none of his kind to be found, not in all the wintry world, and he was working for nothing except his own unnecessary survival. He needed kinship.

He finished the milking and turned the animals out to get exercise. The water tank was frozen over, but Jumbo broke the thin crust with her trunk and they all clustered around to drink. Later in the day the elephant would have to be put to work getting more water from the emergency pump and carrying it to the tank. Jumbo looked quite shaggy now; Brock had never before realized how much hair could grow on an elephant when abrading jungle or the blow torches of human owners didn't remove it.

He himself went over to the haystack outside the sheep fence. He had had to build a board wall around it to keep the flock from breaking through the wire and gorging themselves, but they respected his fences now. The whim of a god – He wondered what sort of strange taboo thoughts went on inside those narrow skulls.

Even before the change, sheep had been animals with personalities of their own, and he knew each of the forty as well as he could know any human.

Bluff, quick-witted Georgina was pushing the timid Psyche away in her haste, fat old Marie Antoinette stood placidly and immovably chewing, Jo-girl did an exuberant dance all by herself in the snow – and there was the old ram, ring-horned Napoleon, magnificently regal, too conscious of supremacy to be arrogant. How could he kill one of them?

Yet there was no help for it. He and Joe and Wuh-Wuh couldn't live on hay, or even the clumsily ground flour and the apples and garden truck in the cellar; Jimmy and Mehitabel could use some broth too – and there were the hides and tallow, the very bones might be worth saving.

Only which one should it be?

He didn't like Georgina much, but she was too good to kill, he needed her blood in his future stock. Jo-girl the glad, Marie who came up and nuzzled his hand, coquettish Margy and shy Jerri and brave-hearted Eleanor – which of his friends was he going to eat?

Oh, shut up, he told himself. *You made your mind up long ago.*

He whistled for Joe and opened the fence gate. The sheep looked curiously at him as they drifted from their completed meal to the shed where they nested. 'Get Psyche over here, Joe,' he said.

The dog was off at once, leaping the drifts like coppery fire. Mehitabel came out of the chicken house and waited quietly for what she had to do. There was a knife in her hand.

Joe nudged Psyche, and the ewe looked at him with a shy sort of wonder. The dog barked, a loud clear frosty noise, and nipped her gently on the flank. She came then, ploughing through the snow and out the gate. There she stood, looking up at Brock.

'Come on, girl,' he said. 'This way.'

He closed the gate and locked it. Joe was urging Psyche around the corner of the chick-house, out of sight of the flock.

The pigs had been tough and clever to start with, and had moreover seen many butcherings of their own kind in earlier days. The sheep didn't know. Brock thought that if a few of their number were led off during the winter and never came back, they would merely accept the fact without worrying about it. Eventually, of course, if man was to go on living off his animals, he would have to inculcate them with some – well, religion – which demanded sacrifices.

Brock shuddered at the thought. He wasn't cut out for the role of Moloch. The human race had been sinister enough without becoming a tribe of blood-drinking gods.

'Over here, Psyche,' he said.

She stood quietly looking at him. He took off his gloves and she licked his palms, her tongue warm and wet against their sweatiness. When he scratched behind her ears, she bleated very softly and moved closer to him.

Suddenly he realized the tragedy of the animals. They had never evolved for this intelligence. Man, with his hands and his speech, must have grown up as a thinking creature, he was at home with his brain. Even this sudden crushing burden of knowledge was not too great for him, because intellect had always been potentially unlimited.

But the other beasts had lived in a harmony, driven by their instincts through the great rhythm of the world, with no more intelligence than was needed for survival. They were mute, but did not know it; no ghosts haunted them, of longing or loneliness or puzzled wonder. Only now they had been thrown into that abstract immensity for which they had never been intended, and it was overbalancing them. Instinct, stronger than in man, revolted at the strangeness, and a brain untuned to communication could not even express what was wrong.

The huge indifferent cruelty of it was a gorge of bitterness in the man's throat. His vision blurred a little, but he moved with savage speed, stepping behind the sheep and throwing her down and stretching her throat out for the knife. Psyche bleated once, and he saw the horror of foreknown death in her eyes. Then the ape struck, and she threshed briefly and was still.

'Take – take –' Brock stood up. 'Take her yourself, Mehitabel, will you?' He found it oddly hard to speak. 'Get Wuh-Wuh t' help you. I got other things to do.'

He walked slowly away, stumbling a little, and Joe and Mehitabel traded a glance of unsureness. To them, this had only been a job: they didn't know why their leader should be crying.

CHAPTER FOURTEEN

Wang Kao was hard at work when the prophet came. It was winter, and the earth lay white and stiff about the village as far as a man could see, but there would be spring again and ploughing to do, and all the oxen had run off. Men and women and children would have to drag the ploughs, and Wang Kao desired to ease their labour as much as could be. He was ripping apart the one fuelless tractor which was the only remnant of the Communists, in search of ball bearings, when the cry rose up that a stranger was approaching across the fields.

Wang Kao sighed and laid down his work. Fumbling through the gloom of the hut which was his smithy, he grasped his rifle and the few remaining cartridges and shrugged on a wadded blue coat. It had been a good friend, that gun, it had seen him through many hundred miles after the army broke up in mutiny and he walked home. There had still been Communist troopers loose then, to say nothing of starved folk turned bandit. Even now, one was never sure what a newcomer might be. The last stranger had come in a shining aircraft simply to bear word that there was a new government under which all men might be free; but that government was remote and feeble as yet, men had to defend themselves when the need arose.

His neighbours were waiting outside, shivering a little in the cold. Some of them had guns like his, the rest were armed only with knives and clubs and pitchforks. Their breath puffed pale from their noses. Behind their line, the women and children and old people stood in doorways, ready to dive for shelter.

Wang Kao squinted across the snow. 'It is just one man,' he said. 'I see no weapons upon him.'

'He rides a donkey, and leads another,' replied his neighbour.

There was something strange here. Who had been able to manage a beast since the great change? Wang Kao felt a prickling along his neck.

It was an elderly man who neared them. He smiled kindly, and one by one the levelled guns sank. But it was odd how thinly he was clad, as if this were summer. He rode up to the line of men and greeted them in a friendly way. No one asked his errand, but the eyes that watched him were question enough.

'My name is Wu Hsi,' he said, 'and I have a message for you which may be of value.'

'Come in, sir,' invited Wang Kao, 'and accept our poor hospitality. It must be bitterly cold for you.'

'Why, no,' said the stranger. 'That is part of my message. Men need not freeze if they have no thick garments. It is all in knowing how not to freeze.'

He crossed one leg over the donkey's shoulders and leaned forward. A small chill breeze ruffled his wispy grey beard. 'I am one of many,' he went on. 'My master taught us, and now we go forth to teach others, and it is our hope that some of those we teach will themselves become prophets.'

'Well, and what is it you teach, sir?' asked Wang Kao.

'It is only the proper use of the mind,' replied Wu Hsi. 'My master was a scholar in Fenchow, and when the great change came he saw that it was a change in men's way of thinking and set himself to search out the best ways of using his new powers. It is but a humble beginning which we have here, and yet we feel that it may be of service to the world.'

'All of us can think more freely and strongly now, sir,' said Wang Kao.

'Yes, I am clearly among worthy men, and yet it may be my poor words will have some newness. Think, people, how often the mind, the will, has mastered the body's weaknesses. Think how men have kept alive during sickness and famine and weariness, when no beast could do aught but die. Then think how much greater such powers must be now, if only a man can use them.'

'Yes.' Wang Kao bowed. 'I see how you have triumphed over the chill of winter.'

'There is not enough cold today to harm a man, if he but know how to keep his blood moving warmly. That is a little thing.' Wu Hsi shrugged. 'A heightened mind can do much with the body; I can, for instance, show you how to tell a wound to stop hurting and bleeding. But the ways of communicating with the beasts, and befriending them; the ways of remembering every tiniest thing one has ever seen or heard; the ways of having no feelings, no wishes, save those the mind says are good; the ways of talking soul to soul with another man, without ever opening the lips; the ways of thinking out how the real world must be, without blundering into vain fancies – these, I humbly feel, may be of more use to you in the long run.'

'Indeed, honoured sir, they would, and we are not worthy,' declared Wang Kao in awe. 'Will you not come in now and dine with us?'

It was a great day for the village, in spite of the news having come so quietly. Wang Kao thought that soon it would be a great day for the whole world. He wondered what the world would look like, ten years hence, and even his patient soul could hardly wait to see.

Outside the viewports, the sky was ice and darkness, a million frosty suns strewn across an elemental night. The Milky Way flowed as a river of radiance, Orion stood gigantic against infinity, and it was all cold and silence.

Space lay around the ship like an ocean. Earth's sun was dwindling as she ran outward towards endlessness, now there were only night and quiet and the titanic shining beauty of heaven. Looking at those stars, each a giant ablaze, and sensing their terrible isolation, Peter Corinth felt the soul within him quail. This was space, reaching out past imagination, worlds beyond worlds and each, in all its splendour, nothing against the mystery that held it.

'*Maybe you need to find God.*'

Well – perhaps he had. He had at least found something more than himself.

Sighing, Corinth turned back to the metallic warmth of the cabin, grateful for finitude. Lewis sat watching the dials and chewing a dead cigar. There was nothing of awe in his round ruddy face, and he hummed a song to himself, but Corinth knew that the huge cold had reached in and touched him.

The biologist nodded ever so slightly. (Works like a charm. The psi-drive, the viewscreens, the gravity, ventilation, servomechanisms – a lovely boat we've got!)

Corinth found a chair and sat down, folding his lanky frame together and clasping his hands over one knee. Starward bound – it was a triumph, perhaps the greatest achievement of history. For it guaranteed that there would always be a history, an outwardness in man so that he could not stagnate forever on his one little planet. Only somehow he, as an individual, did not feel the exultation of conquest. This was too big for trumpets.

Oh, he had always known intellectually that the cosmos was vast beyond comprehension, but it had been a dead knowledge in him, colourless, ten to the umpteenth power quantities and nothing more. Now it was part of his self. He had lived it, and could never again be quite the same man.

Driven by a force more powerful than rockets, freed from Einsteinian speed limits, the ship reacted against the entire mass of the universe, and when travelling faster than light did not have a velocity in the strict sense at all. Her most probable position shifted in an enigmatic way which had required a whole new branch of mathematics to describe. She generated her own internal pseudogravity field, her fuel was mass itself – any mass, broken down into energy, nine times ten to the twentieth ergs per gram. Her view-screens, compensating for Doppler effect and aberration, showed the naked blaze of space to eyes that would never look on it unaided. She carried and sheltered and fed her cargo of frail organic tissue, and they who rode like gods knew their own mortality with a stark and somehow heart-lifting clarity.

For all that, she had an unfinished look. In the haste to complete a thousand years of work in a few months, the builders had left out much they might have installed, computers and robots which could have made the ship altogether automatic. The men aboard could calculate with their changed minds as well and as swiftly as any machine yet built, solving partial differential equations of high order just to get the proper setting for a control. There had been an almost desperate speed in the project, a vague realization that the new humanity had to find a frontier. The next ship would be different, much of the difference founded on data which the first one would bring back.

'Cosmic ray count holding pretty steady,' said Lewis. The ship bristled with instruments mounted outside the hull and its protective warping fields. (I guess that kills off the solar-origin theory for good.)

Corinth nodded. The universe – at least out to the distance they had penetrated – seemed to hold a sleet of charged particles, storming through space from unknown origins to equally unknown destinations. Or did they have any definite points of departure? Maybe they were an integral part of the cosmos, like the stars and nebulae. The professional side of him wanted immensely to know.

'I think,' he said, 'that even the short trips we can make in this little segment of the galaxy are going to upset most of the past astrophysical theories.' (We'll have to build a whole new cosmology.)

'And biology too, I'll bet,' grunted Lewis. (I've been speculating on and off since the change, and now I'm inclined to think that life forms not based on carbon are possible.) 'Well, we'll see.'

We'll see – what a magical phrase!

Even the Solar System would need decades of exploration. The *Sheila* – man was beyond the animism of christening his works, but Corinth remained sentimental enough to think of the ship by his wife's name – had already visited the moon on a flight test; her real voyage had begun with a swing past Venus, ducking down to look at the windy, sandy hell of the poisonous surface, then a stop on Mars where Lewis went wild over some of the adaptations he found in the plant forms, and then outward. In one unbelievable week, two men had seen two planets and gone beyond them. The constellation Hercules lay astern: they meant to locate the fringes of the inhibitor field and gather data on it; then a dash to Alpha Centauri, to see if Sol's nearest neighbour had planets, and home again. All inside of a month!

It will be close to spring when I get back –

The late winter had still held Earth's northern hemisphere when they left. It had been a cold, dark morning. Low-flying clouds blew like ragged smoke under a sky of iron. The sprawling mass of Brookhaven had been almost hidden from them, blurred with snow and haze, and the city beyond was lost to sight.

There had not been many to see them off. The Mandelbaums had been there, of course, hunched into clothes gone old and shabby; Rossman's tall gaunt form was stiff on one side of them; a few friends, some professional acquaintances from the laboratories and workshops, that was all.

Helga had come, wearing an expensive fur coat, melted snow glistening like small diamonds in the tightly drawn blonde hair. Her jewel-hard coolness said much to Corinth, he wondered how long she would wait after the ship was gone to weep, but he had shaken hands with her and found no words. Thereafter she had talked with Lewis, and Corinth had led Sheila around behind the ship.

She looked small and fragile in her winter coat. Flesh had melted from her, the fine bones stood out under the skin and her eyes were enormous. She had become so quiet lately, she sat and looked past him and now and then she trembled a little. The hands that lay in his were terribly thin.

'I shouldn't be leaving you, honey,' he said, using all the words in the old manner and making his voice a caress.

'It won't be for long,' she answered tonelessly. She wore no make-up, and her lips were paler than they should be. 'I think I'm getting better.'

He nodded. The psychiatrist, Kearnes, was a good man, a plump fatherly sort with a brain like a razor. He admitted that his therapy was experimental, a groping into the unknown darknesses of the new human mind, but he had been getting results with some patients. Rejecting the barbarity of brain mutilation by surgery or shock, he felt that a period of isolation from familiarity gave the victim a chance to perform, under guidance, the re-evaluation that was necessary ...

('The change has been an unprecedented psychic shock to every organism possessed of a nervous system,' Dr Kearnes had said. 'The fortunate ones – the strong-willed, the resolute, those whose interests have been by choice or necessity directed outward rather than introspectively, those to whom hard thinking has always been a natural and pleasurable process – they seem to have made the adjustment without too much damage; though I suppose we will all carry the scars of that shock to our graves. But those less fortunate have been thrown into a neurosis which has in many cases become deep psychosis. Your wife, Dr Corinth – let me be blunt – is dangerously close to insanity. Her past life, essentially unintellectual and sheltered, has given her no preparation for a sudden radical change in her own being; and the fact that she has no children to worry about, and no problem of bare survival to occupy her, enabled the whole force of realization to turn on her own character. The old adjustments, compensations, protective forgetfulness and self-deception, which we all had, are no longer of use, and she hasn't been able to find new ones. Worry about the symptoms naturally increased them, a vicious circle. But I think I can help her; in time, when the whole business is better understood, it should be possible to effect a complete cure. How long? How should I know? But hardly more than a few years, at the rate science can expand now; and meanwhile Mrs Corinth should be able to compensate enough for happiness and balance.')

'Well –'

Sudden terror in her eyes: 'Oh, Pete, darling, darling, be careful out there! Come back to me!'

'I will,' he said, and bit his lip.

('Yes, it would be an excellent thing for her – I think – if you went on that expedition, Dr Corinth. Worry about you is a healthier thing than brooding over the shadows her own runaway mind creates for her. It will help wrench her psychic orientation outward where it belongs. She's not a natural introvert ...')

A flurry of snow wrapped them for a moment, hiding them from the world. He kissed her, and knew that in all the years before him he would remember how cool her lips were and how they trembled under his.

There was a deep hollow ringing in the ground, as if the planet itself shuddered with cold. Overhead flared the transatlantic rocket, bound for Europe on some mission of the new-born world order. Corinth's eyes were on Sheila. He brushed the snow from her hair, feeling the softness of it and the childish inward curve of her nape under his fingers. A small sad laughter was in him.

With five words, and eyes and hands and lips, he said to her: 'When I come home again – and what a home-coming that will be, honey! – I expect to find you well and inventing a robot housemaid so you'll be free for me. I don't want anything in all the universe to bother us then.'

And what he meant was: *O most beloved, he be there for me as You have always been, You who are all my world. Let there be no more darkness between us, child of light, let us be together as once we were, or else all time is empty forever.*

'I'll try, Pete,' she whispered. Her hand reached up to touch his face. 'Pete,' she said wonderingly.

Lewis' voice sounded harsh around the flank of the ship, distorted by the wind: 'All aboard that's going aboard!'

Corinth and Sheila took their time, and the others respected that need. When the physicist stood in the air lock waving good-bye, he was well above ground, and Sheila's form was a very small shape against the muddy snow.

Sol was little more than the brightest star in their wake, almost lost in the thronging multitude of suns, out here as far as the orbit of Saturn. The constellations had not changed, for all the leagues that had fled behind them. The huge circle of the Milky Way and the far mysterious coils of the other galaxies glimmered as remotely as they had done for the first half-man who lifted his eyes skyward and wondered. There was no time, no distance, only a vastness transcending miles and years.

The *Sheila* probed cautiously ahead at well under light velocity. On the fringes of the inhibitor field Lewis and Corinth were preparing the telemetered missiles which would be shot into the region of denser flux.

Lewis chuckled with amiable diablerie at the caged rats he meant to send on one of the torpedoes. Their beady eyes watched him steadily, as if they knew. 'Poor little bums,' he said. 'Sometimes I feel like a louse.' He added with a grin, 'The rest of the time I do too, but it's fun.'

Corinth didn't answer. He was looking out at the stars.

'The trouble with you,' said Lewis, settling his bulk into the adjoining chair, 'is that you take life too seriously. You've always done so, and haven't broken the habit since the change. Now me – I am, of course, perfect by definition! – I always found things to swear about and cry over, but there was just as much which was outrageously funny. If there is a God of any kind – and since the change I'm beginning to think there may be, perhaps I've become more imaginative – then Chesterton was right in including a sense of humour among His attributes.' He clicked his tongue. 'Poor old G.K.C.! It's too bad he didn't live to see the change. What paradoxes he would have dreamed up!'

The alarm bell broke off his monologue. Both men started, looking at the indicator light which blinked like a red eye, on and off, on and off. Simultaneously, a wave of dizziness swept through them. Corinth grabbed for the arms of his chair, retching.

'The field – we're approaching the zone –' Lewis punched a key on the elaborate control panel. His voice was thick. 'Got to get outta here –'

Full reverse! But it wasn't that simple, not when you dealt with the potential field which modern science identified with ultimate reality. Corinth shook his head, fighting the nausea, and leaned over to help. *This switch – no, the other one –*

He looked helplessly at the board. A needle crept over a red mark, they had passed light speed and were still accelerating, the last thing he had wished. *What to do?*

Lewis shook his head. Sweat gleamed on the broad face. 'Sidewide vector,' he gasped. 'Go out tangentially –'

There were no constants for the psi-drive. Everything was a variable, a function of many components depending on the potential gradients and on each other. The setting for 'ahead' could become that for 'reverse' under new conditions, and there was the uncertainty principle to reckon with, the uncaused chaos of individual electrons, flattened probability curves, the unimaginable complexity which had generated stars and planets and thinking humans. A train of equations gibbered through Corinth's brain.

The vertigo passed, and he looked at Lewis with a growing horror. 'We were wrong,' he mumbled. 'The field builds up quicker than we thought.'

'But – it took days for Earth to get out of it altogether, man, at a relative speed of –'

'We must have hit a different part of the cone, then, a more sharply defined one; or maybe the sharpness varies with time in some unsuspected manner –' Corinth grew aware that Lewis was staring at him, open-mouthed.

'Huh?' said the other man – how slowly!

'I said – what did I say?' Corinth's heart began thundering in his panic. He had spoken three or four words, made a few signs, but Lewis hadn't understood him.

Of course he hadn't! They weren't as bright as they had been, neither of them.

Corinth swallowed a tongue that seemed like a piece of wood. Slowly, in plain English, he repeated his meaning.

'Oh, yes, yes.' Lewis nodded, too frozen to say more.

Corinth's brain felt gluey. There was no other word. He was spiralling down into darkness, he couldn't think, with every fleeting second he tumbled back towards animal man.

The knowledge was like a blow. They had plunged unawares into the field Earth had left, it was slowing them down, they were returning to what they had been before the change. Deeper and deeper the ship raced, into an ever stronger flux, and they no longer had the intelligence to control her.

The next ship will be built to guard against this, he thought in the chaos. *They'll guess what's happened – but what good will that do us?*

He looked out again: the stars wavered in his vision. *The field*, he thought wildly, *we don't know its shape or extent. I think we're going out tangentially, we may come out of the cone soon – or we may be trapped in here for the next hundred years.*

Sheila!

He bowed his head, too miserable with the physical torment of sudden cellular readjustment to think any more, and wept.

The ship went on into darkness.

CHAPTER FIFTEEN

The house stood on Long Island, above a wide strand sloping to the sea. It had once belonged to an estate, and there were trees and a high wall to screen it off from the world.

Roger Kearnes brought his car to a halt under the portico and stepped out. He shivered a little and jammed his hands into his pockets as the raw wet cold fell over him. There was no wind, no shadow, only the late fall of snow, thick sad snow that tumbled quietly from a low sky and clung to the window-panes and melted on the ground like tears. He wondered despairingly if there would ever again be a springtime.

Well – he braced himself and rang the doorbell. There was work to do. He had to check up on his patient.

Sheila Corinth opened the door for him. She was still thin, her eyes dark and huge in the pale childlike face; but she wasn't trembling any more, and she had taken the trouble to comb her hair and put on a dress.

'Hello, there,' he said, smiling. 'How are you today?'

'Oh – all right.' She didn't meet his eyes. 'Won't you come in?'

She led the way down a corridor whose recent repainting had not quite succeeded in creating the cheerful atmosphere Kearnes wanted. But you couldn't have everything. Sheila could consider herself lucky to have an entire house and a pleasant elderly woman – a moron – for help and companionship. Even nowadays, it meant a lot if your husband was an important man.

They entered the living-room. A fire crackled on the hearth, and there was a view of beach and restless ocean. 'Sit down,' invited Sheila listlessly. She threw herself into an armchair and sat unmoving, her eyes fixed on the window.

Kearnes' gaze followed hers. How heavily the sea rolled! Even indoors, he could hear it grinding against the shore, tumbling rocks, grinding away the world like the teeth of time. It was grey and white to the edge of the world, white-maned horses, stamping and galloping, how terribly loud they neighed!

Pulling his mind loose, he opened his briefcase. 'I have some more books for you,' he said. 'Psychological texts. You said you were interested.'

'I am. Thank you.' There was no tone in her voice.

'Hopelessly outdated now, of course,' he went on. 'But they may give you an insight into the basic principles. You have to see for yourself what your trouble is.'

'I think I do,' she said. 'I can think more clearly now. I can see how cold the universe is and how little we are –' She looked at him with fright on her lips. 'I wish I didn't think so well!'

'Once you've mastered your thoughts, you'll be glad of this power,' he said gently.

'I wish they would bring back the old world,' she said.

'It was a cruel world,' he answered. 'We're well off without it.'

She nodded. He could barely hear her whisper: 'O soldier, lying hollow on the rime, there is frost in your hair and darkness behind your eyes. Let there be darkness.' Before he had time for a worried frown, she continued aloud, 'But we loved and hoped then. There were the little cafes, do you remember, and people laughing in twilight, there were music and dancing, beer and cheese sandwiches at midnight, sailboats, leftover pies, worrying about income taxes, our own jokes, there were the two of us. Where is Pete now?'

'He'll be back soon,' said Kearnes hastily. No use reminding her that the star ship was already two weeks overdue. 'He's all right. It's you we have to think about.'

'Yes.' She knotted her brows together, earnestly. 'They still come to me. The shadows, I mean. Words out of nowhere. Sometimes they almost make sense.'

'Can you say them to me?' he asked.

'I don't know. This house is on Long Island, long island longing island, island of longing, where is Pete?'

He relaxed a trifle. That was a more obvious association than she had sprung on him last time. What had it been? *But when the uttermost hollow-frozen and time so dark that lightlessness is a weight is, then tell me what lies beneath it* … Maybe she was healing herself in the quiet of her aloneness.

He couldn't be sure. Things had changed too much. A schizophrenic's mind went into lands where he could not follow, the new patterns had simply not been mapped yet. But he thought Sheila was acting a little more healthily.

'I shouldn't play with them, I know,' she said abruptly. 'That's dangerous. If you take them by the hand they'll let you guide them for a while, but they won't let go of your hand again.'

'I'm glad you realize that,' he said. 'What you want to do is exercise your mind. Think of it as a tool or a muscle. Go through those drills I gave you on logical processes and general semantics.'

'I have.' She giggled. 'The triumphant discovery of the obvious.'

'Well,' he laughed, 'you're back on your feet enough to make snide remarks, at least.'

'Oh, yes.' She picked at a thread in the upholstery. 'But where is Pete?'

He evaded the question and put her through some routine word-association tests. Their diagnostic value was almost nil – every time he tried them, the words seemed to have taken on different connotations – but he could add the results to his own data files. Eventually he would have enough material to find an underlying pattern. This new n-dimensional conformal-mapping technique looked promising, it might yield a consistent picture.

'I have to go,' he said at last. He patted her arm. 'You'll be all right. Remember, if you ever want help, or just company, in a hurry, all you have to do is call me.'

She didn't get up, but sat there watching him till he was out of the door. Then she sighed. *I do not like you, Doctor Fell*, she thought. *You look like a bulldog that snapped at me once, many hundred years ago. But you're so easy to fool!*

An old song ran through her head:

'He is dead and gone, lady,
   He is dead and gone;
At his head a grass green turf,
   At his heels a stone.'

No, she said to the other one who sang in her head. *Go away.*

The sea growled and grumbled, and snow fell thicker against the windows. She felt as if the world were closing in on her.

'Pete,' she whispered. 'Pete, honey, I need you so much. Please come back.'

CHAPTER SIXTEEN

They flashed out of the field, and the next few minutes were dreadful. Then:
   'Where are we?'

The unknown constellations glittered around them, and the silence was so enormous that their own breathing was loud and harsh in their ears.

'I don't know,' groaned Lewis. 'And I don't care. Lemme sleep, will you?'

He stumbled across the narrow cabin and flopped into a bunk, shaking with wretchedness. Corinth watched him for a moment through the blur that was his own vision, and then turned back to the stars.

This is ridiculous, he told himself sharply. *You're free again. You have the full use of your brain once more. Then use it!*

His body shuddered with pain. Life wasn't meant for changes like this. A sudden return to the old dimness, numb days fading into weeks while the ship hurled herself uncontrollably outward, and then the instant emergence, clear space and the nervous system flaring up to full intensity – it should have killed them.

It will pass, it will pass, but meanwhile the ship is still outward bound, Earth lies farther behind with every fleeting second. Stop her!

He sat grasping the arms of his chair, fighting down the dry nausea.

Calmness, he willed, *slowness, brake the racing heart, relax muscles that jerked against their bones, bank the fires of life and let them build up slowly as they should.*

He thought of Sheila waiting for him, and the image was a steadiness in his whirling universe. Gradually, he felt the strength spreading as he willed it. It was a conscious battle to halt the spasmodic gasps of his lungs, but when that was won the heart seemed to slow of itself. The retching passed away, the trembling stopped, the eyes cleared, and Peter Corinth grew fully aware of himself.

He stood up, smelling the sour reek of vomit in the cabin and activating the machine which cleaned the place up. Looking out the viewscreens, he gathered in the picture of the sky. The ship would have changed speed and direction many times in her blind race through heaven, they could be anywhere in this arm of the galaxy, but –

Yes, there were the Magellanic Clouds, ghosts against night, and that hole of blackness must be the Coal Sack, and then the great nebula in Andromeda – Sol must lie approximately in that direction. About three weeks' journey at their top pseudospeed; then, of course, they'd have to cast about through the local region to find that very ordinary yellow dwarf which was man's sun. Allow a few days, or even a couple of weeks, for that. Better than a month!

No help for it, however impatient he was. Emotion was, casually, a psychophysiological state, and as such ought to be controllable. Corinth willed the rage and grief out of himself, willed calmness and resolution. He went over to the controls and solved their mathematical problem as well as he could with the insufficient data available. A few swift movements of his hands brought the ship's flight to a halt, turned her about, and plunged her towards Sol.

Lewis was unconscious, and Corinth didn't wake him. Let him sleep off the shock of readjustment. The physicist wanted a little privacy for thinking anyway.

He thought back over the terrible weeks in the field. When they had been there, he and Lewis, their lives since Earth had left it had seemed dreamlike. They could hardly imagine what they had been doing; they could not think and feel as those other selves had done. The chains of reasoning which had made the reorganization of the world and the building of the ship possible within months, had been too subtle and ramified for animal man to follow. After a while, their talk and their desperate scheming had faded into an apathy of despair, and they waited numbly for chance to release them or kill them.

Well, thought Corinth on the edge of a mind that was dealing with a dozen things at once, *as it happened, we were released.*

He sat looking out at the stupendous glory of heaven, and the realization that he was bound home and still alive and sane was a pulse of gladness within him. But the new coolness which he had willed into himself overlay him like armour. He could throw it off at the proper time, and would, but the fact of it was overwhelming.

He should have foreseen that this would come. Doubtless many on Earth had already discovered it for themselves but, with communications still fragmentary, had not yet been able to spread the word. The history of man had, in one sense, represented an unending struggle between instinct and intelligence, the involuntary rhythm of organism and the self-created patterns of consciousness. Here, then, was the final triumph of mind.

For him it had come suddenly, the shock of re-emergence into full neural activity precipitating the change which had been latent in him. For all normal humanity, though, it must come soon – gradually, continuously, perhaps, but soon.

The change in human nature and human society which this would bring about was beyond even his imagination. A man would still have motivations, he would still want to do things, but he could select his own desires, consciously. His personality would be self-adjusted to the intellectually conceived requirements of his situation. He would not be a robot, no, but he would not resemble what he had been in the past. As the new techniques were fully worked out, psychosomatic diseases would vanish and even organic troubles ought to be controllable in high degree by the will; no more pain; every man could learn enough medicine to take care of the rest, and there would be no more doctors.

Eventually – no more death?

No, probably not that. Man was still a very finite thing. Even now, he had natural limitations, whatever they might be. A truly immortal man would eventually be smothered under the weight of his own experience, the potentialities of his nervous system would be exhausted.

Nevertheless, a life span of many centuries ought to be attainable: and the spectre of age, the slow disintegration which was senility, could be abolished.

Protean man – intellectual man – infinity!

The star was not unlike Sol – a little bigger, a little redder, but it had planets and one of them was similar to Earth. Corinth sent the ship plunging into the atmosphere of the night side.

Detectors swept the area. No radiation above the normal background count, that meant no atomic energy; but there were cities in which the buildings themselves shone with a cool light, and machines and radio and a world-wide intercourse. The ship recorded the voices that talked through the night, later on the language could perhaps be analysed.

The natives, seen and photographed in a fractional second as the ship went noiselessly overhead, were of the humanoid sort, mammalian bipeds, though they had greenish fur and six fingers to a hand and altogether unhuman heads. Thronging their cities, they were almost pathetically like the crowds in old New York. The form was alien, but the life and its humble desires were the same.

Intelligence, another race of minds, man is not alone in the hugeness of space-time – once it would have marked an epoch. Now it merely confirmed a hypothesis. Corinth rather liked the creatures that walked beneath him, he wished them well, but they were only another species of the local fauna. Animals.

'They seem to be a lot more sensible than we were in the old days,' said Lewis as the ship spiralled over the continent. 'I see no evidence of war or preparations for war; maybe they outgrew that even before they achieved machine technology.'

'Or maybe this is the planet-wide universal state,' answered Corinth. 'One nation finally knocked out all the others and absorbed them. We'll have to study the place a bit to find out, and I, for one, am not going to stop now to do it.'

Lewis shrugged. 'I daresay you're justified. Let's go, then – a quick sweep around the day side, and we'll let it go at that.'

Despite the self-command which had been growing in him, Corinth had to battle down a fury of impatience. Lewis was right in his insistence that they at least investigate the stars which lay near their homeward path. It wouldn't kill anyone on Earth to wait a few weeks more for their return, and the information would be valuable.

A few hours after entering the atmosphere, the *Sheila* left it again and turned starward. The planet fell rapidly behind her driving hull, the sun dwindled and was lost, a whole living world – life, evolution, ages of history, struggle and glory and doom, dreams, hates and fears, hope and love and longing, all the many-layered existence of a thousand million sentient beings – was swallowed by darkness.

Corinth looked out and let the shiver of dismay run free within him. The cosmos was too big. No matter how swiftly men fled through it, no matter how far they ranged in all ages to come and how mightily they wrought, it would be the briefest glimmer in one forgotten corner of the great silence. This single dust mote of a galaxy was so inconceivably huge that even now his mind could not encompass the knowledge; even in a million years, it could not be fully known; and beyond it lay shining islands of stars, outwardness past imagination. Let man reach forth till the cosmos itself perished, he would still accomplish nothing against its unheeding immensity.

It was a healthy knowledge, bringing a humility which the coldness of his new mind lacked. And it was good to know that there would always be a frontier and a challenge; and the realization of that chill hugeness would draw men together, seeking each other for comfort, it might make them kinder to all life.

Lewis spoke slowly in the quiet of the ship: 'This makes nineteen planets we've visited, fourteen of them with intelligent life.'

Corinth's memory went back over what he had seen, the mountains and oceans and forests of whole worlds, the life which blossomed in splendour or struggled only to live, and the sentience which had arisen to take blind nature in hand. It had been a fantastic variety of shape and civilization. Leaping, tailed barbarians howled in their swamps; a frail and gentle race, grey like silver-dusted lead, grew their big flowers for some unknown symbolic reason; a world smoked and blazed with the fury of nations locked in an atomic death clutch, pulling down their whole culture in a voluptuous hysteria of hate; beings of centaur shape flew between the planets of their own sun and dreamed of reaching the stars; the hydrogen-breathing monsters dwelling on a frigid, poisonous giant of a planet had evolved three separate species, so vast were the distances between; the world-civilization of a biped folk who looked almost human had become so completely and inflexibly organized that individuality was lost, consciousness itself was dimming towards extinction as antlike routine took the place of thought; a small snouted race had developed specialized plants which furnished all their needs for the taking, and settled down into a tropical paradise of idleness; one nation, of the many on a ringed world, had scorned wealth and power as motivations and given themselves to a passionate artistry. Oh, they had been many and strange, there was no imagining what diversity the universe had evolved, but even now Corinth could see the pattern.

Lewis elaborated it for him: 'Some of those races were much older than ours, I'm sure. And yet, Pete, none of them is appreciably more intelligent than man was before the Change. You see what it indicates?'

'Well, nineteen planets – and the stars in this galaxy alone number on the order of a hundred billion, and theory says most of them have planets – What kind of a sample is that?'

'Use your head, man! It's a safe bet that under normal evolutionary conditions a race only gets so intelligent and then stops. None of those stars have been in the inhibitor field, you know.

'It ties in; it makes good sense. Modern man is not essentially different from the earliest Homo Sapiens, either. The basic ability of an intelligent species is that of adapting environment to suit its own needs, rather than adapting itself to environment. Thus, in effect, the thinking race can maintain fairly constant conditions. It's as true for an Eskimo in his igloo as it is for a New Yorker in his air-conditioned apartment; but machine technology, once the race stumbles on to it, makes the physical surroundings still more constant. Agriculture and medicine stabilize the biological environment. In short – once a race reaches the intelligence formerly represented by an average I.Q. of 100 to, say, 150, it doesn't need to become smarter than it is.'

Corinth nodded. 'Eventually surrogate brains are developed, too, to handle problems the unaided mind couldn't deal with,' he said. 'Computers, for instance; though writing is really the same principle. I see your point, of course.'

'Oh, there's more to it than that,' added Lewis. 'The physical structure of the nervous system imposes limitations, as you well know. A brain can only get so big, then the neural paths become unmanageably long. I'll work out the detailed theory when I get home, if somebody else hasn't beaten me to it.

'Earth, of course, is a peculiar case. The presence of the inhibitor field made terrestrial life change its basic biochemistry. We have our structural limitations too, but they're wider because of that difference in type. Therefore, we may very well be the smartest race in the universe now – in this galaxy, at least.'

'Mmmmm, maybe so. Of course, there were many other stars in the field too.'

'And still are. New ones must be entering it almost daily. Lord, how I pity the thinking races on those planets! They're thrown back to a submoronic level – a lot of them must simply die out, unable to survive without minds. Earth was lucky; it drifted into the field before intelligence had appeared.'

'But there must be many planets in a similar case,' urged Corinth.

'Well, possibly,' conceded Lewis. 'There may well be races which emerged, and shot up to our present level, thousands of years ago. If so, we'll meet them eventually, though the galaxy is so big that it may take a long time. And we'll adjust harmoniously to each other.' He smiled wryly. 'After all, pure logic mind is so protean, and the merely physical will become so unimportant to us, that we'll doubtless find those beings to be just like ourselves – whatever their bodies resemble. How'd you like to be a partner of a – a giant spider, maybe?'

Corinth shrugged. 'I'd have no objections.'

'No, of course not. Be fun to meet them. And we won't be alone in the universe any more –' Lewis sighed. 'Still, Pete, let's face it. Only a very tiny minority of all the sentient species there must be in the galaxy can have been as fortunate as us. We may find a dozen kindred races, or a hundred – no large number. Our sort of mind is very lonely.'

His eyes went out to the stars. 'Nevertheless, it may be that that uniqueness has its compensations. I think I'm beginning to see an answer to the real problem: what is superbrained man going to do with his powers, what can he find worthy of his efforts? I still wonder if perhaps there hasn't been a reason – call it God – for all this to happen.'

Corinth nodded absently. He was straining ahead, peering into the forward viewscreen as if his vision could leap light-years and find the planet called Earth.

CHAPTER SEVENTEEN

Spring had come late, but now there was warmth in the air and a mist of green on the trees. It was too nice a day to sit in an office, and Mandelbaum regretted his own eminence. It would be more fun to go out and shoot some golf, if the nearest course was dry enough yet. But as chief administrator of the area including roughly the old states of New York, New Jersey, and New England, he had his duties.

Well, when they had gotten the weather-turning force-screens into full production, he'd move his headquarters out in the country somewhere and sit in the open. Till then, he remained in the city. New York was dying, it had no more economic or social purpose and every day some hundreds of people left, but the location was still convenient.

He entered the office, nodded at the staff, and went into his own sanctum. The usual stack of reports waited, but he had barely gotten started when the phone rang. He swore as he picked it up – must be rather urgent if his secretary had bucked it on to him. 'Hello,' he snapped.

'William Jerome.' It was the voice of the superintendent of the Long Island food-factory project. He had been a civil engineer before the change and continued his old work on a higher level. 'I need advice,' he continued, 'and you seem to be the best human-relations idea-man around.'

He spoke a little awkwardly, as did Mandelbaum; both were practising the recently developed Unitary language. It had a maximal logic and a minimal redundancy in its structure, there was a universe of precise meaning in a few words, and it would probably become the international tongue of business and science if not of poetry; but it had only been made public a week before.

Mandelbaum frowned. Jerome's work was perhaps the most important in the world today. Somehow two billion people must be fed, and the food synthesis plants would permit free distribution of an adequate if unexciting diet; but first they had to be built. 'What is it this time?' he asked. 'More trouble with Fort Knox?' Gold was an industrial metal now, valued for its conductivity and inertness, and Jerome wanted plenty of it for bus bars and reaction vats.

'No, they've finally begun delivering. It's the workmen. I've got a show-down on my hands, and it may become a strike.'

'What for? Higher wages?' Mandelbaum's tone was sardonic. The problem of money was still not quite solved, and wouldn't be until the new man-hour credit standard got world-wide acceptance; meanwhile he had established his own local system, payment in scrip which could be exchanged for goods and services. But there was only so much to go around: more money would be a valueless gesture.

'No, they've got over that. But the thing is, they don't want to work six hours a day. It's pretty dull, driving nails and mixing concrete. I've explained that it'll take time to build robots for that sort of work, but they want the leisure immediately. What am I going to do if everybody'd rather accept a minimum standard of living and sit around arguing philosophy in his off hours?'

Mandelbaum grinned. 'Leisure time is part of the standard of living too. What you got to do, Bill, is make 'em want to stay on the job.'

'Yeah – how?'

'Well, what's wrong with setting up loudspeakers giving lectures on this and that? Better yet, give every man a buttonhole receiver and let him tune in on what he wants to hear: talks, symphonies, or whatever. I'll call up Columbia and get 'em to arrange a series of beamcasts for you.'

'You mean broadcasts, don't you?'

'No. Then they'd stay at home and listen. This series will run during working hours and be beamed exclusively at your construction site.'

'Hmmm –' Jerome laughed. 'It might work at that!'

'Sure. You find out what the boys want and let me know. I'll take care of the rest.'

When the engineer had hung up, Mandelbaum stuffed his pipe and returned to his papers. He wished all his headaches could be fixed as easily as that. But this matter of relocation. Everybody and his dog, it seemed, wanted to live out in the country; transportation and communication were no longer isolating factors. That would involve a huge labour of transference and land-scaping, to say nothing of clearing ownership titles. He couldn't resist so strong a demand, but he couldn't do it at once, either. Then there was the business of –

'O'Banion,' said the annunciator.

'Hm? Oh, yes. He had an appointment, didn't he? Send him in.'

Brian O'Banion had been an ordinary cop before the change; during the chaotic period he had worked with the civil police; now he was local chief of Observers. For all that, he was still a big red-faced Irishman, and it was incongruous to hear crisp Unitary coming from his mouth.

'I need some more men,' he said. 'The job's getting too large again.'

Mandelbaum puffed smoke and considered. The Observers were his own creation, though the idea had spread far and would probably be adopted by the international government before long. The smooth operation of society required a steady flow of information, a fantastically huge amount to be correlated every day if developments were not to get out of hand. The Observers gathered it in various ways: one of the most effective was simply to wander around in the guise of an ordinary citizen, talking to people and using logic to fill in all the implications.

'Takes a while to recruit and train 'em, Brian,' said Mandelbaum. 'What exactly do you want them for?'

'Well, first, there's this business of the feeble-minded. I'd like to put a couple of extra men on it. Not an easy job; there are still a lot of 'em wandering around, you know, and they've got to be located and unobtrusively guided the right way, towards one of the little colonies that're springing up.'

'And the colonies themselves ought to be watched more closely and guarded against interference – yeah. Sooner or later, we're going to have to decide just what to do about them. But that'll be part and parcel of what we decide to do about ourselves, which is still very much up in the air. Okay, anything else?'

'I've got a lead on – something. Don't know just what, but I think it's big and I think part of it is right here in New York.'

Mandelbaum turned impassive. 'What's that, Brian?' he asked quietly.

'I don't know. It may not even be criminal. But it's big. I have tips from half a dozen countries around the world. Scientific equipment and materials are going into devious channels and not being seen again – publicly.'

'So? Why should every scientist give us a step-by-step account of his doings?'

'No reason. But for instance, the Swedish Observer corps tracked one thing. Somebody in Stockholm wanted a certain kind of vacuum tube, a very special kind. The manufacturer explained that his whole stock, which was very small because of the low demand, had been bought by someone else. The would-be purchaser looked up the someone else, who turned out to be an agent buying for a fourth party he'd never seen. That got the Observers interested, and they checked every lab in the country; none of them had bought the stuff, so it was probably sent out by private plane or the like. They asked the Observers in other countries to check. It turned out that our customs men had noted a caseful of these same tubes arriving at Idlewild. That put a bee in my bonnet, and I tried to find where those tubes had gone. No luck – the trail ended there.

'So I started asking Observers around the world myself, and found several similar instances. Spaceship parts vanishing in Australia, for example, or a load of uranium from the Belgian Congo. It may not mean anything at all, but, well, if it's a legitimate project, why all this secrecy? I want some more men to help me follow up on it. I don't like the smell of it.'

Mandelbaum nodded. Something like a crazy, unsafe experiment in nucleonics – it could devastate his whole territory. Or there might be a more deliberate plan. No telling as yet.

'I'll see you get them,' he said.

CHAPTER EIGHTEEN

Early summer: the first shy green of leaves has become a fullness enchanted with sunlight, talking with wind; it has rained just an hour ago, and the light cool wind shakes down a fine sparkle of drops, like a ghostly kiss on your uplifted face; a few sparrows dance on the long, empty streets; the clean quiet mass of the buildings is sharp against a luminous blue sky, the thousand windows catch the morning sun and throw it back in one great dazzle.

The city had a sleeping look. A few men and women walked between the silent skyscrapers; they were casually dressed, some almost nude, and the driven feverish hurry of old days was gone. Now and then a truck or automobile purred down the otherwise bare avenue. They were all running off the new powercast system, and the smokeless, dustless air was almost cruelly brilliant. There was something of Sunday about this morning, though it was midweek.

Sheila's heels tapped loudly on the sidewalk. The staccato noise jarred at her in the stillness. But she could only muffle it by slowing her pace, and she didn't want to do that. She couldn't.

A troop of boys, about ten years old, came out of the deserted shop in which they had been playing and ran down the street ahead of her. Young muscles still had to exercise, but it was saddening to her that they weren't shouting. Sometimes she thought that the children were the hardest thing to endure. They weren't like children any more.

It was a long walk from the depot to the Institute, and she could have saved her energy – for what? – by taking the subway. But the thought of being caged in metal with the new men of Earth made her shiver. It was more open and free aboveground, almost like being in the country. The city had served its day, now it was dying, and the bare blind walls around her were as impersonal as mountains. She was alone.

A shadow ran along the street, as if cast by a cloud travelling swiftly overhead. Looking up, she saw the long metallic shape vanish noiselessly behind the skyscrapers. Perhaps they had mastered gravity. What of it?

She passed by two men who were sitting in a doorway, and their conversation floated to her through the quiet:

'– starvish esthetics – the change.'

Swift flutter of hands.

'*Wiedersehen.*' Sigh.

'Negate: macrocosm, un-ego, entropy. Human-meaning.'

She went on a little faster.

The Institute building looked shabbier than the Fifth Avenue giants. Perhaps that was because it was still intensely in use; it did not have their monumental dignity of death. Sheila walked into the lobby. There was no one around, but an enigmatic thing of blinking lights and glowing tubes murmured to itself in a corner. She went over to the elevator, hesitated, and turned off for the staircase. No telling what they had done to the elevator – maybe it was wholly automatic, maybe it responded directly to thought commands, maybe they had a dog running it.

On the seventh floor, breathing a little sharply, she went down the corridor. It hadn't changed, at least – the men here had had too much else to do. But the old fluorescent tubes were gone, now the air itself – or the walls, ceiling, floor? – held light. It was peculiarly hard to gauge distances in that shadowless radiance.

She paused before the entrance to Pete's old laboratory, swallowing a gulp of fear. *Stupid*, she told herself, *they're not going to eat you. But what have they done inside? What are they doing now?*

Squaring her shoulders, she knocked on the door. There was a barely perceptible hesitation, then: 'Come in.' She turned the knob and entered.

The place had hardly changed at all. That was perhaps the most difficult thing to understand. Some of the apparatus was standing in a corner, dusty with neglect, and she did not comprehend the thing which had grown up to cover three tables. But it had always been that way when she visited her husband in the old days, a clutter of gadgetry that simply didn't register on her ignorance. It was still the same big room, the windows opened on a heartlessly bright sky and a remote view of docks and warehouses, a shabby smock hung on the stained wall, and a faint smell of ozone and rubber was in the air. There were still the worn reference books on Pete's desk; his table-model cigarette lighter – she had given it to him for Christmas, oh, very long ago – was slowly tarnishing by an empty ash tray, the chair was shoved back a little as if he had only gone out for a minute and would return any time.

Grunewald looked up from the thing on which he worked, blinking in the near-sighted manner she recalled. He looked tired, his shoulders stooped more than they once did, but the square blond face was the same. A dark young man whom she didn't know was helping him.

He made a clumsy gesture. (Why, Mrs Corinth! This is an unexpected pleasure. Do come in.)

The other man grunted and Grunewald waved at him. (This is) 'Jim Manzelli,' he said. (He's helping me out just now. Jim, this is) 'Mrs Corinth,' (wife of my former boss).

Manzelli nodded. Curtness: (Pleased to meet you.) He had the eyes of a fanatic.

Grunewald went over to her, wiping grimy hands. 'Why' (are you here, Mrs Corinth)?

She answered slowly, feeling her timidity harsh in her throat. (I only wanted to) 'Look around.' (I) 'Won't bother' (you very) 'long.' Eyes, fingers twisting together: Plea for kindness.

Grunewald peered more closely at her, and she saw the expressions across his face. Shock. *You have grown so thin! There is something haunted about you, and your hands are never still.* Compassion: *Poor girl, it's been hard for you, hasn't it? We all miss him.* Conventional courtesy: (I hope you are over your) 'Illness?'

Sheila nodded. (Where is) 'Johansson?' she asked. (The lab doesn't seem the same without his long glum face – or without Pete.)

(He's gone to help out in) 'Africa, I think.' (A colossal job before us, too big, too sudden.)

(Too cruel!)

Nodding: (Yes.) Eyes to Manzelli: (Question.)

Manzelli's gaze rested on Sheila with a probing intensity. She shivered, and Grunewald gave his partner a reproachful look.

(I came up) 'From Long Island today.' Bitterness in her smile, she has grown harder, and a nod: (Yes, they seem to think it's all right to let me loose now. At least, they had no way to compel me, and too much else to do to worry about me in any case.)

A greyness flitted through Grunewald's expression. (You came up to say good-bye, didn't you?)

(I wanted to) 'See' (the) 'place' (once again, only for a little while. It holds so many of his days).

Sudden pleading in her: 'He is dead, isn't he?'

Shrug, pity: (We can't say. But the ship is months overdue, and only a major disaster could have stopped her. She may have run into the) 'Inhibitor field' (out in space, in spite of all precautions).

Sheila walked slowly past him. She went over to Pete's desk and stroked her fingers across the back of his chair.

Grunewald cleared his throat. (Are you) 'Leaving civilization?'

She nodded mutely. *It is too big for me, too cold and strange.*

(There is still) 'Work to do,' he said.

She shook her head. (Not for me. It is not a work I want or understand.) Taking up the cigarette lighter, she dropped it into her purse, smiling a little.

Grunewald and Manzelli traded another look. This time Manzelli made a sign of agreement.

(We have been) 'Doing work' (here which might – interest you), said Grunewald. *Give you hope. Give you back your tomorrows.*

The brown eyes that turned to him were almost unfocused. He thought that her face was like white paper, stretched across the bones; and some Chinese artist had penned the delicate blue tracery of veins across her temples and hands.

He tried awkwardly to explain. The nature of the inhibitor field had been more fully worked out since the star ship left. Even before that time, it had been possible to generate the field artificially and study its effects; now Grunewald and Manzelli had gotten together on a project of creating the same thing on a huge scale. It shouldn't take much apparatus – a few tons, perhaps; and once the field was set up, using a nuclear disintegrator to furnish the necessary power, solar energy should be enough to maintain it.

The project was highly unofficial: now that the first press of necessity was gone, those scientists who chose were free to work on whatever suited their own fancy, and materials weren't difficult to obtain. There was a small organization which helped get what was necessary; all that Grunewald and Manzelli were doing here at the Institute was testing, the actual construction went on elsewhere. Their labour seemed harmless to everyone else, a little dull compared to what was going on in other lines of endeavour. No one paid any attention to it, or reasoned below the surface of Grunewald's public explanation.

Sheila regarded him vaguely, and he wondered about the regions into which her inner self had gone. 'Why?' she asked. 'What is it you're really doing?'

Manzelli smiled, with a harshness over him. (Isn't it obvious? We mean to) 'Build an orbital space station' (and set it going several thousand miles above the surface). 'Full-scale field generators' (in it. We'll bring mankind back to the) 'Old days.'

She didn't cry out, or gasp, or even laugh. She only nodded, as if it were a blurred image of no meaning.

(Retreat from reality – how sane are you?) asked Grunewald's eyes.

(What reality?) she flashed at him.

Manzelli shrugged. He knew she wouldn't tell anyone, he could read that much in her, and that was what counted. If it didn't give her the excited joy Grunewald had hoped for, it was no concern of his.

Sheila wandered over to one side of the room. A collection of apparatus there looked peculiarly medical. She saw the table with its straps, the drawer with hypodermic needles and ampules, the machine which crouched blackly near the head of the table – 'What is this?' she asked. Her tone should have told them that she knew already, but they were too immersed in their own wishes.

'Modified electric-shock treatment,' said Grunewald. He explained that in the first weeks of the change there had been an attempt to study the functional aspects of intelligence by systematic destruction of the cerebral cortex cells in animals, and measurement of the effects. But it had soon been abandoned as too inhumane and relatively useless. 'I thought you knew' (about it), he finished. (It was) 'In the biology of psych departments when Pete (was still here. I remember he) 'protested strongly' (against it. Didn't he gripe to) 'you' (about it too)?

Sheila nodded dimly.

'The change' (made) 'men cruel,' said Manzelli (And) 'Now' (they) 'aren't' (even that, any longer. They've become something other than man, and this world of rootless intellect has lost all its old dreams and loves. We want to restore humanness).

Sheila turned away from the ugly black machine. 'Goodbye,' she said.

'I – well –' Grunewald looked at the floor. 'Keep in touch, won't you?' (Let us know where you are, so if Pete comes back –)

Her smile was as remote as death. (He will never come back. But goodbye, now.)

She went out the door and down the corridor. Near the staircase was a washroom door. It was not marked 'Men' or 'Women,' even the Western world had gone beyond such prudery, and she went in and looked in a mirror. The face that regarded her was hollow, and the hair hung lank and dull to her shoulders. She made an effort with comb and water to spruce up, not knowing or caring why she did. and then went down the stairway to the first floor.

The door to the director's office stood open, letting a breeze find its way between the windows and the building entrance. There were quiet machines inside, probably doing the work of a large secretarial staff. Sheila went past the outer suite and knocked on the open door of the inner office.

Helga Arnulfsen glanced up from her desk. She'd grown a little thin too, Sheila realized, and there was a darkness in her eyes. But even if she was more informally dressed than had once been her habit, she was strong and smooth to look on. Her voice, which had always been husky, lifted a trifle in surprise: 'Sheila!'

'How do you do?'

'Come in,' (do come in, sit down. It's been a long time since I saw you). Helga was smiling as she came around the desk and took Sheila's hand, but her fingers were cold.

She pressed a button and the door closed. (Now we can have) 'Privacy,' she said. (This is the sign I'm not to be bothered.) She pulled up a chair across from Sheila's and sat down, crossing her long trim legs man-fashion. 'Well, good' (to see you. I hope you're feeling well.) *You don't look well, poor kid.*

'I –' Sheila clasped her hands and unclasped them again and picked at the purse in her lap. 'I –' (Why did I come?)

Eyes: (Because of Pete.)

Nod: (Yes. Yes, that must be it. Sometimes I don't know why – But we both loved him, didn't we?)

'You,' said Helga without tone, 'are the only one he cared for.' *And you hurt him. Your suffering was grief within him.*

I know. That's the worst of it. (And still) 'He wasn't the same man,' said Sheila. (He changed too much, like all the world. Even as I held him, he slipped by me, time itself carried him away.) 'I lost him even before he died.'

'No. You had him, it was always you.' Helga shrugged. 'Well, life goes on,' (in an amputated fashion. We eat and breathe and sleep and work, because there is nothing else we can do.)

'You have strength,' said Sheila. (You have endured where I couldn't.)

'Oh, I kept going,' answered Helga.

'You still have tomorrow.'

'Yes, I suppose so.'

Sheila smiled, it trembled on her mouth. (I'm luckier than you are. I have yesterday.)

'They may come back,' said Helga. (There's no telling what has happened to them. Have you the courage to wait?)

'No,' said Sheila. 'Their bodies may come back,' (but not Pete. He has changed too much, and I can't change with him. Nor would I want to be a weight around his neck.)

Helga laid a hand on Sheila's arm. How thin it was! You could feel the bones underneath. 'Wait,' she said. 'Therapy' (is progressing. You can be brought up to) 'Normal' (in – well – a) 'few years, at most.'

'I don't think so.'

There was a touch of contempt, thinly veiled, in the cool blue eyes. *Do you want to live up to the future? Down underneath, do you really desire to keep pace?* 'What else' (can you do) 'but wait? Unless suicide –'

'No, not that either.' (There are still mountains, deep valleys, shining rivers, sun and moon and the high stars of winter.) 'I'll find my adjustment.'

(I've kept in touch with) 'Kearnes.' (He) 'Seemed' (to) 'think' (you were) 'progressing.'

'Oh, yes.' *I've learned to hide it. There are too many eyes in this new world.* 'But I didn't come to talk about myself, Helga.' (I just came to say) 'Good-bye.'

'Where' (are you going? I have to keep in touch with you, if he should come back.)

'I'll write' (and let you know).

'Or give a message to a Sensitive.' (The postal system is obsolete.)

That too? I remember old Mr Barneveldt, shuffling down the street in his blue uniform, when I was a little girl. He used to have a piece of candy for me.

'Look, I'm getting hungry,' said Helga. (Why don't we go have) 'Lunch?'

(No, thank you. I don't feel like it.) Sheila got up. 'Good-bye, Helga.'

'Not good-bye, Sheila. We'll see you again, and you'll be well then.'

'Yes,' said Sheila. 'I'll be all right. But good-bye.'

She walked out of the office and the building. There were more people abroad now, and she mingled with them. A doorway across the street offered a hidden place.

She felt no sense of farewell. There was an emptiness in her, as if grief and loneliness and bewilderment had devoured themselves. Now and then one of the shadows flitted across her mind, but they weren't frightening any longer. Almost, she pitied them. Poor ghosts! They would die soon.

She saw Helga emerge and walk alone down the street, towards some place where she would swallow a solitary lunch before going back to work. Sheila smiled, shaking her head a little. *Poor efficient Helga!*

Presently Grunewald and Manzelli came out and went the same way, lost in conversation. Sheila's heart gave a small leap. The palms of her hands were cold and wet. She waited till the men were out of sight, then crossed the street again and re-entered the Institute.

The noise of her shoes was hard on the stairway. She breathed deeply, trying for steadiness. When she came out on the seventh floor, she stood for a minute waiting for the self-control she needed. Then she ran down the hall to the physical laboratory.

The door gaped ajar. She hesitated again, looking at the unfinished machine within. Hadn't Grunewald told her about some fantastic scheme to –? No matter. It couldn't work. He and Manzelli, that whole little band of recidivists, were insane.

Am I insane? she wondered. If so, there was an odd strength in her. She needed more resolution for what she was going to do than it took to put a gun barrel in her mouth and squeeze a trigger.

The shock machine lay like some armoured animal beside the table. She worked swiftly, adjusting it. Memory of Pete's anger at its early use had, indeed, come back to her in the house of isolation; and Kearnes had been pleased to give her all the texts she asked for, glad that she was finding an objective interest. She smiled again. Poor Kearnes! How she had fooled him.

The machine hummed, warming up. She took a small bundle from her purse and unwrapped it. Syringe, needle, bottle of anaesthetic, electrode paste, cord to tie to the switch so she could pull it with her teeth. And a timer for the switch, too. She had to estimate the safe time for what was necessary, she would be unconscious when the process must be stopped.

Maybe it wouldn't work. Quite likely her brain would simply fry in her skull. What of it?

She smiled out the window as she injected herself. Goodbye, sun, good-bye, blue heaven, clouds, rain, airy song of home-bound birds. Good-bye and thank you.

Stripping off her clothes, she lay on the table and fastened the electrodes in place. They felt cold against her skin. Some of the straps were easy to buckle, but the right arm – well, she had come prepared, she had a long belt that went under the table, around her wrist, a padlock she could snap shut. Now she was immobile.

Her eyes darkened as the drug took hold. It was good to sleep.

Now – one quick jerk with her teeth.

THUNDER AND FIRE AND SHATTERING DARKNESS
RUIN AND HORROR AND LIGHTNING
PAIN PAIN PAIN

CHAPTER NINETEEN

'Hello, Earth. Peter Corinth calling Earth from Star Ship I, homeward bound.'

Buzz and murmur of cosmic interference, the talking of the stars. Earth a swelling blue brilliance against night, her moon like a pearl hung on the galaxy's breast, the sun wreathed in flame.

'Hello, Earth. Come in, come in. Can you hear me, Earth?'

Click, click, zzzzz, mmmmmm, voices across the sky.

Hello, Sheila!

The planet grew before them. The ship's drive purred and rumbled, every plate in the hull trembled with thrusting energies, there was a wild fine singing in the crystals of the metal. Corinth realized that he was shaking too, but he didn't want to control himself, not now.

'Hello, Earth,' he said monotonously into the radio. They were moving well under the speed of light and their signal probed blindly ahead of them, through the dark. 'Hello, Earth, can you hear me? This is Star Ship I, calling from space, homeward bound.'

Lewis growled something which meant: 'Maybe they've given up radio since we left. All these months –'

Corinth shook his head: 'They'd still have monitors of some kind, I'm sure.' To the microphone: 'Hello, Earth, come in, Earth. Anyone on Earth hear me?'

'If some ham – a five-year-old kid, I bet, in Russia or India or Africa – picks it up, he'll have to get the word to a transmitter which can reach us,' said Lewis. 'It takes time. Just relax, Pete.'

'A matter of time!' Corinth turned from the seat. 'You're right, I suppose. We'll make planetfall in hours, anyway. But I did want to have a real welcome prepared for us!'

'A dozen Limfjord oysters on the half shell, with lots of lemon juice,' said Lewis dreamily, speaking all the words aloud. 'Rhine wine, of course – say a '37. Baby shrimp in fresh mayonnaise, on French bread with fresh-churned butter. Smoked eel with cold scrambled eggs on pumpernickel, don't forget the chives –'

Corinth grinned, though half his mind was lost with Sheila, off alone with her in some place of sunlight. It was good, it felt strangely warm, to sit and exchange commonplaces, even if those were overtly little more than a word and a shift of expression. All the long way home, they had argued like drunken gods, exploring their own intellects; but it had been a means of shutting out the stupendous dark quiet. Now they were back to man's hearth fire.

'Hello, Star Ship I.'

They jerked wildly about to face the receiver. The voice that came was faint, blurred with the noise of sun and stars, but it was human. It was home.

'Why,' whispered Lewis in awe, 'why, he's even got a Brooklyn accent.'

'Hello, Star Ship I. This is New York calling you. Can you hear me?'

'Yes,' said Corinth, his throat dry, and waited for the signal to leap across millions of miles.

'Had a devil of a time getting you,' said the voice conversationally, after the time lag had gone by in whining, crackling blankness. 'Had to allow for Doppler effect – you must be coming in like a bat out of Chicago, are your pants on fire or something?' He mentioned nothing of the engineering genius which had made communication possible at all; it was a minor job now. 'Congratulations, though! All okay?'

'Fine,' said Lewis. 'Had some trouble, but we're coming home in one piece and expect to be greeted properly.' He hesitated for a moment. 'How's Earth?'

'Good enough. Though I'll bet you won't recognize the place. Things are changing so fast it's a real relief to talk good old United States once again. Prolly the last time I'll ever do it. What the devil happened to you, anyway?'

'We'll explain later,' said Corinth shortly. 'How are our associates?'

'Okay, I guess. I'm just a technician at Brookhaven, you know, I'm not acquainted. But I'll pass the word along. You'll land here, I suppose?'

'Yes, in about –' Corinth made a swift estimate involving the simultaneous solution of a number of differential equations. 'Six hours.'

'Okay, we'll –' The tone faded away. They caught one more word, – 'band –' and then there was only the stillness.

'Hello, New York, you've lost the beam,' said Corinth.

'Ah, forget it,' said Lewis. 'Turn it off, why don't you?'

'But –'

'We've waited so long that we can wait six hours more. Isn't worthwhile tinkering around that way.'

'Ummmm – well –' Corinth yielded. 'Hello, New York. Hello, Earth. This is Star Ship I signing off. Over and out.

'I did want to talk to Sheila,' he added.

'You'll have plenty of time for that, laddy,' answered Lewis. 'I think right now we ought to be taking a few more observations on the drive. It's got a fluttery note that might mean something. Nobody's ever operated one continuously as long as we have, and there may be cumulative effects –'

'Crystal fatigue, perhaps,' said Corinth. 'Okay, you win.' He gave himself to his instruments.

Earth grew before them. They, who had crossed light-years in hours, had to limp home now at mere hundreds of miles a second; even their new reactions weren't fast enough to handle translight speeds this near a planet. But theirs would probably be the last ship so limited, thought Corinth. At the fantastic rate of post-change technological advance, the next vessel should be a dream of perfection: as if the Wright brothers had built a transatlantic clipper for their second working model. He imagined that his own lifetime would see engineering carried to some kind of ultimate, reaching the bounds imposed by natural law. Thereafter man would have to find a new field of intellectual adventure, and he thought he knew what it would be. He looked at the swelling lovely planet with a kind of tenderness. *Ave atque vale!*

The crescent became a ragged, cloudy disc as they swung around towards the day side. Then, subtly, it was no longer before them but below them, and they heard the first thin shriek of cloven air. They swept over a vastness of moonlit Pacific, braking, and saw dawn above the Sierra Nevada. America fell beneath them, huge and green and beautiful, a strong-ribbed land, and the Mississippi was a silver thread across her. Then they slanted down, and the spires of Manhattan rose against the sea.

Corinth's heart slammed in the cage of his breast. *Be still*, he told it, *be still and wait. There is time now*. He guided the ship towards Brookhaven, where the spacefield was a slash of grey, and saw another bright spear cradled there. So they had already begun on the next ship.

There was a tiny shock as the hull found its berth. Lewis reached over to cut off the engines. When they died, Corinth's ears rang with the sudden quiet. He had not realized how much a part of him that ceaseless drumming was.

'Come on!' He was out of his seat and across the narrow cabin before Lewis had stirred. His fingers trembled as they wove across the intricate pattern of the electronic lock. The inner door swung smoothly open, and then the outer door was open too, and he caught a breath of salt air, blown in from the sea.

Sheila! Where is Sheila? He tumbled down the ladder in the cradle, his form dark against the metal of the hull. It was pocked and blistered, that metal, streaked with curious crystallization-patterns, the ship had travelled far and strangely. When he hit the ground he overbalanced, falling, but he was up again before anyone could help him.

'Sheila,' he cried.

Felix Mandelbaum stepped forth, holding out his hands. He looked very old and tired, burned out by strain. He took Corinth's hands in his own but did not speak.

'Where's Sheila?' whispered Corinth. 'Where is she?'

Mandelbaum shook his head. Lewis was climbing down now, more cautiously. Rossman went to meet him, looking away from Corinth. The others followed – they were all Brookhaven people, no close friends, but they looked away.

Corinth tried to swallow and couldn't 'Dead?' he asked The wind murmured around him, ruffling his hair.

'No,' said Mandelbaum. 'Nor is she mad. But –' He shook his head, and the beaked face wrinkled up. 'No.'

Corinth drew a breath that shuddered in his lungs. Looking at him, they saw the blankness of will descend. He would not let himself weep.

'Go ahead,' he said. 'Tell me.'

'It was about six weeks ago,' Mandelbaum said. 'She couldn't stand any more, I guess. She got hold of an electric-shock machine.'

Corinth nodded, very slowly. 'And destroyed her brain,' he finished.

'No. Not that, though it was touch and go for a while.' Mandelbaum took the physicist's arm. 'Let's put it this way: she is the old Sheila, like before the change. Almost.'

Corinth was dimly aware how fresh and live the sea wind felt in his nostrils.

'Come along, Pete,' said Mandelbaum. 'I'll take you to her.'

Corinth followed him off the field.

The psychiatrist Kearnes met them at Bellevue. His face was like wood, but there was no feeling of shame in him and none of blame in Corinth. The man had done his best, with the inadequate knowledge at his disposal, and failed; that was a fact of reality, nothing more.

'She fooled me,' he said. 'I thought she was straightening out. I didn't realize how much control even an insane person would have with the changed nervous system. Nor, I suppose, did I realize how hard it was for her all along. None of us who endured the change will ever know what a nightmare it must have been for those who couldn't adapt.'

Dark wings beating, and Sheila alone. Nightfall, and Sheila alone.

'She was quite insane when she did it?' asked Corinth. His voice was flat.

'What is sanity? Perhaps she did the wisest thing. Was the eventual prospect of being cured, when we learn how, worth that kind of existence?'

'What were the effects?'

'Well, it was a clumsy job, of course. Several bones were broken in the convulsions, and she'd have died if she hadn't been found in time.' Kearnes laid a hand on Corinth's shoulder. 'The actual volume of destroyed cerebral tissue was small, but of course it was in the most critical area of the brain.'

'Felix told me she's – making a good recovery.'

'Oh, yes.' Kearnes smiled wryly, as if he had a sour taste in his mouth. 'It isn't hard for us to understand prechange human psychology – now. I used the triple-pronged approach developed by Gravenstein and de la Garde since the change. Symbological re-evaluation, cybernetic neurology, and somatic co-ordination treatments. There was enough sound tissue to take over the functions of the damaged part, with proper guidance, once the psychosis had been lifted. I think she can be discharged from here in about three months.'

He drew a deep breath. 'She will be a normal, healthy pre-change human with an I.Q. of about 150.'

'I see –' Corinth nodded. 'Well – what are the chances of restoring her?'

'It will take years, at best, before we're able to recreate nervous tissue. It doesn't regenerate, you know, even with artificial stimulation. We'll have to create life itself synthetically, and telescope a billion years of evolution to develop the human brain cell, and duplicate the precise gene pattern of the patient, and even then – I wonder.'

'I see.'

'You can visit her for a short while. We have told her you were alive.'

'What did she do?'

'Cried a good deal, of course. That's a healthy symptom. You can stay about half an hour if you don't excite her too much.' Kearnes gave him the room number and went back into his office.

Corinth took the elevator and walked down a long quiet hallway that smelled of rain-wet roses. When he came to Sheila's room, the door stood ajar and he hesitated a little, glancing in. It was like a forest bower, ferns and trees and the faint twitter of nesting birds; a waterfall was running somewhere, and the air had the tingle of earth and greenness. Mostly illusion, he supposed, but if it gave her comfort –

He went in, over to the bed which rested beneath a sun-dappled willow. 'Hello darling,' he said.

The strangest thing was that she hadn't changed. She looked as she had when they were first married, young and fair, her hair curled softly about a face which was still a little pale, her eyes full of luster as they turned to him. The white nightgown, a fluffy thing from her own wardrobe, made her seem only half grown.

'Pete,' she said.

He stooped over and kissed her, very gently. Her response was somehow remote, almost like a stranger's. As her hands caressed his face, he noticed that the wedding ring was gone.

'You lived.' She spoke it with a kind of wonder. 'You came back.'

'To you, Sheila,' he said, and sat down beside her.

She shook her head. 'No,' she answered.

'I love you,' he said in his helplessness.

'I loved you too.' Her voice was still quiet, far away, and he saw the dreaminess in her eyes. 'That's why I did this.'

He sat holding himself in, fighting for calm. There were thunders in his head.

'I don't remember you too well, you know,' she said. 'I suppose my memory was damaged a little. It all seems many years ago, and you like a dream I loved.' She smiled. 'How thin you are, Pete! And hard, somehow. Everybody has grown so hard.'

'No,' he said. 'They all care for you.'

'It isn't the old kind of caring. Not the kind I knew. And you aren't Pete anymore.' She sat up, her voice rising a little. 'Pete died in the change. I watched him die. You're a nice man, and it hurts me to look at you, but you aren't Pete.'

'Take it easy, darling,' he said.

'I couldn't go ahead with you,' she said, 'and I wouldn't give you – or myself – that kind of burden. Now I've gone back. And you don't know how wonderful it is. Lonely but wonderful. There's peace in it.'

'I still want you,' he said.

'No. Don't lie to me. Don't you see, it isn't necessary.' Sheila smiled across a thousand years. 'You can sit there like that, your face all frozen – why, you aren't Pete. But I wish you well.'

He knew then what she needed, and let himself go, surrendering will and understanding. He knelt by her bed and wept, and she comforted him as well as she could.

CHAPTER TWENTY

There is an island in mid-Pacific, not far off the equator, which lies distant from the world of man. The old shipping routes and the later transoceanic airlines followed the tracks beyond its horizon, and the atoll had been left to sun and wind and the crying of gulls.

For a brief while it had known humankind. The slow blind patience of coral polyps had built it up, and days and nights had ground its harsh wet face into soil, and the seeds of plants had been blown on a long journey to find it. A few coconuts washed up in the surf, and presently there were trees. They stood for hundreds of years, perhaps, until a canoe came over the world's rim.

Those were Polynesians, tail brown men whose race had wandered far in the search for Hawaiki the beautiful. There was sun and salt on them, and they thought little of crossing a thousand miles of emptiness, for they had the stars and the great sea currents to guide them and their own arms to paddle, *tohiha, hioha, itoki, itoki!* When they drew their boat ashore and had made sacrifice to shark-toothed Nan, they wound hibiscus blooms in their long hair and danced on the beach; for they had looked on the island and found it good.

Then they went away, but the next year – or the year after that, or the year after that, for the ocean was big and time was forever – they came back with others, bringing pigs and women, and that night fires burned tall on the beach. Afterward a village of thatch huts arose, and naked brown children tumbled in the surf, and fishermen went beyond the lagoon with much laughter. And this lasted for a hundred years, or two hundred, before the pale men came.

Their big white-winged canoes stopped only a few times at this island, which was not an important one, but nonetheless faithfully discharged their usual cargo of smallpox, measles, and tuberculosis, so that there were not many of the brown folk left. Afterwards some resistance was built up, aided by Caucasian blood, and it was time for copra planters, religion, Mother

Hubbards, and international conferences to determine whether this atoll, among others, belonged to London, Paris, Berlin, or Washington – large villages on the other side of the world.

A *modus vivendi* was finally reached, involving copra, Christianity, tobacco, and trading schooners. The island people, by this time a mixture of several races, were reasonably satisfied, though they did have many toothaches; and when one of their young men, who through a long chain of circumstances had studied in America, came back and sighed for the old days, the people laughed at him. They had only vague memories of that time, handed down through a series of interested missionaries.

Then someone in an office on the other side of the world decided that an island was needed. It may have been for a naval base, or perhaps an experimental station – the pale men had so many wars, and spent the rest of their time preparing for them. It does not matter any longer why the atoll was desired, for there are no men on it now and the gulls don't care. The natives were moved elsewhere, and spent some quiet years in a sick longing for home. Nobody paid any attention to this, for the island was needed to safeguard the freedom of man, and after a time the older generation died off and the younger generation forgot. Meanwhile the white men disturbed the gulls for a little, putting up buildings and filling the lagoon with ships.

Then, for some unimportant reason, the island was abandoned. It may have been through treaty, possibly through a defeat in war or an economic collapse. The wind and rain and creeping vines had never been defeated, only contained. Now they began the task of demolition.

For a few centuries, men had disturbed the timelessness of days and nights, rain and sun and stars and hurricanes, but now they were gone again. The surf rolled and chewed at the reef, the slow chill sliding of underwater currents gnawed at the foundations, but there were many polyps and they were still building. The island would endure for a goodly fraction of a million years, so there was no hurry about anything. By day fish leaped in the waters, and gulls hovered overhead, and the trees and bamboo grew with frantic haste; at night the moon was cold on tumbling surf and a phosphorescent track swirled behind the great shark who patrolled the outer waters. And there was peace.

The airjet whispered down out of darkness and the high bright stars. Invisible fingers of radar probed earthward, and a voice muttered over a beam. 'Down – this way – okay, easy does it.' The jet bounced to a halt in a clearing, and two men came out.

They were met by others, indistinct shadows in the moon-spattered night. One of them spoke with a dry Australian twang: 'Dr Grunewald, Dr Manzelli, may I present Major Rosovsky – Sri Ramavashtar – Mr Hwang

Pu-Yi –' He went on down the list; there were about a score present, including the two Americans.

Not so long ago it would have been a strange, even impossible group; a
Russian officer, a Hindu mystic, a French philosopher and religious writer,
an Irish politician, a Chinese commissar, an Australian engineer, a Swedish
financier – it was as if all the earth had gathered for a quiet insurrection. But
none of them were now what they had been, and the common denominator
was a yearning for something lost.

'I've brought the control apparatus,' said Grunewald briskly. 'How about
the heavy stuff?'

'It's all here. We can start anytime,' said the Irishman.

Grunewald glanced at his watch. 'It's a couple of hours to midnight,' he
said aloud. 'Can we be ready by then?'

'I think so,' said the Russian. 'It is almost all assembled.'

Walking down towards the beach, he gestured at the bulking shape which
lay black and awkward on the moon-whitened lagoon. He and one comrade
had gotten the tramp steamer months ago and outfitted her with machines
such that they two could sail her around the world. That had been their part
of the job: not too difficult for determined men in the confusion of a dying
civilization. They had sailed through the Baltic, picking up some of their
cargo in Sweden, and had also touched in France, Italy, Egypt, and India on
their way to the agreed destination. For some days, now, the work of assembling the spaceship and her load had progressed rapidly.

The surf roared and rumbled, a deep full noise that shivered underfoot,
and spouted whitely towards the constellations. Sand and coral scrunched
beneath boots, the palms and bamboos rustled dryly with the small wind,
and a disturbed parakeet racketed in the dark. Beyond this little beating of
sound, there were only silence and sleep.

Further on, the ruin of an old barracks mouldered in its shroud of vines.
Grunewald smelled the flowers there, and the heavy dampness of rotting
wood – it was a pungency which made his head swim. On the other side of
the ruin stood some tents, recently put up, and above them towered the
spaceship.

That was a clean and beautiful thing, like a pillar of grey ice under the
moon, poised starward. Grunewald looked at her with a curious blend of
feelings: taut fierce glory of conquest, heart-catching knowledge of her loveliness, wistfulness that soon he would not understand the transcendent logic
which had made her swift designing and building possible.

He looked at Manzelli. 'I envy you, my friend,' he said simply.

Several men were to ride her up, jockey her into an orbit, and do the final
work of assembling and starting the field generator she bore. Then they
would die, for there had not been time to prepare a means for their return.

Grunewald felt time like a hound on his heels. Soon the next star ship would be ready, and they were building others everywhere. Then there would be no stopping the march of the race, and of time. Tonight the last hope of mankind – human mankind – was being readied; there could not be another, if this failed.

'I think,' he said, 'that all the world will cry with relief before sunrise.'

'No,' said the Australian practically. 'They'll be madder'n a nest of hornets. You'll have to allow a while for them to realize they've been saved.'

Well, there would be time, then. The spaceship was equipped with defences beyond the capacity of pre-change man to overcome in less than a century. Her robots would destroy any other ships or missiles sent up from Earth. And man, the whole living race, would have a chance to catch his breath and remember his first loves, and after that he would not want to attack the spaceship.

The others had unloaded the jet from America and brought its delicate cargo to this place. Now they laid the crates on the ground, and Grunewald and Manzelli began opening them with care. Someone switched on a flood-light, and in its harsh white glare they forgot the moon and the sea around them.

Nor were they aware of the long noiseless form which slipped overhead and hung there like a shark swimming in the sky, watching. Only after it had spoken to them did they look up.

The amplified voice had been gentle, there was almost a note of regret in it. 'Sorry to disappoint you, but you've done enough.'

Staring wildly upward, Grunewald saw the steel shimmer above and his heart stumbled within him. The Russian yanked out a pistol and fired, the shots yammering futilely under the steady beat of surf. A gabble came from wakened birds, and their wings flapped loud among the soughing palms.

Manzelli cursed; whirled on his heel, and plunged into the spaceship. There were guns in it which could bring down that riding menace, and – Grunewald, diving for cover, saw a turret in the vessel's flank swing about and thrust a nose skyward. He threw himself on his belly. That cannon fired atomic shells!

From the hovering enemy sprang a beam of intense, eye-searing flame. The cannon muzzle slumped, glowed white. The thin finger wrote destruction down the flank of the ship until it reached the cones of her gravitic drive. There it played for minutes, and the heat of melting steel prickled men's faces.

A giant atomic-hydrogen torch – Grunewald's mind was dazed. *We can't take off now* –

Slowly, the very walls of the crippled spaceship began to glow red. The Swede screamed and pulled a ring off his finger. Manzelli stumbled out of the ship, crying. The force-field died, the machines began to cool again, but there was something broken in the men who stood waiting. Only the heavy sobs of Manzelli spoke.

The enemy craft – it was a star ship, they saw now – remained where it was, but a small antigravity raft floated out of her belly and drifted earthward. There were men standing on it, and one woman. None of the cabal moved as the raft grounded.

Grunewald took one step forward then, and stopped with his shoulders slumping. 'Felix,' he said in a dead voice. 'Pete. Helga.'

Mandelbaum nodded. The single floodlight threw a hard black shadow across his face. He waited on the raft while three quiet burly men, who had been detectives in the old world, went among the conspirators and collected the guns they had thrown away as too hot to hold. Then he joined the police on the ground. Corinth and Helga followed.

'Surely you didn't expect to get away with this,' said Mandelbaum. His voice was not exultant but tired. He shook his head. 'Why, the Observers had your pitiful little scheme watched almost from its beginning. Your very secrecy gave you away.'

'Then why did you let it get so far?' asked the Australian. His tones were thick with anger.

'Partly to keep you out of worse mischief and partly so you'd draw in others of like mind and thus locate them for us,' said Mandelbaum. 'We waited till we knew you were all set to go, and then we came.'

'That was vicious,' said the Frenchman. 'It was the sort of cold-bloodedness that has grown up since the change. I suppose the intelligent, the expedient thing for you now is to shoot us down.'

'Why, no,' said Mandelbaum mildly. 'As a matter of fact, we used a reaction damper along with the metal-heating field, just to keep your cartridges from going off and hurting you. After all, we'll have to find out from you who else has backed you. And then you all have good minds, lots of energy and courage – quite a big potential value. It's not your fault the change drove you insane.'

'Insane!' The Russian spat, and recovered himself with a shaking effort. 'Insane you call us!'

'Well,' said Mandelbaum, 'if the delusion that you few have the right to make decisions for all the race, and force them through, isn't megalomania, them what is? If you really had a case, you could have presented it to the world soon enough.'

'The world has been blinded,' said the Hindu with dignity. 'It can no longer see the truth. I myself have lost the feeble glimpse of the ultimate I once had, though at least I know it was lost.'

'What you mean,' said Mandelbaum coldly, 'is that your mind's become too strong for you to go into the kind of trance which was your particular fetalization, but you still feel the need for it.'

The Hindu shrugged contemptuously.

Grunewald looked at Corinth. 'I thought you were my friend, Pete,' he whispered. 'And after what the change did to your wife, I thought you could see –'

'He's had nothing to do with this,' said Helga, stepping forward a little and taking Corinth's arm. 'I'm the one who fingered you, Grunewald. Pete just came along with us tonight as a physicist, to look over your apparatus and salvage it for something useful.' *Occupational therapy – O Pete, Pete, you have been hurt so much!*

Corinth shook his head and spoke harshly, with an anger new to his mildness. 'Never mind finding excuses for me. I'd have done this alone, if I'd known what you planned. Because what would Sheila be like if the old world came back?'

'You'll be cured,' said Mandelbaum. 'Your cases aren't violent, I think the new psychiatric techniques can straighten you out pretty quick.'

'I wish you'd kill me instead,' said the Australian.

Manzelli was still crying. The sobs tore at him like claws.

'Why can you not see?' asked the Frenchman. 'Are all the glories man has won in the past to go for nothing? Before he has even found God, will you turn God into a nursery tale? What have you given him in return for the splendours of his art, the creation in his hands, and the warm little pleasures when his day's work is done? You have turned him into a calculating machine, and the body and the soul can wither amidst his new equations.'

Mandelbaum shrugged. 'The change wasn't my idea,' he said. 'If you believe in God, then this looks rather like His handiwork, His way of taking the next step forward.'

'It is forward from the intellectual's point of view,' said the Frenchman. 'To a near-sighted, soft-bellied, flatulent professor, this is no doubt progress.'

'Do I look like a professor?' grunted Mandelbaum. 'I was riveting steel when you were reading your first books about the beauties of nature. I was having my face kicked in by company goons when you were writing about the sin of pride and battle. You loved the working man, but you wouldn't invite him to your table, now would you? When little Jean-Pierre, he was a divinity student before the war, when he was caught spying for our side, he held out for twenty-four hours against everything the Germans could do to him and gave the rest of us a chance to escape. Meanwhile, as I recall, you were safe in the States writing propaganda. Judas priest, why don't you ever try those things you're so ready to theorize about?'

The dragging weariness lifted from him as he swung into the old joy of struggle. His voice raised itself in a hard fierce tone, like hammers on iron. 'The trouble with all of you is that one way or another, you're all afraid to face life. Instead of trying to shape the future, you've been wanting a past which is already a million years behind us. You've lost your old illusions and you haven't got what it takes to make new and better ones for yourselves.'

'Including the American delusion of "Progress,"' snapped the Chinese.

'Who said anything about that? That's forgotten too, obsolete junk – another shibboleth born of stupidity and greed and smugness. Sure, all our past has been stripped from us. Sure, it's a terrible feeling, bare and lonely like this. But do you think man can't strike a new balance? Do you think we can't build a new culture, with its own beauty and delight and dreams, now that we've broken out of the old cocoon? And do you think that men – men with strength and hope in them, all races, all over the world – want to go back? I tell you they don't. The very fact you tried this secretly shows you knew the same thing.

'What did the old world offer to ninety per cent of the human race? Toil, ignorance, disease, war, oppression, want, fear, from the filthy birth to the miserable grave. If you were born into a lucky land, you might fill your belly and have a few shiny toys to play with, but there was no hope in you, no vision, no purpose. The fact that one civilization after another went down into ruin shows we weren't fitted for it; we were savages by nature. Now we have a chance to get off that wheel of history and go somewhere – nobody knows where, nobody can even guess, but our eyes have been opened and you wanted to close them again!'

Mandelbaum broke off, sighed, and turned to his detectives. 'Take 'em away, boys,' he said.

The cabal were urged onto the raft – gently, there was no need for roughness and no malice. Mandelbaum stood watching as the raft lifted slowly up into the star ship. Then he turned to the long metal form on the ground.

'What a heroic thing!' he muttered, shaking his head. 'Futile, but heroic. Those are good men. I hope it won't take too long to salvage them.'

Corinth's grin was crooked. 'Of course, we are absolutely right,' he said.

Mandelbaum chuckled. 'Sorry for the lecture,' he replied. 'Old habit too strong – a fact has to have a moral tag on it – well, we, the human race, ought to *get* over that pretty soon.'

The physicist sobered. 'You have to have some kind of morality,' he said.

'Sure. Like you have to have motives for doing anything at all. Still, I think we're beyond that smug sort of code which proclaimed crusades and burned heretics and threw dissenters into concentration camps. We need more personal and less public honour.'

Mandelbaum yawned then, stretching his wiry frame till it seemed the bones must crack. 'Long ride, and not even a proper gun battle at the end,' he said. The raft was coming down again, automatically. 'I'm for some sleep. We can look over this mess of junk in the morning. Coming?'

'Not just yet,' said Corinth. 'I'm too tired.' (I want to think.) 'I'll walk over towards the beach.'

'Okay.' Mandelbaum smiled, with a curious tenderness on his lips. 'Good night.'

'Good night.' Corinth turned and walked from the clearing. Helga went wordlessly beside him.

They came out of the jungle and stood on sands that were like frost under the moon. Beyond the reef, the surf flamed and crashed, and the ocean was roiled and streaked with the cold glimmer of phosphorescence. The big stars were immensely high overhead, but the night sky was like crystal. Corinth felt the sea wind in his face, sharp and salt, damp with the thousand watery miles it had swept across. Behind him, the jungle rustled and whispered to itself, and the sand gritted tinily underfoot. He was aware of it all with an unnatural clarity, as if he had been drained of everything that was himself and was now only a vessel of images.

He looked at Helga, where she stood holding his arm. Her face was sharply outlined against the further darkness, and her hair – she had unbound it – fluttered loosely in the wind, white in the pouring unreal moonlight. Their two shadows were joined into one, long and blue across the glittering sand. He could feel the rhythm of her breathing where she stood against him.

They had no need to speak. Too much understanding had grown up between them, they had shared too much of work and watching, and now they stood for a while in silence. The sea talked to them, giant pulsing of waves, boom where they hit the reef, rush where they streamed back into the water. The wind hissed and murmured under the sky.

Gravitation (sun, moon, stars, the tremendous unity which is space-time)

+ Coriolis force (the planet turning, turning, on its way through miles and years)

+ Fluid friction (the oceans grinding, swirling, roaring between narrow straits, spuming and thundering over rock)

+ Temperature differential (sunlight like warm rain, ice and darkness, clouds, mists, wind and storm)

+ Vulcanism (fire deep in the belly of the planet, sliding of unimaginable rock masses, smoke and lava, the raising of new mountains with snow on their shoulders)

+ Chemical reaction (dark swelling soil, exhausted air made live again, rocks red and blue and ochre, life, dreams, death and rebirth and all bright hopes)

EQUALS

This our world, and behold, she is very fair.

Nevertheless there was a weariness and desolation in the man, and after a while he turned for comfort as if the woman had been his.

'Easy,' he said, and the word and his tones meant: (It was too easy, for us and for them. They had a holy spirit, those men. It should have ended otherwise. Fire and fury, wrath, destruction, and the unconquerable pride of man against the gods.)

'No,' she replied. 'This way was better.' Quietly, calmly: (Mercy and understanding. We're not wild animals any more, to bare our teeth at the fates.)

Yes. That is the future. Forget all red glories.

'But what is our tomorrow?' he asked. (We stand with the wreckage of a world about our feet, looking into a hollow universe, and we must fill it ourselves. There is no one to help us.)

'Unless there is a destiny,' (God, fate, human courage) she said.

'Perhaps there is,' he mused. 'Consciously or not, a universe has been given into our hands.'

She fled from the knowledge, knowing that to answer her he would have to summon up the bravery he needed. Have we the right to take it? If we make ourselves guardians of planets, is that better than Grunewald – blindness of causality, senseless cruelty of chance, the querning in his poor mad head?)

'It would not be thus that we would enter on our destiny,' he told her. 'We would be unseen, unknown guides, guardians of freedom, not imposers of an arbitrary will. When our new civilization is built, that may be the only work worthy of its hands.'

O most glorious destiny! Why should I feel sorrow on this night? And yet there are tears behind my eyes.

She said what had to be said: 'Sheila was discharged a few days ago.' *I weep for you, my darling in darkness.*

'Yes,' he nodded. 'I saw it.' (She ran out like a little girl. She held her hands up to the sun and laughed.)

'She has found her own answer. You still have to find yours.'

His mind worried the past like a dog with a bone. 'She didn't know I was watching her.' *It was a cold bright morning. A red maple leaf fluttered down and caught in her hair. She used to wear flowers in her hair for me.* 'She has already begun to forget me.'

'You told Kearnes to help her forget,' she said. 'That was the bravest thing you ever did. It takes courage to be kind. But are you now strong enough to be kind to yourself?'

'No,' he answered. 'I don't want to stop loving her. I'm sorry, Helga.'

'Sheila will be watched over,' she said. 'She will not know it, but the Observers will guide her wandering. There is a promising moron colony –' *Anguish* '– north of the city. We have been helping it lately without its knowing. Its leader is a good man, a strong and gentle man. Sheila's Wood will be a leaven in their race.'

He said nothing.

'Pete,' she challenged him, 'now you must help yourself.'

'No,' he said. 'But you can change too, Helga. You can will yourself away from me.'

'Not when you need me, and know it, and still cling blind to a dead symbol,' she replied. 'Pete, it is you now who are afraid to face life.'

There was a long stillness, only the sea and the wind had voice. The moon was sinking low, its radiance filled their eyes, and the man turned his face from it. Then he shuddered and straightened his shoulders.

'Help me!' he said, and took her hands. 'I cannot do it alone. Help me, Helga.'

There are no words. There can never be words for this.

The minds met, flowing together, succouring need, and in a way which was new to the world they shared their strength and fought free of what was past.

To love, honour, and cherish, until death do us part.

It was an old story, she thought among the thunders. It was the oldest and finest story on Earth, so it was entitled to an old language. Sea, and stars – why, there was even a full moon.

CHAPTER TWENTY-ONE

Autumn again, and winter in the air. The fallen leaves lay in heaps under the bare dark trees and hissed and rattled across the ground with every wind. Only a few splashes of colour remained in the woods, yellow or bronze or scarlet against greyness.

Overhead the wild geese passed in great flocks, southward bound. There was more life in the sky this year – fewer hunters, Brock supposed. The remote honking drifted down to him, full of wandering and loneliness. It was a clear pale blue up there, the sun wheeled bright and heatless, spilling its coruscant light across a broad and empty land. The wind was strong, flowing around his cheeks and flapping his clothes, the trees were noisy with it.

He went slowly from the main house, scuffing the sere grass under his boots. Joe followed quietly at heel. From the shed came a hammering of sheet iron, Mehitabel and Mac were building their charcoal gas distillator: for them it was too much fun to let be, and the gasoline supplies were very low. Some of the people had gone to town, some were sleeping off their Sunday dinner. Brock was alone.

He thought he might stop in and chatter with Mehitabel. No, let her work undisturbed; her conversation was rather limited anyway. He decided to take a stroll through the woods; it was late afternoon already, and too nice a day to be indoors.

Ella Mae came out of one of the cottages and giggled at him. 'Hello,' she said.

'Uh, hello,' he answered. 'How're you?'

'I'm fine,' she said. 'Want to come inside? Nobody else in here now.'

'No, thanks,' he said. 'I, well, I have to check a fence.'

'I could come along?' she asked timidly.

'Better not,' he said. 'The pigs, you know. They might still be running around in there.'

Ella Mae's watery blue eyes filled with tears, and she lowered her misshapen head. 'You never stop by with me,' she accused.

'I will when I get the chance,' he said hastily. 'It's just that I'm awful busy. You know how it *goes*.' He made his retreat as fast as he could.

Have to get a husband for her, he reflected. *There must be a number of her kind wandering loose even now. I can't have her chasing after me this way, it's too hard on both of us.*

He grinned crookedly. Leadership seemed to be all burden and little reward. He was commander, planner, executive, teacher, doctor, father confessor – and now matchmaker!

He bent over and caressed Joe's head with a big rough hand. The dog licked his wrist and wagged a joyous tail. Sometimes a man could get damnably lonely. Even a friend like Joe couldn't fill all needs. On this day of wind and sharp light and blowing leaves, a day of farewell, when all the earth seemed to be breaking up its summer home and departing down some unknown road, he felt his own isolation like a pain within him.

Now, no more of such thoughts, he reproved himself. 'Come on, Joe, let's take us a walk.'

The dog poised, it was a lovely taut stance, and looked towards the sky. Brock's eyes followed. The flash of metal was so bright it hurt him to look.

An airship – some kind of airship. And it's landing!

He stood with his fists clenched at his sides, feeling the wind chill on his skin and hearing how it roared in the branches behind him. The heart in his breast seemed absurdly big, and he shivered under the heavy jacket and felt sweat on his palms.

Take it easy, he told himself. *Just take it easy. All right, so it is one of Them. He won't bite you. Nobody's harmed us, or interfered with us, yet.*

Quietly as a falling leaf, the vessel grounded nearby. It was a small ovoid, with a lilting grace in its clean lines and curves, and there was no means of propulsion that Brock could see. He began walking towards it, slowly and stiffly. The revolver sagging at his waist made him feel ridiculous, as if he had been caught in a child's playsuit.

He felt a sudden upsurge of bitterness. *Let Them take us as we are. Be damned if I'll put on company manners for some bloody Sunday tourist.*

The side of the aircraft shimmered and a man stepped through it. *Through it!* Brock's first reaction was almost disappointment. The man looked so utterly commonplace. He was of medium height, a stockiness turning plump, an undistinguished face, an ordinary tweed sports outfit. As Brock approached, the man smiled.

'How do you do?'

'How do.' Brock stopped, shuffling his feet and looking at the ground. Joe sensed his master's unease and snarled, ever so faintly.

The stranger held out his hand. 'My name is Lewis, Nat Lewis from New York. Hope you'll pardon this intrusion. John Rossman sent me up. He's not feeling very well or he'd have come himself.'

Brock shook hands, a little reassured by Rossman's name. The old man had always been a decent sort, and Lewis' manner was ingratiating. Brock forced himself to meet the other man's eyes, and gave his own name.

'Yes, I recognize you from Rossman's description,' said Lewis. 'He's quite interested in how you people are making out up here. Don't worry, he has no intention of repossessing this property; it's just a friendly curiosity. I work at his Institute, and frankly, I was curious myself, so I've come to check up for him.'

Brock decided that he liked Lewis. The man spoke rather slowly, it must be a slight effort for him to return to old ways of speech, but there was nothing patronizing about him.

'From what I hear, you've done a marvellous job,' said Lewis.

'I didn't know that you – well – that we –' Brock halted, stammering.

'Oh, yes, a bit of an eye was kept on you as soon as we'd taken care of our own troubles. Which were plenty, believe me. Still are, for that matter. Here, may I offer you a cigar?'

'Hmmm – well –' Brock accepted but didn't smoke it. He had not formed the habit. But he could give the cigar to someone else. 'Thanks.'

'It's not a baby,' Lewis grinned. 'At least, I hope not!' He lit one for himself, using a trick lighter that worked even in the high, noisy wind.

'You've doubtless noticed that the towns around here have all been evacuated,' he said after taking a contented puff.

'Yes, for some months now,' answered Brock. With defiance: 'We've been taking what we needed and could find there.'

'Oh, quite all right. That was the idea; in fact, you can move into any of them if you want. The colony committee just thought it was best to rid you of such, ah, overwhelming neighbours. The people didn't care; at the present stage of their development, one place is about as good as another to them.' Wistfulness flitted across Lewis' face. 'That's a loss of ours: the intimacy of giving our hearts to one small corner of the earth.'

The confession of weakness relaxed Brock. He suspected that it was deliberate, but even so –

'And those who've strayed here to join you have often been unobtrusively guided,' Lewis went on. 'There will be others, if you want them. And I think you could use more help, and they could certainly use a home and security.'

'It's – nice of you,' said Brock slowly.

'Ah, it isn't much. Don't think you've been guarded against all danger, or that all your work was done for you. That was never true, and never will be. We've just – well, once in a while we've thrown a little opportunity your way. But it was up to you to use it.'

'I see.'

'We can't help you more than that. Too much for us to do, and too few of us to do it. And our ways are too different. Your kind and my kind have come to the parting of the roads, Brock, but we can at least say good-bye and shake hands.'

It was a warming speech, something thawed inside Brock and he smiled. He had not relished the prospect of being stamped out by a ruthless race of gods, and still less had he cared to spend his days as anyone's ward. Lewis made no bones about the fact of their difference, but he was not snobbish about it either: there was no connotation of superiority in what he said.

They had been strolling about the grounds as they talked. Lewis heard the clashing hammers inside the shed now, and glanced questioningly at Brock.

'I've got a chimpanzee and a moron in there, making a charcoal apparatus so we can fuel our engines,' Brock explained. It didn't hurt to say 'moron' – not any more. 'It's our day off here, but they insisted on working anyway.'

'How many have you got, all told?'

'Oh, well, ten men and six women, ages from around fifteen to – well, I'd guess sixty for the oldest. Mentally from imbecile to moron. Then a couple of kids have been born too. Of course, it's hard to say where the people leave off and the animals begin. The apes, or Joe here, are certainly more intelligent and useful than the imbeciles.' Joe wagged his tail and looked pleased. 'I draw no distinctions; everyone does what he's best fitted for, and we share alike.'

'You're in command, then?'

'I suppose so. They always look to me for guidance. I'm not the brightest one of the lot, but our two intellectuals are – well – ineffectual.'

Lewis nodded. 'It's often that way. Sheer intelligence counts for less than personality, strength of character, or the simple ability to make decisions and stick by them.' He looked sharply at his bigger companion. 'You're a born leader, you know?'

'I am? I've just muddled along as well as possible.'

'Well,' chuckled Lewis, 'I'd say that was the essence of leadership.'

He looked around the buildings and out to the wide horizon. 'It's a happy little community you've built up,' he said.

'No,' answered Brock frankly. 'It's not.'

Lewis glanced at him, raising his eyebrows, but said nothing.

'We're too close to reality here for snugness,' said Brock. 'That may come later, when we're better adjusted, but right now it's still hard work keeping alive. We have to learn to live with some rather harsh facts of life – such as some of us being deformed, or the need for butchering those poor animals –' He paused, noticed that his fists were clenched, and tried to ease himself with a smile.

'Are you – married?' inquired Lewis. 'Pardon my nosiness, but I have a reason for asking.'

'No. I can't see taking what's available here. No matter, there's enough to do to keep me out of mischief.'

'I see –'

Lewis was quiet for a while. They had wandered over by the corn crib, where a board across two barrels made a seat out of the wind. They sat down, wordlessly, and let the day bluster around them. Joe flopped at their feet, watching them with alert brown eyes.

Presently Lewis stubbed out his cigar and spoke again. He sat looking ahead of him, not facing Brock, and his voice sounded a little dreamy, as if he were talking to himself.

'You and your animals here are making the best of a new situation,' he said. 'So far it's not been a very good one. Would you want to return to the old days?'

'Not I, no,' said Brock.

'I thought not. You're taking this reality which has been given to you, with all its infinite possibilities, and you're making it good. That's what my branch of the race is also trying to do, Brock, and maybe you'll succeed better than we. I don't know. I probably won't ever know – won't live that long.

'But I want to tell you something. I've been out in space – between the stars – and there have been other expeditions there too. We found that the galaxy is full of life, and all of it seems to be like the old life of Earth: many forms, many civilizations, but nowhere a creature like man. The average I.Q. of the whole universe may not be much over a hundred. It's too early to tell, but we have reasons to think that that is so.

'And what are we, the so-called normal humanity, to do with our strange powers? Where can we find something that will try and challenge us, something big enough to make us humble and offer us a task in which we can take pride? I think the stars *are* our answer. Oh, I don't mean we intend to establish a galactic empire. Conquest is a childishness we've laid aside, even now. Nor do I mean that we'll become ministering angels to all these uncounted worlds, guiding them and guarding them till their races get too flabby to stand on their own feet. No, nothing like that. We'll be creating our own new civilization, one which will spread between the stars, and it will have its own internal goals, creation, struggle, hope – the environment of man is still primarily man.

'But I think there will be a purpose in that civilization. For the first time, man will really be going somewhere; and I think that his new purpose will, over thousands and millions of years, embrace all life in the attainable universe. I think a final harmony will be achieved such as no one can now imagine.

'We will not be gods, or even guides. But we will – some of us – be givers of opportunity. We will see that evil does not flourish too strongly, and that hope and chance happen when they are most needed, to all those millions of sentient creatures who live and love and fight and laugh and weep and die, just as man once did. No, we will not be embodied. Fate; but perhaps we can be Luck. And even, it may be, Love.'

The man smiled then, a very human smile at himself and all his own pretences. 'Never mind. I talk too much. Wine-like autumn air, as the old cliché has it.' He turned to Brock. 'What's more to the point, we – our sort – are not going to remain here on Earth.'

Brock nodded silently. The vision before him was too enormous for surprise.

'Your sort won't be bothered,' said Lewis. 'And then in a few years, when things are ready, we'll disappear into the sky. Earth will be left to your kind, and to the animals. And thereafter you will be altogether free. It will be up to you, as to the other kinds of life, to work out your own destiny. And if now and then a bit of luck comes to you – well, that's has always been happening.'

'Thank you.' It was a whisper in Brock's throat.

'Don't thank me, or anyone else. This is merely the logic of events working itself out. But I wish you well, every one of you.'

Lewis stood up and began walking back towards his aircraft. 'I have to go now.' He paused. 'I wasn't quite honest with you when I came. It wasn't Rossman's curiosity that sent me; he could have satisfied that by asking the colony committee, or by dropping in himself. I wanted to check up here personally because – well, you'll be having a new member for your community soon.'

Brock looked at him, wondering. Lewis stopped before his craft.

'She's an old friend,' he said. 'Her story is rather tragic, she'll tell you herself when she feels like it. But she's a good sort, a wonderful girl really, and we who know her want her to be happy.'

The metal shimmered before him. He took Brock's hand. 'Good-bye,' he said simply, and stepped inside. A moment later his vessel was high in heaven.

Brock stared after it till it had vanished.

When he turned back towards the house, the sun was sinking low and the chill bit at him. They'd have to light the fireplace tonight. Maybe they could break out some of the remaining ale if a new recruit was coming, and Jimmy could play the guitar while they all sang. The songs were rowdy, you couldn't expect more of a pioneer people, but there was warmth in them, steadfast-ness and comradeship.

He saw her then, walking up the driveway, and his heart stumbled within him. She was not tall, but her form was sweet and strong under the heavy clothing, and bronze-coloured hair blew around a face that was young and gentle and good to look on. She carried a bundle on her back, and the suns of many days tramping down open roads had tinged her and dusted freckles across the large-eyed face. He stood for a moment without stirring, and then he ran; but when he came up and was before her, he could find no words.

'Hello,' she said shyly.

He nodded awkwardly. It did not occur to him that he was a strong-look-ing man, not handsome, but with something about him that invoked trust.

'I heard talk this was a refuge,' she said.

'Yes,' he replied. 'Have you come far?'

'From New York City.' There was a small shiver in her, and he wondered what had happened there. Or maybe it was just the cold. The wind piped bit-terly now. 'My name is Sheila,' she said.

'I'm Archie – Archie Brock.' Her hand was firm within his. She did not act frightened, and he knew that while she might not be quite as smart as he, she had more than enough intelligence and will to meet this wintering planet. 'You're welcome here. It's always a big event when someone new comes. But you'll find it strange, and we all have to work hard.'

'I'm not afraid of either of those,' she answered. 'I don't think I can ever be afraid again.'

He took her bundle and started back. The western sky was turning red and gold and a thin chill green. 'I'm glad to know you, Miss – what did you say your last name was?'

'Sheila,' she replied. 'Just Sheila.'

They walked up the driveway side by side, the dog and the wind at their heels, towards the house. In there was shelter.

THE BOAT OF A MILLION YEARS

To
G. C. and Carmen Edmondson
Salud, amor, dinero y tiempo para gustarlos.

Chapter III, 'The Comrade,' has appeared in *Analog Science Fiction/Science Fact*, June 1988. Copyright © 1988 by Davis Publications, Inc.

Chapter V, 'No Man May Shun His Doom,' does homage to the late Johannes V. Jensen.

Karen Anderson prepared the epigraph, slightly modifying her translation at my request, and as scholar and critic was invaluable throughout.

The 'CCCP' is due to George W. Price.

For other kinds of help I also thank John Anderson, Víctor Fernández-Dávila, and David Hartwell.

May he go forth in the sunrise boat,
May he come to port in the sunset boat,
May he go among the imperishable stars,
May he journey in the Boat of a Million Years.
                    – *The Book of Going Forth by Daylight*
                    (Theban recension, ca. 18th Dynasty)

I

THULE

1

'To sail beyond the world –'

Hanno's voice faded away. Pytheas looked sharply at him. Against the plain, whitewashed room where they sat, the Phoenician seemed vivid, like a flash of sunlight from outside. It might only be due to the brightness of eyes and teeth or a skin tan even in winter. Otherwise he was ordinary, slender and supple but of medium height, features aquiline, hair and neatly trimmed beard a crow's-wing black. He wore an unadorned tunic, scuffed sandals, a single gold finger ring.

'You cannot mean that,' said the Greek.

Hanno came out of reverie, shook himself, laughed. 'Oh, no. A trope, of course. Though it would be well to make sure beforehand that enough of your men do believe we live on a sphere. They'll have ample terrors and troubles without fearing a plunge off the edge into some abyss.'

'You sound educated,' said Pytheas slowly.

'Should I not? I have traveled, but also studied. And you, sir, a learned man, a philosopher, propose to voyage into the sheerly unknown. You actually hope to come back.' Hanno picked a goblet off the small table between them and sipped of the tempered wine that a slave had brought.

Pytheas shifted on his stool. A charcoal brazier had made the room close as well as warm. His lungs longed for a breath of clean air. 'Not altogether unknown,' he said. 'Your people go that far. Lykias told me you claim to have been there yourself.'

Hanno sobered. 'I told him the truth. I've journeyed that way more than once, both overland and by sea. But so much of it is wilderness, so much else is changing these days, in ways unforeseeable but usually violent. And the Carthaginians are interested just in the tin, with whatever other things they can pick up incidental to that. They only touch on the southern end of the Pretanic Isles. The rest is outside their ken, or any civilized man's.'

'And yet you desire to come with me.'

Hanno in his turn studied his host before replying. Pytheas too was simply

131

clad. He was tall for a Greek, lean, features sharp beneath a high forehead, clean-shaven, with a few deep lines. Curly brown hair showed frost at the temples. His eyes were gray. The directness of their glance bespoke imperiousness, or innocence, or perhaps both.

'I think I do,' said Hanno carefully. 'We shall have to talk further. However, in my fashion, like you in yours, I want to learn as much as I can about this earth and its peoples while I am still above it. When your man Lykias went about the city inquiring after possible advisors, and I heard, I was happy to seek him out.' Again he grinned. 'Also, I am in present need of employment. There ought to be a goodly profit in this.'

'We are not going as traders,' Pytheas explained. 'We'll have wares along, but to exchange for what we need rather than to get wealthy. We are, though, pledged excellent pay on our return.'

'I gather the city is not sponsoring the venture?'

'Correct. A consortium of merchants is. They want to know the chances and costs of a sea route to the far North, now that the Gauls are making the land dangerous. Not tin alone, you understand – tin may be the least of it – but amber, furs, slaves, whatever those countries offer.'

'The Gauls indeed.' Nothing else need be said. They had poured over the mountains to make the nearer part of Italy theirs; a long lifetime ago war chariots rumbled, swords flashed, homes blazed, wolves and ravens feasted across Europe. Hanno did add: 'I have some acquaintance with them. That should help. Be warned, the prospects of such a route are poor. Besides them, the Carthaginians.'

'I know.'

Hanno cocked his head. 'Nevertheless, you are organizing this expedition.'

'To follow knowledge,' Pytheas answered quietly. 'I am fortunate in that two of the sponsors are … more intelligent than most. They value understanding for its own sake.'

'Knowledge has a trick of paying off in unexpected ways.' Hanno smiled. 'Forgive me. I'm a crass Phoenician. You're a man of consequence in public affairs – inherited money, I've heard – but first and foremost a philosopher. You need a navigator at sea, a guide and interpreter ashore. I believe I am the one for you.'

Pytheas' tone sharpened. 'What are you doing in Massalia? Why are you prepared to aid something that is … not in the interests of Carthage?'

Hanno turned serious. 'I am no traitor, for I am not a Carthaginian. True, I've lived in the city, among many different places. But I'm not overly fond of it. They're too puritanical there, too little touched by any grace of Greece or Persia; and their human sacrifices –' He grimaced, then shrugged. 'To sit in judgment on what people do is a fool's game. They'll continue doing it regardless. As for me, I'm from Old Phoenicia, the East. Alexandros destroyed Tyre, and the civil wars after his death have left that part of the world in sorry shape. I seek my fortune where I can. I'm a wanderer by nature anyway.'

'I shall have to get better acquainted with you,' Pytheas said, blunter than he was wont. Did he already feel at ease with this stranger?

'Certainly.' Again Hanno's manner grew cheerful. 'I've thought how to prove my skills to you. In a short time. You realize the need to embark soon, don't you? Preferably at the start of the sailing season.'

'Because of Carthage?'

Hanno nodded. 'This new war in Sicily will engage her whole attention for a while. Agathokles of Syracuse is a harder enemy than the Carthaginian suffetes have taken the trouble to discover. I wouldn't be surprised if he carries the fight to their shores.'

Pytheas stared. 'How can you be so sure?'

'I was lately there, and I've learned to pay attention. In Carthage too. You're aware she discourages all foreign traffic beyond the Pillars of Herakles – often by methods that would be called piracy were it the work of a private party. Well, the suffetes now speak of an out-and-out blockade. If they win this war, or at least fight it to a draw, I suspect they'll lack the resources for some time afterward; but eventually they'll do it. Your expedition will take a pair of years at least, likelier three, very possibly more. The earlier you set forth, the earlier you'll come home – if you do – and not run into a Carthaginian patrol. What a shame, after an odyssey like that, to end at the bottom of the sea or on an auction block.'

'We'll have an escort of warships.'

Hanno shook his head. 'Oh, no. Anything less than a penteconter would be useless, and that long hull would never survive the North Atlantic. My friend, you haven't seen waves or storms till you've been yonder. Also, how do you carry food and water for all those rowers? They burn it like wildfire, you know, and resupplying will be chancy at best. My namesake could explore the African coasts in galleys, but he was southbound. You'll need sail. Let me counsel you on what ships to buy.'

'You claim a great many proficiencies,' Pytheas murmured.

'I have been through a great many schools,' Hanno replied.

They talked onward for an hour, and agreed to meet again on the following day. Pytheas escorted his visitor out. They stopped for a moment at the front door.

The house stood high on a ridge above the bay. Eastward, beyond city walls, hills glowed with sunset. The streets of the old Greek colony had become rivers of shadow. Voices, footfalls, wheels were muted; the air rested in chilly peace. Westward the sun cast a bridge across the waters. Masts in the harbor stood stark against it. Gulls cruising overhead caught the light on their wings, gold beneath blue.

'A lovely sight,' Pytheas said low. 'This coast must be the most beautiful in the world.'

Hanno parted his lips as if to tell about others he had seen, closed them, said finally: 'Let us try to bring you back here, then. It won't be easy.'

2

Three vessels fared by moonlight. Their masters dared not put in at Gadeira or any part of Tartessos – Carthaginian territory – and kept the sea after dark. The crews muttered; but night sailing was not unheard of on familiar lanes, and to be out in the very ocean was a strangeness overwhelming all else.

The craft were alike, so they could more readily travel in convoy. Each was a merchantman, though her principal cargo was well-armed men and their supplies. Narrower in the beam than most of its kind, the black hull swept some hundred feet from the high stern, where the twin steering oars were and a swan's head ornament reared, to the cutwater at the prow. A mast amidships carried a large square sail and a triangular topsail. Forward of it stood a small deckhouse, aft of it lay two rowboats, for towing her at need or saving lives in the worst need. She could get perhaps eighty degrees off the wind, slowly and awkwardly; nimbler rigs existed, but drew less well. Tonight, with a favoring breeze, she made about five knots.

Hanno came forth. The cabin, which the officers shared, was confining for a person of his habits. Often he slept on deck, together with such of the crew as found the spaces below too cramped and smelly. Several of them rested blanket-wrapped on straw ticks along the bulwarks. Moonlight turned planks hoar, cross-barred with long unrestful shadows. Air blew cold, and Hanno drew his chlamys close about him. The wind lulled above whoosh of waves, creak of timbers and tackle. The ship rocked gently, making muscles flex in a dance with her.

A figure stood at the starboard rail, near the forward lookout. Hanno recognized Pytheas' profile against quicksilver moonglade and went to join him. 'Rejoice,' he greeted. 'You can't sleep either?'

'I hoped to make observations,' the Greek replied. 'Nights this clear will be few for us, won't they?'

Hanno looked outward. Brightnesses rippled, sheened, sparked over the water. Foam swirled ghostly. Lanterns hung from the yard scarcely touched his vision, though he saw their counterparts glimmer and sway on the companion ships. Across a distance hard to gauge in this moving mingling of light and night, a vague mass lifted, Iberia. 'We've been lucky thus far in the weather,' Hanno said. He gestured at the goniometer in Pytheas' hand. 'But is that thing of any use here?'

'It would be much more accurate ashore. If only we could – Well, doubt-less I'll find better opportunities later, the Bears will be higher in the sky.'

Hanno glanced at those constellations. They had dimmed as the moon climbed. 'What are you trying to measure?'

'I want to locate the north celestial pole more exactly than has hitherto been done.' Pytheas pointed. 'Do you see how the two brightest stars in the Lesser Bear, with the first star in the tail, form three corners of a quadrangle? The pole is the fourth. Or so they say.'

'I know. I *am* your navigator.'

'I beg your pardon. I forgot for a moment. Too absorbed.' Pytheas chuck-led ruefully, then grew eager. 'If this rule of thumb can be refined, you appreciate what a help that will give seamen. Still more will it mean to geog-raphers and cosmographers. Since the gods have not seen fit to place a star just at the pole, or even especially close, we must make do as best we are able.'

'There have been such stars in the past,' Hanno said. 'There will be again in the future.'

'What?' Pytheas stared at him through the phantom radiance. 'Do you mean the heavens change?'

'Over centuries.' Hanno's hand made a chopping motion. 'Forget it. Like you, I spoke without thinking. I don't expect you to believe me. Call it a sailor's tall tale.'

Pytheas stroked his chin. 'As a matter of fact,' he said, low and slow, 'a corres-pondent of mine in Alexandria, at its great library, has mentioned that ancient records give certain intimations ... It requires deeper study. But you, Hanno –'

The Phoenician formed a disarming grin. 'Perhaps I make lucky guesses once in a while.'

'You are ... unique in several respects. You've actually told me very little about yourself. Is "Hanno" the name you were born with?'

'It serves.'

'You seem without home, family, ties of any kind.' Impulsively: 'I hate to think of you as lonely and defenseless.'

'Thank you, but I need no sympathy.' Hanno mildened his manner. 'You judge me by yourself. Are you already homesick?'

'Not really. Not on this quest that I've dreamt of for years.' The Greek paused. 'But I do have roots, wife, children. My oldest son is married. He should have grandchildren for me when I return.' With a smile: 'My oldest daughter is now marriageable. I left arrangements for her in my brother's hands, with my wife's advice and consent. Yes, my little Danaë too, she may well have a little one of her own by that time.' He shook himself, as if the wind had touched him with cold. 'It won't do to yearn. We'll be long gone at best.'

Hanno shrugged. 'And meanwhile, I've found, barbarian women are usu-ally easy.'

Pytheas regarded him for a silent spell and said nothing about youths already available. Whatever Hanno's tastes might be, he didn't expect the Phoenician would become intimate with any member of the expedition. Behind that genial front of his, how much humanity was in him?

3

All at once, like a blow to the belly, there the Keltoi were. A dozen tall warriors sprang from the forest and started across the grassy slope to the beach, a score, a hundred, two hundred or worse. More swarmed onto the twin headlands sheltering the cove where the ships had anchored.

Mariners yelled, dropped their work of preparing camp, snatched for their weapons, milled about. Soldiers among them, hoplites and peltasts, most still armored, pushed through the chaos to take formation. Helmets, breastplates, shields, swords, pike heads shimmered dully in a thin rain. Hanno ran to their captain, Demetrios, caught him by the wrist, and snapped, 'Don't initiate hostilities. They'd love to take our heads home. Battle trophies.'

The hard visage fleered. 'Do you suppose if we stay peaceful, they'll embrace us?'

'That depends.' Hanno squinted into the dimness before him. The hidden sun at his back had to be near the horizon. Trees made a gray wall behind the oncoming attackers. War cries went saw-edged over the boom of surf outside the little bay, echoed from cliff to cliff, sent gulls shrieking aloft. 'Someone spied us, maybe days ago; sent word to his fellow clansmen; they followed our course, with the woods for a screen; they expected we'd camp at one of the places where the Carthaginians do – we'd see the burnt wood, rubbish, traces, and head in –' He was thinking aloud.

'Why didn't they wait till we were asleep, except for our sentries?'

'They must be afraid of the dark. This can't be their country. And so – Hold fast. Give me – I should have a peeled wand or a green bough, but this may suffice.' Hanno turned about and tugged at the standard. Its bearer clung and cursed him.

'Make him give me this, Demetrios!' Hanno demanded.

The mercenary leader hesitated an instant before he ordered, 'Let go, Kleanthes.'

'Good. Now blow trumpets, bang on shields, raise all the noise you can, but stay where you are.'

The emblem aloft, Hanno advanced. He moved slowly, gravely, staff in right hand, naked sword in left. At his rear, brass brayed and iron thundered.

The Carthaginians had cleared away high growth as far as the spring where they got water, a distance of about an Athenian stadion. New brush sprang up to hinder passage and make it noisy. Thus total surprise was impossible, and the Gauls were not yet in that headlong dash which civilized men dreaded. They trotted forward as individuals or small groups, disorderly and deadly.

They were big, fair-complexioned men. Most flaunted long mustaches; none had shaved lately. Those that did not braid their hair had treated it with a material that reddened it and stiffened it into spikes. Paint and tattoos adorned bodies sometimes naked, oftener wrapped in a dyed woolen kilt – a sort of primitive himation – or attired in breeches and perhaps a tunic of gaudy hues. Their weapons were long swords, spears, dirks; some bore round shields, a few had helmets.

One huge man at the forefront of the roughly semicircular van wore a gilt helmet that flared out in horns. A bronze tore circled his throat, gold helices his arms. The warriors to his right and left were almost as flamboyant. He must be the chief. Hanno moved toward him.

The racket from among the Greeks was giving the barbarians pause, puzzling them. They slowed, looked around, damped their shouts and muttered to each other. Watching, Pytheas saw Hanno meet their leader. He heard horns blow, voices ring. Men sped about, carrying a word he could not understand. The Gauls grumbled piecemeal to a halt, withdrew a ways, squatted down or leaned on their spears, waited. The drizzle thickened, daylight faded, and he saw only shadows yonder.

An hour dragged itself into dusk. Fires blossomed under the forest.

Hanno returned. He walked like another shadow past Demetrios' pickets, between the hushed and huddled sailors, to find Pytheas near the boats, not to flee but because there the water cast off enough light to ease the wet gloom a little.

'We're safe,' Hanno declared. Breath gusted out of Pytheas.

'But we've a busy night ahead of us,' Hanno went on. 'Kindle fires, pitch tents, get the best of the wretched food we have and cook it as well as possible. Not that our visitors will notice the quality. It's quantity that counts with them.'

Pytheas peered, striving to read the half-seen face. 'What's happened?' he asked unevenly. 'What have you done?'

Hanno's tone stayed cool, with a hint of hidden laughter. 'You know I've acquired enough Keltic language to get by, and a fair acquaintance with their customs and beliefs. Those aren't too different from several other wild races'; I can guess my way past any gaps in my knowledge. I went out to them in the style of a herald, which made my person sacred, and talked with their chief. He's not a bad fellow, as such people go. I've known worse monsters in power among Hellenes, Persians, Phoenicians, Egyptians – No matter.'

'What ... did they want?'

'To overcome us before we could escape, of course, take our boats, capture our ships, plunder them. The fact alone showed this isn't likely their native country. Carthaginians have treaties with natives. True, these might have denounced the agreement for some childish reason. However, then they'd have attacked after dark. They brag about their fearlessness, but when it's a question of booty more than glory, they wouldn't care to take unnecessary casualties or risk our being able to stand them off while most of us got away to the ships. Nevertheless they came at us as soon as we were ashore. So they must be afraid of the dark hereabouts – ghosts and gods of the lately slain, not yet appeased. I played on that, among other things.'

'Who are they?'

'Pictones from the east, intending to settle these parts.' Hanno began pacing, to and fro before the eyes of Pytheas. Sand scrunched soddenly underfoot. 'Not much like those tame and half-tame tribes in your Massalian hinterland; but not entirely alien to them, either. They have more respect for skills, for learning, than I've generally found your ordinary Greek does. Their ornament, all their workmanship is beautiful. Not only a herald but a poet, any wise person is sacred. I proved myself a magician, what they call a druid, by various sleight-of-hand tricks and occultistic nonsense. I threatened – oh, very delicately – to lay a satire on them if they offended me. First I'd convinced them I was a poet, by a rough plagiarism of lines from Homer. I'll have to work on that. I've promised them more.'

'You have what?'

Hanno's laugh rang aloud. 'Ready the camp, I say. Prepare the feast. Tell Demetrios' men they're to be an honor guard. We'll have guests at dawn, and I daresay the festivities will brawl on through the whole day. You'll be expected to give pretty lavish gifts, but that's all right, we have ample trade goods along, and honor will require you receive severalfold the value in stuff we can better use. Also, we now have safe conduct for a considerable distance north.' He paused. Sea and land sighed around them. 'Oh, and if we get decent weather tomorrow night, do carry on your star observations, Pytheas. That will impress them no end.'

'And … it's a part of what we're journeying for,' whispered the other man. 'What you've saved.'

4

Behind lay the Dumnonian tin mines, and the harbor to which no Carthaginians would come while the war lasted, and the three ships. Lykias kept a guard on them and saw to their careening and refitting. Demetrios organized overland explorations of the west and south coasts. The interior and north of Pretania Pytheas claimed for himself.

He came with Hanno and a small military escort out of the hills, onto a rolling plain where, here and there, wilderness yielded to plowland and pasture. A gigantic mound inside a fosse and earthworks dominated it. The chalky crater hollowed on top held armed men and their lodgings.

Its commander received the travelers hospitably, once he was sure of their intentions. Folk were always eager for word from outside; most barbarians had pathetically narrow horizons. Talk went haltingly by way of Hanno and a Dumnonian who had accompanied the party this far. Now he wanted to go home. A man by some such name as Segovax offered to replace him and lead the guests to a great wonder nearby.

Autumn was in the wind, chill and loud. Leaves were turning yellow, brown, russet and beginning to fly away. A trail went onto an upland where trees were few. Cloud shadows and pale sunlight sickled across immensities of sallow grass. Sheep flocks afar were lost in loneliness. The Greeks marched briskly, leading the pack ponies they had gotten in Dumnonia. They would not return to the hill fort but push on. One winter was scant time to range this land. Come spring, Pytheas must be back with his ships.

The sight waxed slowly before him. At first it seemed little, and he supposed people made much of it only because they knew nothing better. As he neared, the sense of its mass grew and grew. Within a time-worn earthen rampart loomed a triple ring of standing stones, perhaps seventy cubits wide, the tallest of them well-nigh three man-heights, slabs almost as huge joining them on top, gray, lichenous, weathered, powerful beyond his understanding.

'What *is* this?' he whispered.

'You've seen megalithic works in the South, haven't you?' Hanno's voice was less calm than his words, hushed beneath the wind.

'Yes, but nothing like – Ask!'

Hanno turned to Segovax. Keltic lilted between them.

'He says giants built it in the morning of the world,' Hanno told Pytheas.

'Then his people are as ignorant as we,' the Greek said low. 'We'll camp here, overnight at least. Maybe we can learn something.' It was more a prayer than a hope.

Throughout the rest of the day he devoted himself to his eyes and his instruments. Hanno could give scant help and Segovax hardly any information. Once Pytheas spent a long time finding the exact center of the complex and sighting from there. 'I think,' he said as he pointed, 'that yonder stone outside – the sun will be seen to rise over it on Midsummer's Day. But I cannot be sure, and we cannot wait to find out, can we?'

Night approached. The soldiers, who had snatched the chance to idle, started a fire, cooked food, made ready. Their talk and occasional laughter rattled meaningless. They had no reason to fear attack by mortal men, nor to wonder what ghosts might linger here.

The weather had cleared, and after full darkness Pytheas left the camp to observe, which he did at every opportunity. Hanno came along, bearing a wax tablet and stylus to record the measurements. He had the Phoenician trick of writing without light. Pytheas could use ridges and grooves to read instruments by his fingertips, measurements less close than he wished but preferable to none at all. When a stone had blocked view of flames, they were alone in the ring with the sky.

Titan blacknesses walled them in. Stars flickered between, as if trapped. Overhead curved the Galaxy, a river of mist across which winged the Swan. The Lyre hung silent. The Dragon coiled halfway around a pole strangely high in heaven. Cold deepened with the hours, the vast wheel turned, frost formed hoar on the stones.

'Hadn't we better get some sleep?' Hanno asked at last. 'I'm forgetting what warmth feels like.'

'I suppose so.' Pytheas' answer dragged. 'I've learned as much as I can.' Abruptly, harshly: 'It isn't enough! It never will be. Our lives are a million years too short.'

5

After the long voyage north, past land that grew ever more rugged, ever more girded with holms and reefs, the coast finally bent eastward. These were waters as rough as the ground on which their surf crashed; the ships stood well out and cast anchor at sunset. It was better to huddle tireless than dare those unknown approaches. On the fourth day there appeared above haze the red and yellow heights of an island. Pytheas decided to pass between it and the main shore. His vessels battled their way on until dark.

Men saw no dawn, for air had thickened further. Aft of them a whiteness towered from edge to unseen edge of the world. They had a light breeze and visibility of about a dozen Athenian stadia, so they hoisted dripping sails. The sheer island began to fall behind them, and ahead, to starboard, they spied a murk that ought to be a lesser one. Noise of breakers loudened, an undergroundish thunder.

Then the white wall rolled over them, and they were blind. The breeze died and they lay helpless.

Never had they known or heard of a fog such as this. A man amidships saw neither bow nor stern; vision lost itself in smothering, eddying gray. Over the side he could barely make out turbulence streaked with foam. Water settled on cordage and fell off in a wicked little rain. The deck sheened with it. Wetness weighted hair, clothes, breath, while cold gnawed inward to the bone, as if he were already drowning. The formlessness was full of noise. Seas grew heavier, timbers groaned, the hull swayed crazily. Billows rushed and rumbled, surf roared. Horns hooted, crew wailed themselves hoarse, ship called desperately to unseen ship.

Pytheas, aft by the helm, shook his head. 'What makes the waves rise when we have no wind?' he asked through the tumult.

The steersman gripped his useless tiller and shuddered. 'Things out o' the deeps,' he rasped, 'or the gods o' these waters, angry that we trouble them.'

'Launch the boats,' Hanno advised Pytheas. 'They'll give some warning if we're about to drift onto a rock, and maybe they can pull us clear.'

The steersman bared teeth. 'Oh, no, you don't!' he cried. 'You'll not send men down to the demon-beasts. They won't go.'

'I won't send them,' Hanno retorted. 'I'll lead them.'

'Or I,' Pytheas said.

It became the Phoenician who shook his head. 'We can't risk you. Who else could have brought us this far, or can bring us home? Without you we're all dead. Come help me put spirit into the crew.'

He got his men, because Pytheas' calm words damped the terror in them. They unlashed a boat, dragged it to the side, shoved it over a rail when the deck canted and white-maned waves galloped just beneath. Hanno sprang down, braced calves between two thwarts, took an oar a sailor handed him, fended off while his rowers followed one by one. They fought free at the end of a towline and the next boat came after.

'I do hope the other skippers –' began Hanno. A dash of brine choked off what nobody heard anyhow.

The ship was gone into wet smoke. The boat climbed a comber that was like a moving hillside, hovered on the crest, plunged into a trough where men looked up the heights of water around them. Noise rolled empty of direction. Hanno, at the rudder, could only try to keep the hawser unfouled behind him. 'Stroke!' he bawled. 'Stroke, stroke, stroke!' Men gasped at oars and bailing buckets. The sea lapped around their ankles.

A monstrous grip seized them. They whirled. A cataract leaped out of the fog. It burst over their heads. When they could see again, the ship was upon them. The boat smashed into her hull. The water ground it against the strakes. Wood broke, tore free of nails, shrieked. The boat fell asunder.

Pytheas beheld it. A man flailed arms and legs. The sea dashed him at the ship. His skull split open. Brains, blood, body went under.

'Lines out!' Pytheas shouted. He himself didn't stop to uncoil any from a bollard. He drew his knife and slashed a sheet free of the slack mainsail. When he cast the end overboard, it disappeared in fog and foam. None of the swimmers he glimpsed, lost, glimpsed again had noticed it.

He signalled for another length. The cut sheet still cleated and in his left hand, he slid over the rail. Feet planted on the hull, arm straining to hold the cordage taut and himself in place, he leaned straight out. With his right hand he swung the second line like a whip.

Now he was visible to those he would save, except when the vessel rose onto that side and a wave fountained across him. A man swung past. Pytheas flicked the loose line at his face. The man caught it. Sailors on deck hauled him aboard.

The third whom Pytheas rescued was Hanno, clinging to an oar. After that, his strength was spent. He got back with the help of two mariners and fell in a heap beside the Phoenician. No others attempted his feat; but no more waifs came to sight in the rage around.

Hanno stirred. 'To the cabin, you and me and these two,' he said through clattering teeth. 'Else the cold will kill us. We wouldn't have lived ten minutes in that water.'

In the shelter, men stripped, toweled till blood awoke to stinging life, pulled blankets tightly about themselves. 'You were magnificent, my friend,' Hanno said. 'I wouldn't have supposed you, a scholar – tough, but a scholar – could do it.'

'Nor would I have.' Exhaustion flattened Pytheas' voice.

'You saved us few from the consequences of my folly.'

'No folly. Who could have foreseen the sea in windless air would go so wild so fast?'

'What might have done it?'

'Demons,' mumbled a sailor.

'No,' Pytheas replied. 'It must have been a trick of these enormous Atlantic tides, thrusting through a strait cluttered with isles and reefs.'

Hanno mustered a chuckle. 'Still the philosopher, you!'

'We've a boat left,' Pytheas said. 'And our luck may turn. Beseech your gods if you like, boys.' He lay down on his pallet. 'I am going to sleep.'

6

The ships survived, though one scraped a rock and opened seams. When fog had lifted and waters somewhat calmed, rowers pulled the three to the high island. They found a safe anchorage with a sloping strand where, at low water, they could work to repair damage.

Several families lived nearby: unshorn, skin-clad fishers who kept a few animals and scratched in tiny gardens. Their dwellings were dry-laid stones and turf roofs above pits. At first they fled and watched from afar. Pytheas ordered goods set out, and they timidly returned to collect these. Thereafter the Greeks were their house guests.

That proved fortunate. A gale came from the west. The ships got barely adequate protection from the bluffs around the east-side inlet, but everywhere else the storm ramped unchecked for days and nights. Men could not stand against it. Indoors they must struggle to speak and hear through the racket. Breakers higher than city battlements hurled themselves onto the western cliffs. Stones weighing tons broke from their beds in what had been the shallows. Earth trembled. The air was a torrent of spume, whose salt flayed faces and blinded eyes. It was as if the world had toppled into primordial chaos.

Pytheas, Hanno, and their companions hunched crowded together on dried seaweed strewn over a dirt floor in a cave of gloom. Coals glowed faint red on the hearthstone. Smoke drifted acrid through the chill. Pytheas was another shadow, his words a whisper amidst the violence: 'The fog, and now this. Here is neither sea nor land nor air. They have all become one, a thing like a sea-lung. Farther north can only be the Great Ice. I think we are near the border of life's kingdom.' They saw his head lift. 'But we have not come to the end of our search.'

7

Eastward oversea, four days' sail from the northern tip of Pretania, the explorers found another land. It rose sharply out of the water, but holms protected a great bay. On an arm of this dwelt folk who received newcomers kindly. They were not Keltoi, being even more tall and fair. Their language was kin to a Germanic tongue which Hanno had gotten a little of on an earlier wandering; he could soon make himself understood. Their iron tools and weapons, arts and way of life, did bear a Keltic mark. However, their spirit seemed different, more sober, less possessed by the unearthly.

The Greeks meant to abide a short while, inquire about those realms that were their goal, take on fresh supplies, and proceed. But their stay lengthened. Toil, danger, loss had worn them down. Here they found hospitality and admiration. As they gained words, they won full comradeship, shared in undertakings, swapped thoughts and recollections and songs, sported, made merry. The women were welcoming. Nobody urged Pytheas to order anchors up or asked why he did not.

The guests were no parasites. They brought wonderful gifts. On a ship of theirs they carried men who knew only longboats fashioned of planks stitched together, driven by paddles. Those men learned more about their own waters and communities elsewhere than they had dreamed they might. Trade followed, and visits to and fro for the first time ever. Hunting was excellent in the hinterland, and the soldiers fetched plenty of meat home. The presence of the Greeks, their revelation of an outside world, gave new sparkle to life. They felt themselves taken into brotherhood.

This was the country its people named Thule.

Midsummer came, with the light nights.

Hanno and a lass went to gather berries. Alone under the sweetnesses of birch trees, they made love. The long day tired her, and after they returned to her father's house she fell happily asleep. He could not. He lay for an hour on their bed of hides, feeling her warm against him, hearing her and her family breathe, himself inhaling the fragrance and pungency of the cows stalled at the far end of the single long room. A banked fire sometimes let slip a flame-let, but what made soft dusk was the sky beyond the wickerwork door. Finally he rose, pulled his tunic back over his head, and stole forth.

Above him reached utter clarity, a hue that raised memories of white roses. No more than half a dozen stars could shine through it, atremble, barely see-able. Air rested cool, so quiet that he heard water lap on the bayshore. Dew gleamed on ground that slanted down to the broad argency of it. Inland the terrain climbed toward mountains whose ridges lifted blue-gray into heaven.

He left the village. Its houses nestled together, a double row that ended at a great barn where grain was threshed, in this rainy climate, and which would serve as a fortress in case of attack. Beyond were paddocks, beehives, small fields goldening toward harvest. He drifted from them, beachward. When he came to grass he wiped off his bare feet the muck that free-running pigs and chickens had left in the lane. The moisture caressed him. Farther on he reached shingle, rocks cold and hard but worn smooth. The tide was ebbing, that mighty pulse which the Mediterranean seas scarcely felt, and kelp sprawled along the strand. It gave off odors of salt, depths, mysteries.

Some distance, onward, a man stood looking aloft. Brass gleamed as he pointed his instrument. Hanno approached. 'You too?' he murmured.

Pytheas started, turned about, and replied mechanically, 'Rejoice.' In the luminous twilight it was clear how he must force a smile.

'Not easy to sleep under these conditions,' Hanno ventured. The natives themselves didn't much.

Pytheas nodded. 'I hate to miss a minute of the loveliness.'

'Poor for astronomy, though.'

'Um, by day I've been … gathering data that will yield a better value for the obliquity of the ecliptic.'

'You should have ample by now. We're past the solstice.'

Pytheas glanced away.

'And you sound right defensive,' Hanno pursued. 'Why do we linger here?'

Pytheas bit his lip. 'We've … a wealth of discoveries still to make. It's like a whole new world.'

Hanno's voice crackled: 'Like the land of the Lotus Eaters.'

Pytheas lifted his quadrant as if it were a shield. 'No, no, these are real people, they labor and have children and grow old and die the same as us.'

Hanno regarded him. The waters whispered. Finally the Phoenician said, 'It's Vana, isn't it?'

Pytheas stood mute.

'Many of these girls are beautiful,' Hanno went on. 'Height, slenderness, skin that the summer sun kisses tawny, eyes like the sky around that sun,

144

and those blond manes – oh, yes. And the one who's with you, she's the bonniest of the lot.'

'It's more than that,' Pytheas said. 'She's … free. Unlettered, unaware, but quick and eager to learn. Proud, fearless. We cage our wives, we Greeks. I never thought of it till lately, but … is it not our doing that the poor creatures turn so dull that we're apt to seek sweethearts male?'

'Or whores.'

'Vana is as mettlesome as the liveliest hetaira. But she's not for sale, Hanno. She honestly loves me. A few days ago we decided she must be carrying my child. She came to my arms weeping and laughing.'

'She's a dear person, true. But she's a barbarian.'

'That can be changed.'

Hanno shook his head. 'Don't play tricks on yourself, my friend. It's not like you. Do you daydream about taking her along when we leave? If she survived the voyage, she'd wither and die in Massalia, like any uprooted wildflower. What could she make herself into? What sort of life could you give her? You're too late. Both of you.'

Again Pytheas stood mute.

'Nor can you settle here,' Hanno told him. 'Only think. You, a civilized man, a philosopher, crammed cheek by jowl with other human bodies and cattle into a wretched wattle-and-daub hut. No books. No correspondence. No discourse. No sculptures, no temples, no traditions of yours, nothing of all that's gone to form your soul. She'll age fast, your lady, her teeth will go and her dugs will sag and you'll loathe her because she was the bait that trapped you. Think, I say, think.'

Pytheas' free hand knotted into a fist and smote his thigh, over and over. 'But what can I do?'

'Leave. She'll have no trouble getting a husband who'll raise the child. Her father's well off by their standards, she's proven herself fertile, and every child is precious, as many of them as they lose. Hoist sail and go. We came in search of the Amber Island, remember? Or if it's a myth, then we want to find whatever the reality is. We have these eastern shores and seas to learn a little about. We mean to return to Pretania and finish circumnavigating it, determine its size and shape, for it's important to Europe in a way that Thule can't be for centuries. And then come home to your people, city, wife, children, grandchildren. Do your duty, man!'

'You … speak harshly.'

'Yes. I respect you that much, Pytheas.'

The Greek looked from side to side, to the mountains athwart that sky which hid the stars in its light, down over woodlands and meadows, out across the shining bay toward unseen Ocean. 'Yes,' he said at last. 'You're right. We should have departed long ago. We shall. I'm a graybeard fool.'

Hanno smiled. 'No, simply a man. She brought a springtime you thought you'd lost back into your heart. How often I've seen it happen.'

'Has it to you?'

Hanno laid a hand on his friend's shoulder. 'Come,' he said, 'let's go back and try to sleep. We've work ahead of us.'

8

Weary, battered, faded, and triumphant, three ships neared Massalia harbor. It was a crisp autumn day, the water danced and glittered as if diamond were strewn upon sapphire, but wind was light and bottoms were foul; they moved slowly.

Pytheas beckoned Hanno to him. 'Stand with me here on the foredeck,' he requested, 'for it may be the last quiet talk we shall ever have.'

The Phoenician joined him in the bows. Pytheas was being his own lookout in this final hour of his voyage. 'You can certainly expect a busy time,' Hanno agreed. 'Everybody and his third cousin will want to meet you, question you, hear you lecture, send you letters, demand a copy of your book and insist you write it yesterday.'

Pytheas' lips quirked upward. 'You'll always have a jape, won't you?'

They stood for a bit, watching. Now as the season of the mariners drew to a close, the waves – how small and gentle, in this refuge from the Atlantic – were beswarmed with vessels. Rowboats, lighters, tarry fishers, tubby coastwise merchantmen, a big grain ship from Egypt, a gilt-trimmed barge, two lean warcraft spider-walking on oars, all sought passage. Shouts and oaths volleyed. Sails boomed, yardarms slatted, tholepins creaked. The city shone ahead, a blue-shadowed white intricacy overspilling its walls. Smoke blew in tatters from red tile roofs. Farmsteads and villas nestled amidst brown stubblefields, pastures still green, darkling pines and yellowing orchards beyond. At the back of those hills, a higher range lifted dun. Gulls dipped and soared, mewing, in their hundreds, like a snowstorm of the North.

'You will not change your mind, Hanno?' Pytheas asked.

The other turned grim. 'I cannot. I'll stay till I collect my pay, and then be off.'

'Why? I don't understand. And you won't explain.'

'It's best.'

'I tell you, a man of your abilities has a brilliant future here – boundless. And not as a metic. With the influence I'll have, I can get you Massaliot citizenship, Hanno.'

'I know. You've said this before. Thank you, but no.'

Pytheas touched the Phoenician's hand, which grasped the rail hard. 'Are you afraid people will hold your origin against you? They won't. I promise. We're above that, we're a cosmopolis.'

'I am everywhere an alien.'

Pytheas sighed. 'Never have you ... opened your soul to me, as I have to you. And even so ... I have never felt so close to anyone else. Not even –' He broke off, and both turned their glances aside.

Hanno took on his cool tone again. He smiled. 'We've been through tremendous things together, good and bad, terrible and tedious, frolicsome and frightening, delightful and deadly. That does forge bonds.'

'And yet you will sever them ... so easily?' Pytheas wondered. 'You will merely bid me farewell?'

In a single instant, before Hanno summoned laughter back to himself, something tore apart and the Greek looked into a pain that bewildered him. 'What else is life but always bidding farewell?'

II

THE PEACHES OF FOREVER

To Yen Ting-kuo, subprefect of the Tumbling Brook district, came an inspector from Ch'ang-an, on an errand for the very Emperor. A courier arrived beforehand, giving the household time to prepare a suitable welcome. Next noontide the party appeared, first a dust cloud on the eastern road, then a troop of mounted men, servants and soldiers, attendant on a carriage drawn by four white horses.

Pennons aloft, metal aflash, they made a brave sight. Yen Ting-kuo appreciated it the more against the serenity of the landscape. From his hilltop compound, the view swept down to Millstone Village, earthen walls, roofs of tile or thatch, huddled together along lanes where pigs and peasants fared, but not unsightly – an outgrowth, a part of the yellow-brown loess soil from which men drew their lives. Beyond reached the land. This was early summer, barley and millet intensely green on their terraces, dotted with blue-clad human forms at work. Farmhouses nestled tiny, strewn across distances. Orchards here and there were done flowering, but fruit was set and leaves full of sunlight. Willows along irrigation canals shivered pale beneath a breeze that smelled warmly of growth. Pine and cypress on farther ridges gave dark dignity. Right and left were heights used for pasture, whose contours stood bold out of shadow.

West of the village those hills steepened rapidly and forest covered much of them. The journey remained long and ever more difficult to yonder frontier, to the realms of the Tibetans and Mongols and other barbarians, but already here civilization began thinning out and one treasured it as perhaps no one quite could in its heartland. Yen Ting-kuo murmured:

'*Beautiful are the procession of seasons*
Bequeathed us by the gods
And the procession of ways and rites
Bequeathed us by the ancestors –'

but broke the old poem off and went back through the gate. Ordinarily he would have continued to his house and waited inside. To receive an Imperial envoy he placed himself and his sons, robed in their best, on the porch. Servants flanked the direct way to it across the outer court; elsewhere shrubs made a kind of maze conducting attention to a goldfish pond. Women, children, and menial workers were tucked away in other buildings of the compound.

Stamp, rattle, and clang announced the advent. An equerry did so more formally, dismounting and entering, to be met halfway by the subprefect's chamberlain. They exchanged bows and necessary words. Thereafter the inspector appeared. The servants prostrated themselves, and Yen Ting-kuo gave him the reverence due from a nobleman of lesser rank.

Ts'ai Li responded courteously. He was not of the most impressive, being a short man and rather young for one of such stature, whereas the subprefect was tall and gray. Even the emblems the inspector had donned upon leaving his vehicle showed signs of hard travel. However, many generations of closeness to the throne lived on in his quiet self-assurance. It was to be seen that host and guest took a quick liking to each other.

Presently they could talk alone. Ts'ai Li had been conducted to his quarters, helped to a bath and a change of raiment. Meanwhile arrangements were made for his entourage, assistants and attendants quartered according to rank in the compound, soldiers among the villagers. Savory odors drifted about, a banquet in preparation, spices, herbs, roasting meats – fowl, suckling pig, puppy, turtle – and liquors gently warmed. Sometimes a twang of zither or chime of bell came audibly loud from the house where singers and dancing girls rehearsed.

The inspector had intimated that before thus meeting local officials he wished a confidential talk. It took place in a chamber almost bare except for two screens, fresh straw mats, arm rests, a low table whereon waited wine and rice cakes from the South. Still, the room was bright and airy, its proportions pleasant; the paintings, of bamboo and of a mountain scene, and the calligraphy on the screens were exquisite. Ts'ai Li expressed proper admiration, sufficient to show he appreciated, not enough to require they be given him.

'My lord's slave returns humble thanks,' Yen Ting-kuo said. 'I fear he will find us a somewhat poor and uncultivated lot in these remote parts.'

'Not at all,' replied Ts'ai Li. Long, polished fingernails gleamed as he brought cup to lips. 'Indeed, here seems to be a haven of peace and order. Alas, even near the capital bandits and malcontents are rife, while elsewhere there is actual rebellion and doubtless the Hsiung-nu beyond the Wall look hungrily our way once more. Thus I must perforce have my escort of soldiers.' His tone registered his scorn for that lowliest of the free classes. 'By the favor of Heaven, no need for them arose. The astrologers had indeed found a propitious day for my departure.'

'The presence of the soldiers may have helped,' said Yen Ting-kuo dryly.

Ts'ai Li smiled. 'So speaks the bluff old baron. I gather your family has provided this district with its leaders for a goodly time?'

'Since the Emperor Wu-ti appointed my honored ancestor Yen Chi after his service against the Northern barbarians.'

'Ah, those were the glorious days.' Ts'ai Li breathed forth the least of sighs. 'We impoverished heirs of them can only strive against a rising flood of troubles.'

Yen Ting-kuo shifted on his heels, cleared his throat, looked straight across the table, and said, 'My lord is surely at the forefront in that effort, having made such a long and arduous journey. In what may we help further his righteous purposes?'

'Largely I require information, and perhaps a guide. Word has reached the capital of a sage, a veritable holy man, in your domain.'

Yen Ting-kuo blinked. 'What?'

'Travelers' tales, but we have questioned several such men at length, and the stories agree. He preaches the Tao, and his virtue appears to have brought him great longevity.' Ts'ai Li hesitated. 'Actual immortality? What can you tell me, Sir Subprefect?'

'Oh.' Yen Ting-kuo scowled. 'I understand. The person who names himself Tu Shan.'

'You are skeptical, then?'

'He does not fit *my* idea of a holy man, Sir Inspector,' Yen Ting-kuo growled. 'We get no few who claim to be. Simple countryfolk are all too ready to listen, especially in unsettled times like these. Masterless wanderers, who do no useful work but beg or wheedle their way along. They claim tremendous powers. Peasants swear they have seen such a one cure the sick, exorcise demons, raise the dead, or what have you. I've looked into some cases and found no real proof of anything. Except that often the drifter has availed himself of men's purses and women's bodies, convincing them that is the Way, before moving elsewhere.'

Ts'ai Li narrowed his eyes. 'We know about charlatans,' he said. 'We also know about ordinary wu, folk magicians, honest enough but illiterate and superstitious. Indeed, then-beliefs and practices have seeped into the once pure teachings of Lao-tzu. This is unfortunate.'

'Does not the court follow, instead, the precepts of the great K'ung Fu-tze?'

'Certainly. Yet – wisdom and strength grow scarce, Sir Subprefect. We must seek them where they are to be found. What we have heard of this Tu Shan has led the One Man himself to think that his will be a desirable voice among the Imperial councillors.'

Yen Ting-kuo stared down into his cup as if to seek a comforting revelation therein. 'It is not for the likes of me to question the Son of Heaven,' he said at length. 'And I daresay that fellow can do no serious harm.' He laughed. 'Perhaps his advice will prove no worse than some.'

Ts'ai Li regarded him for a silent while before murmuring, 'Do you imply, Sir Subprefect, that the Emperor has occasionally been misled in the past?'

Yen Ting-kuo paled a little, then flushed and almost snapped, 'I speak no disrespectful word, Sir Mandarin.'

'Of course not. Understood,' said Ts'ai Li smoothly. 'Although, between us, the implication is quite correct.'

Yen Ting-kuo gave him a startled stare.

Ts'ai Li's tone grew earnest. 'Please consider. It is now ten years since glorious Wang Mang received the Mandate of Heaven. He has decreed many reforms and sought in every way to better the lot of his people. Yet unrest waxes. So, be it said, do poverty at home and barbarian arrogance abroad.' He left unspoken: There are those, ever more of them, who declare that the Hsin is not a new dynasty at all but only a usurpation, a product of palace intrigue, and the time is overpast to restore the Han to that power which is rightfully theirs. 'Clearly, better counsel is much needed. Intelligence and virtue often dwell beneath a lowly roof.'

'The situation must be desperate, if you were sent this far to track down a mere rumor,' Yen Ting-kuo blurted. He made haste to add, 'Of course, we are honored and delighted by your exalted presence, my lord.'

'You are most gracious, Sir Subprefect.' Ts'ai Li's voice sharpened. 'But what can you tell me about Tu Shan?'

Yen Ting-kuo looked away, frowned, tugged his beard, and spoke slowly. 'I cannot in honesty call him a rogue. I investigate everything questionable that I hear of, and have no report of him defrauding anyone, or doing any other evil. It is only ... he is not my idea of a holy man.'

'The seekers of the Tao are apt to be, ah, somewhat eccentric.'

'I know. Still – But let me tell you. He appeared among us five years ago, having passed through communities to the north and east, sojourning a while in some. With him traveled a single disciple, a young man of the fanner class. Since then he has acquired two more, and declined others. For he has settled down in a cave three or four hours' walk from here, in the forest upland by a waterfall. There he meditates, or so he claims. I have gone there, and the cave has been turned into a rather comfortable little abode. Not luxurious, but no hardship to inhabit. The disciples have made themselves a hut nearby. They cultivate a bit of grain, catch a few fish, gather nuts and berries and roots. Folk bring other things as gifts, including money. They make the walk in order to hear whatever words he cares to give them, unburden themselves of their woes – he has a sympathetic ear – and receive his blessing, or simply spend a while in his silent presence. From time to time he comes down here for a day or two. Then it is the same, except that he drinks and eats well at our one inn and disports himself in our one joyhouse. I hear he is a mighty lover. Well, I have not heard of him seducing any man's wife or daughter. Nevertheless, his conduct scarcely seems pious to me, nor do such preachments of his as I have heard make much sense.'

'The Tao is not expressible in words.'

'I know. Just the same – well, just the same.'

'And as for making love, I have heard from those learned in the Tao state that by so doing, especially if he prolongs the act as much as possible, a man comes nearer balancing his Yang with the Yin. At least, this is one school of thought. Others disagree, I am told. But we can hardly expect conventional respectability of a person whose goal in life is enlightenment.'

Yen Ting-kuo achieved a sour smile. 'My lord is more tolerant than me, it seems.'

'No, I merely thought I should seek to prepare myself before setting out, that I might hope to understand whatever I may find.' Ts'ai Li paused. 'What of Tu Shan's earlier life? How much truth is in his claim to great age? I hear he has the aspect of a young man.'

'He does, together with the vigor and all else. Should a sage not be, rather, of reverend appearance?' Yen Ting-kuo drew breath. 'Well, but I have made inquiries about those claims of his. Not that he asserts them loudly. In fact, he never mentions the matter unless he must for some reason, as to explain how long-dead Chou P'eng could have been his teacher. But neither has he tried to cover his tracks. I have been able to question people and to visit a few sites myself, when business has taken me in those directions.'

'Please tell me what you have ascertained, that I may compare my own information.'

'Well, it is evidently true, he was born more than a hundred years ago. That was in the Three Great Rocks district, and his class was merely artisan. He followed his father's trade, a blacksmith, married, had children, nothing unusual aside from his not growing old in body. That did gradually make him a neighborhood marvel, but he does not seem to have taken much if any advantage of it. Instead, when his children were married off and his wife had died, he announced he would seek wisdom, the reason for his strange condition and for all else in the world. He set forth, and was not heard of again until he became a disciple of Chou P'eng. When that old sage died in turn, Tu Shan fared onward, teaching and practicing the Tao as he understood it. I do not know how close that is to what Chou P'eng taught. Nor do I know how long Tu Shan proposes to stay here. Perhaps he himself does not. I have asked him, but such people are always skilled in evading questions they do not wish to answer.'

'Thank you. It confirms the reports given me. Now a man of your perspicacity, Sir Subprefect, must see that such a life indicates extraordinary powers of some kind, and –'

A deferential presence appeared in the doorway. 'Enter and speak,' said Yen Ting-kuo.

Ts'ai Li's secretary took a step into the room, bowed low, and announced:

'This underling begs pardon for disturbing his superiors. However, word has just come to him which may have a certain interest and perhaps urgency. The sage Tu Shan is on the western road bound for the village. Has my lord any commands?'

'Well, well,' murmured the subprefect. 'What an interesting coincidence.'

'If it is a coincidence,' answered Ts'ai Li.

Yen Ting-kuo lifted his heavy brows. 'Has he foreseen my lord's arrival and purpose?'

'It need not be a matter of occult abilities. The Tao works to bring events together in harmony.'

'Shall I summon him here, or bid him wait upon my lord's convenience?'

'Neither. I will go to him – much though it pains me to interrupt this fascinating conversation.' At his host's look of surprise, Ts'ai Li added, 'After all, otherwise I would have sought him out in his retreat. If he is worthy of respect, let him be shown respect.'

With a rustle of silk and brocade, he rose from his cushion and started forth. Yen Ting-kuo followed. The inspector's equerry hastened to summon a decent minimum of attendants and bring them after the magnates. They went through the gate and down the hill at a suitably dignified pace.

A wind had arisen. It boomed from the north, cooling the air, driving clouds before it whose shadows went like sickles across the land. Dust whirled yellow off fields and the road. A flock of crows winged past. Their cawing cut through the babble underneath. Folk had clustered at the village well. They were those whose work was not out amidst the crops: tradesmen, artisans, their women and children, the aged and infirm. Soldiers from the envoy's escort crowded roughly in among them, curious.

All were gathered about a man who had stopped at the wellside. His frame, big and broad, wore the same plain blue, quilted jacket and trousers as any peasant's. His feet were bare, thick with calluses. Also bare was his head; stray black locks fluttered free below a topknot. His face was wide, rather flat-nosed, weather-beaten. He had leaned a staff against the coping and taken a small girl child onto his shoulder. Near him stood three young men, as simply garbed as himself.

'Ah, ha, little one!' the man laughed, and chucked the girl under the chin. 'Would you have a ride on your old horsey? Shameless beggar wench.' She squirmed and giggled.

'Bless her, master,' asked the mother.

'Why, what she is, that is the blessing,' replied the man. 'She is still near the Fountainhead of Quietness to which wise men hope they may return. Not that that forbids your desiring a sweetmeat, eh, mei-mei?'

'Can childhood, then, be better than age?' quavered one whose wispy beard fell white from a head bent forward.

'You would have me teach, when my poor throat is choked by the dust of my faring?' responded the man genially. 'No, please, first a cup or three of wine. Nothing in excess, including self-denial.'

'Make way!' cried the equerry. 'Make way for the lord Ts'ai Li, Imperial legate from Ch'ang-an, and for the lord of the district, Yen Ting-kuo!'

Voices halted. People scrambled aside. Frightened, the girl whimpered and reached for her mother. The man gave her to the woman and bowed, politely if not abjectly, as the two robed forms neared him.

'Here is our sage Tu Shan, Sir Inspector,' said the sub-prefect.

'Off with you!' the equerry bade the commoners. 'This is a matter of state.'

'They may listen if they wish,' said Ts'ai Li mildly.

'Their smell should not offend my lord's nostrils,' declared the equerry, and the crowd did shuffle some distance away, to stand in bunches and gape.

'Let us seek back to the house,' Yen Ting-kuo proposed. 'This day you receive a great honor, Tu Shan.'

'I thank my lord most profoundly,' the newcomer answered, 'but we are shabby and unwashed and altogether unfit for your home.' His voice was deep, lacking a cultivated accent though not quite lowly-sounding either. A chuckle seemed to run within it and flicker behind his eyes. 'May I take the liberty of presenting my disciples Ch'i, Wei, and Ma?' The three youths abased themselves until he gave them an unobtrusive signal to rise.

'They can join us.' Yen Ting-kuo failed to hide his distaste entirely.

Did Tu Shan perceive that? He addressed Ts'ai Li: 'Perhaps my lord would care to state his business at once. Then we shall know whether or not pursuing it would waste his time.'

The inspector smiled. 'I hope not, Sir Sage, for I have already expended a great deal of that,' he said. To the baron, the secretary, and the rest who had heard and were shocked: 'Tu Shan is right. He has certainly spared me a doubtless difficult trail to his hermitage.'

'Happenstance,' said the man spoken of. 'Nor does it take supernatural insight for me to guess your errand.'

'Rejoice,' Ts'ai Li told him. 'Word of you has reached the august ears of the Emperor himself. He bade me seek you out and bring you to Ch'ang-an, that the realm have the benefit of your wisdom.'

The disciples gasped before recovering a measure of steadiness. Tu Shan stayed imperturbable. 'Surely the Son of Heaven has councillors beyond counting,' he said.

'He does, but they are insufficient. As the proverb goes, a thousand mice do not equal a single tiger.'

'Perhaps my lord is a bit unfair to the advisors and ministers. They have huge tasks, beyond my poor wits to understand.'

'Your modesty is commendable. It reveals your character.'

Tu Shan shook his head. 'No, I am just a fool, and ignorant. How could I dare so much as see the Imperial throne?'

'You defame yourself,' said Ts'ai Li on a slight note of impatience. 'None can have lived as long as you without being intelligent and without gaining experience. Moreover, you have pondered what you have observed and drawn valuable lessons from it.'

Tu Shan smiled wryly, as though at an equal. 'If I have learned anything, it is that intelligence and knowledge are worth little by themselves. Failing the enlightenment that goes beyond words and the world, they serve mainly to provide us with wonderful reasons for doing what we intend to do regardless.'

Yen Ting-Kuo could not forbear to interject, 'Come, come. You are no ascetic. The Emperor rewards, with Imperial generosity, those who serve him well.'

Tu Shan's manner shifted subtly. It hinted at a schoolmaster with a pupil somewhat slow. 'I have visited Ch'ang-an in my wanderings. Though of course I could not go into the palace grounds, I was in mansions. My lords, there are too many walls there. Every ward is closed off from every other, and when the drums sound from the towers at dusk, their gates are barred to all but the nobility. In the mountains one may go freely beneath the stars.'

'To him who walks in the Way, all places should be alike,' said Ts'ai Li.

Tu Shan inclined his head. 'My lord is well versed in the *Book of the Way and Its Virtue*. But as for me, I am a blunderer, half blind, who would be forever stumbling against those walls.'

Ts'ai Li stiffened. 'I think you make excuses to avoid a duty you would find onerous. Why do you preach to the people, if you care too little about them to lend your thoughts in aid of them?'

'They cannot be aided thus.' Low, Tu Shan's words nonetheless cut through the wind. 'Only they themselves can cope with their troubles, just as every man can only find the Tao by himself.'

Ts'ai Li's voice slid quietly as a dagger: 'Do you deny the Emperor's beneficence?'

'Many Emperors have come and gone. Many more shall.' Tu Shan gestured. 'Behold the flying dust. Once it, too, lived. The Tao alone abides.'

'You risk ... punishment, Sir Sage.'

Sudden laughter pealed. Tu Shan slapped his thigh. 'How can a head removed from its neck give counsel?' He calmed as fast. 'My lord, I meant no disrespect. I say only that I am not fit for the task you have in mind, and unworthy of it. Take me with you, and this will soon be clear. Better that you spare the priceless time of the One Man.'

Ts'ai Li sighed. Yen Ting-kuo, watching the inspector, eased a bit. 'You rascal,' Ts'ai Li said, rueful, 'you use the Book – what is the line? – "Like water, soft and yielding, that wears away the hardest stone –"'

Tu Shan bowed. 'Should we not say, rather, that the stream flows on to its destiny while the stupid rock stays where it was?'

Now Ts'ai Li spoke as to an equal. 'If you will not go, so be it. Forgive me when I report that you proved ... a disappointment.'

Tu Shan nearly grinned. 'How shrewdly you put it.' He bowed to Yen Ting-kuo. 'See, my lord, there is no reason for me to track dirt across your beautiful mats. Best my disciples and I take ourselves from your presence at once.'

'Correct,' said the subprefect coldly.

The inspector cast him a disapproving glance, turned again to Tu Shan, and said, in a voice slightly less than level, 'Yet you, Sir Sage, have lived longer than almost any other man, and show no sign of age. Can you at least tell me how this is?'

Tu Shan became grave. Some might say he spoke in pity. 'I am forever asked that.'

'Well?'

'I never give a clear answer, for I am unable.'

'Surely you know.'

'I have said I do not, but men insist, eh?' Tu Shan appeared to dismiss sadness. 'The story goes,' he said, 'that in the garden of Hsi Wang Mu, Mother of the West, grow certain peaches, and that he whom she allows to eat of these is made immortal.'

Ts'ai Li looked long at him before answering, well-nigh too softly to hear, 'As you wish, Sir Sage.' The watching people drew breath, glanced about, one by one retreated. The inspector bowed. 'I depart in awe.'

Tu Shan bowed likewise. 'Greet the Emperor. He too deserves compassion.'

Yen Ting-kuo cleared his throat, hesitated, then at a gesture followed Ts'ai Li out of the village, back up the hill to the manor house. Their attendants trailed after them. The common folk made reverence, bent above folded hands, and slipped away to the shelter of their homes. Tu Shan and his disciples stood alone by the well. The wind blustered through silence. Shadows came and went.

Tu Shan took his staff. 'Come,' he said.

'Where, master?' Ch'i ventured.

'To our retreat. Afterward –' For an instant, pain crossed the face of Tu Shan. 'I do not know. Elsewhere. West into the mountains, I think.'

'Do you fear reprisal, master?' asked Wei.

'No, no, I trust the word of yonder lord. But it is well to be gone. This wind smells of trouble.'

'The master can tell,' said brash Ma. 'He must have caught that scent often in his many years. Did you indeed taste those peaches?'

Tu Shan laughed a little. 'I had to tell the man something. Doubtless the story will spread, and tales will arise of others who have done the same. Well, we shall be afar.'

He began walking. 'I have warned you aplenty, lads,' he continued, 'and I will warn you again. I have no inspiration, no secrets to impart. I am the most ordinary of persons, except that somehow, for some reason, my body has stayed young. So I searched for understanding, and discovered that this is the only livelihood open to such as I. If you care to listen to me, do. If not, leave with my blessing. Meanwhile, let us see a brisker pace.'

'Why, you said we have nothing to fear, master,' protested Ma.

'No, I did not.' Tu Shan's voice harshened. 'I fear witnessing what will most likely happen to these people, whom I, helplessly, love. The times are evil. We must seek a place apart, and the Tao.'

They walked onward through the wind.

III

THE COMRADE

1

A ship was loading at the Claudian dock. She was big for an ocean-goer, two-masted, her round black belly taking perhaps five hundred tons. The gilt sternpost, curved high over the steering oar fixtures in the form of a swan's neck and head, also bespoke wealth. Lugo went over to inquire about her. Bound more or less this way, he had turned aside with the idea of seeing what went on at the waterfront. He made it his business to keep fully aware of the world around him.

The stevedores were slaves. Though the morning was cool, their bodies gleamed and reeked with sweat as they carried amphoras across the dock and up the gangplank, two men to each great jug. A breeze off the river mingled whiffs of fresh pitch from the ship with their odors. The foreman stood by, and him Lugo could approach.

'The *Nereid*,' he replied, 'with wine, glassware, silks, and I don't know what else, for Britannia. Her skipper wants to catch tomorrow's early tide. Hoy, you!' His whip flicked across a bare back. It was single-stranded and unloaded, but left a mark between shoulder blade and loincloth. 'Move along, there!' The slave gave him a hopeless glower and trudged a little faster to his next burden at the warehouse. 'Got to freshen 'em pretty often,' the foreman explained. 'They get out of shape and lazy, sitting around idle. Not enough to do any more.' He sighed. 'Free men, you could lay off in these wretched times, and call back when you needed them. But if everybody's in his station for life –'

'It's a wonder this vessel is going,' Lugo said. 'Won't she draw pirates like flies to a carcass? I hear the Saxons and Scoti are turning the shores of Armorica into a blackened desert.'

'The House of the Caelii always was venturesome, and I guess there's a big profit to be made when so few dare sail,' the foreman answered.

Lugo nodded, stroked his chin, and murmured, 'M-m, sea rovers usually do seek their plunder on land. No doubt *Nereid* will carry guards as well as her crew being armed. If several barbarian craft came in sight, Scoti probably couldn't climb that tall freeboard out of their currachs, and given any kind of wind, she can show her heels to Saxon galleys.'

'You talk like a mariner yourself. But you don't look like one.' The foreman's glance sharpened. Suspicion was the order of the day. He saw a medium-sized, wiry man of youthful appearance; face narrow and high in the cheekbones, curved nose, slightly oblique brown eyes; black hair and a neatly trimmed beard such as was coming into fashion; clean white tunic, blue raincloak with a cowl shoved back; stout sandals; staff in hand, though he walked lithely.

Lugo shrugged. 'I've been around. And I enjoy talking to people. You, for instance.' He smiled. 'Thanks for satisfying my curiosity, and a good day to you.'

'Go with God,' said the foreman, disarmed, and turned his attention back to the longshoremen.

Lugo sauntered on. When he came opposite the next gate, he stopped to admire the view eastward. His lashes snared sunlight and made bits of rainbow.

Before him flowed the Garumna, on its way to its confluence with the Duranius, their shared estuary, and the sea. Some two thousand shimmering feet across, the water bore several rowboats, a fishing smack bound upstream on oars with its catch, a gaudy spiritsail above a slim yacht. Land on the far side reached low, intensely green; he saw the tawny walls and rosy tiles of two manor houses amidst their vineyards, while smoke blew in tatters from humbler roofs of thatch. Birds winged everywhere, robin, sparrow, crane, duck, a hawk on high, the startling blue of a kingfisher. He heard their calls as an overtone that skipped through the lapping and rustling of the river. It was hard to imagine that heathen Germani raged at the gates of Lugdunum, that the chief city of central Gallia might even now have fallen to them, less than three hundred miles from here.

Or else it was all too easy to imagine. Lugo's mouth tightened. Come along, he told himself. He was more prone to reverie than other men, with less excuse nowadays. This vicinity had been spared so far, but the handwriting on the wall grew plainer for him to read every year, as certain Jews he had known would have phrased it. He turned and reentered the city.

The gate was minor, a sally port in the bulwarks whose towers and battlements stood foursquare around Burdigala. Beside his spear, a sentry leaned half asleep against the sun-warmed stones. He was an auxiliary, a German himself. The legions were in Italy or out toward the frontiers, and mere skeletons of what they had once been. Meanwhile barbarians like this wrung leave from the Emperors to settle in Roman lands. In return, they were supposed to obey the laws and furnish troops; but in Lugdunensis, for example, they had revolted ...

Lugo passed through, across the open pomoerium, into a street that he recognized as Vindomarian Way. It twisted among buildings whose flat sides crowded out all but a strip of sky, the lumpiness of its cobblestones slickened by stinking offal, an obscure lane quite likely going back to ages when only the Bituriges squatted here. However, Lugo had in the course of time taken care to learn the entire city, old as well as new quarters.

Not many people jostled him, and they for the most part shabbily clad. Housewives chattered together while they carried laundry to the river, pails of water from the nearest aqueduct outlet, baskets of vegetables gotten at a local marketplace. A porter came by under a load well-nigh as heavy as what was in the donkey cart he met; he and the driver cursed, trying to get past each other. An apprentice fetching wool for his master had stopped to jape with a girl. Two countrymen in ancient-style coats and breeches, probably cattle drovers, made remarks so accented and full of Gallic words that Lugo could hardly understand what he overheard. A drunken man – a laborer to judge by his hands, out of work to judge by his condition – lurched along in search of a frolic or a fight; unemployment had become rife as the upheavals of the past decade cowed an already decaying commerce. A meretrix in pathetic, bedraggled finery, seeking customers even this early, brushed against Lugo. Except for laying a hand over the purse at his waist he ignored her. A hunchbacked beggar whined for alms in the name of Christ and then, when likewise ignored, tried Jupiter, Mithras, Isis, the Great Mother, and Celtic Epona; finally he screamed maledictions at Lugo's back. Shockheaded children in grimy smocks ran their little errands or played their little games. For them he felt a tug of compassion.

His Levantine features marked him out among them all. Burdigala was cosmopolitan; Italy, Greece, Africa, Asia had poured blood into it. Yet most dwellers remained what their forebears must always have been, strongly built, roundheaded, dark of hair but fair of skin. They spoke Latin with a nasal intonation he had never quite mastered.

A potter's shop, its front open on the wares and whirr of the wheel, showed him where he must turn onto broader Teutatis Street – which, lately, the bishop was trying to make its residents call after St Johannes. It was his quickest route through this maze toward Mother Thorabesom's Lane, where lived the one he sought. Rufus might not be at home, but was certainly not at work. The shipyard had had no orders for well over a year, and its men were now dependent on the state for their bread; circuses amounted to an occasional bear-baiting or the like. If Rufus was out, Lugo was prepared to stroll around inconspicuously till he came back. Lugo had learned patience.

He had gone a hundred yards farther when the new noise reached him. Others heard it too, halted, stiffened, listened with heads cocked and eyes slitted. The majority began retreating. Shopkeepers and apprentices made ready to close doors and shutters. A few men licked their chops and drifted in the direction of the sound. Turmoil called then-kind to itself. The racket loudened, muffled by houses and contorted alleys but unmistakable. Lugo knew it of old, the deep, racking growl, the yelps and hoots. A crowd was hounding somebody.

He realized with a chill who the quarry must be. For a moment he paused. Was it worth the risk? Cordelia, the children, he and his family might have thirty or forty years ahead of them.

Resolution came. He should at least go see whether the situation was hopeless or not. He pulled the hood of his paenula over his head. Sewn to the edge was a veil, which he drew down. He saw reasonably well through the gauze, but it bid his face. Lugo had learned preparedness.

A military patrol might wonder at the sight and stop him for questioning. However, were a patrol in the neighborhood, that pack would not be after Rufus. Instead – Lugo's mouth twisted briefly upward – Rufus might well be under arrest.

Lugo moved to intercept the oncoming tumult, as closely as he could judge. He went a trifle more quickly than the trouble seekers, not quickly enough to draw any special heed. The hood overshadowed the veil and blinkered sight of it; perhaps nobody noticed. Within himself he spoke ancient incantations against danger. Give fear no hold upon you, keep sinews loose and senses open, ready at every instant to flow with the rush of action. Calm, alert, supple; calm, alert, supple –

He came out on Hercules Place just as the hunted man did. A corroded bronze statue of the hero gave the small square its name. Several streets radiated thence. He who burst forth was stocky, his coarse features freckled, his thin hair and unkempt beard an unusual orange-red. The tunic that flapped around stout limbs was drenched and a-reek with sweat. Indeed this must be Rufus, Lugo saw, and 'Rufus' must be a nickname.

The fugitive was built for strength, not speed. His pursuers swarmed close behind. They numbered about fifty, proletarians like him in drab, oft-mended garments. Quite a few were women, locks gone Medusa wild around maenad faces. Most bore what weapons they could snatch, knife, hammer, stick, loose cobblestone. Through their baying tore words: 'Sorcerer! ... Heathen! ... Satan – kill –' A flung rock struck Rufus between the shoulders. He staggered and pounded on. His mouth stretched wide, his chest heaved, his eyes stared as if blinded.

Lugo's gaze flickered. Sometimes he could not wait and see how things went, he must make an instant decision. He gauged the layout, distances, speeds, nature of the throng. Terror thrilled through the hatred they howled. The chance of rescue looked worth taking. If he failed, he might escape with injuries less than fatal; and those would soon heal.

'To me, Rufus!' he shouted. To the pack: 'Halt! Hold off, you lawless dogs!'

The man in the lead snarled at him. Lugo brought hands near the middle of his staff. It was oak. He had drilled holes in the ends and filled them with lead. It whirred and smacked. The man screamed. He reeled aside. A broken rib, likely. Lugo's weapon punched the next under the breastbone. Air whoofed from lungs. Lugo caught a third man across a kneecap. He shrieked his pain and flailed against two at his back. A woman swung a mop. Lugo fended it off and rapped her knuckles. Maybe he cracked a bone or two.

The crowd recoiled on itself, milled, moaned, gibbered. From behind his whirling, half invisible staff, Lugo grinned at them and at the rowdies who had appeared. 'Go home,' he called. 'Dare you take Caesar's law in your own hands? Be off!'

Somebody threw a stone. It missed. Lugo laid a blow on the nearest scalp. He controlled its force. Matters were amply bad without producing corpses; those would provoke immediate official action. Nevertheless the wound bled spectacularly, sudden red brilliance over skin and pavement, a shock to behold.

Rufus' gasps rattled. 'Come along,' Lugo muttered. 'Slow and steady. If we run, they'll be after us again.' He backed off, still twirling the staff, still grinning his most wolfish. At the corner of vision, he saw Rufus sidle on his right. Good. The fellow had kept that much wit.

The hunters mumbled and gaped. The hurt among them ululated. Lugo entered the narrow street he had chosen. It bent around a tenement, and he had no more sight of Hercules. 'Now we move,' he clipped, and turned around. 'No, you fool.' He caught Rufus' sleeve. 'Don't run. Walk.'

Such people as were present looked warily at them but didn't interfere. Lugo ducked into the first alley he knew connected with a different street. When they were alone at the noisome middle of it, he said, 'Stop.' He put his staff beneath an arm and reached for the fibula that held his cloak. 'We'll drape this over you.' He tucked the veil back inside the cowl before he covered his companion's distinctive hair. 'Very well. We are two peaceful men going about our business. Can you remember that?'

The artisan blinked from the hood. Sweat glistened in what light there was. 'Who, who be you?' His voice quavered deep. 'What you want?'

'I would like to save your life,' Lugo said coldly, 'but I don't propose to risk mine any further. Do as I say and we may yet make it to shelter.' When the other began in a dazed fashion to seem doubtful, Lugo added, 'Go to the authorities if you wish. Go at once, before your dear neighbors pluck up courage and come in search. Tell the prefect you're accused of sorcery. He'll find out anyway. While you're being interrogated under torture, you might think how you can prove your innocence. Sorcery is a capital offense, you know.'

'But you –'

'I am no more guilty of it than you are. I have a notion we can help each other. If you disagree, farewell. If not, come with me, and keep your mouth shut.'

Breath shuddered into the burly frame. Rufus drew the cloak close about him and shambled along.

His gait grew easier as they proceeded, for nothing untoward happened. They simply mingled with traffic. 'You may think the world is ending,' Lugo remarked low, 'but it was a purely local fuss. Nobody elsewhere has heard of it, or if anyone has, he doesn't care. I've seen people go on with their everyday lives while the enemy was breaking down the gates.'

Rufus glanced at him, gulped, but preserved silence.

2

Lugo's home was in the northwest quadrant, on the Street of the Sandalmakers, a quiet area. The house was unostentatious, rather old, stucco peeling off the concrete here and there. Lugo knocked. His majordomo opened the door; he kept only a few slaves, carefully chosen and winnowed over the years. 'This man and I have confidential matters to discuss, Perseus,' he said. 'He may be staying with us a while. I do not wish him disturbed in any way.'

The Cretan nodded and smiled his bland smile. 'Understood, master,' he replied. 'I will inform the rest.'

'We can trust them,' Lugo said aside to Rufus. 'They know they have soft berths.' To Perseus: 'As you can see – and smell – my friend has had a strenuous time. We'll lodge him in the Low Room. Bring refreshments immediately; water as soon as you can heat a decent amount, with washcloth and towel; clean garb. Is the bed made up?'

'It always is, master.' The slave sounded a bit hurt. He considered. 'As for raiment, yours will not fit. I'll borrow from Durig. Shall I then purchase some?'

'Hold off on that,' Lugo decided. He might need all the cash he could scrape together in a hurry. Though not the debased small stuff. That was too bulky; one gold solidus equalled about fourteen thousand nummi. 'Durig's our handyman,' he explained to Rufus. 'Otherwise we boast a gifted cook and a couple of maids. A modest household.' Homely details might soothe. He wanted Rufus fit to answer questions as soon as might be.

From the atrium they passed into a pleasant room, equally unpretentious, lighted by sunshine that leaded clerestory windows turned greenish. A mosaic at the center of the floor tiles depicted a panther surrounded by peacocks. Wooden panels set into the walls bore motifs more current, the Fish and Chi Rho among flowers, a large-eyed Good Shepherd. Since the reign of Constantine the Great it had been increasingly expedient to profess Christianity, which hereabouts had better be of the Catholic sort. Lugo remained a catechumen; baptism would have laid inconvenient obligations on him. Most believers put it off till late in life.

His wife had heard and come to meet him. 'Welcome, dear,' she said happily. 'You're back fast.' Her gaze fell on Rufus and grew troubled.

'This man and I have urgent business,' Lugo told her. 'It is highly confidential. Do you understand?'

She swallowed but nodded. 'Hail and welcome,' she greeted in a subdued voice.

Brave girl, Lugo thought. It was hard to look away from her. Cordelia was nineteen, short but deliriously rounded, her features delicate and lips always slightly parted below a lustrous mass of brown hair. They had been married four years and she had borne him two children thus far, both still alive. The marriage brought him certain useful connections, her father being a curial, though no dowry worth mentioning, the curial class being crushed between taxes and civic duties. More important to the couple, they had been drawn to each other, and wedlock became an ever higher delight.

'Marcus, meet Cordelia, my wife,' Lugo said. 'Marcus' was a safely frequent name. Rufus bobbed his head and grunted. To her: 'We must get busy at once. Perseus will see to the necessities. I'll join you when I can.'

She stared after them as he guided his companion off. Did he hear her sigh? Abrupt fear stabbed. He had gone forth with hope aflutter in him, a hope so wild that he must keep denying it, scolding himself for it. Now he saw what the reality might lead to.

No, he would not think about that. Not immediately. One step, two steps, left foot, right foot, that was how to march through time.

The Low Room was downstairs, a part of the cellar that Lugo had had bricked off after he acquired this house. Such hideaways were common enough to draw scant attention. Often they were for prayer or private austerities. In Lugo's line of work, it was clear that he could have use for a place secure from eavesdroppers. The cell was about ten feet square and six high. Three tiny windows just under the ceiling gave on the peristyle garden at ground level. The glass in them was so thick and wavy as to block vision, but the light that seeped through met whitewashed walls, making the gloom not too dense at this moment. Tallow candles lay on a shelf beside flint, steel, and tinder. Furnishings were a single bed, a stool, and a chamber pot on the dirt floor.

'Sit down,' Lugo invited. 'Rest. You're safe, my friend, safe.'

Rufus hunched on the stool. He threw back the cowl but clutched the paenula around his tunic; the place was chilly. His red head lifted with a forlorn defiance. 'Who the muck be you, anyhow?' he growled.

His host lounged back against the wall and smiled. 'Flavius Lugo,' he said. 'And you, I believe, are a shipyard carpenter, unemployed, generally called Rufus. What's your real name?'

An obscenity was followed by: 'What's it matter to you?'

Lugo shrugged. 'Little or nothing, I suppose. You could be more gracious toward me. That rabble would have had the life out of you.'

'And what's that to you?' The retort was harsh. 'Why'd you step in? Look here, I be no sorcerer. I want naught to do with magic or heathendom, me, a good Christian, a free Roman citizen.'

Lugo lifted a brow. 'Have you absolutely never made an offering elsewhere than in church?' he murmured.

'Well, uh, well – Epona, when my wife was dying –' Rufus half rose. He bristled. 'Dung o' Cernunnos! *Be* you a sorcerer?'

Lugo raised a palm. His left hand moved the staff, slightly but meaningfully. 'I am not. Nor can I read your mind. However, old ways die hard, even in the cities, and the countryside is mostly pagan and from your looks and speech I'd guess your family were Cadurci a generation or two ago, back in the hills above the Duranius Valley.'

Rufus lowered himself. For a minute he breathed hard. Then, piece by piece, he began to relax. A smile of sorts responded to Lugo's. 'My parents come o' that tribe,' he rumbled. 'My right name, uh, Cotuadun. Nobody calls me aught but Rufus any more. You be a sharp 'un.'

'I make my living at it.'

'No Gaul you. Anybody might be a Flavius, but what's "Lugo"? Where you from?'

'I've been settled in Burdigala a fair number of years.' A knock on the plank door was handily timed. 'Ah, here comes the excellent Perseus with those refreshments I ordered. I daresay you've slightly more need of them than I do.'

The majordomo brought a tray of wine and water flagons, cups, bread, cheese, olives in a bowl. He put it on the ground and, at Lugo's wave, departed, closing the door behind him. Lugo sat down on the bed, reached, poured, offered Rufus a drink not much diluted. His own he watered well.

'Your health,' he proposed. 'You pretty near lost it today.'

Rufus took a long swallow. 'Ahhh! Bugger me if that don't go good.' He squinted through the dusk at his rescuer. 'Why'd you do it? What be I to you?'

'Well, if nothing else, those proles had no right to kill you. That's the job of the state, after you've duly been found guilty – which I am sure you are not. It behooved me to enforce the law.'

'You knew me.'

Lugo sipped. The wine was Falernian, sweet on his tongue. 'I knew of you,' he said. 'Rumors had reached me. That's natural. I keep track of what's going on. I have my agents. Nothing to frighten you, no secret informers. But street urchins, for example, who earn a coin by bringing me word of anything interesting. I determined to seek you out and learn more. It's lucky for you that that chanced to be exactly when and where I could snatch you from your fellow sons of toil.'

The question soughed through him: How many chances had he missed, by what slender margins, throughout all the years? He did not share the widespread present-day faith in astrology. It seemed likeliest to him that sheer accident ruled the world. Perhaps today the dice had been due to roll in his favor.

If the game was real. *If* anyone like him existed, had ever existed, anywhere under the sky.

Rufus' head thrust forward from the heavy shoulders. 'Why did you?' he grated. 'What the dung be you after?'

He needed calming down. Lugo check-reined the eagerness within himself, that was half fear. 'Drink your wine,' he said. 'Listen, and I'll explain.

'This house may have led you to think I'm a curial, or a mildly prosperous shopkeeper, or something of that kind. I'm not.' Had not been for a long while. Diocletian's decree had supposedly frozen everybody into the status to which they were born, including the middle classes. But rather than be crushed, grain by grain, between the stones of taxation, regulation, worthless currency, moribund trade, more and more were fleeing. They slipped off, changed their names, became serfs or outright slaves, illegal itinerant laborers and mountebanks; some joined the Bacaudae whose bandit gangs terrorized the rural outback, some actually sought to the barbarians. Lugo had made better arrangements for himself, well in advance of need. He was accustomed to looking ahead.

'I'm currently in the pay of one Aurelian, a senator in this city,' he went on.

Hostility sparked. 'I heard about him.'

Lugo shrugged again. 'So he bribed his way into that rank, and even among his colleagues is monumentally corrupt. What of it? He's an able man and understands that it's wise to be loyal to those who serve him. Senators aren't allowed to engage in commerce, you may know, but he has varied interests. That calls for intermediaries who are not mere figureheads. I come and go for him, to and fro, sniffing out dangers and possibilities, bearing messages, executing tasks that require discretion, giving advice when appropriate. There are worse stations in life. In fact, there are less honorable ones.'

'What's Aurelian want with me?' Rufus asked uneasily.

'Nothing. He's never heard of you. Fate willing, he never shall. I sought you out on my own account. We may be of very great value to each other.' Lugo sharpened his tone. 'I make no threats. If we cannot work together but you have done your best to cooperate with me, I can at least get you smuggled out of Burdigala to someplace where you can start over. Remember, you owe me your life. If I abandon you, you're a dead man.'

Sullenness and the gesture of the fig: 'They'll know you hid me here.'

'Why, I'll tell them myself,' Lugo declared coolly. 'As a solid citizen, I did not want you unlawfully slaughtered, but I did feel it incumbent on me to interview you in private, draw you out – Hold!' He had set his cup on the ground as he talked, expecting Rufus might lunge. Now he gripped the staff in both hands. 'Stay right on that stool, boy. You're sturdy, but you've seen what I can do with this.'

Rufus crouched back.

Lugo laughed. 'That's better. Don't be so damned edgy. I really don't want to cause you any harm. Let me repeat, if you'll be honest with me and do as I say, the worst that will happen to you is that you leave Burdigala in disguise. Aurelian owns a huge latifundium; it can doubtless use an extra workman, if I put in a good word, and the senator will cover up any little irregularities for me. At best – well, I don't yet know, and therefore won't make any promises, but it could be glorious beyond your highest-flying childhood dreams, Rufus.'

His words and the lulling tone worked. Also, the wine had begun to. Rufus sat quiet a moment, nodded, beamed, tossed off his drink, held out a hand. 'By the Three, right!' he cried.

Lugo clasped the hard palm. The gesture was fairly new in Gallia, maybe learned from Germanic immigrants. 'Splendid,' he said. 'Just speak fully and frankly. I know that won't be easy, but remember, I have my reasons. I mean to do well by you, as well as God allows.'

He refilled the emptied cup. Behind his jovial façade, tension gathered and gathered.

Rufus drank. His vessel wobbled. 'What d'you want to know?' he asked.

'First, why you got into grief.'

Rufus' pleasure faded. He scowled beyond his questioner. 'Because my wife died,' he mumbled. 'That's what broke the crock.'

'Many men are widowed,' Lugo said, while memory twisted a sword inside him.

The big hand tightened around the cup till knuckles stood white. 'My Livia was old. White hair, wrinkles, no teeth. We'd two kids what grew up, boy and girl. They be married, kids o' their own. And they've gone gray.'

'I thought this might be,' Lugo whispered, not in Latin. 'O Ashtoreth –'

Aloud, using today's language: 'The rumors that reached me suggested as much. That's why I came after you. When were you born, Rufus?'

'How the muck should I know?' The response was surly. 'Balls! Poor folk don't keep count like you rich 'uns. I couldn't tell you who be consul this year, let alone then was. But my Livia was young like me when we got hitched – fourteen, fifteen, whatever. She was a strong mare, she was, popped her young out like melon seeds, though only the two o' them got to grow up. She didn't break down fast like some mares.'

'You may well have reached your threescore and ten, then, or gone beyond,' Lugo said most softly. 'You don't look a day over twenty-five. Were you ever sick?'

'No, 'less you count a couple times I got hurt. Bad hurts, but they healed right up in a few days, not so much as a scar. No toothaches ever. I got three teeth knocked out in a fight once, and they grew back.' The arrogance shriveled. 'People looked at me more and more slanty. When Livia died, that broke the crock.' Rufus groaned. 'They'd been saying I must've made a deal with the Devil. *She* told me what she heard. But what the muck could I do? God give me a strong body, that's all. She believed.'

'I do too, Rufus.'

'When she fell bad sick at last, not many 'ud speak to me anymore. They'd shy from me in the street, make signs, spit on their breasts. I went to a priest. He was scared o' me too, I could see it. Said I ought to go to the bishop, but the bastard stalled about taking me to him. Then Livia died.'

'A release,' Lugo could not help venturing.

'Well, I'd gone to a whorehouse for a long time,' Rufus answered matter-of-factly. Fury flared. 'Now they, them bitches, they told me go away and don't come back. I got mad, raised a ruckus. People heard and gathered around outside. When I came out, the scumswine yelled at me. I decked the loudest mouthed o' them. Next thing I knew, they were on me. I barely fought free and ran. They came after me, more and more o' them.'

'And you'd have died under their feet,' Lugo said. 'Or else presently the rumors would have reached the prefect. The tale of a man who never grew old and was clearly no saint, therefore must be in league with the diabolical. You'd have been arrested, interrogated under torture, doubtless beheaded. These are bad times. Nobody knows what to expect. Will the barbarians prevail? Will we have another civil war? Will plague or famine or a total collapse of trade destroy us? Heretics and sorcerers are objects to take fear out on.'

'I be none!'

'I didn't say you were. I accept you're a common man, as common as I've ever met, aside from – Tell me, have you known or heard of anyone else like you, whom time doesn't appear to touch? Kinfolk, perhaps?'

Rufus shook his head.

Lugo sighed. 'Neither have I.' He mustered resolve and plunged forward. 'And I have waited and tried, searched and endured, since first I came to understand.'

'Uh?' The wine splashed from Rufus' cup.

Lugo sipped out of his own, for what comfort it could give. 'How old do you think I am?' he asked.

Rufus peered before he said at the bottom of his throat: 'You look maybe twenty-five.'

A smile quirked on the left side of Lugo's mouth. 'Like you, I don't know my age for certain,' he answered slowly. 'But Hiram was king in Tyre when I was born there. What chronicles I have since been able to study and figure from show me that that was about twelve centuries ago.'

Rufus gaped. The freckles stood lurid on a skin gone white. His free hand made a sign.

'Don't be afraid,' Lugo urged. 'I'm in no pact with darkness. Or with Heaven, for that matter, or any power, any soul. I am your kind of flesh, whatever that means. I have simply been longer on earth. It is lonely. You have had the barest foretaste of how lonely it is.'

He rose, leaving staff and cup, to pace the cramped floor, hands behind back. 'I was not born Flavius Lugo, of course,' he said. 'That is only the latest name I have taken out of – I've lost count of how many. The earliest was – never mind. A Phoenician name. I was a merchant until the years brought me to trouble much like yours today. Then for a long time I was a sailor, a caravan guard, a mercenary soldier, a wandering bard, any number of trades in which a man may come and go little noticed. That was a hard school I went through. Often I came near dying from wounds, shipwreck, hunger, thirst, a dozen different perils. Sometimes I would have died, were it not for the strange vigor of this body. A slower danger, more frightening as I began to perceive it, was that of drowning, losing my reason, in sheer memories. For a while I did have scant use of my wits. In a way that was a mercy; it blunted the pain of losing everyone I came to care for, losing him and losing her and losing, oh, the children ... Bit by bit I worked out the art of memory. I now have clear recall, I am like a walking library of Alexandria – no, that burned, didn't it?' He chuckled at himself. 'I do make slips. But I have the art of storing what I know until it's wanted, then calling it forth. I have the art of controlling sorrow. I have –'

He observed Rufus' awed regard and broke off. 'Twelve hundred years?' the artisan breathed. 'You seen the *Savior?*'

Lugo forced a smile. 'Sorry, I have not. If he was born in the reign of Augustus, as they say – that would have been, m-m, between three and four hundred years ago – then I was in Britannia at the time. Rome hadn't conquered it yet, but trade was brisk and the southern tribes were cultured in their fashion. And much less meddlesome. That's always a highly desirable feature in a place. Damnably hard to find these days, short of running off to the wild Germani or Scoti or whatever. And even they –

'Another art I've developed is that of aging my appearance. Hair powder, dyes, such things are cumbersome, unreliable. I let everybody talk about how young I continue to look. Some people do, after all. But meanwhile gradually I begin to stoop a little, shuffle a little, cough, pretend to be hard of hearing, complain of aches and pains and the insolence of modern youth. It only works up to a point, of course. Finally I must vanish and start a new life else-where under a new name. I try to arrange things so it will be reasonable to suppose I wandered off and met with misfortune, perhaps because I'd grown old and absent-minded. And as a rule I've been able to prepare for the move. Accumulate a hoard of gold, learn about the home to be, perhaps visit it and establish my fresh identity –'

Some of the weariness of the centuries fell over him. 'Details, details.' He stopped and looked into one of the blind windows. 'Am I going senile? I don't usually gabble this way. Well, you're the first like me I've found, Rufus, the very first. Let's hope you won't be the last.'

'Did you, uh, know about others?' groped the voice at his back.

Lugo shook his head. 'I told you I never did. How could I? A few times I thought I saw a trace, but it gave out or it proved false. Once I may have. I'm not sure.'

'What was that … master? You want to tell me?'

'I may as well. It was in Syracuse, where I based myself for a good many years because of its ties with Carthage. Lovely, lively city. A woman, Althea was her name, fine to look on and bright in the way women sometimes got to be in the later days of the Greek colonies – I knew her and her husband. He was a shipping magnate and I skippered a tramp freighter. They'd been mar-ried for over three decades, he'd gone bald and pot-bellied, she'd borne him a dozen children and the oldest of them was gray, but she might have been a maiden in springtime.'

Lugo fell silent a while before finishing, flat-voiced: 'The Romans captured the city. Sacked it. I was absent. Always make an excuse to clear out when you see that kind of thing coming. When I returned, I inquired. She could have been taken for a slave. I could have tried to find her and buy her free. But no, when I'd tracked down somebody who knew, insignificant enough to've been left unhurt, I learned she was dead. Raped and stabbed, I heard. Don't know if that's true or not. Stories grow in the telling. No matter. It was long ago.'

'Too bad. You should'a got in there first.' Lugo tautened. 'Uh, sorry, master,' Rufus said. 'You don't, uh, don't seem to hate Rome.'

'Why should I? It's eternally the same tale, war, tyranny, massacre, slavery. I've been party to it myself. Now Rome is on the receiving end.'

'What?' Rufus sounded aghast. 'Can't be! Rome is *forever!*'

'As you like.' Lugo turned back to him. 'Apparently I have, at last, found a fellow immortal. At least, here is someone I can safeguard, watch, make certain of. Two or three decades should suffice. Though already I have no real doubt.'

He drew breath. 'Do you see what this means? No, you scarcely can. You've had no time to think about it.' He surveyed heavy visage, low forehead, dis-may yielding to a loose-lipped glee. I don't expect you ever will, he thought. You are a moderately competent woodworker, nothing else. And I'm lucky to have found this much. Unless Althea – but she slipped through my fingers, away into death.

'It means I am not unique,' Lugo said. 'If there are two of us, there must be more. Very few, very seldom born. It isn't in the bloodlines, like height or coloring or those deformities I've seen run in families. Whatever the cause is, it happens by accident. Or by God's will, if you prefer, though I'd think that makes God out to be sheerly capricious. And surely senseless mischance takes off many immortals young, as it takes off ordinary men and women and children. Sickness we may escape, but not the sword or the runaway horse or the flood or the fire or the famine or whatever. Possibly more die at the hands of neighbors who think this must be a demon, magician, monster.'

Rufus cowered. 'My head's all a-spin,' he whimpered.

'Well, you've had a bad time. Immortals need rest too. Sleep if you wish.'

Rufus' expression was glazing over. 'Why couldn't we say we was, uh, saints? Angels?'

'How far would you have gotten?' Lugo gibed. 'Conceivably a man born into royalty – But I don't suppose that's ever happened, as rare as our kind must be. No, if we survive, we learn early on to keep our heads low.'

'Then how shall we find each other?'

Rufus hiccoughed and farted.

3

'Come out with me into the peristyle,' said Lugo.

'Oh, gladly,' Cordelia sang. Almost, she danced at his side.

It was an evening mild and clear. The moon stood over the eastern roof, close to full, in a sky still violet-blue. Westward, heaven darkened and stars trembled forth. City sounds had mostly died out; crickets chirred. Moonlight dappled the flowerbeds, shivered on the water of a pool, brought Cordelia's young face and breast out of shadow into argency.

She and he stood hand in hand a few minutes. 'You were so busy today,' she said at length. 'When you came back early, I hoped – Of course, you had your work to do.'

'I did that, unfortunately,' he replied. 'But these next hours belong to us.'

She leaned against him. Her hair carried a remnant fragrance of sunlight. 'Christians should give thanks for what they get.' She giggled. 'How easy to be a Christian, tonight.'

'How have the children done today?' he asked – his son Julius, no longer stumping about but leaping adventurously everywhere, starting to talk; little, little Dora asleep in her crib, starfish hands curled tight.

'Why, very well,' said Cordelia, a bit surprised.

'I see them too seldom.'

'And you care. Not many fathers do. Not that much.' She squeezed his hand. 'I want to give you lots of children.' Impishly: 'We can begin at once.'

'I have ... tried to be kind.'

She heard how the words dragged, let go of him, widened her eyes in alarm. 'What's wrong, beloved?'

He made himself take hold of her shoulders, look into her face – the moonlight made her searingly beautiful – and answer: 'Between us, nothing at all.' Only the fact that you will grow old and die. And that has happened so often, so often. I cannot count the deaths. There is no measure for the pain, but I think it has not grown any less; I think I have merely learned to live with it, as a mortal can learn to live with an unhealable wound. I thought we could have, oh, thirty, perhaps forty years together before I must leave. That would have been wonderful.

'But I have an unexpected journey to make,' he said.

'Something that man – Marcus – something he's told you?'

Lugo nodded.

Cordelia grimaced. 'I don't like him. Forgive me, but I don't. He's coarse and stupid.'

'He is that,' Lugo agreed. It had seemed wise to him that they let Rufus share their supper. Confinement in the Low Room with nothing but his dreads and animal hopes for company had been breaking what self-control was left him, and he needed it for the time ahead. 'Nevertheless, I got important information from him.'

'Can you tell me what it is?' He heard how hard she tried not to make it a plea.

'I'm sorry, no. Nor can I say where I'm bound or how long I'll be gone.'

She caught both his hands. Her fingers had turned cold. 'The barbarians. Pirates. Bacaudae.'

'Travel has its dangers,' he admitted. 'I've spent a lot of this day making arrangements for you. Just in case, darling, just in case.' He kissed her. The lips that shivered beneath his bore a thin taste of salt. 'You should know this is a matter that may or may not concern Aurelian, but if it does, it must be investigated at once, and he's in Italy. I've told his amanuensis Corbilo as much, and you can collect my pay for your needs from him. I've also left a substantial sum in trust for you at the church. The priest Antoninus took it and gave me a receipt that I'll give you. And you are heir to this property. You'll be all right, you and the children.' If Rome hangs together.

She threw herself against him and clung. He stroked her hair, her back, ruffling the gown, making the caress an embrace. 'There, there,' he crooned, 'this is just in case. Don't be afraid. I'm not running any great risk.' He believed that was true. 'I'll be back.' That was not true, and hurt like fire to utter. Well, no doubt she'd marry again, after he was given up for dead. *Last heard of on the Ordovician coast, about when a Scotic raid occurred ...*

She stood back, hugged herself, swallowed, smiled unsteadily. 'Of course you w-w-will,' she avowed. 'I'll p-pray for you the whole while. And we have this night.'

Until shortly after dawn, when *Nereid* cast off. He'd obtained passage for himself and Rufus. Most of Britannia continued secure, but the barbarians ravaged enough of it that nobody would question a couple of men who appeared in, say, Aquae Sulis or Augusta Londinium with a story of having fled. Given money in hand, they could start afresh; and Lugo had buried a fair supply of honest coins in the island, several generations back.

'If only you could remain,' escaped from Cordelia.

'If only I could.' But Rufus was marked in Burdigala.

Rufus, the male, the oaf, the immortal, who would surely perish miserably without an intelligent man in charge of him. And he must not. However awkward, his was the only help Lugo had toward the ultimate coming together of their kind.

Cordelia heard how the words wrenched themselves from her husband's mouth. 'I will *not* whine,' she declared. 'We do have this night. And many, many more on the far side of your journey. I'll wait for you, I'll always wait.'

No, Lugo thought, you won't. That wouldn't make sense, once you've decided you're a widow, still young but with time at your heels.

Nor could you ever have waited for me always.

I seek for her who shall never have to leave me.

IV

DEATH IN PALMYRA

The caravan to Tripolis would leave at daybreak. Nebozabad, its master, wanted everything ready the evening before. He wanted every man rehearsed in making and breaking camp. Delays not only cost money, they multiplied risk.

So he thought. Some people told him not to fret. Peace was now secure, they said, Syria firmly in Arabian hands. Had not the Khalifa himself passed through Tadmor, on his way to holy Jerusalem, three years ago? Nebozabad was less trustful. Throughout his life he had seen too much war, with the disruption of trade, breakdown of order, and upsurge of banditry that soon followed. He meant to use every hour of opportunity that God granted him.

Therefore his charges bedded down not in a caravanserai but on a ground beyond the Philippian Gate. He went about, speaking to camel drivers, guards, traders, lesser folk, issuing commands where needed, piecemeal giving turmoil a shape and a meaning. Night was well upon him before he was done.

He paused, then, to enjoy a moment alone. Air had gone cool, with a tinge of smoke from the small fires that glimmered in the camp. Otherwise it was a huddle of darkness. He made out the peaks of a few tents, pitched by the more prosperous among his travelers, and sometimes light flickered off the spearhead of a sentry on his rounds. Nebozabad wanted all routines working from the outset. A murmur reached his ears, talk of men who sat up late, occasionally the soft whicker of a horse or the rumble and gurgle in a camel's throat.

Stars glittered brilliant, beyond counting. From the west a gibbous moon cast light down the shallow valley. It frosted hills, palm fronds, the tower tombs that rose out of shadow, the turrets and battlements of the city wall. That wall loomed sheer, gray-white, as if a piece of the steppe surrounding this basin had been turned on end. It seemed as eternal, too, its massiveness never to be breached, the life that now slept behind its shelter to pulse every day forever.

The thought made Nebozabad bite his lip. Much too well did he know otherwise. In his own lifetime the Persians had driven out the Romans, and later the Romans had driven out the Persians, and today both nations were in retreat before the sword of Islam; and while trade routes still bore wealth into Tadmor and forth again, the city was long past her glory. Ah, to have lived then, when she – Palmyra on Latin and Greek tongues – was the queen of Syria, before Emperor Aurelian crushed Zenobia's bid for freedom –

Nebozabad sighed, shrugged, turned about and started back. A city, like a man, must bear whatever fate God decrees. In that much, at least, the Muslims were right.

On his way, he heard and answered several greetings. 'Christ be with you, master.' 'And his spirit be with you.' Everyone recognized his stocky form in the plain djellabah, his rather heavy features bared to the sky. Moonlight touched white streaks in hair and short-cropped beard.

Presently he neared his own tent. It was of good material though modest size; he never took along weight that could, instead, be in articles of value. Lamplight glowed faint yellow around a flap hanging loose.

A hand clutched his ankle. He stopped short, sucked in a breath, closed fingers on knife hilt. 'Quiet,' whispered frantically. 'By God's mercy, I pray you. I mean no harm.'

Nonetheless chill tingled through him as he peered. Someone crouched, flattened close to the ground, a paleness amidst the shadows. Naked? 'What is this?' he hissed.

'I need help,' came back at him. 'Can we speak alone? Behold, I am unarmed.'

He believed he knew that voice. Often had he had to make quick decisions. 'Abide,' he said low. The imploring hand released him. He stepped around to the front of his tent and slipped past the flap, with care that little light flash forth. Within, the camel's-hair fabric enclosed a measure of warmth. A clay lamp dimly showed his bedroll spread out for him, water pitcher and basin and two or three other minor comforts ready, his body servant hunkered down. That person brought knees, hands, and brow to earth in salutation and asked, 'What is my master's desire?'

'I expect a visitor,' Nebozabad told him. 'Depart cautiously, as I arrived. When I have secured the entrance, let no one else seek to me, nor ever speak a word of this.'

'On my head be it, master.' The slave glided off. Nebozabad had chosen and trained him well; he was wholly loyal. When he was gone, Nebozabad looked out for a moment, murmured, 'Come now,' and drew back again.

The other scuttled through, straightened, confronted him. Despite his half knowledge, he gasped. A woman indeed. Oh, woman's very self!

He remembered the danger, muttered a curse, hastened to secure the entrance. Then he dared try to deal with her.

She had lowered herself to knees and toes, hands laid across her lap. Midnight tresses flowed over shoulders, down past her breasts. He guessed flittingly that that was not quite by chance. Nothing else had she for garment, except grime, a streak of clotting blood on the left forearm, sweat that shimmered in the lamplight, and the gloom. Her body might have belonged to an ancient goddess, lithe, firm-bosomed, slim-waisted, round-hipped. The face she turned to him was broad across the cheekbones, straight of nose, lips full above the cleanness of chin and jawline. Her skin was faintly golden and the great eyes, beneath arching brows, were hazel. In her, Roman of the West, Roman of the East, Hellene, and Persian had mingled with Syria.

He stared down at the sight. She seemed a maiden, no, a youthful matron, no, something for which he had no name. But he knew her.

Her voice trembled husky. 'O Nebozabad, old friend, there is no hope left me save in you. Help me, as once my house helped you. You have known us all your life.'

Forty-odd years. The thought struck like a dagger. His mind flew back across more than thirty of them.

1

Aliyat both longed for Barikai's return and dreaded it. She would have the solace of his embrace and of giving him her own upbearing love. So had they stood together when they lost other children; but those were infants. First, though, she must tell him what had happened.

He was elsewhere in Tadmor, talking with the merchant Taimarsu. News from the front was evil, the Persians inflicting defeat after defeat upon the Romans, thrusting into Mesopotamia, with Syria's defenses thin on their left. More and more, commerce with the seaboard pulled into its shell and awaited the outcome. Caravan masters such as Barikai suffered. Most were, themselves, chary of venturing anywhere. He, bolder, went off to persuade the traffickers that they should not let goods molder in warehouses.

She imagined his heartiness, his laughter: 'I'll convey them. Prices in Tripolis or Berytus will be at a peak! Rewards are for the brave.' She had encouraged it. Daughter of a man in the same trade, she was closer to her husband than most wives, almost a partner as well as his mate and the mother of his children. It eased the wistfulness that tugged at her whenever she stood on the city wall and watched his train move off beyond the horizon.

But today – A female slave found her in the garden and said, 'The master is here.' Aliyat's spirit twisted within her. She called up courage as women must, in childbed or by deathbed, and hastened. Her skirts rustled through a silence full of eyes. All the household knew.

It was a fair-sized household in a good-sized building. Until lately Barikai, like his father before him, had done well. Aliyat hoped it would not become necessary to sell off any slaves; she was fond of them. She was instituting frugality … What mattered such things?

The atrium lay dim with eventide. Her glance fell on the image of the Virgin that stood in a niche, its blue and gold aglow against whitewash. For a little while she had knelt before it, silently praying that the news not be true. The image had merely stared, changeless.

Barikai had just given his cloak to a servant. Beneath it he wore a robe decorated with gold thread, to show power, confidence. Time had grizzled the dark hair and furrowed the lean face, but he still walked springily. 'Christ be with you, my lady,' he began, as was seemly in the presence of attendants. His gaze sharpened. He reached her in three long strides and took her by the shoulders. 'What is wrong?'

She must swallow twice before she could beg, 'Come with me.' His mouth drew tight. Wordlessly he followed her back into the garden.

Enclosed by the house, it was a place of cool calm, refuge from the world. Jasmine and roses grew around a pool where water lilies floated. Their fragrances drenched the air. Overhead, heaven had gone royal blue as the sun went below the roof. Here two people could be alone.

Aliyat turned to Barikai. She doubled her fists at her sides and forced out, 'Manu is dead.'

He stood unmoving.

'Young Mogim brought the word this morning,' Aliyat told him. 'He was among the few who escaped. The squadron was on patrol south of Khalep. A Persian cavalry troop surprised them. Mogim saw Manu take an arrow in his eye, fall from the saddle, go down under the hoofs.'

'South of Khalep,' Barikai croaked. 'Already. Then they are coming into Syria.'

She knew that man-thought was only the first poor shield he could lift. She saw it break in his grasp. 'Manu,' he said. 'Our first-born. Gone.' The hand shook with which he crossed himself, over and over. 'God have mercy on him. Christ take him home. Help him, holy Georgios.'

I too should pray, Aliyat thought, and knew with a wan surprise that any wish to do so had withered.

'Have you told Aqmat?' Barikai asked.

'Of course. Best, I think, best leave her and her children in peace for a while.' Manu's young wife had lived in terror of this since he was called to war. The fact had fallen on her like a hammer.

'I sent a messenger to Hairan, but his master has dispatched him to Emesa on some business,' Aliyat went on. The younger of their sons worked for a dealer in wine. 'The sisters mourn at home.' Their three living daughters were married, well enough that she was glad of the earlier struggle to amass good dowries for them.

'I think now – to carry on my trade – I think I will take Nebozabad to apprentice,' Barikai mumbled. 'You know him, do you not? Son of the widow Hafsa. Only ten years old, but a likely lad. And it would be a kindness. It might make the saints smile a little on Manu's soul.'

Abruptly he seized her, painfully hard. 'But why do I chatter like this?' he yelled. 'Manu is gone!'

She loosened his hands, guided his arms around her, held him very close. They stood thus for many heartbeats, while shadows rose in the garden and light drained from the sky.

'Aliyat, Aliyat,' he whispered at last, shakenly, into her hair, 'my love, my strength. How can it be that you are what you are? Wife of mine, mother, grandmother, and yet you could well-nigh be the girl I made my bride.'

2

When the Persians occupied Tadmor, they first levied a heavy tribute. Thereafter they were not bad overlords – no worse than the Romans, thought Aliyat in secret. Zarathushtrans who held fire sacred, they let everybody worship according to belief, and in fact kept Orthodox Christians, Nestorian Christians, and Jews from molesting each other. Meanwhile their firm control of the territories they won allowed trade to resume, also with their own country. After a dozen years, people heard that they were advancing farther, had taken Jerusalem and presently Egypt. Aliyat wondered if they would go on to Old Rome, but decided, from what men told about Italy, that that raddled land, divided among Lombard chiefs, the Catholic Pope, and remnant Imperial garrisons, would be no prize.

Word trickled in: a new Emperor, Heraklios, reigned in Constantinople and was said to be energetic and able. However, he had woes close to home. Barely did he cast the wild Avars back from the capital city.

In Tadmor such events seemed remote, not quite real. Aliyat was nearly the sole woman there who even heard of them. One had one's private life to cope with. For her, too, the days and the years blurred together. A grandchild born, a friend dying, rose into reality and stood afterward in memory like lone hills espied on a long caravan trek.

So matters were at the hour that ended them.

She set forth with a sturdy female attendant for the agora. They left early in the morning, to finish her bargaining and carry back her purchases before the heat of the day drove folk indoors to rest. Barikai bade her a farewell she could barely hear. He had been weak of late, with bouts of pain in the chest and shortness of breath, he who was hitherto so strong. Neither prayers nor physicians availed much.

Aliyat and Mara followed their winding street to the Colonnade and walked on along it. The great double row of pillars gleamed triumphant between the arches at either end, bursting into florescence where the capitals challenged heaven. From a ledge on each, a statue of some famous citizen looked down, centuries of history at attention. Below them the ways were crowded with shops, trading offices, chapels, joyhouses, humanity. Smells eddied thick, smoke, sweat, dung, perfume, aroma of spices and oils and fruits. Noise rioted, footfalls, hoofbeats, wheel-creak, hammer-clang, chant, shout, speech, mostly the Aramaic of this country but also Greek, Persian, Arabic, and tongues of lands more distant yet. Colors swirled, a cloak, a robe, a veil, a headdress, a pennon streaming from a lance, an ornament, a charm. A rug seller sat amidst the rich hues of his wares. A wine vendor held his leather bottle aloft. A coppersmith made clangor. An oxcart slogged through the crowds, laden with dates from the oasis. A camel grunted and shambled beneath bales of silk from beyond Aliyat's ken. A squad of Persian horsemen trotted behind a trumpeter who warned the throng to clear the way; their armor flashed, their plumes rippled. A litter bore a wealthy merchant, another a bedizened courtesan, who both looked out with indolent insolence. A black-clad Christian priest drew aside from an austere magus and crossed himself once the latter was past. Drovers who had brought sheep in from the arid steppe wandered wide-eyed among enticements that would likely send them back to their tents penniless. A flute piped, a small drum thumped, somebody sang, high-pitched and quavery.

This was her city, Aliyat knew, these were her people, and nonetheless she was ever more estranged from them.

'Lady! Lady!'

She stopped at the call and glanced about. Nebozabad forced a path toward her. The persons whom he shoved aside shook their fists and cursed him. He went on unhearing until he reached her. She read his countenance and foreknowledge became a boulder in her breast.

'Lady, I hoped I could overtake you,' the young man panted. 'I was with my master, your husband, when – He is stricken. He uttered your name. I sent for a physician and myself started after you.'

'Lead me,' said Aliyat's voice.

He did, loudly, roughly, quickly. They returned beneath the brightening, uncaring sky to the house. 'Wait,' Aliyat commanded at the door of the bedchamber, and went in alone.

She need not have hurt Nebozabad by leaving him out in the corridor. She had not been thinking. Of course several slaves were there, standing aside, awed and helpless. But likewise, already, was their remaining son Hairan. He leaned over the bed, holding fast to him who lay in it. 'Father,' he pleaded, 'father, can you hear me?'

Barikai's eyes were rolled back, a hideous white against the blueness that crept below the skin. Froth bubbled on his lips. The breath shuddered in and out of him, ceased, came raggedly anew, ceased again. Beadwork curtains across the windows tried to obscure the sight. For Aliyat they only made a twilight through which she saw him the starker.

Hairan looked up. Tears ran into his beard. 'I fear he is dying, mother,' he said.

'I know.' She knelt, brushed his hands aside, laid her arms about Barikai and her cheek on her man's bosom. She heard, she felt the life go away.

Rising, she closed his eyes and tried to wipe his face. The physician arrived. 'I can see to that, my lady,' he offered.

She shook her head. 'I will lay him out,' she answered. 'It is my right.'

'Fear not, mother,' Hairan said unevenly. 'I will provide well for you – you shall have a peaceful old age –' The words trailed off. He stared, as did the physician and the slaves. Barikai, caravan master, had not reached his full threescore and ten, but he seemed as if he had, hair mostly white, visage gaunt, muscles shriveled over the bones. His widow who stood above him could have been a woman of twenty springtimes.

3

Unto Hairan the wine merchant was born a grandson, and great was the rejoicing in his house. The feast that he and the father gave for kinfolk and friends lasted far into the night. Aliyat withdrew early from the women's part of it, into the rear of the building where she had a room. No one thought ill of this; after all, however much respect her years entitled her to, they were a burden.

She did not seek rest as everybody supposed. Once alone, she straightened her back and changed her shuffling gait. Fast, supple, she went out a back door. The voluminous black garments that disguised her figure billowed with her haste. Her head was covered as usual, which hid the blackness of her locks. Family and servitors often remarked on how amazingly youthful her face and hands were; but now she lowered a veil.

She passed a slave going about his duties, who recognized her but simply made salutation. He would not babble about what he had seen. He too was old, and knew that one must bear with the old if sometimes they grow a trifle strange.

The night air was blessedly cool and fresh. The street was a gut of shadow, but her feet knew every stone and she found her way easily to the Colonnade. Thence she strode toward the agora. A full moon had cleared surrounding roofs. Its brilliance hid the stars close to it, though lower down they swarmed and sparkled. The pillars lifted white. Her footfalls slithered loud in the silence. Most folk were abed.

She took some risk, but it was slight. Mostly, the city guards had continued under the Persians to maintain law and order. Once she hid behind a column while a squad tramped past. Their pikeheads sheened like liquid in the moonlight. Had they seen her, they might well have insisted on bringing her home – unless they took her for a harlot, which would have led to questions for which she lacked answers.

'Why do you prowl about after dark?' She could not say, she did not know, yet she *must* get away for a while or else begin screaming.

This was not the first such time.

At the Street of the Marketers she turned south. The grace of the theater fountained upward on her right. On her left, the portico and wall around the agora lay ghostly under the moon. She had heard that they were but fragments of what formerly was, before desperate men quarried them for fortification material as the Romans closed in on Zenobia. That suited her mood. She passed through an unbarred gateway onto the broad plaza.

Remembrance of its liveliness by day made it feel all the more empty. Statues of former high officials, military commanders, senators, and, yes, caravan leaders ringed it in like sentinels around a necropolis. Aliyat walked through the moonlight to the center and stopped. Her heartbeat and breath were the only sounds she heard.

'Miriamne, Mother of God, I thank you –' The words died on her lips. They were as hollow as the place where she stood, they would be mockery did she finish them.

Why was she barren of gladness and gratitude? A son had been born to the son of her son. The life that was in Barikai lived on. Could she call his dear shade out of the night, surely it would be smiling.

A shudder went through her. She could not raise the memory. His face had become a blur; she had words for its lineaments, but no vision any longer. Everything receded into the past, her loves died and died and died, and God would not let her follow them.

She should praise Him with song, that she was hale and whole, untouched by age. How many, halt, gnarled, toothless, half blind, afire with pain, longed for death's mercy? Whereas she – But the fear of her gathered year by year, the glances askance, whispers, furtive signs against evil. Hairan himself saw in the mirror his gray hair and lined brow, and wondered about his mother; she knew, she knew. She held as much apart as she could, not to remind her kin, and understood what an unspoken conspiracy was theirs, to avoid speaking of her before outsiders. And so she became the outsider, the one forever alone.

How could she be a great-grandmother, she in whose loins burned lust? Was that why she was punished by this, or what dreadful childhood sin of hers had she forgotten?

The moon moved onward, the stars turned their wheel. Slowly, something of heaven's bleak tranquility came to her. She started homeward. She would not surrender. Not yet.

4

The war devoured a generation, but in the end Heraklios prevailed. He drove the Persians before him until they sued for peace. Two-and-twenty years after they left, the Romans re-entered Tadmor.

On their heels was a new resident, Zabdas, a dealer in spices from Emesa. That was a somewhat larger city, nearer the seaboard, therefore wealthier and more closely governed. Zabdas' family firm had an affiliate in Tadmor. After the chaos of battle and the latest change of overlords it needed reorganization, a cunning hand on the reins and a shrewd eye out for such opportunities as might appear. He arrived and took charge. That required making acquaintances, alliances, among local people. He was handicapped in this by being newly widowed, and therefore soon began looking for a wife.

Nobody told Aliyat about him, and indeed when he first visited Hairan it was on business. The dignity of the house, the guest, and herself required that she be among the women who bade him welcome before the men supped. Out of sheer rebelliousness, or so she vaguely thought, she left off her shapeless grandam's clothes and dressed in modest but becoming wise. She saw his startlement on learning who she was; eyes met eyes; a thrill that she fought to control went through her. He was a short man of about fifty, but erect, alert, the white hairs few and the visage well-molded. They exchanged ritual courtesies. She went back to her room.

Though she often found it hard to pluck a single memory out of the multitude that crowded her, certain experiences repeated themselves frequently enough that she gained skill from them. She could well read the meaning of Hairan's glances when he thought she didn't notice, the words he spoke to her and the words he did not. She could sense a rising current of excitement in the wives and slaves, even the older children. Her sleep became broken, she paced and paced or stole out by dark, the comfort that she had sometimes found in books now vanished.

It was no surprise when at length Hairan asked her to see him privately. That was in winter's early night, after most of the household had gone to bed. He admitted her when she knocked, escorted her to a cushioned stool, sat down cross-legged on the rug behind a table on which stood wine, dates, cakes.

For a space there was quiet. Bronze lamps sheened in the light that their flames threw soft. It picked out floral patterns of frescos, reds and blues and browns of carpet, the folds of his robe and the furrows in his face. He was wholly gray and had grown a pot belly. He blinked dim-sightedly at her slimness. The brocade of green and gold that she had chosen lay close over curves; above her head covering, a wreath of gold wire enclosed the clear brows.

'Will you take refreshment, mother?' he invited finally, very low.

'Thank you.' She reached for a goblet. The wine glowed on her tongue. Drink and food, those were comforts too. They had not lost their savor as she aged, nor had she become fat.

'You should not thank me.' He looked away. 'It is my duty to provide for your well-being.'

'You have been a dutiful son.'

'I have tried my best.' In a rush, never meeting her gaze: 'You, though, you are unhappy with us. True? I am not blind or deaf so far, not quite. You seldom if ever complain, but I cannot help knowing.'

She commanded her body to be still, her voice to be level: 'True. No fault of yours, nor of anyone else.' She must force herself to hurt him. 'I daresay you feel you are a young man trapped in flesh growing old. Well, I am an old woman trapped in flesh that stays young. Why this is, only God knows.'

He twined fingers together. 'You are – how old? Threescore and ten? Well, some people do carry their years well and reach great ages. If you lived for a hundred years in good health, it would not be unheard of. May God grant you do so.' She marked how he evaded mention of the fact that except for teeth showing wear she bore no trace of the time that had passed.

Let her encourage him to say what he intended to say. 'You will understand how my uselessness makes me restless.'

'It need not!' burst from him. He lifted his eyes. She saw sweat on his skin. 'Hark. Zabdas, a respectable man, a merchant, has asked for your hand in marriage.'

I knew this, she thought; and aloud: 'I know whom you speak of.' She said naught about the cautious inquiries she had contrived to make. 'But he and I met just a single time.'

'He has queried people about you, and talked repeatedly with me, and – He is, I say, an honorable man, well off and with excellent prospects for the future, a widower in need of a wife. He realizes that you are older than him, but feels this is no barrier. He has children grown, grandchildren coming, what he wants is a helpmate. Believe me, I have made sure of this.'

'Do you wish the union, Hairan?' Aliyat asked quietly.

She sipped while he stuttered, fumbled with his goblet, looked to and fro, before he said, 'I would never compel you, mother. It simply appears to me … it may be in your best interests. I will not deny, he offers certain business agreements that would … help. My enterprise has fallen on hard times.'

'I know.' He showed surprise. Aliyat whetted her tone: 'Did you think *me* blind or deaf? I worked closely with your father, Hairan, as you never let me work with you.'

'I – mother, I did not mean –'

She laughed a little. 'Oh, you have been as kindly as you know how. Let us put such things behind us. Tell me more.'

5

The wedding and the celebration that followed were an occasion small, almost subdued. Finally the bride was escorted to the groom's bedchamber and left with a maidservant.

The room was not large, its walls merely whitewashed, its furnishings austere. Some garlands had been hung around it. A screen blocked off one corner. A three-branched candelabrum gave light. Laid across the bed were two nightgowns.

Aliyat knew she was expected to change into hers. Mutely, she let the attendant help her. She and Barikai had frolicked naked, with wicks burning bright. Well, times changed, or perhaps it was people who differed. She had been too long cut off from gossip to say.

When she stood briefly unclad, Zabdas' slave cried: 'But my lady is beautiful!'

Aliyat stroked hands down her flanks. The touch tingled. She barely stopped short of her groin. Tonight she would again know the true pleasure that had haunted her for – how many years? She smiled. 'Thank you.'

'I, I heard you were old,' the girl stammered.

'I am.' Aliyat's manner imposed fear and silence.

She had an hour or two by herself in bed. Thoughts tumbled through her head, out of control. Now and then she shivered. At least her days in the house of her son had been predictable. That, though, was what had become the horror of them.

She sat up with a start when Zabdas entered. He closed the door behind him and stood for a moment watching her. In festival garb, he was ... dapper. Her gown was of rather thick material, loosely cut, but her bosom swelled it outward. 'You are more fair than I knew,' he said in his careful way.

She lowered her lashes. 'I thank my lord,' she replied around the tightness in her throat.

He advanced. 'Still, you are a woman of discretion, with the wisdom of your years,' he said. 'Such a one do I require.' He halted before the icon of St Ephraem Syrus that was the chamber's sole fixed ornament and crossed himself. 'Grant us a satisfactory life together,' he prayed.

Taking his nightshirt, he went behind the screen. She saw how neatly he hung his clothes over the top. When he returned dressed for sleep, he bent over, cupped a hand behind each candle in turn, and blew them out. He got into bed with his usual economy of motion.

He is my husband, pulsed in Aliyat. He is my liberation. Let me be good to him.

She reached out. Her arms enclosed, her mouth went seeking. 'What?' Zabdas exclaimed. 'Be at ease. I shall not hurt you.'

'Do, if you like.' She pressed against him. 'How may I please you?'

'Why, why – This is – Kindly lie still, my lady. Remember your years.'

She obeyed. Sometimes she and Barikai had enjoyed playing master and slave. Or youth and whore. She felt Zabdas raise himself to an elbow. His free hand tugged at her gown. She pulled it up and spread her thighs. He climbed between. He rested his full weight on her, which Barikai had not, but then Zabdas was much lighter. She reached to guide him. Briskly, he took care of that himself, grasped her breasts through the cloth, and thrust. He did not seem to notice how her arms and legs clasped him. It was quickly over.

He got off and lay until his breathing was again even. She could barely see him as a deeper shadow in the night. He sounded troubled: 'How wet you were. You have the body of a young woman, as well as the face.'

'For you,' she murmured.

Through the mattress she felt him tauten. 'What is your age in truth?' So Hairan had avoided saying it outright; but Zabdas had perhaps avoided asking.

Fourscore and one, she knew. 'I have never kept count,' was the safest reply. 'But there has been no deception, my lord. I am Hairan's mother. I … was quite young when I bore him, and you have seen that I carry my years better than most.'

'A wonder.' His voice was flat.

'Uncommon. A blessing. I am unworthy, but –' It must out: 'My courses have not yet ended. I can bear you children, Zabdas.'

'This is –' He searched for a word. 'Unexpected.'

'Let us thank God together.'

'Yes. We should. But now best we sleep. I have much to do in the morning.'

6

To Zabdas came the caravan master Nebozabad. They must discuss a proposed shipment to Darmesek. A journey of that length could no longer be lightly undertaken. News was too ominous, of the Arabian onslaught against Persia and threat to New Rome.

The merchant received his guest well, as he did all who were of consequence, and bade him dine. Aliyat insisted on serving them with her own hands. As they sat over then-dessert, Zabdas excused himself and was gone for a while. He suffered from an occasional flux of the bowels. Nebozabad waited alone.

The room was the best furnished in the house, with embroidered red hangings, four seven-branched candelabra of gilt bronze, a table of teakwood carven in foliate patterns and inlaid with nacre, the ware upon it of silver or the finest glass. A pinch of incense in a brazier made the air, on this warm eventide, a little cloying.

Nebozabad looked up when Aliyat came in with a tray of fruits. She stopped across from him, in dark garments that muffled sight of more than hands, countenance, the big hazel eyes. 'Sit down, my lady,' he urged.

She shook her head. 'That would be unseemly,' she answered in a near whisper.

'Then I will stand.' He rose from his stool. 'Far too long has it been since last I saw you. How fares it?'

'Well enough.' She took on expression; her words leaped. 'And how is it with you? And Hairan and, oh, everybody? I hear very little.'

'You do not see much of anyone, do you, my lady?'

'My husband feels it would be ... indiscreet ... at my age. But how goes it, Nebozabad? Tell me, I beg you!'

He repeated her phrase: 'Well enough. Another grandchild born to him, a girl, have you heard? As for myself, I have two living sons and a daughter, by the grace of God. Business –' He shrugged. 'This is what I've come about.'

'Is the danger from the Arabs great?'

'I fear so.' He paused, tugged his beard. 'In your days with master Barikai, may he be happy in Heaven, you knew everything that went on. You took a hand in it yourself.'

She bit her lip. 'Zabdas feels differently.'

'I suppose he wishes to keep rumors down, and that is why he never has Hairan, or any kinsman of yours, here – Forgive me!' He had seen what crossed her features. 'I should not pry. It's only that, that you were my master's lady when I was a boy, and ever gracious to me, and –' His voice trailed off.

'You are good to be concerned.' She jerked her head as if to keep it from drooping. 'But I have fewer sorrows than many do.'

'I heard your child died. I'm sorry.'

She sighed. 'That was last year. Wounds heal. We will try again.'

'You have not already? – No, again I spoke badly. Too much wine. Forgive me. Seeing how beautiful you still are, I thought –'

She flushed. 'My husband is not too old.'

'Yet he – No. Aliyat, my lady, if ever you should need help –'

Zabdas returned and she, having set down her tray, said good night and departed.

7

While Roman and Persian bled each other to exhaustion, afar in Makkah Muhammad ibn Abdallah saw visions, preached, must flee to Yathrib, prevailed over his enemies, gave his refuge the new name Medinat Rasul Allah, the City of the Apostle of God, and died as master of Arabia. His Khalifa, Successor, Abu Bekr suppressed rebellion and launched in earnest those holy wars that united the people and carried the faith out across the world.

Six years after the troops of Emperor Heraklios reclaimed Tadmor, the troops of Khalifa 'Omar took it. The year after that they were in Jerusalem, and the year after that the Khalifa visited the holy city, passing triumphant through a completely subjugated Syria while couriers brought accounts of Islamic banners carried deep into the Persian heartland.

On the day he spent in Tadmor, from her rooftop Aliyat witnessed magnificence, gallant horses, richly caparisoned camels, riders whose helmets and mailcoats, lances and shields turned sunlight into flame, cloaks like windblown rainbows, trumpet and drum and deep-voiced chant. The streets surged, the oasis boiled with the conquerors. Yet she noticed that the far greater number of them were lean and roughly clad. Likewise was their garrison here, and their officials lived simple lives, five times daily humbling themselves before God when the muezzin's call wailed across the sky.

Nor were they bad rulers. They levied tribute, but it was not unbearable. They turned a few churches into mosques, but otherwise left Christians and Jews in the peace that they sternly enforced. The qadi, their chief justice, held court beneath the arch at the east end of the Colonnade, near the agora, and even the lowliest could appeal directly to him. Their irruption had been too swift to damage trade much, and it soon began reviving.

Aliyat was not altogether surprised when Zabdas said to her, in the tone that meant he would banish her to a rear room if she gave him any dispute: 'I have reached a great decision. This household shall embrace Islam.'

Nonetheless she stood a while quiescent, amidst the shadows with which the single frugal lamp filled their bedchamber. When she spoke it was slowly, and her eyes searched him. 'This is indeed a matter of the first importance. Have they compelled you?'

He shook his head. 'No, no. They do not – except pagans, I am told.' He formed his thin brief smile. 'They would rather most of us remain Christian, so we may own land, which believers may not, and pay tribute for it as well as the other taxes. My talks with the imam whom I approached have been difficult. But of course he may not refuse a sincere convert.'

'You'll gain many advantages.'

He reddened. 'Do you call me a hypocrite?'

'No, no, certainly not, my lord.'

Zabdas turned mild. 'I understand. To you this is a terrible shock, you who have been raised to worship Christ. Think, though. The Prophet never denied that Jesus was also a prophet. He was simply not the last one, the one to whom God revealed the full truth. Islam sweeps away the superstition about countless saints, the priests who come between a man and his God, the witless commandments and restrictions. We have but to acknowledge that there is one God and Muhammad is His Prophet. We have but to live righteous lives.' He lifted a forefinger. 'Think. Could the Arabs have borne everything before them as they have done, as they are doing and shall do, were theirs not the cause that is blessed, the faith that is true? I am bringing us to the truth, Aliyat.' He squinted, peering. 'You welcome the truth, do you not? It cannot harm you, can it?'

Recklessly, she cast across the space between them: 'I hear a man who becomes a Muslim must suffer what Jewish boys do.'

'It will not disable me,' he snapped. Curbing temper again: 'I do not expect a woman to understand these deep things. Only trust in me.'

She swallowed, willed ease upon herself, moved toward him. 'I do, my lord, I do,' she murmured. Maybe she could cause him to beget a third child on her, and maybe that one would survive to give meaning back to her life. He seldom took her to him, mostly when she made herself coax him in that same hope. It was almost as if, more and more, he feared her.

As for the change of religion, that mattered less than he supposed. What had the saints done to help, throughout the endless years?

8

She had not foreknown what the change meant. Islam burst upon Syria too suddenly. Zabdas studied it before he made his move. Only when the thing was done did she learn.

The Prophet had laid upon women of the faith the ancient usages of Arabia. In public they must wear the yashmak, the heavy veil hiding everything but the eyes, and likewise at home in the presence of any man but father, brother, husband, or son. Unchastity was punished by death. Quarters for men and women were separate, like an invisible wall built through the house, to whose door its master had the single key. Submission of wife to husband was not bounded by law and custom as it was among Christians and Jews; while a marriage lasted it was total, his the right to mutilate or kill the disobedient. Aside from such tasks as marketing, she had nothing to do with the outside world; he, his children by her, and his dwelling were to be her universe. For her there was no church, and whatever Paradise she might hope for would not be his.

So Zabdas explained, piecemeal as occasion arose. Aliyat was not sure the Law was quite that one-sided. She was entirely sure that in most families, practice softened it. But be that as it may, she was a prisoner.

She was even denied the solace of wine. That might be just as well, she decided once the first rage had faded. She had been resorting to it much oftener than was wise.

Oddly, however, as the Muslim months passed, she found herself less alone than hitherto. Thrust together, the females of the household – not only she and the slaves, but the wives and girl-children of two of Zabdas' sons who had joined him in Tadmor – at first quarreled viciously, then began to confide in each other. Her position and her freedom from aging had set her apart. Those who now saw her sharing their helplessness discovered they could overlook these things, and if they told her their troubles she would do what little she could to aid them.

For her part, she learned bit by bit that she was not utterly isolated. In some ways, she touched more of the city than she had done since Barikai's death. She might be confined, but lesser females must needs go out on various errands; and they had kinfolk with whom they gossiped at every opportunity; and nobody cared to be strict with the humble, nor stopped to think that they too possessed sharp ears, open eyes, and inquiring minds. As the touch of a fly quivers through the web to the spider that sits at its middle, so did flickers of information reach Aliyat.

She was not present when Zabdas sought the qadi soon after his conversion; but in view of what was overheard and passed on, and what happened later, eventually she believed she could reconstruct it almost as well as if she had been invisibly listening.

Normally the qadi heard pleas in the open. Everybody was free to come. She could have done so, had she had any real plaint. She thought of it, and concluded drearily that she did not. Zabdas was never abusive. He provided adequately. If he no longer came to her bed, what should a woman close to her ninetieth year expect – whether or not she had again borne him a child, and this one did keep on living? The very thought was obscene.

He asked for a private audience and the qadi granted it. The two sat in the house of Mitkhal ibn Dirdar and sipped chilled pomegranate juice while they talked. Neither paid heed to the eunuch who waited on them; but he had acquaintances outside, who in their turn knew people.

'Yes, of course you may divorce your wife,' Mitkhal said. 'It is easily done. However, under the Law she retains all property that was hers, and I gather she brought a fair amount to this marriage. In every event, you must see to it that she does not become destitute or lack for protection.' He bridged his fingers. 'Moreover, do you wish to offend her kinfolk?'

'Hairan's goodwill is worth little these days,' Zabdas clipped. 'His business fares poorly. Aliyat's other children – by her first marriage – scarcely know her any more. But, hm, the requirements you describe, those could prove awkward.'

Mitkhal regarded him closely. 'Why do you wish to put this woman from you? In what is she at fault?'

'Proud, resentful, sullen – No,' said Zabdas beneath that gaze, 'I cannot in honesty call her contumacious.'

'Has she not given you a child?'

'A girl. The two before, they soon died. The girl is small and sickly.'

'That is shabby ground for blame, my friend. Old seed gives thin fruit.'

Zabdas chose to misunderstand. 'Old, yes, by … by the Prophet! I have inquired. I should have done so at the first, but – Sir, she nears the hundred-year mark.'

The qadi's lips formed a soundless whistle. 'And yet – one hears rumors – is she not yet fair? And you tell me she remains healthy and fertile.'

Zabdas leaned forward. Sunlight fell through the grille over a window to dapple his balding head. Behind sparse whiskers, the wattles under his jaw wabbled as he cried in a high-pitched, cracking voice: 'It's unnatural! Lately she lost a tooth or two and I believed at last, at last – But new ones are growing out, as if she were a child of six or seven! She must be a witch, or an ifrit, a demon, a – That's what I beg for. That's what I ask for, an investigation, a – an assurance I can cast her out and – not have to fear her vengeance. Help me!'

Mitkhal raised a palm. 'Hold, hold.' His words flowed soft. 'Be calm. Truly we have a marvel here. Yet all things are possible to God the Omnipotent. She has not been impious or sinful in any way, has she? You may have done right to keep her as secluded as you could – since you, her husband, have had this terror brewing within you. If the tale went abroad and spread panic, she might have been set on in the streets. Beware of that.' Severely: 'Ancient patriarchs lived close to a thousand years on earth. If God the Compassionate sees fit to let – Aliyat, is that her name? – linger for close to a hundred, ageless, who are we to question His will or divine His purpose?'

Zabdas stared at his lap. What teeth remained to him gritted together. 'Nevertheless,' he mumbled.

'My counsel is that you keep her as long as she does no evil, for this is both justice for her and prudence for you. My decree, upholding the Law, is that you offer her no harm when she has offered none, nor make accusations that are baseless.' Mitkhal reached for his cup, sipped, smiled. 'But, true, if coupling with a crone strikes you as indecent, that is a matter of your choice. Have you considered taking a second wife? You are allowed four, you know, besides concubines.'

In these latter years of his, Zabdas was quick to cool down from both his angers and his fears. He sat a moment silent, looking into a corner of the room. Then his mouth tilted upward and he murmured, 'I thank my lord for his wise and merciful judgment.'

9

The day came when he summoned Aliyat to his office.

It was a chamber bare and cramped. A window opened on the inner court, but was too high up to afford sight of water or flowers. A niche gaped white where once the image of a saint stood. At the far end, a dais held a table bestrewn with letters, records, and writing materials. Behind it, he sat on a bench.

She entered. He laid aside a papyrus sheet, which crackled, and pointed downward. She went to knees and toes on the bare tiles before him. Silence stretched.

'Well?' he snapped.

She kept her eyes lowered. 'What is my lord's desire?'

'What have you to say for yourself?'

'What must your handmaiden defend?'

'Mock me not!' he shouted. 'I've had my fill of your insolence. Now you have struck my wife in the face. It is too much.'

Aliyat looked up, caught his glance, held fast. 'I thought Furja would go whimpering to you,' she said steadily. 'What tale did she bear? Fetch her and let me hear.'

His fist struck the desk. 'I will settle this. I am the master. I am being kind. I am giving you your chance to explain why you should escape a whipping.'

She drew breath. This had been foreseeable since the thing happened; she had had a pair of hours wherein to marshal words. 'My lord must know that his new bride and I are apt to quarrel.' Stupid, weak-chinned, spiteful creature, forever seeking to squirm herself into the man's favor and shrill herself into sovereignty over the harem. 'Alas that this should be. It is wrong.' That tasted foul but had better be said. 'Today she gave me an intolerable insult. I smote her once, open-handedly, across the chops. She wailed and fled – to you, who have things of importance to deal with.'

'She has often complained to me. You have been overbearing ever since she came into my house.'

'I have demanded no more than the respect due your senior wife, my lord.' I will *not* become a slave, a dog, a thing.'

'What was this insult?' asked Zabdas.

'It was vile. Must I take it in my mouth?'

'Um-m ... describe it.'

'She shrieked that I keep my looks and strength by – means unspeakable in decent company.'

'Um! Are you certain? Women have flighty memories.'

'I suppose if you haled her in and put the question, she would deny it. Not her first lie.'

'Word against word.' Zabdas sighed loudly. 'What is a man to believe? When shall he find peace to get on with his work? Women!'

'I think men, too, would grow jangle-witted, were they shut away forever with nothing to do that was worth the doing,' said Aliyat, for she felt she had little to lose.

'If I have left you … undisturbed, it has been out of consideration for your age.'

'And yours, my lord?' she dared purr.

He paled. The brown spots on his skin stood plain to see. 'Furja does not find me wanting!'

Not quite every night of the month, Aliyat thought. And, in sudden, sur-prising pity: *He fears that his uneasiness about me would unman him; and likely that very fear would.*

But they were moving toward deadly ground. She drew back: 'I pray my lord's pardon. No doubt some of the blame does fall on me, his servant. I simply hoped to explain to him why squabbles trouble his harem. If Furja will show me courtesy, I will do likewise.'

Zabdas rubbed his chin and stared beyond her. She had a brief, eerie feel-ing that somehow this was a chance for which he had waited. At length he regarded her and said, his tone strained, 'Life was different for you in your young days. Old people find it hard to change. At the same time, this vigor you have kept makes it impossible for you to resign yourself. Am I right?'

She swallowed. 'My lord speaks truth,' she answered, amazed that he showed any insight.

'And I have heard that you were helpful to your first husband in his busi-ness,' he went on.

She could only nod.

'Well, I have given you much thought, Aliyat,' he said faster. 'My duty under God is to provide for your welfare, which should include your spirit's. If time has become empty for you, if our daughter is not enough – well, per-haps we can find something more.'

Her heart sprang. Blood thundered in her ears.

Again he looked past her. 'What I have in mind is irregular,' he said, cau-tiously now. 'No violation of the Law, understand, but it could cause gossip. I am willing to hazard this for your sake, but you must do your part, you must exercise the utmost discretion.'

'Wha-whatever my lord commands!'

'It will be a beginning, a trial. If you acquit yourself well, who knows what may follow? But hark.' He wagged his forefinger. 'In Emesa is a youth, a distant kinsman of mine, who is eager to go into the business. His father will be pleased if I invite him here and train him. I, though, I lack time to teach him the ins and outs, the rules and customs and traditions peculiar to Tadmor, as well as the basic practicalities – especially where it comes to making shipments, to dealing with caravaneers. I could assign a man of mine to his instruction, but I can ill spare anyone. You, however; I suppose you remember. Of course, the utmost discretion is essential.'

Aliyat prostrated herself. 'Trust me, my lord!' she sobbed.

10

Bonnur was tall, broad in the shoulders, slim in the waist. His beard was the merest overlay of silk across the smooth features, but a man's strength rested in the hands. His movements and his eyes were like a gazelle's. Though he was Christian, Zabdas received him cordially before sending him to find a bed among the other young men who served and learned here.

A twelvemonth back, the merchant had bought a lesser building adjacent to his home. He set workers to erect walls and roof joining the pair together, then knock out what separated them and make them one. Thus he would gain added offices, storerooms, and quarters for an expanded staff; his trade was burgeoning. Lately he had ordered a halt to the construction. He declared it was better to wait and see what effect the ongoing conquest of Persia would have on the traffic with India. The addition therefore stood unfurnished, unoccupied, dusty, and silent.

When he led her into it, Aliyat was astonished to find a room at the far end had been swept and outfitted. A plain but thick wool carpet softened the floor. Hangings flanked the second-story window. A table held a water carafe, cups, papyrus, ink, pens. Two stools waited nearby. And Bonnur did. Though Aliyat had been introduced to him earlier, her pulse quickened.

He salaamed deeply. 'Be at ease,' said Zabdas with unaccustomed cordiality, 'at ease, my dears. If we are to be a little irregular, we may as well enjoy it.'

He took a turn around the room, talking: 'For my wife to explain things to you, Bonnur, and for you to ask of her, you need freedom. I am not the dry stick people take me for. I know that the folkways, the subtleties of a city cannot be entered in a ledger or parsed like a sentence. Stares and sniggers and the constraint you would feel, did you sit conferring in plain sight of every fool, those would bind your tongues, your minds. The task would become difficult, prolonged, perhaps impossible. And, to be sure, I would be considered eccentric at best for setting you to it. Men might wonder if I was near my dotage. That would be bad for trade, oh, yes.

'Therefore this retreat. At such times as I deem right, when your services are not required elsewhere, Bonnur, I will send word. You will leave the house and enter this section by its back door, on the lane behind. And I will give you a signal, Aliyat. You will betake yourself directly here. In fact, sometimes you will come here to be alone. You have desired to help me; very well, you may look over such reports and figures as I shall lend you, undisturbed, and offer me your opinions. This will be common knowledge. At other times, unbeknownst to anyone else, you will meet Bonnur.'

'But sir!' Red and white went in waves over the boyish face. 'The lady and I and nobody else? Surely a maidservant, a eunuch, or – or –'

Zabdas shook his head. 'The protestation does you honor,' he replied. 'However, a watcher would defeat my whole purpose, which is to give you a true feel of conditions in Tadmor while avoiding derision and insinuations.' He looked from one to the other of them. 'I never doubt I can trust my kinsman and my first wife.' With a flick of a smile: 'She is, after all, aged beyond the usual span of life.'

'What?' Bonnur exclaimed. 'Master, you jest! The veil, the gown, they cannot hide –'

'It is true,' said Zabdas, a low sibilation. 'You shall hear of it from her, along with things less curious.'

11

A day approached sunset. 'Well,' said Aliyat, 'best we stop. I have duties still before me.'

'And I. And I should think upon what you have revealed to me this time.' Bonnur's voice dragged.

Neither of them rose from the stools on which they sat facing. Abruptly he colored, dropped his gaze, and blurted, 'My lady has a wonderful intelligence.'

It felt like a caress. 'No, no,' she protested. 'In a long life, even a stupid person learns a few things.'

She saw him break down a barrier so that he could meet her eyes. 'Hard to believe you are, are old.'

'I carry my years well.' How often had she said it precisely thus? How mechanical it had become.

'All you have seen –' Reckless impulse: 'The change of faith. That you were forced away from Christ!'

'I have no regrets.'

'Do you not? If only for, for the freedom you have lost – the freedom your friends have lost, the simple freedom to look upon you –'

For an instant she was about to hush him. Nothing closed off the doorway but a bead curtain. However, such a thing muffled sound somewhat, and deserted corridors and rooms stretched between it and the inhabited part, and he had spoken softly, deep in his throat, while tears glimmered on his lashes.

'Who cares to see a hag?' she fended, and knew she was teasing.

'You are not! You shouldn't have to cower behind that veil. I've noticed when you forgot to stoop and shamble.'

'You have watched me closely, it seems.' She fought a dizziness.

'I cannot help myself,' he confessed miserably.

'You are too curious.' As if a different creature used her tongue, her hands: 'Best we quench that. Behold.'

She drew the yashmak aside. He gasped.

She dropped it back and stood up. 'Are you satisfied? Keep silence, or we shall have to end these meetings. My lord would mislike that.' She left him.

Her daughter met her in the harem. 'Mama, where have you been? Gutne won't let me play with the lion doll.'

Aliyat groped after patience. She ought to love this child. But Thirya was whimpery, and sick half the time, and resembled her father.

12

Sometimes the sameness of the days broke, when Zabdas gave Aliyat materials to study and report on. In the room that was apart, she tried to grasp what she read, but it slipped and wriggled about like a handful of worms. Twice she met there with Bonnur. The second time she took off her veil at the outset, and she had dressed in a gown of light material. 'The weather is blazing hot,' she told him, 'and I am only an old granny, no, great-grandmother.' They accomplished little. Silences kept falling between them.

More days flowed sluggishly together. She lost count of them. What difference did their number make? Each was just like the last, save for bickerings and nuisances and, at night, dreams. Did Satan brew certain of those for her? If so, she owed him thanks.

Then Zabdas summoned her to his office. 'Your counsel has gone worthless,' he said peevishly. 'Does your dotage come upon you at last?'

She bit back rage. 'I am sorry, my lord, if no thoughts have occurred to me of late. I will try to do better.'

'What's the use? No use in you any more. Furja, now, Furja warms my bed, and surely soon she'll be fruitful.' Zabdas waved a hand in dismissal. 'Well, be off. Go wait for Bonnur. I'll send him. Perhaps at least you can persuade him to mend those woolgathering ways he's taken on. By all the saints – by the beard of the Prophet, I regret my promises to both of you!'

Aliyat stalked through the empty part of the house with fists clenched. In the room of meetings she prowled back and forth, back and forth. It was a cage. She halted at the window and stared out through the grille. From there she could look over the walls around the ancient temple of Bel. Its limestone seemed bleached under a furious sun. The bronze capitals of the portico columns blazed. Heat-shimmer made the reliefs on the cella waver. Long had it stood unused, empty, like herself. Now it was being refurbished. She had heard at fourth or fifth hand that the Arabs planned to make a fortress of it.

But were those Powers entirely dead? Bel of the storm, Jarhibol of the sun, Aglibol of the moon – Ashtoreth of begettings and births, terrible in beauty, she who descended into hell to win back her lover – unseen, they strode across the earth; unheard, they shouted throughout heaven; the sea that Aliyat had never known thundered behind her breasts.

A footstep, a click of beads, she whirled about. Bonnur halted. Sweat sheened on him. She caught the smell of it, filling the heat and silence, man-smell. She was wet with her own; the dress clung to her.

She unfastened her veil and cast it to the floor.

'My lady,' he choked, 'oh, my lady.'

She advanced. Her hips swung as if of themselves. Breath loudened. 'What would you with me, Bonnur?'

His gazelle eyes fled right and left, trapped. He backed off a step. He raised his hands against her. 'No,' he begged.

'No, what?' she laughed. She stopped before him and he must needs meet her look. 'We've things to do, you and I.'

If he is wise, he will agree. He will sit down and begin asking about the best way to bargain with a caravaneer.

I will not let him be wise.

13

'I have business in Tripolis,' Zabdas said. 'It may keep me several weeks. I shall go with Nebozabad, who leaves a few days hence.'

Aliyat was glad she had left her veil on after reaching his office. 'Does my lord wish to say what business it is?'

'No sense in that. You've grown barren of advice, as of everything else. I am informing you privately so that I can state what should be obvious, that in my absence you are to abide in the harem and occupy yourself with a wife's ordinary duties.'

'Of course, my lord.'

She and Bonnur had thus far had two afternoons together.

14

Thirya stirred. 'Mama –'

Aliya pushed fury down. 'Hush, darling,' she breathed. 'Go to sleep.' And she must wait while the child tossed and whined, until finally the bed was quiet.

Finally!

Her feet remembered the way through the dark. She clutched her nightgown to her lest it brush against something. The thought flitted: Like this do the unrestful dead steal from their graves. But it was to life that she was going. Already the juices of it ran hot. Her nostrils drank the cedary odor of her desire.

Nobody else woke, and there was no guard on as small, as drab a harem as this. Her fingers touched walls, guiding her, until she reached the last dear corridor. No, do not run, make no needless sound. The beads in the doorway snaked around her. The window framed stars. A breeze from the cooling desert drifted through it. Her pulse racketed. She pulled off the gown and tossed it aside.

He came. Her toes gripped the carpet.

'Aliyat, Aliyat.' The rough whisper echoed in her head. Bonnur stumbled, knocked a stool over, panted. She gurgled laughter and slipped to him.

'I knew you would come, beloved,' she sang. His arms enclosed her. She clawed herself tight to him. Her tongue thrust between his lips.

He bore her down, they were on the carpet, the thought flashed that she must take care it show no stains, he groaned and she reached after him.

Lantern light glared. 'Behold!' Zabdas cackled.

Bonnur rolled off Aliyat. Both sat up, crouched back, crawled to their feet. The lantern swung in Zabdas' hand. It sent huge misshapen shadows adance over the walls. She saw him in fragments, eyeballs, nose, wet snags of teeth, wrinkles, hatred. Right and left of him were his two sons. They bore swords. The steel gleamed.

'Boys, seize them!' Zabdas shouted.

Bonnur reeled. He lifted his hands like a beggar. 'No, master, my lord, no.'

It tumbled through Aliyat: Zabdas had planned this from the first. He had no passage arranged with the caravan. These three waited in another room, their light muffled, for that which he knew would happen. Now he would be rid of her, and keep her property, and believe that even an ifrit – or whatever inhuman thing she might be – would not return from the punishment for adultery.

Once she would have welcomed an ending. But the weariness of the years was burned out of her.

'Bonnur, fight!' she screamed. 'They'll tie us in a sack and the people will stone us to death!' She laid her hands on his back and shoved him forward. 'Are you a man? Save us!'

He howled and leaped. A man swung sword. Unpracticed, he missed. Bonnur caught that arm with one hand. His fist crunched into the nose behind. The second brother edged around, awkwardly, afraid of hitting the wrong body. The struggle lurched past Aliyat. It left a smear of blood on her. She bounced clear.

Zabdas blocked the doorway. She snatched the lantern from the old man's feeble grasp and dashed it to the floor. Oil flared in yellow flame. He staggered aside. She heard him shriek as the fire licked his ankle.

She fled past the beads, down hall and stairway, out the rear door, from the lane into ghost-gray streets between blank walls. The Philippian Gate stayed open after dark when a caravan was making ready. If she took care, if she moved slowly and kept to the shadows, its sentries might not see her.

Oh, Bonnur! But she had no breath or tears to spare for him, not yet, not if she wanted to live.

15

Those in the caravan who glanced behind them saw the towers of Tadmor catch the first sun-gleam. Then they were up the valley and out on the steppe. Ahead of them the sky also brightened until the last stars faded away.

Signs of man were sparse on that day's travel. After Nebozabad left the Roman road on a short cut across the desert, there was nothing but a trail worn by the generations before him who had fared likewise. He called halt for the night at a muddy pool where the horses could drink. Men contented themselves with what they carried along in skins, camels with what scrawny shrubs were to be found.

The master strode through the bustle and hubbub to a certain driver. 'I will take that bale, now, Hatim,' he said. The other grinned. Like most in this trade, he considered smuggling to be a part of it, and never asked unnecessary questions.

The bale was actually a long bundle tied together with rope, which had been nestled into the load on the camel. Nebozabad's slave carried it back, into the master's tent, laid it down, salaamed, and went to squat outside, forbidding intruders. Nebozabad knelt, undid the knots, unrolled the cloth.

Aliyat crept forth. Sweat plastered her hair and the djellabah he had lent to the curves of her. The countenance was hollow-eyed, the lips cracked. Yet once he had given her water and a bite of food, she recovered with eerie quickness, well-nigh minute by minute as he watched.

'Speak low,' he warned. 'How have you fared?'

'It was hot and dry and gut-wrenching bumpy,' she answered in a voice husky more than hoarse, 'but I shall forever thank you. Did a search party come?'

He nodded. 'Soon after we left. A few Arabian soldiers, rousted out – after Zabdas gained himself ill will by waking the qadi, I gather. They were sleepy and uninterested. We need not have hidden you so well.'

She sighed where she sat, knees drawn up, ran fingers through her matted tresses, gave him a smile that shone and lingered in the lamplit dusk. 'You cared, dear friend.'

Cross-legged before her, he scowled. 'Reckless was I. It might cost me my head, and I've my family to think of.'

She reached to stroke fingers across his wrist. 'Rather would I die than bring harm on you. Give me a waterskin and a little bread, and I will strike off across the desert.'

'No, no!' he exclaimed. 'That would be a slower death. Unless the nomads found you, which would be worse. No, I can take you along. We'll swaddle you well in garments too large, keep you offside and unspeaking. I'll say you're a boy, kin to me, who's requested a ride to Tripolis.' He grinned sourly. 'Those who doubt the "kin" part of that will snicker behind my back. Well, let them. My tent is yours to share while the journey lasts.'

'God will reward you, where I cannot. Barikai in Paradise will intercede for your soul.'

Nebozabad shrugged. 'I wonder how much good that will do, when it's the escape of a confessed adulteress I'm aiding.'

Her mouth trembled. A tear ran down the sweat and grime dried on her cheeks. 'It's right, though,' he said in haste. 'You told me what cruelties drove you from your wits.'

She caught his nearer hand in both hers and clung.

He cleared his throat. 'Yet you must understand, Aliyat, I can do no more than this. In Tripolis I must leave you, with what few coins I can spare, and thereafter you are alone. Should I be charged with having helped you, I will deny all.'

'And I will deny I saw you. But fear not. I'll vanish from sight.'

'Whither? How shall you live, forsaken?'

'I will. I have already seen ninety years. Look. Have they left any mark on me?'

He stared. 'They have not,' he mumbled. 'You are strange, strange.'

'Nonetheless – simply a woman. Nebozabad, I, I can do somewhat to repay a morsel of your kindness. The only things I have to offer are memories, but those you can bring home with you.'

He sat motionless.

She drew closer. 'It is my wish,' she whispered. 'They will be my memories too.'

16

And gladsome they are, she thought when afterward he lay sleeping. I could almost envy his wife.

Until he grew old, and she did. Unless first a sickness took one or the other off. Aliyat had never in her life been ill. Her flesh had forgotten the abuse of the day and the night that were past. A pleasant languor pervaded it, but if perchance he should awaken, she would instantly arouse to eagerness.

She smiled in the dark. Allow the man his rest. She would like to go out and walk about a while, under the moon and the high desert stars. No, too risky. Wait. Wait. She had learned how.

Pain twinged. Poor Bonnur. Poor Thirya. But if ever she let herself weep for any of the short-lived, there would be no end of weeping. Poor Tadmor. But a new city lay ahead, and beyond it all the world and time.

A woman who was ageless had one way, if none else, to live onward in freedom.

V

NO MAN SHUNS HIS DOOM

It is told in the saga of Olaf Tryggvason how Nornagest came to him when he was at Nidharos and abode some while in the king's hall; for many and wonderful were the tales that Gest bore. Evening after lengthening evening as the year drew toward winter, men sat by the fires and hearkened. Tales they heard from lifetimes agone and the far ends of the world. Often he gave them staves as well, for he was a skald, and was apt to strum a harp underneath the words, in English wise. There were those who muttered he must be a liar, asking how any man could have fared so widely or been so old. But King Olaf bade these be still, and himself listened keenly.

'I was living on a farm in the Uplands,' Gest had said to him. 'Now my last child yonder has died, and again I am weary of my dwelling – wearier than ever, lord. Word of you reached me, and I have come to see whether it is true.'

'What you have heard that is good, is true,' answered the priest Conor. 'By God's grace, he is bringing a new day to Norway.'

'But your day first broke very long ago, Gest, did it not?' murmured Olaf. 'We have heard of you again and again. Everyone has – though none but your neighbors in the mountains have seen you for many years, and I supposed you must be dead.' When he looked at the newcomer he saw a man tall and lean, straight in the back, gray of hair and beard but with few lines across the strong bones of his face. 'You are not really aged after all.'

Gest sighed. 'I am older than I seem, lord.'

'Gest of the Norns. A strange and heathenish nickname, that,' said the king slowly. 'How did you come by it?'

'You may not want to hear.' And Gest turned the talk elsewhere.

Right well did he understand the craft of doing so. Over and over, Olaf urged him to take baptism and be saved. Yet the king did not make threats or order death, as he did with most who were stubborn about this. Gest's tales were so gripping that he wanted to keep the wanderer here.

Conor pressed harder, seeking Gest out almost daily. The priest was eager in the holy work. He had come with Olaf when the latter sailed from Dublin to Norway, overthrew Hákon Jarl, and won the land for himself. Now the king was calling in missionaries from England and Germany as well as Ireland, and maybe Conor felt a bit left out.

Gest gave him grave heed and soft answers. 'I am no stranger to your Christ,' Gest said. 'I have met him often, or at least his worshippers. Nor am I plighted to Odin and Thor.' His smile was rueful. 'I have known too many different gods.'

'But this is the true and only God,' Conor replied. 'Hang not back, or you will be lost. In just a few years a full thousand will have passed since his birth among men. Belike he will come back then, end the world, and raise the dead for judgment.'

Gest stared afar. 'It would be good to believe I can meet my dead anew,' he whispered; and he let Conor talk on.

At eventide, however, after meat, when the trestle tables had been taken from the hall and women carried the drinking horns forth, he had other things to talk about, yarns to spin, verses to chant, questions to meet. Once a couple of guardsmen happened to speak of the great battle at Bravellir. 'My forebear Grani from Bryndal was among the Icelanders who fought for King Sigurdh Ring,' one boasted. 'He cut his way close enough to see King Harald War-Tooth fall. Starkadh himself had not strength to save the Danes that day.'

Gest stirred. 'Forgive me,' he said. 'There were no Icelanders at Bravellir. Norsemen had not yet found that island.'

The warrior bristled. 'Have you never heard the lay that Starkadh made?' he flung back. 'It names all the worthies who came to the fray on either side.'

Gest shook his head. 'I have heard, and I do not call you a liar, Eyvind. You passed on what you were told. But Starkadh never made any such lay. Another skald did, lifetimes afterward, and put it in his mouth. Bravellir was bloodied –' He sat a few heartbeats thinking, while the fires in the trenches guttered and crackled. 'Was it three hundred years ago? I have lost track.'

'Do you mean Starkadh was not there, and you were?' gibed the guardsman.

'Oh, he was,' said Gest, 'though he was not much like the stories men tell of him now, nor lamed and half blind with age when at last he went to his death.'

Stillness fell anew. King Olaf peered through shifting shadows at the speaker before he asked low, 'Did you, then, know him?'

Gest nodded. 'I did. Indeed, it was right after Bravellir that we met.'

1

His staff was a spear, for no man traveled unarmed in the North; but over the small pack on his back hung a harp in its case, and he offered harm to none. When at nightfall he found a homestead, he slept there, repaying hospitality with songs and tales and news from outside. Otherwise he rolled up in his cloak, and by dawnlight drank from a spring or brook and ate of whatever bread and cheese his latest host had given him. Thus had he fared through most of his years, from end to end of the world.

This day was cool beneath a wan sky where clouds were scant and the sun swung southward. The woods that decked the hills of Gautland stood hazed and hushed. Birches had begun to turn yellow, and the green of oak and beech was less bright than erstwhile. Firs lifted darkling among them. Ripe currants glowed in the shade. Smells of earth and damp filled every breath.

Gest saw it all, widely, from a ridge he had climbed. Below him the land rolled off to an unclear edge of sight. Mostly it was tree-clad, but meadows and plowed fields broke it here and there. He spied two houses and their outbuildings, distance-dwindled; smoke rose straight upward from the roofs. Close by, a stream glistened on its way to a lake that shone in the offing.

He had come far enough from the battlefield that the wreckage and the dead strewn across it were blurred together in his eyes. Carrion birds swarmed aloft and about and back down, a whirling blackness, but also gone tiny for him. He could barely hear their cries. Sometimes the howl of a wolf lifted, to hang above the hills for what seemed a long while before dying away in echoes.

Living men had withdrawn, bound home. They took wounded kindred and friends along, but could merely throw a little earth over such of the fallen as they knew. A band of them whom Gest had come upon this morning did tell him that King Sigurdh had borne off the body of his foe King Harald, to give it a barrow and grave goods at Uppsala for the sake of his own honor.

Gest leaned on his spear, shook his head, and smiled sadly. How often had he beheld the like of this, after young men stormed forth to cast their lives from them? He did not know. He had lost the number somewhere in the waste of the centuries. Or else he had never had the heart to try keeping count. He was not sure which, any more. Yet as always, he felt the need to say a farewell, the only thing he or anyone else could now give the young men.

It was no skaldic drapa that came to his lips. The words were Northern, so that the dead would understand if they could hear, but he lacked all wish to praise bravery and recall mighty deeds. The verse form that he chose was from a country thousands of miles toward the sunrise. There a short, slanty-eyed folk knew much and fashioned things of wondrous beauty, though there too the sword ranged free.

'The summer fading,
Chill shall slash the leaves bloody
And the geese trek – where?
Already this ground went red
While the wind called souls away.'

A brief spell more Gest lingered, then turned and departed. Those Danes he met earlier had seen the one whom he sought leave soon after half a dozen Swedes did and follow them eastward. Thereupon Gest had gone to Bravellir and cast about until his woodsman's eye lighted on what he thought must be the tracks. He had better hurry. Nonetheless he kept to his everyday stride. It looked lazy, but in the course of a day it left as much behind it as a horse might, or more; and it let him stay aware of everything around him.

He was on a game trail. The kings had set Bravellir as their meeting place because it was a broad meadow through which a road ran north and south, about halfway between Harald in Scania and Sigurdh in Sweden. However, the land round about was thinly settled. The six going this way must be headed for the Baltic shore, where lay the ship or ships that had brought them. That they were so few bespoke how terrible the battle had been. It would be remembered, sung about, made even larger in the minds of men, for hundreds of years to come. And those who plowed yonder fields would molder forgotten.

Gest's shoes scuffed softly on soil. Branches were a roof overhead, through which sunbeams fell to make spatters of light on the shadowy hallway before him. A squirrel ran like a flame up a tree. Somewhere a dove moaned. Brush rustled on the left, a great dim shape slipped off, an elk. Gest let his soul drift into the sweet-smelling reaches. Meanwhile, though, he kept reading the traces. That was easy, footprints, broken twigs, torn spiderwebs, marks on mossy logs where men had sat down to rest. They were no hunters by trade, as he had been through much of his life. Nor was the one who followed them, never stopping, closing the gap between. Those feet were huge.

Time passed. The sunbeams lowered, lengthened, took on a golden hue. A bit of cold crept into the air.

Suddenly Gest halted. He leaned forward, head cocked, listening. Faintly to him came a noise he thought he knew.

He quickened his pace to a lope. Muffled at first by leaves, the sound swelled fast, clang and clatter, shouts, soon crackling, snapping, and harsh breath. Gest brought his spear to the ready and glided on as quietly as might be.

A slain man sprawled across the trail. He had fallen into a bush that snagged the upper half of him. Blood dripped from its stems and pooled below, screamingly bright. A blow had cloven him from the left shoulder through the breastbone. Pieces of rib and lung poked out of him. Fair hair clung sweat-matted to cheeks whereon no beard grew, just the down of a boy. He stared and gaped emptily.

Gest drew aside and found himself treading on another body. Close by, brush churned with combat. He glimpsed men, iron, blood and more blood. Weapon banged on weapon, scraped across helmets, thudded against wooden shields. Another fighter toppled. A thigh spouted red; he threshed about and shrieked. It was the kind of noise a human throat ought not to make. A fourth warrior dropped and lay sodden in a patch of nettles. The head was nearly off him.

Gest got behind a young fir. It screened him, and he could see between its limbs. Two were left of the band that the newcomer had overtaken and attacked. Like their mates, they wore only sarks, coats, breeks. If any owned mail, he had not thought to put it on until too late. Both these did have kettle hats. One carried sword and shield, one an ax.

Their lone foe was fully outfitted, in knee-length byrnie, conical helmet with noseguard, an iron-rimmed shield in his left grip and a sword of uncommon size in his right. He was more than big, overtopping Gest's goodly height by a head, shoulders as wide as a doorframe, arms and legs like oak boughs. An unkempt black beard reached to his chest.

The pair had recovered from the shock of his onslaught. They worked together, barking words to and fro. The swordsman went straight at the giant. Blades clashed, agleam when they rose into a sunbeam, a blur as they hissed downward or sideways. The Swede caught a blow on his shield that made him lurch, but stood fast and struck back. The axman circled behind their enemy.

The huge man must have known it. Blindingly fast, he spun on his heel and plunged at the axman, offside, so that the stroke missed him by inches. His blade whipped. The axman staggered, dropped his weapon, stared at a right forearm laid open and bone-shattered. The giant leaped on past him. There was a grassy patch between him and the other swordsman. At its end he turned and burst into a run at that fellow. Shields boomed together, with weight and speed behind his. Overborne, the Swede went on his back. Somehow he kept hold of his sword and got his shield up. The giant sprang high and landed on him. Shield was driven against ribs. Gest thought he heard them crack. Breath whoofed out. The giant straddled the writhing body and made his kill in two strokes.

He glared around. The wounded axman was in flight, blundering off among the boles. The winner dashed after and cut him down.

The shrieks of the thigh-slashed man ebbed off to cawing, to rattling, to silence.

Laughter boomed from a cavern of a breast. The huge man rammed his blade thrice into the earth, wiped it clean on the shirt of a fallen, and sheathed it. His breathing eased. He doffed helmet and coif, dropped them, swept a hairy hand over the sweat that runneled off his brow.

Gest came out from behind the fir. The giant snatched at his hilt. Gest leaned spear in the crotch of a tree and spread his palms. 'I am peaceful,' he said.

The warrior stayed taut. 'But are you alone?' he asked. His voice was like heavy surf on a strand of stones.

Gest looked into the rugged face, the small ice-blue eyes, and nodded. 'I am. Besides, after what I have just seen, I would not think Starkadh need be wary of anyone or anything.'

The warrior grinned. 'Ah, you know me. But we have not met erenow.'

'Everybody in the North has heard of Starkadh the Strong. And ... I have been in search of you.'

'You have?' Surprise turned into a glower. 'Then it was a nithing's trick to stand aside and give me no help.'

'You had no need,' said Gest in his mildest tone. 'Also, the battle went so fast. Never have I seen such weapon-wielding.'

Pleased, Starkadh spoke friendlier. 'Who are you that seek me?'

'I have borne many names. In the North it has oftenest been Gest.'

'What would you of me?'

'That is a long tale. May I first ask why you hounded these men down and slew them?'

Starkadh's gaze went elsewhere, toward the sun whose light shot in yellow beams between trees turning dark against heaven. His lips moved. After a bit he nodded, met Gest's look again, and said:

> 'Here shall wolves not hunger.
> Harold fed the ravens.
> Honor won we. Only
> Odin overcame us.
> Ale I lack, but offer
> All these foes to Harald.
> Never was he niggard.
> Now I've shown I'm thankful.'

So it was true what they said, Gest thought. As well as being the foremost of warriors, Starkadh had some gift as a skald. What else might he be?

'I see,' Gest acknowledged slowly. 'You fought for Harald, and wished to avenge your lord after he fell, though the war be done with.'

Starkadh nodded. 'I hope I have gladdened his ghost. Still more do I hope I have gladdened his forebear King Frodhi, who was the best of lords and never stinted me of gold or weapons or other fine things.'

A tingle went through Gest, a chill along his backbone. 'Was that Frodhi Fridhleifsson in Denmark? They say Starkadh was of his household. But he died lifetimes ago.'

'I am older than I seem,' answered Starkadh with renewed roughness. He shook himself. 'After this day's work, thirst is afire in me. Would you know where there is water?'

'I know how to find water, if you will come with me,' Gest told him. 'But what of these dead men?'

Starkadh shrugged. 'I'm no scaldcrow to pick them clean. Leave them for the ants.' Flies buzzed around blind eyes, parched tongues, clotting blood. Stenches hung heavy.

Gest had grown used to such sights, but he was ever happy to lay them behind him, and tried not dwell on thoughts of widows, children, mothers. The lives he had shared were short at best, the merest blink of years, and afterward, for most, a span hardly longer before they were wholly forgotten by all but him. He took his spear and led the way down the trail.

'Will you be returning to Denmark?' he asked.

'I think not,' rumbled Starkadh at his back. 'Sigurdh will make sure the next king in Hleidhra is beholden to him, and that the under-kings are at odds with each other.'

'Chances for a fighting man.'

'But I'd mislike watching the realm fall asunder that Frodhi built and Harald War-Tooth rebuilt.'

Gest sighed. 'From what I have heard, the seed of something great died at Bravellir. What will you do?'

'Take ships that I own, gather crews for them, and go in viking – eastward to Wendland and Gardhariki, I think. Is that a harp you bear above your pack?'

Gest nodded. 'I've put my hand to sundry kinds of work, but mainly I am a skald.'

'Then come with me. When we reach a lord's hall, make a drapa about what I wrought this day. I'll reward you well.'

'We must talk about that.'

Silence fell between them. After a while Gest saw the signs he had been awaiting and took a side trail. It opened on a glade starred with clover. A spring bubbled up at the middle; water trickled off through the grass, to lose itself under the trees. They made a wall around, dark beneath, still golden-green on top where the last sunbeams touched them. The eastern sky was violet-blue. A flight of rooks winged homeward.

Starkadh cast himself belly down and drank with mighty slurps. When at length he raised his dripping beard, he saw Gest busy. The wanderer had lain down his cloak, opened his pack, spread things out. Now he gathered dead-wood below the trees and bushes that surrounded the glade. 'What are you doing?' Starkadh asked.

'Making ready for night,' Gest told him.

'Does nobody dwell nearby? A swineherd's hut would do.'

'I know not, and belike darkness would overrun us while we searched. Besides, here is better rest than on a dirt floor breathing smoke and farts.'

'Oh, I've slept under the stars often enough, and gone hungry too. I see you've a little food with you. Will you share?'

Gest gave the warrior a close look. 'You'd not simply take it from me?'

'No, no, you are neither foeman nor quite a stranger.' Starkadh laughed. 'Nor a woman. Too bad.'

Gest smiled. 'We'll halve what there is, though it's not much for a man your size. I'll set snares. By morning, with luck, we'll have voles to cook, or even a squirrel or hedgehog.' He paused. 'Would you like to help me? If you'll work as I show you, we can make ourselves snug before nightfall.'

Starkadh rose. 'Do you think me a coalbiter? Of course I'll take a hand. Are you a Finn, or have you dwelt among Finns, to know these woodsrunner's tricks?'

'No, I was born in Denmark like you – a long time ago. But I learned the hunter's craft in my boyhood.'

Gest found, unsurprised, that he must pick his words with care when giving orders. Starkadh's haughtiness was likely to flare. Once he roared, 'Am I a thrall?' and half drew blade. He resheathed it, smacked fist into palm, and did as he was bidden. For that moment, pain had twisted his face.

Daylight drained from the west. More and more stars glittered forth. When dusk had seeped upward to fill the glade, the men had their camp ready. A brushwood shelter, bracken and boughs heaped within, would allow rest free of dew, night mists, and rain if any fell. Turfs piled outside its mouth cast back into it the warmth of a fire that Gest had kindled with a drill. Besides nuts and berries, he had found pine cones, sedges, and roots to eke out the bread and cheese. After he had roasted them in the ways that were needful, he and Starkadh would bed down fairly full.

He hunkered at the fire, with his knife whittling a green stick into part of a cooking tool. It was a fire more low than the warrior would have built, softly sputtering, its slight smoke savory of resin. Though air cooled fast at this season, Starkadh learned he could stay comfortable by sitting close. The red and yellow flames cast wavery light over Gest's cheekbones and nose; it glinted from his eyes and made shadows in the gray beard. 'These are good skills you own,' Starkadh said. 'Indeed you shall fare with me.'

'We will talk of that,' Gest answered, watching his work.

'Why? You told me you were in search of me.'

'Yes, I was.' Gest drew breath. 'Long and long had I been away, until at last memories of the North overwhelmed me and I must come back to see if the aspens still quivered in the light nights of midsummer.' He did not speak of a woman who died after he and she fared thirty years together over the vast plains of the East with her herder tribesfolk. 'I had lost hope in my quest, I had stopped seeking – until as I walked through the woods and over the heaths of Jutland and the old tongue reawakened in me, not too much changed since I left, I began to hear about Starkadh. Him I must meet! I followed word of him to Hleidhra, where they said he had gone across the Sound to join King Harald and thence onward to war. I followed that trail to Bravellir, and reached it at sunset when the day's slaughter had ended. In the morning I found men who had seen him go from it, and I took the way they pointed, and here we are, Starkadh.'

The huge man shifted about. 'What would you of me?' he growled uneasily.

'First I would ask for the tale of your life. Some of the stories I heard were wild.'

'You're a news-greedy one.'

'I have sought knowledge throughout the world. M-m-m ... how shall a storyteller repay a night's lodging or a skald make staves for chieftains, unless he have something word-worthy behind his teeth?'

Starkadh had unbuckled his sword, but dropped hand to knife. 'Is this the beginning of witchcraft? Uncanny are you, Gest.'

The wanderer locked gaze with the warrior and answered, 'I swear to cast no spell. What I am after is more strange than that.'

Starkadh quelled a shiver. As if charging at fear to trample it underfoot, he said in a rush: 'What I have done is well known, though belike no man save me knows all of it. But sooth it is, wild and sometimes ugly tales have mushroomed over the years. I am *not* of Jotun birth. That's old wives' chatter. My father was a yeoman in the north of Zealand, my mother came of honest fisher folk, and they had other children who – grew up, lived like anybody else, grew old, and were laid in howe, those that battle or sickness or the sea had spared – also like anybody else.'

'How long have they lain in the earth?' Gest asked softly.

Starkadh ignored the question. 'I was big and strong, as you see. From childhood I lacked wish to muck and plow the fields or haul nets full of stinking fish. Twelve years old, I went off in viking. Some neighborhood men had a ship in common. They met with other ships and harried a while along the Norse shores. When they went back for hay harvest, I stayed behind. I sought out a skipper who was going to stay the winter; and thereafter my fame waxed fast.

'Shall I tell you of battles, reavings, burnings, feasts, hunger, cold, shipmates, women, offerings to the gods, strife against storm and bad luck when the gods grew angry with us, kings we served and kings we overthrew? The years lie jumbled and awash in me like flotsam on a skerry.

'Frodhi, king at Hleidhra, took me in after I suffered shipwreck. He made me the head of his household troops, and I made him the greatest of lords in his day. But his son Ingjald proved a weakling, sluggard, glutton. I upbraided him and quit the land in disgust. Yet from time to time I have been back and wielded blade for worthier men of the Skjoldung house. Harald was the best of them, he became first among kings through all of Denmark and Gautland

and well into Sweden; but now Harald is fallen, and his work broken, and I am alone again.'

He cleared his throat and spat. That may have been his way of not weeping.

'They told me Harald was aged,' Gest said. 'He must ride to Bravellir in a wagon, and was well-nigh blind.'

'He died like a man!'

Gest nodded and spoke no further, but busied himself with the food. They ate wordlessly. Afterward they slaked their thirst anew at the spring and went aside, left and right, to piss. When Starkadh came back to the fire he found Gest already there, squatting on his haunches. The night was wholly upon them. Thor's Wain gleamed enormous, barely over treetops, the North Star higher like a spearpoint.

Starkadh loomed above the fire, legs astraddle, fists on hips, and nearly snarled, 'Too long have you slyly fended me off, you. What do you want? Out with it, or I'll hew you down.'

Gest looked up. The light slipped to and fro along the shadows in his face. 'A last question,' he said. 'Then you shall know. When were you born, Starkadh?'

The giant coughed forth a curse. 'You ask and ask and ask, and naught do you give! What kind of being are you? You sit on your hams like a Finnish warlock.'

Gest shook his head. 'I learned this much farther east,' he replied mildly, 'and many things else, but none of them are wizardry.'

'You learned womanishness, you who took care to arrive late at the battle-field and stood by while I fought six men!'

Gest rose, straightened his back, stared across the flames, and said in a voice like steel sliding from sheath: 'That was no war of mine, nor would I have hunted men who boded me no further harm.' In the dim and restless light, under the stars and Winter Road, suddenly he seemed of a tallness with the warrior, or in some way taller still. 'A thing I heard said about you is that though you be foremost in battle, you are doomed to do ill deeds, nithing's work, over and over and over. They say Thor laid this on you because he hates you. They say the god who bears you good will is Odin, father of witchcraft. Could this be true?'

The giant gasped. It was as if he shrank back. He raised hands and thrust at air. 'Empty talk,' he groaned. 'Naught more.'

Gest's words tramped against him. 'But you have done treacheries. How many, in those lifetimes that have been yours?'

'Hold your jaw!' Starkadh bellowed. 'What know you of being ageless? Be still, ere I smite you like the dayfly you are!'

'That might not be so easy,' Gest purred. 'I too have lived a long time. Far longer than you, my friend.'

The breath rattled in Starkadh's throat. He could merely gape.

Gest's tone went dry. 'Well, nobody in these parts would keep count of years, as they do in the South or the East. What I heard was that you have lived three men's lifetimes. That must mean simply that folk remember their grandfathers telling of you. A hundred years is a good enough guess.'

'I – have thought – it was more.'

Again Gest's eyes caught Starkadh's and held them. His voice softened but Weakened, trembled the least bit, like a night breeze. 'I know not myself how old I am. But when I was a boy, they did not yet ken metal in these lands. Of stone did we make our knives, our axheads and spearheads and arrowheads, our burial chambers. It was not Jotuns who raised those dolmens that brood over the land. It was us, your own forebears, laying our dead to rest and offering to our gods. Though "we" are no more. I have outlived them, I alone, as I have outlived all the generations of men after – until today, Starkadh.'

'You have grayed,' said the warrior in a kind of sob, as if that could be a denial.

'I went gray in my young manhood. Some do, you know. Otherwise I have not changed. I have never been sick, and wounds heal swiftly, without scars. When my teeth wear out, new ones grow. Is it the same for you?'

Starkadh gulped and nodded.

'Belike you've taken more hurts than me, such a life as you've led,' said Gest thoughtfully. 'Myself, I've been as peaceful as men let me be, and as careful as a roamer may. When the charioteers rolled into what these days we call Denmark –' He scowled. 'That is forgotten, their wars and their deeds and their very speech. Wisdom lasts. It is what I have sought across the world.'

Starkadh shuddered. 'Gest,' he mumbled. 'I remember now, in my own youth there went tales of a wayfarer who – *Nornagest*. Are you he? I thought he was but a story.'

'Often have I left the North for hundreds of years. Always it called me home again. My last stay here ended maybe fourscore years ago. Less of an absence than formerly, but –' Once more Gest sighed. 'I feel myself grow ever wearier of roving the earth among the winds. So folk remembered me for a while, did they?'

Starkadh shook his head dazedly. 'And to think that I, I was alive then. But I must have been faring about ... Is it true that the Norns told your mother you would die when a candle burned down, and she snuffed it out and you carry it still?'

Gest grinned. 'Do you yourself believe you have your lifespan from Odin?'

He turned grave: 'I know not what has made us twain what we are. That is a riddle as dark as the death of all other mankind. Norns or gods in truth? The hunger to know drove me to the far ends of the world, that and the hope of finding more like myself. Oh, seeing a beloved wife wither into the grave, and seeing our children follow her – But nowhere did I come on any else whom time spares, nor did I come on any answer. Rather, I heard too many answers, I met too many gods. Abroad they call on Christ, but if you fare southward long enough it is Muhammad; and eastward it is Gautama Buddha, save where they say the world is a dream of Brahm, or offer to a host of gods and ghosts and elves like ours in these Northlands. And almost every man I asked told me that *his* folk know the truth while the rest are benighted. Could I but hear a word I felt even half sure of –'

'Fret not yourself about that,' said Starkadh, boldness rising anew in him. 'Things are whatever they are, and no man shuns his doom. His freedom is to leave a high name behind him.'

'I wondered if I was altogether alone, and my deathlessness a curse laid on me for some horrible guilt I have forgotten,' Gest went on. 'That seemed wrong, though. Strange births do happen. Oftenest they are weak or crippled, but now and then something springs up that can flourish, like a clover with four leaves. Could we ageless be such? We would be very few. Most could well die of war or mischance before discovering they are different. Others could well be slain by neighbors who come to fear they are witches. Or they may flee, take new names, learn how to hide what they are. I have mostly done this, seldom abiding at length in any single place. Once in a while I have met folk who were willing to take me for what I am – wise men in the East, or raw backwoods dwellers like my Northerners – but in the end there was always too much sorrow, too heavy a freight of memories, and I must leave them also.

'Never did I find my own sort. Many and many a trail did I follow, sometimes for years, but each led to naught. At last hope faded out of me, and I turned my footsteps homeward. At least the Northern springtime is forever young.

'And then I heard about you.'

Gest came around the fire. He reached to lay hands on Starkadh's shoulders. 'Here my quest ends, where it began,' he said. Tears trembled on his lashes. 'Now we are two, no more alone. And by this we *know* there must be more, women among them. Together, helping and heartening each other, we can search till we begin to find. Starkadh, my brother!'

The warrior stood unmoving before he said, 'This … comes … suddenly.'

Gest let go. 'It does that. I've had the whole while to think since the first word I got about you. Well, take your time. We have more time than most men, you and I.'

Starkadh stared off into the dark. 'I thought someday I must grow old and strengthless like Harald,' he breathed. 'Unless first I fell in battle, and I thought I would see to it that I did … But you tell me I shall always be young. Always.'

'A load that on me has often felt well-nigh unbearable,' Gest told him. 'Shared, though, it will be light.'

Starkadh clenched oak-burl fists. 'What shall we do with it?'

'Ward the gift well. It may, after all, be from Beyond, and those who bear it singled out for deeds that will change the world.'

'Yes.' Glee began to throb in Starkadh's voice. 'Fame undying, and I alive to enjoy it. War-hosts to rally round me, kingdoms to take, royal houses to found.'

'Hold, hold,' said Gest. 'We're not gods, you know. We can be slain, drowned, burned, starved like any other men. I've stayed on earth these uncounted years by ganging warily.'

Starkadh gave him a cold look. Scorn snorted: 'I understand that. Do you understand honor?'

'I don't mean we should skulk. Let us make sure of our safety, both in strength and in boltholes, lest luck go awry. After that we can make known what we are, piece by piece, to such folk as we can trust. Their awe of us will help, but that is not enough; to lead, we must serve, we must give.'

'How can we give unless we have gold, treasures, a hoard such as deathless vikings can heap up?'

Gest frowned. 'We draw near to quarreling. Best we speak no further tonight, but sleep on it. Tomorrow, refreshed, we'll think more clearly.'

'You can sleep – after this?'

'What, are you not worn out?'

Starkadh laughed. 'After reaping a goodly harvest.' He failed to see how Gest winced. 'As you wish. To bed.'

However, in the shelter he thrashed and muttered and flung his arms around. Finally Gest slipped back outside.

He found a dry spot close to the spring, but decided he would take his rest in meditation rather than sleep. Having assumed the lotus position, he raised calm within himself. That came easily. He had far surpassed his gurus in lands east of the sunrises over Denmark: for he had had centuries to practice the disciplines of mind and body that they taught. Yet without those teachings, he doubted he could have endured his lot. How fared those masters, those fellow chelas? Had Nadha or Lobsang at last won free of the Wheel?

Would he ever? Hope bound him. He could never quite bring himself to loosen it. Did that mean he spurned the faith? 'Om mani padme hum.' No such words had seized him by the soul; but was that because he would not let them? Could he only find a God to Whom he could yield –

At least he had become like the sages in control of the body and its passions. Rather, in this he had won to the power for which they had striven; Breath and heartbeat dwindled at his command until he was unaware of them. Chill ceased to be a thing invading his skin; he was of it, he was the night world, he became the stave that unfolded.

'Slowly the moon
Slides aloft.

Keen is its edge,
Cutting the dark.
Stars and frost,
As still as the dead,
Warn of another
Waning year.'

A noise recalled him. Hours had passed. The east stood gray above the trees. Dew spread the only brightness in a hueless half-light. Mists smoked above it and along men's breath. The clear gurgle of the spring sounded much louder than it was.

Starkadh hunched at the shelter. He had knocked it apart, blundering out. He carried the sheathed sword that had lain across his doffed mail. A blood-shot and dark-rimmed gaze jumped about until it landed on Gest. He grunted and stalked that way.

Gest rose. 'Good morning,' he greeted.

'Did you spend the night sitting?' Starkadh wondered. His voice grated. 'Sleep fled me too.'

'I hope you got some rest anyway. I'll go see what's in the snares.'

'Wait. Ere I take more at your hands –'

Cold pierced Gest from within. 'What's wrong?'

'You. Your slippery tongue. I tossed as in a nightmare, fighting to grasp what you meant yesterday. Now you'll make it plain to me.'

'Why, I thought I did. We are two ageless men. Our loneliness is at an end. But there must be others, women among them, for us to find and … and hold dear. For this, we'll swear oaths, become brothers –'

'Of what kind?' rasped Starkadh. 'I the chieftain, later the king; you my skald and redesman – But that's not what you said!' He swallowed. 'Or do you also want to be a king?' Brightening: 'Surely! We can divide the world between us.'

'We would die trying.'

'Our fame will never die.'

'Or worse, we would fall out with each other. How shall two stay together when always they deal in death and betrayal?'

At once Gest saw his mistake. He had intended to say that such was the nature of power. Seizing it and holding it were alike filthy. But before he could go on, Starkadh clapped hand to hilt. The rocky face went dawn-pale. 'So you besmirch my honor,' he said from the bottom of his gullet.

Gest lifted a hand, palm outward. 'No. Let me explain.'

Starkadh leaned close. His nostrils flared. 'What have you heard about me? Spew it out!'

Gest knew starkly that he must. 'They tell how you took one small king captive and hanged him for an offering to Odin, after you had promised him his life. They tell how you murdered another in his bath house, for pay. But –'

'I had to!' Starkadh yelled. 'Ever was I an outsider. The rest were, were too young, and –' He uttered a bawl like an aurochs bull's.

'And your loneliness lashed you till you struck back, blindly,' Gest said. 'I understand. I did when first I heard about you. How often have I felt thus? I remember deeds of mine that hurt me worse than fire. It's merely that I am not a killer.'

Starkadh spat on the ground. 'Right. You've hugged your years to you like a crone wrapping herself in her blanket.'

'But don't you see,' Gest cried, 'things have changed for us both? Now we've better work to do than attack folk who never harmed us. It was the lust for fame, wealth, power that brought you to dishonor.'

Starkadh screamed. His sword flew free. He hewed.

Gest shifted like a shadow. Nonetheless the edge ripped down his left arm. Blood poured forth, drenched the cloth, dripped into the streamlet that ran from the spring.

He drifted back, drew his knife, halted in half a crouch. Starkadh stood fast. 'I should ... chop you in twain ... for what you said,' he panted. Gulping air: 'But I think you will die soon enough of that stroke.' Laughter clanked. 'A shame. I did hope you'd be a friend. The first real friend of my life. Well, the Norns will it otherwise.'

Our natures do, Gest thought. And: How easily I could kill you. How open you stand to a hundred martial tricks I know.

'Instead, I shall have to go on as erstwhile,' said Starkadh, 'alone.'

Let it be so, thought Gest.

With the fingers of his right hand he searched below his torn shirt and pushed together the lips of his wound. Pain he made into something apart from himself, like the mists that broke under the strengthening light. He gave his mind to the blood flow.

Starkadh kicked the shelter aside, fetched his mail, drew it over the under-padding in which he had spent the night. He donned coif and helmet, belted on sword, picked up shield. When he was ready to leave, he stared in aston-ishment at the other man. 'What, are you still on your feet?' he said. 'Shall I make an end of you?'

Had he tried that, it would have been the end of him. But he stopped, shivered, turned away. 'No,' he mumbled. 'This is all too spooky. I'm off to my own doom, Nornagest.'

He lumbered up the trail, into the woods and beyond sight.

Then Gest could sit down and bring a whole heed to the steering of his body. He had stopped the bleeding before he suffered overmuch loss, though he would be weak for a few days. No matter. He could stay here until he was fit to travel; the earth would provide for him. He began to hasten the knitting of the flesh.

He dared not wish he were able to heal the wound inside.

2

'However, we only met fleetingly, Starkadh and I,' Gest went on. 'Afterward hearsay about him reached me now and then, until I went abroad again; and when I came back he was long dead, slain as he had wanted.'

'Why have you fared so widely?' asked King Olaf. 'What have you sought?'

'What I never found,' Gest answered. 'Peace.'

No, that was not wholly right, he thought. Over and over had he been at peace, in the nearness of beauty or wisdom, the arms of a woman, the laughter of children. But how short the whiles! His latest time as a husbandman, in the Uplands of Norway, seemed already the dream of a single night: Ingridh's youthful gladness, its rebirths in the cradle he had carved, her heart that stayed high while she grew more gray than he, but then the shriveling years, and afterward the burials, the burials. Where now wandered Ingridh? He could not follow, not her nor any of those who glimmered on the rim of memory, not that first and sweetest of all, garlanded with ivy and in her hand a blade of flint ...

'In God is peace,' said the priest.

It could be, it could be. Today church bells rang in Norway, as they had done for a lifetime or more in Denmark, yes, above that halidom of the Mother where he and the garland girl had offered flowers ... He had seen the charioteers and their storm gods come into the land, he had seen bronze and iron, the wagon trains bound south for Rome and the viking ships bound west for England, sickness and famine, drought and war, and life patiently beginning anew; each year went down into death and awaited the homecoming of the sun that would bring it to rebirth; he too could let go if he would, and drift away on the wind with the leaves.

King Olaf's priest thought that soon every quest would end and the dead arise. How good if that was true. Ever more folk believed so. Why should not he?

Come unto me, all ye that labour and are heavy laden, and I will give you rest.

Days later, Gest said, 'Yes, I will take your baptism.' The priest wept for joy. Olaf whooped.

But when it was done, that evening in the hall Gest took forth a candle and lighted it at a torch. He lay down on a bench where he could see it. 'Now I may die,' he told them.

Now I have yielded.

He let the candle flame fill his vision, his being. He made himself one with it. The light waxed for him until he almost thought it shone on those lost faces, brought them back out of the dark, nearer and nearer. His heartbeat heeded him, slowing toward quietness.

Olaf and the young warriors stood dumb with awe. The priest knelt in shadow and prayed without uttering the words aloud.

The candleflame flickered to naught. Nornagest lay still. Through the hall sounded a wind of the oncoming winter.

VI

ENCOUNTER

From afar the gold shone like a daylight evenstar. Sometimes trees hid it, a woodlot or a remnant of forest, but always as the travelers moved west they saw it again, brilliant in a vastness of sky where a few clouds wandered, above a plain where villages and freshly greening croplands lay tiny beneath the wind.

Hours wore on, sunbeams now tangled themselves in Svoboda Volodarovna's brows, and the hills ahead loomed clear, the city upon the highest of them. Behind its walls and watchtowers lifted domes, spires, the smoke from a thousand hearths; and over all soared the brightness. Presently she heard chimes, not the single voice of a countryside chapel but several, which must be great ones to sound across this distance, ringing together in music such as surely sang among the angels or in the abode of Yarilo.

Gleb Ilyev pointed. 'The bell tower, the gilt cupola, belongs to the cathedral of Sviataya Sophia,' he said. 'That's not any saint's name but means "Holy Wisdom." It comes from the Greeks, who brought the word of Christ to the Rusi.' A short, somewhat tubby man with a pug nose and a scraggly beard turning gray, he was given to self-importance. Yet leathery skirt bespoke many years of faring, often through danger, and goodly garb told of success won by it.

'Then all this is new?' asked Svoboda in amazement.

'Well, that church and certain other things,' Gleb replied. 'Grand Prince Yaroslav Vladimirovitch has built them since these lands fell to him and he moved his seat here from Novgorod. But of course Kiyiv was already great. It was founded in Rurik's time – two centuries ago, I believe.'

And to me this was only a dream, Svoboda thought. It would have been less real than the old gods that we suppose still haunt the wilderness, did not merchants like Gleb pass through our little settlement once in a while, bringing their goods that few of us can afford but also their tales that everyone is eager to hear.

She clucked to her horse and nudged it with her heels. These lowlands near the river were still wet after the spring floods, and the mire of the road had wearied the horse. Behind her and her guide trailed his company, half a dozen hirelings and two apprentices leading the pack animals or driving a pair of laden wagons. Here, safe from bandits or Pecheneg raiders, they had laid weapons aside and wore merely tunics, trousers, tall hats. Gleb had put on good clothes this morning, to make a proper show when he arrived; a fur-trimmed cloak was draped over a brocaded coat.

Svoboda was well-clad too, in a gown of gray wool bordered with embroideries. Hiked up across the saddle, her skirts revealed finely stitched boots. A headcloth covered flaxen braids. Weather had only tinged her with bronze, work had built strength without stooping the back or coarsening the hands. Well-figured enough that the big bones did not stand forth, she looked at the world out of blue eyes set widely in a face of blunt nose, full mouth, square chin. Lineage and fortune showed; her father had been headman of the village in his day, and each of her husbands had been better off than most men – blacksmith, hunter-trapper, horse breeder and dealer. Nonetheless she must keep herself reined in if she would appear calm, and the heart in her breast kept breaking free of that grip.

When she came in clear sight of the Dniepr, she could not help catching her breath. Brown and mighty rolled the river: easily five hundred paces across, she guessed. To her right a low, grassy island divided it. Lesser streams flowed in from either side. The far shore was surprisingly much forested, though houses and other buildings led up from the water to the city and clustered around its ramparts, while orchards or small farmsteads and pastures nestled elsewhere in the hills.

On this bank was just a muddy huddle of dwellings. Its laborers and peasants gave the travelers scant heed; they were used to such. What did draw some stares and mutters was her. Few women accompanied any traders, and those who did were seldom of an honorable kind.

A ferry waited. Its owner hastened to meet Gleb and chaffer with him, then went about calling for crew to man the sweeps. Three trips would be necessary. The gangway was steeply pitched, for the wharf was built high against the yearly rise. Gleb and Svoboda were among the first to cross. They took stance near the bows, the better to watch. Voices barked, wood creaked, water lapped and splashed, the vessel started off. The breeze was cool, wet, full of silty smells. Fowl winged about, ducks, geese, lesser birds, once a flight of swans overhead, but not so many as at home; here they were hunted more.

'We come at a busy time,' Gleb warned. 'The city is crammed with strangers. Brawls are common, and worse than that can befall, despite everything the Grand Prince does to keep order. I shall have to leave you alone while I attend to my work. Be very careful, Svoboda Volodarovna.'

She nodded impatiently, barely hearing words he had spoken over and over, her gaze and her heed aimed forward. As they approached the west bank, the ships gathered there seemed to breed until they were past counting.

She caught hold of her senses and told herself that now the outer hulls, riding at anchor, did not hide those at the docks from her, and the number must be scores rather than hundreds. It took away none of the wonder. Here were no barges such as she was on, nor rowboats and dugout punts such as her own folk used. These were long and lean, clinker-built, gaudily painted, many with stemposts carved into fantastic figureheads. Oars, yards, and unstepped masts lay on trestles above the benches. How their sails must spread like wings when they came to the sea!

'Yes, the famous merchant fleet,' said Gleb. 'Most likely all are now gathered. Tomorrow, perhaps, they leave for Constantinople, New Rome.'

Again Svoboda scarcely listened. She was trying to imagine that sea the ships would find at the river's end. It reached farther than a man could look; it was rough and dark and salt of taste; huge snakes and people who were half fish beset its waves. So the tales went. She strove to form the vision, but failed. As for the city of the Basileus, how could the claim be true that it made Kiyiv, *Kiyiv*, look small and poor?

To go and find out, to be there!

She sighed once, then shoved longing aside. Quite enough newness lay straight ahead. What she might gain and what she might suffer were alike unforeseeable. Even in fireside stories, no woman had ever ventured this that she was venturing. But none had ever been driven by a need like hers.

Memories flitted through her, secret thoughts that had come when she was alone, working in house or garden, gathering berries or firewood in the outskirts of the forest, lying wakeful in the night. Could she also be special, a princess stolen from the crib, a girl chosen for destiny by the old gods or the Christian saints? No doubt every child nursed daydreams of that sort. They faded away as one grew up. But in her they had slowly rekindled –

No prince came riding, no fox or firebird uttered human words, life simply went on year by year by year until at last she broke free; and that was her own, altogether ordinary doing. And here she was.

Her heart quickened afresh. It hammered fear out of her. Wonders in truth!

The ferry knocked against bollards. Its crew made fast. The passengers debarked into racket and bustle. Gleb pushed through the crowd of workers, hawkers, sailors, soldiers, idlers. Svoboda stayed close at his side. She had always taken care to uphold self-command in his presence, bargain rather than appeal, be friendly rather than forlorn; but today he knew what he did while she was bewildered. This was nothing like a fair at the town she knew, which was little more than a fort for villagers to take refuge in.

She could watch, though, hearken, learn. He talked to a man of the harbormaster's and a man of the Prince's, he left orders with a man of his about where to bring the rest of his band, and finally he led her up the hill into the city.

Its walls were massive, earthen, whitewashed. An arched gateway, flanked by turrets and crowned with a tower, stood open. Guards in helmet and chain mail leaned on their pikes, no hindrance to the traffic that thrust to and fro, on foot, on horseback, donkey cart, ox-drawn wagon, sometimes sheep or cattle herded toward slaughter, once a monstrous beast, like a thing out of nightmare, that Gleb called a camel. Beyond, streets twisted steep. Most of the vividly painted buildings that lined them were timber, below roofs of mossy shingle or blossoming turf. Often they stood two, even three stories high. In the windows of those that were brick, there gleamed glass. Above them she glimpsed the golden cupola where the bells dwelt, surmounted by a cross.

Noise, smells, surge and push of bodies overwhelmed Svoboda. Gleb must raise his voice when he pointed out some new kind of person. The priests she knew at once, black-gowned and long-bearded, but a man more coarsely clad was a monk, sent into town from his nearby cave on an errand, while a magnificently robed elder borne in a litter was a bishop. Townsfolk – housewives who dickered on a market square overflowing with goods and people, portly merchants, common workers, slaves, children, peasants from the hinterland – wore an endlessness of different garbs, and nowhere the dear decorations of home. Tarry sailors, tall blond Northmen, Poles and Wends and Livonians and Finns in their various raiments, high-cheeked tribesmen off the steppes, a pair of Byzantines clothed with elegance and disdain, she was lost among them, and at the same time she was upraised, carried along, drunk on marvel.

At a house near the south wall, Gleb halted. 'This is where you will stay,' he said. She nodded. He had told her about it. A master weaver, whose daughters had married, earned extra money by taking in trustworthy lodgers.

A maidservant answered Gleb's knock. The goodwife appeared. Gleb's followers brought in Svoboda's baggage, and he paid the woman. They went to the room that would be hers. Cramped, it held a narrow bed, stool, pot, basin, water jug. Above the bed hung a picture, a man with a halo, letters around him to spell out a name that the wife said was St Yuri. 'He slew a dragon and saved a maiden,' she explained. 'A fine guardian for you, my dear. You have come to be married, I believe?' The sharp, hasty accent forced Svoboda to listen closely.

'So we trust,' Gleb replied. 'Arranging the betrothal will take days, you understand, Olga Borisovna, and then there will be the wedding preparations. Now this lady is tired after a long, hard journey.'

'Of course, Gleb Ilyev. What else? Hungry too, I'm sure. I will go see that the soup is hot. Come to the kitchen when you are ready, both of you.'

'I must be straightway off, myself,' he said. 'You know how a trader has to watch and pounce at this season, like a sparrowhawk, if he would strike any bargains worth half his trouble.'

The woman bustled off. So did his men, at a gesture from him. For a moment he and Svoboda were alone.

Light was dim; this room had only a small window covered by membrane. Svoboda searched Gleb's face as best she could, where he stood in the doorway. 'Will you meet Igor Olegev today?' she asked low.

'I doubt that,' he sighed. 'He is an important man, after all, his voice strong in the folkmoot, and – and very busy while the fleet is here, not just as a chandler but – well, when you deal with men of many nations, it becomes politics and schemes and –' He was not wont to speak thus awkwardly. 'I'll leave word, and hope he can receive me tomorrow. Then we'll set a time for you to meet with him, and – and I'll pray for a good outcome.'

'You said that was sure.'

'No, I said I think it likely. He is interested. And I know him and his situation well. But how could I make you any outright promise?'

She sighed in her turn. 'True. At worst, you said, you can find somebody less well off.'

He stared down at the rushes on the floor. 'That ... need not happen either. We are friends of old, you and I. Right? I could – look after you – better than, than you have thus far let me do.'

'You have been more than kind to me,' she said gently. 'Your wife is a lucky woman.'

'I had better go,' he mumbled. 'Get my whole party together, everyone quartered, wares stored, and then – Tomorrow, whenever I can, I'll stop here and give you the news. Until then, God be with you, Svoboda Volodarovna.' He turned and hurried off.

She stood a while, her thoughts atumble, before she found her way to the kitchen. Olga gave her a bowl of rich beef broth, crowded with leeks and carrots, black bread and ample butter on the side. She settled herself on the bench across the table and chattered away. 'Gleb Ilyev has told me so much about you –'

With a wariness that the years had taught her, Svoboda steered the talk. Just how much had the man said? It was a relief to learn he had been as shrewd as usual. He had described a widow with no dependent children alive and no prospect of remarriage in her distant, rude neighborhood. Out of charity, and in hope of earning credit in Heaven, Gleb had suggested her to the chandler Igor Olegev of Kiyiv, himself lately left bereaved among several youngsters. The prospect appeared good; a woodlander could learn city ways if she was clever, and this woman had other desirable qualities as well. Therefore Gleb helped Svoboda convert her inheritance to cash, a dowry, and took her along on his next trip.

'Ah, poor darling, poor little one.' Olga dabbed at tears. 'No child of yours above the earth, and no man to wed one so young and beautiful? I cannot understand that.'

Svoboda shrugged. 'There was ill feeling. Please, spare me talking about it.'

'Yes, village feuds. People can indeed get nasty, hemmed in by themselves all their lives. And then, pagan fears prey on them. Do they imagine you're unlucky, cursed by a witch perhaps, just because you've had many sorrows? May God now, at last, prosper your life.'

So Gleb had told truth, while holding back truth. A trader skill. For an instant, Svoboda wondered about him. They got along well together, she and he. They could do more than that, if this marriage scheme fell through. Let the priests call it sin. Kupala the Joyous would not, and maybe the old gods did linger on earth ... But no. Gleb was already gray. Too little time remained for him that she could bring herself to hurt the wife whom she had never met. She knew how loss felt.

Having eaten, and Olga gone back to a housewife's work, Svoboda sought her room. She unpacked, stowed her possessions, and wondered what to do next. There had always been some task, if only to spin thread. But she had left the things of home behind, with home itself. Nor could she just sink into blessed idleness, savoring it, or into sleep, as countryfolk were apt to when the rare, brief chance came. That was not the way of a headman's daughter, wife to a man of weight.

Restlessness churned in her. She paced the floor, flung herself onto the bed, bounced up again, yawned, glowered, paced anew. Should she go help Olga's household? No, she wouldn't know her way about. Moreover, Igor Olegev might well think it demeaned his bride. If anything was to come of that. What was he like? Gleb called him a good fellow, but Gleb would never see him from a woman's side, not even well enough that what he said of Igor's looks called forth anything real for Svoboda.

St Yuri, there on the wall, she could at least take the measure of, gaunt, big-eyed – She knelt before him and tried to ask his blessing. The words stuck in her throat. She had been dutiful but not devout, and today proper meekness was beyond her.

She paced. Decision came slowly. Why must she stay penned between these walls? Gleb had told her to be careful, but she had often gone alone into the woods, fearless of wolf or bear, and taken no harm. Once she caught a runaway horse by the bridle and dragged him to a stop, once she killed a mad dog with an ax, once she and her neighbors crowded into the stockaded town and stood off a Pecheneg raid. Besides, while the hours dribbled away here, life pulsed out there, newness, wonder. The bell tower shone tall ...

Of course! The church of the Holy Wisdom. There, if any place, she could feel prayerful; there God would hear and help.

Yes, surely.

She threw a cloak on, pinned it fast, drew up the hood, glided forth. Nobody could forbid her to leave, but it would be best if she went unnoticed.

She did pass a servant, maybe a slave, but he gave her a dull glance and continued scrubbing out a tile stove in the main room. The door closed behind Svoboda. The street swept her off.

For a while she wandered, shyly at first, then in a daze of delight. Nobody offered her any rudeness. Several young men did stare, and a couple of them grinned and nudged each other, but that just made her tingle. Now and then somebody jostled her by chance. It was less often than earlier, the ways were less thronged, as the sun sank westward. Finally she got a clear sight of the cathedral and steered by it.

When she saw St Sophia full on, she caught her breath. Sixty paces long it was, she guessed dizzily, rising white and pale green in walls and bays, arched doorways and high glass windows, up and up to, yes, ten domes in all, six bearing crosses and four spangled with stars. For a long time she could only stand and look. At last, mustering courage, she went on past workmen who were adding to the splendor. Her heart thudded. Was this forbidden? But besides priests, commoners went in and out. She passed the entrance.

After that, for a time during which time was not, she drifted like a rusalka beneath the water. Almost she wondered if she too had drowned and become such a spirit. Twilight and hush enfolded her, windows glowed with colors and images, walls with gold and images ... but no, that stern strange face overhead was Christ, Lord of the World, in the ring of his apostles, and yonder giantess made of little stones was his Mother, and ... the song, the deep moaning tones that finally lifted from behind a carven screen, while bells rang high above, those were in praise of his Father ... She prostrated herself on cold flags.

Awareness seeped into her much later. The church had become a cavern of night; she was alone, except for a few clergy and many candles. Where had the day gone? She crossed herself and hastened out.

The sun was down, the sky still blue but swiftly darkening, the streets full of dusk between walls in whose windows flame light fluttered yellow. They were well-nigh deserted. Her breath, footfalls on cobbles, rustle of skirts sounded loud in the quiet. Turn right at this corner, left at the next – no, wait, that was wrong, she had never seen yonder house with the rafter ends carved into heads – She was lost.

She stopped, filled her lungs and eased them again, grinned wryly. 'Fool,' she whispered. 'At your age you should have known better.' She glanced about. Roofs stood black against a heaven gone almost as dark, where three stars trembled. Opposite, paleness crept upward, the moon rising. So, west and east. Her lodging stood near the south wall. If she kept on that way, as closely as these crooked lanes allowed, she should reach it. Then she could knock on a door and ask directions. No doubt Olga would make a fuss and tomorrow Gleb would chide her.

She stiffened her back. She was headman Volodar's daughter. Picking her steps carefully, gown held above ankles, to avoid the worst muck, she set off.

Twilight thickened toward night. Air lay chilly. The moon gave wan light when she saw it, but mostly it was still behind roofs.

Lampglow, smoke, smells of kvass and cookery, spilled from a half-open door. Voices barked, laughter bayed. She scowled and went by on the far side of the street. An inn, where men were getting drunk. She had seen that sort of thing when she visited the town with a husband. Rostislav had grown too fond of it, he'd reel back to her, all stench and sweat –

Boots thudded behind her, louder, nearer.

She quickened her steps. The other did too, and drew alongside. 'Ha,' he growled, 'greeting to you.' She could barely understand him.

They entered a patch of moonlight and he became more than a shadow. A head taller than she, he blocked the gathering western stars out of her sight. She saw a pate shaven except for a lock on the right side, a bristle of mustache under a nose that had once been broken, tattoos over the shaggy breast and down the thick arms. He wore a shirt half unlaced, broad trews, short cloak, everything stiff with old grease. The knife at his belt was nearly of sword size, a weapon forbidden to everyone but the Prince's guards within this city.

A demon! flashed ice-sharp through her, and then: No, a Varyag. I've heard about them, Northmen and Rusi who ply the rivers, walking stormwinds – She pulled her look from him and sought to go on.

A hand clamped on her right arm. 'Now, now, not be hasty,' he laughed. 'You out for fun this late, no? I give you fun.'

'Let me be!' she cried, and tugged at the grip. He wrenched. Pain stabbed sickeningly through her shoulder. She stumbled. He held her fast.

'Come,' he said, 'there's an alley, you like it.' The smell of him caught at her gorge. She must gag before she could scream.

'Quiet, you! Nobody come.' His free hand cuffed. Her head rocked. Darkness roared through. Nonetheless, somehow, she dug her heels down and screamed again.

'Quiet or I – Ha-a-a.' He cast her to the cobbles. When she could see upward, he had turned to meet two others.

They must have been on a side street and heard, she thought amidst the dizziness. Let them help me. Christ, Dazhbog, Yarilo, St Yuri, help them help me.

The Varyag's knife was out. 'Go,' he snarled. 'No need you. Go.' She realized that he was drunk, and that that made him the more dangerous.

The smaller of the two men advanced, cat-footed. 'I think best you go cool that noggin of yours, friend,' he replied mildly. His own knife slipped forth. It was a tool for eating and ordinary cutting, a sliver against that great blade. Nor did its bearer seem any kind of warrior. His slender frame bore a fur-lined coat and trousers smoothly tucked into soft boots. Svoboda made out that much because his companion carried a lantern, which threw a dull glow on them both and a puddle of it at their feet.

The Varyag grinned beneath the moon. 'Dainty lordling and cripple,' he jeered. 'You tell me what to do? Scoot, or I find how white your tripes be.'

The second new man put down the lantern. It had been in his left hand. His right was missing. From a leather cup strapped to that forearm reached an iron hook. Otherwise he was muscular, his garb stout but plain. He drew his small knife. 'We two,' he rumbled. 'You alone. Cadoc say go, you go.' Unlike the slim man, he could barely speak Russian.

'Two cockroaches!' the Varyag yelled. 'Perun thunder me, enough!'

He made a long step forward. His weapon flashed. The slim man – Cadoc? – swayed aside. He thrust out an ankle and gave a push. The Varyag tripped, crashed to the stones. The man with the hook laughed. The Varyag roared, sprang up, charged him.

The hook slashed. Its curve ended in a point that went deep into the attacker's upper arm. The Varyag yelled. The opponent's knife cut his wrist. His own iron clattered loose. Cadoc danced in and, half playfully, seized his hairlock and sliced it across. 'The next trophy comes from between your legs,' Cadoc said with a leer. The Varyag howled, whirled, fled. Echoes died away.

Cadoc hunkered down by Svoboda. 'Are you well, my lady?' he asked. 'Here, lean on me.' He helped her rise.

His companion stooped for the Varyag's knife. 'No, leave that,' Cadoc ordered. His Russian must be for her benefit. 'I wouldn't want the guard to find it on us. That oaf's carcass would scarcely be as inconvenient. Let's get away. The racket may well have drawn attention we can do without. Come, my lady.'

'I, I'm unhurt.' The breath sobbed in Svoboda's throat. She had, in fact, suffered nothing but possible bruises. A measure of daze remained. She went blindly along, Cadoc's hand on her elbow.

The man with the lantern and the hook asked something that must mean, 'Where to?'

'Our lodging, of course,' Cadoc snapped in Russian. 'If we should meet a patrol, then nothing has happened, we've simply been out for a little drink and merriment. Will you agree to that, my lady? You do owe us something, and we'd hate to miss the fleet's departure tomorrow because Yaroslav's officers wanted to question us.'

'I must get home,' she pleaded.

'You shall. We'll see you safely back, never fear. But first –' Shouts lifted to the rear. 'Hark! Somebody did come. They've found the knife, and if they have a lantern too, they'll have seen the blood and scuffled offal. Here.' Cadoc led them into an alley, a tunnel of murk. 'Round about, but it avoids trouble. We'll lie low for an hour or two and then escort you, my lady.'

They emerged on a broad street, moon-bright. Svoboda's wits had returned. She wondered how far she could trust the pair. Might it be wisest to insist she go back to Olga's at once? If they refused, she could strike out by herself, no worse off than earlier. But that had not been well off at all. And – a throbbing, a warmth – never had she known anybody like this. Never again would she, perhaps. They were to sail in the morning and she, she was once more to become a wife.

Then Cadoc plucked his companion's sleeve and said merrily, 'Whoa, Rufus. Don't go on past.' A house bulked before them. The door was unbarred. They wiped their feet and trod through, into a space where she could barely see tables, benches, a couple of night lamps burning. 'The common room,' said Cadoc in her ear. 'This is a hostel for those who can afford it. Quiet, please.'

She peered. Rufus' lantern showed him to be lumpy-featured, freckled, the dense whiskers and thin hair a bright yellowish-red. Cadoc was altogether foreign, his face narrow and aquiline, the eyes slightly aslant like a Finn's but large and brown, hair shoulder-length and as raven-black as the beard he kept trimmed to a point. A golden finger ring was equally alien in its workmanship, a snake that bit its tail. Seldom had she met as ready a smile as was his.

'Well, well,' he murmured. 'I had no idea that the lady in distress was so comely.' He bowed, as if she were a princess. 'Fear not, I repeat. We'll take proper care of you. Alas for your raiment.' Glancing down, she saw filth smeared over it.

'I, I could tell people I fell,' she stammered. 'That is true.'

'I think we can do better,' Cadoc said.

Rufus followed them upstairs to a second-floor chamber. It was large, wainscoted, drapes by a glazed window and a rug on the floor, with four beds, a table, several stools, and whatever else comfort required. Rufus took the candle from his lantern and used it to light the tapers in a seven-branched brass holder. His deftness told Svoboda he must have lost his hand long ago, to have learned so well how to do without it.

'We are the only two,' Cadoc told Svoboda. 'It's worth the cost. Now –' He squatted by a chest, took a key from his pouch, opened the lock. 'Most of our goods are on our ship, naturally, but here are some especially valuable, whether from abroad or acquired in Kiyiv. They include –' He rummaged. 'Ah, yes.' The fabric he drew out shone in the candlelight. 'I regret we can't prepare a hot bath at this hour, my lady, but yonder you'll find a basin, water jug, soap, towels, slop jar. Make free, and afterward don. this. Meanwhile, of course, Rufus and I will absent ourselves. If you'll open the door a crack and hand out your soiled things, he'll see what he can do toward cleansing them.'

The redbeard made a mouth. He grumbled in an unknown tongue. Cadoc replied and, somehow, jollied him till he nodded. They took single candles in holders and left.

Svoboda stood alone with her bewilderment. Did she dream? Had she blundered into elvenland, or had she met a pair of gods, here in this Christian stronghold? Suddenly she laughed. Whatever befell, it was new, it was a wonder!

She unfastened brooches and laces, pulled clothing over her head, held it around the door as Cadoc had suggested. Somebody took it. She closed the door again and went to wash. The cloth caressed a nakedness that the cool air seemed to flow across. She dawdled at the task. When a knock sounded, she called, 'Not yet,' and hurried to dry herself. The garment, tossed onto a bed, drew a gasp from her. It was a robe of sheening, baby-smooth material, gold-trimmed blue, secured by silver buttons. Her feet were now bare. Well, peeping from beneath the skirt, they would catch glances, she thought, and flushed hot. Quickly she combed locks fallen astray around her coiled braids, and knew their amber color would show well above the dress. 'Enter,' she said, not quite evenly.

Cadoc appeared, a tray balanced on his left hand. He shut the door behind him and put the tray on the table. It bore a flagon and two cups. 'I never knew silk could be this beautiful,' he said.

'What?' asked Svoboda. She wished her pulse would slow.

'No matter. I'm often rather brash. Please sit and enjoy a stoup with me. I woke the potboy to give me of the landlord's choicest. Take your ease, recover from that foul experience.'

She lowered herself to a stool. Before he did likewise, Cadoc poured out a red liquid with a summery odor. 'You are very kind,' she whispered. As Gleb is kind, she thought; then, unwillingly: No, Gleb is a countryside trader growing old. He can read and write, but what else does he know, what has he seen and done beyond his narrow rounds? 'How can I repay you?' Immediately: That was a foolish thing to say!

However, Cadoc only smiled, raised his cup, and replied, 'You can tell me your name, my lady, and whatever else you care to. You can gladden me with your company for a short while. That is ample. Drink, I pray you.'

She sipped. Deliciousness flowed over her tongue. This was no berry wine of the backwoods, it was – was – 'I, I am –' Almost, she gave him her baptismal name. But of course that would be unwise. She believed she could trust this man, but if a sorcerer somehow learned it she would be open to spells. Besides, she seldom thought about it. 'Svoboda Volodarovna,' the name she used at home. 'From … afar. Where is your friend?'

'Rufus? Oh, I've put him to getting your clothes as clean as possible. Afterward he won't disturb us. I gave him a flagon of his own to keep him company. A loyal man, brave, but limited.'

'Your servant, then?'

Did a shadow flit across his face? 'An associate of mine for a long, long time. He lost his hand fighting once, warding my back, when a gang of Saxons ambushed us. He kept on fighting, left-handed, and we escaped.'

What were Saxons? Robbers? 'Such a wound should have disabled him, at least. Most men would soon have died of it.'

'We're a tough pair. But enough. How did you happen to be abroad after dark, Svoboda Volodarovna? You're clearly not the kind who ordinarily would. It was sheer luck that Rufus and I were in earshot. We'd been having a last cup with a Rus factor I've come to know; bade him goodnight since we must rise betimes tomorrow, set off, and then – Ah, it seems God would not let a lady such as you come to sordid grief.'

The wine glowed and thrilled in her blood. She remembered caution, but did find herself blurting out as much as Gleb had revealed on her behalf to Olga Borisovna and ... and, as her voice ran on, to Igor Olegev. Cadoc's shrewd, quiet questions made it easy.

'Ah,' he murmured at length. 'Thank the saints, we did save you from ruin. That besotted mercenary would have left you in no state to hide what had befallen, if he left you alive at all.' He paused. 'Whereas you can tell your landlady, and afterward that man who's playing father to you, that you stayed too late at the church, lost in prayer. It's nothing unusual hereabouts.'

She bridled. 'Shall I give them a falsehood? I have my honor.'

He grinned. 'Oh, come now. You're not fresh out of a cloister.' She didn't know what that might be, but caught his drift. 'How often in your life has a lie been more than harmless, been a shield against hurt? Why put the good Gleb in an awkward position, when he has worked so hard on your behalf?' Impudently: 'As the go-between who brought Igor the chandler a superb new wife, Gleb can await excellent business deals. Spoil it not for him, Svoboda.'

She covered her confusion by draining her cup. He refilled it. 'I understand,' he said. 'You are young, and the young are apt to be idealistic. Nevertheless, you have imagination and boldness beyond your years, more than most men do, that you would set forth into an altogether different life. Use that wisdom.'

Sudden desolation welled up in her. She had learned how to turn it into mirth of a sort. 'You talk as my grandfather might have,' she said. 'How old are *you*?'

His tone bantered. 'Not yet worn out.'

Eagerness to know surged like lust. She leaned forward, aware of his awareness of her bosom. The wine buzzed, bees in a clover meadow. 'You've told nothing of yourself. What are you?' A prince or boyar, ending his father's name not in 'ev' but in 'vitch'? The byblow of a forest god?

'A merchant,' he said. 'I've followed this route for years, building my wealth till I own a ship. My stock is fine things: amber and furs from the North, cloths and delicacies from the South, costly without being too bulky or heavy.' Maybe the drink had touched him a bit also, for he added, puzzlingly, half under his breath, 'It lets me meet people of many different kinds. I am curious about them.'

'Where are you from?'

'Oh, I came through Novgorod, as traders from my parts do, by river, lake, portage, to here. Ahead lie the great Dniepr and its falls – hardest of the portages, that, and our military escort much needed in case of raiders off the steppe – then the sea, and at last Constantinople. Not that I make the journey every year. It's long both ways, after all. Most cargoes are transshipped here at Kiyiv. I return to Swedish and Danish ports, or ofttimes to England. However, as I said, I want to travel as much as I'm able. Have I answered you windily enough?'

She shook her head. 'No. I meant, what is your nation?'

He spoke with more care. 'Rufus and I – Cymriu, the dwellers call that country. It is part of the same island as England, is the last of the ancient Britain, best for me because nobody there would mistake me for English. Rufus doesn't matter, he's my old retainer, he's gone by the nickname so long that he's well-nigh forgotten any else. I, though – Cadoc ap Rhys.'

'I've never heard of those lands.'

'No,' he sighed, 'I didn't expect you had.'

'I've a feeling you've traveled more than you just said.'

'I have wandered quite widely, true.'

'I envy you,' burst from her. 'Oh, I envy you!'

He raised his brows. 'What? It's a hard life, often dangerous, always lonely.'

'But free. Your own master. If I could fare like you –' Her eyes stung. She swallowed hard and tried to lay hold on the tears before they broke loose.

Turned grave, he shook his head in his turn. 'You do not know what becomes of camp followers, Svoboda Volodarovna. I do.'

Understanding washed over her. 'Y-you are a lonely man, Cadoc,' she said around a thickness. 'Why?'

'Make the best of that life you have,' he counselled. 'Each in our own way, we are all of us trapped in ours.'

'You too.' Your strength must fade, your pride shall crumble, in one more blink of time you will go down into the earth and soon after that your very name will be forgotten, dust on the wind.

He winced. 'Yes. Thus it seems.'

'I'll remember you!' she cried.

'What?'

'I – Nothing, nothing. I am shaken and weary and, and I think a little drunk.'

'Do you wish to sleep till your clothes are ready? I'll stay quiet – Svoboda, you weep.' Cadoc came around the table, stooped over her, laid an arm across her shoulders.

'Forgive me, I'm being weak and, and foolish. Not myself, please believe me, not myself.'

'No, certainly not, dear venturer. I know how you feel.' His lips brushed her hair. Blindly she turned her head toward him, and knew he would kiss her. It was gentle. Her tears made it taste like the sea.

'I am an honorable man, of sorts,' he said against her cheek. How warm were his breath, his body. 'I'd not force you to anything.'

'You need not,' she heard through the great soft thunders.

'I depart shortly after dawn, Svoboda, and your marriage awaits you.'

She gripped him hard, nails into his coat. 'Three husbands I have had already,' she told him, 'and sometimes, at the lakeside, the spring feast of Kupala – Oh, yes, Ca-doc.'

For an instant she saw that she had let out too much. Now she must some-how answer his questions, with her head awhirl … But he gave her his hand, it was as if he lifted her to her feet, and went by her side to a bed.

Thereafter she was again in a dream. Her wanting him had come over her as a torrent. If she foresaw anything whatsoever, it was a slaking. He was not a big man, but he might be strong, he might take a while to finish, long enough, and then she could topple into sleep. Instead, he took the robe from her through a time that swayed on and on, and guided her to help him off with his garb, always his fingers and his mouth knowing what to do, what to evoke; and though the bed was narrow, when he brought her down upon it he still stroked and touched and kissed until she wailed for him to open the heavens and unloose the suns.

Afterward they caressed, laughed, japed, spread two straw ticks on the floor that they might have real room to move about, played, loved, his head rested between her breasts, she urged him anew and yet anew, he swore he had never known the match to her and the believing of him was a tall fire.

The glass in the window grayed. Candles had burned down to stubs. The smoke of them drifted bitter through a chill that she finally began to feel.

'I must see you to your lodging,' he said in her arms.

'Oh, not at once,' she begged.

'The fleet leaves soon. And you have your own world to meet. First you will need rest, Svoboda, dear.'

'I am weary as if I'd plowed ten fields,' she murmured. A giggle. 'But you did the plowing. You rascal, I'm hardly able to walk.' She nuzzled the silky beard. 'Thank you, thank you.'

'I'll sleep soundly on the ship, myself. Afterward I'll wake and remember you. And long for you, Svoboda. But that is the price, I suppose.'

'If only –'

'I told you, the trade I follow these days is a bad one for a woman.'

'You come home from it after the season, don't you?'

He sat up. His face seemed as gray as the light. 'I have no home any more. I dare not. You couldn't understand. Come, we must hurry, but we needn't ruin this that we've had.'

Dumbly, she waited while he dressed and went to get her clothes from Rufus. The thought trickled through her: He's right, the thing is impossible, or at least it would be too brief and become too full of pain. He does not know, however, why he is right.

Her garments were wet after washing. They hung clammily. Well, with luck she could get to her room unnoticed. 'I wish I could give you the silk robe,' Cadoc said. 'If you can explain it away – No?' Maybe he would think of her when it passed to some girl somewhere else. 'I also wish I could feed you. We're under time's whip, you and I. Come.' Yes, she was hungry, faint with hunger and weariness and ache. That was good. It pulled her spirit back down to where she belonged.

Fog hazed and hushed the streets. The sun had belike risen, but barely, in the east that Svoboda had forsaken. She walked hand in hand with Cadoc. Among the Rusi, that simply meant friendship. Nobody outside would know when the clasp tightened. Few people were around thus far, anyhow. From a passerby Cadoc learned the way to Olga's dwelling.

They stopped before it. 'Fare gladly, Svoboda,' he said.

'And you,' was all she could answer.

'I will remember you –' his smile twisted – 'more than is wise.'

'I will forever remember you, Cadoc,' she said.

He took both her hands in his, bowed above them, straightened, let her go, turned, and walked off. Soon he was lost in the fog.

'Forever,' she said into the emptiness.

A while she remained standing. The sky overhead was clear, brightening to blue. A falcon, early aloft, caught the light of the hidden sun on his wings.

Maybe it's best that this was what it was and nothing more, she thought. A moment snatched free, for me to keep beyond the reach of the years.

Three husbands have I buried, and I think that was release, to pray them goodbye and see them shoveled under, for by then they had wasted and withered and were no longer the men who proudly stood beside me at the weddings. And Rostislav had peered at me, wondered, accused, beaten me when he got drunk … No, burying my children, that was the worst. Not so much the small ones, they die and die and you have no time to know them except as a brightness that goes by. Even my first grandchild, he was small. But Svetlana, now, she was a woman, a wife, it was my great-grandchild who killed her in the birthing.

At least that was the final sorrow. The villagers, yes, my living children, they could no longer endure this thing that is I, that never grows decently old. They fear me, therefore they hate me. And I could no longer endure, either. I might have welcomed the day when they came with axes and clubs to make an end of the thing.

Gleb Ilyev, ugly, greedy little Gleb – he has the manhood to see past strangeness, see the woman who is neither child of the gods nor creature of Satan but is the most lost and bewildered of any. I wish I could reward Gleb with better than silver. Well, I wish for much that cannot be.

Through him, I have found how to stay alive. I will be the best wife to Igor Olegev that I am able. But as the years pass, I will befriend somebody else like Gleb, and when the time comes, he will find a new place, a new beginning for me. The widow of *one* man can marry again, in some town or on some farm well distant, and nobody she knew will think it is altogether outlandish, and nobody she comes to know will think of questions she dares not answer. Of course, the children must be left provided for, such as are not grown. I will be the best mother that I am able.

A smile winged by.

Who can tell? A few husbands of mine may even be like Cadoc.

Her dress clung and dripped. She felt how cold she was, shivered, and walked slowly to the door of the house.

VII

THE SAME KIND

1

Habit dies hard, and then from time to time will rise from its grave. 'What do you really know about this drab, Lugo?' asked Rufus. He spoke in Latin such as had not been heard for centuries, even among churchmen of the West.

Nor had Cadoc used that name for a span longer yet. He replied in Greek: 'Practice your living languages more. Get your terminology right. The word you used scarcely fits the most fashionable and expensive courtesan in Constantinople.'

'A whore be a whore,' said Rufus stubbornly, though he did change to the modern tongue of the Empire. 'You been, uh, in-vest-igating her, talking with people, sounding 'em out, damn near since we got here. Weeks. And me left to twiddle my thumb.' He glanced down at the stump of his right wrist. 'When're we going to *do* something?'

'Perhaps quite soon,' Cadoc answered. 'Or perhaps not. It depends on what further I can learn about the lovely Athenais, if anything. And on much else, to be sure. I am not only overdue for a change of identity, we are both overdue for a change of occupation. The Rus trade is spinning faster and faster toward ruin.'

'Yah, yah, you've said that plenty often. I've seen for myself. But what about this woman? You haven't told me nothing about her.'

'That is because patience in disappointment is not among your excellences.' Cadoc paced to the single window and stared out. It stood open on summer air, odors of smoke and tar and dung and hinted fragrances, noise of wheels and hoofs and feet and voices. From this third-floor inn room the view swept over roofs, streets, the city wall, the gate and harbor of the Kontoskalion. Masts raked upward from the docks. Beyond glittered the Sea of Marmora. Craft danced on its blueness, everything from bumboats shaped like basins to a freighter under sail and a naval dromond with oars in parade-ground step. It was hard to imagine, to feel, the shadow under which all this lay.

Cadoc clasped his hands behind his back. 'However, I may as well inform you now,' he said. 'Today I have hopes that I'll reach the end of the trail, or find that it was a false scent. It's been maddeningly vague, as you'd expect. So-and-so tells me that somebody else once told him this-and-that. With difficulty, because he's moved, I track down Kyrios Somebody Else to verify it, and to the best of his dim recollection that is not quite what he told So-and-so, but from a third party he did once hear – Ah, well.

'Basically, "Athenais" is the latest name the lady has taken. No surprise there. Name changes are quite usual in her profession; and of course she prefers to obscure her origins, the fact that she was not always the darling of the city. I've established that, earlier, she worked as Zoë in one of the better brothels over in Galata; and I am practically certain that before then she was on this side of the Golden Horn, in the Phanar quarter, as a less elegant girl calling herself Eudoxia. Beyond that, the information is slight and unreliable. Too many people have died or otherwise disappeared.

'The pattern has been the same, though, an outwardly affable but actually secretive woman who avoids pimps – at worst, formerly, she paid off as necessary – and spends no more on fanciments than she must. Instead, she saves – invests, I suspect – with an eye to moving up another rung on the ladder. Now she is independent, even powerful, what with her connections and the things she doubtless knows. And –' Despite the dull houndwork that lay behind, despite the coolness he kept in his tone, a tingle went along Cadoc's backbone, out to his scalp and fingertips. 'The trail reaches at least thirty years into the past, Rufus. It may well be fifty or more years long. Always she is youthful, always she is beautiful.'

'I knew what you was after,' said the redbeard, unwontedly low, 'but I'd stopped thinking you'd ever find it.'

'I too, almost. Seven centuries since I came on you, and nobody before and nobody afterward, for all my searching. Yes, hope wears thin. Maybe today, at last –' Cadoc shook himself, turned about, and laughed. 'I'm soon due at her place. I dare not tell you what a few hours there cost!'

'Have a care,' Rufus grunted. 'A whore be a whore. I go find me a cheap 'un, ha?'

Impulsively, Cadoc reached into his pouch and gave him a fistful of silver miliarisions. 'Add this to your own coins and enjoy yourself, old fellow. A shame that the Hippodrome isn't open just now, but you must know several odeions where the performances are bawdy enough for your less elevated moments. Just don't talk too loosely.'

'You taught me that, you did. Have fun. I hope she turns out to be what you want, master. I'll use a bit o' the money to buy you a good-luck spell.' That seemed to be about as much as the prospect could move Rufus' stolidity. But then, Cadoc thought, he lacks the wit to understand what it will mean to find another immortal – a woman. At least, immediately; it may dawn on him later.

I don't suppose I quite understand it yet myself.

Rufus went out. Cadoc took an embroidered mantle off its hanger and fitted it over the fine linen sakkos and bejeweled dalmatic that enrobed him. On his feet were curly-toed shoes from far Cordova. Even for an afternoon appointment, one went to Athenais appropriately dressed.

He had already gotten his hair cut short and his beard shaven off. Fluent in Greek and familiar, after much prowling, with the byways of the city, he could pass for Byzantine. Not that he would try to do so unnecessarily. It wasn't worth the risk. Rus merchants were supposed to stay in the St Mamo suburb on the Galata side of the Horn, crossing the bridge to the Blachernae Gate by day and returning at evening. He was still listed among them. It had taken a substantial bribe as well as persuasive chatter to get permission to take lodging here. He was not actually a Rus, he told the officials, and he was ready to retire from the trade. Both statements were true. He had gone on, mendaciously but persuasively, about certain new arrangements he had in mind, which would be to the profit of local magnates as well as himself. In the course of generations, given an innate talent for it, one learns how to convince. Thus he won freedom to pursue his inquiries with maximum efficiency.

The streets throbbed and clamored with traffic. He followed their steepnesses to the Mesè, the avenue that, branching, ran from end to end of the city. Down its width on his right he spied the column that upbore Justinian's equestrian statue in the Forum of Constantine and beyond it, just glimpsed, the walls of the Imperial palace grounds, senate house, law courts, Hippodrome; the domes of Hagia Sophia; the gardens and shining buildings on the Acropolis: glories raised through lifetime after transient lifetime.

He turned left. Brilliance flowed with him and glowed from the arcades that lined the thoroughfare. Plainness was nearly lost in it, workmen, porters, carters, farmers in from the countryside, priests of the lower orders. Even hawkers and strolling entertainers flaunted fantastic colors as they shouted what wonders they offered; even slaves wore the liveries of great households. A nobleman passed by in his palanquin, young dandies whooped in a wineshop, a troop of guardsmen tramped with mail agleam, a cavalry officer and his attendant cataphracts cantered haughtily behind a runner who shouted and elbowed people aside, banners flew, cloaks and scarfs billowed in a brisk wind off the sea, New Rome seemed immortally young. Religion yielding to commerce and diplomacy, foreigners were plentiful, be they suave Muslim Syrians, boorish Catholic Normans, or from lands farther and stranger yet. Cadoc was content to vanish into the human flood.

At the Forum of Theodosius he crossed over to its northern corner, ignoring the sellers who cried their wares and the beggars who cried their need. Where the Aqueduct of Valens overlooked the roof-decked hollow it spanned, he paused for a moment's breath. The view swept before him, down to rampart and battlements, the Gate of the Drungarii, the Golden Horn full of its own tarings, and across those waters hills green with growth, white with the houses of Pera and Galata. Gulls yonder made a living snowstorm. You can tell a rich harbor by its gulls, thought Cadoc. How much longer will this many fly and mew here?

He thrust sadness from him and continued north, downhill, until he found the house he wanted. Outwardly it was an unpretentious three-story building, hemmed in by its neighbors, the façade rosy-plastered. But that was ample for one woman, her servants, and the revelries over which she presided.

A bronze knocker was made in the form of a scallop shell. Cadoc's heart skipped step. Had she recalled that this Western Christian emblem of a pilgrim once belonged to Ashtoreth? The fingers with which he rattled it were damp.

The door opened and he confronted a huge black man in Asian-like shirt and trousers – an entire male, likelier hireling than slave, well able to remove anyone whom his employer found objectionable. 'Christ be with you, kyrie. May I ask what is your desire?'

'My name is Cadoc ap Rhys. The lady Athenais awaits me.' The visitor handed over a piece of parchment bearing the identification, given him when he paid the price to her broker. That woman had had to decide first that he was suitably refined, and still she had told him no time was available for a week. Cadoc slipped the doorman a golden bezant – a little extravagant, perhaps, but impressiveness might help his chances.

It certainly got him deference. In a twittering cloud of pretty girls and two eunuchs he passed through an anteroom richly furnished, its walls ornamented with discreetly erotic scenes, up a grand staircase to the outer chamber of a suite. This was hung in red velvet above a floral Oriental carpet. Chairs flanked a table of inlaid ebony whereon stood a flagon of wine, figured glass goblets, plates of cakes, dates, oranges. Light fell dim through small windows, but candles burned in multiple holders. Sweetness wafted from a golden censer. A lark dwelt in a silver cage. Here Athenais was.

She put aside the harp she had been strumming. 'Welcome, Kyrie Cadoc from afar.' Her voice was low, scarcely less musical than the strings had been – carefully trained. 'Twice welcome, bearing news of marvels, like a fresh breeze.'

He bowed. 'My lady is too gracious to a poor wanderer.'

Meanwhile, keenly as if she were an enemy, he assessed her. She sat on a couch, displaying herself against its white-and-gold back, in a gown that enhanced rather than revealed. Her jewelry was a bracelet, a pendant, and three rings, small but exquisite. It was her person, not her wealth, and her spirit more than her person, that she had the intelligence to emphasize. Her figure was superb in a voluptuous Eastern fashion, but he judged that suppleness and strength underlay it. Her face he would simply have called handsome: broad, straight-nosed, full-lipped, eyes hazel beneath arching brows, blue-black hair piled thick around the tawny complexion. It was not looks that had brought her to this house, it was knowledge, skill, perception, the harvest of – how long an experience?

Her laugh chimed. 'No poor man enters here! Come, be seated, take refreshment. Let us get to know each other.'

She never rushed to the bedroom, he had heard, unless a patron insisted, and such a one was seldom allowed back. Conversation and flirtation beforehand were part of a delight that was said to have a climax unrivalled.

'Marvels have I seen,' Cadoc declared, 'but the finest of them today.' He let a servant remove his upper garment and sat down beside her. A girl knelt to fill their glasses. At a tiny gesture from Athenais, all attendants bowed out.

She gave him a subtle flutter of lashes. 'Certain men of Britannia are more polished than news of it led me to expect,' she murmured. 'Have you come directly from there?' He observed the sharpness of the demure glance and knew she was taking his measure. If he wanted a woman who had more in her head than a mouth, that was what she would provide.

Therefore –

His pulse stammered. The self-control of centuries underlay the calm wherewith he regarded her, took a sip of the estimable wine, and smiled. 'No,' he said, 'I have not been in Britannia, or England and Wales as they call it nowadays, for a rather long time. But then, though I told your ancilla that is my country when she asked, I am not really a native of it. Or of anywhere else, any longer. On my last visit here I heard rumors about you. They caused me to return as soon as possible.'

She half shaped a reply, aborted it, and sat cat-watchful, too wise to exclaim, 'Flatterer!'

He calculated his grin. 'I daresay your ... callers ... number some with various peculiarities. You gratify them or not according to your inclination. It must have been a cruel struggle to win this independence. Well, then, will you indulge my whim? It is perfectly harmless. I only wish to talk for a short span. I would like to tell you a story. You may find it amusing. That is all. May I?'

She failed to quite hide her tautness. 'I have heard many stories, kyrie. Do continue.'

He leaned back and let the words flow easily while he looked before him, observing her from the corner of an eye. 'Call it the kind of yarn that sailors spin during calm watches or in taverns ashore. It concerns a mariner, though afterward he did numerous different things. He thought himself an ordinary man of his people. So did everybody else. But bit by bit, year by year, they noticed something very odd about him. He never fell sick and he never grew old. His wife aged and finally died, his children turned gray and then white-haired, their children begot and raised children and likewise fell prey to time, but everything in this man since the third decade of his life stayed change-less. Was that not remarkable?'

He had her, he saw, and exulted. Her gaze was utterly intent.

'At first it seemed he might be blessed of the gods. Yet he showed no other special powers, nor did he do any special deeds. Though he made costly sac-rifices and later, approaching despair, consulted costly magicians, to him came no revelation, nor any solace when those he loved went down into death. Meanwhile the slow growth of awe among the people had, with equal slowness, become envy, then fear, then hatred. What had he done to be thus condemned, or what had he sold to be thus spared? What *was* he, sorcerer, demon, walking corpse, what? He barely evaded attempts on his life. Finally the authorities moved to investigate him and he fled, for he suspected they would question him under torture and put him to death. He knew he could be wounded, although he recovered fast, and felt sure that the worst injuries would prove as fatal to him as to anybody else. Despite his loneliness, he kept a young man's desire for life and the savoring of it.

'For hundreds and hundreds of years he was a rover on the face of the earth. Often he let his yearnings overcome him and settled down somewhere, married, raised a family, lived as mortals do. But always he must lose them, and after a single common lifetime disappear. Between whiles, which was mostly, he plied trades where a man can come and go little remarked. His old seamanship was among these, and it took him widely across the world. Ever he sought for more like himself. Was he unique in the whole creation? Or was his kind simply very rare? Those whom misfortune or malice did not destroy early on, they doubtless learned to stay hidden as he had learned. But if this be the case, how was he to find them, or they him?

'And if his was a hard and precarious lot, how much worse must it be for a woman? What could she do? Surely none but the strongest and cleverest survived. How might they?

'Does that conundrum interest my lady?'

He drank of his wine, for whatever tranquility might lie within it. She stared beyond him. Silence lengthened.

At last she drew breath, brought her look back to engage his, and said slowly, 'That is a curious tale indeed, Kyrie Cadoc.'

'A tale only, of course, a fantasy for your amusement. I do not care to be locked up as a madman.'

'I understand.' A smile ghosted across her countenance. 'Pray continue. Did this undying man ever come upon any others?'

'That remains to be told, my lady.'

She nodded. 'I see. But say more about him. He's still a shadow to me. Where was he born, and when?'

'Let us imagine it was in ancient Tyre. He was a boy when King Hiram aided King Solomon to build the Temple in Jerusalem.'

She gasped. 'Oh, long ago!'

'About two thousand years, I believe. He lost count, and later when he tried to consult the records they were fragmentary and in disagreement. No matter.'

'Did he – meet the Savior?' she whispered.

He sighed and shook his head. 'No, he was elsewhere at that time. He did see many gods come and go. And kings, nations, histories. Perforce he lived among them, under names of their kind, while they endured and until they perished. Names he lost track of, like years. He was Hanno and Ithobaal and Snefru and Phaon and Shlomo and Rashid and Gobor and Flavius Lugo and, oh, more than he can remember.'

She sat straight, as if ready to spring, whether from him or at him. Low in her throat, she asked, 'Might Cadoc be among those names?'

He kept seated, leaned back, but eyes now full upon hers. 'It might,' he answered, 'even as a lady might have called herself Zoë, and before that Eudoxia, and before that – names which are perhaps still discoverable.'

A shudder passed through her. 'What do you want of me?'

He set his glass down, most carefully, smiled, spread his hands, palms up, and told her in his softest voice, 'Whatever you choose to give. It may be nothing. How can I compel you, supposing that were my desire, which it is not? If you dislike harmless lunatics, you need never see or hear from me again.'

'What ... are you ... prepared to offer?'

'Shared and lasting faith. Help, counsel, protection, an end of loneliness. I've learned a good deal about surviving, and manage to prosper most of the time, and have my refuges and my hoards against the evil days. At the moment I command modest wealth. More important, I stay true to my friends and would rather be a woman's lover than her overlord. Who knows but what the children of two immortals will themselves prove deathless?'

She studied him a while. 'But you always hold something back, don't you?'

'A Phoenician habit, which a rootless life has strengthened. I could unlearn it.'

'It was never my way,' she breathed, and came to him.

2

They lounged against pillows at the headboard of the huge bed. Talk grew between them like a blossoming plant in spring. Now and then a hand stroked across flesh gone cool again, but those were gentle caresses. A languor possessed them, as if part of the lingering odors of incense and love. Their minds roused first. The words were calm, the tone tender.

'Four hundred years ago I was Aliyat in Palmyra,' she said. 'And you, in your ancient Phoenicia?'

'My birthname was Hanno,' he answered. 'I used it the oftenest, afterward, till it died out of every language.'

'What adventures you must have had.'

'And you.'

She winced. 'I would rather not speak of that.'

'Are you ashamed?' He laid a finger under her chin and brought her face around toward his. 'I would not be,' he said gravely. 'I *am* not. We have survived, you and I, by whatever means were necessary. That's now behind us. Let it drift into darkness with the wreckage of Babylon. We belong to our future.'

'You ... do not ... find me sinful?'

He laughed a bit. 'I suspect that if we both grew quite candid about our pasts, you'd be the one shocked.'

'Nor do you fear God's curse?'

'I have learned much in two thousand years, but nothing about any gods, except that they too arise, change, age, and die. Whatever there is beyond the universe, if anything, I doubt it concerns itself with us.'

Tears trembled on her lashes. 'You are strong. You are kind.' She nestled close. 'Tell me of yourself.'

'That would take a while. I'd grow thirsty.'

She reached for a bell on an end table and rang it. 'That we can do something about,' she said with a flash of smile. 'You're right, however. We have the whole future wherein to explore our past. Tell me first of Cadoc. I do need to understand him, that we may lay our plans.'

'Well, it began when Old Rome departed from Britannia – No, wait, I forgot, in all this joy. First I should tell you about Rufus.'

A maidservant entered. She dipped her glance, otherwise seemed unperturbed by the two naked bodies. Athenais ordered the wine and refreshments brought in from the anteroom. While this was done, Cadoc marshalled his thoughts. When they were alone, he described his companion.

'Poor Rufus,' she sighed. 'How envious he will be.'

'Oh, I expect not,' Cadoc replied. 'He's grown used to being my subordinate. In return, I do his thinking for him. Give him adequate food, drink, and swiving, and he's content.'

'Then he has been no balm for your aloneness,' she said softly.

'Not much. But I owe my life to him, several times over, and therefore this day's magnificence.'

'Glib scoundrel.' She kissed him. He buried his visage in her fragrant hair until she guided him to a glassful, a sweet cake, and sober discourse.

'– the western Britons preserved some vestige of civilization. Yes, I frequently thought of making my way here, where I knew the Empire continued.

But for a long time, the likelihood of arriving with any money, or arriving at all, was slight. Meanwhile life among the Britons was not too bad. I had come to know them. It was easy to move among identities and to stay reasonably well-off. I could wait for the English, the Franks, the Northmen to acquire milder ways, for civilization to be reborn throughout Europe. After that, as I've mentioned, the Rus trade route let me make a good living and meet a variety of people, both along it and down here in the Mediterranean world. You understand that that seemed my only hope of finding anyone else like me. Surely you've cherished the same hope, Athenais – Aliyat.'

He could barely hear: 'Until it grew too painful.'

He kissed her cheek, and she brought her lips to his, and presently she crooned, 'It has ended. You have found me. I keep striving to believe that this is real.'

'It is, and we'll keep it so.'

With that practicality which bespoke her intelligence, she asked, 'What do you propose we do?'

'Well,' he said, 'it was about time anyhow for me to finish with Cadoc. He's been in sight longer than he should have been; some old acquaintances must be starting to wonder. Besides, since the Norman duke made himself king of England, more and more young English, ill content, have been coming south to join the Emperor's Varangian Guard. Those who happened to hear of Cadoc would know how unlikely it is that a Welshman be a trader of his sort.

'Worse, when the Rus lord Yaroslav died his realm was divided among his sons, and they are now falling out with each other. The barbarian plainsmen take advantage. The routes grow dangerous. Fresh Rus attacks on Constantinople are quite conceivable, and could hurt the trade even more. I well remember what difficulties previous forays caused.

'So, let Athenais and Cadoc retire from their businesses, move away, and drop out of touch with everybody they knew. First, naturally, Aliyat and Hanno will have liquidated their possessions.'

She frowned. 'You talk as if you meant to leave Constantinople. Must we? It is the queen of the world.'

'It will not remain that,' he told her grimly.

She gave him a startled glance.

'Think,' he said. 'The Normans have taken the last Imperial outpost in Italy. The Saracens hold everything south of there from Spain through Syria. They have not been totally hostile of late. However – the Imperial defeat at Manzikert last year was more than a military disaster that led to an abrupt change of Emperors. The Turks had already taken Armenia from you, remember. Now Anatolia lies open to them. It will be touch and go whether the Empire can hold the Ionian littoral against them. Meanwhile the Balkan provinces chafe and the Normans venture east. Here at home, commerce shrinks, poverty and unrest grow, corruption at court vies for mastery with incompetence. Oh, I daresay the catastrophe will be a while in coming full upon New Rome. But let us get out well ahead of it.'

'Where? Is any place safe and, and decent?'

'Well, certain of the Muslim capitals are brilliant. Far eastward, I hear, an emperor reigns over a realm vast, peaceful, and glorious. But those are alien folk; the ways to them are long and beset. Western Europe would be easier, but it's still turbulent and backward. Also, since the churches openly split apart, life there has been hard for people from Orthodox countries. We'd have to make a show of conversion to Catholicism, and we'd best avoid conspicuousness like that. No, on the whole I'd say we should stay within the Roman Empire for another century or two. In Greece, nobody knows us.'

'Greece? Hasn't it gone barbarian?'

'Not quite. There's a heavy population of Slavs in the north and Vlachs in Thessaly, while the Normans are plaguing the Aegean Sea. But such cities as Thebes and Corinth remain well off, well defended. A beautiful country, full of memories. We can be happy there.'

Cadoc raised his brows. 'But haven't you given thought to this yourself?' he went on. 'You could only have continued as you are for another ten years at best. Then you'd have had to withdraw, before men noticed that you don't grow old. And as much in the public eye as you've been, you could scarcely stay on in these parts.'

'True.' Athenais smiled. 'I meant to announce I'd had a change of heart, repented my wickedness, and would retire afar to a life of poverty, prayer, and good works. I've already made arrangements for the quick, quiet transport of my hoard – against any sudden need to escape. After all, that has been my life, to drop from one place and start afresh in another.'

He grimaced. 'Always like this?'

'Need forces me,' she answered sadly. 'I'm not fit by nature to be a nun, a she-hermit, any such unworldly being. I often call myself a well-to-do widow, but at last the money is spent, unless some upheaval – war, sack, plague, whatever – brings ruin first. A woman cannot very well invest her money like a man. Whatever pulls me down, usually I must begin again among the lowliest and ... work and save and connive to become better off.'

His smile was rueful. 'Not unlike my life.'

'A man has more choices.' She paused. 'I do study things beforehand. I agree, on balance Corinth will be best for us.'

'What?' he exclaimed, sitting straight in his astonishment. 'You let me rattle on and on about what you perfectly well knew?'

'Men must show forth their cleverness.'

Cadoc whooped laughter. 'Superb! A girl who can lead me, *me*, by the nose like that is the girl I can stay with forever.'

He sobered: 'But now we'll make the move as soon as may be. At once, if I had my wish. Out of this … filth, to the first true home we've either of us had since –'

She laid fingers across his tips. 'Hush, beloved,' she said low. 'If only that could be. But we can't simply disappear.'

'Why not?'

She sighed. 'It would rouse too much heed. A search for me, at least. There are men, highly placed men, who care for me, who'd be afraid I'd met with foul play. If then we were tracked down – No.' A small fist clenched. 'We must go on with our pretenses. For another month, perhaps, while I prepare the ground with talk of, oh, making a pilgrimage, something like that.'

A little while passed before he could say, 'Well, a month, set against centuries.'

'For me, the longest month I ever knew. But we'll see each other during it, often, won't we? Say we will!'

'Of course.'

'I will hate making you pay, but you can see I must. Never mind, the money will be ours once we are free.'

'Hm, we do need to lay plans, make arrangements.'

'Let that wait till next time. This while we have today is so short. Then I must make ready for the next man.'

He bit his lip. 'You cannot tell him you've fallen sick?'

'I'd best not. He's among the most important of them all; his good will can spell the difference between life and death. Bardas Manasses, a manglabites on the staff of the Archestrategos.'

'Yes, someone that high in the military, yes, I understand.'

'Oh, my dearest, inwardly you bleed.' Athenais embraced him. 'Stop. Forget everything but the two of us. We still have an hour in Paradise.'

She was wholly as knowing, as endlessly various and arousing, as men said.

3

A miniature procession crossed the bridge over the Horn and approached the Blachernae Gate. They were four Rusi, two Northmen, and a couple in the lead who were neither. The Rusi carried a chest that was plainly heavy, suspended on two poles. The Northmen were off-duty members of the Varangian Guard, helmed and mailed, axes on their shoulders. Though it was clear that they were earning some extra pay by shepherding a valuable freight, it was also clear that this was with official permission, and the sentries waved the party through.

They went on by streets under the city wall. Heights soared above them to battlements and heaven. The morning was yet young and shadow lay deep, almost chill after the brightness on the water. Mansions of the wealthy fell behind and the men entered the humbler, busier Phanar quarter.

'This be muckwit,' grumbled Rufus in Latin. 'You've even sold your ship, haven't you? At a loss, I'll bet, so fast you got rid of everything.'

'Turned it into gold, gems, portable wealth,' Cadoc corrected merrily. He used the same language. While he had no reason to distrust their escort, caution was alloyed with his spirit. 'We're leaving in another pair of weeks, or had you forgotten?'

'Meanwhile, though –'

'Meanwhile it'll be stored safely, secretly, where we can claim it at any hour of the day or night and no beforehand notice. You've been too much sulking when you weren't off bousing, old fellow. Have you never listened to me? Aliyat arranged this.'

'What'd she tell their high and mightinesses, to make the way so smooth for us?'

Cadoc grinned. 'That I let slip to her what a glorious deal I stand to make with certain other high and mightinesses – a deal which these men can have a slice of if they help me. Women, too, can learn how to cope with the world.'

Rufus grunted.

The building in which Petros Simonides, jeweler, lived and had his shop was unprepossessing. However, Cadoc had long had some knowledge of what trade went through it, besides the owner's overt business. Several members of the Imperial court found it sufficiently useful that the authorities turned a blind eye. Petros received his visitors jovially. A pair of toughs whom he called nephews, though they resembled him not in the least, helped bring the chest to the cellar and stow it behind a false panel. Money passed. Cadoc declined hospitality on the grounds of haste and led his own followers back to the street.

'Well, Arnulf, Sviatopolk, all of you, my thanks,' he said. 'You may go where you like now. You will remember your orders about keeping silence. That need not keep you from drinking my health and fortune.' He dispensed a second purseful. The sailors and soldiers departed gleefully.

'You didn't think Petros' food and wine be good?' asked Rufus.

'They doubtless are,' said Cadoc, 'but I really have need to hurry. Athenais keeps this whole afternoon for me, and first I want to get myself well prepared at the baths.'

'Huh! Like this whole while since you met her. Never seen you lovesick before. You could as well be fifteen.'

'I feel reborn,' said Cadoc softly. His vision dwelt on distances beyond the bustle and narrowness around. 'You will too, when we've found you your true wife.'

'With my luck, she'll be a sow.'

245

Cadoc laughed, clapped Rufus on the back, and slipped a bezant into his single palm. 'Go drown that gloom of yours. Or better yet, work it off with a lively wench.'

'Thanks.' Rufus showed no change of mood. 'You do toss money these days.'

'A strange thing about pure joy,' Cadoc murmured. 'One wants to share it.'

He sauntered off, whistling. Rufus stood with hunched shoulders and stared after him.

4

Stars and a gibbous moon gave light enough. The streets, gone mostly quiet, were swept clean. Occasionally a patrol marched by, lantern-glow shimmering on metal, embodiment of that power which held the city at peace. A man could walk easy.

Cadoc drank deep of the night air. Heat had yielded to mildness, and smoke, dust, stenches, pungencies lain down to rest. As he neared the Kontoskalion, he caught a ghost of tar on the breeze, and smiled. How smells could rouse memories. A galley lay at the Egyptian Harbor of Sor, weathered and salt-streaked by fabulous seas, and his father towered over him, holding his hand … He raised that same hand to his nostrils. The hair on it tickled his lip. A scent like jasmine, Aliyat's perfume, and was there still some of her own sweetness? That had been such a long farewell kiss.

And so happily weary. He chuckled. When he arrived, she told him a message had come from the great Bardas Manasses, he was unable to visit her this evening as planned, she and her dearest had that added time as a free gift of Aphrodite. 'I have discovered what immortal strength means,' she purred at the last, close against his breast.

He yawned. Sleep would be very welcome. If only it were at her side – But her servants already saw how she favored this foreigner. Best not give them further cause for wonderment. Gossip might reach the wrong ears.

Soon, though, soon!

Abruptly darkness deepened. He had turned into a lesser street near the harbor and his lodging. Brick walls hulked on either side, leaving just a strip of sky overhead. He slowed, careful lest he stumble on something. Silence had also grown thick. Were those footfalls behind him? It crossed his mind that he had several times glimpsed the same figure in a hooded cloak. Bound the same way by mere chance?

Light gleamed, a lantern uncovered in an alley as he passed it. For an instant he was dazzled. 'That's him!' struck through. Three men came out of the gut into the street. A sword slipped free.

Cadoc sprang backward. The men deployed, right, left, in front. They had him boxed, up against the opposite wall.

His knife jumped forth. Two of the attackers were armed like him. He wasted no breath in protest or scream for help. If he couldn't save himself, he'd be dead in minutes. His left hand ripped his mantle loose from its brooch.

The swordsman swung back to strike. The lantern, set down at the alley mouth, made him a featureless piece of night, but Cadoc saw light ripple along his hip. He was mail-clad. The steel whirred. Cadoc swayed aside. He snapped the mantle at the unseen face. It drew a curse and tangled the weapon. Cadoc leaped right. He hoped to dodge past the foeman there. That wight was too skillful. His bulk stepped in the way. His dagger thrust. Cadoc would have taken it in the belly, had he possessed less than immortal vigor. He parried with his own knife and retreated.

Bricks gritted against his shoulder blades. He was trapped anyhow. He showed teeth and feinted, side to side. The daggermen prowled beyond his reach. The swordsman prepared to hew afresh.

Sandals thudded on stones. Light glimmered on a coppery beard. Rufus' hook caught the swordsman's throat. It went in. Rufus worked it savagely. The man dropped his blade, clawed at the shaft, went to his knees. He croaked through the blood.

Cadoc scrambled, snatched up the sword, bounced back erect. He was no grand master of this weapon, but he had tried to acquire every fighting art that the centuries brought. A knifeman scuttered clear. Cadoc whirled in time to smite the second, who was nearly at his back. The blade struck an arm. Through the heavy impact, Cadoc thought he felt bone give. The man shrieked, stumbled, and fled.

Snarling, Rufus pulled his hook out and went for the first stabber. That one vanished too, down the street and into night. Rufus halted. He turned about. 'You hurt?' he panted.

'No.' Cadoc was as breathless. His heart banged. Yet his mind had gone wholly cold and clear, like ice afloat in the sea off Thule. He glanced at the mailed man, who writhed and moaned and bubbled blood. 'Let's go ... before somebody ... comes.' He discarded the telltale sword.

'To the inn?'

'No.' Cadoc trotted away. His wind returned to him, his pulse slowed. 'They knew me. Therefore they knew where to wait and must know where I'm staying. Whoever sent them will want to try again.'

'I guessed it might be a good idea to tail after and keep an eye on you. That be a pile o' treasure you left with that Phanariot son of a pig.'

'I shouldn't pride myself on my wits,' said Cadoc bleakly. 'You showed a barrelful more than I did.'

'Haw, you be in love. Worse'n drunk. Where should we go? I s'pose the main streets be safe. Maybe we can wake 'em at another inn. I've still got money on me, if you don't.'

Cadoc shook his head. They had emerged on a thoroughfare, bare and dim under the moon. 'No. We'll slink about till sunrise, then mingle with people bound out of the city. Those can't have been common footpads, or even killers for hire. Armor, sword – at least one of them was an Imperial soldier.'

5

Vsevolod the Fat, who stood high among the Rus merchants, owned a house in St Mamo. It was small, since he only used it when he was at Constantinople, but furnished with barbaric opulence and, during his stays, a wanton or two. The servants were young kinsmen of his, whose loyalty could be relied on, and upstairs was a room whose existence was not obvious.

He entered it near the close of day. Gray-shot, his beard fell to the paunch that swelled his embroidered robe. A fist clutched a jug. 'I brought wine,' he greeted. 'Cheap stuff, but plenty. You will want plenty, and not care how fine it is. Here.' He shoved it toward Cadoc.

The latter rose, paying it no heed. Rufus took it instead and upended it over his mouth. He had snored for hours, while Cadoc prowled to and fro between the barren walls or stared out a window at the Golden Horn and the many-domed city beyond.

'What have you found, Vsevolod Izyaslavev?' Cadoc asked tonelessly, in the same Russian.

The merchant plumped his bottom down on the bed, which creaked. 'Bad news,' he rumbled. 'I went to the shop of Petros Simonides and met guards posted. It cost me to get an honest answer out of them, and they don't know anything anyhow. But he is arrested for interrogation, they said.' A sigh like a steppe wind. 'If that is true, if they don't let him off, there goes the best smuggling outlet I ever had. Ah, merciful saints, help a poor old man earn the bread for his little wife and darling children!'

'What about me?'

'You understand, Cadoc Rhysev? I dared not push too hard. I am not young like you. Courage has leaked out with youth and strength. Remember now the Lord, in these high days of your life, before age and woe come on you too. But I did talk with a captain in the city guard that I know. Yes, it is as you feared, they want you. He does not know just why, but spoke of a brawl near your rooming place and a man killed. Which I knew already, from you.'

'I thought as much,' said Cadoc. 'Thank you.'

Rufus lowered the jug. 'What do we do?' he grated.

'Best you stay here, where you have sought refuge,' Vsevolod replied. 'Before long I go home to Chernigov, you know. You can ride with me. The Greeks shall not know you in my ship. Maybe I disguise you as a beautiful Circassian slave girl, Rufus, ha?' He guffawed.

'We don't have the cost of our passage,' Cadoc said.

'No matter. You are my friend, my brother in Christ. I trust you to pay me back later. Thirty percent interest, agreed? And you tell me more about how you got into this trouble. That might forewarn me.'

Cadoc nodded. 'Once we're outbound, I will.'

'Good.' Vsevolod's eyes flickered between his guests. 'I thought we would have a jolly time tonight, get drunk, but you are not in the mood. Yes, a terrible sorrow, all that money gone. I will have your supper sent up. We shall meet tomorrow. God cheer your sleep.' He rose and lumbered out. The panel slid shut behind him.

Constantinople was a blue shadow above golden-shining water, against golden-red sunset. Dusk filled the room in St Mamo like smoke. Cadoc raised the wine jug, swallowed, set it down again.

'You really going to tell him?' wondered Rufus.

'Oh, no. Not the truth.' Now they spoke Latin. 'I'll invent a story that he'll believe and that will do him no harm. Something about an official who decided to get rid of me and seize my gold rather than wait for his share of the profit.'

'The swine could've been jealous o' you, too,' Rufus suggested. 'Vsevolod might know you was seeing that Athenais.'

'I have to make up a story in any case.' Cadoc's voice cracked. 'I can't understand what happened, myself.'

'Hunh? Why, plain's a wart on your thumper. The bitch put one o' her customers onto it. Shut your mouth for aye – they'd've gone after me next – and divvy your money. Maybe she's got a hold on a fellow high in the gover'ment, like something she knows about him. Or maybe he was just glad to oblige her and take his share. We was lucky and lived, but she's won. The hunt is out for us. If we want to stay alive, we won't come back for twenty-thirty years.' Rufus took the wine and glugged. 'Forget her.'

Cadoc's fist struck the wall. Plaster cracked and fell. 'How could she? How?'

'Ah, 'twas easy. You wove the snare for her.' Rufus patted Cadoc's shoulder. 'Don't feel bad. You'll swindle yourself another chest o' gold inside a ge-ne-ration.'

'Why?' Cadoc leaned against the wall, face buried in arm.

Rufus shrugged. 'A whore be a whore.'

'No, but she – immortal – I offered her –' Cadoc could not go on.

Rufus' mouth drew tight, invisibly in the gloom. 'You ought to could see. You can think better'n me when you put your mind to it. How long's she been what she be? Four hundred years, you said? Well, now, that be a lot o' men. A thousand a year? Maybe less these days, but likely more than that earlier.'

'She told me she, she takes as ... much freedom from the life ... as she can.'

249

'Shows you how fond she be of it. You know the sort o' things a lot o' fellows want from a whore. And all the times a girl gets roughed up, or robbed, or kicked out, or knocked up and left to handle that however she can – leave it on a trash heap, maybe? Four hundred years, Lugo. How d'you s'pose she feels about men? And she'd never've got to watch you growing old.'

VIII

LADY IN WAITING

Rain fell throughout the day. It was very light, soundless, and lost itself in the mists that smoked over the ground; but it closed off the world like sleep. From the verandah Okura looked across a garden whose stones and dwarf cypresses had gone dim. Water dripped off the shingles above her and filmed the whitewash of the enclosure wall. There sight ended. Though the broad south gate stood open, she barely glimpsed the avenue outside, a puddle, a leafless cherry tree. Fog had taken away the minor palace beyond. All Heian-kyo might never have been.

She shivered and turned back toward her quarters. The two or three servants whom she passed by were bulky in wadded garments. Her overlapping kimonos kept some warmth of their own and the carefully matched winter colors preserved a forlorn elegance. Breath drifted ghostly. When she entered the mansion, twilight enfolded her. It was as if cold did also. Shutters and blinds could hold off wind, but dankness seeped through and braziers availed little.

Yet comfort of a sort awaited her. Masamichi had been kind enough to allot her a sleeping platform to herself in the west pavilion. Between the sliding screens that marked the room off, a pair of chests and a go table hunched on the floor. She had a fleeting fancy that they wished they could creep under the thick tatami that covered the platform. No one else was about, so its curtains were drawn back. By the flicker of a few tapers, futon and cushions lay as black lumps.

She opened the cupboard where her koto stood. It was among the heirlooms not yet removed; its name was Cuckoo Song. How right for such a day as this, she thought: the bird that is the inconstant lover, that can bear word between the living and the dead, that embodies the ineluctable passage of time. She had in mind a melody well-liked when she was a girl. Afterward she had sometimes played it for her men – those two among her lovers whom she truly cared for – But no, she remembered that the instrument was now tuned for a winter mode.

A maid came into the section, approached, bowed, and piped, 'A messenger has arrived from the noble Lord Yasuhira, my lady.' Her manner took it for granted. The liaison between Chikuzen no Okura, lady in waiting in the household of Ex-Emperor Tsuchimikado, and Nakahari no Yasuhira, until lately a Minor Counselor to self-re-proclaimed Emperor Go-Toba, went back many years. Her own name for him was Mi-yuki, Deep Snow, because that had been his first excuse for staying the night with her.

'Bring him.' Okura's pulse quivered.

The maid left. She returned as the courier showed himself on the verandah. With the light from outside at his back, Okura could not only see through the translucent blind that he was a boy, she made out that his brocade coat was dry, his white trousers hardly sullied. Besides wearing a straw cape, he must have gone on horseback. The least of smiles touched her lips. Deep Snow would preserve appearances until the end.

Her smile died. The end was upon them both.

With proper ritual, the messenger reached that which he carried under the blind to the maid and knelt, waiting for the reply. The maid brought the letter to Okura and went out. Okura released and unrolled it. Yasuhira had used a pale green paper, tied to a willow switch. His calligraphy was less fine than erstwhile; he had grown farsighted.

'With dismay I learn that you have lost your position at court. I hoped the Ex-Emperor's consort would shelter you from the wrath that has fallen on your kinsman Chikuzen no Masamichi. What shall become of you, deprived of his protection when I too am made well-nigh helpless? This is a sorrow such as only Tu Fu could express. To my own poor attempt I add the wish that we may at least meet again soon.

'In the waning year
My sleeves, which lay over yours,
Are wet as the earth,
Though the rain on them is salt
From a sea of grief for you.'

His poetry was indeed not to be named with any line of the great Chinese master, Okura thought. Nevertheless a desire for his presence struck with astonishing suddenness. She wondered why. Whatever ardor they once felt had long since cooled to friendship; she could not recall just when they had last shared a mattress.

Well, seeing one another might strengthen them by the knowledge that each was not uniquely alone in misfortune. True, she had heard that the new military governor was confiscating thousands of estates from families who had supported the Imperial cause; but that was a mere number, as unreal as the inner life of a peasant or laborer or dog. True, this house would be taken over by a follower of the Hojo clan; but to her it had simply meant lodging given her out of a sense of duty toward common ancestors. Her dismissal was the sword-cut she actually felt. It lopped her from her world.

Still, she would shortly have left in any case. Surely Yasuhira's isolation was worse. Let them exchange what solace they could.

One must cling to form, even in answering what she recognized as an appeal. Okura knelt silent, thinking, composing, deciding, before she called for a servant. 'I will have a sprig of plum,' she instructed. That should complement her reply more subtly than cherry. From her writing materials she selected a sheet colored pearl-gray. By the time she had the ink mixed, her words stood clear before her. They were only another poem.

'Blossoms grew fragrant,
Then faded and blew away,
Leaving bitter fruit.
It fell, and on bare branches
Twig calls to twig through the wind.'

He would understand, and come.

She prepared the package with the artistry it deserved and gave it to a maid to bring to the courier. He would fare swiftly across the city, but his master's ox-drawn carriage, the only suitable conveyance for a nobleman, would take the better part of an hour. Okura had time to prepare herself.

Holding a taper close, she examined her face in a mirror. It had never been beautiful: too thin, cheekbones too strong, eyes too wide, mouth too large. However, it was properly powdered, the brows well plucked, the cosmetic brows painted just sufficiently far up the forehead, the teeth duly blackened. Her figure also left much to be desired, more bosom and less hip than should be there. It did carry its clothing well; the silks flowed gracefully when she walked with the correct gait. Her hair redeemed many faults, a jet cataract trailing on the floor.

Thereafter she ordered rice wine and cakes made ready. Her karma and Yasuhira's could not be altogether bad, for she was alone with a few of the servants precisely now. Masamichi had taken his wife, two concubines, and children to settle in with a friend who offered them temporary shelter. Their private possessions were going along for storage. He had said Okura and hers could come too, but was noticeably relieved when she told him she had her own plans for the future. Well-bred, the family had never said anything unseemly about the men who called on her and sometimes spent the night. Nonetheless, the fact that somebody who mattered was bound to overhear things would have inhibited conversation on this day when, of all days, it must be either frank or useless.

With the clepsydra taken away and the sun obscured, it was impossible to tell time. Okura guessed that Yasuhira's arrival occurred about midday, the Hour of the Horse. Because of the servants, she had one of them place her screen of state conveniently, and upon hearing his footsteps on the verandah she knelt behind it. Also for his sake, she thought wryly. Their world falling to pieces around them, the old proprieties mattered perhaps more than ever.

He and she spent a while in formalities and small talk. Thereupon she broke convention and pushed the screen aside. Once that would have implied lovemaking to come. Today a poetic reference or two among the banalities had made it clear that such was the intent of neither. They only wished to speak freely.

The maids Kodayu and Ukon might well be more taken aback by this than by any union of bodies so daylit blatant. They preserved blank deference and brought in the refreshment. Good girls, Okura thought as they went away. What would become of them? Slightly surprised, she found herself wishing the new master would keep the staff on and treat them gently. She feared he would not, being the kind of creature he was.

She and her visitor settled onto the floor. While Yasuhira courteously contemplated the floral pattern on his wine cup, she thought how he seemed to have aged overnight. He went gray years ago, but moon face, slit eyes, bud of a mouth, tiny tuft of beard had remained as handsome as in his youth. Many a lady sighed and compared him to Genji, the Shining Prince of Murasaki's two-hundred-year-old story. Today rain had streaked the powder and blurred the rouge, revealing darkened lower lids, blotchy sallowness, deepened lines, and his shoulders were slumped.

He had not lost the courtier grace with which, in due course, he sipped. 'Ah,' he murmured, 'that is most welcome, Asagao.' – Morning Glory, the name for her that he used in private. 'Savor, aroma, and warmth. "Resplendent light –"'

She was compelled to cap the literary allusion by saying, 'But not, I fear, "everlasting fortune,"' and whetted that a little by adding, 'As for Morning Glory, at my age might not Pine Tree be better?'

He smiled. 'So I have kept some of my touch in guiding conversation. Shall we get unpleasant topics out of the way at once? Then we can discourse of former times and their joys.'

'If we have the heart to.' If *you* do, she meant. I never had any choice but to make myself strong.

'I had hoped the Lord Tsuchimikado would retain you.'

'Under these circumstances, dismissal may be less than the worst thing that could happen to me,' she said. He failed to completely hide puzzlement. She explained: 'Without a family holding rice land, I would be scarcely more than a beggar, lacking even a place of my own like this to retire to when off duty. The others would despise and soon abuse me.'

'Indeed?'

'Women are as cruel as men, Mi-yuki.'

He nibbled a cake. She realized that was cover for the collecting of his thoughts. At length he said, 'I must confess, the knowledge of the situation made thin my expectations for you.'

'Why so?' She knew the answer perfectly well, but also knew that explaining to her would help him.

'It is true that Lord Tsuchimikado stayed at peace during the uprising,' he said, 'but if he did not work against the Hojo chieftains, neither did he assist them. Now I daresay he feels a need to curry favor, the more so because they may then make one of his line the next Emperor when our present sovereign dies or abdicates. Ridding himself of every member of any family that was in revolt seems a trivial gesture. Just the same, it is a gesture, and Lord Tokifusa, whom they have set as military governor over Heian-kyo, will take due note of it.'

'I wonder what sin in a past life caused Lord Go-Toba to try to seize back the throne he had quitted,' Okura mused.

'Ah, it was no madness, it was a noble effort that should have succeeded. Remember, his brother, the then Emperor Juntoku, was with him in it, and so were not only families like ours and their followers, but soldiers of the Taira who would fain avenge what the Minamoto did to their fathers; and many a monk also took up arms.'

A bleakness passed through Okura. She knew how the monks of Mount Hiei repeatedly descended on this city and terrorized it, not only by threats but by beatings, killings, looting, burning. They came to enforce political decisions they wanted; but were they any better than the outright criminal gangs who effectively ruled over the entire western half of the capital?

'No, it must have been because of our own former sins that we failed,' Yasuhira continued. 'How far have we fallen since the golden days! We might have won to an Emperor who truly ruled.'

'What do you mean?' asked Okura, sensing how he needed to express his bitterness.

It erupted: 'Why, what has the Emperor been for generations but a doll in the hands of the mighty, enthroned as a child and made to step down and retire into a life of idleness when he reached manhood? And meanwhile the clans have made earth sodden with blood as they fought out who should name the Shogun.' He gulped for air and explicated in the same rush of words: 'The Shogun is the military head in Kamakura who is the real master of the Empire. Or who was. Today – today the Hojo have won the clan wars; and *their* Shogun is himself a boy, another doll who says what their lords want him to say.'

He reined himself in and apologized: 'I beg Asagao's pardon. You must be shocked at my bluntness; and needlessly, for of course a woman cannot understand these things.'

Okura, who had kept her ears open and her mind awake amply long enough to know everything he had told her, replied, 'True, they are not for her. What I do understand is that you grieve over what we have lost. Poor Mi-yuki, what shall become of you?'

Somewhat calmed, Yasuhira said, 'I was in a better position to bargain for leniency than Masamichi or most others. Thus I have leave to occupy my mansion in Heian-kyo for a short time yet. After I must depart, it will be to a farm in the east, well beyond Ise, that I am allowed to keep. The tenants will support me and my remaining dependants.'

'But in poverty! And so far away, among rude countryfolk. It will be like passing over the edge of the world.'

He nodded. 'Often will my tears fall. Yet –' She could not readily follow his quotation, having had scant opportunity to practice spoken Chinese, but gathered that it was about maintaining a serene spirit in adversity. 'I hear there is a view of the sacred mountain Fuji. And I can take some books and my flute with me.'

'Then you are not wholly destroyed. That is one bright dustmote in the dark air.'

'What of you? What has happened to this household?'

'Yesterday came the baron who will take possession here. The worst kind of provincial, face unpowdered and weathered like a peasant's, hair and beard abristle, uncouth as a monkey and growling a dialect so barbarous that one could barely comprehend him. As for the soldiers in his train, oh, they could almost have been wildfolk of Hokkaido. Yes, knowledge of what I leave behind may temper my longing for Heian-kyo. He gave us a few days to make our preparations.'

Yasuhira hesitated before he said, 'Mine will be no fitting existence for a well-born lady. However, if you have nothing else, come with my party. For the rest of our days we can strive to console each other.'

'I thank you, dear old friend,' she answered mutedly, 'but I do have my own road before me.'

He emptied his cup. She refilled it. 'Indeed? Let me be glad on your account, not disappointed on mine. Who will take you in?'

'No one. I will seek the temple at Higashiyama – that one, for I have often been there with the Ex-Imperial consort and the chief priest knows me – I will go and take vows.'

She had not expected him to show dismay. He almost dropped his cup. Wine slopped forth to stain his outer robe. 'What? Do you mean full vows? Become a nun?'

'I think so.'

'Cut off your hair, your beautiful hair, don coarse black raiment, live – How will you live?'

'The fiercest bandit dares not harm a nun; the poorest hovel will not deny her shelter and some rice for her bowl. I have in mind to go on perpetual pilgrimage, from shrine to shrine, that I may gain merit in whatever years of this life are left me.' Okura smiled. 'During those years, perhaps I can call on you from time to time. Then we will remember together.'

He shook his head, bemused. Like most courtiers, he had never traveled far, seldom more than a day's journey from Heian-kyo. And that had been by carriage – to services that for his kind were occasions more social than religious; to view blossoms in the springtime countryside or the maple leaves of autumn; to admire and make poems about moonlight on Lake Biwa … 'Afoot,' he mumbled. 'Roads that wet weather turns into quagmires. Mountains, gorges, raging rivers. Hunger, rain, snow, wind, fiery sun. Ignorant commoners. Beasts. Demons, ghosts. No.' He set down his cup, straightened, firmed his voice. 'You shall not. It would be hard for a young man. You, a woman, growing old, you will perish miserably. I won't have it.'

Rather than remind him that he lacked authority over her, for his concern was touching, she asked gently, 'Do I seem feeble?'

He fell silent. His eyes searched, as if to pierce the garments and look at the body that had sometimes lain beneath his. But no, she thought, that would never cross his mind. A decent man, he found nudity disgusting, and in fact they had always kept on at least one layer of clothing.

Finally he murmured, 'It is true, it is eerie, the years have scarcely touched you, if at all. You could pass for a woman of twenty. But your age is – what? We have known each other for close to thirty years, and you must have been about twenty when you came to court, so that makes you only a little younger than me. And my strength has faded away.'

You speak aright, she thought. Bit by bit I have seen you holding a book farther from your eyes or blinking at words you do not quite hear; half your teeth are gone; more and more fevers come upon you, coughs, chills; do your bones hurt when you rise in the mornings? I know the signs well, and well I should, as often as I have watched them steal over those I loved.

The impulse had seized her days before, when the bad news broke and she began to think what it meant and what to do. She had curbed it, but it stayed restlessly alive. If she yielded, what harm? She could trust this man. She was unsure whether it would help or hinder him against his sorrow.

Let me be honest with him, she decided. At least it will give him something to think about besides his great loss, in the solitude that awaits him.

'I am not the age you believe, my dear,' she said quietly. 'Do you wish the truth? Be warned, at first you may suppose I have gone mad.'

He studied her before replying with the same softness, 'I doubt that. There is more within you than you have ever manifested. I was vaguely but surely conscious of it. Perhaps I dared never inquire.'

Then you are wiser than I believed, she thought. Her resolution crystallized. 'Let us go outside,' she said. 'What I have to tell is for no ears but yours.'

Not troubling about cloaks, they went forth together, onto the verandah, around this pavilion, and along a covered gallery to a kiosk overlooking the pool. Near its placidity rose a man-high stone in whose ruggedness was chiseled the emblem of the clan that had lost this home. Okura halted. 'Here is a good spot for me to show you that no evil spirit uses my tongue to speak falsehoods,' she said.

Solemnly, she recited a passage she had chosen from the Lotus Sutra. Yasuhira's manner was as grave when he told her, 'Yes, that suffices me.' He was of the Amidist sect, which held that the Buddha himself watches over humankind.

They stood gazing out at things of chaste beauty. Mist from the rain filled the kiosk and covered hair, clothes, eyelashes with droplets. The cold and the silence were like presences, whose awareness was remote from them.

'You suppose I am about fifty years old,' she said. 'I am more than twice that.'

He caught a breath, looked sharply at her, looked away, and asked with closely held calm, 'How can this be?'

'I know not,' she sighed. 'I know only that I was born in the reign of Emperor Toba, through whom the Fujiwara clan still ruled the realm so strongly that it lay everywhere at peace. I grew up like any other girl of good birth, save that I was never ill, but once I had become fully a woman, all change in me ceased, and thus it has been ever since.'

'What karma is yours?' he whispered.

'I tell you, I know not. I have studied, prayed, meditated, practiced austerities, but no enlightenment has come. At last I decided my best course was to continue this long life as well as I was able.'

'That must be ... difficult.'

'It is.'

'Why have you not revealed yourself?' The voice trembled. 'You must be holy, a saint, a Bodhisattva.'

'I know I am not. I am troubled and unsure and tormented by desire, fear, hope, every fleshly evil. Also, as my agelessness first came slowly to notice, I have encountered jealousy, spite, and dread. Yet I could never hitherto bring myself to renounce the world and retreat to a life of sacred poverty. So whatever I am, Mi-yuki, I am not holy.'

He pondered. Beyond the garden wall swirled formlessness. Eventually he asked her, 'What did you do? What have your years been like?'

'When I was fourteen, an older man – his name no longer matters – sought me out. He being influential, my parents encouraged him. I cared little for him, but knew not how to refuse. In the end he spent the three nights at my side and thereafter made me a secondary wife. He also got me a position at the court of Toba, who by then had abdicated. I bore him children, two of whom lived. Toba died. Soon after, my husband did.

'By then the wars between the Taira and the Minamoto had broken out. I made an occasion to retire from the service of Toba's widow and, taking my inheritance, withdrew to the family from which I sprang. It helped that a lady not at court lives so secluded. But how empty an existence!

'At last I confided in a lover I had gotten, a man of some wealth and power. He brought me to a rural estate of his, where I spent several years. Meanwhile he got my daughter married off elsewhere. He took me back to Heian-kyo under her name – such people as remembered marveled at how much she resembled her mother – and through his patronage I came again into service at a royal household. Gradually I outlived the scorn they have for provincials; but when they gradually observed how I kept my youth –

'Do you wish to hear it all?' she asked in an upsurge of weariness. 'This has been my third such renewal. The tricks, the deceptions, the children I have borne and, one way or another, managed to have adopted elsewhere, lest it become too plain that they grow old while I do not. That has hurt most. I wonder how much more I could endure.'

'Therefore you are leaving everything behind,' he breathed.

'The time was already overpast. I hesitated because of the strife, the uncertainty about what would become of my kindred. Well, that has been settled for me. It feels almost like a liberation.'

'If you take nun's vows, you cannot return here as you did before.'

'I have no wish to. I have had my fill of the petty intrigues and hollow amusements. Fewer are the midnight stars than the yawns I have smothered, the hours I have stared into vacancy and waited for something, anything to happen.' She touched his hand. 'You gave me one reason to linger. But now you too must go. Besides, I wonder how much longer they can keep up the pretense in Heian-kyo.'

'You choose a harder way than I think you imagine.'

'No harder, I think, than most in times to come. It is a cruel age we are bound into. At least a wandering nun has people's respect, and ... nobody questions her. Someday I may even win to understanding of why we suffer what we do.'

'Could I ever show courage like hers?' he asked the rain.

Once more she touched his hand. 'I feared this tale might distress you.'

Still he looked before him, into the silvery blindness. 'For your sake, perhaps. It has not changed you for me. While I live, you will remain my Morning Glory. And now you have helped me remember that I am safely mortal. Will you pray for me?'

'Always,' she promised.

They stood a while in silence, then went back inside. There they spoke of happy things and summoned up happy memories, pleasures and lovelinesses that had been theirs. He got a little tipsy. Nevertheless, when they said farewell it was with the dignity becoming a nobleman and a lady of the Imperial court.

IX

GHOSTS

Did smoke rouse her? Bitter in her nostrils, sharp-edged in her lungs, at first it was all that was. She coughed. Her skull flew asunder. The shards fell back with a crash. They ground against each other like ice floes on a lake under storm. Again she coughed, and again. Amidst the noise and the sword-blade hurt she began to hear a crackling that loudened.

Her eyes opened. The smoke savaged them. Through it, blurrily, she saw the flames. That whole side of the chapel was coming ablaze. Already the fire licked up to the ceiling. She could not make out the saints painted there, nor any icons on the walls – were they gone? – but the altar abided. As the smoke drifted and the half-light leaped, its bulk wavered in her sight. She had a wild brief sense that it was adrift, would soon reach her and crush her under its weight or else float away forever on the smoke.

Heat billowed. She crept to hands and knees. For a while she could not lift her head. It was too heavy with pain. Then something at the edge of vision drew her in a slow shamble. She slumped above and groped after comprehension.

Sister Elena. Sprawled on her back. Very still, more than the altar was, altogether empty of movement. Eyes open, firelight ashimmer in them. Mouth agape, tongue half out of it, dry. Legs and loins startlingly white against the clay floor and the habit pulled up over them. White flecks likewise catching the light across her groin. Blood-spatters bright on thighs and belly.

Varvara's insides writhed. She threw up. Once, twice, thrice the vomit burst forth. The surges ripped through her head. When they were done, though, only the foul taste and the burning left in her, more awareness had awakened. She wondered in a vague way whether this had been the final violation or a sign of God's grace, covering the traces of what had been done to Elena.

You were my sister in Christ, Varvara thought. So young, oh, how young. I wish you had not been in such awe of me. Your laughter was sweet to hear. I wish we could sometimes have been together, only the two of us, and told secrets and giggled before we went to prayers. Well, you have won martyrdom, I suppose. Go home to Heaven.

The words wavered over pain and throbbing and great swoops of dizziness. The fire roared. Its heat thickened. Sparks danced through the smoke. Some landed on her sleeves. They winked out, but she must flee, or else burn alive.

For a moment, weariness overwhelmed her. Why not die, here with little Elena? Make an end of the centuries, now when everything else had come to an end. If she breathed deeply, the agony would be short. Afterward, peace.

Sunlight struck long, brass-yellow, through haze and whirling soot. While she wondered about death, her body had crawled out the door. Astonishment jolted her more fully back to herself. She swung her gaze to and fro. Nobody was nigh. Mostly wood, the cloister buildings were afire all around. Somehow she got to her feet and stumbled from them.

Beyond the enclosure, animal wariness took hold. She crouched back down, next to a wall, and peered. Monastery and nunnery stood a distance from the town, as was usual. The religious should have found shelter behind the defenses. They had not had time. The Tatars arrived too soon, were *there*, horses between them and safety. They scrambled back and beseeched the Virgin, the saints and angels. Presently some of the wild men came to them, yelping like dogs.

It made no difference, Varvara saw. Pereyaslavl had fallen. No doubt the Tatars stormed it before they troubled about the house of the Virgin. A monstrous black cloud rose from its walls, up and up into the sky, where it broke apart into smears across eventide purity. Flames stabbed into view beneath. They tinged the gloom with restless red. She remembered dimly how the Lord went before the Israelites as a pillar of smoke by day and a pillar of fire by night. Did His voice roar like the pyre that had been Pereyaslavl?

Here and there across the rolling farmlands, villages burned too, smaller darknesses taking flight. The Tatars seemed to be assembling near the town. Squads galloped through grainfields toward the main body of horsemen. Warriors afoot herded captives along, not many – but then, Varvara saw, the invaders were no huge army, not the locust swarm of rumor, several hundred perhaps. They weren't steel-clad either, it was mostly leather and fur on those stocky forms, now and then a blink but that was likelier off a weapon than a helmet. One at their van bore the standard, a pole from whose cross-arm hung – tails of oxen? The mounts were just ponies, dun-colored, shaggy, longheaded.

Yet these men had come as a runaway blaze over the land, driving all before them or trampling it down. Even cloister dwellers had heard, years ago, how the Pechenegs themselves fled to the Rusi, begging for succor. Riders who attacked like a single dragon with a thousand thunderous legs, arrows that flew like a sleetstorm –

Otherwise the countryside reached green, outrageously peaceful, eastward from the sun. Light streamed into the Trubezh, so that the river became a flow of gold. Flocks of waterfowl winged toward the marshes along its shores.

Yonder is my refuge, Varvara knew, my one tiny hope.

How to reach it? Her flesh was a lump of pain, splintered in places with anguish, and her bones were weights. Nevertheless, with the fire at her back, go she must. Knowledge made up for awkwardness. She could advance a bit, freeze, wait till it appeared safe to gain a few more feet. That meant a long time till she reached her goal, but time remained to her, oh, yes. She choked off a crazy laugh.

At first a cloister orchard gave concealment. How often had these trees blossomed amazing pink and white in spring, rustled green in summer, offered crisp sweetness in autumn, stood skeletally beautiful against winter's gray, for her sisters and her? The number of years was lost somewhere in Varvara's head. Certain of their people flitted through, Elena, shrewish Marina, plump and placid Yuliana, Bishop Simeon grave behind his huge bush of beard – dead, today or years since, ghosts, she herself perhaps dead too but denied quietness, a rusalka creeping back to its river.

Beyond the orchard was pasture. Varvara thought for a while she would do best to wait among the trees for nightfall. Terror whipped her onward. She found herself slipping along more and more snakishly. Skill returned, indeed it did, when you had gained it in your girlhood. Before Christ came to the Rusi, and for generations afterward, women often ranged the forest as freely as men. Not the deep forest, no, it was dark, trackless, a place where beasts and demons prowled: but the verge, where sunlight reached and you could gather nuts and berries.

That lost greenwood felt closer than the cloister. She had no recollection of what happened after the enemy drew near the sanctuary.

At a sudden thudding, she went flat in the grass. Despite utter weariness, her heart banged and a thin singing lifted between her temples. It was well she had not stayed in the orchard. Several Tatar horses trotted among the trees and out onto the slope. She glimpsed one rider clearly, his broad brown face, slant slit eyes, wispy whiskers. Did she know him? Had he known her, back in the chapel? They passed close by but onward, they had not noticed her.

Thanks welled in her breast. Only later did she recall that they had not been to God or any saint but to Dazhbog of the Sun, the Protector. Another ancient memory, another strong ghost.

Dusk softened horizons by the time she reached the marsh for which she aimed. Fitful reddenings still touched the smoke of Pereyaslavl; the outlying villages must be entirely ash and charcoal. Tatar campfires began to twinkle in ordered clusters. They were small, like their masters, and bloody.

Mud oozed cool over Varvara's sandals, between her toes, up her ankles.

She found a hummock where the grass was merely damp and sank down, curled onto its springiness. Her fingers dug into the turf and the sod beneath. Earth, Mother of All, hold me close, never let me go, comfort your child!

The first stars glimmered forth. She grew able to weep.

Thereafter she pulled off her clothes, layer by layer. A breeze nuzzled her nakedness. Having left the garments bundled, she pushed through reeds till she waded in the stream. Here she could wash out her mouth and gullet, drink and drink. The water was slow to reach every parched finger-end. Meanwhile she crouched and scrubbed herself, over and over. The river laved, licked, caressed. She squatted and opened her loins to it. 'Make me clean,' she begged.

Light of stars and the Heaven Path gleamed off its current, enough for her to find her way back. She stood on the hummock so the breeze could dry her. That made her shiver but didn't take long. Her lips quirked for a moment – cropped hair was a legacy of the cloister, useful tonight. Afterward she took up her clothes, and nearly retched. Now she caught their stench of sweat, blood, Tatar. It took almost the last of her strength to put them back on. Maybe she couldn't have, were it not for the overlay of smoke-smell. Another legacy, another remembrance. She must keep covered against the night chill. Though she had never been sick in her life, she might well be too weakened to stave off a fever.

Slumping back onto the hummock, she dropped into a half-sleep wherein ghosts gibbered.

Dawn roused her. She sneezed, groaned, shuddered. However, as brightness lengthened across the land, the same cold clarity waxed within. Cautiously moving about her hiding place, she felt the stiffness work out of her joints, the aches dwindle. Wounds still hurt, but lesseningly as day warmed them; she knew they would heal.

She kept well down amidst the reeds, but from time to time ventured a look outward. She saw the Tatars water their horses, but the river blotted up any filth before it reached her. She saw them ride from horizon to horizon. Often they returned with burdens, loot. When the shifting masses at camp chanced to part before her eyes, she spied the captives, huddled together under mounted guard. Boys and young women, she supposed, those worth taking for slaves. The rest lay dead in the ashes.

She still lacked memory of her last hours in the cloister. A blow to the head could do that. She had no wish for the knowledge. Imagination served. When the raiders broke in, the religious must have scattered. Quite likely Varvara seized Elena's hand and led her, a dash into the chapel of St Eudoxia. It was small and offside, without treasures, the devils might overlook it. Of course they hadn't.

But what then? How had Elena died? Varvara – well, she dared hope she had fought, forced three or four to hold her down by turns. She was big, strong, a survivor of much, used to looking after herself. At last, she guessed, a Tatar, maybe when she bit him, smashed her head against the floor. Elena, though, Elena was slight and frail, gentle, dreamy. She could only have lain where she was while the thing went on and on and on. Maybe the last man, seeing what his fellow did to punish Varvara, had grinned and done the same to Elena. It killed her. Did they take her companion for dead also, belt up their breeches, and go? Or did they simply not care?

At least they hadn't used knives. Varvara would not have outlived that. Indeed, while her skull seemed amply hard, she might not have roused in time to escape, save for the vitality that kept her ageless. She should thank God for it.

'No,' she breathed, 'first I thank You for letting Elena die. She would have been broken, haunted all her days, hounded all her nights.'

Further gratitude slipped her mind.

The river and the hours muttered past. Birds clamored. Flies buzzed thick as smoke, drawn by her stinking garb. Hunger began to gnaw. She recollected another old skill, lay belly down in the mud by a backwater that some drifted brushwood had formed, waited.

She was no longer alone. Ghosts crowded close. They touched and tugged at her, whispered, beckoned. At first they were horrible. They took her against her will, drunken husbands and two different ruffians who had caught her during the years when she wandered. With a third she had been lucky and gotten a knife into him first. 'Burn in hell with those Tatars,' she snarled. 'I outlived you. I shall outlive them.'

Yes, and the memories of them. If nothing else, she would humble the new ghosts as she had overcome the old ones. It might take years – she had years – but at last the strength that had kept her alive this long would again make her able to live gladly.

'Good men, come back to me. I miss you. We were happy together, were we not?'

Father. White-bearded Grandfather, from whom she could wheedle anything. Elder brother Bogdan, how they used to fight but how splendid he later grew, before a sickness ravaged his guts and tore him down. Younger brother, yes, and sisters, who teased her and became dear to her. Neighbors. Dir, who kissed her so shyly in a clover meadow where bees buzzed; she was twelve years old, and the world wobbled. Vladimir, first of her husbands, a strong man until age gnawed him hollow but always gentle with her. Husbands later, those she had liked. Friends who stood by her, priests who consoled her, when sorrow returned to her house. How well she recalled ugly little Gleb Ilyev, but then, he was the first of those who helped her escape when a home turned into a trap. Oh, and her sons, her sons, grandsons, daughters and granddaughters too, great-grandchildren, but time took them away. Every ghost had a face that changed, grew old, finally was the mask that the dead wear.

No, not quite every one. Some she had known too fleetingly. Strange, how vivid remained that trader from abroad – Cadoc, his name? Yes, Cadoc. She was glad she had not watched him crumble – when? Two hundred years, more or less, since their night in Kiyiv. Of course, he might have perished early, in the beauty of his youth.

Others were misty. Certain among them she was unsure of, whether they had been real or were fragments of dreams that had clung to memory.

With a splash and splatter, a frog jumped from among the rushes, onto the brushwood. He settled himself, fat, green-white, to lurk for flies. Varvara stayed moveless. She saw his attention turn from where she lay. Her hand pounced.

He struggled, cool and slippery, till she knocked him on the head. Then she plucked him apart, gnawed and sucked his meat off the bones, cast them into the river with muttered thanks. Ducks bobbed in midstream. She could have shed her clothes, slid into the water, swum carefully underneath to seize one by the legs. But no, the Tatars might glimpse it. Instead, she grubbed sedges of a kind with edible roots. Yes, the forest skills lived on in her, had never really faded.

Otherwise – She supposed it was a growing despair, a sense of her soul slipping from her, that brought her to the sanctuary. No, that wasn't the whole reason. She had said too many farewells. In the house of God was refuge that would endure.

Surely there was peace, around her if not always within. The lusts of the flesh refused to die, among them the wish to feel again a small warmth in her arms, a small mouth milking her. She reined them in, but then sometimes they kicked up mockeries of the Faith, memories of old earthy gods, longings to see beyond walls and fare beyond horizons. And petty sins too, anger at her sisters, impatience with the priests and the endlessly same tasks. Nonetheless, on the whole, peace. Between the chores, the chafings, and the puzzled search for sanctity were hours in which she could bit by bit, year by year, rebuild herself. She discovered how to order memories, have them at her beck rather than let them fade to nothing or else overwhelm her with their manyness. She tamed her ghosts.

A wind made the sedges rustle. She shivered likewise. What if she had failed? If she was not alone in the world, was the common fate of her kind to go mindless and perish helpless?

Or was she in truth alone, whether blessed or damned? Certainly the cloister had no record of such folk, ever, since the Methuselan morning of the world. Not that she had told anybody beforehand. The caution of centuries forbade. She came as a widow, taking the veil because the Church encouraged widows to do so.

To be sure, when the decades slipped by and her flesh continued young –

Noise thrust into the marsh, shouts, whinnies, drumbeats. She scuttered to look. The Tatars had trussed up their loot and marshalled their ranks. They were departing. She saw no captives, but guessed they were bound astride pack horses with the rest of the baggage. Smoke still blew thinly out of the blackened, broken walls of Pereyaslavl.

The Tatars were headed northeasterly, away from the Trubezh, toward the Dniepr and Kiyiv. The great city was a day's march in that direction, less on horseback.

O Christ, have mercy, were they off to take Kiyiv?

No, they were too few.

But others must be raging elsewhere across the Russian land. Their demon king must have a plan. They could join together, resharpen swords blunted by butchery, and go on as a conquering horde.

In the house of God I sought eternity, passed through Varvara. Here I have seen that it also has an end.

I too?

Yes, I can die, if only by steel or fire or famine or flood; therefore someday I shall die. Already, to those among whom I was ageless, those that live, I am a ghost, or less than a ghost.

First the nuns, later the monks and secular priests, finally the layfolk began to marvel at Sister Varvara. After some fifty years, peasants were appealing to her for help in their woes and pilgrims arriving from places quite far. As she had feared from the outset, there was no choice but to tell her confessor the truth about her past. With her reluctant leave, he informed Bishop Simeon. The latter planned to inform the Metropolitan. If they did not have an actual saint in the cloister of the Virgin, and Sister Varvara said she could not possibly be one, they had a miracle.

How was she to live with that?

She would never have to. The bishop, the priests, the believers were dead or fled. The annals of the cloister were burned. Anything elsewhere was likewise destroyed, or soon would be, or was doomed to molder away forgotten now when people had so much death to think about. A memory of her might linger in a few minds, but seldom find utterance, and it would die with them.

Had the Tatars come as God's denial, His decision that she was unworthy – or as His release from a burden no child of Adam should bear – or was she, defiled and torn, nonetheless so full of worldly pride that she dared imagine she mattered?

She clung to the hummock. Earth and sun, moon and stars, wind and rain and human love, she could understand the old gods better than she understood Christ. But they were forsaken by man, remembered only in dances and feasts, fireside tales and fireside spirits; they were ghosts.

Yet lightning, thunder, and vengeance forever walked the skies above Russia, be they of Perun or of St Yuri the dragonslayer. Varvara drank strength from the soil as a babe drinks milk. When the Tatars were out of sight, she sprang to her feet, shook her fist after them, and shouted, 'We will abide! We will outlast you, and in the end we will crush you and take back what is ours!'

Calmer, then, she removed her clothes, washed them in the river, spread them on a slope to dry. Meanwhile she cleansed herself again and gathered more wild food. Next morning she sought the ruins.

Ash, charred timber, snags of brick and stone lay silent under heaven. A pair of churches were left, foul with soot. Inside them sprawled corpses. The slain outside were many more, and in worse condition. Carrion birds quarreled over them, flying off with a blast of wingbeats and shrieks whenever she approached. There was nothing she could do but offer a prayer.

Searching about, she found clothes, shoes, an undamaged knife, and suchlike needs. Taking each, she smiled and whispered, 'Thank you' to its owner's ghost. Her journey would be hard and dangerous at best. She did not mean it to end until she had reached the kind of new home she wanted – whatever that was.

In the dawn that followed, before setting forth, she told the sky: 'Remember my name. I am Varvara no more. I am again Svoboda.' Freedom.

X

IN THE HILLS

1

Where mountains began their long climb toward Tibet, a village nestled. On three sides its dell lifted steeply, making horizons high and close. A stream from the west rushed through upper woods of cypress and dwarf oak, gleamed as a waterfall, passed among the buildings, and lost itself in bamboo and ruggedness eastward. The people cultivated wheat, soybeans, vegetables, melons, some fruit trees on the floor of the vale and on small terraces above. They kept pigs, chickens, and a fishpond. This, their score or so of turf-roofed earthen houses, and they themselves had been there so long that sun, rain, snow, wind, and time had made them as much a part of the land as the pheasant, the panda, or the wildflowers in spring.

On the east the view opened, a wrinklescape manifoldly green and tawny with forest, to right and left a sight of snowpeaks afloat in heaven. Through it wound a road, scarcely more than a track, the village its terminus. Traffic was sparse. Several times a year, men undertook a journey of days, to market in a little town and home again. There they also paid taxes in kind. Thus the governor very seldom thought to send a man to them. When he did, the inspector only stayed overnight, inquired of the elders how things were going, received ritual answers, and departed eagerly. The place had a somewhat uncanny reputation.

That was in the eyes of orthodox outsiders. To others it was holy. Because of this awe, whether vague or devout, as well as its loneliness, war and banditry had passed the village by. It followed its own ways, enduring no more than the ordinary sorrows and calamities of life. Once in a while a pilgrim overcame the obstacles – distance, hardship, danger – to visit it. In the course of generations, a few among those had remained. The village took them into its peace. Thus things were. Thus had they always been. Their beginnings were unknown save to myth and the Master.

Great, therefore, was the excitement when a herdboy came running and shrilled that a traveler was on the way. 'Shame, bad, that you left your ox unattended,' chided his grandfather, but gently. The boy explained that he had first tethered the beast; and, after all, no tiger arrived. He was forgiven. Meanwhile folk bustled and shouted about. Presently a disciple struck the gong in the shrine. A metal voice toned forth, rang off the hillsides, mingled with shush of waterfall and murmur of wind.

Autumn comes early in the high hills. Woodlands were dappled brown and yellow, grass was turning sere, fallen leaves crunched underfoot near puddles left by last night's rain. Overhead the sky arched unutterably blue, empty of all but wings. Bird cries drifted faint through air flowing down the mountainside. Smoke from hearthfires sharpened its chill.

As the stranger trudged up the last stretch of road, the gathered villagers saw with astonishment that this was a woman. Threadbare and oft mended, her gown of coarse cotton had faded to gray. Her boots were equally near the end of their service, and use had worn smooth the staff that swung in her right hand. From her left shoulder hung a rolled-up blanket, just as wayworn, which held a wooden bowl and perhaps one or two other things.

Yet she was no beggar granny. Her body was straight and slim, her stride firm and limber. Where a scarf fluttered loose, one could see hair like a crow's wing, hacked off just below the earlobes; and her face, though weathered, drawn close over the bones, was unlined. Never had such a face appeared in these parts. She did not even seem of quite the same breed as the lowlanders from whose country she fared.

Elder Tsong trod forward. For lack of a better thought, he greeted her according to the ancient rite, despite every newcomer hitherto having been male. 'In the name of the Master and the people, I bid you welcome to our Morning Dew Village. May you walk in the Tao, in peace, and the gods and spirits walk with you. May the hour of your advent prove lucky. Enter as a guest, depart as a friend.'

'This humble person thanks you, honorable sir,' she replied. Her accent was like none that anybody had heard before, but that was no surprise. 'I come in search of … enlightenment.' The word shook. Fervent must her hope be.

Tsong turned and bowed toward the shrine and the Master's house behind it. 'Here is the home of the Way,' he said. Some persons smiled smugly. *Their* home.

'May we know your name, that it be borne to the Master?' Tsong asked.

She hesitated, then: 'I call myself Li, honorable sir.'

He nodded. The wind ruffled his thin white beard. 'If you have chosen that, you have likely chosen well.' In her pronunciation, it could mean the measure of distance. Ignoring whispers, mutters, and stirrings among the folk, he forbore to inquire further. 'Come. You shall take refreshment and stay with me.'

'Your … leader –'

'In due course, young miss, in due course. Pray come.'

Her features settled into an aspect no one could fathom, something between resignation and an ageless determination. 'Again, my humble thanks,' she said, and accompanied him.

The villagers moved aside. Several uttered words of goodwill. Beneath a natural curiosity, they were as alike in their mildness – the very children were – as in their padded garments and work-hardened hands. Alike, too, were many faces, broad and rather flat-nosed above sturdy frames. After Tsong, his family, and Li disappeared, they chatted for a while, then piece-meal went back to their cookfires, handmills, looms, tools, animals, all that kept them alive as it had kept their ancestors alive from time out of mind.

Tsong's oldest son, with wife and offspring, lived with him. They stayed in the background, except for serving tea and food. The house was larger than most, four rooms inside rammed-earth walls, darksome but comfortably warm. While homes were poorly and rudely furnished, there was no real want; rather, contentment and cheerfulness prevailed. Tsong and Li sat on mats at a low table and enjoyed broth flavored with ruddy peppercorns, fragrant amidst the savors of other foodstuffs hung under the roof.

'You shall wash and rest before we meet with my fellow elders,' he promised.

Her spoon trembled. 'Please,' she blurted, 'when may I see the teacher? I have come, oh, a long and weary way.'

Tsong frowned. 'I understand your desire. But we really know nothing about you, ah, Miss Li.'

Her lashes lowered. 'Forgive me. I think what I have to tell is for his ears alone. And I think – I, I pray he will want to hear me soon. Soon!'

'We must not be overhasty. That would be irreverent, and maybe unlucky. What do you know about him?'

'Hardly more than rumors, I confess. The story – no, different stories in different places as I wandered. At first they sounded like folk tales. A holy man afar in the west, so holy that death dares not touch him – Only as I came nearer did anyone tell me that *this* is his dwelling ground. Few would say that much. They seemed afraid to speak, although … I never heard ill of him.'

'No ill is there to hear,' said Tsong, softened by her earnestness. 'You must have a great soul, that you ventured the pilgrimage. Quite alone, too, a youthful woman. Surely your stars are strong, that you took no harm. That bodes well.'

Dim of eye and in smoky dusk, he failed to see how she winced. 'Nevertheless our wizard must read the bones,' he continued thoughtfully, 'and we must offer to the ancestors and spirits, yes, hold a purification; for you are a woman.'

'What has the holy man to fear, if time itself obeys him?' she cried.

His tone calmed her somewhat: 'Nothing, I daresay. And certainly he will protect us, his beloved people, as he always has. What do you wish to hear about him?'

'Everything, everything,' she whispered.

Tsong smiled. His few stumps of teeth glistened in what light passed through a tiny window. 'That would take years,' he said. 'He has been with us for centuries, if not longer.'

Again she tautened. 'When did he come?'

Tsong sipped his tea. 'Who knows? He has books, he can read and write, but the rest of us cannot. We tally the months, but not the years. Why should we? Under his good sway, lifespans are alike, as happy as the stars and the spirits may grant. The outside world troubles us never. Wars, famines, pestilences, those are gnat-buzz borne in from the market town, which itself hears little. I could not tell you who reigns in Nanking these days, nor do I care.'

'The Ming drove out the foreign Yuan some two hundred years ago, and the Imperial seat is Peking.'

'Ah, learned, are you?' the old man chuckled. 'Yes, our forebears did hear about invaders from the north, and we know they are now gone. However, the Tibetans are much closer, and they have not attacked these parts for generations, nor ever our village. Thanks be to the Master.'

'He is your true king, then?'

'No, no.' The bald head shook. 'To rule over us would be beneath his dignity. He counsels the elders when we ask, and of course we heed. He instructs us, during our childhoods and throughout our lives, in the Way; and of course we gladly follow it as well as we are able. When someone falls from it, the chastisement he orders is gentle – though quite enough, since real evildoing means expulsion, exile, homelessness for life and ever afterward.'

Tsong shuddered slightly before going on: 'He receives pilgrims. From among them and from among our own youths who wish it, he accepts a few disciples at a time. They serve his worldly needs, listen to his wisdom, strive to attain a small part of his holiness. Not that this keeps them from eventually having households of their own; and often the Master honors a family, any family in the village, with his presence or his blood.'

'His blood?'

Li flushed when Tsong answered, 'You have much to learn, young miss. Male Yang and female Yin must join for the health of the body, the soul, and the world. I am myself a grandson of the Master. Two daughters of mine have borne him children. One was already married, but her husband kept from her until they were sure it would indeed be a child of Tu Shan that blessed their home. The second, who is lame in one leg, suddenly needed only a bedspread for her dowry. Thus is the Way.'

'I see.' He could barely hear her. She had gone pale.

'If you cannot accept this,' he said kindly, 'you may still meet him and receive his blessing before you leave. He forces no one.'

She gripped the spoon in her fist as if its handle were a post to which she clung lest she be whirled off the earth. 'No, I will surely do his will,' stumbled from her throat, 'I who have been seeking over all these li, all these years.'

2

He could have been a peasant man of the village – but then, every one of them was closely or distantly descended from him – with the same strong frame clad in the same thick coat and trousers, the same grime and calluses on feet that indoors were bare. His beard hung thin, youthfully black, his hair was drawn into a topknot. The house he inhabited with his disciples was as big as any, but no bigger, also of plain earth above a clay floor. The room to which one of the young men admitted her before bowing and leaving was scarcely better furnished. There was a bedstead, wide enough for him and whatever woman might attend him; straw mats, stools, table; a calligraphic scroll, gone brown-spotted and flyspecked, on the wall above a stone altar; a wooden chest for clothing, a smaller brass one that doubtless held books; a few bowls, cups, cloths, and other everyday things. The window was shuttered against a blustery wind. A single lampflame did little to relieve murkiness. Coming in from outdoors, Li was first aware of the smell. It was not unpleasant, but it was heavy, blent of old smoke and grease, manure tracked in on shoes, humanity, centuries.

Seated, he lifted a hand in benison. 'Welcome,' he said in the hill dialect. 'May the spirits guide you along the Way.' His gaze was shrewd. 'Do you wish to make offering?'

She bowed low. 'I am a poor wanderer, Master.'

He smiled. 'So they have told me. Fear not. Most who come here believe gifts will win them the favor of the gods. Well, if it helps uplift their souls, they are right. But the seeking soul itself is the only real sacrifice. Be seated, Lady Li, and let us come to know each other.'

As the elders had instructed her, she knelt on the mat near his feet. His look searched her. 'You do that otherwise than any woman I have seen before,' he murmured, 'and you talk differently, too.'

'I am but newly in these parts, Master.'

'I mean that you do not talk like a lowlander who has picked up some of the highland form of speech.'

'I thought I had learned more than one Chinese tongue well, as long as I have been in the Middle Kingdom,' broke from her.

'I've been widely about, myself.' He shifted to the idiom of Shansi or

Honan, though it was not quite what she remembered from the wealthy, populous northeastern provinces and he used it rustily. 'Will you be more at ease talking this?'

'I learned it first, Master.'

'It's been long since I – But where are you from, then?'

She raised her face toward his. Her heart thuttered. With an effort like reining in a wild horse, she kept her voice level. 'Master, I was born across the sea, in the country of Nippon.'

His eyes widened. 'You have come far in your search for salvation.'

'Far and long, Master.' She drew breath. Her mouth had gone dry. 'I was born four hundred years ago.'

'*What?*' He leaped to his feet.

She rose too. 'It is true, it is true,' she said desperately. 'How could I dare lie to you? The enlightenment I seek, have sought, oh, that was to find someone like myself, who never grows old –'

She could hold back the tears no more. He laid his arms around her. She clung close and felt how he also trembled.

After a time they drew apart and, for another while, stared at one another. The wind boomed outside.

A strange calm had fallen on her. She blinked her lashes clear and told him, 'You have only my word for this, of course. I learned quite early to be nobody that anybody was … much concerned about or would … especially remember.'

'I believe you,' he answered hoarsely. 'Your presence, you, a foreigner and a woman, that speaks for you. And I think I am afraid to disbelieve you.'

A laugh sobbed. 'You will have time aplenty to make certain.'

'Time,' he mumbled. 'Hundreds, thousands of years. And you a woman.'

Old fears awoke. Her hands fluttered before her. She forced herself to stand where she was. 'I am a nun. I took vows to Amida Butsu – the Buddha.'

He nodded, against straining muscles. 'How else could you travel freely?'

'I was not always safe,' she wrung out of her lips. 'I have been violated in wild lands of this realm. Nor have I always been true. I have sometimes taken shelter with a man who offered it, and stayed with him till he died.'

'I'll be kind,' he promised.

'I know. I asked … of certain women here … But what of those vows? I thought I had no choice before, but now –'

His laughter gusted louder than needful. 'Ho! I release you from them.'

'Can you?'

'I am the Master, am I not? The people aren't supposed to pray to me but I know they do, more than to their gods. Nothing bad has come of it. Instead, we've had peace, lifetime after lifetime.'

'Did you … foresee that?'

He shrugged. 'No. Myself, I am – maybe a thousand and a half years old. I don't remember just when I came here.'

The past took possession of him. He looked beyond her and the wall, he spoke low and rapidly:

'The years blur together, they become one, the dead are as real as the living and the living as unreal as the dead. For a while, long ago, I was mad, in a waking dream. Some monks took me in, and slowly, I'm not sure how, slowly I grew able to think again. Ah, I see that something like that happened to you too. Well, for me it still is often hard to be sure what I truly remember, and I forget much.

'I had found, like you, the safest thing was to be a footloose religious person. I only meant to stay here a few years, after they'd made me welcome. But time went on and on, this was a snug den and foes feared to come, once word of me had drifted about, and what else, what better, was there? I've tried to do my people no harm. I think, they think I do them good.'

He shook himself, trod forward, caught both her hands. His were big, strong, but less hard than other men's. She had heard that he lived off their labor, at most diverting himself with his ancient trade of blacksmith. 'But who are you, Li? What are you?'

In sudden weariness, she sighed. 'I have borne many names, Okura, Asagao, Yukiko – names did not matter among us, they changed as our positions changed, and we might use a different nickname for every friend. I was an attendant at a court that became a shadow. When no more pretense of being mortal was possible, and I feared to proclaim what I was, I turned nun and begged my way from shrine to shrine, place to place.'

'It was easier for me,' he admitted, 'but I too found I'd better keep moving, and stay clear of anybody powerful who might want me to linger. Until I found this haven. How did you come to leave … Nippon, you call that land?'

'I was forever hoping to find someone like me, an end to the loneliness, the – meaninglessness; for I had tried to find meaning in the Buddha, and no enlightenment ever came. Well, the news reached us that the Mongols – they who had conquered China and tried to invade us, but the Divine Wind wrecked their ships – they had been driven out. The Chinese were sailing far and wide, also to us. This land is … our motherland in spirit, the mother of civilization.' She saw puzzlement, and recalled that he was of lowly birth and had lived withdrawn since before she came into the world. 'We knew of many holy sites in China. I thought, as well, there if anywhere would be other … immortals. So I took passage as a pilgrim, the captain gained merit by carrying me, and on these shores I set off afoot … I did not then know how vast the country is.'

'Have you never wished to go home?'

'What is home? Besides, the Chinese have stopped sailing. They have destroyed all their great ships. It is forbidden on pain of death to leave the Empire. You had not heard?'

'We're free of overlords here. Welcome, welcome.' His tone deepened, strengthened. He let go her hands and once more laid arms about her waist, but now the clasp was strong and his breath turned musky. 'You've found me, we're together, you, my wife! I waited and waited, prayed, offered, cast spells, till at last I gave up hope. Then you came. Li!' His mouth sought hers.

She turned her cheek, protested faintly, no, this was too fast, unseemly. He paid no heed. It was not an assault, but it was an overwhelming. She surrendered as she might have surrendered to a storm or a dream. While he had her, she tried to bring her thoughts under control. Afterward he was drowsy and gentle for a while, then wildly merry.

3

Winter struck with blinding snow on wind that rampaged among the houses and stretched fingers through every crack around door or shutter. The calm that followed was so cold that silence seemed to ring, with stars uncountable above a white hardness that gave back their glitter. Folk went into the weather no more than they needed, to tend their livestock and get fuel. At home they crouched over tiny hearth-fires or slept the hours away within heaped sheepskins.

Li felt sick. She always did in the mornings during the first part of a pregnancy. That she had become fruitful was no surprise, as often as Tu Shan lay with her. Nor did she regret it. He meant well, and bit by bit, without letting him know what happened, she schooled him in what pleased her, until sometimes she too flew off into joy and came back down to lie happily wearied in the warmth and odor of him. And this child they had gotten together might also be ageless.

Still, she wished she could exult over it as he did. On her best days she was free of forebodings, no more. If only she had something to do. At least in Heian-kyo there had been color, music, the round of ceremonies, the often vicious but oftener titillating intrigues. At least on the road there had been changing landscape, changing people, unsureness, small victories over trouble or danger or despair. Here she could, if she liked, weave the same cloths, cook the same meals, sweep the same floors, empty the same muck buckets – though the disciples expected to do the menial tasks – and swap the same and the same words with women whose minds ranged as far as next year's kitchen gardening.

Their men took interest in a little more than that, some of them, though not much more. However, they felt ill at ease with her. They knew her for the chosen of the Master and accorded her respect, in a clumsy fashion. Yet they also knew her for a woman; and she was soon taken for granted, sacred but a part of everyday life, like Tu Shan; and women did not sit in the councils of men.

Li gathered that this was no great loss to her.

One day of that winter stood forth in memory, an island at the middle of an abyss that swallowed all the rest. The door swung open on dazzlingly sun-lit, blue-shadowed drifts. A wave of chill, poured through. Tu Shan's bulk blotted the light. He entered and closed the door. Gloom clapped down again. 'Hoo!' he whinnied, stamping the snow off his boots. 'Cold enough to freeze a fire solid and the anvil with it.' She must have heard him say that a hundred times, and a few other favorite expressions.

Li looked up from the mat on which she knelt. Bright spots danced before her. They were due to reflection off the brass chest, which the disciples wor-shipfully kept polished. She had been staring at it for – an hour? two hours? – while sunken in the half-doze that was her retreat from these empty months.

A thought smote. The suddenness of it made her catch her breath. Next she wondered why it had not occurred to her before, then supposed that was because the newness of this life had driven everything else out of her mind until the life went stale, and she was saying: 'Horseshoe,' the pet name she had given him, 'I have never looked in yonder box.'

His mouth was open, he had been about to speak. He left it hanging thus for a moment before he replied slowly, 'Why, uh, those are the books. And, uh, scrolls, yes, scrolls. The holy writings.'

Eagerness thrilled through her. 'May I see them?'

'They're not for, uh, ordinary eyes.'

She rose and told him fiercely, 'I too am immortal. Have you forgotten?'

'Oh, no, no.' He waved his hands, a vague gesture. 'But you're a woman. You can't read them.'

Li's mind leaped back across centuries. Ladies of the court in Heian-kyo were literate in the vernacular but seldom in Chinese. That was the classical language, which only men could properly comprehend. Nevertheless she had contrived to study the writing, and sometimes in China had found a chance, a span of rest in a tranquil place, to refresh that knowledge. Moreover, these texts were most likely Buddhist; that faith had intermingled here with Tao-ism and primitive animism. She would recognize passages.

'I can,' she said.

He gaped. 'You can?' He shook his head. 'Well, the gods have singled you out ... Yes, look at them if you want. But handle them carefully. They're quite old.'

Joyful, she went to the chest and opened it. At first she saw it only full of shadow. She fetched the lamp and held it above. Wan light flickered and fell.

The chest gaped across rot, mildew, and fungus.

She moaned. Barely did she keep from letting hot grease spill onto the corruption. With her free hand she groped, caught hold of something, lifted a gray tatter up to view.

Tu Shan bent over. 'Well, well,' he muttered. 'Water must have gotten in. How sad.'

She dropped the shred, replaced the lamp, rose to confront him. 'When did you last look into that box?' she demanded most quietly.

His glance shifted elsewhere. 'I don't know. No reason to.'

'You never read the sacred texts? You have them perfectly by heart?'

'They were gifts from pilgrims. What are they to me?' He summoned bluster. 'I don't need writings. I am the Master. That's enough.'

'You cannot read or write,' she said.

'They, well, they suppose I can, and – What harm? What harm, I ask you?' He turned on her. 'Stop nagging me. Go. Go into the other rooms. Leave me be.'

Pity overcame her. He was, after all, so vulnerable – a simple man, a common man, whom karma or the gods or the demons or blind accident had made ageless for no know-able reason. With peasant shrewdness he had survived. He had acquired the sonorous phrases that a saint should utter. And he had not abused his position here; he was a god-figure that required little and returned much, assurance, protection, oneness. But the unchanging cycle of season after season after season, world without end, had dulled his wits and even, she saw, sapped his courage.

'I'm sorry,' she said, laying a hand on his. 'I meant no reproach. I'll tell nobody, of course. I'll clean this out and from now on take care of such things for you – for us.'

'Thank you,' he replied uncomfortably. 'Still, well, I meant to tell you you'll have to stay in the back rooms till nightfall.'

'A woman is coming to you,' she said in a voice as leaden as the knowledge.

'They expect it.' His own voice loudened. 'So it's been since – since the beginning. What else was there for me? I can't suddenly withhold my blessing from their households. Can I?'

'And she's young and pretty.'

'Well, when they aren't, I've been kind to them anyhow.' He forced indignation. 'Who are you to call me faithless? How many men have you been with in your time, and you a nun?'

'I said nothing against you.' She turned around. 'Very well, I go.' She felt his relief like radiance at her back.

The four disciples huddled together in one room of their quarters, blurs of darkness by lamplight, and played a game with sticks tossed on the floor.

They sprang to their feet when Li entered, bowed awkwardly, stood in abashed silence. They knew quite well why she was here, but could not think what to say.

How young they were, she thought. And how handsome Wan, at least, was. She imagined his body on hers, lithe, hot, delirious.

Perhaps later. There would be boundless later. She smiled at them. 'The Master wants me to rehearse you in the Diamond Sutra,' she told them.

4

It was raining when the village buried the first child of the Master and the Lady. They had hoped for sunshine but the wizard and the tiny corpse both told them they could not auspiciously wait longer than they had done. Spring that year had come late. Its bleakness and damp stretched on into the summer. They slipped through to the lungs of the girl-child, who gasped for a few days before she lay still. Oh, very still, when she cried and sucked and snuggled no more.

With Tu Shan, Li watched the wizard lower the coffin into a hole where water sloshed. The disciples stood close, the rest of the people in a rough ring. Beyond them she saw mists, shadowy hints of hillside, grandeur dissolved in this formless gray that tapped on her face and dripped off her hat and weighted her hair. Wet wool stank. Her breasts ached with milk.

The wizard rose, took up the rattle tucked under his rope belt, and shook it as he pranced around the grave screaming. Thus he warded off evil spirits. The disciples and those few others who had prayer wheels spun them. Everybody swayed to and fro. The chant sounded as raw as the air, '– honored ancestors, great souls, honored ancestors, great souls –' over and over, rite of a heathendom that the Tao and the Buddha had barely touched.

Tu Shan raised his arms and intoned words more fitting, but blurred and mechanical. He had spoken them too often. Li hardly noticed. She likewise had known too many deaths. She could not at the moment count the number of infants she had borne and lost. Seven, eight, a dozen? It hurt more to watch children grow old. But farewell, daughter of mine. May you not be lonely and afraid, wherever you have gone.

What Li felt now was the final hard freezing of resolution within herself.

Things ended. Folk mumbled words and went back to their work. The wizard remained. His task was to fill the grave. At her back, through his ongoing quavery song, Li heard clods fall on the coffin.

The disciples sought their parents' homes for the nonce. Li and Tu Shan entered an empty house. He left the door ajar for light. Coals aglow on the hearth had somewhat warmed the room. He shucked his coat and tossed it on the bed. A sigh gusted from him. 'Well,' he said. 'That's done.'

After a span, into her silence: 'The poor wee girl. But it happens. Better luck next time, eh? And maybe a son.'

She tensed. 'There will be no next time, here,' she answered.

'What? He lumbered around to stand before her. His arms dangled at his sides.

She met his stare full on. 'I will not stay,' she told him. 'You should leave with me.'

'Are you crazed?' Fear crossed the usually firm countenance. 'Has a demon gotten into you?'

She shook her head. 'Only an understanding, and it has been growing for months. This is simply no life for us.'

'It's peaceful. It's happy.'

'So you see it, because you've lain in it so long. I say it is stagnant and squalid.' She spoke calmly, the least bit sadly. 'At first, yes, after my wanderings, I believed I had come to a sanctuary. Tu Shan,' – she would not give him his endearment name until he yielded, if ever he did – 'I have learned what you should have seen an age ago. Earth holds no sanctuaries for anyone, anywhere.'

Amazement made his anger faint. 'You want back to your palaces and monkey courtiers, eh?'

'No. That was another trap. I want … freedom … to be, to become whatever I am able to. Whatever *we* are able to.'

'They need me here!'

She must first put down scorn. If she showed hers for these half-animals, she could well lose him. And, true, in his liking for them, his concern and compassion, he was better than she was. Second she must muster all the will at her command. If she surrendered and abided, she would likewise slowly become one with the hillfolk. That might aid her toward selflessness, toward ultimate release from the Wheel; but she would give up every imaginable attainment that this life held. What escape, except through random violence, did she have from it?

'They lived much the same before you,' she said. 'They will do so after you. And with or without you, it cannot be for always. The Han people press westward. I have seen them clearing forest and breaking earth. Someday they will take these lands.'

He fell into bewilderment. 'Where can we go? Would you be a beggar again?'

'If need be, but then only for a short while. Tu Shan, a whole world lies beyond this horizon.'

'We kn-know nothing about it.'

'I know something.' Through the ice of her resolve shone a strengthening fire. 'Foreign ships touch the shores of China. Barbarians thrust inward. I have heard about mighty stirrings to the south, on the far side of the mountains.'

'You told me … it's forbidden to leave the Empire –'

'Ha, what does that mean to us? What watchmen stand on those paths we can find? I tell you, if we cannot seize the opportunities that beckon everywhere around, we do not deserve our lives.'

'If we become famous, they … would notice we don't grow old –'

'We can cope with that. Change rushes through the world unbridled. The Empire can no more stay forever locked into itself than this village can. We'll find advantages to take. Perhaps just setting money out at interest for a long time. We'll see. My years have been harder than yours. I know how full of secret places chaos is. Yes, we may well go under, we may perish, but until then we will have been wholly alive!'

He stood dazed. She knew she would need months wherein to prevail, if indeed she could. Well, she had the patience of centuries to draw upon, when there was something for which to work.

Clouds thinned, light broke through, the rain in the doorway gleamed like flying arrows.

5

Springtime came back, and that year it was mild, overwhelmingly bright, full of fragrances and the cries of wildfowl returned. Gorged with snow melt, the stream sprang white amidst hillside leaves, brawled through the dell, plunged into the bamboo forest, bound for the great river and so at last the sea.

A man and a woman followed it on the road. They were clad for travel. Staves swung in their hands. On his back was a load of needful goods, on hers a swaddled baby boy who gurgled lustily and happily as he looked around him at wonders.

The people stood gathered together behind, where their homes came to an end, and wept.

XI

THE KITTEN AND THE CARDINAL

Armand Jean du Plessis de Richelieu, cardinal of the Church, first minister to His Most Christian Majesty Louis XIII, who had created him duke, gave his visitor a long regard. The man was altogether out of place in this chamber of blue-and-gilt elegance. Though decently clad for a commoner, he seemed unmistakably the seafarer he proclaimed himself. Of medium height, he had the suppleness of youth, and the dark hawk face was unlined; but something about him – perhaps the alert steadiness of the look he gave back – bespoke a knowledge of the world such as it takes many years in many corners to gain.

Windows stood open to summer fragrances blowing from the fields and woodlands of Poitou. The river Mable clucked past an ancestral castle lately rebuilt as a modern palace. Sunlight, reflected off the water, danced in shards among the cherubs and ancient heroes that adorned the ceiling. At a little distance from the cardinal's thronelike chair, a kitten played with its shadow across the parquetry.

Richelieu's thin fingers stroked the parchment on his lap. Its age-spotted dun made his robe appear blood-bright. For this meeting he had put on full canonicals, as though to shield against demons. But when he spoke, his voice held its wonted wintry calm.

'If this be not falsified, today shall perhaps see the strangest audience I have ever granted.'

Jacques Lacy bowed with more grace than would have been awaited. 'I thank your eminence for it, and assure him all is true.' His speech was not quite of the region nor of any in France. Did it still bear a lilt of Ireland, or of some land farther yet? Certainly it showed that, if not formally educated, he had read many books. Where did a skipper plying between the Old World and the New find time?

'You may thank the bishop who prevailed upon me,' said Richelieu dryly.

'After the priest of St Félix had prevailed upon another, Your Eminence.'

'You are a bold one indeed, Captain Lacy. Have a care. This matter is dangerous enough already.'

'I humbly beg Your Eminence's pardon.' The tone was by no means insolent, but neither was it contrite.

'Well, let us get on with your business.' Even away from Paris, hours were precious; and the future might not hold a large store of them. Nevertheless Richelieu considered for a minute, stroking the beard that brought the gauntness of his features to a point, before ordering: 'Describe exactly what you said to the priest and caused him to do.'

Surprise slightly shook Lacy's self-command. 'Your Eminence knows.'

'I will compare the accounts.' Richelieu sighed. 'And you may spare the honorifics hereafter. We are alone.'

'I thank Your – Well.' The mariner drew breath. 'I sought him out at his church in St Nazaire after I heard that … monsieur would grace these parts, no enormous distance to travel from there, with his presence for a while. I told him of the casket. Rather, I reminded him, for he knew about it in a half-forgotten way. Naturally, that caught his attention, for nobody else remembered. It had simply gathered dust in the crypt these past four hundred years.'

The kitten pounced at Lacy's foot. A smile in its direction flickered across the cardinal's lips. His eyes, huge and feverishly luminous, turned back to the man. 'Did you relate how it came to be there?' he pursued.

'Certainly, monsieur. That was evidence for my good faith, since the story had not become part of folklore.'

'Do so again.'

'Ah … in those days a Breton trader named Pier, of Ploumanac'h, settled in St Nazaire. It was hardly more than a village – not that it's major these days, as monsieur doubtless knows – but on that account a house cost little, and the location was handy for the small coastwise vessel he acquired. Men could more easily change their homes and trades then than now. Pier prospered modestly, married, raised children. At last, widowed, he declared he'd enlist in the crusade – the final one, as it turned out – that King Louis the Saint was launching. By that time he was old, but remarkably well-preserved. Many people said he still looked downright youthful. He was never seen afterward, and folk supposed he had died.

'Before he left, he made a substantial donation to the parish church. That was common when someone was about to go on a long journey, let alone off to war. However, to this gift he attached a condition. The church was to keep a box for him. He showed the priest that it contained nothing more than a rolled-up parchment, a document of some importance and confidentiality; whereupon he sealed it. One day he or an heir would return to claim it, and the parchment itself would validate that claim. Well, a request of this kind was not unheard of, and the priest duly entered it in the annals. Lifetimes went by. When I appeared, I expected I'd have to find the record for today's priest; but he's an antiquarian and had browsed through the books.'

Richelieu lifted the parchment and read it for perhaps the seventh time, repeatedly glancing at Lacy. 'Yes,' he murmured, 'this declares that the rightful heir will look just like Pier de Ploumanac'h, whatever name he bears, and describes him in full. Excellently crafted, that description.' The cardinal fancied himself a man of letters, and had written and produced several dramas. 'Furthermore, there is this verse in supposed nonsense syllables that the claimant will be able to recite without looking at the text.'

'Shall I do so for monsieur?'

'No need – thus far. You did for the priest, and later for his bishop. The proof was sufficient that he in turn wrote to the bishop of this diocese, persuading him to persuade me to see you. For the document concludes by declaring that the ... heir ... will carry tidings of the utmost importance. Now why did you refuse any hint of their nature to either prelate?'

'They are only for the greatest man in the land.'

'That is His Majesty.'

The visitor shrugged. 'What chance would I have of admission to the king? Rather, I'd be arrested on suspicion of – almost anything, and my knowledge tortured out of me. Your eminence is known to be more, m-m, flexible. Of an inquiring mind. You patronize learned and literary men, you've founded a national academy, you've rebuilt and generously endowed the Sorbonne, and as for political achievements –' His words trailed off while he waved his hands. Clearly he thought of the Huguenots curbed, yet kept conciliated; of the powers of the nobles patiently chipped down, until now their feudal castles were for the most part demolished; of the cardinal's rivals at court outwitted, defeated, some exiled or executed; of the long war against the Imperialists, in which France – with Protestant Sweden, the ally that Richelieu obtained – was finally getting the upper hand. Who really ruled this country?

Richelieu raised his brows. 'You are very well informed for a humble sea captain.'

'I have had to be, monsieur,' replied Lacy quietly.

Richelieu nodded. 'You may be seated.'

Lacy bowed once more and fetched a lesser chair, which he placed before the large one at a respectful distance, and lowered himself. He sat back, seemingly at ease, but a discerning eye recognized readiness to explode into instant action. Not that there was any danger. Guards stood just outside the door.

'What is this news you bear?' Richelieu asked.

Lacy frowned. 'I do not expect Your Eminence to believe upon first hearing it. I gamble my life on the supposition that you will bear with me, and will dispatch trusty men to bring you the further evidence I can provide.'

The kitten frolicked about his ankles. 'Chariot likes you,' the cardinal remarked, a tinge of warmth in his voice.

Lacy smiled. 'They say monsieur is fond of cats.'

'While they are young. Go on. Let me see what you know about them. It will tell me something about you.'

Lacy leaned forward and tickled the kitten around the ears. It extended tiny claws and swarmed up his stockings. He helped it to his lap, chucked it under the chin and stroked the soft fur. 'I've had cats myself,' he said. 'Afloat and ashore. They were sacred to the ancient Egyptians. They drew the chariot of the Norse goddess of love. They're often called familiars of witches, but that's nonsense. Cats are what they are, and never try like dogs to be anything else. I suppose that's why we humans find them mysterious, and some of us fear or hate them.'

'While some others like them better than their fellow men, God forgive.' The cardinal crossed himself in perfunctory fashion. 'You are a remarkable man, Captain Lacy.'

'In my way, monsieur, which is quite different from yours.'

Richelieu's gaze intensified. 'I obtained a report on you, of course, when I heard of your wish,' he said slowly. 'But tell me about your past life in your own words.'

'That you may judge them – and me, monsieur?' The mariner's look went afar, while his right hand continued as the kitten's playmate. 'Well, then, I'll tell it in a curious way. You'll soon understand the reason for that, which is that I do not want to lie to you.

'Seumas Lacy hails from northern Ireland. He can't readily say when he was born, for the baptismal record is back there if it's not been destroyed; but on the face of it, he must be around fifty years old. In the year 1611 the English king cleared the Irish from the best parts of Ulster and settled it with Scottish Protestants. Lacy was among those who left the country. He took a bit of money along, for he came of a mildly well-to-do seafaring family. In Nantes he found refuge with old-established Irish trading folk, who helped him regularize his status. He took the French form of his Christian name, became a French subject, and married a French woman. Being a sailor, he made long voyages, as far as Africa, the West Indies, and New France. Eventually he rose to shipmaster. He has four children alive, their ages from thirteen to five, but his wife died two years ago and he has not remarried.'

'And when he heard that I would be in Poitou for several weeks, he went downstream to St Nazaire and opened the casket that his ... ancestor had left in the church,' Richelieu said low.

Lacy looked straight at him. 'Thus it is, Your Eminence.'

'Presumably you always knew about it.'

'Obviously I did.'

'Although you are Irish? And no member of your family claimed the thing for four centuries. You yourself lived almost thirty years in nearby Nantes before you did. Why?'

'I had to be sure of the situation. At that, the decision was hard.'

'The report states that you have an associate, a redheaded man with a missing hand who goes by the name of MacMahon. Lately he has disappeared. Why?'

'No disrespect intended, Your Eminence, but I sent him off because I couldn't foresee what would come of this, and it was wrong to risk his life also.' Lacy smiled. The kitten tumbled about his wrist. 'Besides, he's an uncouth sort. What if he gave offense?' He paused. 'I took care not to know just where he's gone. He'll find out whether I've returned safely home.'

'You show a distrustfulness that is ... scarcely friendly.'

'On the contrary, monsieur, I'm putting a faith in you that I've put in none but my comrade for a very long time. I stake everything on the belief that you will not immediately assume I'm a madman, an enemy agent, or a sorcerer.'

Richelieu gripped the arms of his chair. Despite the robe, it could be seen how his wasted frame tautened. His eyes never wavered. 'What, then, are you?' he asked tonelessly.

'I am Jacques Lacy from Ireland, your eminence,' the visitor replied with the same levelness. 'The only real falsehood about that is that I was born there, for I was not. I did spend more than a century in it. Outside the English-held parts people have a large enough measure of freedom that it's rather easy to change lives. But I fear they are all doomed to conquest, and the plantation of Ulster gave me an unquestionable reason for departing.

'I came back to where I had once been Pier de Ploumanac'h – who was not a Breton born. Before and after him I've used other names, lived in other places, pursued other trades. It's been my way of surviving through the millennia.'

Breath hissed between teeth. 'This is not a total surprise to me. Since I first heard from the bishop, I have been thinking ... Are you the Wandering Jew?'

The head shook; the kitten sensed tension and crouched. 'I know about rascals who've pretended they were him. No, monsieur, I was alive when Our Lord was on earth, but never saw him, nor knew about him till much later. Once in a while I have passed myself off as a Jew, because that was safest or simplest, but it was pretense, same as when I've been a Mussulman.' The mouth formed a grim grin. 'For those roles, I had to get circumcised. The skin slowly grew back. On my kind, unless a wound is as great as the loss of a hand, it heals without scars.'

'I must think anew.' Richelieu closed his eyes. Presently his lips moved. They shaped the Paternoster and the Ave, while his fingers drew the Cross, over and over.

Yet when he was done and looked back upon the world, down at the parchment, he spoke almost matter-of-factly. 'I saw at once that the verse here is not actually nonsense. It bears a certain resemblance to Hebraic, transcribed in Roman letters, but it is different. What?'

'Ancient Phoenician, Your Eminence. I was born in Tyre when Hiram was its king. I'm not sure whether David or Solomon was reigning in Jerusalem just then.'

Again Richelieu closed his eyes. 'Two and a half millennia ago,' he whispered. He opened them wide. 'Recite the verse. I want to hear that language.'

Lacy obeyed. The rapid, guttural words rang through sounds of wind and water, through the silence that filled the chamber. The kitten sprang off his lap and pattered to a corner.

Stillness prevailed for half a minute before Richelieu asked, 'What does it mean?'

'A fragment of a song, the sort men sang in taverns or when camped ashore during a voyage. *Black as the sky of night is my woman's hair, bright as the stars are her eyes, round and white as the moon her breasts, and she moves like Ashtoreth's sea. Would that my sight and my hands and myself lay upon all!'* I'm sorry it's so profane, monsieur. It was what I could remember, and at that, I had to reconstruct it.'

Richelieu quirked a smile. 'Yes, I daresay one forgets much in thousands of years. And in … Pier's day, clerics, too, were less refined than they are now.' Shrewdly: 'Though did you expect that something like this would go a little way toward authenticating you, since it is the kind of thing that would stick in a man's mind?'

'I am not lying to Your Eminence. In no particular.'

'In that case, you have been a liar throughout the ages.'

Lacy spread his palms. 'What would monsieur have had me do? Imagine, if you please, even in this most enlightened of eras and countries, imagine I proclaimed myself openly. At best I'd be taken for a mountebank, and be lucky to escape with a scourging. I could easily go to the galleys, or hang. At worst I'd be condemned as a sorcerer, in league with Satan, and burned. Evil would befall me without my saying a word if I just stayed in one place, living on and on while they buried my sons and grandsons and I never showed signs of age. Oh, I've met folk – many live at this moment in the New World – for whom I could be a holy man or a god; but they've been savages, and I prefer civilization. Besides, civilization sooner or later overruns the savages. No, best I arrive at a new home as a plausible outsider, settle down a few decades, and at last move onward in such wise that people take for granted I've died.'

'What brought this fate upon you?' Richelieu signed himself anew.

'God alone knows, Your Eminence. I'm no saint, but I don't believe I was ever an especially terrible sinner. And, yes, I am baptized.'

'When was that?'

'About twelve hundred years ago.'

'Who converted you?'

'I'd been a Christian catechumen a long time, but customs changed and – May I ask leave to defer telling how it happened?'

'Why?' demanded Richelieu.

'Because I must convince Your Eminence that I'm telling the truth, and in this case the truth looks too much like invention –' Before those eyes, Lacy broke off, threw up his hands, laughed, and said, 'Very well, if you insist. It was in Britain after the Romans were gone, at the court of a warlord. They called him Riothamus, their High King, but mainly he had some cataphracts. With them he staved off the English invaders. His name was Artorius.'

Richelieu sat motionless.

'Oh, I was no knight of his, merely a trader who came by on my rounds,' Lacy stated. 'Nor did I meet any Lancelot or Gawain or Galahad, nor see any glittering Camelot. Little of Rome lingered there. In fact, it's only my guess that this was the seed corn of the Arthur legend. But monsieur will understand why I was reluctant to mention it at all. I was tempted to concoct a prosaic falsehood.'

Richelieu nodded. 'I do understand. If you continue a liar, you are as skillful a one as I have found in a wide experience.' He forbore to inquire whether the Phoenician had embraced Christ out of expediency, the same as when he did homage to numerous other gods.

Lacy's tone became wry. 'I shan't insult you by denying that I've given a great deal of beforehand thought to this interview.'

Richelieu plucked the parchment from his lap and cast it to the floor. It struck with a small rattling noise that drew the notice of the kitten. So much of a bodily gesture did the cardinal permit himself. He leaned forward, fingertips pressed together. Sunlight glistened off a great ring of gold and emerald. 'What do you want from me?' he snapped.

'Your protection, monsieur,' Lacy replied, 'for myself and any like me.' Color came and went in his lean cheeks, above the closely trimmed beard which had not a single silver hair.

'Who are they?'

'MacMahon is one, as your eminence must have guessed,' Lacy told him. 'We met in France when it was still Gaul. I've encountered or heard of three more whom I wondered about, but death by mischance took them before I could be certain. And another I did feel sure of, but that person – disappeared. Our kind must be very rare, and shy of revealing themselves.'

'Vanishingly rare, as the learned doctor Descartes might put it,' said Richelieu with a flash of bleak humor.

'Some, over the centuries, may have tried to do what I am trying this day, and come to grief. No record of them would likely remain, if any was ever made.'

The kitten advanced cautiously toward the parchment. Richelieu sat back. Lacy had stayed well-nigh immobile, hands folded on the sober-hued knee breeches. 'What more evidence have you to offer?' the cardinal asked.

Lacy gazed away at nothing visible. 'I thought about this for lifetimes before I took the first measures.' His voice was methodical. 'One gets into the habit of taking forethought and biding one's time. Perhaps too much so. Perhaps opportunities slip by and it's again too late. But one has learned, sometimes at a high price, monsieur, one has learned that this world is dangerous and nothing in it abides. Kings and nations, popes and gods – no irreverence meant – all go down in the dust or up in the flames, all too soon. I have my provisions, piecemeal made over the centuries, hoards buried here and there, tricks for changing identities, a tool chest of assorted skills, and ... my reliquaries. They are not all in churches, nor are they all of them caskets containing parchments. But throughout Europe, northern Africa, hither Asia lie the tokens I planted whenever I could. My idea was that if and when a hope came along, I'd go to the nearest of those caches and retrieve what it held. That should give me my opening wedge.

'Now, if Your Eminence likes, I can describe quite a few that will be accessible to his agents. I can say exactly what the nature of each is, and where it reposes. In several cases, at least, it will definitely have been there for a long while. In every case, they can verify that Captain Jacques Lacy could not possibly have made the arrangements at any time in the half century that men have known him.'

Richelieu stroked his beard. 'And meanwhile you expect to wait in custody, hostage to this material,' he murmured. 'Yes. I have little doubt that it exists, for you show no signs of madness. Therefore you cannot be an impostor either, of any sort known to criminal justice. Unless, indeed, you really are a sorcerer, or an actual demon.'

A film of sweat shone on Lacy's brow, though he responded steadily: 'Holy water or exorcism won't hurt me. You could have me put to the question. You'd find me healing quite fast from anything that didn't kill or totally mutilate. I came here because everything I could find out made me think you are too wise – I do not say "merciful," monsieur, I say "wise, enlightened, intelligent" – to resort to that.'

'Others will urge me to do so.'

'Your Eminence has the power to refuse them. That's another reason why I sought you. I've waited centuries for such a man at such a crux in history.'

The kitten arrived at the parchment, reached out, patted it. Curled back into a loose roll, it rustled and moved. Delighted, the kitten bounced to and fro.

Richelieu's look smoldered. 'Have you never before had a protector?'

Lacy sighed. 'Once, monsieur. About three hundred years after my birth, in Egypt.'

'Tell me.'

'Like a number of Phoenicians – I'd resumed that nationality – I sailed in the service of Pharaoh Psammetk. You may have read of him under the name Psammetichus. He chanced to be strong and wise, like you, a man who saved his country from disaster and made it once more secure. Oh, I'd planned nothing, except to depart in my usual way when the time came. But it also chanced this king lived long, reigning for more than fifty years. And I – well, it was a good service I was in; and when my first Egyptian wife died I married another and we were … uncommonly happy. So I lingered, till the king saw past the mannerisms by which I feigned encroaching age. He persuaded me to confide in him, and took me under his wing. To him I was sacred, chosen by the gods for some purpose unknown but surely high. He set inquiries afoot throughout his realm and as far abroad as possible. Nothing came of them. As I said, my kind must be very rare.'

'What finally happened?'

'Psammetk died. His son Necho succeeded him, and had no love for me. Nor hatred, I suppose; but most of the priests and courtiers did, seeing me as a threat to their positions. It grew plain that I wouldn't last in the royal compound. If nothing else, an assassin would get me. But the new king denied me leave to go. I think he feared what I might be able to do.

'Well, talk rose about dispatching a Phoenician crew to try sailing around Africa. I used what little influence was left me to help make that come about, and be named to it. An immortal man might prove valuable in unknown countries.' Lacy shrugged. 'At the first opportunity, I jumped ship and made my way to Europe. I never found out whether the expedition succeeded. Herodotus said it did, but he was often careless about his information.'

'And I assume any record of you in Egypt has decayed, if your enemies didn't expunge it,' Richelieu said. 'Not that we can read those glyphs.'

'Please understand, monsieur,' Lacy urged, 'I've seldom been in the presence of greatness. Psammetk, Artorius, two or three others, but usually insignificantly; and now Your Eminence. I've glimpsed more, but only when I was in a crowd. It's almost always been wisest to stay obscure. Besides, I'm just an old sailor, with nothing special to offer.' Eagerly: 'Except my memories. Think what I can mean to scholars. And if, under your protection, I draw other immortals to us – think, my lord, what that will mean to … France.'

Silence fell again, except for the wind, the river, a ticking clock, and the kitten that made a toy of the parchment. Richelieu brooded. Lacy waited.

At last the cardinal said: 'What do you truly want of me?'

'I told you, monsieur! Your protection. A place in your service. The proclamation of what I am, and the promise that anyone like me can come to the same safe harbor.'

'Every rogue in Europe will swarm here.'

'I'll know what questions to ask, if your learned men don't.'

'M-m, yes, I daresay you will.'

'After you've made a few examples, that nuisance should end.' Lacy hesitated. 'Not that I can foretell what the immortals will each prove to be like. I've admitted, my MacMahon is a crude sort. The other whom I was sure of is, or has been, a prostitute, if she still lives. One survives as best one can.'

'But some may well be decent, or repent. Some may in truth be holy – hermits, perhaps?' Richelieu's momentarily dreamy tone sharpened. 'You have not sought for any new patron after that Egyptian king, more than two thousand years ago?'

'I told Your Eminence, one grows wary.'

'Why have you now at last let down your guard?'

'In part because of you,' Lacy answered at once. 'Your Eminence hears much flattery. I needn't go into detail about what's the plain truth. I've already spoken it.

'But you by yourself wouldn't have been enough. It's also that I dare hope the times are right.'

The parchment jammed against a leg of the chair of state and resisted further attempts. The kitten mewed. Richelieu looked down and half reached. 'Does my lord wish –?' Lacy sprang to pick up the animal and proffer it. Richelieu took the small fuzzy form in both hands and placed it on his lap where the parchment had rested. Lacy bowed and resumed his seat.

'Continue,' the cardinal said while he caressed his pet.

'I have watched the course of things as well as a man can who's in the middle of them,' Lacy said. 'I've read books and listened to philosophers, and to common folk with native wit. I've thought. Immortality is lonely, monsieur. One has much time for thinking.

'It seems to me that in the past two or three centuries, a change has been coming upon the world. Not just the rise or fall of another empire; a change as great as the change from boy to man, or even worm to butterfly. Mortals feel it too. They speak of a Renaissance that began perhaps fourteen hundred years after Our Lord. But I see it more clearly. Pharaoh Psammetk – how far could his couriers go? How many could they find who'd understand my question that they bore, and not cower from it, ignorant and frightened? And he was as powerful a king as any in his age. The Greeks, the Romans, the Byzantines, the Persians, all the rest, they were little better as regards either knowledge or range. Nor did I ever again have access to a ruler I trusted; nor had I then thought to prepare myself for such a meeting. That came later.

'Today men have sailed around the globe; and they know it *is* a globe. The discoveries of such as Copernicus and Galileo –' He saw the slight frown. 'Well, be that as it may, men learn marvelous things. Europe goes forth into a whole new hemisphere. At home, for the first time since Rome fell, we begin to have good roads; one can travel swiftly, for the most part safely, over hundreds of leagues – thousands, once this war is over. Above all, maybe, we have the printing press, and more people every year who can read, who can be reached. At last we can bring the immortals together!'

Richelieu's fingers amused the kitten, which was becoming drowsy, while his brows again drew downward. 'That will take a considerable time,' he said.

'Oh, yes, as mortals reckon – Forgive me, Your Eminence.'

'No matter.' Richelieu coughed. 'With none but Chariot to hear, we can speak plainly. Do you indeed believe mankind – here in France, let us say – has attained the security that you found to be such a delusion through all prior history?'

Taken aback, Lacy stammered, 'N-no, monsieur, except that – I think France will be strong and stable for generations to come. Thanks largely to Your Eminence.'

Richelieu coughed afresh, his left hand to his mouth, his right reassuring the kitten. 'I am not a well man, Captain,' he said, hoarsened. 'I never have been. God may call me at any moment.'

Lacy's visage took on a somehow remote gentleness. 'I know that,' he said softly. 'May He keep you with us for many years yet. But –'

'Nor is the king in good health,' Richelieu interrupted. 'Finally, finally he and the queen are blessed with a child, a son; but the prince is not quite two years old. About when he was born, I lost Father Joseph, my closest councillor and ablest helper.'

'I know that also. But you have this Italian-born Mazarin, who's much like you.'

'And whom I am preparing to be my successor.' Richelieu's smile writhed. 'Yes, you have studied us carefully.'

'I must. I've learned how, during my span on earth. And you too think far ahead.' Lacy's words quickened. 'I beg you, think. You'll need a while to take this in, as well as to verify my story. I'm amazed how calmly you've heard me out. But – an immortal, in due course a gathering of immortals, at the service of the king – today's king, and afterward his son, who should reign long and vigorously. Can you imagine what that will mean to his glory, and so to the glory and power of France?'

'No, I cannot,' Richelieu snapped. 'Nor can you. And I have likewise learned wariness.'

'But I tell you, Your Eminence, I can give you evidence –'

'Silence,' Richelieu commanded.

He rested left elbow on chair arm, chin on that fist, and stared into space, as if beyond the walls, the province, the kingdom. His right hand gently stroked the kitten. It fell asleep, and he took his fingers away. The wind and the river rustled.

At last – the clock, on which Phaeton careered desperately in Apollo's runaway sun chariot, had snipped off almost a quarter of an hour – he stirred and looked back at the other man. Lacy had gone Orientally impassive. Now his countenance came alive. The breath shivered in and out of him.

'I need not trouble myself with your tokens,' Richelieu said heavily. 'I assume you are what you assert. It makes no difference.'

'I beg Your Eminence's pardon?' Lacy whispered.

'Tell me,' Richelieu went on, and he came to sound nearly amiable, 'do you, in the teeth of what you have seen and suffered, do you really believe we have won to a state of things that will endure?'

'N-no,' Lacy admitted. 'No, I think instead everything is changing, everything, and this will go on and on, and nobody can guess what the end will be. But – because of it – we and the generations to come, our lives will be unlike any that ever were lived before. The old bets are off.' He paused. 'I've grown weary of being homeless. You cannot dream of how weary. I'll snatch at any chance of escape.'

Richelieu ignored the informal language. Perhaps he did not notice it. He nodded, and said as he might have crooned to one of his pets, 'Poor soul. How brave you are, to have ventured this. Or else, as you say, how weary. But you have just your single life to lose. I have millions.'

Lacy's head lifted stiffly. 'My lord?'

'I am responsible for this realm,' Richelieu said. 'The Holy Father is old and troubled and never had any gift of statecraft. Thus I am also responsible to a certain extent for the Catholic faith, which is to say Christendom. A good many people think I've given myself over to the Devil, and I confess to scorning most scruples. But in the end, I am responsible.

'You see this as an age of upheaval, but also of hope. You may be right, perhaps, but if so, you look on it with an immortal eye. I can only, I may only, see the upheaval. War devastating the German lands. The Empire – our enemy, yes, nevertheless the Holy Roman Empire that Charlemagne founded – bleeding to death. Protestant sect after sect springing up, each with its own doctrine, its own fanaticism. The English growing back to power, the Dutch growing newly to it, voracious and ruthless. Stirrings in Russia, India, China. God knows what in the Americas. Cannon and muskets bringing down the ancient strongholds, the ancient strengths – but what will replace them? To you, the discoveries of the natural philosophers, the books and pamphlets that pour from the printing presses, those are wonders that will bring a new era. I agree; but I, in my position, must ask myself what that era will be like. I must try to cope with it, keep it under control, knowing the entire while that I shall die unsuccessful and those who come after me will fail.'

His question lashed: 'How then dare you suppose I would ever allow, yes, encourage and trumpet the knowledge that persons exist whom old age passes by? Should I – the doctor Descartes might say – throw yet another, wholly unknown and unmanageable factor into an equation already insoluble? "Unmanageable." Indeed that is the right word. The sole certainty I have is that this spark would ignite a thousand new religious lunacies and make peace in Europe impossible for another generation or worse.

'No, Captain Whatever-you-are,' he ended, glacial again in the way the world had come to fear, 'I want no part of you or your immortals. France does not.'

Lacy sat equally quiet. He had had his reverses often before. 'May I try to persuade Your Eminence otherwise, over the next few days or years?' he asked.

'You may not. I have too much else to occupy my mind, and too damnably little time left for it.'

Richelieu's manner mildened. 'Be at ease,' he said with half a smile. 'You shall depart freely. Caution enjoins me to have you arrested and garroted within this hour. Either you are a charlatan and deserve it or a mortal danger and require it. However, I deem you a sensible man who will withdraw to his obscurity. And I am grateful to you for a fascinating glimpse of – what is best left alone. Could I have my wish, you would stay a while and we would talk at length. But that would be risky to me and unkind to you. So let us store this afternoon, not among our memories, but among our fantasies.'

Lacy sat silent for a bit, until he drew breath and answered, 'Your Eminence is generous. How can you tell I won't betray your trust and seek elsewhere?'

Richelieu chuckled. 'Where else? You have called me unique. The queen of Sweden has a penchant for curious characters, true. She is still a minor, though, and when she does take power, well, everything I know about her makes me warn you most sincerely to stay away. You are already aware of the hazards in any other country that matters.'

He bridged his fingers. 'In all events,' he continued, didactic, 'your scheme was poor from the beginning, and my advice is that you abandon it forever. You have seen much history; but how much of it have you *been?* I suspect that I, in my brief decades, have learned lessons in which your nose was never rubbed.

'Go home. Then, I strongly suggest, make provision for your children and disappear with your friend. Take up a new life, perhaps in the New World. Remove yourself, and me, from temptation, remembering what my temptation is. For you dream a fool's dream.'

'Why?' Lacy croaked.

'Have you not guessed? Really, I am disappointed in you. Hope has triumphed over experience. Hark back. Remember how kings have kept wild animals in cages – and freaks at court. Oh, if I accepted you I might be honest in my intentions, and Mazarin might be after me; but what of young Louis XIV when he comes to his majority? What of *any* king, any government? The exceptions are few and fleeting. Even if you immortals were a race of philosophers who also understood how to rule me – do you suppose those who do rule would or could share power with you? And you have admitted you are only extraordinary in your lifespans. What can you become but animals in the royal menagerie, endlessly watched by the secret police and disposed of if ever you become inconveniently articulate? No, keep your freedom, whatever it costs you.

'You begged me to think about your proposal. I tell you to go and think about my counsel.'

The clock ticked, the wind blew, the river flowed.

From down in his throat, Lacy asked, 'Is this Your Eminence's last word?'

'It is,' Richelieu told him.

Lacy rose. 'Best I leave.'

Richelieu's lips contorted. 'I do wish I had more time to give you,' he said, 'and myself.'

Lacy approached. Richelieu extended his right hand. Lacy bowed and kissed it. Straightening, he said, 'Your Eminence is as great a man as I have ever met.'

'Then God have mercy on humankind,' Richelieu replied.

'I shall never forget you.'

'I will bear that in mind for as long as is granted me. Farewell, wanderer.'

Lacy went to the door and knocked. A guard opened it. Richelieu signalled him to let the man by and close it again. Thereupon he sat with his thoughts. The sunlight lengthened. The kitten woke, scrambled down his robe, and frisked off in its own life.

XII

THE LAST MEDICINE

Over the plain from the north the young men came a-gallop. The haste and rhythm of it were like the ripples that went through the grass beneath the wind. Sunflowers here and there swayed the same, lofty, petals as hot yellow as the light pouring across the world. Land and sky reached both unbounded, green seemed to meet blue but that was only at the edge of sight, distance went on and on farther than dreams could fly. A hawk rode the airflows, dipping and soaring, his wings twin flames. A flight of marshfowl lifted, so many that they darkened their quarter of heaven.

Children set to keep crows out of the fields were first to see the young men. The oldest boy among them ran back to the village, filled with importance; for Deathless had ordered that he be told of the return. Yet when the boy had passed inside the stockade and was among the houses, his courage faltered. Who was he to speak to the mightiest of all shamans? Dared he risk interrupting a spell or a vision? Women at their work saw him stand forlorn. One hailed him, 'Ohé, Little Hare, what is in your heart?' But they were only women, the old men he glimpsed were only old men, and surely this was a thing of terrible power if Deathless cared so much about it.

The boy gulped and made for a certain house. Its dun sod loomed over him. When he came around its length to the front, the doorway gaped on a nightful cave where a single banked fire glimmered red. The families that shared it were elsewhere, doing their tasks or, if they had none, taking their ease down by the river. One did remain, the person for whom Little Hare had hoped, a man dressed in woman's clothes, grinding corn. He looked up and asked in his mild way, 'What do you wish, lad?'

Little Hare gulped. 'The hunters come back,' he said. 'Will you go tell the shaman, Three Geese?'

The noise of stone against stone ceased. The berdache rose. 'I will,' he replied. Such as he had some power against the unseen, perhaps because the spirits made up to them for their lack of manliness. Besides, he was a son of Deathless. He dusted meal off his buckskin, uncoiled his braids, and departed at a dignified pace. Little Hare gusted relief before he started back to his duty. Eagerness tingled in him. What a brave sight the riders would be when they went by!

The shaman's house stood next to the medicine lodge at the middle of the village. It was smaller than the rest because it was only for him and his family. He was there just then with his wives. Copperbright, mother of Three Geese, sat on the ground outside, watching over the two small daughters of Quail Wing while they played in the sun. Bent, half-blind, she was glad she could still help this much at her great age. In the doorway, Rain At Evening, who had been born the same winter as the berdache, helped a daughter of her own, Dawn Mist, ornament a dress with dyed quills for the maiden's forthcoming marriage. She greeted the newcomer and, at his word, went inside to call her husband. Deathless came forth after a short while, still fastening his breech-clout. Young Quail Wing peeped out from within, looking rumpled and happy.

'Ohé, father,' said Three Geese with due respect but not the awe that was in the likes of Little Hare. After all, this man had dandled him when he was a baby, taught him to know the stars and how to set snares and everything else needful or delightful – and, when it grew clear that the youth was not going to become fully a man, never lessened his love but accepted the fact with the calm of one who had watched hundreds of lives blow past on the wind. 'They have seen Running Wolf's party on the way back to us.'

Deathless stood quiet for a bit. When he frowned, a single wrinkle spread on his face. Sweat made his skin gleam over the springy muscles like dew upon rock; his hair was like the rock itself, polished obsidian. 'Are they sure that is who it is?' he asked.

'Why, who else?' replied Three Geese, astonished.

'Enemies –'

'Raiders would not come so openly, in broad daylight. Father, you have heard about the Pariki and their ways.'

'Oh, true, I have,' the shaman muttered, as if he had forgotten and needed reminding. 'Well, I must make haste now, for I want to speak to the hunters alone.'

He went back into his house. Berdache and women exchanged looks where foreboding stirred. Deathless had spoken against the buffalo hunt, but Running Wolf had gotten his band together and left too swiftly for any real talk about it. Since then Deathless had brooded, and sometimes taken elders aside, who afterward kept silence themselves. What did they fear?

Soon Deathless reappeared. He had donned a shirt with strong signs burnt into the leather. White swirls of paint marked his countenance; a cap made from the pelt of a white mink encircled his brows. In his left hand he bore a gourd rattle, in his right a wand topped with a raven's skull. The rest stood aside, even the children gone silent. This was no longer the kindly, rather quiet husband and father they knew; this was he in whom a spirit dwelt, he who never grew old, he who during the ages had guided his folk and made them unlike any other.

The hush followed him as he walked among the dwellings. Not every eye watched with the ancient reverence. Especially in the heads of boys, several smoldered.

Through the open gate of the stockade he passed, and through the patches of corn, beans, and squash outside. The village stood on a bluff overlooking a broad, shallow river and the cottonwoods along the banks. Northward the ground sloped into gently rolling hugeness. Hereabouts short-grass prairie gave way to tall-grass plain. Shadows went mysterious over green waves. The hunters were now quite near. Earth drummed to hoofbeats.

When he recognized the man afoot, Running Wolf signalled halt and reined in. His mustang whinnied and curvetted before standing quiet. Leggings held close against ribs, the rider sat the beast as if he had grown from it or it from him. His dozen followers were nearly as skillful. Under the sun, men and horses alike blazed with life. In some hands were lances, on some shoulders hung bows and quivers. A knife of the finest flint rested at each waist. Headbands bore patterns of lightning bolt, thunderbird, hornet. From Running Wolf's, feathers of eagle and jay thrust upward – did he think someday he would fly?

'Ohé, great one,' he said reluctantly. 'You honor us.'

'How went the chase?' asked Deathless.

Running Wolf gestured backward at the pack animals. They bore hides, heads, haunches, humps, entrails, umbles, lavishness that strained against rawhide lashings. Already, as they rested, the grease and clotted blood were drawing flies. Exultance surged in his voice: 'Never was such sport, never such slaughter! We left more than this behind for the coyotes. Today the people feast, no, they gorge.'

'The spirits will punish wastefulness,' Deathless warned.

Running Wolf squinted at him while retorting, 'What, is Coyote not pleased that we feed his kind so well too? And the buffalo are as many as the blades of grass.'

'A fire can blacken the land –'

'And with the first rain it springs green anew.'

Breath hissed between teeth when the leader thus dared interrupt the shaman; but none of the band were really shocked. Two grinned.

Deathless ignored the breach, save that his tone grew harder still: 'When the buffalo come by, our men go forth to take of them. First they offer the proper dances and sacrifices. Afterward I explain our need to the ghosts of the quarry, that they be appeased. So it has always been, and we have prospered in peace. Ill must come from leaving the ancient, proven path. I will tell you what atonement you can make, and lead you in it.'

'And shall we then return to waiting until a herd drifts within a day's walk of here? Shall we try to cut a few out and kill them without any man getting gored or trampled? Or if we are lucky, may we stampede the whole herd over a drop, and see most meat rot before we can eat it? If our fathers brought home little, it was because they *could* do no more, nor could the dogs draw much on their wretched travois.' Running Wolf's words came in spate, never hesitating. Clearly he had awaited this encounter sometime upon his return, and planned what he would say.

'And if the new ways are unlucky,' exclaimed Red Hawk, 'why do the tribes that follow them flourish so mightily? Shall they take everything, and we pick the carrion bones?'

Running Wolf frowned at his follower and beckoned for silence. Deathless sighed. His response was almost gentle: 'I foreknew you would speak like this. Therefore I sought you out where nobody else can hear. It is hard for a man to admit he has been wrong. Together we shall find how you can set things right and still keep your pride. Come with me to the medicine lodge, and we will seek a vision.'

Running Wolf straightened, sheer against the sky. 'Vision?' he cried. 'I have had mine, old man, under the high stars after a day when we raced with the wind. I saw riches overflowing, deeds men will remember longer than you yourself have lived and will live, glory, wonder. New gods are in the land, fiery from the hands of the Creator, and – they ride on horses whose hoofs drum thunder and strike forth lightning. It is for you to make peace with them!'

Deathless lifted his wand and shook his rattle. Unease crossed faces. The mounts felt it and snorted, shied, stamped.

'I meant no offense, great one,' Running Wolf said quickly. 'You wish us to talk free of fear and boasting alike, no? Well, if I got too loud, I'm sorry.' He tossed his head. 'Nevertheless, the dream did come to me. I have told my comrades, and they believe.'

The magical things sank earthward in the shaman's grasp. He stood for a little while unmoving, dark amidst the sunlight and grass, before he said low, 'We must talk further and try to learn the meaning of what has happened.'

'Indeed we must.' Relief made Running Wolf's tone kindly. 'Tomorrow. Come, great one, let me lend you this, my prize stallion, and I will walk while you ride into the village, and you will bless us there as you have always blessed the returning hunters.'

'No.' Deathless went from them.

They sat mute, troubled, until Running Wolf laughed. He sounded like his namesake in wooded eastern country. 'The joy among our people will be blessing enough,' he said. 'And ah, for us the women, hotter than their fires!'

Most of them had to force an echo of his mirth. However, the act heartened them. He at the forefront, they struck heels to flanks and pounded whooping ahead. When they passed the shaman, they never glanced his way.

Upon his own entry, he found tumult. Folk seethed about the party, shouted, capered, exulted. Dogs clamored. The abundance was more than meat. It was fat, bone, horn, gut, sinew, all they needed to make nearly all they wanted. And this was the barest beginning. The hides would become coverings for tipis – those that were not traded eastward for poles – and then whole families could range as far and as long as they wished, hunt, butcher, tan, preserve on the spot, before going on to the next kill and the next …

'Not overnight,' Running Wolf cautioned. Though he spoke weightily, his voice carried through the racket. 'We have few horses yet. And first we must care for these that have served us.' Victory rang: 'But we shall soon have more. Every man of us shall have his herd.'

Somebody howled, somebody else did likewise, and then the tribe was howling – his sign, his name, his leadership to be.

Deathless went around them. Few noticed him. Those looked away, abashed, before throwing themselves the more wildly back into jubilance.

The wives and youngest children of Deathless stood fast outside his house. There they could not see the crowd, but the cheers broke across them. Quail Wing's gaze kept drifting yonder, wistfully. She was hardly more than a girl. He halted, confronted them. Lips parted but nobody had words.

'You were good to wait here,' he said at length. 'Now you may as well go join the rest, help cook the food, share in the feast.'

'And you?' asked Rain At Evening low.

'I have not forbidden it,' he said bitterly. 'How could I?'

'You counselled against the horses, you counselled against the hunt,' quavered Copperbright. 'What madness is in them, that they no longer heed you?'

'They will learn better,' Rain At Evening avowed.

'I am thankful I shall soon be snug in death.' Copperbright reached a gnarled hand toward Deathless. 'But you, poor darling, you must live through that lesson.'

Quail Wing regarded her children and shuddered a little.

'Go,' said the man. 'Have pleasure. Also, it will be wise. We must not let the folk feel divided. That could well destroy them. I always strove to keep my people together.'

Rain At Evening considered him. 'However, you will stay away?' she asked.

'I will try to think what can be done,' he answered, and went into the medicine lodge. They lingered a bit, troubled, before leaving. His unsureness, the defiance of him, struck at the heart of everything by which they had lived.

With its entrance toward sunrise, the lodge had at this time of day gone gloomy. Light from doorway and smoke-hole lost itself in shadows brimming the circle of floor and walls. Things magical were blurs, gleams, hunched lumps. Deathless laid buffalo chips in the firepit at the center. He worked with drill and tinder until flames licked small. After he had banked the fire, he put tobacco that traders bore from afar into his calumet, kindled it, breathed deep, let the sacred dizziness whirl him off toward meditation.

Insight escaped him. He was wanly glad when a form darkened the door-way. By then the sun was on the horizon he could not see. Light tinged with yellow the smoke that drifted thick and savory off cookfires. The din of cele-bration was at once loud and remote, only half real.

'Father?' came a shy whisper.

'Enter,' said Deathless. 'Be welcome.'

Three Geese stooped, passed through, settled on the opposite side of the pit. His face was barely visible, webbed and gullied with encroaching age, full of the concern that a berdache need not be ashamed to show. 'I hoped you would give me refuge here, father,' he said.

'From what?' asked Deathless. 'Has anyone abused you?'

'No, no. Everybody is gleeful.' Three Geese winced. 'That is what hurts. Even the old men seem to have cast their doubts from them.'

'Save for you.'

'And perhaps a few others. How should I know? More of the women are with us in their hearts, but the men sweep them along. And it *is* a mighty gain that Running Wolf and his followers have made.'

'He promises unboundedly much in the future.'

Three Geese grunted an affirmative.

'Why do you not share these hopes?' Deathless asked.

'You are my father, who was always kind to me,' said the berdache. 'I fear there will be scant kindness in the morrow that Running Wolf brings.'

'From what we know about the tribes who have gone the way of the horse, that is so.'

'I have heard men say – when I happened to be in earshot of man-talk – that some are forced to it.'

'True. They are thrust from their ancient homes, the eastern woodlands, out onto the prairie, by invaders from farther east. They say those invaders bear horrible weapons that shoot lightning. They get them from pale-skinned foreigners such as we hear rumors of. But others, like the Pariki, have freely taken to the horse, and spill out of the west, out of the mountains yonder.'

'They did not have to. We do not have to. I have spoken with travelers, traders, whoever bears news from outside. North of us the Arikara, Hidatsa, and Mandan still live in olden wise. They remain strong, well-off, content. I would have us do the same.'

'I have talked with two or three of those young men who brought horses despite your counsel, father,' said Three Geese. 'One of them went forth with Running Wolf, first to practice, later on this buffalo hunt. They say – he says – they intend no disrespect, no overthrow of anything. They only want for us whatever is good in the new ways.'

'I know. I also know you cannot pick and choose. Change is a medicine bundle. You must refuse it altogether, or take the whole thing.'

Sorrow thinned the voice of Three Geese: 'Father, I do not question your wisdom, but I have heard some who do. They wonder if you can understand change, you who live outside of time.'

Deathless smiled sadly through the dusk. 'Strange, my son, strange that only now, when you near the end of your days, do we truly confide in each other.' He drew breath. 'Well, I seldom speak of my youth. It was so long ago that it seems a half-forgotten dream. But as a boy I listened to my grandfather tell about the drought of many years that at last made our people trek eastward from the uplands, to find a better home here. We were still learning how to be plainsfolk when I became a man. I had no idea then of what I was. No, I expected to grow old and lie down to rest in the earth like everyone else. When, slowly, we came to see that this was not happening – what more soulshaking change than that can you imagine? Since it was clear the gods had singled me out, I must seek the shaman, have him teach me, change from man to disciple, finally from housefather to shaman myself. And the years flew by faster and faster. I saw girls born whom I wed when they were grown and buried when they had died, along with the children, the children. I saw more tribes pour onto the plains, and war begin among them. Do you know it was only in your mother's girlhood that we decided we must build a stockade? True, a certain awe of me has helped keep enemies off, but – Running Wolf has had a vision of new gods.'

He laughed wearily. 'Yes, my son, I have known change. I have felt time rush by like a river in flood, bearing the wreckage of hopes downstream out of sight. Now do you understand why I have tried to bulwark my people against it?'

'They must heed you,' Three Geese groaned. 'Make a medicine that will open their eyes and unstop their ears.'

'Who can make a medicine against time?'

'If anyone can, father, that one is you.' The berdache hugged himself and shivered, though the air was still mild. 'This is a good life we have, a gentle life. Save it for us!'

'I will try,' said Deathless. 'Leave me alone with the spirits.' He held out his arms. 'But first come and let me embrace you, my son.'

The old cold body trembled against the firm warm flesh, then Three Geese said farewell and departed.

Deathless sat unmoving as embers faded and night welled up out of the earth. Noise continued, drum-throb, chants, feet stamping around an extravagant fire. It grew louder when the doorway brightened again. A full moon had risen. That gray went black as the moon climbed higher, though the ground outside remained hoar. At last the merrymaking dwindled until silence laid its robe over the whole village.

No vision had come. Perhaps a dream would. He had heard that men of nomad tribes often tortured themselves in hope that that would call the spirits to them. He would abide with the ancient unforced harmonies. On a few heaped skins, one atop him, he slept.

Stars fared across heaven. Dew glittered in deepening chill. The very coyotes had quieted. Only the river murmured, along the banks, under the cottonwoods, around the sandbars, on and on in retreat from the sinking moon.

Slowly, eastern stars dimmed as their part of the sky turned pale.

The hoofs that neared scarcely broke the stillness. Riders dismounted, left their animals in care of chosen companions, approached on foot.

They meant to steal the horses hobbled outside the stockade. A boy on watch saw them and sped for the gate. He screamed his warning till a warrior overtook him. A lancethrust cast him to hands and knees. Little Hare gobbled around the blood that welled into his mouth. He threshed about till he fell in a heap that looked very small. War cries ripped the dawn.

'Out!' roared Running Wolf before his house. 'It's an attack! Save the horses!'

He was the first to dash forth into the open, but men swarmed after him, mostly naked, clutching whatever weapons they had snatched. The strangers sprang at them. Alien words yowled. Arrows whirred. Men screamed when struck, less in pain than in fury. Running Wolf bore a tomahawk. He sought the thick of the foe and hewed, snarled, a tornado.

Bewildered, the villagers nevertheless outnumbered the raiders. The Pariki leader yelled commands. His men rallied to him, where he shook his lance on high. In a body, they beat the defenders aside and poured through the opened gate.

Dawnlight strengthened. Like prairie dogs, women, children, old folk fled back into houses. The Pariki laughed and pursued them.

Running Wolf lost time getting his dismayed fighters together. Meanwhile the Pariki made their quick captures – a woman or child seized, hauled outside, or fine pelts grabbed, a buffalo robe, a shirt with colorful quillwork – and regathered in the lane that went straight to the gateway.

One warrior found a beautiful young woman with an aging one and a crone in the smallest of the houses, next to a round lodge. She wailed and clawed at his eyes. He pinned her wrists at her back and forced her along, regardless of struggles or of the others who sought to hinder him. A man bounded from the lodge. He was unarmed apart from a wand and a rattle. When he shook them, the warrior hooted and swung a tomahawk at him. The man must dodge back. The raider and his prey joined the rest of the war band.

Running Wolf's men milled in the entrance. At their backs, those Pariki who had kept the horses arrived at a gallop, with the free beasts on strings. The villagers scattered. The forayers seized manes, got on with a single leap, dragged booty or captives up after them. The men who had already been riding helped injured comrades mount and collected three or four dead.

Running Wolf bayed, egged his people on. Their arrows were spent, but enough of them finally came at his heels that the foe made no further try for their herd. Instead the Pariki rode west, bearing their prizes. Dazed with horror, the villagers did not give chase.

The sun rose. Blood glowed brilliant.

Deathless sought the battle place. Folk were getting busy there. Some mutilated two corpses the enemy had not recovered, so that the ghosts must forever drift in the dark; these persons wished aloud for live prisoners to torture to death. Others tended their own slain. Three Geese was among those who worked on the wounded. His hands eased anguish; his low voice helped men bite back any cries. Deathless joined him. The healing arts were part of a shaman's lore.

'Father,' said the berdache, 'I think we need you more to make medicine against fresh misfortune.'

'I know not if any power to do that is left in me,' Deathless replied.

Three Geese pushed a shaft deeper into a shoulder, until the barbed head came out the rear and he could pull the entire thing free. Blood welled, flies buzzed. He packed the hole with grass. 'I am ashamed that I was not in the fight,' he mumbled.

'You are long past your youth, and fighting was never for you,' Deathless said. 'But I – Well, this took me by surprise; and I have forgotten whatever I once knew about combat.'

Running Wolf stalked around, tallying the harm that had been done. He overheard. 'None of us knew anything,' he snapped. 'We shall do better next time.'

Three Geese bit his lip. Deathless went impassive.

Afterward he did undertake his duties as the shaman. With his disciple, who yesterday had never come near him, he led rites for the lost, cast spells for the clean mending of wounds, made offerings to the spirits. An elder mustered courage to ask why he did not seek omens. 'The future has become too strange,' he answered, and left the man standing appalled. By eventide he could take a short span to console Quail Wing's children for the taking of their mother, before he again went alone into the medicine lodge.

Next morning the people buried the dead. Later they would dance in their honor. First, though, the hale men gathered at a place which had known happier meetings. Running Wolf had demanded it – no council of elders calmly finding their way toward agreement, but every man who could walk – and none cared to gainsay him.

They assembled before a knoll near the bluff edge. Standing on it, a man could look south to the broad brown river and its trees, the only trees anywhere in sight; east to the stockade, the fields clustered about it, gravemounds both raw and time-worn; elsewhere across grass that billowed and shimmered, green and white, under a shrill wind. Clouds flew past, trailing shadows through a sunlight gone harsh. Thunderheads loomed blue-black in the west. From here the works of man seemed no more than anthills, devoid of life. Nothing but the horses moved yonder. They chafed at their hobbles, eager to be off and away.

Running Wolf mounted the knoll and raised an arm. 'Hear me, my brothers,' he called. Wrapped in a buffalo robe, he seemed even taller than he was. He had gashed his cheeks for mourning and painted black bars across his face for vengefulness. The wind fluttered the plumes in his headband.

'We know what we have suffered,' he told the eyes and the souls that sought him. 'Now we must think why it happened and how we shall keep it from ever happening again.

'I say to you, the answers are simple. We have few horses. We have hardly any men who are good hunters upon them, and we have no skilled warriors at all. We are poor and alone, huddled within our miserable walls, living off our meager crops. Meanwhile other tribes ride forth to garner the wealth of the plains. Meat-fed, they grow strong. They can feed many mouths, therefore they breed many sons, who in turn become horseman hunters. They have the time and the mettle to learn war. Their tribes may be strewn widely, but proud brotherhoods and sisterhoods, oath-societies, bind them together. Is it then any wonder that they make booty of us?'

His glance fell hard on Deathless, who stood in the front row under the hillock. The shaman's gaze responded, unwavering but blank. 'For years they stayed their hand,' Running Wolf said. 'They knew we had one among us who was full of spirit power. Nonetheless, at last a band of young men resolved to make a raid. I think some among them had had visions. Visions come readily to him who rides day after day across empty space and camps night after night beneath star-crowded skies. They may have urged each other on. I daresay they simply wanted our horses. The fight became as bloody as it did because we ourselves had no idea of how to wage it. This too we must learn.

'But what the Pariki have found, and soon every plains ranger will know, is that we have lost whatever defense was ours. What new medicine have we?'

He folded his arms. 'I ask you, Deathless, great one, what new medicine you can make,' he said. Slowly, he stepped aside.

Indrawn breath whispered among the men, beneath the damp chill that streaked from the stormclouds. They stared at the shaman. He stood still an instant. Thereafter he climbed the knoll and confronted Running Wolf. He had not adorned himself in any way, merely donned buckskins. Against the other man, he seemed drab, the life in him faded.

Yet he spoke steadily: 'Let me ask you first, you who take leadership from your elders, let me ask you and let you tell us what you would have the people do.'

'I did tell you!' Running Wolf declared. 'We must get more horses. We can breed them, buy them, catch them wild, and, yes, steal them ourselves. We must go win our share of the riches on the plains. We must become skilled in the arts of war. We must find allies, enroll in societies, take our rightful place among folk who speak Lakotan tongues. And all this we must begin upon at once, else it will be too late.'

'Thus is your beginning,' said Deathless quietly. 'The end is that you will forsake your home and the graves of your ancestors. You will have no dwellings save your tipis, but be wanderers upon the earth, like the buffalo, the coyote, and the wind.'

'That may be,' replied Running Wolf with the same levelness. 'What is bad about it?'

A gasp went from most listeners; but several young men nodded, like horses tossing their heads.

'Show respect,' quavered an aged grandson of the shaman. 'He is still the Deathless one.'

'He is that,' acknowledged Running Wolf. 'I have spoken what was in my heart. If it be mistaken, tell us. Then tell us what we should do, what we should become, instead.'

He alone heard the answer. The rest divined it, and some wrestled with terror while others grew thoughtful and yet others shivered as if in sight of prey.

'I cannot.'

Deathless turned from Running Wolf, toward the gathering. His voice loudened, though each word fell stone-heavy. 'I have no further business here. I have no more medicine. Before any of you were born, rumors came to me of these new creatures, horses, and of strange men who had crossed great waters with lightnings at their command. In time the horses reached our country, and that which I feared began to happen. Today it is done. What will come of it, nobody can foretell. All that I knew has crumbled between my fingers.

'Whether you must change or not – and it may well be that you must, for you lack the numbers to keep a settlement defended – you *will* change, my people. You want it, enough of you to draw the rest along. I no longer can. Time has overtaken me.'

He raised his hand. 'Therefore, with my blessing, let me go.'

It was Running Wolf who cried, Go? Surely not! You have always been ours.'

Deathless smiled the least bit. 'If I have learned anything in my lifetimes of years,' he said, 'it is that there is no "always."'

'But where would you go? How?'

'My disciple can carry out what is needful, until he wins stronger medicine from warrior tribes. My grown sons will see to the welfare of my two old wives and my small children. As for myself – I think I will fare alone in search of renewal, or else of death and an end of striving.'

Into their silence, he finished: 'I served you as well as I was able. Now let me depart.'

He walked down the knoll and away from them. Never did he look back.

XIII

FOLLOW THE DRINKING GOURD

A thunderstorm flamed and boomed during the night. By morning the sky was clear, everything asparkle, but the fields were too wet for work. That didn't matter. Crops were coming along fine, alfalfa so deep a green you could nearly hear the color and corn sure to be knee-high by the Fourth of July. Matthew Edmonds decided that after chores and breakfast he'd fix up his plow. The colter needed sharpening and there was a crack in the whip-pletree. If he reinforced it, he could get yet another season's use out of it before prudence called for replacement. Then Jane had a long list of tinker-ings around the house for him.

When he closed the kitchen door, he stopped and drew a breath on the top step. The air was cool and damp, rich with smells of soil, animals, growth. On his right the sun had just cleared the woods behind the bam; the rooster wea-thervane there threw the light back aloft into a blue that had no end. The yard was muddy, but puddles shone like mirrors. He let his eyes run left, across silo, pigsty, chickenhouse, over his acres that rolled away beyond them bear-ing the earth's abundance. Could he, could any man ever make any real return for the blessings of the Lord?

Something flickered at the edge of sight. He turned his head fully left. You could see the county road from here, about a hundred yards off along the west edge of the property. On the other side lay Jesse Lyndon's land, but his house was to the north, hidden from this by its own patch of woods. The Edmonds' drive was also screened from sight, lined with apple trees whose fruit was starting to swell among pale-bright leaves. Out from between them ran a woman.

Chief, the half-collie, was helping ten-year-old Jacob take the cows to pas-ture. That was just as well. The woman acted scared when Frankie bounded forth barking at her, and he was only a fox terrier. At least, she shied from him and made fending motions. She kept on running, though. No, she stag-gered, worn out, close to dropping. All she had on was a thin dress that had once been yellow, halfway down her shins. A shift, would the ladies call it? Ragged, filthy, and drenched, it clung to a skin from under which the flesh had melted away. That skin was the shade of weak coffee.

Edmonds sprang down the steps and broke into a run himself. 'You, Frankie, quiet!' he hollered. 'Shut up!' The little dog skipped aside, wagged his tail, and lolled his tongue.

Man and woman met near the corncrib, stopped, stared at each other. She looked young, maybe twenty, in spite of what hardship had done to her. Feed her up and she'd be slender and tall instead of skinny. Her face was different from the usual, narrow, nose curved and not very wide, lips hardly fuller than on some whites, big eyes with beautiful long lashes. Hair, cut short, wasn't really kinky; it would bush out if ever she let it grow. Edmonds thought with a pang how a slaveowner must have forced her mother or her grandmother.

The wind went raw in her throat. She tried to straighten, but a shiver took hold of her. 'Peace,' Edmonds said. 'Thee is with friends.'

She stared. He was a big sandy man, wearing clothes darker than most and a hat that was flat of crown, broad of brim. After a moment she gasped, 'Yo' Massa Edmonds?'

He nodded. 'Yes.' His voice stayed easy. 'And thee, I think, is a fugitive.'

She half lifted her hands. 'Please, suh, please, dey's aftuh me, right behin' me!'

'Then come.' He took her arm and led her across the yard to the kitchen door.

The room beyond was large and sunny, clean-scrubbed but still full of sweet odors. Jane Edmonds was spooning oatmeal into Nellie, not quite one, while four-year-old William stood on a stool and manfully pumped water into a kettle fresh off the stove. Its earlier load steamed in a dishpan. Everybody stopped when Father and the Negress appeared.

'This girl needs shelter, and quickly,' Edmonds told his wife.

Herself fine-boned, hair peeping red from beneath a scarf, she dropped the spoon and clutched fist between fingers. 'Oh, dear, we haven't any real hiding place ready.' Decision: 'Well, the attic must serve. Nothing in the basement to hide behind. Maybe the old trunk, if they search our house –'

The Negress leaned against the counter. She didn't pant or shake now, but wildness still dwelt in her eyes. 'Go with Jane,' Edmonds told her. 'Do what she says. We'll take care of thee.'

A brown hand snaked out. The big butcher knife almost flew from the rack into its grasp. 'Dey ain' gon' take me 'live!' she yelled.

'Put that down,' Jane said, shocked.

'Child, child, thee must not be violent,' Edmonds added. 'Trust in the Lord.'

The girl crouched back, blade bright in front of her. 'Ah don' wanna hurt nobody,' she answered, raspy-voiced, 'but dey fin' me, Ah kill mahse'f 'fo' dey take me back, an' fust Ah kill one o' dem if'm de Lawd he'p me.'

308

Tears stood forth in Jane's eyes. 'What have they done, to drive thee to this?'

Edmonds cocked his head. 'Frankie's barking again. Don't wait, let her keep the knife, just get her out of sight. I'll go talk to them.'

Since his boots were muddy, he went straight out and around the corner of the house to the front porch on the west side. The drive branched off where the apple trees ended, an arm leading south. Edmonds hushed the dog and placed himself on the step before the screen door, arms folded. When the two men saw him, they cantered that way and drew rein.

Their horses were splashed but fairly fresh. At each saddle was sheathed a shotgun, at each belt hung a revolver. One rider was burly and blond, one gaunt and dark. 'Good day, friends,' Edmonds greeted them. 'What can I do for ye?'

'We're after a runaway nigger woman,' said the blond man. 'You seen her?'

'How does thee suppose I should know?' Edmonds replied. 'Ohio is a free state. Any person of color passing by should be as free as thee or me.'

The dark man spat. 'How many like that you got around here? They're all runaways, and you damn well know it, Quaker.'

'I do not, friend,' said Edmonds with a smile. 'Why, I could name thee George at the feed store, Caesar in the blacksmith shop, Mandy who keeps house for the Abshires –'

'Stop stallin' us,' snapped the blond man. 'Listen, this mornin' early we seen her ourselves, way off. She ducked into some woods and shook us, but this here's jest about the only way she could come, and we've found barefoot tracks in the road.'

'And up your drive!' crowed his companion.

Edmonds shrugged. 'It's getting to be summer. Children leave off their shoes whenever we let them.'

The blond man narrowed his eyes. 'All right, suh,' he murmured. 'If you're so innocent, you won't mind us lookin' through your place, will you?'

'She could'a snuck in without you knowin',' suggested the other. He forced a smile. 'You wouldn't like that, you with a wife and kids, I'll bet. We'll jest make sure for you.'

'Yeh, you wouldn't break the law,' said the first. 'You'll co-op-erate, sure. C'mon, Allen.'

He moved to dismount. Edmonds raised a thick, hard hand. 'Wait, friend,' he called softly. 'I am sorry, but I cannot invite either of ye in.'

'Huh?' grunted the blond man.

Allen snickered. 'He's skeered o' what his wife'll do if we track up her floor, Gabe. Don't you worry, suh, we'll wipe our feet real good.'

Edmonds shook his head. 'It grieves me, friends, but neither of ye is welcome. Please go.'

'Then you are harborin' the nigger!' Gabe exploded.

'I did not say that, friend. I simply do not wish to talk further with ye. Please get off my land.'

'Listen, you. Helpin' a runaway, that's a federal crime. Could cost you a thousand dollars or six months in jail. Law says you got to help *us*.'

'An iniquitous ordinance, as wrong as President Pierce's designs on Cuba, plain contrary to God's commandments.'

Allen drew his pistol. 'I'll give you a commandment,' he snarled. 'Stand aside.'

Edmonds didn't stir. 'The Constitution grants my family and me the right to be secure in our home,' he told them with the same calm.

'By God –' The weapon lifted. 'You wanna get shot?'

'That would be a pity. Thee would hang, thee knows.'

Gabe gestured. 'Put that away, Allen.' He straightened in the saddle. 'Aw right, Mr Niggerlover. 'Tain't far to town. I'm goin' right in there and git me a warrant and a deppity sheriff. Allen, you watch and see nobody sneaks out o' here while I'm gone.' He squinted back at Edmonds. 'Or you wanna be reasonable? Your last chance, boy.'

'Unless the Lord show me otherwise,' Edmonds said, 'I believe I am the reasonable man here and ye, friends, are terribly mistaken.'

'Aw right! About time we started makin' some examples. Watch close, Allen.' Gabe wheeled his horse and struck spurs to flanks. In a shower of mud, he galloped away. Frankie's barking sounded thin against the hoofbeats.

'Now, friend, kindly remove thyself,' Edmonds said to Allen.

The slavecatcher grinned. 'Oh, I think I'll jest ride around, this fine mornin'. Won't hurt nothin', won't poke in nowheres.'

'Thee will nevertheless be trespassing.'

'I don't think the jedge'll call it that, you a lawbreaker and all.'

'Friend, we in this family have always done our humble best to observe the law.'

'Yeah, yeah.' Allen unlimbered his shotgun and laid it across his saddle-bow. He clucked to the horse and jogged off, around the yard, on patrol.

Edmonds went back inside. Jane was on hands and knees, cleaning tracks off her floors. She rose and stood quietly while her husband told her what had happened. 'What shall we do?' she asked.

'I must think,' he answered. 'Surely the Lord will provide.' His gaze sought William. 'My son, thee is happy, because thee is too young to know about evil. However, thee can help us. Pray keep silent, unless thee needs something for thyself, and then speak only to thy mother. Say no word to anybody else till I tell thee. Can thee do that?'

'Yes, father,' piped the boy, delighted by the responsibility.

Edmonds chuckled. 'At thy age, it won't be so easy. Later I'll tell thee a story about another boy named William. He became famous for keeping still. To this day they call him William the Silent. But thee'd better hold thyself aside. Thee may go play with thy toys.'

The lad pattered off. Jane wrung her hands. 'Matthew, must we endanger the children?'

Edmonds took both her hands in his. 'A deal more dangerous it'd be to let wickedness go unresisted ... Well, thee see to Nellie. I'd better catch Jacob on his way back. And we all have our work to do.'

His older son, tanned and towheaded, came into sight from behind the barn as the man stepped out again. Edmonds walked unhurriedly to meet him. Allen saw from a distance and rode toward them. The big dog, Chief, sensed trouble and growled.

Edmonds quieted him. 'Jacob,' he said, 'go clean up.'

'Of course, father,' replied the boy, surprised.

'But don't head for school. Wait in the house. I think I'll have an errand for thee.'

The blue eyes widened, went to the approaching stranger, back to the parent, kindled with understanding. 'Yes, sir!' Jacob scampered from them.

Allen halted. 'What you been talkin' about?' he demanded.

'Can't a man speak to his son any more in these United States?' The smallest bit of harshness touched Edmonds' tone. 'I almost wish my religion would let me kick thee off my grounds. Meanwhile, at least leave us alone in our business. *It* doesn't hurt anybody.'

In spite of his weapons, Allen looked uneasy. Edmonds stood bear-powerful. 'I got my livin' to make, same as you,' the slavecatcher mumbled.

'Plenty of honest jobs around. Where is thee from?'

'Kentucky. Where else? Gabe Yancy and me, we been trackin' that coon for days.'

'Then the poor creature must be half dead from hunger and weariness. The Ohio's a wide river. Thee does not think she could swim across, does thee?'

'I dunno how, but them niggers got their ways. Some-body'd seen her yestiddy on t' other bank, like she meant to cross. So we ferried over this mornin', and sure 'nough, found somebody else who'd spotted what had to be her. And then we seen her ourselves, till she went into the woods. If only we'd'a had a dawg or two –'

'Brave men, chasing unarmed women like animals.'

The rider leaned forward. 'Listen,' he said, 'she ain't jest any old runaway off a plantation. They's somethin' queer about her, somethin' real wrong. That's how come Mr Montgomery was fixin' to sell her south. He wants her back for more'n the money she's worth.' He wet his lips. 'And don't you forget, if she gits away, you got a thousand dollars owin' to him, 'sides the fine and jail.'

'That's if they can prove I had anything to do with her escape.'

Anger flashed: 'You won't lie your way out o' this.'

'Lying is against the principles of the Society of Friends. Now kindly let me get on with my work.'

'So you don't lie to nobody, huh? You ready to swear you ain't hidin' any nigger?'

'Swearing is against our religion too. We don't lie, that's all. It doesn't mean we have to make conversation.' Edmonds turned his back and walked off. Allen didn't pursue him, but after a minute took up his rounds again.

In the dimness of the wagon shed, Edmonds began to repair his plow. His mind wasn't really on it. At last he nodded to himself and returned to the house. Allen's look followed his every step.

Inside, he asked Jane, 'How's our guest?'

'I took some food up to her,' she said. 'Starved, she is. This is the first station she's found.'

'She struck off entirely on her own?'

'Well, naturally she'd heard about the Underground Railroad, but only that it exists. She lived on roots, grubs, a few times a meal in a slave cabin. Swam the river last night during the storm, with a piece of driftwood to keep her afloat.'

'If ever anybody earned freedom, she has. How did she find us?'

'Came on a Negro man and asked. From what she told me, I think it must have been Tommy Bradford.'

Edmonds frowned. 'I'd better speak to Tommy. He's a steady fellow, but we'll have to be more careful in future ... Well, we're pretty new in this traffic. Our first passenger.'

'Too soon,' she said fearfully. 'We should have waited till thee had the hidey-hole dug and furnished.'

'This duty can't wait, dear.'

'No, but – What shall we do? Those dreadful anti-Abolitionists in the neighborhood – they would be glad to see us ruined –'

'Speak no evil of people. Jesse Lyndon is misguided, but he's not a bad man at heart. He'll come to the light eventually. Meanwhile, I have a notion.' Edmonds raised his voice. 'Jacob!'

The boy entered the plainly, comfortably furnished parlor. 'Yes, father?' Excitement danced in his tone, his whole being.

Looming over him, Edmonds laid a hand on his shoulder. 'Listen carefully, son. I have an errand for thee. We have a guest today. For reasons that thee doesn't need to know, she's staying in the attic. Her dress isn't fit to be seen in. It was all she had, but we will provide her decent clothes. I want thee to take the foul old garment elsewhere and get rid of it. Can thee do that?'

'Uh, y-yes, sure, but –'

'I told thee to listen close. Thee may go barefoot, which I know thee enjoys, and carry a basket. Pick up some dead-wood for kindling on thy way home, eh? Keep the dress down in the basket. We don't want anybody offended. There is no hurry. Go across the road to the Lyndons' woods. Do not gather sticks there, of course; that would be stealing. Saunter about, take pleasure in God's beautiful creation. When thee is by thyself, put on a black kerchief thy mother will give thee to cover thy hair from the sun. It's pretty muddy. Thee would do well to roll up thy sleeves and trousers, and pull the dress over them. A smock to keep thine own clothes clean, understand? Just the same, I suppose thee'll get thy head and arms and legs mired up. Downright black, even. Well, I remember how I liked that when I was a kid.' Edmonds laughed. 'Till I came back and my mother saw me! But this is a holiday for thee, so that such carelessness will be allowable.' He paused. 'If perchance thee pass near the Lyndon house, so they spy thee, don't linger. Don't give them a good look, but run past quickly. They'd be scandalized to know young Jacob Edmonds was dressed and mucked like that. Dash back into the woods and bury the dress somewhere. Then circle back to our land and collect that kindling. Thee may take several hours all told.' He squeezed the shoulder and smiled. 'How's that sound, hm?'

His son had strained breathless at his words. Eagerness blazed: 'Yes, sir! Wonderful! I can do it!'

Jane touched her man's arm. 'Matthew, dear, he's only a child,' she protested.

Jacob reddened. Edmonds raised a palm. 'There should be no danger to him if he's as smart as I think he is. And thee,' he said sternly to the face below his, 'remember Jesus doesn't like bragging. Tomorrow I'll give thee a note to the schoolmaster, that I needed thy help here today. That's all that either of us has to tell anybody, ever. Got me?'

Jacob stood very straight. 'Yes, sir, I do.'

'Good. I'd better get back to work. Have fun.' Edmonds stroked his wife's cheek, softly and briefly, before he went out.

As he crossed the yard, Allen rode over and exclaimed, 'What you been doin'?'

'Minding my own business,' Edmonds said. 'We have a farm to run, if thee has not heard.' He went on into the shed and took up his task again.

It was near midday and he was growing hungry – Jacob doubtless wolfing the sandwiches Jane would have made – when the dogs barked and Allen whooped. Edmonds strolled into the warm sunlight. Alongside Gabe rode a man with curly brown hair and troubled youthful face. The three of them brought their horses to meet the farmer.

'Good day, friend Peter,' said Edmonds cheerily.

'Hi.' Deputy Sheriff Frayne bit the greeting off. He struggled a few seconds before he could go on. 'Matt, I'm sorry, but this man's gone to Judge Abshire and got a search warrant for your place.'

'That was not very neighborly of the judge, I must say.'

'He's got to uphold the law, Matt. I do too.'

Edmonds nodded. 'Everybody should, when it is at all possible.'

'Well, uh, they claim you're hiding a fugitive slave. That's a federal offense, Matt. I don't like it, but it's the law of the land.'

'There is another Law, Peter. Jesus Christ spoke it in Nazareth. *"The spirit of the Lord is upon me, because he hath anointed me to preach the gospel to the poor; he hath set me to heal the broken-hearted, to preach deliverance to the captives, and recovering of sight to the blind, to set at liberty them that are bruised."'*

'No more o' your preachin', Quaker!' Gabe shouted. He was tired, sweaty, on edge after so much faring to and fro. 'Deppity, do your duty.'

'Search as thee will, thee will never find a slave on this land,' Edmonds declared.

Frayne stared. 'You swear to that?'

'Thee knows I can't give an oath, Peter.' Edmonds stood silent for a spell. Then, in a rush: 'But it'd bother my wife and frighten our little ones, having ye ransack the house. So I'll confess. I did see a Negro woman today.'

'You *did?*' Allen yelled. 'And didn't tell us right off? Why, you son of a bitch –'

'That'll do, fellow!' Frayne rapped. 'Any more and I'll run you in for abuse, threat, and menace.' He turned to Edmonds. 'Can you describe what you saw?'

'She was wearing a ragged yellow dress, badly stained, and it was clear she was traveling north. Before ye spend valuable time here, why not ask the people in that direction?'

Frayne scowled. 'Um, yeah,' he said reluctantly, 'the Lyndons are about a mile off, and they … don't like Abolitionists.'

'They might have seen something too,' Edmonds reminded him. 'They wouldn't keep it from thee.'

'The tracks we followed –' Allen began.

Edmonds chopped air with his hand. 'Bah! Barefoot tracks are every-where. Look, if ye find nothing, hear nothing, yonder, ye can come back and search us. But I warn ye, it'll take hours, as many possible hiding places as a big farm has got, and meanwhile a fugitive who was not here would get clean away.'

Frayne stared hard at him. Gabe opened his mouth. 'He's right,' the deputy said. 'Let's go.'

'I dunno –' Gabe muttered.

'You want my help or not? I been hauled from my business in town for this. I'm not about to lose another half a day watching you bumble around if it's needless.'

'You go ask,' Gabe told Allen. 'My turn to guard this place.'

'I'll come along,' Frayne said, and rode off with the warrant in his pocket.

Jane appeared on the kitchen steps. 'Dinner!' she hailed.

'I regret we cannot invite thee to share our table,' Edmonds said to Gabe. 'A matter of principle. However, we'll send food out.'

The slavecatcher shook his head, furiously, and swatted at a fly. 'To hell with you,' he grated, and trotted to a vantage point.

Edmonds took his time washing up. He had barely finished saying grace when the dogs barked once more. Glancing out a window, he and Jane saw the deputy ride back into the yard and over to Gabe. After they had talked a minute, Gabe spurred his horse and disappeared between the apple trees. Soon he came back to sight on the road, northbound in a hurry.

Edmonds went onto the steps. 'Will thee come eat with us, friend Peter?' he called.

The deputy rode to him. 'Thanks, but, uh, I'd better get on back,' he replied. 'Another time, or you folks come in to Molly and me, hey? Maybe next week?'

'I thank thee. We'll be in touch. Did the Lyndons have news?'

'Yeah, Jesse told as how he glimpsed what's got to be her. We've seen the last of those two boys for a while, I guess.' Frayne hesitated. 'I never thought you'd give out information like that.'

'I really didn't want my house invaded.'

'N-no, but still –' Frayne rubbed his chin. 'You said nobody'd ever find a slave on your land.'

'I did.'

'Then I s'pose you haven't joined the Railroad after all. There was some rumors.'

'It's better not to listen to gossip.'

'Yeah. And better not wonder too much.' Frayne laughed. 'I'm off. Give your missus my best.' He turned serious. 'If you did ever tell a lie – if you ever do – I'm sure it's in a rightful cause, Matt. I'm sure God will forgive you.'

'Thee is kind, but thus far falsehoods haven't been necessary. Not but what I don't have plenty of other sins to answer for. Good day, friend, and give thy Molly our love.'

The deputy tipped his hat and departed. When he was out of earshot, Edmonds stated, 'There *are* no slaves. It's against Christ's teaching that human beings should be property.'

He went back in. Jane and William cast him expectant looks. Nellie gurgled. He smiled as widely as a mouth could stretch. 'They are gone,' he said. 'They took the bait. Let us give thanks to the Lord.'

'Mr Frayne?' asked his wife.

'He's gone home.'

'Good. I mean, he'd be welcome, but now we can bring Flora down to eat with us.'

'Oh, is that her name? Well, certainly. I should have thought of that myself.'

Jane left the kitchen, set the ladder against a wall, climbed it, opened the trapdoor, murmured. In a short while she returned with Flora at her heels. The colored girl walked warily, eyes darting to and fro. A gown of the wife's rustled about her ankles. The knife quivered in her hand.

'Thee can surely put that from thee now,' Edmonds told her. 'We're safe.'

'We really is?' Her gaze searched his. She laid the knife on the counter.

'Thee should never have taken it up, thee knows,' Edmonds said.

A measure of strength had risen in the worn body. Pride rang: 'Ah wasn' goin' back there nohow. Ah'd die fust. Hope Ah'd kill fust.'

'"*Dearly beloved, avenge not yourselves, but rather give place unto wrath; for it is written, Vengeance is mine; I will repay, saith the Lord.*"' Edmonds shook his head sadly. 'I dread His punishment of this sinful land when it comes.' He stepped forward and took the swart hands in his. 'But let's not talk of such things. On second thought, we should eat right away and give thanks later, when we can feel properly joyful.'

'What then, massa?'

'Why, Jane and I will see to it thee get a hot bath. Later thee'd better sleep. We can't risk keeping thee here. The hunters might be back tomorrow. As soon as it's dark, thee and I'll be off to the next station. Have no fears, Flora. Thee ought to reach Canada in another month or less.'

'Yo's mighty good, massa,' she breathed. Tears trembled on her lashes.

'We try our best here to do what the Lord wants, as well as we can understand it. And by the way, I'm nobody's master. Now for pity's sake, let's eat before the food gets cold.'

Shyly, Flora took Jacob's chair. 'Ah don' need much, thank yo', ma – suh an' ma'm. The lady done gimme somethin' awready.'

'Well, but we've a plenty of meat to get onto those bones of thine,' answered Jane, and heaped her plate for her – pork roast, mashed potatoes, gravy, squash, beans, pickles, cornbread, butter, jam, tumbler on the side full of milk that had sat in the cool of the springhouse.

Edmonds kept up a drumfire of talk. 'Here's somebody who hasn't heard my jokes and stories a score of times,' he said, and finally coaxed a few slight laughs from his guest.

After pie and coffee the grownups left William in charge of Nellie and retired to the parlor. Edmonds opened the family Bible and read aloud while they stood: '– *And the Lord said, I have surely seen the affliction of my people which are in Egypt, and have heard their cry by reason of their taskmasters; for I know their sorrows; and I am come down to deliver them out of the hand of*

*the Egyptians, and to bring them up out of that land and unto a good land and
a large, unto a land overflowing with milk and honey –'*

Flora shivered. The tears ran free down her cheeks. 'Let mah people go,'
she whispered. Jane hugged her and cried too.

When they had prayed together, Edmonds regarded the girl a while. She
met his look, flinching no longer. A sunbeam through a window turned her
darkly aglow. For the first time today he felt unsure of himself. He cleared his
throat. 'Flora,' he said, 'thee needs rest before nightfall, but maybe thee would
sleep better for having told us something about thyself. Thee doesn't have to.
It's just, well, here we are, if thee would like to talk to friends.'

''Tain't much to tell, suh, an' some of it's too awful.'

'Do sit,' Jane urged. 'Never mind me. My father is a doctor and I'm a farm
wife. I don't flinch easy.'

They took chairs. 'Did thee have far to go?' Edmonds asked.

Flora nodded. ''Deed Ah did, suh. Don' know how many miles, but Ah
counted de days an' nights. Sebenteen o' dem. Often thought Ah was gonna
die. Didn' min' dat too much, long's dey didn' catch me. Dey was gonna sell
me down de ribber.'

Jane laid a hand over hers. 'They were? What on earth for? What were you
doing there? I mean, your duties –'

'Housemaid, ma'm. Nuss to Massa Mon'gom'ry's chillun, like Ah was to
hisself when he little.'

'What? But –'

''Twasn' too bad. But dey sell me, Ah knowed Ah'd be a field han' ag'in, or
wuss. B'sides, Ah'd been thinkin' 'bout freedom a long time. We heahs things
an' passes dem on to each othah, us black folks.'

'Wait a minute,' Edmonds broke in. 'Did thee say thee was a – a mammy to
thy master when he was a child? But thee can't be that old.'

As Flora answered, he thought that already she bore herself like one free
and, yes, proud. Maybe too proud. 'Oh, Ah is, suh. Dat's why dey was fixin' to
sell me. Wasn' nothin' Ah did wrong. But yeah by yeah, Ah saw how Massa
an' Missus was watchin' me mo' an' mo' strange, same as ever'body else. Den
when she died – well, Ah knowed he couldn' stan' habbin' me dere no mo'.
Could yo' of?'

Both the Edmondses sat silent.

'Happened befo',' Flora went on after a minute during which the grandfather clock had seemed to tick as loud as doom. 'Dat's how come Ah knows
what it's like bein' a field han'. Not jes' watchin' an' feelin' sorry fo' dem. No,
Ah been dere. When dat ol' Massa sol' me to Massa Mon'gom'ry's father, he
didn' say nothin' 'bout mah age den. So Ah figgered dere was mah chance.'
She stopped, swallowed, looked at the carpet. 'Better not tell yo' how Ah
got'm to notice me an' git me trained fo' de big house.'

Edmonds felt his cheeks go fiery. Jane patted the hand beneath hers and murmured, 'Thee needn't tell, dear. What choice has a slave ever had?'

'None, ma'm, an' dat's a fack. Ah was 'bout fo'teen de fust time Ah was sol', away from mah father an' mother, an' dat man an' bofe his sons –' Flora's glance touched the Bible on its stand. 'Well, we s'pose fo'gibe, ain't we? Po' young Marse Brett, he done get killed in de waw. Ah saw his pappy when de wuhd come, an' would'a felt sorry fo' him 'cep' Ah was too tired fum wuhk.'

A chill went along Edmonds' backbone. 'What war?'

'De Rebolution, it was. Yay, eben us slabes heard 'bout dat.'

'But then thee – Flora, no, it can't be! That would make thee … about a hundred years old.'

Again she nodded. 'Ah buried mah men, mah real men, an' Ah buried chillun, when dey wasn' sol' off fum me, an' –' Suddenly her firmness broke. She reached out toward him. 'It's been too long!'

'Were you born in Africa?' Jane asked low.

Flora fought for calmness. 'No, ma'm, in a slabe cabin. But mah dad, he was stolen away fum dere. Used to tell us young'uns 'bout it, de tribe, de foe-rest – said he was part Ay-rab, an' –' She stiffened. 'He daid. Dey all daid, and nebba free, nebba free. Ah swo' to mahse'f Ah was gonna be, in deir names Ah was. So Ah followed de Drinkin' Gourd an' – an' heah Ah is.' She buried her face in her hands and wept.

'We must be patient,' Jane said across the bowed head. 'She's overwrought.'

'Yes, what she's been through, I suppose that would drive anybody kind of crazy,' Edmonds agreed. 'Take her away, dear. Give her that bath. Put her to bed. Sit with her till she sleeps.'

'Of course.' They went their separate ways.

Though Jacob came home jubilantly, supper was quiet. His parents had decided to leave Flora resting as long as possible. Jane would pack a basket of food for the next stage of the journey. Once she said, 'Matthew, I wonder what she meant by following the Drinking Gourd. Does thee know?'

'Yes, I've heard,' he answered. 'It's the Big Dipper. The one constellation nobody can mistake. They have a song about it, the slaves, I believe.'

And he wondered what other songs went secretly through the land, and what songs might awaken in the future. Battle hymns? No, please, God, of Thy mercy, no. Withhold Thy wrath that we have so richly earned. Lead us to Thy light.

As dusk fell, he and Jacob rolled forth the buggy and harnessed Si to it. 'Can I come along, father?' the boy asked.

'No,' Edmonds said. 'I'll be gone till nearly sunrise. Thee has school tomor-row after chores.' He rumpled the bright head. 'Be patient. Man's work will come on thee quite soon enough.' After a moment: 'Thee made a fine start today. I can only hope the Lord won't later want far more.'

Well, but Heaven waited, the reward that has no bounds. Poor half-mad Flora. What if somebody really did have to live on and on like that, in bondage or hunted or – whatever menial thing she could become in Canada? Edmonds shuddered. God willing, as she met friendship along the Underground Railroad, she ought to recover her wits.

A lantern glowed. Jane brought the fugitive out and helped her into the buggy. Edmonds mounted to the driver's seat. 'Good night, my dear,' he said, and gently touched whip to horse. Wheels creaked down the drive and onto the road. The air was still fairly warm, though a touch of oncoming cold went through it. The sky ranged from purple in the west to velvety black in the east. Stars were blinking forth. The Big Dipper stood huge. Presently Edmonds made out the Little Dipper and Polaris in it, that guided north toward freedom.

XIV

MEN OF PEACE

1

The ranch house was small, a one-room sod cabin, but the more defensible for that. Its two windows had heavy inside shutters and each wall a pair of loopholes. Picket stakes surrounded it, six deep. Men built like this in the west Texas cattle country – such of them as weren't dead or fled.

'Lord, but I wish we'd cleared out in time,' Tom Langford said. 'You and the kids, at least.'

'Hush, now,' replied his wife. 'You couldn't run the spread without me, and if we gave up we'd lose everything we've worked for.' She leaned across the table, over the firearms and ammunition that covered it, to pat his arm. A sunbeam through a hole on the east side struck through the gloom within and made living bronze of her hair. 'All we got to do is hold out till Bob brings help. Unless the redskins quit first.'

Langford kept himself from wondering whether the vaquero had gotten clean away. If the Comanches had spied him and sent pursuit with remounts, he must already lie scalped. No telling. Though you could see a long ways around here, by day, the war band had appeared at dawn, when folks were just getting started on the chores, and arrived faster than you might believe. Of the hands, only Ed Lee, Bill Davis, and Carlos Padilla had made it to the house with the family, and not before a bullet smashed Ed's left arm.

Susie had set and bandaged that limb as best she was able after the warriors recoiled from gunfire and withdrew out of sight. At the moment Ed had Nancy Langford on his lap. The three-year-old clung hard to him, terrified. Bill kept watch at the north end, Carlos at the south, while Jim flitted between east and west in the pride and eagerness of his own seven years. A sharpness of powder still hung in the air, and some smoke seemed to have drifted in from the barn as well. The Indians had torched it, the only wooden building on the place. The roar of its burning reached the defenders faintly, like a noise in a nightmare.

'They're comin' back!' Jim shrilled.

Langford grabbed a Winchester off the table and sprang to the west wall.

Behind him he heard Lee say, 'Bill, you help the missus reload. Carlos, you be with Tom. Jim, you go 'round and tell me where I'm needed.' The voice was ragged with pain but the man could work a Colt.

Langford peered through his loophole. Sunlight brightened the bare ground outside. Dust puffed and swirled ruddy from the hoofs of oncoming mustangs. He got a brown body in his sights, but then the pony veered and the rider vanished, except for one leg. Indian trick, hang yourself down the other side. But a Comanche without a horse was only half himself. Langford's rifle cracked and nudged his shoulder. The mustang reared, screamed, went over, kicked. The warrior had thrown himself clear. He was lost in the dust and rampage. Langford realized he had pretty much wasted that shot, and picked his next target with care. The bullets had to last.

Riders would never take this house. They'd learned as much, first time. They galloped around and around, whooping, firing. One toppled, another, another. I didn't get them, Langford knew. Carlos did. A real marksman, him. Brave, too. Could likely have gotten away from where he was when they showed up, but stuck with us. Well, I never did hold with looking down on a man just because he's Mexican.

'Comin' on foot, over here!' Jim cried.

Yes, of course, the mounted braves provided covering fire, distraction, for those who snaked amongst the pickets. Langford allowed himself a glance backward. Bill Davis had left the table to join Ed Lee on the north. The black cowhand wasn't the best with a gun in these United States, but his targets were close, slowed down by the barrier, scornful of death. He blasted away. Susie brought him a reloaded rifle, took his emptied weapon back, fetched Ed a fresh pistol. The screams, hoofquake, shooting went on and on, world without end. You weren't scared, no time for that, but at the back of your head you wondered if there had ever been anything else or ever would be.

Suddenly it was over. The wild men gathered up their dead and wounded and pulled off again.

In the silence that followed, the clock sounded nearly as loud as – a hammer nailing down a coffin lid. It was a big old grandfather clock, the single treasure from her parents' home that Susie had wanted carted out here. The dial glimmered through a blue haze. Langford squinted eyes which the powder smoke stung and whistled softly. Just about ten minutes since the attack began. No more, dear God?

Nancy had crawled into a corner. She huddled hugging herself. Her mother went to give whatever comfort she could.

2

The wind across the high plains still bore much winter in it. This range wasn't as bleak as the Llano Estacado, over which the travelers had come, but the spring rains had not started in earnest and only a breath of green touched endless sere grass. Trees – willow or cottonwood clumped by whatever streams ran through these miles, the occasional lonesome oak – reached bare limbs into a bleached sky. Game was plentiful, though. It wasn't buffalo, except for white bones, the work of white hunters; buffalo were fast getting scarce. However, pronghorn, peccary, jackrabbit ran everywhere, with wolves and cougars to prey on them, while elk, bear, and cougar haunted the canyons. Jack Tarrant's party hadn't seen any cattle since well before they left New Mexico. Twice they passed abandoned ranches. The red terror woke to all its old fury while the states were at each other's throats, and the Army had a lot of quelling yet to do, seven years after Appomattox.

Sunlight dazzled eastward vision. At first Tarrant couldn't see what Francisco Herrera Carillo pointed at. '*Humo*,' the trader said. '*No proviene de ningún campamento.*' He was a pale-brown man with sharp features; even on the trail he kept his chin shaven, mustache trimmed, clothes neat, as if to remind the world that among his forefathers were Conquistadores.

Tarrant looked a bit like him, given aquiline nose and large, slightly oblique eyes. After a moment he too made out the stain rising athwart heaven. 'Not from a camp, when it's visible from below the horizon,' he agreed slowly in the same Spanish. 'What, then? A grass fire?'

'No, that would be wider spread. A building. I think we have found your Indians.'

Burly and redbearded, hook newly strapped on to stick out of his right sleeve, Rufus Bullen stumped over to join them. 'Christ!' he growled. Two missing front teeth made his English slightly slurred. If others than Tarrant noticed the new growth that had begun to push stubs through the gums, they had said nothing about it. 'You mean they've set fire to a ranch?'

'What else?' Herrera replied coolly, holding to his own language. 'I have not been in these parts for some time, but if I remember right and have my bearings, that is the Langford property. Or was.'

'What're we waiting for? We can't let 'em –' Rufus broke off. His shoulders sagged. '*Inutilis est*,' he mumbled.

'We will probably arrive too late, and can certainly do nothing against a war band,' Tarrant reminded him, also in Latin.

Herrera shrugged. He had grown used to the Yanquis dropping into that lingo. (He recognized an occasional word from the Mass, but no more, especially since they spoke it differently from the priests.) This quest of theirs was mad anyway. 'You wish to speak with the Comanches, no?' he observed. 'You can hardly do that if you fight them. Come, let us eat and be on our way. If we're lucky, they will not have moved on before we get there.'

His sons Miguel and Pedro, young but trailwise, had wakened at dawn and gotten busy. A coffeepot steamed and two pans sizzled on a grill above a fire of buffalo chips – an abundance of which remained – and mesquite. As hard as the seekers pushed, without time off to hunt, no bacon was left except fat for cooking, but they kept plenty of corn meal to make tortillas and two days ago the father had had the good luck to knock down a peccary. It had been quite a ways off. Every Comanchero was necessarily a crack shot.

The travelers ate fast, cleaned camp gear, obeyed nature, left soap and razors till later, hit the saddle and set off. Herrera varied the pace between trot and canter, now and then a walk. The two whom he guided had learned to heed him. Easy though it seemed, this sparing of horseflesh covered many miles a day. Besides, the remuda amounted to just a pair of ponies each and three pack mules.

The sun climbed, the wind sank. Warmth crept into the air and drew sweet sweat odors from the mounts. Hoofs thudded, leather creaked. The tall dry grass rustled aside. For a while the smoke rose higher, but presently it thinned, blew apart, faded away. Wings as black wheeled where it had been. 'You can usually tell a Comanche camp from afar,' Herrera remarked. 'The vultures wait for the leavings.'

It was hard to tell whether Rufus flushed. Hats failed to keep skin like his from reddening and chapping. His voice did grate: 'Dead bodies?' That was in Spanish, which he could speak after a fashion.

'Or bones and entrails,' Herrera replied. 'They have always been hunters, you know, when they are not at war.' A minute went by. 'Your buffalo killers destroy their livelihood.'

'Sometimes I think you like them,' Tarrant murmured.

'I have dealt with them since I was Pedro's age, as did my fathers before me,' Herrera said. 'One comes to a little understanding, whether one will or no.'

Tarrant nodded. Comancheros had been trading out of Santa Fe for a century, since de Anza fought the tribes to a standstill and made a peace that endured because he had gained their respect. It was a peace with the New Mexicans alone. Spaniards elsewhere, any other Europeans, the Mexicans who ruled later, the Americans – Texan, Confederate, Yankee – who despoiled the Mexicans, those remained fair game; and indeed by now there had been such bloodshed and cruelty on both sides that truce between Comanches and Texans was no more thinkable than it was between Comanches and Apaches.

Tarrant forced his mind back to his horse. He and Rufus had gotten fairly good at riding range style; but damn it, what they really were was seamen. Why couldn't their search have led them into the South Pacific, or along the shores of Asia, or anywhere but this unbounded emptiness?

Well, the search might be near an end. No matter how often he had thought it before, that coursed through his blood and shivered up his spine. O Hiram, Psammetk, Pytheas, Althea, Athenais-Aliyat, Armand Cardinal Richelieu, Benjamin Franklin, how far has the River borne me from you! And all the lesser ones, beyond counting, down in dust, wholly forgotten save for whatever might glimmer in him, a comrade of decades or a drinking companion in a tavern, a wife and the children she bore him or a woman chance-met for a single night –

Herrera's shout slammed him back into the day: *'¡Alto!'* and a rush of alien gutturals. Rufus dropped left hand to pistol. Tarrant gestured him from it. The boys brought the pack animals to a stop. Their eyes darted around, they were new to this and nervous. Despite his earlier times between jaws ready to snap shut, Tarrant's flesh prickled.

Two men had come around a brush-grown hillock where they must have been on watch. Their scuffy-looking mustangs closed the distance in a few pulsebeats. They checked the gallop with invisible touch of knees and twitch of hackamore; seated merely on blankets, they seemed parts of the beasts, centaurs. Their own frames were stocky, bandy-legged, swarthy, clad in breechclouts, leggings, and moccasins. Midnight hair hung in twin braids past broad faces painted in the red and black of death. Leather sunshades had been left behind and the war bonnet of the northern plains was unknown here. One man had stuck a few feathers into a headband. The other bore a great shaggy cap or helmet from which sprang buffalo horns. He carried a Henry repeating rifle. A bandolier of cartridges crossed his chest. His companion nocked an arrow to a short bow. Archers were rare of late, or so Tarrant had heard. Maybe this warrior was poor, maybe he preferred the ancestral weapon. No matter. That barbed iron head could punch through ribs to the heart, and more shafts waited in their quiver.

Herrera talked on. Buffalo Horns grunted. The bowman slacked his string. Herrera turned in the saddle to regard his employers. 'The fight is not ended,' he told them, 'but the Kwerhar-rehnuh will receive us. Chief Quanah himself is here.' Moisture glistened on his face. He had gone a bit pale around the nostrils. In English he added, for many Comanches knew some Spanish: 'Be ver-ree careful. Sey 'ave much anger. Sey can easy kill a w'ite man.'

3

The ranch buildings had already been visible. As he drew closer, they seemed to Tarrant, if anything, more small and lonesome in the middle of immensity. He recognized what must be the owners' home, a bunkhouse, and three lesser outbuildings. Sod, they were little damaged. A barn was smoldering ashes and charred fragments; the family had doubtless spent a lot of money and hope on getting the lumber hauled to them. A couple of wagons had been pushed into the flames. A chicken coop had been emptied and smashed. Hoofs had trampled saplings that were to have grown into shelter against sun and wind.

The Indians were camped where a windmill stood skeletal by the cattle trough for which it pumped water. That put them out of rifleshot from the house and, probably, sight through loopholes. About thirty tipis lifted their gaudily decorated buffalo hide cones across what had been a pasture. At a fire near the middle, women in buckskin gowns prepared captured, butchered steers for eating. They were rather few. The braves numbered maybe a hundred. They loafed about, napped, shot dice, cleaned firearms or whetted knives. Some sat grim in front of lodgings from within which sounded keening; they mourned kinsmen slain. A few, mounted, kept an eye on the many horses that grazed in the distance. They were as tough as their masters, those mustangs that could keep going on winter's grass.

When the newcomers caught the notice of the camp, excitement kindled. Most people ran to crowd around and jabber. The stoic reserve of Indians was a myth, unless they were in pain or dying. Then a warrior's pride was that not the most prolonged and agonizing torture his captors or their women could think of would make him cry aloud. It was an ill thing to fall into such hands.

Buffalo Horns shouted and pushed his pony through the ruck. Herrera called greetings to men he knew. The smiles and waves that he got in return made Tarrant feel easier. If they took due care, his party ought to outlive this day. After all, to these folk hospitality was sacred.

Close by the windmill was a tipi whereon were painted signs that Herrera whispered were powerful. A man too dignified to leave it for curiosity's sake stood outside, arms folded. The travelers drew rein. Tarrant realized that he looked on Quanah, half-white war chief of the Kwerhar-rehnuh. The name of that band meant 'Antelopes' – an American misnomer for the pronghorn, like 'buffalo' for bison or 'corn' for maize; and curious it seemed for the lords of the Staked Plains, the fiercest of all those Comanches whom the United States had yet to conquer.

Save for lightning-like bands of yellow and ocher, he wore simply loincloth and moccasins, with a Bowie knife sheathed on a belt. Yet there could be no mistaking him. From his mother's race he took straight nose and a height that towered, thickly muscled, over his followers. However, he was even darker than most of them. His regard of the strangers was lion-calm.

Herrera greeted him deferentially in the tongue of the Nermernuh, the People. Quanah nodded. 'Bienvenidos,' he rumbled forth, and continued in accented but fluent Spanish. 'Dismount and come in.'

Tarrant felt relieved. In Santa Fe he had learned some of the Plains Indian sign language, but used it haltingly; and Herrera had told him that few Comanches were adept in it anyway. The trader had said Quanah might or might not condescend to speak Spanish with Americans. He had a certain grasp of English too, though he would scarcely handicap himself with it when he didn't have to. 'Muchas gracias, señor,' Tarrant said, to establish that he was the head of this band. He wondered whether he should have used the honorific 'Don Quanah.'

Herrera left the remuda in charge of his sons and accompanied Tarrant and Rufus into the tipi behind the chief. Its outfit was sparse, little more than bedrolls; this was a war band. The light within fell gentle after the glare outside, the air smelled of leather and smoke. The men settled cross-legged in a circle. Two wives left, posting themselves at the entrance in case of a task for them.

Quanah was not about to smoke any peace pipe, but Herrera had said it would be okay to offer cigarettes. Tarrant did while introducing himself and his friend. Deftly left-handed, Rufus took a matchbox from his pocket, extracted and struck a stick, lighted the tobacco. To have such a formidable-seeming man serve them honored both the principals.

'We have come a weary way in the wish of finding you,' Tarrant added. 'We thought the Antelopes would be on their home grounds, but you had already left, so we must ask anyone we met, and the earth itself, where you were gone.'

'Then you are not here to trade,' said Quanah in Herrera's direction.

'Sr Tarrant engaged me in Santa Fe to bring him to you, when he had learned I would be able to,' the trader answered. 'I did pack along some rifles and ammunition. One will be a gift to you. As for the rest, well, surely you have taken many cattle.'

Rufus sucked in a sharp breath. It was notorious that New Mexican ranchers wanted stock and would buy without questions. Comancheros got small detachments of Indians to drive herds they had lifted out of Texas to that market, in exchange for arms. Tarrant laid a hand on the redhead's knee and muttered in Latin, against the outrage he saw, 'Stay quiet. You knew this.'

'Make your camp with us,' Quanah invited. 'I expect we will be here until tomorrow morning.'

Hope quivered in Rufus' tone: 'Uh, you will spare them in yonder house?'

Quanah scowled. 'No. They have cost us comrades. The enemy shall never boast that any defied us and lived.' He shrugged. 'Besides, we have need of a short rest, as hard as we have fared – the better to fight the soldiers afterward.'

Yes, Tarrant understood, this was not really a plundering expedition, it was a campaign in a war. His inquiries had informed him of a Kiowa medicine man, Owl Prophet, who called for a great united thrust that would forever drive the white man from the plains; and last year such horror erupted that Washington's attempts at peace came to an end. In fall Ranald Mackenzie took the black troopers of his Fourth Cavalry into these parts, against the Antelopes. Quanah led a retreat that was a running fight, brilliantly waged – Mackenzie himself received an arrow wound – high up onto the Llano Estacado until winter forced the Americans to withdraw. Now he was returning.

The stern gaze shifted to Tarrant. 'What do you want with us?'

'I too bear gifts, senor.' Clothing, blankets, jewelry, liquor. Despite his remoteness from this conflict, Tarrant could not bring himself to convey weapons; nor would Rufus have stood for it. 'My friend and I are from a distant land – California, by the western waters, which I'm sure you have heard of.' In haste, because that territory belonged to the foe: 'We have no quarrel with anyone here. The races are not foredoomed to blood feud.' A risk that he deemed he should take: 'Your mother was of our people. Before setting forth, I learned what I could about her. If you have any questions, I will try to answer them.'

Stillness fell. The hubbub outside seemed faint, distant. Herrera looked uneasy. Quanah sat expressionless, smoking. Time passed before the chief said, heavily: 'The Tejanos stole her and my small sister from us. My father, Peta Nawkonee the war chief, mourned for her until at last he took a wound in battle that got inflamed and killed him. I have heard that she and the girl are dead.'

'Your sister died eight years ago,' Tarrant replied low. 'Your mother soon followed her. She too was sick with grief and longing. Now they rest at peace, Quanah.'

The tale had been easy enough to obtain, a sensation remembered to this day. In 1836 an Indian band attacked Parker's Fort, a settlement in the Brazos valley. They slew five men and mutilated them as was Indian wont, preferably before death. They gang-raped Granny Parker after a lance pinned her to the ground. Two of the several other women they violated were left with injuries almost as bad. Two more women they carried away, together with three children. Among these was nine-year-old Cynthia Anne Parker.

The women and boys were eventually ransomed back. Though this was by no means the first time the Comanches took females for slaves, the tale of just what those two suffered came to stand for hundreds; and the Texas Rangers rode with vengeance in their hearts.

Cynthia Anne fared better. Capriciously adopted, raised as a girl of the Nermernuh, she forgot English, forgot well-nigh everything of her early childhood, became an Antelope and presently a mother. By all accounts, hers was a happy marriage; Peta Nawkonee loved his wife and wanted no woman after he lost her. That was in 1860, when Sul Ross led a Ranger expedition in retaliation for a raid and fell upon the Comanche camp. Its men were off hunting. The Texans shot what women and children fled too slowly, and a Mexican slave whom Ross believed to be the chief himself. Barely in time, a man saw, through dirt and dung-grease, that the hair of one squaw was golden.

The Parker clan and the state of Texas did everything they could for her. It was no use. She was Naduah, who only yearned back to the prairie and the People. Repeated attempts to escape finally forced her kinfolk to keep a guard on her. When disease robbed her of her daughter, she howled, tore and slashed her own flesh, sank into silence and starved herself to death.

Out on the plains, her younger son perished as wretchedly. Sickness dwelt always among the Indians, tuberculosis, arthritis, worms, ophthalmia, the smallpox that Europeans brought, a litany of ills without end. But her older son flourished, gathered a war band, became headman of the Antelopes. He refused to sign the Medicine Lodge treaty that would put the tribes on a reservation. Instead, he carried terror along the frontier. He was Quanah.

'Have you seen their graves?' he asked levelly.

'I have not,' Tarrant said, 'but if you wish, I can visit and tell them of your love.'

Quanah smoked for a while longer. At least he didn't outright call the white man a liar. Finally: 'Why have you sought me?'

Tarrant's pulse quickened. 'It is not you, chief, great though your fame be. Word has come to me of somebody in your following. If I have heard aright, he hails from the north and has traveled widely and long. Yes, very long, longer than anybody knows, though he never seems to grow old. His must be a strange power. On your home grounds, uh, Nermernuh who stayed behind told us that he came along on this faring. My desire is to speak with him.'

'Why?' demanded Quanah. The bluntness, unlike an Indian, betokened tension below the iron surface.

'I believe he will be glad to talk with me.'

Rufus puffed hard on his cigarette. Laid across his lap, the hook trembled.

Quanah raised his voice to the squaws. One of them left. Quanah returned his look to Tarrant. 'I have sent for Dertsahnawyeh. Peregrino.' – the Spanish for the Comanche name: Wanderer.

'Do you hope he will teach you his medicine?' he went on.

'I have come to find out what it is.'

'I do not think he could tell you, if he were willing, which I do not think he would be.'

Herrera peered at Tarrant. 'You only told me you wanted to find out what might lie behind those rumors,' the trader said. 'It is dangerous to meddle in warriors' affairs.'

'Yes, I call myself a scientist,' Tarrant snapped. To Quanah: 'That is a man who seeks for whatever truth lies hidden behind things. How do the sun and the stars shine? How did the earth and life come to be? What really happened in the past?'

'I know,' replied the chief. 'Thus you whites have found ways to do and make many terrible things, and the railroad runs where the buffalo grazed.' Pause. 'Well, I suppose Dertsahnawyeh can take care of himself.' Starkly: 'As for me, I must think how to capture yonder house.'

There was nothing more to say.

The tipi entrance darkened. A man trod in. While clad like the rest, he bore no war paint. Nor was he a native of these lands, but tall, slender, lighter-hued. When he saw who sat with Quanah he spoke gently in English. 'What do you want of me?'

4

They walked over the prairie, Tarrant, Peregrino, Rufus trailing a step or two behind. Light spilled out of vastness, a measure of warmth lifted from soil. Dry grass rattled. Camp and buildings soon vanished among the tall tawny stalks. Smokes continued in sight, rising straight and slow toward the vultures.

Revelation was strangely subdued. Or perhaps it wasn't strange. They had waited so long. Tarrant and Rufus had felt hope grow into near certainty while they quested. Peregrino had nurtured an inner peace to which any surprise was like a passing breath of air. Thus he endured his loneliness, until he outlived it.

'I was born almost three thousand years ago,' Tarrant said. 'My friend is about half as old.'

'I never counted time until lately,' said Peregrino. They might as well use that name, out of the many he had had. 'Then I guessed five or six hundred years.'

'Before Columbus – What changes you've seen!'

Peregrino smiled as a man might at a graveside. 'You more. Have you come on any like us, besides Mr Bullen?'

'Not quite. A woman once, but she disappeared. We've no idea whether she's still alive. Otherwise, you're my first since him. Did you ever?'

'No. I tried but gave up. For all I knew, I was solo. How did you get on my trail?'

'That's kind of a story.'

'We got plenty time.'

'Well –' Tarrant drew a tobacco pouch from his pants and, from his shirt, the briar pipe it would have been unwise to smoke before Quanah. 'I'll start with Rufus and me arriving in California in '49. You've heard about the Gold Rush? We got rich off it. Not as miners, as merchants.'

'You did, Hanno,' said the man at his heel. 'I tagged along.'

'And damn useful you've been, in more tight spots than I can list,' Tarrant declared. 'Eventually I dropped from sight for a few years, then showed up in San Francisco under my present alias and bought a ship. I've always favored the sea. By now I own several; the firm's done right well.'

Having loaded his pipe, he laid fire to it. 'Whenever I could afford to, I've hired men to look for signs of immortals,' he proceeded. 'Naturally, I don't tell them that's what they're after. By and large, those of our kind who survive must do it by staying obscure. These days I'm an eccentric millionaire interested in lineages. My agents figure me for an ex-Mormon. They're supposed to locate – oh, individuals who seem much like others that dropped from sight earlier, and are apt to appear carrying a pretty fair grubstake – that sort of thing. What with railroads and steamships, I can at last spread my net across the world. Of course, it's not that big yet, and the mesh is awfully coarse, which may be why it's caught nothing except a few that turned out false.'

'Until today,' said Peregrino.

Tarrant nodded. 'A scout of mine, exploring around Santa Fe, caught rumors about a medicine man among the Comanches, who didn't really belong to them – the description sounded like a Sioux or a Pawnee or whatever – but he'd gained a good deal of authority and … he'd been heard of elsewhere, earlier, several different times and places. Not that any civilized person had pieced this together. Who'd take the fancies of savages seriously? Uh, pardon me, no offense. You know how whites think. My agent didn't suppose it was worth pursuing. He noted it in a couple of sentences in his report just to show me how industrious he was.

'That was last year. I decided to follow it up myself. Lucked out and found two aged people, an Indian and a Mexican, who remembered – Well, it seemed, if he existed, he'd joined Quanah. I hoped to find the Comanches in winter quarters, but as was, we had to track them.' Tarrant laid a hand briefly on Peregrino's shoulder. 'And here we are, my brother.'

Peregrino halted. Tarrant did. For a space they looked into each other's eyes. Rufus stood aside, bemused. At last Tarrant formed a wry grin and murmured, 'You're wondering whether I'm a liar, aren't you?'

'How do you know I speak truth?' the Indian replied as low.

'Tactful fellow, you. Well, in the course of time I've cached evidence, as well as getaway gold, here and there. Come with me and I'll show you enough of it. Or you can simply watch me for twenty or thirty years. I'll provide for you. Meanwhile, why else on earth should I spin you a yarn like this?'

Peregrino nodded. 'I believe you. But how do you know I'm not out to swindle you?'

'You couldn't have foreseen my arrival, and you did leave many years' worth of trail. Not on purpose. No white who didn't know what to look for would ever have suspected. The tribes – what do they make of you, anyway?'

'That depends.' Peregrino's gaze went over miles where grass waved above buffalo skulls, on beyond the horizon. When he spoke slowly, often stopping to form a sentence before he uttered it, his English became a language other than what he had been using. 'Each lives in its own world, you know; and those worlds are changing so fast.

'At first I was a medicine man among my birth-people. But they took to the horse and everything that went with that. I left them and drifted for – winter after winter, summer after summer. I was trying to find what it meant, all that I lived through. Sometimes I settled down a while, but it always hurt too much, seeing what was happening. I even tried the whites. At a mission I got baptized, learned Spanish and English, reading and writing. Afterward I went deep into Mexican and Anglo country both. I have been a market hunter, trapper, carpenter, wrangler, gardener. I talked with everybody who would talk with me and read every printed word that came my way. But that was no good either. I never belonged there.

'Meanwhile tribe after tribe got wiped out – by sickness, by war – or broken and herded onto a reservation. Then if the whites decided they wanted that land too, out the redskins went. I saw the Cherokees at the end of their Trail of Tears –'

The quiet, almost matter-of-fact voice died away. Rufus cleared his throat. 'Well, that's how the world is,' he grated. 'I seen Saxons, vikings, Crusaders, Turks, wars o' religion, witches burned –' Louder: 'I seen what Injuns do when they get the upper hand.'

Tarrant frowned him to silence and asked Peregrino, 'What brought you here?'

The other sighed. 'I finally thought – oh, I was slow about it – this life of mine that went on and on and on, with nothing to show for it but graves – it must have some purpose, some use. And maybe that was just in the long experience, and being ageless would make folks listen to me. Maybe I could help my people, my whole race, before they went under, help them save something for a new beginning.

'About thirty years ago, I came back to them. The Southwest was where free tribes were likely to hang on the longest. The Nermernuh – you do know

"Comanche" is from Spanish, don't you? – they had driven out the Apaches; they had fought the Kiowas as equals and made allies of them; for three hundred years they had stood off the Spanish, the French, the Mexicans, the Texans, and carried war to the enemy in his home country. Now the Americans aim to crush them once for all. They've earned better than that. Haven't they?'

'What are you doing?' Tarrant's question seemed to hover like the dark wings overhead.

'To tell the truth, I was among the Kiowas first,' Peregrino said. 'They are more open in their minds than the Nermernuh, also about long life. Comanches believe a real man dies young, in battle or the hunt, while he is strong. They don't trust their old ones and treat them bad. Not like my birth-people, so long ago … I let my … my reputation grow with time. It helped that I know some things to do for the wounded and the sick. I never set myself up as a prophet. Those crazy preachers have been the death of thousands, and the end is not yet. No, I just went around from band to band, and they came to think I was holy. I did whatever I could for them in the way of healing or advice. Always I counselled peace. Finally – it's a long story – I joined up with Quanah, because he was becoming the last great chief. Everything will turn on him.'

'Peace, did you say?'

'And whatever we can save for our children. The Comanches have nothing left from their ancestors, nothing they can truly believe in. That eats them out from the inside. It leaves them wide open for the likes of Owl Prophet. I found a new faith among the Kiowas and I'm bringing it to the Nermernuh. Do you know the peyote cactus? It opens a way, it quiets the heart –'

Peregrino stopped. A tiny laugh fluttered in his throat. 'Well, I don't mean to sound like a missionary.'

'I'll be glad to listen later,' said Tarrant, while he thought: I have seen so many gods come and go, what's one more? 'Also to any ideas you may have about making peace. I told you I have money. And I've always made a point of getting wires in my hands. You savvy? Certain politicians owe me favors. I can buy others. We'll work out a plan, you and I. But first we've got to get you away from here, back to San Francisco with us, before you take a bullet in your brain. Why the hell did you come along with these raiders anyway?'

'I said I have to make them listen to me,' Peregrino explained wearily. 'It's uphill work. They're suspicious of old men to start with, and when their world is falling to pieces around them they're afraid of magic as strange as mine and – They've got to understand I'm not unmanly, I am on their side. I can't leave them now.'

'Wait a minute!' Rufus barked.

They stared at him. He stood foursquare, legs planted wide apart, hat pushed back from roughened red face. The hook that had pierced foemen looked suddenly frail under this heaven. 'Wait a minute,' stumbled from him. 'Boss, what're you thinking? The first thing we got to do is save those ranchers.'

Tarrant moistened his lips before it dragged out of him: 'We can't. We're two against a hundred or worse. Unless –' He cast a glance at Peregrino.

The Indian shook his head. 'In this the People would not heed me,' he told them, dull-voiced. 'I would only lose what standing I have.'

'I mean, can we ransom that family? Comanches often sell prisoners back, I've heard. I've brought trade goods along, besides what was intended for presents. And Herrera ought to turn his stock over to me if I promise him payment in gold.'

Peregrino grew thoughtful. 'Well, maybe.'

'That's giving those devils the stuff to kill more whites,' Rufus protested.

Bitterness sharpened Peregrino's tone. 'You were telling as how this sort of thing is nothing new on earth.'

'But, but the barbarians in Europe, they were *white*. Even the Turks – Oh, you don't mind. You ride with these animals –'

'That'll do, Rufus,' Tarrant clipped. 'Remember why we've come. Saving a few who'll be dead anyway inside a century is not our business. I'll see if I can, but Peregrino here is our real kinsman. So pipe down.'

His comrade whirled about and stalked off.

Tarrant watched him go. 'He'll get over it,' he said. 'Short-tempered and not very bright, but he's been loyal to me since before the fall of Rome.'

'Why does he care about … dayflies?' the medicine man wondered.

Tarrant's pipe had gone out. He rekindled it and stared into the smoke as it lost itself beneath the sky. 'Immortals get influenced by their surroundings, too,' he said. 'We've mostly lived in the New World these past two hundred years, Rufus and I. First Canada, when it was French, but then we moved to the English colonies. More freedom, more opportunity, if you were English yourself, as of course we claimed to be. Later we were Americans; same thing.

'It affected him more than me. I owned slaves now and then, and shares in a couple of plantations, but didn't think much about it either way. I'd always taken slavery for granted, and it was a misfortune that could happen to anybody, regardless of race. When the War Between the States ended it and a great deal else, to me that was simply another spin in history's wheel. As a shipowner in San Francisco I didn't need slaves.

'But Rufus, he's a primitive soul. He wants something to cling to – which is what immortals never can have, right? He's gone through a dozen Christian faiths. Last time he got converted was at a Baptist revival, and a lot of it still clings to him. Both before and after the war he took seriously what he kept hearing about the white race's right and duty to lord it over the colored.'

Tarrant chuckled unmerrily. 'Besides, he's been without a woman since we left Santa Fe. It was a terrible disappointment to him when he found on the Staked Plains that Comanche women don't free-and-easy receive outsiders like they do, or used to do, farther north. There must be a white woman or two in yonder cabin. He doesn't imagine he lusts after them himself – oh, he wouldn't dream of anything except being respectful and gallant and getting adoring looks – but the thought of redskin after redskin on them seems to be more than he can bear.'

'He may have to,' Peregrino said.

'Yes, he may.' Tarrant grimaced. 'I must admit I don't relish it, nor the idea of ransoming them with guns. I'm not quite as case-hardened as … I must behave.'

'I think nothing will happen for hours.'

'Good. I have to give Quanah my presents, go through any formalities – you'll advise me, won't you? – but not right away, hm? Let's walk on. We've a lot of talking to do, you and me. Three thousand years' worth.'

5

Warriors gathered around. Now they were still, in wildcat dignity, for this was a ceremonial occasion. The westering sun cast gleams over obsidian hair and mahogany skin; on the eastern side it lit flames in eyes.

Between the ranks, before his tipi, Quanah received Tarrant's gifts. He made a speech in his father's language, lengthy and doubtless full of imagery in his fathers' wise. Standing by the visitor, Peregrino said in English when it was done: 'He thanks you, he calls you friend, and tomorrow morning you will pick out of his horses whichever you like best. That is generous for a man on the warpath.'

'I know,' Tarrant said. To Quanah, in Spanish: 'My thanks to you, great chief. May I ask a favor, in the name of the friendship you so kindly give us?'

Herrera, in the front row though well back, started, tautened, and squinted. Tarrant hadn't stopped by him upon returning, but had collected his presents and gone straight here. Word flew quickly about, and when he saw the braves assemble, Herrera came for politeness and wariness.

'You may ask,' said Quanah, impassive.

'I wish to buy free those folks you hold trapped. They are useless to you. Why should you spend more time and men on them? We will take them away with us. In exchange we will pay a good price.'

A stir went through the Comanches, a rustle, a buzz. Those who understood whispered to those who had not. Hands tightened on hafts, here and there on a firearm.

A man near the chief uttered a string of harsh words. He was gaunt, scarred, more deeply lined in the face than was common even for aged Indians. Others near him muttered as if in agreement. Quanah lifted a hand for attention and told Tarrant, 'Wahaawmaw says we have our fallen to avenge.'

'They fell, uh, honorably.'

'He means all our fallen, through all the years and lifetimes, deathtimes we have suffered.'

'I didn't think you people – thought that way.'

'Wahaawmaw was a boy in that camp where the Tejanos took Quanah's mother,' Peregrino related. 'He found cover and escaped, but they shot down his own mother, brother, two little sisters. A while back he lost his wife and a small son; the soldiers were using a howitzer. The same has happened, different places, to many who are here.'

'I'm sorry,' Tarrant said to any who would listen. 'But those people yonder had nothing to do with that, and – well, I carry plenty of fine things like those I've given your chief. Wouldn't you rather have them than a few stinking scalps?'

Wahaawmaw claimed the right to speak. He went on for minutes, snarling, hissing, flinging up his hands and crying aloud to heaven. Anger answered in a surf-noise. When he was done and had folded his arms, Peregrino scarcely needed to translate: 'He calls this an insult. Shall the Nermernuh sell their victory for blankets and booze? They'll take more loot than they can carry off the Tejanos, and the scalps as well.'

He had warned Tarrant to expect this kind of outcome. Therefore Tarrant looked straight at Quanah and said, 'I can make a better offer. We have rifles with us, boxes full of cartridges, things you need as you need horses if you are to wage war. How much, for those poor lives?'

Herrera took a step forward. 'No, wait,' he called.

Quanah forestalled him. 'Are these in your baggage? If so, good. If not, you are too late. Your companion has already agreed to trade his for cattle.'

Tarrant stood moveless. Wahaawmaw, who must have gotten the gist, crowed at him. 'I could have told you,' Herrera said through the rising crowd-noise.

Quanah brought that down while Peregrino breathed in Tarrant's ear, 'I will see whether I can talk them into changing the deal. Keep your hopes on a tight rein, though.'

He launched into oratory. His fellows responded likewise. For the most part they spoke soberly. The effort always was to reach a consensus. They had no government. Civil chiefs were little more than judges, mediators, and even war chiefs only commanded in battle. Quanah waited out the debate. Toward the end, Herrera had something to say. Soon after that, Quanah pronounced what he took to be the verdict, and assent passed among his followers like an ebb-tide wave. The sun stood low. Wahaawmaw cast Tarrant a triumphant glare.

Sadness dulled Peregrino's English. 'You have guessed, no? It did not work. They have not gotten much blood yet, and are thirsty for it. Wahaawmaw claimed it would be bad luck to give quarter, and quite a few were ready to believe that. They can spare the half a dozen to round up this ranch's herd and bring it to New Mexico. They enjoy that trip. And the Comanchero told them he is not a man to pull out of a bargain once it's been struck. That made them extra touchy about their own honor. Also … Quanah didn't argue either way, but they know he has an idea for taking the house that he would like to try, and they are curious what it may be.' He stood silent for part of a minute. 'I did my best. I really did.'

'Of course,' Tarrant answered. 'Thanks.'

'I want you to know I don't like what will happen, either. Let's ride off and not come back till morning, you and me – Rufus if he wants.'

Tarrant shook his head. 'I've a notion I'd better stay around. Don't worry. I've seen enough sacks in the past.'

'I suppose you have,' said Peregrino.

The meeting broke up. Tarrant gave Quanah his respects and walked among knots of warriors, whose looks on him ranged from sullen to gleeful, toward Herrera's camp. It was several yards from the nearest tipi. The New Mexican found men to talk with and thus delayed himself.

His sons had a fire started. They were busy with preparations for supper, before the quick prairie dark should fall. Long sunbeams trailed through smoke. Bedrolls waited. Rufus sat idle, hunched, a bottle in his single fist. He looked up when Tarrant approached and asked, needlessly once he had seen, 'What happened?'

'No dice.' Tarrant lowered himself to the trampled grass and reached out. 'I'll take a swig of that whiskey. Not much, and you'd better watch it closer.' Its bite went beneficent down his gullet. 'I've failed altogether. Peregrino won't leave the Comanches, and they won't take ransom.' Curtly he described the situation.

'That son of a bitch,' Rufus breathed.

'Who? Quanah? He may be enemy, but he's honest.'

'No, Herrera. He could have –'

The trader glided into view. 'Did I hear my name?' he asked.

'Yeah.' Rufus lurched to his feet, bottle in hand. He stayed with English, except for, '*Vipera es.* You snake. You greaser. You could'a – could'a – sold Hanno – sold the boss those guns an' –'

Herrera's right hand moved toward his Colt. His sons edged left and right, not yet drawing their knives. 'I could not change a bargain that had been made,' he said. Spanish was too soft a language to convey the full coldness. 'Not unless they agreed, and they refused. That would have hurt my reputation, damaged my business.'

'Sure, you breed, you're always ready for sellin' white men, white women, sellin' 'em for – for money. Blood money.' Rufus spat at Herrera's feet.

'We will not speak of blood,' said the trader most quietly. 'I know who my father was. And I saw him weep when the Yanquis robbed our country from us. Now I must step aside for them in the streets of Santa Fe. The priest tells me I should not hate them, but need I care what becomes of them?'

Rufus groaned. His hook slashed. Herrera slipped back in time. The pistol sprang forth. Tarrant jumped to his feet and caught Rufus by the arms before the redbeard could try to draw. Slowly, the boys sheathed their blades.

'Behave yourself,' Tarrant panted. 'Sit down.'

'Not with these!' Rufus coughed in Latin. He shook free of the grasp on him. 'And you, Hanno. Can't you remember? Like that woman we saved, way back when in Russia. And that was just a single man, and he wouldn't have cut her belly open afterward, or given her to the females with their knives and torches –' He stumbled off, away from everybody, still gripping the bottle.

Looks followed him for a little. Then Tarrant said to Herrera, 'Let him be. He'll get his wits back. Thanks for your patience,' with less than total sincerity.

<h1 style="text-align:center">6</h1>

Twice during the afternoon, Tom Langford ventured outside. When he saw the encampment, he stepped quickly in again and rebarred the door. Toward evening he said, 'I s'pect they'll try a night attack. Why else would they hang around this long? Maybe again at dawn, but could be any time. We'll just have to keep alert. If we stand 'em off then, they ought to up and go. Injuns don't know how to lay a siege.'

Bill Davis laughed softly and richly. 'We ain't wuth it,' he opined.

'*Los vecinos vendrán indudablemente a ayudarnos* –'Elp weell come,' Carlos Padilla ventured.

'I dunno how fast, if ever,' Langford sighed. 'S'posin' Bob got through, the neighbors are scattered pretty thin these days. Maybe a cavalry troop is somewhere close enough.'

'We are in the hands of God,' Susie declared. She smiled at her husband. 'Yours too, dear, and strong hands they are.'

Ed Lee tossed and muttered on the Langfords' bed. His injury had lit a fever in him. The children were more than ready for sleep.

First there was supper, cold beans, bread, the last milk. They had no firewood to speak of, and little water. Langford asked his wife to say grace. Nobody minded when Carlos crossed himself. Afterward the men one by one and bashfully went behind a sort of curtain Susie had rigged in a corner to hide the bucket all must share. Langford had emptied it whenever he stepped out. He hoped nobody more would have any real business there till the Indians were gone. That would be kind of nasty, in these close quarters with a woman and a girl. The privy was sod, it ought to be around yet. If not, well, they'd have the tall grass for walls, the freedom of these acres for which he had saved and toiled and now fought.

Dusk thickened to night. A single candle burned on the table amidst the guns. The Langfords and the hale men stood watches, two peering out loopholes taken in turn while two caught naps, on the floor or alongside poor Ed. Stars crowded what they glimpsed of sky. The ground was gray-black vague. A waning sliver of moon would be scant help when it rose shortly before the sun. Meanwhile the cold and the stillness gnawed away.

Once the wife whispered from her side of the room, 'Tom?'

'Yeah?' He allowed himself a look at her. In this dim light he couldn't see dirt, exhaustion, hollowed cheeks and black-rimmed eyes. She was the girl of his courting days, from whose front porch he'd walk home on the rainbow.

'Tom, if – if they do get in and you have the chance –' She must take a breath. 'Would you shoot me – first?'

'Christ, no!' he choked, and could taste the horror.

'Please. I'd bless you.'

'You might live, honey. They do sell prisoners to our people.'

She stared at the floor, then quickly, remembering her duty, out a loophole. 'I wouldn't want to live. Not after –'

'Do you s'pose I'd ever turn my back on you? Reckon you don't know me as well as I thought.'

'No, but you – I'd be without you on earth. Why not together in Heaven, at once?'

He knew the redskins wouldn't spare his life. Unless he was lucky, he wouldn't be a man when he died. Not that knives and fire, or being staked out under the sun with his eyelids cut off, would leave him in shape to think much about that. 'Well, you might still manage to get the kids through.'

Again her head drooped. 'Yes. I'm sorry. I clean forgot. Yes, I was bein' selfish.'

'Aw, don't you fret, sweetheart,' he said as cheerfully as he was able. 'Nothin' bad's goin' to happen. Next week our biggest worry will be how we can keep from braggin' too loud.'

'Thank you, darlin'.' She turned her attention outward.

The night wore on. They had divided it into four watches, then all to be afoot in advance of dawn, when attack was likeliest. About three in the morning by the grandfather clock, the Langfords finished their second trick, roused the hands, and stretched themselves out, he on the floor, she beside Ed. Should the hurt man stir from the heavy sleep into which he had dropped, she'd know it and see to whatever need was his. The other men would shoot better, the more well rested they were.

A shotgun blast kicked Langford awake.

Bill thudded against the wall and fell. The lead had sleeted across the cabin and taken him in the back. By candlelight and monstrous flickery shadows the blood that gushed from him shone blacker than his skin.

Carlos crouched on the north side, rifle aimed and useless. Two broad muzzles thrust in by the west loopholes. One smoked. It withdrew. Instantly another took its place. Meanwhile the second roared.

Langford jumped to the bedside and Susie. Sick understanding billowed through him. Hostiles, just three or four, had crawled under cover of night, slowly, often stopping, shadows in the gloom, till they were among the stakes and under the eaves. When they shoved their guns through, maybe they hoped they'd fire straight into an eye.

No matter. Shooting blind, wedging the barrels to and fro, they made defense impossible.

Whoops lifted, nearer and nearer. Thunder beat on the door. No tomahawks, Langford knew; that was a regular woodcutting ax, probably his. Panels splintered. A gust blew out the candle. Langford fired and fired, but he couldn't see anything for sure. The hammer clicked on emptiness. Where the hell were the loaded guns? Susie screamed. Maybe he should have saved a bullet for her. Too late. The door was down and the dark full of warriors.

7

The racket brought Tarrant and the Herreras from their bedrolls, hands to weapons. Tumult went murky among the tipis. 'El ataque,' the trader said beneath yowls and shots.

'What're they doing?' Tarrant grated. 'Another frontal assault, in the dead of night? Crazy.'

'I do not know,' Herrera said. The noise rose rapidly to crescendo. He bared teeth, a dim flash under the stars. 'Victory. They are taking the house.' Tarrant bent to put on his boots. 'Where do you go? Stay here. You could too easily get killed.'

'I've got to see if I can do anything.'

'You cannot. Myself, I stay, not out of fear but because I do not want to see what comes next.'

Tarrant's pain lashed: 'You told me you don't care.'

'Not much,' Herrera admitted. 'But it would be evil to gloat, nor have I the heart for it. No, my sons and I will pray for them.' He plucked the other man's sleeve. You slept fully clad in such a place as this. 'Do stay. You, somehow, I like.'

'I'll be careful,' Tarrant promised, and loped off.

He skirted the Comanche camp. More and more torches came to life there, flared, bobbed, streamed sparks on their hasty way. Sight of them dimmed the stars that in their uncountable thousands gleamed frost-bright across black. Nevertheless he had light enough to turn the soil gray for him.

Where the devil was Rufus? Probably snoring out on the prairie alongside the empty bottle. Just as well. No matter how self-controlled, a white man took a risk, showing himself to red men in blood-rut.

So why did he, Hanno, Lugo, Cadoc, Jacques Lacy, William Sawyer, Jack Tarrant, a hundred different aliases, behave like this? He knew he couldn't save the ranchers, and didn't mean to try. They must perish as star-many had perished before them and would in the future, over and over, world without end. History chewed them up and spat them out and soon most rotted forgotten, might as well never have been. Maybe the Christians were right and mankind was like that, maybe it was simply in the nature of things.

His intention was practical. He hadn't survived this long by hiding from the terrible. Rather, he kept alert, aware, so he'd know which way to jump when the sword swung. Tonight he'd observe from the fringes. If an impulse arose to wipe out his party too, he could talk it down, given help from Peregrino and maybe even Quanah, before it got out of control. In the morning he'd start back toward Santa Fe.

The chief stood huge near the cabin, a long-helved ax on his shoulder. Torchlight guttered across painted face and body, horned headdress; it was as if he flickered in and out of hell. The braves were mostly less clear, blobs of night that swarmed, pranced, screeched, waved their brands like battle flags. Squaws capered with them, knives or sharpened sticks in hand. The doorway gaped hollow.

They kept clear a space in front of it. Three dead men sprawled at the threshold, dragged forth. The Anglo's left arm was splinted; someone had cut his throat before stopping to think about sport. Rib ends stuck out of a hole torn in the Negro's back. A third seemed Mexican, though he was so slashed and pulped it was hard to be sure; he had gone down fighting.

Lucky bastards. Two squaws held fast a small boy and a smaller girl who screamed, blind with fear. A tall Anglo sat slumped. Blood matted his hair and dripped onto clothes and earth. He was stunned. Two warriors locked the arms of a young woman who writhed, kicked, cursed them and called on her God.

A man bounded from the ruck. A torch swung near him for a moment and Tarrant recognized Wahaawmaw. He had slung his rifle to free his hands. The right gripped a knife. He laughed aloud, caught the collar of the woman's dress in his left, slashed downward. The cloth parted. Whiteness gleamed, and a sudden string of blood-beads. Her captors forced her down on her back. Wahaawmaw fumbled at his breechclout. The man prisoner stirred, croaked, struggled to regain his feet. A brave gave him a gun butt in the stomach and he sagged, retching.

A grizzly bear growl resounded. From around the cabin stormed Rufus. His Colt was drawn. He swept his hook back and forth. Two Indians stumbled aside, faces gashed open. He reached the woman. The men who pinned her sprang up. He shot one through the forehead. He hooked an eye from the other, who recoiled shrieking. His boot smashed into Wahaawmaw's groin. That warrior tumbled, to squirm by the white man. He sought to choke down agony, but it jerked past his lips.

Flambeau flare made Rufus' beard its own hue. He stood with his legs on either side of the woman, hunched forward, swaying a little, flaming drunk but the Colt rock-steady before him. 'Aw right,' he boomed, 'you filthy swine, first o' you makes a move, I'll plug him. She's gonna go free, an' –'

Wahaawmaw straightened on the ground and rolled over. Rufus didn't see. There was too much else for him to watch. 'Look out!' Tarrant heard himself yell. The Indian howls drowned his voice. Wahaawmaw unslung his rifle. Prone, he fired.

Rufus lurched back. The pistol fell. Wahaawmaw shot again. Rufus crumpled. His weight sank onto the woman and held her fast.

Wild, Tarrant shoved men aside. He sprang into the clear space and went on his knees beside Rufus. '*O sodalis, amice perennis –*' Blood bubbled from the mouth and into the red beard. Rufus gasped. For an instant it seemed he grinned, but Tarrant couldn't really know in the shifty torchlight or even by the light of the stars. He clasped the big body to him and felt life ebb away.

Only then did he hear what a silence had fallen. He looked aloft. Quanah stood above him, the ax held out like a roof or a buffalo-hide shield. Had he roared his folk into quietude? They were a massive blur, well back from him and the dead, the wounded, the captive. Here and there a blaze briefly picked out a face or made eyeballs glisten.

Tarrant hauled Rufus off the woman. She stirred, stared, mewed. 'Easy,' he murmured. She got to hands and knees, made her way thus to the man. Squaws had let go of the children, who were already at his side. He'd regained consciousness. At least, he could sit straight and lay his arms around them all.

The warriors Rufus injured had joined the crowd, except for the slain one and Wahaawmaw. He had risen but leaned on his rifle, shakily, holding himself where the pain was.

Tarrant got up too. Quanah lowered his ax. The pair of them regarded each other.

'Bad is this,' said the chief at last. 'Very bad.'

A skipper from Phoenicia learned how to snatch at every chance, no matter how thin a shred. 'Yes,' Tarrant answered. 'A man of yours has killed a guest of yours.'

'He, your man, broke murdering into our midst.'

'He had a right to speak, to be heard in your council. When your Nermer-nuh would bar his way and likely attack him, he acted in self-defense. He was under your protection, Quanah. At worst, you could have had him seized from behind, as many men as you command. I think you would have done that if you had gotten the chance, for everyone calls you a man of honor. But this creature shot him first.'

Wahaawmaw groaned outrage. Tarrant didn't know how much he had understood. The argument was weak, almost ridiculous. Quanah could dismiss it out of hand. And yet –

Peregrino stepped forth. He overtopped the chief by a couple of inches. He carried a medicine bundle and a wand on which hung three buffalo tails, things he must have brought from his tipi. A hiss and mumble went through the crowd. Torches wavered. Dertsahnawyeh, the undying one, had power to raise awe in the fiercest heart.

'Stay where you are, Jack Tarrant,' he said quietly, 'while Quanah and I go talk.'

The chief nodded. He spoke certain commands. Wahaawmaw snarled but hobbled obediently off to lose himself in the throng. Several warriors came rifles in hand to keep guard on the whites. Quanah and Peregrino departed into the night.

Tarrant went over to the prisoners and hunkered down. 'Listen,' he said low, 'we may be able to get you free. Keep still, don't make any fuss. This band's had a shock that cooled them down some, but don't do anything to remind them they meant to destroy you.'

'I got you,' the man answered, clearly if not quite firmly yet. 'Whatever happens, we owe you our prayers, you and your partner.'

'He came like a knight of King Arthur,' the woman whispered.

He came like a goddamned drunken idiot, Tarrant thought. I could have headed him off if I'd known. I would have. Oh, Rufus, old buddy, you always hated to be alone, and now you are, forever.

The man offered his hand. 'Tom Langford,' he said. 'My wife Susan. Nancy. Jimmy, uh, James.' For out of grime and drying tears and the start of a bruise, the boy had cast his father a reproachful look. Tarrant wanted to hoot laughter.

He choked it down, shook hands, gave his name, and finished, 'We'd better not talk more. Besides, the Indians expect me to see to my dead.'

Rufus lay about ten feet from the Langfords. It might have been ten thousand miles. Tarrant couldn't wash him, but he straightened the body, closed the eyes, bound up the jaw with a bandanna. He drew his pocket knife and cut himself in the face and along bared arms and chest. Blood welled and dripped, nothing serious but it impressed the watchers. This was their way of mourning, not the white man's. Surely therefore the dead was mightily important, to be avenged with cannon and saber unless his friends were appeased. At the same time, the friend who was here did not wail over him, and that too was eerie. By ones and twos and threes, the Nermernuh melted off toward the comfort of their camp.

Well, Rufus, you did have fifteen hundred years, and you enjoyed just about every day of them. You wenched and fought and sang and gorged and swilled and adventured, you were a hard worker when we needed work done and a better yet man to have at my back when we needed that and in your rough gruff style a pretty good husband and father whenever we settled down a while. I could have done without your stupid practical jokes, and by ourselves for any length of time your conversation got so boring it was physically painful, and if you saved my life now and then, I staked my own as often to pull you out of some scrape you'd blundered into, and – and a lot of gusto went out of my world tonight, Rufus. A lot of love.

False dawn chilled the east. Quanah and Peregrino were dim in sight until they reached the cabin and halted. Tarrant rose. The guards glided deferentially aside. From the ground the Langfords stared dull-eyed, wrung dry, their children uneasily asleep.

Tarrant stood waiting.

'It is decided,' said Quanah. The deep voice rolled like hoofs over the plains. Breath blew ghost-white in the cold. 'Let all men know that the Nermernuh are generous. They will heed my wishes in this matter. You, the trader, and his sons may go home. You may take these captives along. They are in exchange for your comrade. He brought his death on himself, but since he was a guest, let that be his price, because the Nermernuh set high their honor. Nor shall his body be harmed, but we will give him decent burial, so that his spirit may find its way to the afterworld. I have spoken.'

A shudder passed below Tarrant's skin. He had more than half awaited worse than this. Somehow he kept it hidden and said, 'I thank you much, señor, and I will tell my people that the soul of Quanah is large.' He believed he meant it.

For an instant the chief let his stateliness drop. 'Thank Peregrino. He persuaded me. Begone before sunrise.'

He beckoned to the guards. They followed him toward the Comanche camp.

A mortal might have crumbled to pieces as the pressure came off, cackled and gibbered and swooned. An immortal had more reserves, more bounce. Nonetheless Tarrant's words trembled. 'How did you do it, Peregrino?'

'I pushed your argument as far as it would go.' Again the Indian took time to build and weigh each English sentence. 'He wasn't unwilling to take it. He isn't a fiend, you know; he's fighting for the life of his people. But he must convince them also. I had to … call in all my chips, call on the spirits, finally tell him that either he released you or I left him. He does value my advice as well as … my medicine. After that it wasn't hard to get him to release this family too. I will help him convince the warriors that was a good idea.'

'He was right when he told me to thank you,' Tarrant said. 'I will for as many centuries as I've got left.'

Peregrino's smile was as bleak as the eastern light. 'You need not. I had my reasons and I want my price.'

Tarrant swallowed. 'What is it?'

The tone mildened. 'I admit I did have to save you. Maybe you and I are the only immortals in the world, now. We must join together sometime. But meanwhile –'

Peregrino reached out and caught Tarrant's arm. 'Meanwhile, here are my people,' throbbed from him. 'I wasn't born to them, but they are almost the last of us who were born to this land and are still free. They won't be much longer. Soon they will be broken.' Even as Tyre and Carthage were, Gallia and Britannia, Rome and Byzantium, Albigensians and Hussites, Basques and Irish, Quebec and the Confederacy. 'I told you yesterday out on the prairie, I have to stay with them to the end, reason with them, help them find a new faith and hope. Else they'll dash themselves to pieces, like buffalo over a cliff. So I will be working among them for peace.

'I want you to do the same. As I told Quanah, letting these few go can earn us a little good will. More will die, horribly, but here is a talking point for you. You claim you are rich and have the ear of powerful men. All right, my price for these lives is that you work on your side for peace, a peace that my people can live with.'

'I'll try my best,' said Tarrant. He truly meant that. If nothing else, the day would come when Peregrino held him to account.

They clasped hands. The Indian strode off. False dawn died away and he was quickly into the shadows.

'Follow me,' Tarrant called to the Langfords. 'We have to hit the trail at once.'

What sum of years had Rufus bought for these four? Two hundred, maybe?

8

In far Western eyes, the Wichita Mountains were hardly more than hills; but they rose steeply, treeless, yet under the spring rains turning deeply green and starred with wild-flowers. In its valley among them a big house and its outbuildings reigned over many acres of cropland, pasture, cattle, and horses, horses.

Grass shone wet after a shower and clouds drifted white when a hired carriage left the main road for the drive to the homestead. A farmhand on a pony, who had been inspecting fences, saw it and rode to inquire. Mr Parker wasn't here, he said. The driver, who was likewise an Indian, explained that his passenger's business was actually with Mr Peregrino. Startled, the worker gave directions and stared after the vehicle. It was almost as strange to him as the autos that occasionally stuttered by.

A side track brought it to a frame cabin surrounded by flowerbeds, kitchen garden in back. On the porch a man clad in dungarees and sandals sat reading. He wore his hair in braids but was too tall and slender to be a Comanche. As the carriage approached he laid his book aside, sprang down the steps, and stood waiting.

It stopped. A white man climbed out. His clothes bespoke prosperity only if you looked closely at material and tailoring. For a moment he and the dweller were still. Then they ran to grip hands and look into each other's eyes.

'At last,' Peregrino said, not quite evenly. '*Bienvenido, amigo.*'

'I'm sorry to have been this long about coming,' Tarrant answered. 'It happened I was in the Orient on business when your letter reached San Francisco. After I got home, I thought a telegram might draw too much notice. You'd written to me years ago, when I sent you my address, that just that bit of mail set tongues wagging. So I simply caught the first train east.'

'It's all right. Come in, come in.' With long practice behind it the English flowed easily, colloquially. 'If your driver wants, he can go on to the big house. They'll take care of him. He can cart us to town – how about day after tomorrow? I've things of my own to see to, including stuff I'd like shipped after me. If that's okay with you.'

'Of course, Peregrino. Damn near anything you may want is.' Having spoken to the other man, Tarrant took a Gladstone bag from the carriage and accompanied his host inside.

The cabin held four rooms, neat, clean, sunny, austerely furnished except for a substantial number of books, a gramophone, a collection of mostly classical records, and, in the bedchamber, certain articles of religion. 'You'll sleep here,' Peregrino said. 'I'll roll up in the back yard. No, not a peep out of you. You're my guest. Besides, it'll be kind of like old days. I often do it anyway, in fact.'

Tarrant glanced around. 'You live alone, then?'

'Yes. It seemed wrong to me, getting married and having kids when I knew that in the end I'd fake something and desert them. Life among the free tribes was different. How about you?'

Tarrant's mouth pinched together. 'My latest wife died last year, young. Consumption. We tried a desert climate, everything, but – Well, we had no children, and this identity has been around nearly as long as is safe. I'm making ready for a change.'

They settled themselves in the front room on wooden chairs. Above Peregrino's head a chromolithograph gazed from its frame at Tarrant, a Rembrandt self-portrait. Bad though the copy was, mortal sorrow lingered in those eyes. From his bag Tarrant had taken a bottle of Scotch. Illegally, he filled both glasses his host had fetched. He also offered Havana cigars. Mere creature comforts are still comforts.

'How've you been doing otherwise?' Peregrino inquired.

'Busy,' Tarrant said. 'Not sure how rich I am – I'd have to go through the books of several aliases – but it's a heap, and bigger every day. One thing I want you for, besides yourself, is to help me think what's most worth spending it on. How about you?'

'Peaceful, on the whole. I cultivate my patch of land, make things in my woodworking shop, counsel my congregation – native church, so I'm not really like a white minister – and teach in a school. I'll be sorry to leave that. Oh, and I read a lot, trying to learn about your world.'

'And I suppose you're Quanah's advisor.'

'Well, yes. But look, don't think I'm the power behind his sad little throne or anything like that. He's done it all himself. He's a remarkable man. Among whites he'd have been a Lincoln or Napoleon. The most I can claim credit for is making some things possible, or at least easier, for him. He went ahead and did them.'

Tarrant nodded, remembering – The grand alliance of Comanche, Kiowa, Cheyenne, and Arapaho, Quanah its paramount chief. The bloody repulse at Adobe Walls, the year of warfare and manhunt that followed, and the last starvelings, led by Quanah, going onto the reservation in 1875. The good intentions of an Indian agent three years afterward, when he arranged for the Comanches to ride out under military escort on a final buffalo hunt, and no buffalo remained. And yet, and yet –

'Where is he now?' Tarrant asked.

'In Washington,' Peregrino said. Receiving a look of surprise: 'He goes there fairly often. He *is* our spokesman, for all our tribes. And, well, too bad about Mr McKinley, but that did put Theodore Roosevelt in the White House. He and Quanah know each other, they're friends.'

He smoked for a while in silence. The ageless are seldom hurried. At length he went on: 'Among us Quanah's more than a rather wealthy farmer. He's a headman and judge, he holds us together. The whites don't like the peyote nor his clutch of wives, but they put up with it because he doesn't just keep us going, by doing so he keeps their consciences at ease. Not that he's any sobersides. A genial sort, apt to tell stories or use language that'd make a sailor blush. But he is … reconciliation. He calls himself Quanah Parker, in memory of his mother. Lately he talks about having her bones and his sister's moved here, so they can rest beside his. Oh, I don't blinker myself. We Indians have a steep, tough road to walk, and a lot of us will fall by the wayside. But Quanah's gotten us started.'

'And you brought him to that,' Tarrant said.

'Well, I worked against the prophets, I used what influence I had toward getting peace into the minds of the People. And you, from your side, kept your promise.'

Tarrant grinned crookedly. It had cost. You couldn't simply buy politicians, you had to buy or push men who in their turn could strike deals with the grim incorruptibles. But Quanah did not go to jail or hang.

'I suspect you're too modest,' Tarrant said. 'Never mind. We've done our work. Maybe we've justified our long lives; I don't know. So you're ready to travel?'

Peregrino nodded. 'I can't do anything more here that others can't whom I've helped train. And I have been on this reservation more than a quarter century. Quanah's covered for me, kept me pretty much tucked in a corner, discouraged those who remember from talking to outsiders about me. But it isn't like the prairie. Folks are wondering. If any real word leaked to the newspapers – ah, that worry's at an end. I'll leave him a letter, and my blessing.'

He looked out the window. It faced west. His hand lifted to his lips the brew of a people who themselves were once barbarians, southward raiding, northward retreating in war after war for their freedom. He said, 'It's time for me to start over.'

XV

COMING TOGETHER

1

Rain roared. It washed away heat and grime, turned the air into flying, stinging gray. When lightning flashed, the hue became brief mercury, while thunder trampled down noise of motors, horns, water spurting from wheels. One bolt stabbed the new Empire State Building, but dissolved in the steel web under the masonry. Though the hour was early afternoon, headlights glimmered on cars and buses. Even midtown, pedestrians became few, trudging hunched beneath umbrellas or dodging from marquee to awning. Taxis were not to be had.

Uptown, Laurace Macandal's street lay altogether bare. Ordinarily it bore life enough, and after dark bustled and glittered. Several night clubs had sprung up among the neighborhood's modest tenements, small shops, and this old mansion she had renovated. Hard times or no, white folks still came to Harlem for jazz, dance, comedy, a little freedom from care such as they told each other Negroes were born to. Just now, everybody was inside, waiting out the weather.

She glanced at a clock and beckoned to one of the maids. 'Listen well, Cindy,' she said. 'You haven't been long in service, and something very important will happen today. I don't want you making mistakes.'

'Yes, Mama-lo.' Awe shivered in the girl's voice.

Laurace shook her head. 'That, for instance. I have told you before, I am only "Mama-lo" at holy times.'

'I, I'se sorry, … ma'm.' Tears blurred sight of the woman who stood before the girl – a woman who looked young and yet somehow old as time; tall, slim, in a maroon dress of quiet elegance, a silver snake bracelet on her left wrist and at her throat a golden pendant whose intertwined circle and triangle surrounded a ruby; too dark to be called high yellow, but with narrow face, arched nose, hair straight and stiff. 'I keeps forgettin'.'

Laurace smiled and reached to pat the maid's hand. 'Don't be afraid, dear.' Her voice, which could be a trumpet, sang like a violin. 'You're young, with much to learn. Mainly I want you to understand that my visitor today is special. That's why no men will be around except Joseph, and he's to stay with the car. You will help in the kitchen. Don't leave it. No, there is nothing wrong with the way you serve at table, and you're prettier than Conchita, but she ranks higher. Rank must be earned, by service as well as faith and study. Your time will come, I'm sure. Mainly, Cindy, you are to keep silence. You may not speak a single word to anybody, ever, about who my guest was or anything else you might happen to see or hear. Do you understand?'

'Yes, ma'm.'

'Good. Now be off with you, child. Oh, and do work harder on your English. You'll never get anywhere in the world unless you sound educated. Are educated. Master Thomas tells me you aren't doing so well at arithmetic, either. If you need extra help, ask him for it. Teaching isn't just his job, it's his calling.'

'Y-yes, ma'm.'

Laurace inclined her head and half closed her big eyes, as if listening. 'Your good angel hovers near,' she said. 'Go in peace.'

The girl trotted off, pert in her starched uniform, radiant in her sudden joy.

Alone, Laurace prowled about, picked up objects, fiddled with them, put them down again. She had made this room Victorian, oak wainscots, heavy furniture, thick carpet and drapes, glass-fronted cabinets for carefully chosen curios, a shelf of books still more select, on top of which rested the white bust of a man who had been black. Electric bulbs in a glass chandelier were dim; rain's twilight crowded close. The effect was impressive without being overly strange.

When, from a bow window, she saw the car she had dispatched arrive at the curb, she set restlessness aside and straightened. Most would depend on what impression she herself made.

The chauffeur got out, unfolded a large umbrella, came around to the right side and opened the rear door. He escorted his passenger to the porch, where he rang the bell for her. Laurace didn't see that, but she heard and knew. She likewise knew of the two maids who received the visitor, took her coat, and guided her down the hall.

As she entered the room, Laurace went to meet her. 'Welcome, welcome,' she said, and clasped both hands in hers.

Clara Rosario's fingers responded only slightly, as did her mouth to the smile offered her. She seemed alien, her own finery a little too bright-colored. Though her hair was marcelled midnight, skin tawny, lips full, she was of white race, hazel-eyed, straight-nosed, wide across the cheekbones. Laurace stood three inches higher. Nonetheless Clara carried herself boldly, as well she might, given a figure like hers.

'Thank you,' she said, with a staccato accent. Glancing about: 'Quite a place you got here.'

'We'll be private in the sanctum,' said Laurace. 'It has a liquor cabinet. Or would you prefer tea or coffee? I'll order it brought.'

'Uh, thanks, but I could use a drink right now.' Clara laughed nervously.

'You can stay for dinner, can't you? I promise you a *cordon bleu* meal. By then we should have completed our ... business, and be able to relax and enjoy it.'

'Well, not too late. They expect me there, you know? I jolly them along and – Could be trouble, too, for me to head off. Men are kind of on edge these days, wondering what's going to go wrong next, you know?'

'Besides, we don't want anybody wondering what you're up to,' Laurace agreed. 'Don't worry. I'll send you back in plenty of time.' She took Clara's arm. 'This way, please.'

When the door had shut behind them, Clara stood a while, tensed. Between curtained windows, the smaller room was wholly foreign. Straw mats covered the floor, leopard pelts the curiously shaped chairs. Two African masks dominated one wall. On a shelf between them rested a human skull. Opposite stretched an eight-foot python skin. At the farther end stood a marble altar. Upon its red-bordered white cloth were a knife, a crystal bowl full of water, and a bronze candlestick with seven twisty branches. Lighting was from a single heavily shaded lamp on a table beside silver boxes for cigarettes and matches and an incense holder whose smoke turned breath pungent. Almost lost in their everydayness were the cabinet and console radio that flanked the entrance, or the coffee table which near the middle held glasses, ice bucket, seltzer, carafe, ashtrays, small dishes of delicacies.

'Don't be alarmed,' said Laurace. 'You must have seen magicians' lairs in the past.'

Clara nodded. 'A few times,' she gulped. 'You mean you –'

'Well, yes and no. These things aren't for use; they're meant to convey sacredness, power, mystery. Also,' Laurace added matter-of-factly, 'nobody would dare open that door without my leave, under any circumstances whatsoever. We can talk in perfect safety.'

Clara rallied. She would not have endured through her centuries without ample courage; and her hostess offered nothing but friendship, of a sort and provided it be possible. 'I guess we've gone mighty different ways, you and me.'

'Time we bring them together. Would you like some music? I can get two good stations.'

'No, let's just talk.' Clara grimaced. 'I don't need music all the time, you know? I run a high-class house.'

'Poor dear.' Much sorrow was in the gentleness. 'You don't have it so easy, do you? Have you ever?'

Clara lifted her head. 'I get by. How about that drink?'

She chose a strong bourbon-and-branch, together with a cigarette, and settled onto the sofa before the table. Laurace poured a glass of Bordeaux and sat down on a chair across from her. For a space there was silence, apart from the dulled noise of the rainstorm.

Then Clara said, half defiantly, 'Well, what about it? What are we going to talk about?'

'Suppose you start,' Laurace answered, her words continuing soft. 'Whatever you want. This is just the first of our real meetings. We'll need many more. We have everything to learn about each other, and decide, and finally do.'

Clara drew breath. 'Okay,' she said fast. 'How did you find me? When you showed up at my apartment and, and told me you're immortal, *too* –' It had not brought on hysteria, but Laurace had soon realized she'd better go. Afterward it had been a matter of three careful telephone conversations, until now. 'I thought at first you were crazy, you know? But you didn't act it and how could a crazy person have found out? Later I wondered if you wanted to blackmail me, but that didn't make sense either. Only ... all right, how do you know what I am, and how can I know you really are what you claim?' She raised her glass in a jerky motion and drank deep. 'I don't want to offend you, but, well, I've got to be more sure.'

'Naturally you're cautious,' Laurace said. 'Do you think I'm not? We've both had to be, or die. But look around you. Would something like this belong to any criminal such as you ever knew?'

'N-no ... Unless the prophet of a cult – But I never heard of you, and I would have, as rich as you must be.'

'I'm not. Nor is the organization I lead. It does require me to maintain the appearance of, m-m, solidity. As to your questions, though.' Laurace sipped of her wine. Her voice grew slow, almost dreamy:

'I don't know when I was born. If any record was made, I couldn't tell where to find it, and probably it's long lost. Who cared about a pickaninny slave? But from what I remember, and what I deduced after I began to study, I must be about two hundred years old. That isn't much, set against your age. Fourteen hundred, did you say? But of course I wondered, more and more desperately, whether I was quite alone in the world or not.

'Any others like me must be hiding the fact like me. Men can go into a variety of occupations, lives. Women have fewer opportunities. When at last I had the means to search, it made sense to begin with the trade that a woman might very well, even most likely, be forced into.'

'Whoredom,' said Clara starkly.

'I told you before, I pass no judgments. We do what we must, to survive. One such as you could have left a trail, a trail often broken but perhaps possible to follow, given time and patience. After all, she wouldn't expect anybody would think to try. Newspaper files, police and court records, tax rolls and other registers where prostitution had been legal, old photographs – things like that, gathered, sifted, compared. Some of my agents have been private detectives, some have been … followers of mine. None knows why I wanted this information. Slowly, out of countless fragments, a few parts fitted together. It seemed there had been a woman who did well in Chicago back in the nineties till she got into some kind of trouble, curiously similar to one in New York later, in New Orleans later still, again in New York –'

Clara made a slicing gesture. 'Never mind,' she snapped. 'I get the idea. I should have remembered, in fact. It happened before.'

'What?'

'Back in Konstantinopolis – Istanbul – oh, Lord, nine hundred years ago, it must have been. A man tracked me down pretty much the same way.'

Laurace started to rise, sank back, leaned forward. 'Another immortal?' she cried. 'A man? What became of him?'

'I don't know.' Belligerently: 'I wasn't glad to be found then, and I'm not sure I am now. You are a woman, I guess that makes a difference, but you've got to convince me, you know?'

'A man,' Laurace whispered. 'Who was he? What was he like?'

'Two. He had a partner. They were traders out of Russia. I didn't want to go off with them, so I shook them, and never heard anything since. Probably they're dead. Let's not talk it about it yet, okay?'

The rain-silence descended.

'What a horror of a life you have had,' Laurace finally said.

Clara grinned on the left side of her mouth. 'Oh, I'm tough. Between the times I work, when I live easy on what I've earned and saved – or sometimes, yeah, I've married money – it's good enough that I want to keep going.'

'I should think – you told me you've mostly been a madam since you came to America – isn't that better than it … used to be for you?'

'Not always.'

2

She hated sleeping where she worked. In Chicago she had an apartment five blocks away. Usually she could go home about two or three a.m., and the afternoons were her own; then business was slack enough for Sadie to manage. She'd go shopping downtown, or enjoy the sunshine and flowers in Jackson Park, or visit one of the museums built after the Columbian Exposition, or ride a trolley out into the countryside, all sorts of things, maybe with a couple of the girls, maybe by herself, but always ladylike.

Gas lamps flared. Pavement stretched ash-gray, empty as the moon. Lightly though she walked, her footfalls sounded loud in her ears. The two men who came out of an alley were like more shadows until they fell in on either side of her.

She choked down a gasp. Fear chilled and keened. He on the right was a hulk, bristle-chinned and smelly. He on the left was hardly more than a boy. He had no color in his face except for the pus yellow the lamps gave it, and from time to time he giggled.

'Hello, Mrs Ross,' the big man said. His voice was gritty. 'Nice evening, ain't it?'

Fool, she raged at herself, fool, I should have been careful, I should have spent what a bodyguard would cost, but no, I couldn't be bothered, I had to save every cent toward my next years of freedom – In a way that was ancient with her, she killed the fear. She couldn't afford it.

'I don't know you,' she said. 'Let me be.'

'Aw, we know you. Mr Santoni, he showed us on the street when you was passing by. He asked us we should have a little talk with you.'

'Go, before I call a policeman.'

The boy tittered. 'Shut up, Lew,' said the big man. 'You get too impatient.' To her: 'Now don't be like that, Mrs Ross. All we want to do is talk with you a while. You just come along quiet.'

'I'll talk to your boss, Mr Santoni, I'll speak to him again if he insists.' Buy time. 'Later today, yes.'

'Oh, no. Not so soon. He says you been real unreasonable.'

He wants to add my business to his string, he wants to end every independent house in the city, we're to do his will and pay him his tribute. Christ, before it's too late, send us a man with a sawed-off shotgun!

It was already too late for her. 'He wants Lew and me should have a little talk with you first. He can't waste no more of his time arguing, you got me? Just come along quiet now, and you'll be all right. Lew, put that goddamn shiv back.'

She tried to run. A long arm snapped her to a halt. The way they pinioned her was effective; further resistance could have led to a dislocated shoulder. Around the next corner waited a cabriolet and driver. The horse hadn't far to go before it reached a certain building.

Several times the big man must restrain the boy. Afterward he would sponge her, speak soothingly, give her a smoke, before they resumed. Drawing on past experience, she avoided damage that would be permanent, on her if not on a mortal. They actually let her out of the cab in front of a doctor's house.

The hospital staff were amazed at how fast she healed, quite without marks. While they did not interrogate her, they understood more or less what had happened and expected it would be a very meek, obliging, frequently smiling person who left them. Well, a body so extraordinary might generate a personality equally resilient.

Just the same, Carlotta Ross cut her losses, sold whatever she could and dropped from sight. She had never heard of the rival who later bushwhacked Santoni. She seldom bothered taking revenge. Time did that for her, eventually. She was content to start over elsewhere, forewarned.

3

'I get along, though. I'm used to the life. Pretty good at it, in fact.' Clara laughed. 'By now, I'd better be, huh?'

'Do you loathe all men?' Laurace asked.

'Don't pity me! ... Sorry, you mean well, I shouldn't've flared up. No, I've met some that I guess were decent. Not usually in my line of work, though, and not for me. I don't have to take them on any more myself; just take their money. I couldn't have anybody for real anyway. Can I? Can you?'

'Not forever, obviously. Unless someday we find others of our kind.' Laurace saw the expression before her. 'Others we like.'

'Mind if I have a refill of this drink? I'll help myself.' Clara did, and took a cigarette from her purse. Meanwhile she asked, no longer aggressive, almost shy: 'What about you, Laurace? How do you feel? You were a slave once, you've said. That must have been as bad as anything I ever knew. Maybe worse. Christ knows how many slaves I've seen in my life.'

'Sometimes it was very bad. Other times it was, oh, comfortable. But never free. At last I ran away. White people who were against slavery got me to Canada. There I found work as a housemaid.'

Clara studied Laurace before murmuring, 'You don't talk or behave like a servant.'

'I changed. My employers helped me. The Dufours, they were: kindly, mildly prosperous, in Montreal. When they saw I wanted to better myself, they arranged schooling for me – after working hours, and servants worked long hours in those days, so it took years – but I'll always be grateful to the Dufour family. I learned correct English, reading, writing, arithmetic. On my own, consorting with *habitants*, I picked up French of a sort. I turned into quite a bookworm, as far as circumstances allowed. That gave me a patchwork education; but as the years went on, I gradually filled many of the gaps in it.

'First I had to master memory. I was finding it harder and harder to pull whatever I wanted out of such a ragbag of recollections. It was becoming hard to *think*. I had to do something. You faced the same problem, I dare say.'

Clara nodded. 'Awful, for maybe fifty years. I don't know what I did or how, can't recall much and everything's jumbled. Might have gotten into real trouble and died, except – okay, I fell into the hands of a pimp. He, and later his son, they did my thinking for me. They weren't bad guys, by their lights, and of course my not growing old made me special, maybe magical, so they didn't dare abuse me, by the standards of the, uh, eighth century Near East, it must have been. I think they never let on to anybody else, but moved me to a different city every few years. Meanwhile, somehow, bit by bit, I got myself sorted out, and when the son died I felt ready to strike off on my own again. I wonder if most immortals aren't that lucky. Somebody insane or witless wouldn't last long without a protector, most times and places. Would she?'

'I've thought that myself. I was luckier still. By the early twentieth century we had a science of psychology. Crude, largely guesswork, but the idea that the mind can be understood and fixed makes a huge difference. I found auto-hypnosis did wonders – We'll talk about this later. Oh, we have so much to talk about.'

'I guess you never got too badly confused, then.'

'No, I kept control throughout. Of course, I moved around. It hurt to leave the Dufours, but people were wondering why I didn't age like them. Also, more and more I wanted independence, true independence. I went from job to job, acquired skills, saved my money. In 1900 I moved back to the States. There a colored person was less conspicuous, and here in New York you can go as unnoticed as you care to. I opened a small cafe. It did well – I am a good cook – and in time I was able to start a larger place, with entertainment. The war boomed business. Afterward Prohibition made profits larger yet. White customers; I kept another, less fancy den for blacks. One of my white regulars became a friend. At City Hall he saw to it that I didn't pay off exorbitantly or have to worry about the mob muscling in.'

Clara considered her surroundings. 'You didn't buy this with the proceeds from two speakeasies,' she said.

Laurace smiled. 'Shrewd, aren't you? Well, the truth is that presently I took up with a pretty big-time rumrunner. White, but –'

4

Donald O'Bryan loved wind and water. At home he filled shelves with books about sailing ships, hung pictures of them on the walls, built models of them whose exquisite detail seemed impossible for such large hands. Besides the power cruiser he used in his business, he kept a sloop on Long Island Sound. When he started taking his black 'housekeeper' on day trips, she went unchallenged by members of the yacht club. Everybody liked Don but nobody who was smart messed with him.

Heeled over on a broad reach, the boat rushed through swoosh and spar-kle. Gulls soared white above the wake, into which he had merrily cast scraps from lunch. When you ran before the wind, its booming was hushed to a cradle song and the air grew almost snug, so that you caught the live salt smell of it.

Reaching, a steersman must be careful. Don had secured the boom against an accidental jibe, but control remained tricky. He managed without effort. His body belonged where he was. His being had turned elsewhere.

Between watch cap and pea jacket, the snub-nosed face had lost its earlier cheerfulness. '*Why* won't you marry me?' he pleaded. 'I want to make an honest woman of you, really I do.'

'This is honest enough for me,' she laughed.

'Flora, I love you. It's not only that you're grand in bed, though you are, you are. It's … your soul. You're brave and dear and a thousand times more bright than me. It's proud I'd be to have you bear my children.'

Humor died. She shook her head. 'We're too different.'

'Was the Queen of Sheba too different from King Solomon?'

'In this country she would be.'

'Is it the law you fret about? Listen, not every state forbids marriage between the races, and the rest have to respect it once it's happened where it's allowed. That's in the Constitution.'

The same Constitution that says a man can't take a glass of beer after a hot day's work, she thought. 'No, it's what we'd have to live with. Hatred. Isolation from both your people and mine. I couldn't do that to our children.'

'Not everywhere,' he argued. 'Listen, you've heard me before, but listen. I won't keep my trade forever. In a few more years I'll have more money piled together than we could spend in a hundred. Because I am really a careful, saving man, in spite of liking a good time. I'll take you to Ireland. To France. You always wanted to see France, you've said, and what I saw made me want to go back, during the war though it was. We can settle down wherever we like, in some sweet country where they don't care what the color of our skins may be, only the color of our hearts.'

'Wait till then, and we'll talk about this.' Maybe by then I can bring myself to it, to seeing time eat him hollow. Maybe I'll be sure by then that he won't grow bitter when I tell him – because I can never deceive him, not in any way that matters – and will even be glad to have me there in my strength, holding his hand as he lies on his deathbed.

'No, now! We can keep it secret if you want.'

She stared across the dancing waves. 'I can't do that either, darling. Please don't ask me to.'

He frowned. 'Is it you fear being the wife of a jailbird? I swear to God they'll never take me alive. Not that I expect they'll catch me at all.'

She looked back at him. A lock of hair curled brown from beneath the cap and fluttered across his brow. How like a boy he seemed, a small boy full of love and earnestness. She remembered sons she had borne and buried. 'What difference would it make whether a justice of the peace mumbled a few words over us, if we aren't free to stand together in sight of everybody?'

'I want to give you my vows.'

'You have given them, dearest. I could weep for the joy of that.'

'Well, there is this too,' he said, rougher-toned. 'I don't plan on dying, but we never know, and I want to make sure I leave you provided for. Won't you give my heart that ease?'

'I don't need an inheritance. Thank you, thank you, but I don't.' She grimaced. 'Nor do I want more to do with lawyers and the government than I can possibly help.'

'Um. So.' He gnawed his lip for a minute. 'Well, I can understand that. All right.' His smile burst forth like the sun between clouds. 'Not that I'm giving up on making you Mrs O'Bryan, mind you. I'll wear you down, I will. Meanwhile, however, I'll make arrangements. I don't trust bankers much anyway, and this is a profitable time to liquidate my real estate holdings. We'll put it in gold, and you'll know where the hoard is.'

'Oh, Don!' The money was nothing, the wish was the whole world and half the stars. She scrambled to her knees in the cockpit and pressed herself against him.

He bent over. His left arm closed around her shoulders, his mouth sought hers. 'Flora,' he said huskily. 'My beautiful strange Flora.'

5

'– We loved each other. I've never been afraid to love, Clara. You should learn how.'

The other woman stubbed out her cigarette and reached for a fresh one. 'What happened?'

Voice and visage grew blank. 'A revenue boat intercepted him in 1924. When he bade fair to outrun them, they opened fire. He was killed.'

'Oh. I'm sorry.'

Laurace shook herself. 'Well, we're familiars of death, you and I.' Once more calm: 'He left me a quarter million in negotiable instruments. I needed to get away, sold my night clubs and spent the next four years traveling. First Ireland, England, France. In France I improved my French and studied about Africa. I went there, Liberia, then the colonies along that coast, hoping to discover something about my ancestors. I made friends in the bush and added to what I'd learned from books, more of how those tribes live, what they live by, faith, ritual, secret societies, tradition. That caused me to return by way of Haiti, where I also spent a while.'

Clara's eyes widened. 'Voodoo?'

'Voudun,' Laurace corrected. 'Not black magic. Religion. What has sustained human beings through some of the cruelest history on earth, and still does in. some of its most hideous poverty and misrule. I remembered people here at home, and came back to Harlem.'

'I see,' Clara breathed. 'You did start a cult.'

Momentarily, Laurace was grim. 'And you're thinking, "What a nice racket." It isn't like that in the least.'

'Oh, no. I didn't mean –'

'You did.' Laurace sighed. 'Never mind. A natural thought. I don't blame you. But the fact is, I had no need to prey on superstition. Investments I'd made before going abroad had done well. I didn't like the look of the stock market, and pulled out in time. Oh, by myself I'd be quite comfortably off.' Seriously: 'There were my people, though. There was also the matter of my own long-range survival. And, now, yours.'

Clara showed near-bewilderment. 'What've you done, then, if you haven't founded a church?'

Laurace spoke quickly, impersonally: 'Churches and their leaders are too conspicuous, especially if they achieve some success. Likewise revolutionary movements. Not that I wish for a revolution. I know how little bloodshed ever buys. That must be still more true of you.'

'I never gave it your kind of thought,' Clara said humbly. Her cigarette smoldered unnoticed between her fingers.

'What I am organizing is – call it a society, somewhat on the African and Haitian model. Remember, those outfits aren't criminal, nor are they for pleasure; they are parts of the whole, the cultures, bone and muscle as well as spirit. Mine does contain elements of both religion and magic. In Canada I was exposed to Catholicism, which is one root of voudun. I don't tell anybody what church he should go to; but I open for him a vision of being not only a Christian, but belonging to the whole living universe. I don't lay curses or give blessings, but I say words and lead rites in which I am – not a goddess or Messiah, not even a saint, but she who is closer than most to understanding, to power.

'Oh, we have a practical aspect too. A Haitian would know what I mean by the surname I've taken. But I don't call for gaining control – not by vote, like the Republicans and Democrats, or by violence, like the Communists, or by persuasion, like the Socialists. No, my politics is individuals quietly getting together under leadership they have freely accepted, helping each other, building a life and a future for *themselves*.'

Clara shook her head. 'I'm sorry, I can't quite see what you mean.'

'Don't worry.' Warmth was in the reply. 'For the time being, think of it on the spiritual side as offering my followers something better than booze and coke. As for the material part, now that breadlines have gotten long, more and more hear about us and come to us, black, white, Puerto Rican, every race. Openly, we're just another among hundreds of volunteer groups doing poor relief. Quietly, as newcomers prove trustworthy and advance through our degrees of initiation – we take them into a community they can belong to, work in, believe in, modestly but adequately and with hope. In return, when I ask for it, they help me.'

Laurace paused before continuing: 'I can't explain it much better than that, today. You'll learn. Truth to tell, I'm learning too. I never laid out any grand scheme, I fumbled my way forward, and still do. Maybe this will crash to ruin, or decay. But maybe – I can't foresee. Immortal leadership ought to make an important difference, but how to use it, I'm not yet sure. About all that I feel reasonably sure of is that we have to keep ourselves from being noticeable.'

'Can you?'

'We can try. "We" includes you, I trust.' Laurace lifted her wine glass. 'Here's to tomorrow.'

Clara joined in the toast but remained troubled. 'What're your plans for … for the near future?'

'Considerable,' Laurace answered. 'And you can do a great deal. You save your money, right? Well, we, the society, we're stretched thin. We badly need operating capital. Opportunities go begging. For instance, since the crash, stocks are at rock-bottom prices.'

'Because we've got a depression. I thought you said you left the market.'

Laurace laughed. 'If I'd foreseen exactly what would happen two years ago October, I'd have sold short at the right point and now own Wall Street. But I am not a sorceress – nor do I claim to be – and I've learned to play cautious. That doesn't mean timid or unthinking. Look, depressions don't last forever. People will always want homes, cars, a thousand different good, solid things; and sooner or later, they'll again be able to buy them. It may take fifty years to collect our profit, but immortals can wait.'

'I see.' Clara's features came aglow. 'Okay. With that to look forward to, I can stand another fifty years in the life.'

'You needn't. Times are changing.'

'What men want won't change.'

'No, though the laws may. No matter. Clara, shake free of that sordidness as fast as you can unload.'

'What for? What else can I do? I don't know anything except –' With forlorn determination: 'I will not turn into a parasite on you. I won't.'

'Oh, no,' Laurace answered. 'We take no parasites in. Quite aside from the money you contribute, you'll earn your keep. You may not appreciate it yet, but you have fourteen hundred years of experience behind you, with the insight, the intuition, that must have brought. Yours may well be a bitter wisdom, but we need it.'

'What for?'

'For the building of our strength.'

'Huh? Wait, you said –'

'I said I do not intend to overthrow the government, take over the country, anything stupid and ephemeral like that,' Laurace declared. 'My aim is the exact opposite. I want to build something so strong that with it we can say "No" to the slavers, the lynch mobs, and the lords of state.

'Men seized my father, bore him away in chains, and sold him. They hounded me when I escaped, and would have caught me if other men had not broken their law. A few years ago, they shot down the man I loved, for nothing worse than providing a pleasure they said nobody must have. At that, he was lucky. He might have died earlier, in their damned useless war. I could go on, but why? You could tell more, as much longer as you've lived.

'What's brought this death and misery, but that men have had power over other men?

'Don't mistake me. I am not an anarchist. Human beings are so made that the few will always rule the many. Sometimes they mean well – in spite of everything, I believe the founders of the United States did – but that doesn't long outlive them.

'The only partial security we who want to lead our own lives will ever have, we must create from within us. Oneness. Ongoing resolution. The means to live independent of the overlords. Only by guiding the poor and helpless toward this can we immortals win it for ourselves.

'Are you with me?'

XVI

NICHE

The hotel was new and rather soulless, but it stood near Old Town, with a fine tenth-floor view of roofs and narrow streets climbing to the stones of the Citadel. That mass stood darkling athwart stars dimmed by lamps and lightful panes. On the west side, the corner suite overlooked modern Ankara, Ulus Square, the boulevard, radiance glaring and flashing, opulent storefronts, crowded sidewalks, hasty automobiles. Heat of a day in late summer lingered, and the windows stood open to catch whatever coolness crept in off the river and hinterland. Height muffled traffic noise, even car horns, to an undertone hardly more loud than the large fan whirring on its stand.

For the American patron and his dinner guest, room service had set an elegant table and carried up an excellent meal. Through most of it they had sparred with small talk. The language in which they could most readily converse turned out to be Greek. Now they were at the stage of cheese, coffee, and liqueurs.

Oktay Saygun leaned back, held his Drambuie to the light before he sipped, creased his jowls with a smile. He was a stocky, paunchy man, his nose the single impressive thing about him. While not shabby, his business suit had clearly been years in use and inexpensive when bought. 'Ah,' he murmured, 'delicious. You are a most knowledgeable gentleman, Kyrie McCready.'

'I am glad you enjoyed this,' replied the other. 'I hope you feel more at ease with me.'

Saygun cocked his head in birdlike fashion, if the bird be a well-fed owl or parrot. David McCready was two or three centimeters taller than he, lean and limber. Though the dark hawk visage showed only geniality, the eyes – oddly Levantine for the name he bore – met his own and searched. 'Did I give you the opposite impression?' Saygun asked. 'I'm sorry. What a poor return for your hospitality. Not my intention at all, I assure you.'

'Oh, I don't blame you. A telephone call, an invitation from a perfect stranger. I might want to lure you into some criminal scheme. Or I might be a foreign agent, a spy. These days they must swarm in every capital.'

Saygun chuckled. 'Who would bother to subvert a little bureaucrat in the purely civilian archives? If anything, you would be the endangered one.

Think. You have had your dealings with our bureaucracy. It is impossible not to, especially if one is a foreigner. Believe me, when we set our minds to it we can tangle, obstruct, and bring to a dead halt a herd of stampeding elephants.'

'Still, this is an uneasy time.'

Saygun turned grave. His look wandered out the window, nightward. 'Indeed,' he said low. 'An evil time. Herr Hitler was not content with engulfing Austria, was he? I fear Mister Chamberlain and Monsieur Daladier will let him work his will on Czechoslovakia too. And nearer home, the ambitions of the Tsars live on in Red Russia.' He turned his attention back, took forth a handkerchief, wiped his narrow brow and sleeked down his black hair. 'Pardon me. You Americans prefer optimism always, not so? Well, whatever happens, civilization will survive. It has thus far, no matter what changing guises it wears.'

'You are quite well-informed, Kyrie Saygun,' McCready said slowly. 'And something of a philosopher, it seems.'

The Turk shrugged. 'One reads the newspapers. One listens to the radio. The coffee shops have become a Babel of politics. I seek occasional relief in old books. They help me tell the transient from the enduring.'

He drained his glass. McCready refilled it and asked, 'Cigar?'

'Why, yes, thank you very much. That humidor of yours appears to hold promise.'

McCready fetched two Havanas, a clipper which he offered first to his guest, and a lighter. As he settled himself again, his voice shivered the least bit. 'May I get to my business now?'

'Certainly. You would have been welcome to do so earlier. I assumed you wished to become acquainted. Or, if I may put it thus, to feel me out.'

McCready's grin was wry. 'You did the better job of that, on me.'

'Oh? I simply enjoyed a pleasant conversation with an interesting person. Everybody is fascinated by your wonderful country, and your career as a businessman has been remarkable.'

McCready started his visitor's cigar for him and became occupied with his own. 'We went on at length about me, when talk didn't ramble over ordinary matters. The upshot was that scarcely anything got said about you.'

'There was nothing to say, really. I am as dull and insignificant a man as you will ever find. I cannot imagine you maintaining any interest in me.' Saygun drank smoke, rolled it around his tongue, exhaled luxuriously, chased it with a taste of liqueur. 'However, at the moment I am glad. Pleasures like this seldom come to a minor official in a routine-bounded department of government. Turkey is a poor country, and President Atatürk was rather ruthless about corruption.'

McCready's tobacco kindled less smoothly. 'My friend, you are anything but dull. You've proved yourself very shrewd, very skillful at hiding whatever you want to hide. Well, it's no great surprise. People in our situation who don't have those qualities, or can't acquire them, probably don't last long.'

Beady eyes widened. '"Our" situation? What might that be?'

'Still cautious, are you? Understandable. If you are what I hope, that's an old, old habit. If not, then you are wondering whether I am a confidence man or a madman.'

'No, no. Please. Your newspaper advertisement last year attracted me. Enigmatic, but somehow ... genuine. Indeed, wonderfully phrased.'

'Thank you. Though composing it was largely the work of my partner. He has a gift for words.'

'I take it you placed the advertisement in many places around the world?' McCready nodded and Saygun continued: 'I suppose not only the language but the text, the message, varied according to region. Here – how did it go? – "Those who have lived so long that our forefathers are like brothers and comrades to them –" yes, that appeals to a Near Easterner, a citizen of an ancient land. Yet the average person who chances to see it gets the impression that a scholar is interested in meeting old people who have studied and meditated upon history, with a view to exploring whatever wisdom may be theirs. Did many respond?'

'No. Most who did were not quite right in the head or tried to cadge money. You were the only one in this country whom my agent decided I might care to follow up.'

'It has taken you a considerable time. I had begun to think your organization was not serious, perhaps a hoax.'

'I had to study a number of reports. Most I discarded. Then I started off around the world. This is my third interview.'

'I gather an agent of yours met those who answered the advertisements everywhere that they were placed. Clearly, you have substantial resources, Kyrie McCready. For a purpose you have yet to reveal to me and, I daresay, have told none of the agents.'

The American nodded. 'I gave them certain secret criteria to apply.' Peering through the smoke: 'The most important was that a respondent look young and in good health, even though the call seemingly was for old people. I explained that I don't want the fact publicized but I am searching for natural-born geniuses, with knowledge and insight far beyond their years, especially in history. With minds like that from different civilizations brought into contact, we may found a real science of it, beyond anything that thinkers like Spengler and Toynbee have proposed. The agents doubtless consider me a crackpot on this subject. However, I pay well.'

'I see. Have the previous two whom you met proven satisfactory?'

'You know that isn't what I am really searching for,' McCready said.

Saygun laughed. 'In the present case, that is just as well. I am no genius of any kind. No, a total mediocrity. And content with it, which shows I am doubly dull.' He paused. 'But what about those other two?'

McCready chopped air with his cigar. 'Damnation,' he exclaimed, 'must we shilly-shally all night?'

Saygun leaned back in his chair. The broad face and small bland smile could be a visor over wariness, glee, anything. 'God forbid I repay your generosity with discourtesy,' he said. 'Perhaps it would be best if you took the lead and made a forthright statement.'

'I will!' McCready sat half crouched. 'If I'm wrong about you, you won't take me for merely eccentric, you'll believe I'm a raving lunatic. In that case, I suggest you go home and never speak of this evening to anybody; because I'll deny everything and you'll be the one to look silly.' In haste: 'That's not a threat. For the convenience of us both, I request your silence.'

Saygun elevated his glass. 'From your viewpoint, you are about to take a risk,' he replied. 'I understand. I promise.' He drank as if in pledge.

McCready stood up. 'What would you say,' he asked softly, 'if I told you I am not an American by birth – that I was born in these parts, nearly three thousand years ago?'

Saygun gazed into his drink a while. The city mumbled. A drape stirred ever so slightly to the first night breath off the plateau of Anatolia. When he raised his eyes, he had gone expressionless. 'I would call that a most unusual statement.'

'No miracles, no magic,' McCready said. 'Somehow it happens. Once in ten million births, a hundred million, a billion? The loneliness – Yes, I am a Phoenician, from Tyre when Tyre was new.' He began pacing, to and fro on the carpet. 'I've spent most of all that time seeking for others, any others like me.'

'Have you found them?'

McCready's tone harshened. 'Three certain, and of them a single one is still alive to my knowledge, my partner whom I mentioned. He's tracked down two possibilities himself. As for the other two, we don't age, you know, but we can be killed the same as anybody else.' Savagely, he ground his cigar out in an ashtray. 'Like that.'

'Then I suppose the two you have spoken with on this journey, they were disappointments?'

McCready nodded. He slammed fist into palm. 'They're what I am officially after, highly intelligent and thoughtful … young people. Maybe I can find a place for them, I do have my enterprises, but –' He stopped on the floor, legs wide apart, and stared. 'You're taking this very calmly, aren't you?'

'I admitted I am a dull person. Phlegmatic.'

'Which gives me reason to think you're different from them. And my agent did make a quiet investigation. You could pass for a man in his twenties, but you've held your present job more than thirty years.'

'My friends remark on it. Not with much envy; I am no Adonis. Well, some individuals are slow to grow wrinkled and gray.'

'Friends – You're neither sociable nor unsociable. Affable, but never intimate. Effective enough at your desk, promoted according to seniority, but unambitious; you do everything by the book. Unmarried. That's uncommon in Turkey, but not unheard of, and nobody is interested enough in you to wonder seriously.'

'Your judgment is less than flattering.' Saygun didn't sound offended. 'Reasonably accurate, though. I have told you, I am content to be what I am.'

'An immortal?' McCready flung at him.

Saygun lifted a palm, cigar between fingers. 'My dear sir, you leap to conclusions.'

'It fits, it fits. Listen, you can be honest with me! Or at least bear with me. I can show you evidence that's convinced men more intelligent than either of us, if you'll cooperate. And – How can you just sit there like that?'

Saygun shrugged.

'If nothing else, even if I'm wrong about you and you suppose I'm crazy, you ought to show some excitement,' McCready snapped. 'A desire to escape, if nothing else. Or – But I think you are ageless yourself, you can join us and together we can – *How old are you, anyway?*'

Into the stillness that followed, Saygun said, a new steel in his tone: 'Credit me with some brains, if you please. I have told you I read books. And I have had a year to consider what might lie behind that curious, evasive procedure of yours; and conceivably before then I have speculated about these matters. Would you mind taking your seat again? I prefer to talk in civilized wise.'

'My ... apologies.' First McCready went to the sideboard. He mixed a stiff Scotch and soda. 'Would you like this?'

'No, thank you. Another Drambuie, if I may. Do you know, it never came to my attention before tonight. But then, only recently has Turkey become a modern, secular state. Marvelous stuff. I must lay some in before the next war makes it unobtainable.'

McCready overcame interior tumult and returned to the table. 'What do you want to say?' he asked.

Saygun barely smiled. 'Well,' he replied, 'things were growing hectic, weren't they? To be expected, no doubt, when you made such extraordinary claims. Not that I deny them, kyrie. I am no scientist, to decide what is and is not possible. Nor am I so rude as to call my host deluded, let alone a liar. But we should calm down. May I tell you a story?'

'By all means,' McCready rasped, and drank deep.

'Perhaps I can better label it a speculation,' Saygun said. 'A flight of fancy, like some works of Mr H. G. Wells. What *if* such-and-such were true? What consequences?'

'Go on.'

Saygun relaxed, smoked, sipped, let his voice amble. 'Well, now, shall we imagine a man born rather long ago? For example, in Italy toward the end of the Roman Republic. Family of the equestrian class, undistinguished, its men seldom much interested in war or politics, seldom succeeding or failing greatly in commerce, often making careers in the civil service. The state and its conquered provinces had grown swiftly, enormously. There was need for clerks, registrars, annalists, archivists, every class of those workers who provide a government with its memory. Once Augustus had taken control, procedures were soon regularized, organization made firm, order and predictability instilled. For a peaceful man, the lower and median ranks of the civil service were a good place to be.'

McCready inhaled sharply. Saygun ignored it: 'Next I would like to borrow your imaginative concept of the occasional person who never grows old. Since you have obviously considered every ramification, I need not spell out the difficulties that the years must bring to such a man. Perforce, when he reaches the normal retirement age, he gives up his position and moves away, telling his acquaintances that it will be to someplace with a mild climate and a low cost of living. Yet if he is entitled to a pension, he dares not draw it forever; and if pensions are not customary, he cannot live forever on savings, or even on investments. He must go back to work.

'Well, he seems youthful and he has experience. He reenters the bureaucracy in a different city, under a different name, but quickly proves his worth and earns promotion from junior grade to about the middle of the hierarchy among the record-keepers. In due course he retires again. By then sufficient time has gone by that he can return to, say, Rome and start over.

'Thus it goes. I shan't bore you with details, when you can readily visualize them. For example, sometimes he marries and raises a family, which is pleasant – or if it happens not to be, will pass, so all he needs is patience. This does complicate his little deceptions, hence he spends other periods in tranquil bachelorhood, varied by discreet indulgences. He is never in any danger of being found out. His position in the archives enables him to make cautious but adequate insertions, deletions, emendations. Nothing to harm the state, nothing to enrich himself, no, never. He simply avoids military service and, in general, covers his tracks.' Saygun snickered. 'Oh, now and then he might slip in something like a letter of recommendation for the young recruit he plans to become. Please remember, though, that he does do honest work. Whether he puts stylus to wax, pen to paper, nowadays types or dictates, he helps maintain the memory of the state.'

'I see,' McCready whispered. 'But states come and go.'

'Civilization continues,' responded Saygun. 'The Principate hardens into the Empire and the Empire begins to crack like drying mud, but people go on getting born and getting married, they ply their trades and die, always they pay taxes, and whoever rules must hold the records of this or he has no power over the life of the people. The usurper or the conqueror may strike off heads at the top, but he will scarcely touch the harmless drudges of the civil service. That would be like chopping off his own feet.'

'It has happened,' McCready said bleakly.

Saygun nodded. 'True. Corruption rewards its favorites with jobs. However, certain jobs are not especially tempting, while at the same time their holders would be hard to dispense with. Then occasionally barbarians, fanatics, megalomaniacs attempt to make a clean sweep. They cause desolation. Nevertheless, more often than not, some continuity endures. Rome fell, but the Church preserved what it could.'

'I suppose, though,' McCready said, word by word, 'this man ... you are imagining ... had moved to Constantinople.'

Saygun nodded. 'Of course. With Constantine the Great himself, who necessarily expanded the government offices in his new capital and welcomed personnel willing to transfer. And the Roman Empire, in its Byzantine incarnation, lasted another thousand years.'

'After which –'

'Oh, there were difficult times, but one manages. Actually, my man was stationed in Anatolia when the Osmanlis overran it, and did not get back to Constantinople until they had taken it too and renamed it Istanbul. Meanwhile he had fitted into their order of things without many problems. Changed his religion, but surely you can sympathize with that, and with a certain recurring necessity that an immortal Muslim or Jew faces.' Saygun half grinned. 'One wonders about possible women. Recurrent intactness?'

His mien went back to mock professorial: 'Physically, this man would stay inconspicuous. The original Turks were not very unlike the people here, and soon melted into them the same as Hittites, Gauls, Greeks, Romans, countless nations had done before. The sultans reigned until after the World War. In name, at any rate; frequently not in fact. It made small difference to my man. He simply helped maintain the records.

'Likewise under the republic. I must confess I – my man prefers Istanbul and looks forward to his next period of working there. It is more interesting, and alive with ghosts. But you know that. However, by now Ankara has become quite liveable.'

'Is that all he wants?' McCready wondered. 'Shuffling papers in an office, forever?'

'He is used to it,' Saygun explained. 'Perhaps it actually has a trifle more social value than soaring hopes and high adventure. Naturally, I wanted to hear what you had to say, but – forgive me – the situation you describe is ill-suited to one of my temperament. Let me wish you every good fortune.

'May I have your card? Here is mine.' He reached in his pocket. McCready did likewise. They exchanged. 'Thank you. We can, if you so desire, mail new cards to each other as occasion arises. The time may possibly come when we have reason to communicate. Meanwhile, absolute confidentiality on both sides, agreed?'

'Well, but listen –'

'Please. I detest disputes.' Saygun glanced at his watch. 'My, my. Time flies, eh? I really must go. Thank you for an evening I will never forget.'

He rose. McCready did too and, helplessly, shook hands. Having bade goodnight, the bureaucrat, still relishing his cigar, departed. McCready stood in the hall door till the elevator bore him off, down into the city and its crowds of the anonymous.

XVII

STEEL

This was not the forest of old, but there was cover aplenty for a hunter, oh, yes, and all too much quarry. First, though, Katya had open ground to cross. She went from the battered yellow brick of the Lazur Chemical Plant on her belly. The pavement beneath her was as rough, after nearly three months of war. It felt colder against her palms than did the wind on her face. Clouds and a little snow had slightly warmed the November air.

She slipped forward a meter or so at a time, stopped, peered about, before the next advance. Heaven rested heavy, hiding the sun behind its gray. Sometimes it let fall a thin white flurry for the gusts to scatter. On Katya's left the ground sloped to the Volga. Ice floes drifted, bumped together, churned and turned on their way down its steel-hued stream. No boats dared moved among them. Scant help could come to the Russians from the east until the river froze hard. The shore opposite seemed deserted, steppe reaching, wan with winter, on and on into Asia.

To her right, beyond the railroad tracks, Mamaev Hill rose a hundred meters aloft. Its slopes were black. Shells and boots quickly beat snow into mud. She identified two or three gun emplacements. Silence brooded. The soldiers who had contested that height for weeks must be catching their breath or a few moments' sleep, briefly brothers in exhaustion and wretchedness, before the next combat erupted.

The stillness foreboded. It was abnormal to hear no fire, anywhere, for this long a stretch. War waited – eyes and gunsights wholly upon her?

Nonsense, she snapped to herself, and moved onward. Nevertheless, when she came in among walls, breath shuddered from a breast cage that had begun to ache.

She rose and stood crouched. These were not truly walls, after what had happened to them. Concrete blocks still lifted sheer, but doorless doorways and glassless windows yawned on emptiness. A heap of rubble had spilled into the street.

Rifles cracked. A submachine gun chattered. A grenade popped, another, another. Shouts ripped raw. She couldn't make out words. The sounds were unhuman. Her own rifle was off her shoulder and she inside the shell of a building as the first echoes died.

Boots thudded. They hit without rhythm, and too often a shard rattled from them. Whoever drew near stumbled and staggered more than he ran. Katya risked a peek around the doorjamb. From behind a ruin some twenty meters south, a man lurched into the intersection of this street and the one down which he fled. He wore a Red Army uniform and helmet, but carried no weapon. Blood smeared his right hand and dripped down that leg. He stopped. She saw how he panted. He swung his head to and fro. Almost, she called to him, but checked herself. After a few seconds he continued his weaving way in the same direction, out of her view.

She brought her rifle up.

Two more men appeared, at a lope that should soon overtake him. Squarish helmets and gray-green garb proclaimed them Germans. Either could easily have lifted his own firearm and shot the fugitive. So their officer must have told them to bring him back for interrogation. That looked safe, a short run through an area believed to be free of life.

It had stabbed through Katya: Let the thing happen. I mustn't compromise my mission. But she knew too well what awaited that fellow. Also, what he could tell might prove as valuable as anything she would observe.

Decision was nearly instant. Sometimes she weighed a matter for years before she settled on what to do. Sometimes she could simply wait several decades and let time wear the problem away. Yet she had not stayed alive this long by being always hesitant. At need, she leaped with the unheeding energy of youth.

She fired. A German spun on his heel and flopped bonelessly down. His companion yelled and threw himself prone. His rifle barked. He probably hadn't seen her, but knew at once, more or less, whence that shot had come. Quick-witted. Not for the first time, the thought stirred in Katya that maybe among the invaders was one of her kind, as full of centuries and solitude as she was.

She barely noticed the thought, afar at the back of her skull. She had pulled inside straightway after shooting. A windowframe beckoned. She closed her eyes for three breaths while she considered the geometry of what she had seen. The enemy must be *there*. Quick, before he moves elsewhere. She stepped to the hole and squeezed trigger even as she aimed.

The butt gave her a stiff, friendly nudge. The soldier screamed. He let go his rifle and lifted his torso on hands that spread white, helpless, upon asphalt. She had gotten him in the back. Best silence him. Those yells would call his mates. She drew a bead. His face exploded.

Extraordinary marksmanship. By far the most shots in battle went wild. Comrade Zaitsev would be proud of her. She wished the German would lie still like the first, not writhe and kick and gush blood. Well, he was quiet now.

She hadn't time to cringe. Surely the rest understood something had gone wrong. No matter how cautious, they would find this place within minutes.

Katya dashed forth, over the rubble, up the street, past her prey. Horrible, when it was human. Of course, then it hunted you likewise. She turned left down the cross street.

The Soviet soldier had not gone far. Her ambush had been quick, while he slowed still more. In fact, he was shuffling by a wrecked tram, leaning on it. Katya wondered if he would prove such a burden that she must abandon him. She sped in pursuit. 'Stop!' she cried. 'I'm your help!' Her voice sounded small and hollow among the ruins, beneath the leaden sky.

He obeyed, turned around, braced himself against the metal, slumped. She drew close and halted. He was quite young, she saw, not shaven lately but with just a dark fuzz over the skin. Otherwise his face was old, pinched, white as the snowflakes that drifted about and powdered his shoulders. His eyes stared and his jaw hung slack. Shock, she realized. That hand of his was pretty badly mangled. A grenade, no doubt.

'Can you follow me?' she asked. 'We'll have to move fast.'

His left forefinger rose and wobbled in the air, as if to trace her outline. 'You are a soldier,' he mumbled. 'Like me. But you are a woman.'

'What of it?' Katya snapped. She took hold of his forearm and shook him. 'Listen. I can't stay. That's death. Come along if you're able. Do you understand? Do you want to live? Come!'

He shuddered. Breath went raggedly down his throat. 'I ... can ... try.'

'Good. This way.' Katya shoved him around and forward. Turn right at the next corner, left at the next after that, put a maze between yourself and the enemy. This district was smashed, like the city center toward which she aimed – snags, debris, choked lanes, masonry still fire-blackened in spots, a wilderness where you could shake your hunters. Despite lacking sun or shadows, she kept her sense of direction ... A growl resounded.

'Take cover!' Katya ordered. The youth joined her beneath a rusted metal sheet which stuck out of a vast heap of wreckage like an awning. A stench hung beneath, oozing from bricks, beams, broken glass, thick and sickly-sweet even in the chill. A shell or bomb must have made a direct hit, bringing this whole tenement down on everybody inside. Children, their mothers, their babushkas? No, most who couldn't fight were evacuated early on. Likeliest it was soldiers who rotted here. Any building could become a fort when defenders fought invaders street by street. Which had these been? ... It didn't matter, least of all to them.

Her companion retched. He must have recognized the smell. That was a hopeful sign. He was coming out of his daze.

The aircraft swept low above rooflessness. She had a glimpse of it, lean, swift, swastika on its tail, then it was gone. Reconnaissance, or what? Probably the pilot wouldn't have noticed them, or troubled about them if he did. But you could never tell. The fascists had strafed crowds of evacuees waiting for ferries across the river. Two Soviet soldiers were game more fair.

The throbbing receded. Katya heard no other. 'Let's go,' she said.

The young man accompanied her for some paces before he exclaimed weakly, 'Is this right, comrade? I think we're headed south.'

'We are,' she told him.

'B-but, but the enemy has that part. Our people, they're in the north end of town.'

'I know.' She took his elbow and hurried him onward. 'I have my orders. Turn back if you wish. I doubt you'll get far. Or you may come with me if you can. If you can't, I'll have to leave you. If you make a noise, or any kind of trouble for me, I must kill you. But I do believe it's your only chance.'

He clenched his usable fist. 'I'll try,' he whispered. 'Thank you, comrade.'

She wondered whether Zaitsev would thank her. This mission was worth more lives than a single cripple's. Well, sharpshooters must rely on their own judgment oftener than not. And supposing she did get this private back to his unit, her superiors needn't know. Unless he really could tell something worthwhile –

The street ended at Krutoy Gully. On the opposite side of the ravine, buildings were equally damaged but more high and massive than here. That was where the central city began. 'We have to get across,' Katya said. 'No bridge. We crawl down and creep up. You go first.'

He nodded, jerkily, nevertheless a nod. Stooping, he scuttled over the open space and wriggled out of sight. She had been prepared to let him draw any fire. She hadn't wanted a stalking horse, but there he was, and if he proved hopelessly clumsy she couldn't let him destroy her too. Instead, he did well enough. So he'd been rather lightly shocked, and was shaking that off with the vitality of youth.

Rifle in hand, every sense honed, she followed. Dirt gritted, leafless bushes scratched. After they started up, his strength flagged. He scrabbled, slid back a way, sank together and sobbed for air. She slung her weapon and went on all fours to his side. He gave her a desperate look. 'I can't,' he wheezed. 'I'm sorry. Go on.'

'We're nearly there.' Her left hand clasped his. 'Now, work, damn you, *work*.' She clambered backward, boot heels dug into soil, straining like a horse at a mired field gun. He set his teeth and did what he was able. It sufficed. They reached the top and found shelter by a heap of bricks. Her tunic was dank with sweat. Wind chilled her to the bone.

'Where ... are we ... bound?' coughed from him.

'This way.' They got to their feet. She herded him along, keeping them next to walls, halting at each doorway or corner to listen and peer. A couple of fighters flew sentinel well above. Their drone fell insect-faint over the desolation. She began to hear a deeper rumble, artillery. A duel somewhere out on the steppe? Mamaev remained quiet. The whole city did, it seemed, one great graveyard that waited for the thunders of doomsday.

Her destination wasn't far. That would have been madness. She would not have been sent even this deep into the German-held sector, had she not repeatedly shown she could get about unseen as well as any commando – and, she knew, those expert killers were less expendable than she. If the recommended site proved unduly dangerous and she couldn't quickly find a better, she was to give up and make her way back to the Lazur.

From behind one of the trees that still lined a certain boulevard, she gazed across a bomb crater and two crumpled' automobiles. The building she wanted did appear safe. It belonged to a row of tenement houses, slab-sided and barrack-like. Though in sorry shape, it rose above what was left of its neighbors, a full six floors. The windows were blind holes.

Katya pointed. 'Yonder,' she told the young man. 'When I signal, get over there and inside fast.' She took her binoculars from the case hung about her neck and searched for signs of enemy. Only broken panes, smudges, pockmarks came into view. Snow whirled dry on a gust that whistled. She chopped her hand downward and led the sprint. In the empty doorway she whirled about and crouched ready to fire at anything suspicious. The snow flurry had stopped. A scrap of paper tumbled along before the wind.

Flights of concrete stairs went steeply upward. Their wells were full of gloom. On the lower landings, doors blown off hinges lay in a chaos of things and dust. Above, they remained shut. On the top floor, she tried a knob. If necessary, she would shoot out the lock, but that door creaked faintly as it yielded.

Here the dimness was less. Smashed windows admitted light as well as cold. The apartment had been fairly good, two rooms plus a kitchen alcove. To be sure, the bathroom was a flight down, shared by the tenants of three floors. Concussion had cracked plaster off lath and spread chunks and powder across furniture and threadbare carpet. Rain blowing in had made a slurry, now hardened, under the sills. Mildew speckled what was left on the walls. The stains also marked drapes, bedclothes, a sofa. Blast had acted as capriciously as usual. A Stakhanovite poster clung garish and two framed photographs were likewise unfallen: a young couple at their wedding, a white-bearded Uncle Vanya who might be the grandfather of bride or groom. Three or four others had crashed. Some strewn books and magazines moldered. A small radio lay among them. A clock had gone silent on its table. Flowers in pots were brown stalks.

Apart from utensils and the like, Katya didn't notice more personal possessions. Maybe they had been meager enough for the family to take along at evacuation. She had no wish to investigate, when she might turn up a little girl's doll or a little boy's bear. She could merely hope the owners had escaped, all of them.

She went through the rooms. People had slept in both. The first faced approximately north, the second east. With the door open between them, she could scan a full half circle, springing from window to window. That vision covered a dozen streets in both directions, because most of the vicinity was a crumbled wasteland. Yet it had never occurred to the enemy either to occupy or to dynamite such a watchpost. Well, everybody got stupid now and then, especially in war. This time Soviet intelligence had spied a Nazi blindness.

Returning to the room of entry, she found the infantryman hunched on the sofa. He had taken off his helmet and outer coat. The sweat in his shirt was rank. (Well, Katya thought, I'm scarcely a rose garden myself. When did I last have a proper bath? Ages ago, that night in the forest when I went to earth in a peasant's hut –) His hair was curly. A hint of color had risen in his face.

'Beware taking a chill, comrade,' she warned. 'We'll be here a while.' She set her rifle down and unshipped her canteen. 'You must need water worse yet than I do, so you go first, but don't take much. Swish it around in your mouth before you swallow. It has to last us.'

While he did, she squatted, took his injured hand in both hers, shook her head and clicked her tongue. 'Nasty,' she said. 'Those bones are a mess. At least no major blood vessel was cut. I can do something for it. Hold still. This will hurt.'

He caught his breath repeatedly when she cleaned and wrapped the wounds. Thereafter she gave him a piece of chocolate. 'We'll share my rations too,' she promised. 'They're scant, but hunger is a joy set beside our real problems, no?'

The bite revived him somewhat. He managed a shaky smile. 'What is your name in Heaven, you angel?' he quavered.

She checked both the windows. Nothing, except the distant cannon fire. 'Me an angel?' she replied meanwhile with a grin. 'What kind of Communist are you?'

'I'm not a Party member,' he said humbly. 'I should have joined, my father wanted me to, but – Well, after the war.'

She put a chair in front of him and settled down. There was no sense in constantly staring out. She'd hear any important movement, as quiet as things were. A glance every few minutes would serve. 'What are you, then?' she asked.

'Pyotr Sergeyevitch Kulikov, private, Sixty-Second Army.'

A tingle passed through her spine. She whistled softly. 'Kulikov! What a perfectly splendid omen.'

'Eh? Oh ... oh, yes. Kulikovo. Where Dmitri Donskoi smote the Mongols.' He sighed. 'But that was ... six hundred years ago, almost.'

'True.' I remember how we rejoiced when the news reached our village. 'And we aren't supposed to believe in omens any longer, are we?' She leaned forward, interested. 'So you know the exact date of that battle, do you?' Even now, exhausted, in pain, penned up to wait for possible death. 'You sound educated.'

'My family in Moscow is. I hope someday to become a professor of classics.' He tried to straighten. His voice took on a ghost of resonance. 'But who and what are you, my rescuer?'

'Ekaterina Borisovna Tazurina.' The latest of my names, my self-created identities.

'A woman soldier –'

'We exist, you know.' She mastered her annoyance. 'I was a partisan before the fighting swept me here. Then they put me in uniform – not that that's likely to make any difference if the Germans catch me – and when I'd passed Lieutenant Zaitsev's course, they raised me to sergeant because a sharp-shooter needs some freedom of action.'

Pyotr's eyes widened. They had heard about Zaitsev from end to end of the Soviet Union. 'This must be a special mission for you, not just sniping.'

Katya nodded. 'Word came from Pavlov's House. Do you know what I mean?'

'Of course. A building hereabouts, right in among the Germans, that Sergeant Pavlov and a few heroes have held since – the end of September, hasn't it been?'

She forgave him repeating the obvious. He was hurt, bewildered, and oh, how young. 'They maintain communication with us,' she explained. 'Certain things they've noticed give reason to believe the enemy plans a major thrust into our end of town. No, I wasn't told what things, no need for me to hear, but I was sent to watch from this point and report whatever I see.'

'And you happened to pass by when – Incredible luck for me.' Tears welled. 'But my poor friends.'

'What happened?'

'Our squad went on patrol. My unit's currently in a block of detached houses well south of Mamaev. We didn't expect trouble, as quiet as it's gotten.' Pyotr drew an uneven breath. 'But all at once it was shooting and screaming and – My comrades dropped, right and left. I think I was the last one alive after … a few minutes. And with this hand. What could I do but run?'

'How many Germans? Where did they come from? How were they equipped?'

'I c-couldn't tell. Everything went too fast.' He sank his face into his left palm and shuddered. 'Too terrible.'

She gnawed her lip, angry. 'If you're with the Sixty-Second, you've had months of combat experience: The enemy drove you back from – Ostrov, was it? All the way across the plain to here. And still you couldn't pay attention to what was going on around you.'

He braced himself. 'I can, can try to remember.'

'That's better. Take your time. Unless something dislodges us first, we'll be sitting where we are till we've seen what headquarters ought to know about. Whatever that may be.'

She checked the windows, came back, sat down again before him, took his good hand. Now that he was out of immediate danger, nature wanted him to sleep and sleep and sleep, but that couldn't be allowed. What he had suffered wasn't overpoweringly severe, he was young and healthy, and when she spoke soothingly she saw how her femaleness helped rouse him.

Fragment by fragment, a half-coherent story emerged. It appeared the Germans had been reconnoitering. Their force was small, but superior to the Russian squad. Knowing themselves to be in hostile territory, they had kept totally alert and seen an opportunity to ambush Pyotr's group. Yes, clearly they wanted prisoners to take back. Katya knew a grim hope that he was in fact the single survivor.

A scouting mission was a strong indication of a major attack in the works. She wondered if she ought to consider that this information fulfilled her task, and return with it at once. Of course, when the squad failed to report, the officer who dispatched it would guess the truth; but that might not be for a considerable time. No, probably the story wasn't worth as much as the possibility of her gaining more important knowledge here.

Send Pyotr? If he didn't make it, the Red Army wouldn't have lost much. Unless he blundered into captivity. Could he hold out a while under torture, or would his broken body betray him into betraying her? It wasn't a chance she wanted to take. Nor was it fair to him.

Helping him summon forth what his whole being cried out to forget – that wrought a curious intimacy. In the end, while they shared water and bread, he asked shyly, 'Are you from hereabouts, Katya Borisovna?'

'No. Far to the southwest,' she answered.

'I thought so. You speak excellent Russian, but the accent – Though it isn't quite Little Russian either, I think.'

'You've a sharp ear.' Impulse seized her. Why not? It was no secret. 'I'm a Kazak.'

He started. Water spluttered from his lips. He wiped them, a clumsy, shaken gesture, and said, 'A Cossack? But you, you're well educated yourself, I can hear that, and –'

She laughed. 'Come, now. We're not a race of horse barbarians.'

'I know –'

'Our schooling is actually better than average. Or used to be.' The ray of mirth vanished behind winter clouds. 'Before the Revolution, most of us were farmers, fishers, merchants, traders who went far into Siberia. We did have our special institutions, yes, our special ways.' Low: 'Our kind of freedom.'

That was why I drifted toward them after I ceased teaching embroidery at the cloister school in Kiev. That is why I have been with them and of them, almost from their beginnings, these four hundred years. A scrambling together of folk from Europe and Asia, down along the great rivers and over the unbounded steppes of the South, armed against Tatar and Turk, presently carrying war to those ancient foes. But mainly we were smallholders, we were a free people. Yes, women also, not as free as men but vastly more than they had come to be everywhere else. I was always a person in my own right, possessed of my own rights, and it was never very hard to start a new life in another tribe when I had been too long in one.

'I know. But – Forgive me,' Pyotr blurted. 'Here you are, a Soviet soldier, a patriot. I heard that, well, that Cossacks have gone over to the fascists wholesale.'

'Some did,' Katya admitted starkly. 'Not most. Believe me, not most. Not after what we saw.'

At first we had no knowledge. The commissars told us to flee. We stayed fast. They pleaded with us. They told us what horror Hitler wreaks wherever his hordes go. 'Your newest lie,' we jeered. Then the German tanks rolled over our horizon, and we learned that for once the commissars had spoken truth. It didn't happen only to us, either. The war threw me together with people from the whole Soviet Ukraine, not Cossacks, ordinary Little Russians, little people driven to such despair that they fight side by side with the Communists.

Even so, yes, true, thousands and thousands of men have joined the Germans as workers or soldiers. They see them as liberators.

'After all,' she went on hastily, 'it's in our tradition to resist invaders and rise against tyrants.'

The Lithuanians were far away, they mostly left us alone and were content with the name of overlords. But the Polish kings goaded us into revolt, over and over. Mazeppa welcomed the Great Russians in and was made a prince of the Ukraine, but soon he found himself in league with the Swedes, hoping they might set us free. We finally made our peace with the Tsars, their yoke was not unbearably heavy any more; but later the Bolsheviks took power.

Pyotr frowned. 'I've read about those Cossack rebellions.'

Katya winced. Three centuries fell from her, and she stood again in her village when men – neighbors, friends, two sons of hers – galloped in after riding with Chmielnicki and shouted their boasts. Every Catholic or Uniate priest they or the serfs caught, they hanged in front of his altar alongside a pig and a Jew. 'Barbaric times,' she said. 'The Germans have no such excuse.'

'And the traitors have less yet.'

377

Traitors? Vasili the gentle blacksmith, Stefan the laughterful, Fyodor the fair who was a grandson of hers and didn't know it – How many millions of dead there they seeking to avenge? The forgotten ones, the obliterated ones, but she remembered, she could still see starvation shrivel the flesh and dim the eyes, children of hers had died in her arms; Stalin's creatures shot her man Mikhail, whom she loved as much as the ageless can love any mortal, shot him down like a dog when he tried to take for his family some of the grain they were shipping out in cram-full freight trains; he was lucky, though, he didn't go on another kind of train, off to Siberia; she had met a few, a few, who came back; they had no teeth and spoke very little and worked like machines; and always you went in fear. Katya could not hold herself in. She must cry, 'They had their reasons!'

Pyotr gaped at her. 'What?' He fumbled through his mind. 'Well, yes, kulaks.'

'Free farmers, whose land that they had from their fathers was torn from them, and they herded onto kolkhozes like slaves.' Promptly: 'That was how they felt, you understand.'

'I don't mean the honest peasants,' he said. 'I mean the kulaks, the rich landowners.'

'I never met any, and I traveled rather widely. Some were prosperous, yes, because they farmed wisely and worked hard.'

'Well, I – I don't want to offend you, Katya, you of all people, but you can't have traveled as much as you think. It was before your time, anyway.' Pyotr shook his head. 'No doubt many of them meant well. But the old capitalist regime had blinded them. They resisted, they defied the law.'

'Until they were starved to death.'

'Ah, yes, the famine. A tragic … accident?' He ventured a smile. 'We're not supposed to call it an act of God.'

'I said – No matter.' I said they *were* starved to death. The harvests never failed. The state simply took everything from us. That brought us at last to submission. 'I only wanted to say that many Ukrainians feel they have a grievance.' They never quite gave up hope. In their hearts, they resist yet.

Indignation flashed. 'They are stupid!'

Katya sighed. 'They certainly made a bad mistake, those who went over to the Nazis.'

God help me, I might have myself. If Hitler had been willing, no, if he had been able to treat us as human beings, he would have had us all. This day he would hold Moscow, Leningrad, Novosibirsk; Stalin would cower among his gulags in the farthest corner of Siberia, or be a refugee with the Americans. But no, the fascists burned, raped, slew, tortured, they dashed out the brains of babies and laughed while they machine-gunned children, women, the old, the unarmed, they bayoneted for sport, they racked prisoners apart or doused them with gasoline and set them alight, oh, it sickens me to think of them in holy Kiev!'

'You knew what was right, and did it,' Pyotr said softly. 'You are braver than I.'

She wondered if fear of the NKVD had kept him from deserting. She had seen the corpses the Green Hats left along the roads by the thousands, for a warning.

'What made you join the partisans?' he asked.

'The Germans occupied our village. They tried to recruit men from among us, and killed those who refused. My husband refused.'

'Katya, Katya!'

'Luckily, we were newly married and had no children.' I was rather newly arrived there, bearing a fresh name. That has grown difficult under the Communists. I have to search out slovenly officials. But they are common enough. Poor Ilya. He was so glad, so proud of his bride. We could have been happy together for as long as nature allowed.

'Luckily?' Pyotr knuckled fresh tears. 'Regardless, you were very brave.'

'I am used to looking after myself.'

'As young as you are?' he marveled.

She couldn't help smiling. 'I'm older than I look.' Rising: 'Time for another survey.'

'Why don't we each take a window?' he suggested. 'We could watch almost without a break. I feel much better. Thanks to you,' he ended adoringly.

'Well, we could –' Thunder grumbled. 'Hold! Artillery! Stay where you are.'

She sped to the north room. Early winter dusk was falling, the wreckage gone vague among shadows, but Mamaev still bulked clear against the sky. Fire flickered there. The crashing waxed, widely about. 'Our half-truce is over,' she muttered when she came back to look east. 'The big guns are busy.'

He stood at the middle of the floor, his features hard to see in the quickly thickening murk but his voice uncertain. 'Did the enemy begin it?'

Katya nodded. 'I think so. The start of whatever they have planned. Now we earn our pay, I hope.'

'Really?' The question trembled.

'If we can get some idea of what is going on. How I wish we had a moon tonight.' She chuckled dryly. 'But I wouldn't expect the Germans to pick their weather to oblige us. Keep quiet.'

She shuttled between windows. Dark deepened. Thin snow on untrafficked streets was slightly helpful to eyes and night glasses. The cannonade mounted.

Abruptly breath hissed between her teeth. She risked leaning out for a better view. Cold fell around her like a cloak.

'What is it?' Pyotr tried to whisper.

'Hush, I told you!' She strained to be sure. Black blots on the next street over from this, headed straight north … A hunter could interpret traces for a soldier. Those were perhaps a hundred men, afoot, therefore infantry, but they dragged several carts on which rested faintly sheening shapes that must be mortars …

They passed. She lowered her glasses and groped through the apartment till she found Pyotr. He had sat down, maybe in his weariness he had fallen asleep, but he sprang to his feet when she touched him.

Tautness keened within her. 'Germans bound for Kratoy Gully,' she said into his ear. 'Got to be, on that route. If they wanted to go fight near the hill, they'd be headed westerly and I might never have seen them.'

'What … do they intend?'

'I don't know, but I can guess. It's surely part of a general offensive against our sector. The cannon – and maybe armor, attacking from the side – those should hold our people's attention. Meanwhile yonder detachment establishes itself in the ravine. It has the makings of a strongpoint. Our headquarters was in Tsaritsa Gorge, farther south, till the Germans took it, at heavy cost. If they take and hold the Kratoy, why, troops can scramble straight through it, or their engineers might throw a new bridge across.'

'Do you mean we could lose the whole city?'

'Oh, that alone won't do it. We have our orders, directly from Stalin. Here, at this place he renamed in his own honor, here we stand. We die if need be, but the enemy shall not pass one centimeter beyond us. 'Every little thing counts, though. It would surely cost us hundreds of lives. This is what I came for. Now I go back and tell.'

She felt him shiver. 'We go!'

A dead man's hand clenched around her throat. She swallowed twice before she could say: 'Not together. It's too important. This whole district will be aswarm. I'll have all I can do to get through alive, and I'm experienced. You must try by yourself. Wait here till – tomorrow night? – till it looks safer.'

Between her hands, he straightened. 'No. My comrades are fighting. I ran away once. Not again.'

'What use will you be, with that wound of yours?'

'I can carry ammunition. Or – Katya, you might not make it. I might, by sheer luck, and let them know.' He laughed, or sobbed. 'A tiny, tiny chance, but who can say for certain?'

'Oh, God. You idiot.'

'Every little thing counts, you said.'

Yes, each scrap thrown into the furnace, it does become part of the steel. 'I mustn't delay, Pyotr. Give me, well, half an hour till you start, so I can get clear. Count to, uh –'

'I know some old songs and about how long they take. I'll sing them in my head. While I think of you, Katya.'

'Here.' She undid objects and tossed them on the sofa. 'Food, water. You'll need strength. No, I insist; I'm not injured. God keep you, lad, you – you Russian.'

'We'll meet again. Won't we? Say we will!'

Instead, she cast her arms about him and laid her mouth on his. Just for a minute. Just for a memory.

She stepped back. He stood. His breath went like flaws of wind in the dark (springtime wind?) amidst the hammering of the guns. 'Do be careful,' she said. Taking up her rifle, she felt her way to the door.

And down the stairs. And into the streets.

Tanks roared somewhere on her left. Would the Germans mount a night attack? Likelier a feint. But she was no strategist, merely a sharpshooter. Flashes etched skeletal buildings against a reddened sky. She felt the racket through her bootsoles. Hers was simply to deliver a message.

Or to survive? What had she to do with the cruel follies of mortals? Why was she here?

'Well, you see, Pyotr, dear, I am a Russian too.'

A park, a piece of openness between these jagged walls, glimmered white before her. A solitary tree was left, the rest were stumps and splinters around a crater. She skirted it, keeping to shadows. Likewise would she skirt the ravine, and be most cautious when she came to the railroad tracks that led to the Lazur. She must arrive with her word.

She doubted Pyotr would. Well, if not, he'd stop a bullet or two that might otherwise have gone into somebody more effective. If somehow he kept alive – Maria of the mercies, let him, help him! – of course they'd never see each other, or hear, or anything. Suppose two grains of dust are whirled together for a moment when a storm runs over the steppe. Will it bring them back?

Certainly never her to him. She would be changing identities again before long. Whenever the Four Horsemen rode across the world, they opened easy ways for doing that. She could not have stayed much more with the Cossacks anyhow.

But first –

The guns boomed louder. Given the news she bore, the Soviet artillery would take aim at Kratoy Gully. It would blast the Germans out of there before they could dig in. That would be that, while the war went on.

Work, you guns. Bring down the wrath of Dazhbog and Perun, of St Yuri the dragonslayer and St Alexander Nevsky. Here we stand. The thing that bestrides all Europe shall come no farther than us. If we fight in the name of a monster, that makes no difference. And we don't really. Once this Stalingrad was Tsaritsyn. It can become something else someday in the future. But good for now to think that we hold fast in the City of Steel.

We will endure, and prevail, and abide the day of our freedom.

XVIII

JUDGMENT DAY

1

At first it was as if half a century had never been. Snow-peaks gleamed against unutterable blue; in this clarity they seemed almost near enough to touch, though any of them might be fifty miles remote. A road that was little more than a track rose, fell, writhed through a darkness of deodars and gnarly wild fruit trees where langurs scampered. Then the forest opened onto pasture strewn with boulders, intensely green after the rains. Sheep and cattle grazed among stone threshing-floors. Tiny terraces carved from the valley walls bore maize, amaranth, buckwheat, barley, potatoes. A westering sun breathed a ghost of purple across the heights that looked into it, while across from them shadows lengthened, intricate over the wrinkles of the land. The air smelled of grass and glaciers.

As his mule brought him nearer the village, Wanderer began to see how much it had in fact changed. It had grown. Most of the new houses were not earth-roofed stone but timber, two or three stories high, with carved and painted galleries; it was curious to find something so like Swiss chalets here on the knees of the Himalayas. Wires ran from a former dwelling which must house a generator, and the fuel tanks outside it also supplied a battered truck. A satellite receiver dish quite likely served more than a single communal television set. The folk were still Bhutias, essentially Tibetan stock, and men still generally wore the traditional long woolen coat, women the sleeved cloak; but he spied occasional sneakers or blue jeans, and he wondered how many people held by the mingled Buddhism, Hinduism, and animism that had been the faith of their fathers.

Herders and workers in the fields swarmed to meet him, soon joined by those who had been at home. Excitement capered and shouted. Any visit from outside was an event, and this newcomer was extraordinary. His two attendants were simply Gurkhas, familiar enough, guides to manage the animals and serve his needs, but he himself rode altogether strange, clad like a white man but broad of face and bronze of skin, his nose jutting yet his hair and eyes and cheekbones akin to theirs.

One woman, shriveled and toothless with age, made an abrupt sign against evil and scuttled from the crowd into a house. One man, equally old, drew a sharp breath before he bowed very low. They remembered his earlier call on them, Wanderer knew – when they were children and he just the same as today.

His senior Gurkha spoke with another woman, large and strong, who must be something like the mayor. She in turn addressed the villagers. A sort of calm descended. They eddied around the party, silent or talking in undertones, while it made its way through the lanes to a house at the northern edge of the settlement.

This seemed much as it had been. It remained the biggest, of stone and wood, an alien grace to its lines. Glass shone in the windows. Graveled paths twisted about the shrubs, dwarf trees, bamboo, and stones of a small, exquisite garden at the rear. The servants who emerged were of a new generation, but the man and woman who trod onto the verandah and waited were not.

Wanderer dismounted. Slowly, under awed stares and a hush, he walked to the steps and up. He bowed before the two, and they returned the gesture with equal gravity.

'Welcome,' said the man, and 'Oh, boundlessly welcome!' the woman. He was Chinese, powerfully built, rather flat of countenance and without guile in it. She was Japanese, well-formed in a petite fashion, cat-alert beneath the schooled serenity. Both wore robes, simple though of the best material.

They had used Nepali, of which Wanderer had but a few words. 'Thank you,' he replied in Mandarin Chinese. 'I have returned as I promised.' He smiled. 'This time I took the trouble to learn a language you understand.'

'Fifty years,' the woman breathed, using that tongue. 'We could not be sure, we could only wait and wonder.'

'At last, at last,' the man said as shakily. He raised his voice in the tribal dialect. 'I told them we will hold a feast of rejoicing tomorrow,' he explained. 'Our servants will see to your men. Please come inside where we can be alone and honor you rightfully, sir – uh –'

'John Wanderer,' the American supplied.

'Why, that is what you called yourself before,' the woman said.

Wanderer shrugged. 'What difference, after so long and in a foreign country? I like the name, take it again and again, and otherwise usually a version of it. Who are you being?'

'What does that matter any more?' It came as a bass cry from the man's throat. 'We are what we are, together for always.'

The room where they conferred was gracious, the furniture Chinese, a variety of objects on shelves. The pair had adventured widely before they raised up this home. That was in 1810, as nearly as Wanderer could figure from the calendar they employed. Subsequently they had absented themselves from time to time for years on end, gone to oversee the businesses that kept them prosperous, brought souvenirs back. Those included books; Tu Shan found his diversion mainly in handicrafts, but Asagao was quite a reader.

In the presence of their fellow immortal, they chose to recall those ancient names. It was as if they snatched for a handhold, now when once more their world was falling to pieces.

Nevertheless joy overrode uneasiness. 'We hoped so, hoped you really were what you seemed to be,' Asagao said. 'How we hoped. More than an end to loneliness. Others like us, why, that gives meaning to these lives of ours. Does it not?'

'I can't say,' Wanderer replied. 'Besides you, my friend and I know of only one who is certainly alive, and he refuses to associate himself with us. We may be mere freaks.' From the end table next his chair he lifted a cup and took a sip of the pungent local *chong*, followed by a mouthful of tea. They comforted.

'Surely we are on earth for a reason, however mysterious,' Asagao insisted. 'At least, Tu Shan and I have tried to serve some purpose beyond surviving.'

'How did you find us, fifty years ago?' the man asked in his pragmatic way.

No real conversation had been possible then, when everything passed through an interpreter who had better not realize what meaning lay behind the words he rendered. Wanderer could just hint. Presently he thought these two had caught his intent and were doing likewise. They made it clear that they had no wish to depart, nor did they invite him to prolong his stay. Yet they were abundantly courteous, and when he risked his guide's astonishment and suggested that he return in fifty years, their answer throbbed with eagerness. Today they all knew, past any doubt, what they were.

'I was always restless, never fond of cities, for I began as a wild plainsman,' Wanderer related. 'After the first World War I set off around the world. My friend Hanno – he uses different identities, but between us he is Hanno – he had grown rich in America and gave me ample money, hoping I might come on the track of somebody like us. Nepal was not easy to reach or enter in those days, but I guessed that on that account it could harbor such persons. In Katmandu I caught rumors of a couple in the uplands who lived a kind of baronial existence among tribespeople whose benefactors and teachers they were. In spite of treating themselves well, they were considered holy. The story went that when they grew old they left on pilgrimage, and their son and his wife reappeared in their place. Imagine how such a tale drew me.'

Asagao laughed. 'Things were never so simple, of course,' she said. 'Our people aren't fools. They keep up the fiction about us because that is plainly what we want, but they know quite well that the same two come back to them. They don't fear or envy us, their nature is to accept various lots in life.

To them, yes, we are sacred and full of power, but we are also their friends. We sought long and far to find ourselves a home like this.'

'Besides,' Tu Shan grunted, 'they don't care to be overrun by worshippers, curiosity seekers, and the government and its tax collectors. At that, we have to deal with several visitors a year; more than that lately. Stories do get about. Only our distance from everything keeps them faint enough to protect us.'

Wanderer nodded. 'I would probably have ignored them if I hadn't been on the lookout. But nevertheless the modern world seems to be moving in.'

'We cannot forbear to bring what is good,' Asagao murmured. 'Literacy, medicine, awareness, whatever lightens these hard lives without corrupting them too much.'

Wanderer bleakened. 'It would have happened anyway, wouldn't it? You are losing control, aren't you?'

'I said we get more strangers all the time,' Tu Shan snapped. 'And inspectors from the king. Such hardly ever sought us out before. Nor did they ask as many questions.'

'We know the country is changing, the whole world is in upheaval,' Asagao sighed. 'Dear has this place been to us, but we understand that we must eventually disappear from it forever.'

'Or else become known for what you are,' Wanderer agreed low. 'Do you wish that? If so, tell me. I'll leave tomorrow, and in America change my name.' He left unspoken that he had not uttered any modern name of Hanno's.

'We have thought of it,' Tu Shan admitted. 'Sometimes in the past we made no pretense.' He paused. 'But that was always among simple countryfolk, and we could always withdraw and hide again when danger threatened. I am not sure we can do that any longer.'

'You cannot, once you are found out. They will track you down if you try, for they have many means these days to hunt men. Afterward you will be slaves, no doubt well-housed and well-fed but never set free, animals for them to study.'

'Is it really that bad?'

'I fear it is,' Asagao said. To Wanderer: 'We have spoken much about it, Tu Shan and I. The king of Nepal might treat us kindly, as his pet animals, but what if the Red Chinese or the Russians demand our persons?'

'At least keep your freedom,' Wanderer urged. 'You can proclaim yourselves when the times look auspicious to you, but I do not think they are yet, and once you have done so, there will be no more choices.'

'Do you mean for us to go away with you?'

'I hope you will, or at any rate follow me soon. Hanno will provide for you – whatever you need that is in his power to get, and his power is great.'

'We could go,' she said slowly. 'As I told you, we know how much people move about these days, and news leaps across thousands of miles. We have seen foreigners pass by and felt how they wondered about us. Even more do we feel the growing presence of the government. So in the last few decades we have begun making ready, as we did over and over in the past. We have taken care to have no children throughout that time. Our last living ones are long since settled down – we always reared them elsewhere – and believe us dead. We never enlightened them about us.' She winced. 'That would have hurt too much.'

'Then the children born to two immortals are themselves mortal?' Wanderer whispered. She nodded. He shook his head, in pain of his own. 'Well, Hanno and I often speculated about that.'

'I hate to go,' Tu Shan said heavily.

'Go someday we must,' Asagao answered. 'We knew that from the start. Now finally we can fly straight to shelter, companionship, help. The sooner the better.'

He shifted in his chair. 'I still have things to do. Our villagers will miss us, and we will miss them.'

'Always have we lost to death all those we loved. Let us instead remember these as they are today, alive. Let their memory of us fade gently into a legend that nobody else believes.'

The windows were turning blue with dusk.

2

Corinne Macandal, Mama-lo of the Unity and known to it as the daughter of its founder Laurace, halted her pacing when Rosa Donau entered. For a space the two women stood as if in confrontation. Shades drawn, the Victorian room was murkily lighted; eyeballs shone brighter than its glass or silver. Silence weighted the air, somehow made heavier by an undertone of traffic on the street outside.

After a moment Rosa said unsurely, 'I'm sorry to be this late. I was out for hours. Is this a bad time? Your message on my machine was that I should come right away, without calling back.'

'No, you did well,' Corinne told her.

'What's the matter? You look all tensed up.'

'I am. Come.' The black woman led the white into the adjoining chamber, where nobody dared enter unbidden. She ignored the arcane objects that crowded it and went directly to the coffee table. Rosa turned as usual to face the altar and touched brow, lips, breast. She had spent too many centuries appealing to saints and appeasing demons to be certain that no real power dwelt in things called holy.

Corinne picked up a magazine that lay open on the table. She handed it to the other and pointed. 'Read that,' she ordered.

Also here, the light was dim. The journal was one of respectable popular scholarship, like *Smithsonian* or *National Geographic*. Corinne indicated an advertisement near the back. Under the heading LONGEVITY STUDIES stood four column inches of text. The format was staid, the words discreet; most persons who noticed would find them dry, of interest to none except specialists. They leaped at Rosa: '– very long-lived individuals in excellent health ... young but prospectively long-lived are of similar interest ... scientific studies ... recollections of history as actually experienced ...'

Her hands began to shake. 'Not again,' broke from her.

Corinne started, recovered, gave her a searching look, but asked merely, 'What do you make of it?'

Rosa dropped the magazine and stared down at its cover. 'Probably nothing,' she mumbled. 'I mean, just what it says, somebody wants to, uh, examine and talk with folks who've gotten really old, or who might.'

'*How* old?'

Rosa lifted her glance. 'I tell you, it can't have anything to do with us!' she shrilled. 'There are scientists trying to get a handle on what aging is, you know?'

Corinne shook her head. 'The way this is phrased, somehow it doesn't quite fit that,' she said slowly. 'And how better might immortals try to get in touch with others like them?'

'It could be a scam. Or a trap.' Desperation chattered. 'Don't write to that box number, Laurace. Don't. We've got too much to lose.'

'Or to gain? What are you afraid of?'

'What could happen to us. And our work, everything we're doing.' Rosa aimed a jerky gesture at the curtained windows. 'The Unity'll fall apart without us. What'll become of everybody that trusts us?'

Corinne's gaze went in the same direction, as if it pierced through to the swamp of horrible decay in which this house stood like an island. 'I'm not sure we're doing much of anything any longer.'

'We are, we are. We're saving some, at least. If we – tell anybody what we are – that's the end. Nothing will ever be the same again.'

Corinne swung her vision back to Rosa, tautened, and pounced. 'You've seen something like this already, haven't you?'

'No.' The Syrian made fending motions. 'I mean, well –'

'It escaped you. It's written on you. Neither of us has stayed alive without getting pretty good at body language. Speak, or by God, I – I will contact this Willock fellow.'

Rosa shuddered. Resistance collapsed. She swiped at tears. 'I'm sorry. Yeah, yes, I did. Had almost forgotten, it was so long ago. Nothing more came of it, so I thought there was nothing to it. Till now.'

'When? Where?'

'In the papers, then. I don't remember the date, but it was shortly before the war, World War Two, that is.'

'About fifty years ago. Maybe exactly fifty years? Go on.'

'Well, it was an ad sort of like this. Not just the same, but, well, I wondered.'

'And you kept silent? You never called it to my attention.'

'I was scared!' Rosa screamed. 'Like I am now!' She stumbled to a chair, sank onto its zebra hide, and wept.

After a little while Corinne went to her, bent down, laid arms about the bowed shoulders and cheek close to cheek. 'I understand, Aliyat, dear,' she murmured. 'You hadn't been with me but a few short years. You had finally, barely won to something good, something hopeful. After those dreadful centuries – yes, of course you were terrified of any change, and the change here would have been unforeseeable. Oh, I forgive you. You may even have been right.'

She straightened. 'Still,' she said most softly, 'that fifty-year interval is strong evidence for another immortal. Isn't it? He or she wouldn't risk a continuous campaign. The short-lived would be too likely to start wondering. Our kind has time, and learns patience.'

'How do you know what they're like?' Rosa pleaded. 'They could be bad. I told you how I met two men and – well, we didn't get along. If they're still alive, if they're behind this, I wouldn't put anything past them.'

Corinne's tone parched. 'I gather you made enemies of them. You had better pull yourself together and explain, at long last, what did happen.' She waved a hand. 'Not today, as overwrought as you are. And ... yes, we must certainly stay cautious. I'll see what I can discover about Mr Willock before deciding whether to contact him – and how, if I do.'

She gentled again: 'Meanwhile, don't worry too much, dear. We have resources. I haven't told you in any detail. Secrecy does become a habit, doesn't it? Besides, this kind of thing isn't your *métier*. But over the years I've developed my own connections, including a few persons in key official positions.' The voice clanged. 'We won't stay passive. We're not alone any more? Then we've got to claim our share in the world, or else make ready to defend what is ours.'

3

The tax examiner ruffled several sheets of paper and frowned across his desk. 'I think we ought to see your client in person,' he said.

'I believed I mentioned to you, Mr Tomek is vacationing abroad,' Hanno replied with studied edginess. 'I've shown you my power of attorney in this matter.'

'Yes, yes. However. Naturally, you may accompany him, Mr Levine, if he wants legal counsel at his side.'

'Why? Have you any reason to suspect wrongdoing? I assure you, each detail in each one of his enterprises is in order. Haven't I been able to answer every single question you've put, these past two hours?'

'We have barely begun, Mr Levine. I have never seen so complicated a web of transactions and interlocking arrangements.'

'Go ahead and trace them out. If you turn up anything unlawful, I'll be totally surprised, but I'll be on call.' Hanno drew breath. 'Mr Tomek is an old man. He's earned a long rest and as much pleasure as is possible at his age. I don't think you can make any case for calling him in, and if you try, I intend to protest formally, as high up the ladder as necessary.' He left implied: Your superiors won't thank you for that.

Nasty young corporation mercenary, said the examiner's attitude, before he sagged a bit and his gray head bent. Fleetingly, Hanno pitied him. What a hell of a way to have spent the few worthwhile decades nature doled out, harassing people in their business and always with paper, never with more than a ghost of whatever blood-joy stirred in village busybody, religious inquisitor, state secret policeman.

Hanno dismissed the feeling: He's making me waste this afternoon, and yes, doubtless the dreariness has just started. He calculated his conciliation. 'No offense. You have your duty to do. And you'll find us entirely cooperative. But –' try for a laugh – 'I guarantee you won't make wages.'

The auditor smiled sourly. 'I admit you've given me what we need to conduct a preliminary check. You understand, don't you, we accuse nobody. It would be easy to make honest mistakes in this, uh, cat's cradle.'

'Mr Tomek's staff keeps close track, you know. Now if you have no further need of me today, perhaps I should leave you to your work.'

He ought to be calmer, inside as well as outside, Hanno thought when he left. There was nothing worse to fear than a dismal nuisance, because Charles Tomek's affairs were in truth defensible. Every last one of the many steps by which a gross income of millions became a taxable income of some hundred thousands, was legal. Let IRS try its meanest. Not only governments could use computers. Human beings could.

And Washington had no state income tax yet. That had been one strong reason among many for moving to Seattle. For that matter, he hadn't really shot the afternoon. Thinking he might, he had made no other commitments; much of the long summer day remained for him to enjoy.

Nevertheless the session rankled. He knew why. I've been spoiled, he thought. Once this was a free country. Oh, I always knew that couldn't last, that here too things were bound to grind back to the norm – masters and serfs, whatever names they go by. And so far we continue happier than most of the world ever was. But damn, modern democracy has the technology to regiment us beyond anything Caesar, Torquemada, Suleyman, or Louis XIV dared dream of.

He sighed, standing in the elevator, suppressing the wish for a smoke although he was alone. Quite apart from the laws that multiplied around him like bacteria, he owed consideration to the lungs of poor, vulnerable mortals. Indeed, he hadn't brought his tax liability down as far as he could have. A man who lived in a country ought to contribute his fair share to its mainten-ance and defense. Everything else was extortion.

John Wanderer disagrees, Hanno reflected. *He speaks of human needs, threatened biosphere, scientific mysteries, and says it's romanticism to sup-pose private enterprise can cope with them all. No doubt he's right to some extent. But where do you draw the line?*

Maybe I've been around too long, maybe it's prejudiced me. But I remem-ber, for example, those glorious public works that government gave to Egypt, century after century, and how they benefitted the people – pyramids, statues of Rameses II, grain tribute to Rome, Aswan Dam. I remember small shops I've closed, men and women thrown out of jobs, because the regulations and required recordkeeping changed them to losing propositions.

He came forth into downtown. A wind, strong and cold, thrust odors of salt water through automobile stench. Sunlight spilled from heaven. Crowds bustled. A street musician fiddled a tune he liked, to judge by his stance and his face. The wind flapped the skirts of a particularly delicious girl, as brave a sight as Old Glory on her staff above one building. The vitality caught at Hanno, blew the darkness out of him.

For a minute, practicality lingered. He must consider seriously, and soon, phasing out Charles Tomek. Death and cremation abroad, widower, child-less, assets willed to various individuals and certain foundations ... In due course Tomek's pet lawyer had better move away, drop out of sight. That would be much simpler to arrange; hundreds or thousands of men in the United States must bear the name Joseph Levine ... And the dozen add-itional identities in four different countries, ranging from magazine publisher to day laborer, yes, they all needed attention. Those which he had created as boltholes, mere camouflage, against a day of need, probably remained safe. Others, though, were for diversification, so he could be active, carry out his undertakings and investments, without making any of them unduly notice-able; and by now some of them, such as Tannahill, were becoming so. How long could he keep up the dance?

How long did he actually wish to? He well understood that his resentment of the modern state sprang in large part from its erosion of privacy; and priv-acy, like liberty, was a pretty new and fragile idea. Gods damn it, he was a seaman, he wanted a deck again under his feet. But for most of the twentieth century he had only been able to operate, if he would keep his secret, in offices, by mail and wire and telephone and computer, chasing paper profits, hardly better off – except for his yachts, women, feasts, luxuries, travels, and the hunt that was his ultimate purpose in life – hardly better off than that poor publican, his enemy.

To what end? Wealth? It was a Phoenician's way to strength. But how much strength would he ever find use for? No amount of money would stave off a nuclear warhead. At best, it would buy refuge for him and his, and the means to start over once the ashes had settled. For that, a million or two dollars were ample. Meanwhile, why not shut down his businesses in the course of the next ten or a dozen years, then take a holiday for whatever time this civilization hung together? Didn't he deserve it?

Did his comrades want that, though? They were so earnest in their different ways, those three. And, of course, any day his renewed search might turn up others. Or anything else might happen.

The wind whooped. Suddenly Hanno laughed aloud with it. He ignored the stares he got. Maybe living through history had made him a touch paranoid. Yet he had also learned from it that every hour of freedom was a precious gift, to be savored in fullness and stored away where thieves could not break in and steal. Here half a beautiful afternoon and a whole evening had fallen into his hands. What to do with them?

A drink in the revolving bar on the Space Needle? The view of mountains and water was incomparable, and Lord knew when the next clear day would happen along. No. This past interview had driven him too much into himself. He desired companionship. Natalia was still at work, pridefully and wisely declining to let him support her. Tu Shan and Asagao were afar in Idaho, John Wanderer in the Olympics on one of his backpacking trips. He could drop into, say, Emmett Watson's for a beer and some oysters and general friendliness – no, the danger of meeting a self-appointed poet was too great. Jokes aside, he didn't feel like chitchat with somebody he'd never see again.

That left a single possibility; and he hadn't visited Giannotti's lab for quite a spell. Nothing spectacular could have happened there or he'd have been notified, but it was always interesting to get a personal progress report.

By the time of that decision, Hanno had reached the lot where he left the Buick registered to Joe Levine. He considered driving straight to his destination. Surely no one had put a tail on him. But accidents could happen, and sometimes did. Immortality made caution a habit. Moreover, he intended to end up with Natalia. Therefore he bucked through traffic to Levine's place near the International District. It had parking of its own. In the apartment he opened a concealed safe and exchanged Levine's assorted identification cards for Robert Cauldwell's. A taxi brought him to a public garage where

Cauldwell rented a space. Entering the Mitsubishi that waited, he returned to the streets.

He liked this tightly purring machine much better. Damn, it seemed only yesterday that Detroit was making the best cars for their price on earth.

His goal was a plain brick building, a converted warehouse, in a light-industry section between Green Lake and the University campus. A brass plate on its door read RUFUS MEMORIAL INSTITUTE. Those who asked were told that Mr Rufus had been a friend of Mr Cauldwell, the ship-owner who endowed this laboratory for fundamental biological science. That satisfied their curiosity. The work being done interested them much more, emphasizing as it did molecular cytology and the effort to discover what made living beings grow old.

It had been a plausible way for Cauldwell to dispose of his properties and retire into obscurity. Two magnate identities were more than Hanno could maintain after the government got thoroughly meddlesome. Tomek was pulling in the most money by then, and leaving less of a trail. Besides, this might offer a hope –

Director Samuel Giannotti was at his workbench. The staff was small though choice, administration was kept to an unfussy minimum, and he continued to be a practicing scientist. When Hanno arrived, he took time to shut down his experiment properly before escorting the founder to his office. It was a book-lined room as comfortably rumpled-looking as his large, bald-headed self. A swivel chair stood available for each man. Giannotti fetched Scotch from a cabinet, ice and soda from a fridge, and mixed mild drinks while Hanno charged his pipe.

'I wish you'd give that foul thing up,' Giannotti said, settling down. His voice was amicable. The seat creaked to his weight. 'Where'd you get it, any-way? From King Tutankhamen?'

'Before my time,' Hanno drawled. 'Do you mind? I know you've quit, but I didn't expect you'd take the Christer attitude of so many ex-smokers.'

'No, in my line of work we get used to stenches.'

'Good. How's that line go from Chesterton?'

'"If there is one thing worse than the modern weakening of major morals it is the modern strengthening of minor morals,"' quoted Giannotti, who was a devotee. 'Or else, later in the same essay, "It is the great peril of our society that all its mechanism may grow more fixed while its spirit grows more fickle." Not that I've often heard you worry about morals or the spirit.'

'I don't worry aloud about the oxygen supply, either –'

'Obviously.'

'– or the other necessities of survival. It would annoy me less that we're heading into a new puritanical era if the puritanism concerned itself about things that matter.' Hanno struck match to tobacco and drew the fire alight.

'Well, I worry about you. Okay, your body has recovered from traumas that would have finished off any of us ordinaries, but that doesn't mean your immortality is absolute. A bullet or a swig of cyanide would kill you as easily as me. I'm not at all convinced your cells can stand that kind of chemical insult forever.'

'Pipe smokers don't inhale, and for me cigarettes are *faute de mieux*.' Hanno's brows knotted slightly. 'Just the same ... do you have any solid scientific reason for what you said?'

'No,' Giannotti admitted. 'Not yet.'

'What are you turning up lately, if anything?'

Giannotti sipped from his glass. 'We've learned of some very interesting work in Britain. Fairweather at Oxford. It looks as though the rate at which cellular DNA loses methyl groups is correlated with lifespan, at least in the animals that have been studied. Jaime Escobar here is setting up to pursue this line of inquiry further. I myself will re-examine cells of yours from the same viewpoint, with special reference to glycosylation of proteins. On the QT, of course. I'd like fresh material from the four of you, blood, skin, biopsy sample of muscle tissue, to start new cultures for the purpose.'

'Any time you want, Sam. But what does this signify, exactly?'

'You mean "What might it signify, at a guess?" We know little thus far. Well, I'll try to sketch it out for you, but I'll have to repeat stuff I've told you before.'

'That's all right. I am a simon-pure layman. My basic thought habits were formed early in the Iron Age. Where it comes to science, I can use plenty of repetition.'

Giannotti leaned forward, caught up in his quest. 'The British themselves aren't sure. Maybe the demethylation is due to cumulative damage to the DNA itself, maybe the methylase enzyme becomes less active in the course of time, maybe something else. In any event, it may – at the present stage this is only a suggestion, you understand – it may result in deterioration of mechanisms that hitherto kept certain other genes from expressing themselves. Maybe those genes become free to produce proteins that have poisoning effects on still other cellular processes.'

'The checks and balances begin to break down,' Hanno said mutedly, through a cloud of blue smoke.

'Probably true, but that's so vague and general a statement, practically a tautology, as to be useless.' Giannotti sighed. 'Now don't imagine that we have more than a single piece of the jigsaw puzzle here, if we have that much. And it's a puzzle in three dimensions, or four, or *n*, with the space not necessarily Euclidean. For instance, your regeneration of parts as complex as teeth implies more than freedom from senescence. It indicates retention of juvenile, even fetal characteristics, not in the gross anatomy but probably on the molecular level. And that fantastic immune system of yours must tie in somehow, too.'

'Yeah.' Hanno nodded. 'Aging isn't a single, simple thing. It's a whole clutch of different ... diseases, all with pretty much the same symptoms, like flu or cancer.'

'Not quite, I think,' Giannotti replied. They had been over the same ground more than once, but the Phoenician was right about his need for that. He must have won to a terrifying degree of knowledge about himself, Giannotti sometimes thought. 'There does appear to be a common factor in the case of every mortal organism with more than a single cell – and maybe the unicellulars too, maybe even the prokaryotes and viruses – if only we can find what it is. Conceivably this demethylation phenomenon gives us a clue to it. Anyhow, that's my opinion. I concede my grounds are more or less philosophical. Something as biologically fundamental as death ought to be in the very fabric of evolution, virtually from the beginning.'

'Uh-huh. Advantage to the species, or, I should say, the line of descent. Get the older generations out of the way, make room for genetic turnover, allow more efficient types to develop. Without death, we'd still be bits of jelly in the sea.'

'There may be something to that.' Giannotti shook his head. 'But it can't be the whole story. It doesn't account for humans outliving mice by an order of magnitude, for instance. Or species that live indefinitely, like bristlecone pines.' Weariness dragged at his smile. 'No, most likely life has adapted itself to the fact, made the best it could of the fact, that sooner or later, one way or another, entropy will ring down the curtain on its wonderful chemical juggling act. Whether your kind represents the next step in evolution, a set of mutations that created a fail-safe system, I can't say.'

'But you don't think so, do you?' Hanno asked. 'We don't breed true.'

'No, you don't,' Giannotti said with a barely perceptible wince. 'However, that may come. Evolution is cut-and-try. If I may anthropomorphize,' he added. 'Often it's hard not to.'

Hanno clicked his tongue. 'You know, when you say things like that, I have trouble believing you're a believing Catholic.'

'Separate spheres,' Giannotti answered. 'Ask any competent theologian. And I wish you would, for your own sake, you poor lonely atheist.' Quickly: 'The point is, the material world and the spirit world are not identical.'

'And we'll outlive the galaxies, you and I and everybody,' he had said once toward dawn, when the bottle was low. 'You may spend ten thousand years, or a million or a billion, in the flesh, but it will hardly mean more, then, than the three days that a premature baby had. Maybe less; the baby died innocent ... But this is a fascinating problem, and it does have unlimited potentialities for the whole world, if we can solve it. Your existence cannot be a mere stochastic accident.'

Hanno didn't argue, though he preferred their everyday banter, or straight-forward talk about the work. He had found after years of acquaintance that here was one of the rare people whom he could trust with his secret; and in this case it might, just possibly, bring an end to the need for secrecy. If Sam Giannotti could endure knowing of lives that went on for millennia, and keep silent about them even with his wife, because of a faith whose elements Hanno remembered as having been ancient in Hiram's Tyre – so be it.

'But never mind,' the scientist went on. 'What I wish more, right now and always, is the same as ever. That you'd release me from my promise and let me make known – or better, make known yourself – what you are.'

'Sorry,' Hanno said. 'Must I repeat why not?'

'Cast off that suspiciousness, can't you? I forget how many times I've told you, the Middle Ages are behind us. Nobody will burn you for a witch. Show the world the proofs you showed me.'

'I've learned to be leery of doing anything irrevocable.'

'Will I never make you understand? I'm shackled. I can't so much as tell my staff the truth. We piddle around and – If you come out of the closet, Bob, discovering the immortality mechanism will become the human race's top priority. Every resource will go to it. The knowledge that it is possible is half the battle, I swear. They might crack it inside of ten years. Meanwhile, can't you see the dying down of war, arms races, terrorism, despotism, given such a prospect before everyone? How many needless deaths can you stand to have on your conscience?'

'And I've told *you* before, I doubt the outcome would be anything like that sweet,' Hanno snapped. 'Three thousand years of experience, as close as makes no difference, say otherwise. An overnight revelation like that would upset too many applecarts.'

He had no cause to repeat how he controlled the veto. If and when necessary, he would dispose of the things he had used to convince Giannotti. John Wanderer, Tu Shan, and Asagao were accustomed to following his lead, he far and away their senior. Should one of them rebel and reveal, that person possessed no evidence of the kind that Hanno had assembled. After forty or fifty years of observation, people might take the claim seriously; but why would an immortal spend so great a while in custody? Richelieu had been right, three and a half centuries ago. The risks were too large. If your body stayed youthful, you kept a young animal's strong desire to live.

Giannotti sank back into his chair. 'Oh, hell, let's not rehash a stale argument,' he muttered. Louder: 'I do ask you to put that pessimism and cynicism of yours aside and think again. When everybody can have your lifespan, you'll have no more reason to hide.'

'Sure,' Hanno agreed. 'Why d'you suppose I founded this place? But let the change come gradually, with forewarning. Give me and my friends and the world time to prepare. Meanwhile, you said it, the argument has long since gone moldy.'

Giannotti laughed, as a man may laugh when he can lower a burden from his shoulders. 'Okay. Shop talk and gossip. What's new with you?'

Time goes fast in congenial company. The hour was past six when Hanno pulled up in front of Cauldwell's house.

The unpretentious building on Queen Anne Hill had a magnificent view. He stood for a minute and savored it. Beneath a westering sun the distant mountains seemed to glimmer only half real, as if they rose in a dream or in elfland. Southward, beyond the slim silhouette of the Space Needle, the light turned Elliot Bay to molten silver and touched treetops with gold. Farther on, Rainier bulwarked heaven, blue rock-mass and white purity. Air went cool into breath. Traffic noises were a whisper, and a robin loosed scraps of melody. Yes, he thought, this was a lovely planet, an Aladdin's hoard of wonders. Too bad how humans mucked it up. Nevertheless he intended to stick around.

A bit reluctantly, he went inside. Natalia Thurlow was there and the door not locked. She sat before the television watching the news. A jowly face and beaky nose filled the screen. The voice was lubricated, sonorous:

'– join in your noble cause. It is the cause of men and women of good will everywhere. This squandering of untold wealth on weapons of mass destruction, while human beings go hungry and homeless, must end, and end soon. I pledge myself –' The view panned back to show a packed auditorium. On the stage, American and Soviet flags flanked Edmund Moriarty. The United Nations banner was spread directly behind, and a streamer above read CONCERNED CITIZENS' COMMITTEE FOR PEACE.

'Judas priest!' Hanno groaned. 'Do you want me to barf on our nice new carpet?'

Natalia turned the set off and came to give him a hug and a kiss. He responded energetically. She was a rangy blond in her mid-thirties who knew well how to please him, not least by being an independent sort.

Having disengaged, she ran fingers through the hair he had rumpled. 'Hey, big boy, you came out of that bad mood in a hurry,' she laughed. 'Not quite so fast, if you please. Dinner won't wait for more than a short drink. I expected you earlier.' Usually she cooked. Hanno was good at it, but she found it relaxing after a day of working on computer software. She cocked her head. 'Of course, afterward –'

'Well, all I want is a beer,' he said. 'Sam and I hoisted a couple at the lab.'

'What? I thought you had less fun in prospect.'

'So did I, but I got out of the Internal Reaming Service sooner than I feared.' He had mentioned he was in for such a session, though not the identities actually involved. He sought the kitchen. She had already poured herself a sherry.

Returning with his mug of Ballard Bitter to sit down on the couch beside her, he found she had gone serious, half angry. 'Bob,' she said, 'I insist you quit making nasty cracks about the government. Sure, it has its faults, including heavy-handedness, but it is ours.'

'"Government of the people, by the people, and for the people." Yeah. Trouble is, the three classes of people aren't the same.'

'I've heard you on the subject before, in case you've forgotten. If you're right about that being the nature of government, why bitch at this one? It is the only thing that stands between us and what is far worse.'

'Not if Senator Moriarty has his way.'

'Wait a minute,' she said sharply. 'You're entitled to call him mistaken, but not to call him … a traitor, the way I've heard you imply. He speaks for millions of perfectly decent Americans.'

'So they imagine. His real constituency is industries that vote their tariff protections and subsidies, bums who vote their handouts, and intellectuals who vote their slogans. As for this new-found pacifism of his, that's the current fashion. Before, his breed was always hell-bent to get us into foreign wars, except that we mustn't win any that were fought against Communists. Now he's picking up extra votes – someday they may help him into the White House – by telling us that violence never settles anything. If only the city fathers of Carthage could talk to him.'

She put irritation aside and riposted with a grin, 'Plagiarizing Heinlein, are you?'

He had come to admire the deftness with which she could defuse a quarrel. They'd had too many lately. Chuckling, he relaxed. 'You're right, I am a fool to waste good drinking time on politics, especially when it's in the company of a sexy woman.'

Inwardly there passed through him: He may have delivered himself into my hands, though. I'll get a tape of the proceedings tomorrow. If they went as I imagine, well, the next issue of *The Chart Room* is almost ready to go to press. I barely have time to pull Tannahill's editorial and slip in another that'll be pure *Schadenfreude* to write.

Natalia laid a hand over his. 'You're pretty sexy yourself, for your information,' she said. 'Horrible old reactionary, but if word got around about what you're like in bed, I'd have to fight the women off with a shillelagh.'

Her smile faded. She sat quiet a while before adding softly, 'No, I take that first part back. I think you're down on governments because you've seen victims of their blunders and, yes, cruelties. It would be better if you were in charge. Under that crusty exterior, you're fine and considerate.'

'And too smart to want power,' he interpolated.

'And you are not old, either,' she went on. 'Not in any way that counts.'

'Sixty-seven, last time I looked.' At Robert Cauldwell's birth certificate.

'I could be your father, or your grandfather if my son and I had been a tad precocious.' I could be your hundredfold-great-grandfather. Quite possibly I am.

He felt her gaze on him, but didn't meet it. 'When *I* look, I see a person who appears younger than me. It's eerie.'

'Persistent ancestors, I've told you.' A bottle of hair dye, to pretend indulgence of that small vanity. 'I've also told you you should start shopping for a newer model. I honestly don't want it to get too late for you.'

'We'll see.' A single time in their three-year union had she suggested marriage. Were he using a different, younger personality he might well have gone through with it. As was, he couldn't explain what a dirty trick on her it would be.

The thought flitted through him that if he did make known what he was and Giannotti's estimate of the rate of progress thereafter proved right, Natalia could become immortal herself. Probably rejuvenated, too; given such a command of biochemistry, that ought to be easy. But while he was fond of her, he had not permitted himself to fall really in love for centuries; and he didn't feel ready to unleash incalculable consequences on the world. Not this evening, at least.

She put on gaiety. 'Who's your Danish pen pal?'

He blinked. 'What?'

'In today's mail. Otherwise nothing special – Hey, important, is it?'

His heart thudded. 'I'll see. Excuse me a minute.'

He'd not thought about the post. It lay on a corner table. As he took the envelope postmarked Copenhagen, he saw the printed name and address of a hotel and, hand-written above it, 'Helmut Becker.'

His agent in Frankfurt, receiving responses to an advertisement published throughout northern Europe, then following up on any that seemed to come from a person who might fit his requirements – of course, Becker had merely been told that the Rufus Lab wanted to contact members of long-lived families; if they were young but showed intelligence, as evinced by an interest in history, that was ideal –

Hanno forced his mouth and hands into steadiness. He opened the letter. It was in stilted English, but there was no reason Natalia shouldn't read it. She knew about the project, considered the approach unscientific but tolerated it together with the rest of his eccentricities. In fact, he should give her every appearance of openness, to hide the excitement that roared within him. 'Apparently I've got a little trip ahead of me,' he told her.

4

They were friendly folks in the Lost River country, and besides, Chinese farmers had always done well throughout Idaho. So when Mr and Mrs Tu became tenants of the property that Tomek Enterprises owned, neighbors made them welcome. Their background was interesting to hear about, he a small landowner in Taiwan, she the daughter of a Japanese trade representative there. Marriages like that faced problems in Asia, even this long after the war. Also, they had some difficulties with the Kuomintang government, nothing terrible but enough to make them feel restricted and harassed. Through her family they met Mr Tomek himself, who arranged for them to come to America. At first their English was broken, but they soon became pretty good at it.

Still, they never quite fitted in. They managed the fields and herds well. They kept the house spic and span, and if some things in it were kind of odd, you had to expect that. They were well-behaved, polite, helpful. However, they held themselves back, joined no church or social club or anything, got along in company but didn't really open up, repaid invitations with fine food and pleasant conversation but took no lead in sociability. Well, they *were* Orientals, and maybe that made them feel sensitive about having had no children.

After six years they did stir gossip and uneasiness. They'd gone off on vacations from time to time, like most people, except that they said practically nothing about where it was to or what they'd done. Now they came back with a pair of youngsters from Chicago, slum kids, been in trouble, one of them black. It wasn't an adoption, the Tus explained; they simply aimed to see what a real home in a healthy environment could do. They had letters to show this was okay with the authorities.

Their neighbors worried about mischief, misleading of their own children, maybe drugs. Edith Harmon, who was a forceful lady, took it upon herself to call when Shan was away and have a heart-to-heart talk with Asagao. 'I understand your feelings, dear, and it's kind of you, but we have so much do-gooding these days.'

Asagao smiled and asked, 'Is do-badding better?' She went on at once: 'I promise you it will be all right. My husband and I have guided lives before now.'

'Really?'

'It gives meaning to ours. Or perhaps you have heard about the Buddhist concept of acquiring merit. Here, let me warm that coffee for you.'

And it did succeed. There was a little friction at first, especially in school. The boy got into a couple of fights, the girl was caught shoplifting. Their fosterers straightened them out fast and thoroughly. Shan might not be the smartest man alive, but he was no dummy either, and he had a way of getting others to do what he wanted that did not come just from great physical strength. Asagao was quiet, gentle, and – the neighborhood discovered – sharp as a tack. The kids worked hard on the ranch and soon worked hard in school. They became popular. After four years they left, of an age and qualified to take jobs waiting for them elsewhere. Folks missed them, and didn't object to the new waifs who then arrived. Instead, the community felt proud.

The Tus didn't go looking for children. They told how they had been appalled at what they read or saw on TV, afterward witnessed for themselves. Inquiring around, they came on an outfit, small but with branches in several big cities, that tried to make placements. Mutual trust developed. The original experience showed what they had to offer and what sort of kids would likely benefit from it. After that, the organization chose and sent.

Shan and Asagao figured three at a time was as much as they could rightly handle, and not if those all came at once. So two years had passed when they got the third member of the second group. She was a fourteen-year-old from New York. They met her at the Pocatello airport and drove her back to their place.

To start with, Juanita was a handful and a half, nervous as a trapped bobcat, often sullen, sometimes exploding in screams and curses that shocked the ranch hands. They had learned patience and firmness, though. The youngsters already there had gotten to a point where they too were a steadying, calming force. Above all, the married couple was, and also the beautiful land, open air, honest labor, hearty food. It helped that this was summer; Juanita didn't have school to cope with as well. Soon she was turning into quite the little lady.

One day Asagao asked her to come along, the two of them alone, and help pick berries in a hidden nook of the hills, more than an hour away on horseback. They packed a lunch and took their time. On the way home, shy young dreams began to reach lips. Asagao well knew how to keep talk aflow without pushing.

Yesterday a thunderstorm had broken a hot spell. The air was full of wayward breezes and soft smells. Light was lengthening from the west, but still held that upland brilliance which made the mountains seem almost next door and yet left you feeling what a vastness you looked across. Clouds towered white into dizzying depths of blue. The valley rolled in a thousand shades of green, twinkly with irrigation, on and on toward the orchards and ranch buildings. Red-winged blackbirds darted and cried over the pasture, and cattle near the fence line lifted large eyes to watch the horses pass. Leather squeaked, hoofs plopped, riding was oneness in a lazy sweet rhythm.

'I really would like to learn about your religion, Mrs Tu,' Juanita said. She was a dark, thin girl who walked with a limp. Her father used to beat her, as he did her mother, till at last she put a kitchen knife in his shoulder and ran off. In the saddle she was on her way to centaurhood, and corrective surgery was scheduled for later this year. Meanwhile she did her share of chores, assigned to allow for the handicap. 'It must be wonderful if –' she flushed, glanced aside, dropped her voice – 'if it's got believers like you and Mr Tu.'

Asagao smiled. 'Thank you, love, though we are quite ordinary, you know. I think you had better get back into your own church. Of course we'll be glad to explain what we can. All our children have been interested. But what we live by can't actually be put in words. It's very alien to this country. It might not even be a religion by your standards, but more a way of life, of trying to get in harmony with the universe.'

Juanita gave her a quick, searching regard. 'Like the Unity?'

'The what?'

'The Unity. Where I come from. Except they – they couldn't take me. I asked a guy who belongs, but he said it's ... a lifeboat as full as it can carry.' A sigh. 'Then I got lucky and got found by – for – you. I think prob'ly this is better. You'll fix me to go live anyplace. The Unity, you stay with it. I think. But I don't know much about it. They don't talk, the members.'

'Your friend must have, if you heard about it.'

'Oh, word gets around. The dope dealers, now, they *hate* it. But I guess it's only in the New York area. And like I said, the higher you go in it, the less you tell. Manuel, he's too young. He grew up in it, his parents did too, but they say he's not ready yet. He doesn't know much except about the housing and education and – well, members help each other.'

'That sounds good. I have heard of such organizations.'

'Oh, this isn't a co-op exactly, and it's not like, uh, the Guardian Angels, except for what they call sentinel stance, and – It's sort of like a church, except not that either. Members can believe anything they want, but they do have – services? Retreats? That's how come I wondered if this was like the Unity.'

'No, can't be. We're simply a family. We wouldn't have any idea how to run anything larger.'

'I guess that's why the Unity stopped growing,' Juanita said thoughtfully. 'Mama-lo can only keep track of so much.'

'Mama-lo?'

'The name I've heard. She's kind of a – a high priestess? Except it isn't a church. But they say she's real powerful. They do what she wants, in the Unity.'

'Hm. How long has this been going on?'

'I don't know. A long time. I heard the first Mama-lo was the mother of this one, or was she the grandmother? A black woman, though I hear she's got a white woman works close with her, always has had.'

'This is fascinating,' Asagao said. 'Do go on.'

– Evenings after dinner were usually for being together. Foster parents and children talked, played games, sat quietly reading. Sometimes they watched the single television set, but only by mutual consent, subject to adult over-rule. A person who wished to be alone could withdraw to his or her room with a book or pursue a hobby in the little workshop. Thus the hour was late when Tu Shan and Asagao walked out. They ranged widely and were gone long. Nevertheless they spoke in Chinese. To be sure, their dialect of it still came most easily to them of the tongues they had mutually mastered in their centuries.

Night lay cool and still. Land reached shadowy, treetops loomed darkling beneath the extravagant stars of the high West. Once an owl hooted, repeatedly, before ghosting past.

'They could so well be our kind.' Asagao's tone shivered. 'Something built up slowly, over generations, yet centered on one or two individuals, who talk about being mother and child but remain mysterious and work in the same style. We two were chiefs, under one title or another, of different villages; our businesses in the cities were incidental. Hanno made his businesses into his power, protection, and disguise. Here may be a third way. Down among the poor, the rootless, the disinherited. Give them leadership, counsel, purpose, hope. In return they will provide you your little kingdom, or queendom; and there you can live safe, hidden, for mortal lifetimes.'

'It may be,' Tu Shan replied in the slow fashion that was his when he thought hard. 'Or perhaps not. We will write to Hanno. He will investigate.'

'Or should we do that?'

'What?' He checked his stride, startled. 'He knows how. We are country-folk, you and I.'

'Will he not keep these immortals underground, as he has kept Wanderer and us, as he would keep that Turk did the man not stay aside on his own account?'

'Well, he has explained why.'

'How sure are we that he is right?' Asagao demanded. 'You know how I have studied. I have talked with that learned man, Giannotti, whenever he examined us again. Do we truly need to go on beneath our masks? It was not always necessary for us in Asia. It never was for Wanderer among his wild Indians. Is it in America today? Times have changed. If we made ourselves known, it could well mean immortality for everyone within a few years.'

'Maybe it would not. And what then would people do to us?'

'I know. I know. And yet – Why must we take it for granted that Hanno is right? Why shouldn't we decide for ourselves whether he is the wisest because he is the oldest, or else has grown set in his ways and now is making a horrible mistake, out of needless fear and ... utter selfishness?'

'M-m-m –'

'At worst we die.' Asagao lifted her head against the stars. 'We die like everybody else, except that we have had so many, many years. I am not afraid to. Are you?'

'No.' Tu Shan laughed a bit. 'I dislike the thought, yes, I admit that.' Sobering: 'We do have to tell him about this Unity thing. He has the means, the knowledge, to find out. We don't.'

Asagao nodded. 'True.' After a moment: 'But once we have learned whether or not these are like us –'

'We owe Hanno much.' Entry to this nation, through Tomek's influence over a certain Congressman. Help in getting acquainted with it. Establishment here, once they realized that American cities would never be for them.

'We do. We also owe humanity much, I think. And ourselves. Freedom to choose is our right too.'

'Let us see what happens,' Tu Shan proposed.

They walked on a while in silence. A bright rapid star rose in the west and crossed the lower constellations. 'Look,' Tu Shan said. 'A satellite. This *is* an age of marvels.'

'I believe that is Mir,' she answered slowly.

'What? … Oh, yes. The Russian one.'

'The space station. The only space station. And the United States, since *Challenger* –' Asagao had no further need to speak. As long as they had lived together, they could each often follow what was in the other's mind. Dynasties flourish and fall. Empires do, nations, peoples, destinies.

5

'– And may holiness be with your good angels. Let the Fire burn strong and the Rainbow bear peace. Go now toward God. Fare you well.'

Rosa Donau raised her hands in benediction, brought them over her bosom, and bowed to the cross that stood on the altar before her between the red and the black candles in their lily-shaped holders. Opposite, her fellow celebrants did likewise. They were a score, male and female, mostly dark of skin and gray of hair, elders of the families that would be living here. The service had lasted an hour, simple words, chants to a drum-beat, a sacred dance, hypnotic in its very restraint and softness. The gathering departed without speaking, though several threw her wide smiles and a number signed themselves.

She remained for a time, sought a chair and a deeper calm. As yet, the chapel was sparsely furnished. Behind the altar hung a picture of Jesus, more gaunt and stern than was common although his hand was upraised in blessing. Painted directly on plaster, the Serpent of Life encircled him. It was flanked by emblems that could be of the loas or the saints, however you wished. The symbols right and left could be luck, magic, sanctity, or – just encouragement, she knew; lift up your heart, honor with bravery the life that is in you.

Here was no doctrine but the sacredness of creation because of the Creator's presence in it, no commandment but loyalty to your kindred of the spirit. The animistic, pantheistic imagery was only a language for saying that. The rites were only to evoke it and to bind the kindred together. You could believe whatever else you thought must be true. Yet not since she was a maiden, fourteen hundred years ago, had Aliyat felt such power as lingered here.

Within her, if not in the altar or the air. Hope, cleansing, purpose, something she could *give* instead of forever taking or squandering. Was that why Corinne had asked her to lead the consecration of this building?

Or was Corinne simply too occupied with the question of who, or what, laired behind that innocent-seeming call to the long-lived? She had certainly gone close-mouthed. Aliyat knew merely that she soon learned the Willock named was no more than an agent under the impression he was handling matters for a scientific outfit. (Could that even be true?) Maybe Corinne had asked those contacts of hers in the government, police, FBI, whoever and wherever they were, to look into the matter. No, probably not; too dangerous; it might alert them to the fact that Mama-lo Macandal was not all she seemed ...

Well, not to worry, she had said; and a hard life did teach a girl how to concentrate on what was close to hand. Aliyat sighed, rose, blew out the candles, turned off the lights as she left. The chapel was on the second floor. Besides making it fit for use, workers had rebuilt the rotting staircase to the hallway outside it; but otherwise, so far they were occupied elsewhere. A naked bulb glared on peeling, discolored plaster. This was a nasty district, way down on the lower west side. However, here the Unity could cheaply acquire an abandoned tenement house for its members to restore to decency. She couldn't help wondering whether there would ever be more such undertakings. Let it get bigger and it would become too noticeable, and beyond the control of that pair whose cover and stronghold it was. Nonetheless, people who belonged were bound to grow up, marry, have children.

She descended to a jumble of equipment and materials in the lobby. The night watchman rose to greet her. Another man got up too, young, big, ebony-hued. Aliyat recognized Randolph Castle. 'Good evenin', Missus-lo Rosa,' he rumbled. 'Peace an' strength.'

'Why, hello,' she replied, surprised. 'Peace and strength. What are you doing here so late?'

'Thought I'd walk you back. Figured you might stay on after the rest had left.'

'That's very kind of you.'

'Just bein' careful,' he said grimly. 'We don't wanna lose you.'

They bade the watchman goodnight and went out. The street was poorly lit, its murk apparently empty, but you never knew what might wait in those shadows and taxis didn't cruise the area. Her place wasn't far, a light house-keeping room in the Village. However, she was glad to have formidable company.

'Wanted to talk with you anyway,' he said once they had started off. 'If you don't mind.'

'No, of course not. That's a main part of what I'm for, isn't it?'

He must force the words out. 'No pers'nal troubles this time. It's for ever'body. Only I don't know as how we can tell Mama-lo.'

Aliyat brushed fingers across his clenched fist. 'Go on,' she urged gently. 'Whatever you say will be safe with me.'

'I know. Oh, I know.' She had heard his confession of wrongdoing and helped him set matters right. After a number of hollowly thudding footfalls: 'Look, Mama-lo don't re'lize how bad this area is. None of us did, or I guess we wouldn't've bought into it. But I been findin' out.'

'Crime, drug dealing. We've handled those before. What else?'

'Nothin'. But these dealers, they're mean. They know 'bout us an' they don't intend we should get no foothold here, no ways.'

Chill struck through her. She had met absolute evil in century after century, and knew its power.

Once she had laughed this presence of it off. 'Who cares, as long as we keep our own people clean?' she said. 'Let others wreck themselves if they want. You smuggled in booze and ran speakeasies during Prohibition. I did pretty much the same. What's the difference?'

'I'm surprised you don't know better than to ask that,' Corinne answered. She paused. 'Well, you've been trying hard to steer clear of everything wicked. Listen, dear. The stuff that's coming in these days is different. We say nothing in the Unity against taking an occasional drink, we use wine in some of our ceremonies, but we teach our members not to get drunk. You cannot not lose your mind to stuff like crack. And ... the old gangsters could get vicious enough, I'm not sure now that I should ever have condoned their business, but compared to the dealers today they were the Holy Innocents.' Her fingers writhed together. 'Today it's like the slave trade come back.'

That was years ago, when things were only starting to get bad. Aliyat had learned since then. And the Unity took action at each of its settlements. A solid band of dwellers who kept watch, called the police whenever they had information, set an example, helped the lost find the way home to humanness, and stood together in half-military wise: they could make a neighborhood unprofitable, actually dangerous, for pushers.

'I been threatened, myself,' Castle said. 'Other guys have too. I think, we really think, if we don't pull out, the mob's gonna try an' blow us away.'

'We can't abandon the project,' she told him. 'We've sunk more than we can afford to lose into it. The Unity isn't rich, you know.'

'Yeah, I know. So what can we do?' He straightened. 'Fight back, tha's what we can do.'

'People aren't allowed to defend themselves in New York City,' she snapped.

'Uh-huh. Only – well, sure, we can't tell Mama-lo. We can't let her know. She'd have to forbid, wouldn't she? No matter what we'd lose. But if some of us was ready to fight back, an' word o' that got aroun' underground, why, maybe we'll never have to. How 'bout that? You been aroun' a lot. What do you think?'

'I'll need to hear a great deal more. And, yes, think hard.' Already Aliyat suspected what her decision would be.

'Sure. We'll talk whenever you can spare the time, Missus-lo Rosa. We're dependin' on you.'

On me! she thought, and pride thrilled.

They walked mute thereafter to the entrance of her home building. She gave him her hand. 'Thanks for being so honest, Randy,' she said.

'Thank you, Missus-lo.' In this brighter illumination, his smile gleamed. 'When can we meet again?'

Temptation blazed. Why not at once? He was strong and handsome in his rugged fashion, and it had been a long time, and ... she wondered if she had at last become able to give of herself, whole-heartedly, without hate or contempt or even suspicion.

But no. He might be shocked. Certainly many members would be., if they found out. Better not chance it.

'Soon,' she promised. 'Right now I have some record-keeping chores to finish. In fact, I'd better put in a couple of hours tonight, before I go to sleep. Soon, though.'

6

From the lounge where he sat, turning over the pages of a British magazine without the text especially registering on his mind, Hanno could see into the foyer. Twice a woman entered and his heart jumped; but she went on toward the elevator. The third time proved the charm. She spoke with the clerk at the desk, turned, and moved hesitantly his way. At once he rose from the leather of the armchair. It crossed his mind that long residence in this country might not have given a Russian Western habits of punctuality; and a Russian perhaps hundreds of years old –

She came in and halted. His vision flashed across her. Becker's description was sketchy, and the German had been under orders not to ask for photographs, lest a prospect take alarm. She was about as tall as Hanno, which put her on the short side among modern Nordics though average among her own kind. A full figure, lithely and erectly borne, gave the impression of more height. Her features were broad, blunt, comely. Blond hair in a Dutch bob framed fair skin. Quietly dressed, she wore low shoes and carried a shoulder bag.

Her brows lifted. Tongue touched lips. If she was nervous, which would be more than understandable, she mastered it gamely. 'Mr … Cauldwell?'

How could that husky voice sound familiar? Just *déjà vu*, no doubt. Hanno bowed. 'At your service, ah, Dr Rasmussen,' he said. 'Thank you for coming.'

She constructed a smile for him. 'Miss Rasmussen will do, if you please. You will remember I am a veterinarian, not a physician.' Her English came readily, though the heavy accent was more Slavic than Danish. 'I am sorry to be late. It is because of an emergency in my office.'

'That's okay. You couldn't leave an animal to suffer.' He recalled how much they made of shaking hands here and extended his. 'I am glad you could, and would, come at all.'

Her grip was firm. The blue gaze intensified upon him, no longer shy. Not forward, either; watchful; he thought of a hunter. Yes, but it was also – puzzled, more than this curious meeting warranted? 'Your agent made it sound … interesting,' she said. 'I can promise nothing until I have heard more.'

'Of course. We need to talk quite a lot; and then, if I am not presuming, I would like the pleasure of your company at dinner.' Win or lose, he would. Why did she excite him so? 'The talk should be private. This hotel doesn't have a bar, but we can find one close by, or a coffee shop or anything you wish, as long as we won't be distracted or overheard.'

She went straighter to business than he had dared hope. 'I think you are a gentleman, Mr Cauldwell. Let us use your room.'

'Wonderful!' Old manners returned and he offered her his arm. She took it with a natural grace making up for the fact that she had obviously not had much practice.

They were silent in the elevator, never quite looking at each other. Damn, he thought, something about her haunts me. Could I have seen her before? Hardly possible. Oh, I have visited Denmark now and then, but while she's sightly, she wouldn't stand out in a crowd of such women as they've got here.

He had taken a top-floor suite. The hotel was fairly old, far from Copenhagen's loftiest, but these windows gave a view over bustling downtown and lovely, soaring spires. Furnishings were comfortable, a little faded, reminiscent of a gentility well-nigh vanished from the world. She smiled more easily than at first. 'You have good taste in places to stay,' she murmured.

'This is a favorite of mine,' he said. 'Has been for a long time.'

'Do you travel much?'

'Going to and fro in the earth, and walking up and down in it. Please be seated. What would you like to drink? I have a small refrigerator, beer, akvavit, Scotch, soda, or I'll be glad to send down for anything else.'

'Coffee, thank you.'

A cautious choice. He rang. Turning around, he saw that she hadn't taken cigarettes from her bag. Probably then, unlike most Danes, she didn't smoke. He wished for his pipe to soothe him but decided against it and settled facing her.

'I am not sure how much Becker made clear to you,' he began.

'Very little. I am frank about that. He told of the … Rufus Institute? … in America and how it wanted to study persons who … can expect to live for many years. The interest in history – there are more measures of intelligence than that. I went away feeling very unsure. When you telephoned from across the ocean, I wondered whether to make this appointment. But I will hear you, Mr Cauldwell.'

'I am the man who founded the Institute.'

She studied him. 'You must be rich.'

He nodded. 'Yes.' Himself alert for any clue whatsoever: 'I am a great deal older than I look.'

Did the breath hiss inward between her teeth? 'To me you seem young.'

'As you do to me. May I ask your age?'

'I told Mr Becker.' Starkness stood forth. 'No doubt he, or you, or a detective of yours checked the public records.'

He lifted a palm. 'Hold on. Please. We both need to be honest, but let's not push ahead too hard. Allow me a few questions. You are Russian by birth?'

'Ukrainian. I reached Denmark in 1950. By now I am naturalized.'

He made his lips shape a soundless whistle. 'Almost forty years ago, and you must have been adult then.'

Her grin was taut. 'You are searching for people who age slowly, no? How old are *you*, Mr Cauldwell?'

'I wonder if we shouldn't postpone that subject a while,' he said carefully.

'Perhaps … we … should.' Both of them shivered.

'I don't want to pry,' he said, 'but I had better know. Are you married? I am not, currently.'

The flaxen head shook. 'Nor I. I have not married in this country. I got permission to change my last name. "Olga" is common enough in Denmark, but the rest of it, nobody could spell or pronounce.'

'And "Rasmussen" here is like "Smith" in the USA. You didn't want to be more conspicuous than you could help, did you?'

'Not at first. Things have changed since.' She sighed. 'I have wondered lately if I might even go back, now when they say the terror has been ended. Never a day but I have longed for my motherland.'

'You could have too much explaining to do.'

'Probably. I did go away as a refugee, an outlaw.'

That was not precisely what I meant, he thought; and I suspect she realizes it.

'The Danish government knows, down in its archives,' she proceeded. 'I said little to Mr Becker, but you may as well hear. During the war I was a soldier in the Red Army. Many Ukrainians wanted to be free – of Stalin or of the Soviet Union itself, because we are the old, true Russians. Kiev was the seed and the root of the whole Russian nation. The *Moskaly* came later. Many of us welcomed the Germans for liberators. That was a terrible mistake, but how could anybody know, when for more than twenty years all we heard was lies or silence? Some men enlisted with Hitler. I never did, I tell you. One resists the invader, whoever he is. But when the Germans retreated, they left parts of the Ukraine in revolt. Stalin needed years to crush it. Have you heard this?'

'I know something about it,' he said bleakly. 'If I remember aright, the resistance movement had a headquarters in Copenhagen. Just the same, hardly a word about what was happening got into the liberal –' no, in Europe 'liberal' retained its original meaning – 'the Western establishment press.'

'I had been discharged, but I had friends, kinsmen, people of mine in the rebellion. Some openly fought, some were sympathizers who gave what help they could whenever they dared. I knew I was under suspicion. If I did not soon betray somebody to Stalin's secret police, they would come for me. Then it would be the labor camp or the bullet in the head or worse.' Anguish reawakened. 'But how could I join the rebels? How could I shoot at Russian soldiers, my comrades of the war? I fled. I made my way to the West.'

'That was an awesome doing,' he said, altogether sincerely. It had meant hunger, thirst, hiding, running, walking, slipping past guard posts, surviving on what scraps of food she chanced to find, for a thousand miles and more.

'I am strong,' she replied. 'I had my sharpshooter skills. And I had prepared myself.' Fingers gripped the arms of her chair. 'It was not my first time like that.'

Thunder racketed in his skull. 'I have ... had adventures ... of my own ... in the past.'

A knock sounded. Hanno got up and admitted a bellboy, who brought a tray with urn, cups, sugar, cream, and *kringler*. While he oversaw its placement and tipped the man, he said, because lightness was necessary but stillness impossible, 'You've had a peaceful time since, I gather.'

He felt the same need was driving her. 'I got asylum in Denmark.' From what officials, and how? he wondered. Not that it mattered. If you knocked around in the world long enough, you learned the ways of it, and the byways. 'I wanted that because of the Ukrainian connection, but I came to love this country. They are dear people, and the land is so mild. I worked on a farm, decided I would like to be a veterinarian, went to school, studied English and

German also, to talk with foreigners who might bring me their pets. Now I have a practice out in Kongens Lyngby, a nice suburb.'

The bellman had left. Hanno walked back to stand above her. 'But you are of retirement age, or nearly,' he said. 'Your friends marvel at how you still appear young. They tease you about a fountain of youth. They begin to wonder, though, why you don't retire. The government does too. Where will you go, Olga?'

She gazed steadily up at him. 'Yes, they keep excellent records in Denmark. Where would you suggest that I go? And what is *your* real name?'

His pulse hammered. 'All right,' he said, 'no more pussyfooting. I didn't want to scare you off. However, I believe I can come right out with the truth after all.' He resumed his chair, not to seem threatening or attempting of dominance. One like her would react fiercely to that, he judged. 'What I am about to tell you will sound like insanity, or some wild confidence game, unless you are what I'm pretty sure you are. Do not take fright. Listen to me. Go open the door and stand by it if you wish.'

She shook her head. Her breasts rose and fell.

'As close as makes no difference,' Hanno said, 'I am three thousand years old. Do you care to tell me – What?'

She had gone wholly white. For a moment she sagged back in her chair. He half rose to help and reassure. She straightened. 'Cadoc,' she whispered.

'Huh?'

'Cadoc. You. It comes back to me. The trader in Kiev. Kiyiv, we called it then. When was that? Nearly one thousand years past, I think.'

Memory smote like a sudden look into the sun. 'You ... your name –'

'I was Svoboda then. In my heart I always am. But who are you really?'

Of course, he thought in his daze, neither would remember a briefly met mortal for very long, out of an uncountable myriad gone down into dust. But neither had ever quite forgotten, either. He called to mind now the phantom that had stirred in him at moments strewn through the centuries.

'S-Svoboda, yes,' he stammered. 'We rescued you.'

'And the night was golden. We could have had more!'

They left their chairs and stumbled into each other's arms.

7

Outside, the District of Columbia stewed in its summer. Air conditioning breathed coolness through Moriarty's office. The heat that he felt was dry, a fire. He slapped the magazine down onto his desk. The noise cracked. 'You bastard,' he mumbled. 'You evil, malignant –'

The intercom chimed. 'Mr Stoddard to see you, Senator,' announced his receptionist's voice.

Moriarty caught a breath and gusted it back as a laugh. 'Perfect timing!' he exclaimed. 'Send him right in.'

The man who entered was short, undistinguished-looking, and coldly competent. Sweat from outdoors glistened on his cheeks. He carried a brief-case. 'How do you do, sir,' he greeted. His glance went from face to desk and back again. 'You've been reading the latest, I see.'

'Of course,' Moriarty snapped. 'Sit down. Have you seen it?'

'Not yet.' Stoddard took a chair. 'I've been busy investigating the person responsible, you know.'

The fleshy man behind the desk picked up the magazine again and placed it under his dashingly styled reading glasses. 'Listen to this. The editorial. Deals with my speech in aid of the CCCP. I'm taking a paragraph at random, more or less.' Trained, his voice shed the throb of indignation and recited methodically:

'"The senator was introduced by peace and disarmament activist Dr Fulvia Bourne. He dealt with the embarrassment in masterly fashion. Rather than refer to her speech at the previous day's banquet, whether to endorse or dis-avow such colorful phrases as 'the Pentagon, a pentacle crowded with the demons of nuclear madness,' or 'the CIA – the Children Immolation Agency,' he made an unspeech of it and simply called her a modern Joan of Arc. That St Joan took arms in the cause of liberation became an unfact. Thence it was an easy transition to the necessity for statesmanship, for 'patience abroad but impatience at home.' Evidently the patience is to be with the likes of Srs Cas-tro and Ortega. After all, the senator's esteemed party colleague, the Reverend Nahaliel Young, addresses both these gentlemen as 'Dear Comrade.' We are to have no patience whatsoever with, say, South Africa. As for domestic pol-icy, an impatience to complete the destruction of the productive classes in America –"'

'Arrh!' he erupted. 'Why go on? Read it for yourself, if you can stand to.'

'May I ask a question, Senator?' Stoddard murmured.

'Certainly. I've always stood for free and open dialectic.'

Stoddard's gaze weighed Moriarty. 'Why do you let this Tannahill get your goat? He isn't writing anything that other opponents of yours don't.'

The broad countenance reddened. 'He puts no bounds on his nastiness. Opposition is different from persecution. You know how he tries not just to make trouble nationally, but to drive a wedge between me and my constituency.'

'Oh, he does operate out of New England and make a lot of regional refer-ences, but he's not in your state, Senator. And really, *The Chart Room* has a small circulation.'

'It only takes a small dose of virus, slipped to the right people, to infect a whole population. Tannahill's getting attention not just from old-line conservatives and neo-fascists, but on campuses, among the young.' Moriarty sighed. 'Oh, yes, the snake has his First Amendment rights, and I admit his gibes at me hurt more than they ought. I should be used to cruelty.'

'If I may say so, you often leave yourself open to the likes of him. I'd have advised you against addressing that rally.'

'In politics you take what allies you can find, and make the best of them.'

'Like South Africa? Sorry.' Stoddard didn't sound repentant.

Moriarty frowned but continued: 'The Committee does include some extremists, but damn it, they're extremists in a good cause. We need their energy and dedication.' He cleared his throat. 'Never mind. Let's get to business. The business of discovering who this Tannahill is and who's behind him. What can you tell me?'

'Nothing much, I'm afraid. As far as my investigators have dug, and they're good at their work, he's clean. True, they didn't manage to dig to the very bottom.'

'Oh?' Moriarty leaned forward. 'He remains the mystery man on that estate of his?' The remark was irresistible: 'He would have settled in New Hampshire, wouldn't he? "Live free or die." He may even believe it.'

'He's not a Howard Hughes-like recluse, if that's what you mean, Senator,' Stoddard replied. 'In fact, what makes him hard to learn about is that he's seldom at his place. He gets around – everywhere, maybe, though for the most part my men couldn't find out where he does go. Neither his household servants nor his magazine staff were any help to speak of. They're two handfuls of hand-picked individuals, long with him, loyal to him, close-mouthed. Not that they keep any shameful secrets.' He chuckled. 'No such luck. They simply don't know what the boss does away from them, and they have an antiquated Yankee notion that it's nobody's business.'

Moriarty gave his assistant a sharp glance. Sometimes he wondered whether Stoddard was not aiding him strictly for the pay. However, the fellow performed well enough that one must put up with his occasional impudence. 'What have you found?' Moriarty asked. 'No matter if you repeat things I already know.'

'I'm afraid that's what I'll mainly be doing.' The other man drew a sheet of paper from his briefcase and consulted the notes on it. 'Kenneth Alexander Tannahill was born 25 August 1933 in Troy, Vermont, a little town near the Canadian border. His parents moved away shortly afterward. A former neighbor, to whom they wrote a couple of letters, said they'd gone to Minnesota, but he couldn't remember precisely where. A North Woods hamlet. Everything's shadowy, nothing on record but the bare minimum of official stuff and a few old stories in an upstate newspaper.'

Excitement tingled in Moriarty. 'Do you mean this could be an assumed identity? Suppose the real Tannahills all died, say in an accident. A man with money, who wanted to cover his tracks, could set a detective agency to locating such a deceased family, one that suited his needs.'

'Maybe.' Stoddard sounded skeptical. 'Damn hard to prove.'

'Draft records from before the end of conscription?'

'I'd rather not try springing anything like that loose for you, Senator.'

'No, I suppose not. Unless we can turn up clues that justify it to the proper authorities.'

'Tannahill has never claimed he was ever in the service. We got that much. But a lot of men his age never were, in spite of Korea and Vietnam, for a variety of reasons. He's given no hints as to why he wasn't. Uh, it isn't that he acts evasive or secretive. Associates describe him as a genial sort with a ready fund of jokes and quips; though he does require competence from his employees, and gets it. He simply has a knack for turning conversation away from himself.'

'He would. Go on. Never married, I believe?'

'No. Not homosexual or impotent. There have been a few women over the years whom we've identified. Nothing especially serious, and none of them bear him any grudge.'

'Too bad. What kind of trail has he left on the West Coast?'

'Essentially zilch. He first surfaced in New Hampshire, bought his house and grounds, started his magazine, all as a – not exactly an employee of Tomek Enterprises. "Associate" or "agent" might be a better word. At any rate, Tomek finances him, and I'd guess that a lot of his trips are for purposes of reporting back to the old man.'

'Who's pretty shadowy himself, isn't he?' Moriarty stroked his chin. It puffed out a bit under his fingers. 'I've been thinking more and more that that line may well be worth pursuing.'

'Senator, my advice to you is to drop this whole business. It's expensive as hell, it takes up staff time you badly need in an election year, and I'm ninety-nine percent convinced it could never produce anything politically useful.'

'Do you think I am only a politician, Hank?'

'I've heard you describe your ideals.'

Moriarty reached decision. 'You're right, we can't go on chasing ghosts. At the same time, I feel it in my bones, something here won't bear the light of day. Yes, I have personal motivations too. Exposing it would be a coup; and I'm sick of Tannahill's baiting and want to lash back. We'll have to leave off the effort to get background information, I suppose, but I won't give up entirely.' He bridged his fingers and peered over them. 'Where is he at the moment?'

Stoddard shrugged. 'Someplace this side of the moon ... probably.'

Moriarty bit his lip. *The Chart Room* had been extra vicious about the decline of the American space program. 'Well, he'll have to come back eventually. I want his house and his office under surveillance. When he does show up, I want a twenty-four-hour tail on him. Understand?'

Stoddard began to form an answer, swallowed it, and nodded. 'Can do, if you don't mind paying what it costs.'

'I have money,' Moriarty said. 'My own if necessary.'

8

'What *is* wrong?'

Natalia Thurlow's question cut – or probed, like a sword early in an engagement. Hanno realized that she would no longer be denied. Nonetheless he stood for a while yet, staring out of Robert Cauldwell's living room window. The late summer dark had fallen. Where his body staved off reflections he saw lights in their thousands, down the hill and through the lower city to the peace that lay mightily upon the waters. Thus had Syracuse basked in wealth and happiness, with the greatest mechanicians of the age to perfect her defenses; and meanwhile the austere Romans prepared themselves.

'You came home yesterday like a man in a dream,' Natalia went on at his back. 'Then today you left practically at dawn, and haven't returned till now, still locked up inside yourself.'

'I told you why,' he said. 'Business accumulated while I was gone.'

'What do you mean? Except for your interest in the Rufus Lab, what do you do any longer, locally?'

The challenge made him turn around. She stood rigid, fists at her sides. The pain that he saw hurt him too; the rising anger that he heard was a kind of balm.

'You know I have things going elsewhere,' he reminded her. She had seen the modest downtown office he maintained. He had never described just what it was for.

'Indeed. Whenever I tried to call you, your machine answered.'

'I had to get around. What did you want? I phoned the machine here to say you shouldn't wait dinner for me.'

In point of fact, throughout the day he had mostly been Joe Levine, briefing a couple of other attorney-accountants on Charles Tomek's tax audit so that they could take over while he was gone for some unpredictable time on some unspecified matter. They already knew the general situation and many details, of course. No single agent could cope with Uncle Sam. (And what did those hordes of paper shufflers produce that was of any value to any living soul?) However, there were certain tricky points they needed to understand.

At that, it could prove costly, leaving them to their own devices. Not that they might reveal illegalities. None existed. Hanno knew better than to allow such a crack in his defenses against the state. But he couldn't explain to them why Mr Tomek must not be found on his travels and brought back to help cope.

Ephemera. Expendable. Svoboda would soon arrive, to be the fifth in the fellowship.

And beyond her – Despite himself, his pulse thuttered.

'I thought we could meet for dinner at a restaurant,' Natalia was saying.

'Sorry. That wouldn't have worked. I grabbed a sandwich.' Untrue. He could not have stayed calm in her company. He wasn't quite the poker player he had supposed. Maybe Svoboda had thawed something within him, or shaken it till it began to crack.

'You refuse me the reason you were so rushed, don't you?' Natalia sighed. 'You're a wily one. Only now does it really dawn on me how little you've ever let slip about what you do, about anything meaningful that concerns you.'

'Look, let's not fight,' he urged. 'You know I'm, uh, taciturn by nature.'

'No, you're not. That's the trouble. You talk and talk, glib, interesting, but aside from those Neanderthal politics of yours, how much do you seriously say?' Before he could reply, she raised a hand to hush him. 'In spite of that, I've discovered how to read certain clues. Whoever you met in Denmark, it wasn't the "promising subject" you spoke of so vaguely. And then when we got home from the airport and you looked through the mail, that one letter in it that rocked you back – You couldn't completely hide your reaction. But I foresaw you wouldn't show it to me or speak a single word about it.'

Assuredly not, Hanno thought. Especially since Asagao, the naive little sweetheart, had penned it in her awkwardly precise English. 'It's private, confidential.'

'A person in Idaho, as well as Denmark?'

Damn! She'd noticed the return address. He should have cautioned the Asian pair about communicating with him. But they knew his Cauldwell identity from the Rufus connection, and they were timid about the Tomek complex – an unfamiliar kind of thing, where perhaps strangers would intercept messages – and it had never before occurred to him that they, of all people on earth, might bumble onto a fresh scent.

As it was, Natalia had been honorable and not steamed the envelope open. Well, he'd made sure of her character before taking up with her more than casually.

Did he indeed understand her, though? She was a bright and complicated person. That was what had attracted him. She might have had fewer surprises to spring on him if he'd been more forthcoming with her.

Too late now, he thought. The sadness that crossed him was half weariness. Even for a creature of his vitality, this had been an exhausting day.

He roughened his language: 'Get off my back, will you? Neither of us owns the other.'

She stiffened further. 'No, you haven't wanted any commitment, have you? What am I to you, besides a sexual convenience?'

'Oh, for God's sake, stop this nonsense!' He made a step in her direction. 'What we've had was, was splendid. Let's not ruin it.'

She stood unstirring, save that her eyes grew very wide. 'Was?' she whispered.

He had wanted to tell her in kindlier wise. Maybe this was better. 'I have to take off again. Not sure when I'll be back.'

Fly east. As Tannahill, engage a private detective to collect the basic information about those Unity people, take a few surreptitious photos, provide him the basis for deciding whether to approach them directly or not. Meanwhile Svoboda would have wound up her affairs in Europe, obtained her visa and ticket, boarded a plane. She'd be landing in New York. The seclusion of the Tannahill property offered a chance to get genuinely acquainted, to catch up on the past millennium.

'And you won't tell me why,' Natalia said, flat-voiced.

'I am sorry, but I can't.' He had long since learned to avoid elaborate fictions.

She looked past him, or through him. 'Another woman? Maybe. But more to it than that. Else you'd just cast me off.'

'No, listen – Look Nat, you're welcome to keep on living here, in fact I hope you do, and –'

She shook her head. 'I have my pride.' Her gaze sharpened. 'What are you up to? Who are you conspiring with, and why?'

'I say again, this is a personal matter.'

'Maybe it is. Considering the attitudes you've expressed, I can't be sure.' She lifted her hand anew. 'Oh, I won't go bearing tales, especially since you give me nothing to go on. But I've got to cover my ass. You understand that, don't you? If the cops ever question me, I'll tell them what little I know. Because I don't owe you any loyalty any longer.'

'Hey, wait!' He reached to take hold of her. She warded him off. 'Let's sit down and have a drink and talk this out.'

She considered him. 'How much more will you actually have to say?'

'I – well, I care about you and –'

'Never mind. You can make up the Hide-a-Bed for yourself. I'll pack my things tomorrow.'

She went from him.

I would have had to depart before long in any case, he could not cry after her. *It should have been easier than this. At least I'll occupy no more of the years that are left you.*

He wondered if she, once alone tonight, would weep.

9

Rain fell slowly through windlessness, almost a mist. Its tarnished silver hid the slabs of apartment buildings and muffled every noise. There were only wet grass, dripping leaves, glimmer of marshwater along the walkway. Nobody else was about on such a midweek afternoon in northwest Copenhagen. Having left his place and gone the short distance to Utterslev Mose Park, Peter Astrup and Olga Rasmussen had the world to themselves.

Beneath his cap, droplets glinted on the round young face like tears. 'But you cannot leave just like this,' he pleaded.

She looked straight ahead. Both her hands, after he let go, she had jammed into the pockets of her coat. 'It is sudden,' she admitted.

'Brutally sudden!'

'That's why I asked you to take the day off so I could meet you. Time is short, and I have much to do first.'

'After I hadn't seen or heard from you since –' He seized her arm. 'What were you doing? Who have you been with?'

She edged aside. He felt the unspoken command and released her. He was always gentle, she thought, sympathetic, yes, he may be the sweetest lover I have ever had or ever will. 'I don't want to hurt you more than I must, Peter,' she said low. 'This way seems best.'

'But what of our holiday in Finland?' He gulped. 'Pardon me, that was an idiotic thing to ask ... now.'

'Not really.' She made herself regard him again. 'I was looking forward the same as you. This opportunity, though, is too great.'

'Is it?' he demanded desperately. 'To go haring off to America and – and what? You haven't made that at all clear.'

'It's confidential. Scientific research. I promised to say nothing about it. But you know how interested I am.'

'Yes. Your mind, your reach of knowledge, I believe that drew me to you more than your beauty.'

'Oh, come,' she tried to laugh. 'I realize I'm rather plain.'

He stopped. Perforce she did likewise. They faced each other in the chilly gray. Because he was still youthful, he blurted, 'You are mysterious, you hide something, I know you do, and you are, are incomparable as a woman.'

And Hanno, she thought, has also passed many mortal lifetimes in learning.

'I, I love you, Olga,' Peter stammered. 'I've told you before. I do again. Will you marry me? With papers and, and everything.'

'Oh, my dear,' she murmured. 'I'm old enough to be –' Abruptly she could not say, 'Your mother.' Instead: 'I am too old for you. I may not look it, but I have told you. We've enjoyed this past couple of years.'

We have, we have. And Hanno – what do I truly know of Hanno? What can I await from him? He and I have both lived too long in secret, it has surely misshaped us in ways we don't feel, but he prowled the world for thrice the time that I abided in my Russia. He has been fascinating and challenging and, yes, fun; but already I have glimpsed a ruthlessness. Or is it an inward loneliness? How much is he able to care for anyone or for anything beyond naked survival?

Through the confusion she heard herself finish: 'We knew from the first that it couldn't last. Let's end it cleanly, while it's still happy.'

He stood slumped. 'I don't care how old you are,' he said. 'I love you.'

Exasperation stirred. You're being babyish, she kept from saying. Well, what could I expect from a person not yet thirty? You have nothing left for me to discover. 'I'm sorry.' No doubt I should have declined you at the beginning, but the flesh has its demands and liaisons here are easy come, easy go. With Hanno and those others – Is an immortal marriage possible? I don't think I'm actually in love with him yet, or he with me. Perhaps we never will be. But that's no foundation for an enduring partnership anyway. Certainly not by itself. We'll have to see what happens.

We'll *see*. What *happens*.

'Don't take it this hard,' she said. 'You'll get over it, and find the right girl.'

And settle down to raise children who will grow up into the same comfortable narrowness and crumble into the same dust. Unless we are on the verge of fire and slaughter and a new dark age, as Hanno thinks we may well be.

Svoboda smiled at Peter. 'Meanwhile,' she said quietly, 'we might go back to your apartment and give ourselves a grand farewell.'

After all, it would only be until tomorrow.

10

Corinne Macandal received her caller in the Victorian living room. 'How do you do,' she said, and offered her hand. His was sinewy, unexpectedly hard, the clasp light but firm. He bowed over hers with an archaic assurance. 'Please be seated. Would you like a cup of coffee or tea?'

Kenneth Tannahill kept his feet. 'Thank you,' he replied, 'but could we please talk in confidence, where nobody can overhear?'

Surprised, she looked closer at him. Her immediate thought was: How old is he, anyway? Black hair, smooth skin, supple frame spoke of youth, but more than the leanness of the countenance suggested a man who had seen many years and much of the world. The signs were too subtle for her to name, nonetheless real. 'Indeed? I thought you wanted an interview for your magazine.'

His smile was somehow feline. 'That isn't exactly what my note asked for, though it did give that impression, didn't it?'

Wariness laid hold of her. 'What do you want, then? I must confess I'm not familiar with your, m-m, *Chart Room*.'

'It's not a big publication. Nor sensationalistic, may I add. Mostly it runs articles, or essays, on current events. We often go into history or anthropology, trying to put things in perspective.'

'It sounds interesting.' Macandal drew breath. 'However, I'm afraid I must decline an interview or anything like that. I don't want publicity. It's distasteful to me personally, and it might harm the Unity.'

'Really? I should think if the work you people are doing – evidently in many ways a unique approach – if it became widely known, you'd get more support, cooperation, everything you need. Others might be inspired to imitate you.'

'I doubt they could, successfully. We *are* unique. One of the things that makes it possible for us to do what we do is precisely our smallness, our intimacy. Being stared at could destroy that.'

Tannahill's large, half oblique eyes sought hers and held steady. 'I suspect it's less important than you yourself, my lady,' he said in almost an undertone. 'And your associate, Ms. Donau.'

Alarm stabbed. Macandal drew herself up and raised her voice a bit. 'What are you after? Will you please come to the point?'

'My apologies. No offense intended. On the contrary. But I do believe we should talk in complete privacy.'

She came to a decision. 'Very well. Wait a minute and I'll issue instructions about that.'

Stepping into the hall, she found a maid and whispered, 'The gentleman and I will be in the sanctum. Tell Boyd and Jerry to stand by, and come in at once if I ring.'

The girl gaped. 'You 'spec' trouble, ma'am?'

'Not really,' Macandal reassured her. 'But just in case.' You didn't keep going immortally by omitting precautions.

She returned and led Tannahill in among the things that stood for power. He seemed to scan them thoroughly in the moment that it took her to shut the door. 'Now do sit down,' she told him, more curtly than she had intended.

He obeyed. She took a chair across the coffee table. 'I'd appreciate your explaining your errand as quickly as possible,' she said.

He couldn't quite hide the tension that was also in him. 'Forgive me if I don't,' he answered. 'What I'm here about is tremendous. I have to be sure of you before I dare let you in on it. Let me start by promising you there will be no threats, demands, attempts to make you do anything wrong. I belong to an unusual class of people. I have reason to think you and Ms. Donau do too. If so, we'll invite you to join us, for purposes of mutual help and companionship.'

Can he be – ? Briefly, the dimness of the chamber hazed before her and a roaring was in her ears. Through it she heard:

'I'll be honest, and hope you won't get angry. I've had a detective agency prepare a report on you two and your organization for me. They did not pry. They simply went around for about a week, chatted with persons who were willing, took a few snapshots, otherwise looked through newspaper files and relevant public records. It was only for purposes of briefing me, so that I could come today prepared to talk intelligently and not waste your time.' Tannahill smiled a bit. 'You, the individual, remain as enigmatic as ever. I know practically nothing about you except that according to those files and the recollections of two or three aged Unity members, your mother founded this group which you head, and you resemble her. On the other hand, if I'm not mistaken, I have somewhat more information about Rosa Donau.'

Macandal summoned composure. Her heart wouldn't stop racing, but her mind ran smoothly and every sense was whetted. If this truly was an immortal, need that be a menace, be aught but joy? Of course, if he wasn't – Yes, she too must tread with care. 'Then why haven't you approached her first?' she asked.

'She might not like that. Can't you see, I'm trying not to arouse fears.' Tannahill leaned forward, hands on knees. 'May I tell you a story? Call it a piece of fiction if you like. Or a parable; you're obviously well-read.'

She nodded.

'Once upon a time,' he began slowly, 'a woman lived in what is now Istanbul. In those days they called it Constantinople, and it was the capital of a great empire. The woman wasn't born there, but in Syria. She'd had a hard life, knocked around a lot in the world and taken many cruel knocks from it. Yes, she was much older than she appeared. Not as old as her profession, for which she needed that youthful-looking body. She did well in it, though at intervals she had to pull up stakes and relocate under a different name. To her, at last, came a man who was also older than he seemed. He and his partner had wandered far and wide. At present they were traders, on the Russian river route.'

Always he watched her. She couldn't take it any more. 'Stop!' she cried. Drawing breath: 'Mr … Tannahill, are you by any chance associated with … a gentleman named Willock?'

The fingers whitened on his knees. 'Yes. That is, I know of him. He may not have heard of me. A longevity research foundation engaged him to find people who carry – the genes for long life. Extremely long life.'

'I see.' Strange how calm she suddenly was, how detached. It was as if somebody else spoke. 'Rosa and I saw his advertisement. We found it interesting.'

'But you didn't respond.'

'No. We have to be careful. The Unity works among, and against, some bad types. We have our enemies, and they have no scruples.'

'So I've gathered. I swear to you, uh, Miss Macandal, this group I belong to is decent. In fact, we were alerted to your existence because two among us do human rehabilitation themselves. And we are few. Oh, very few,' he ended.

'Nevertheless, you must give me time to consider this. You've learned about us. What do we know about you?'

Tannahill sat silent for the better part of a minute before he nodded. 'That's reasonable. Ask anything you like.'

She lifted her brows. 'Do you guarantee to answer every single question, truthfully and in full?'

He threw back his head and laughed. 'No. Good for you!' Turning serious: 'Not before we fully trust each other. Let me do whatever I can toward that.'

'For the moment, nothing. I want to run an independent check on you. Read a few issues of your magazine. Find out how you live, what your neighbors think of you, that sort of thing. What you did to us. It shouldn't take long. Then Rosa and I will plan our next move.'

He smiled, visibly easing. 'What you're telling me is, "Don't call us, we'll call you." Okay. On my side we have both time and patience. We know how to wait. Nothing will happen till you want it to.'

He reached in a pocket and offered his card to her. 'That's my New Hampshire address. My friend and I – I'm not in town alone – we'll return there tomorrow. Phone whenever you wish, or write if you prefer. If we go away, I'll tell the staff how to get in touch with me, and should be able to come back here on a day's notice.'

'Thank you.'

He came near winning her over at once by promptly rising and saying, 'No, my thanks to you. I look forward to hearing at your convenience.' He paused. 'Please tell my fable to Ms. Donau, and add the happy ending. The man in it stopped long ago being angry at the woman. He hopes she'll enjoy meeting him again.'

'I'll tell her,' Macandal agreed. They clasped hands afresh, a touch that clung the least bit, but neither spoke while she saw him to the door.

Her gaze followed him till he had disappeared down the mean street, walking briskly and fearlessly. Well, she thought, he can take care of himself, he's been in worse places than Harlem by daylight ... Damn, what a charmer!

Or am I just reading that into him? Aliyat may well be right, an immortal man is not necessarily a good man.

If he is, though – if *they* are – She still hasn't explained to me exactly what she's got against him –

What am I waiting for? Why am I hanging back? My God, he's a man. There are probably other men.

Cool it, girl!

The flood of lust receded. It left her atremble, but able to laugh at herself, and that was a cleansing. Celibacy had been the price she must pay; Mama-lo could not take a series of lovers and dared not take a husband. She thought: I was proud of my self-control, and overlooked how self-important I was getting. Down underneath, honey, you're just another raunchy, limited, woundable human being.

One who's got responsibilities, though.

She went inside again and upstairs to a room that served as a private office. Its prosaic furnishings and equipment brought her further down from dizziness. She had work to do.

Macandal settled at the desk and reached for the phone. Among the numbers keyed in were three for certain police officers and one for a middle-rank agent of the Federal Bureau of Investigation. The Unity had saved those men when they were children. Restless, they had not stayed, but by then it had equipped them to handle the world and they remembered. Not that any of them would betray his trust; nor would she ever ask him to. However, more than once they had looked into matters for her, taking for granted that her unspecified reasons were legitimate. Through them she could quickly find out a great deal about Kenneth Tannahill – perhaps even some things he himself didn't know.

11

The cab driver had taken on a grim expression when Aliyat gave him the address. He was plainly glad to let her out there and be gone. For a moment she felt forsaken.

Twilight lingered in the sky, but the rotting walls around her closed most of it off and night already possessed the street. What lampglow fell dully on it showed bare pavement, cracked sidewalks, scraps of paper and plastic, shards of glass, empty cans, cigarette butts, refuse less describable. A few windows, not boarded up, glowered at her. She saw nobody looking from them. It was as if she could smell the fear, one more stench among those that loaded an air still hot.

She hastened to the Unity's tenement. The facade was as dingy as the rest, refurbishing must wait its turn, but she ought to find freshness well advanced within. The workmen had gone home hours ago. Had the neighborhood shown life while they and their cheerful clatter were on hand?

The door was locked. It hadn't been on her last visit. She glanced over her shoulder as she leaned on the buzzer, and gripped her purse tightly against her ribs.

A dark outline appeared in the safety-webbed glass. The man was studying her through a peephole. He took what felt like a long time to let her in. She recognized him but not the other standing nearby, though each wore the badge of a security volunteer. Well, she could not know every member any more. Neither man was he whom she had expected.

'Missus-lo!' the first exclaimed. 'What're you doin' here, this late?'

'I need to see Randy Castle,' she said fast. 'I was told he's staying here now.'

'Yeah, he is.' A tongue clicked. 'You shouldn't of come, Missus-lo. 'Speci'lly not alone.'

I realized that as soon as I arrived, she kept from admitting. Instead: 'Well, he works all day.' – for a hauling company, which kept him on the move, unavailable to her. 'I thought he'd be at Hope Flower.' – the Unity complex where he had an apartment, in a safer district than this. 'When he didn't answer my calls, after I'd tried for hours, I rang his parents and they told me where he was. We need him for a job and he hasn't any phone here.'

'We do.' The guard gestured at the instrument on a table amidst the clutter left by the carpenters. 'I'd of fetched him.'

'No, I'm sorry, this is a confidential matter.'

'I see.' His trust was instant and absolute. 'Well, he's right down the hall, Number Three.' As he pointed, he forced a smile. 'Don't you worry none, Missus-lo. We'll get you home okay.'

'One way or t'other,' muttered his companion.

Beyond the lobby, the corridor had been restored, awaiting only paint and a carpet. She knocked on a new door. The big man flung it open. 'What?' he growled, and then, seeing her: 'Hey, what's goin' on?'

'I have to talk with you,' Aliyat said.

With awkward, touching deference he ushered her in and closed the door again. The apartment was neatly finished but barely furnished, no tenants having been expected yet. Several books rested on a table beside a hotplate, and he had been covering notepaper with scrawled exercises. Like most young folk of the Unity, he was improving his education; his dream was to become an engineer. 'Make yourself to home, Missus-lo,' tumbled from his lips. 'Glad to see you, but wish you hadn't come, know what I mean? What can I do for you?'

Because he wanted her to, she took the single chair. He offered to make coffee. She shook her head, and he sat down on the floor at her feet. 'What's wrong?' she inquired. 'Why have you moved? Where's Gus?' – the former night watchman.

Starkness replied. 'Laid up, Missus-lo. Bunch o' punks came in, uh, four nights ago an' beat him pretty bad.'

'Has Mama-lo heard?' she asked, appalled.

'N-not yet. We figured might be best to tell you first, get your 'pinion.' The disciples trying to protect the saint, Aliyat thought. And Corinne might, after all, order abandonment of the project rather than grappling with violence. Men who have learned to be proud don't easily retreat. 'Only you was out of town.'

'Yes, this past couple of weeks. I'm sorry, I should have left word where I could be reached, but I never thought there'd be an emergency like this.'

'Sure,' he said, quite sincerely. 'You couldn't of known. You needed a vacation bad, you did. We noticed how tired you was gettin'.'

Not really, she thought. At least, not in the flesh. Still, it's true, administration and treasury and accounting and counseling and – everything I do for us, mostly by myself because we can't afford a proper staff – it does wear me down. No matter how much the Unity means to me, I cannot make it my whole life. I don't have the spirit, the goodness, for that. From time to time I've got to get away, take what I've saved out of my little paychecks and go elsewhere under a different name, enjoy a bit of luxury, glamour, fun, have an affair if I meet somebody attractive. (And mostly, these past several years, that's been a man, not a woman; the Unity has washed away a lot of bitterness and started many sores healing.) Why am I talking to myself like this? To push away guilt, that I was absent? 'How is Gus?'

'He'll be all right. Healer Jules fixed him up neat as any regular doctor could have, and they're takin' care of him at his place.'

'You didn't notify the police, then?'

'What use? Just put ourselves to a lot o' trouble.'

'Listen,' Aliyat rapped, 'how often must Mama-lo and I explain, the police are not our enemies? The criminals are.' I'm only half a hypocrite, she thought. Mostly, I guess, the cops mean well. But they're saddled with laws that breed crime worse than Prohibition ever did.

'Well, if nothin' else, they're stretched too thin,' Castle said defensively. 'They can't post a round-the-clock watch for us, can they? And Gus told us those scumbags promised worse if we don't clear out. Maybe firebombing, even. We decided we'd strengthen night-time security. That ought to discourage 'em. It's why me and some other men are stayin' here.'

Chill crept along Aliyat's backbone. The street outside was bare and quiet. So quiet. Had word gone around that something was in the works?

What could she do? Nothing, unless later. 'Do be careful,' she begged. 'None of this is worth losing a single life.' You might have fifty or sixty years left you, Randy, dear.

'Um, you too, Missus-lo. Don't you risk comin' here again after dark. Not till we got the quarter cleaned up.' He sat straight, quickly eager. 'What you want? How can we help you?'

That wakened the thrill that had coursed through when she spoke with Corinne upon her return today. It flamed the sordid surroundings out of her. She couldn't sit still, she sprang to her feet. 'I have to take a long drive, up into New Hampshire. I'll be needing a driver and – let's hope not, but maybe a bodyguard. Someone strong and completely reliable, including able to keep his mouth shut. I thought right away of you. Are you willing?'

He likewise had risen, to loom above her and exult: 'At your service, Missus-lo, an' thank you!'

'You probably needn't lose time from work. Now that I know I can count on you, I'll write ahead and tell them to expect me.' She didn't really think mail would be intercepted, but she'd use a private express service to be safe, and to make sure of overnight delivery. Tannahill could reply in the same fashion. 'We'll leave early Saturday morning. If everything goes well, we can return Sunday evening. Or I might stay a while and you come back alone.' If I decide I dare trust them there.

'Sure.' He grew troubled. 'You mentioned a bodyguard. Could it turn dangerous? I wouldn't feel right about takin' you into danger.'

'No, I don't expect any physical threats.' Is that absolutely true? she wondered. With a grin: 'It might help my errand if you're in the background being huge. My purpose will be to convey a message and then, I think, confer.'

The message being that Corinne has learned Kenneth Tannahill is under close surveillance, apparently on behalf of a United States senator. She had just about decided to mail him the warning when I arrived. I told her that if I deliver it in person, that ought to rock him back enough that I can grab the initiative and – and what? Take his measure?

Cadoc, Hanno, it can only be him, whom I robbed and tried to get killed. He told her he's forgiven me, and nine hundred years would be a long time to carry a grudge, unless it's festered that whole while. We've got to decide whether to join with him and whoever else is in his band; and how to join, on what terms, if we do. I think I can recognize a crook or a monster sooner, more certainly, than Mama-lo.

'This will be kind of peculiar, though, Randy,' she said. 'I need to enter the place and leave it unbeknownst to – well, whoever might be watching from outside. I'll figure out some sort of disguise. Maybe cut my hair short, make my face up dark, dress like a man, and we carry tool kits, to seem like workers sent to do some repair job. The car we'll drive is old and plain, and I'll get hold of New Hampshire plates.' Though the Unity shunned crime, you were bound to learn who in town could supply what for a price. 'We'll switch along the way.'

An excitement she had well-nigh forgotten overrode forebodings. Shoot the dice and to hell with the authorities. Am I still an outlaw at heart?

But here stands this boy. 'I'm sorry,' she finished. 'We can't let you sit in on our talks, and I can't tell you anything. All I can do is swear this is honest business.'

'I wouldn't doubt that for one second, Missus-lo,' he answered.

Her fingers closed on the brown hand before her. 'You *are* a darling.'

Through the door went a crash and a scream.

'Hoy! Them?' Castle plunged across the room. Racket resounded. 'Stay put, Missus-lo!' he yelled. From a carton on the floor he pulled an object darkly metallic and sped for the door. 'I'm comin', brothers! Hang on!'

'No, wait, drop that thing, don't, Randy –' Aliyat had no time to think. She followed the man who grasped the pistol that was forbidden to common folk.

Down the hall. Beyond the lobby Aliyat saw safety glass shattered. Smoke eddied against the night. Half a dozen men, youths, creatures were in. The guards – Two invaders held one watchman hard against the wall. Where was his companion? Others of the Unity boiled forth at Aliyat's back.

'Halt, you bastards!' Castle roared. His gun barked, a warning shot aloft.

An attacker responded, straight.

Castle lurched, reeled back, somehow fired levelly before he fell. Aliyat glimpsed the blood that spouted from his throat.

The hammer smote her.

12

Moriarty was at breakfast when Stoddard called. The senator kept a phone in that room too. Even in this his summer home, in his own secure state, he must always be ready; and the number was unlisted, which gave some protection.

The voice immediately yanked his full awareness to it. Once he whistled, once he breathed, 'My God.' He finally snapped, 'Hop the first plane you can get out of National. Take a cab at this end, never mind what that costs. Bring all the material you have to date. I need the background. Been on the trail, you know, hitting the hustings ... Okay. It does sound good, doesn't it? ... Hurry. 'Bye.'

He hung up. 'What was that about?' asked his wife.

'Sorry, top secret,' he replied. 'Uh, will you see to rescheduling my appointments today?'

'Including the Garrisons' party? Remember who'll be there.'

'Sorry. This is that important. You go, offer my regrets, and charm the socks off the VIPs.'

'I'll do my best.'

'Which is mighty fine, my love.' What a First Lady she'd make – someday, someday, when his destiny blossomed. She wouldn't mind the other women much, then. 'Excuse me if I eat and run. I've a lot to clear away in less time than I was counting on.'

He did, in truth. Congress had adjourned, but constituents never set their problems aside and he couldn't offend the key interests. And the convention had left him with several cans of worms to get rid of before the election. And meanwhile his speech day after tomorrow needed more work. It was merely at the dedication of a high school, but if he said the right things in striking new phrases, the media might pick one up. He *must* find an identifying motto, like FDR's '– the only thing we have to fear is fear itself.' Or JFK's 'Ask not what your country –'

He received Stoddard a few hours later in his study. It was an airy room with a view over salt water that danced and glittered and upbore white wings of sailboats. Autographed photos of himself in the company of famous persons did not cover the walls as they did those of his Washington office. Instead there were a few family portraits, a landscape painted by his daughter, a horsemanship trophy from prep school days, a case of books for reference and recreation rather than display. He looked up from the desk, greeted, 'Hello. Sit down,' realized how brusque he had been. 'Excuse me. I guess I'm more on edge than I knew.'

Stoddard took a swivel chair, leaned back, laid his briefcase across his lap. 'Me too, Senator. Mind if I smoke?'

'No.' Moriarty sketched a rueful smile. 'Wish I dared.'

'We're alone.' Stoddard held the pack toward him.

Moriarty shook his head. 'No, thanks. Quitting was too hard. I wonder what Churchill would have made of a society where you can't take a puff any longer if you hope for national office.'

'Unless you're from a tobacco state.' A match scritted. 'Otherwise, yes, what one does is vote price supports, subsidies and export assistance for the tobacco industry, while calling for a war on dangerous addictive drugs.'

Damn the son of a bitch! Too bad he was so useful. Well, that jape had cost him the offer of a drink. 'Let's get cracking. How much detail do you have on this affair?'

'How much do you, sir?'

'I read the piece in the *Times* after you called. It wasn't very informative.'

'No, I suppose not. Because on the surface, it isn't much of a story. Another little shootout among the socially deprived of New York City.'

Glee exploded. 'But it has a connection to Tannahill!'

'Maybe,' Stoddard cautioned. 'All we're sure of is that members of the Unity were involved, and Tannahill visited its head last month, and it's a rather strange outfit. Not underground, but … reclusive? We'd have to spend quite a while digging for information, and it might well prove to be a wild goose chase. Tannahill could have seen the head-woman for some completely unrelated reason, like wanting to write an article. He was definitely at home during the incident. Still is, last I heard.'

Moriarty quelled the interior seething. Is this actually ridiculous? he wondered. Why am I turning the heavy artillery on a gadfly?

Because an instinct that my calling has honed tells me there is something big behind this, big, big. Uncovering it could do more than silence a noisy reactionary. It could lift me into orbit. Four years hence, eight at most, I could be bringing that new dawn which Tannahill and his night-spooks dread.

He sat back into well-worn, accepting, creaky leather, and set a part of his mind to telling one muscle after the next that it should slack off. 'Look,' he said, 'you know I haven't had time to stay abreast of your efforts. Brief me. Begin at the beginning. Never mind if you repeat this or that I've heard before. I want the facts arranged orderly for inspection.'

'Yes, sir.' Stoddard opened the case and took out a manila folder. 'Suppose I give you a quick summary, from the start, before we go into particulars.'

'Fine.'

Stoddard checked his notes. 'I did tell you when Tannahill reappeared in New Hampshire, you remember. We've had a tail on him since then. As per your instructions, I notified the FBI of that. The agent I talked to was a little annoyed.'

'He considered me officious, no doubt.' Moriarty laughed. 'Better that than seem furtive. And it has planted a bee in their bonnet. Go on.'

'Shortly after his return – do you want dates? Not yet? – shortly afterward, Tannahill went down to New York, took a hotel room, and met a plane from Copenhagen at Kennedy airport. A young woman, uh, flew to his arms when she'd cleared customs, and they were shacked up in that hotel for several days. It looked like a honeymoon situation, sightseeing, fancy restaurants, you know the bit. We checked back, of course. Her name is Olga Rasmussen, Danish citizen but actually from Russia, a refugee. Some puzzling things about her, but it's hard to do detail work internationally, and expensive. You decide whether we should.

'Meanwhile Tannahill dropped in at Unity headquarters. He didn't stay long and hasn't been in touch again, unless he's got a secret line.' Stoddard said nothing about the legality of any wire taps and Moriarty didn't inquire. 'He and Rasmussen went north to his place. They've been there since, not going out much nor doing anything unusual in public. Except ... lately they drove to the nearest airport and brought home a man who's now their house guest or whatever. We haven't been able to trace him, apart from indications that he's from the West Coast. Native American, to judge by his appearance.'

'What sort?' Moriarty asked. 'They don't all look alike.'

'Huh? Well, he's tall and hawk-faced. Tannahill introduced him to shopkeepers and such in the village as John Wanderer.'

'Hm. West Coast ... Well, what about the violence last night?'

'Apparently the local drug baron in that section of New York had his goons make a raid on a tenement that Unity is fixing for its members. He seems to have been trying to force it out before it gets established on his turf. It's too apt to choke off businesses like his.'

Moriarty searched his memory. 'I may have heard a little about Unity before the story today, but I'm not sure. Tell me.'

'They're obscure,' Stoddard said. 'I gather that's by choice. Stay compact, controllable; keep a low profile. It's a kind of self-help organization in the poverty classes, but not like any other. Not a church, though it has a religious element – ceremonies, anyhow. Not a militant group, though the members stick together, including on patrols that are more than simple neighborhood watches. However, hitherto they've avoided breaking any laws where anybody could see. The president, high priestess, whatever her title is, she's quite the mystery woman. Black, name of Corinne Macandal. She has a white associate, Rosa Donau, who's the one involved in the shooting. And that's about all we've turned up so far on Unity.'

'Tell me about the affair,' Moriarty urged. 'The account in the paper was so sketchy.'

'I'm afraid mine will be, too. Donau was at this restoration project when the gang broke in. One of the Unity men had a firearm. Shots were exchanged. He was killed, but not before he'd done for an enemy. Donau was seriously wounded.'

Moriarty nodded. 'Saturday night specials. Bullets spraying around. And nevertheless the rednecks quack about the Second Amendment ... Continue. Any more casualties?'

'Two unarmed night watchmen had been roughed up. Several other men from Unity were staying at the place, but they had only clubs – well, a couple of permissible-type knives.'

'Bad enough. None of them were hurt?'

'No, nor engaged. After those few shots, the attackers fled. Obviously they hadn't expected that kind of resistance. My guess is that they intended vandalism, destruction. The Unity people called the police. The dead men went to the morgue, Donau to the hospital. Shot through the chest. Condition serious but stable.'

'M-m-m.' Moriarty tugged his chin and squinted out across the sunlit waters. 'I daresay the head honcho – Macandal, is that her name? – she'll issue a statement expressing shock and disavowing those vigilantes.'

My impression is they'll swear it was strictly their own idea.'

'Which might be true. Donau should know more, if she survives. A material witness, at the very least ... Yes, I think this was not simply another brawl in the slums.' Triumph trumpeted. 'I believe we can find grounds for me to demand a federal investigation of Unity and everybody who's ever touched it.'

13

'Actually, by and large, Indian men worked as hard as their women,' Wanderer said. 'It was just that the division of labor was sharper than among whites, and the women's share was what a visitor in camp saw.'

'But wasn't the men's part more fun?' Svoboda asked. 'Hunting, for instance.' Her expression was rapt. Here she sat in the presence of a man who had been of those fabulous tribes, had experienced the Wild West.

Hanno considered lighting his pipe. Better not. Svoboda disliked it and he'd cut back on that account. Probably soon she'd make him quit altogether. Meanwhile, he thought grumpily, why doesn't she aim a few of her questions my way? I saw a bit of the American frontier too. I knew this land we're on when it was wilderness.

His gaze went out the nearer window of the living room. Afternoon sunlight glowed across the lawn. At the edge of grass a flowerbed flaunted red, violet, gold below the burglar-alarmed chain link fence that surrounded the property. From here he couldn't see the driveway sweep in from the county road, through an electrically controlled gate and between stately beech trees to the mansion. Visible instead behind the fence were second-growth woods whose leafage billowed and twinkled under the wind.

A lovely place, this, the ideal retreat after New York, peacefulness in which he and Svoboda could explore each other more deeply and she could get to know Wanderer. But he must return to Seattle and affairs neglected. She'd come along, she'd enjoy the city and adore its hinterland. Wanderer ought to stay behind a while, in case of a message from Macandal ... Would those two women ever stop dithering, or whatever they were at? ... Svoboda was anxious to meet Asagao and Tu Shan ... He, Hanno, should not think in terms of distracting her from Wanderer. He didn't own her, he had no right to be jealous, and anyway, there was nothing serious between those two, so far –

The phone rang. Wanderer stopped in mid-sentence. 'Go on,' Hanno invited. 'It may not need any response.'

The answering machine recited its instructions aloud and beeped. A female voice came, rapid, not quite steady: 'Madame Aliyat must speak with Mr Tannahill. It's urgent. Don't call straight back –'

Aliyat! Hanno was already across the room. He snatched the receiver from the antique table. 'Hello, Tannahill here, is that *you?*'

No, he recognized Macandal's tones. *'Parlez-vous français?'*

What? His mind leaped. *'Oui.'* He had maintained his French in serviceable if less than perfect condition, updating as the language evolved, for it was often a valuable tool. *'Désirez-vous parler comme ci? Pourquoi, s'il vous plait?'*

She had had less practice in recent decades, talked slowly and haltingly, sometimes required his help in making clear what she meant. Fallen silent, Wanderer and Svoboda heard his speech grow steely, saw his visage stiffen.

'– *Bien. Bonne chance. Au revoir, espérons-nous.*'

He put the receiver back and turned to his companions. For a moment only the wind outside gave utterance. Then he said, 'First I'll make sure nobody overhears,' and went out. The household staff didn't eavesdrop, nor interrupt unless necessary, but English was the sole common tongue today.

Returning, he stood arms akimbo before the chairs they swung around and stated into their stares: 'That was Corinne Macandal – finally, and not with glad tidings. I wish now I had the *New York Times* delivered here.' Harshly, he told them about the disaster of night before last.

'Oh, terrible.' Svoboda got up, reaching for him. He didn't notice. Wanderer stayed where he was, lynx-alert.

'I've worse yet,' Hanno said. 'Macandal has friends in certain government departments, especially police.' He recognized the unspoken question on the woman's lips and threw her a wintry grin. 'No, you can't call them moles. They give her information or early warning, at her request, which is seldom. Nothing for bad purposes, merely so she won't be caught off base. The sort of precaution an immortal would naturally take. I used to myself, till I got into a position where it was better to steer as clear of government as possible.

'Well, after I'd seen her, she wanted to know about me before committing herself to any course of action, or inaction – know more than I might be willing to reveal. So she inquired of those contacts and discovered that I've been under detective surveillance since shortly before our meeting. It's at the behest of Edmund J. Moriarty. Yes, Neddy, the senator, my *bête noire*. Apparently I've become his.'

He sighed. 'I should have left him alone. I thought I was doing a public service, badgering him; that I owed the United States this slight help, because I honestly doubt it could survive his Presidency. My mistake. I should have concentrated on our own survival. Too late.'

Svoboda had whitened. 'The secret police?' she whispered.

'No, no.' Hanno patted her shoulder. 'You should know better, after your years in the West, or have you been listening to European leftists? The Republic hasn't decayed that far yet. I daresay Moriarty has been fishing, in hopes he'll find something to discredit or incriminate Kenneth Tannahill Macandal doesn't see it that way. I gather she admires him, because he's supposedly done things for the poor. She's been too busy to learn much history. The revelation that he was after me caused her to hang back from further contact. Might I actually be evil? She does have a hell of a lot to lose, not money but a whole life-work.'

'Never mind,' Wanderer said. 'Plain to see, in this crisis she felt she had to tip you off regardless.'

'It's more than that,' Hanno replied. 'We talked very circumspectly. A lot of what I tell you, I deduce logically from her indirect words, on the basis of what I knew before. But she checked again with her Washington sources and found she's now under the eye too. After that gunfight, Moriarty may very well succeed in getting the FBI on the case. That's the Federal Bureau of Investigation, Svoboda, a sort of national police. The drug connection, if nothing else. Even though Unity's fought the narcotics traffic more effectively than any branch of government – well, could Tannahill be in it, could he have masterminded that assault? Also, the unfortunate fact is that the member who was killed had a pistol and used it. In New York that's more illegal than mugging a grandmother. Since the Goetz case, the liberals have been out for blood. Macandal should be able to prove her innocence, but she'll have a devil of a time first, and ... anything might come out in the course of the investigation.'

'Not to mention that other woman, Aliyat, being in the hospital.'

'Yeah. She hasn't been interrogated, in her condition, but when they do go to work on her, the fat could be in the fire. During her whorehouse days she was repeatedly arrested. You know the drill, spasm of public morality, hustle the girls off to show your zeal for law enforcement, then let them right back out. She was fingerprinted, over and over, through the years. And the FBI has accumulated the world's largest collection of fingerprints.'

Wanderer grunted as if hit in the belly. Svoboda caught her lip between her teeth.

'Well, Macandal had already decided she should stop hesitating, get in touch with me, try to find out for herself what kind of a guy I am,' Hanno continued. 'Aliyat was to come this weekend as her representative and, hm, scout. An acid test, considering what last happened between us two.

'First they had in mind an express message to set up the meeting, me to reply the same way. But the shooting cut that off. Now she saw she'd better put her suspicions aside and confer in earnest. An exchange of written communications would obviously be too slow and cumbersome. A personal visit would give away too much, and we can't manage a clandestine one in a hurry. Our phones are quite likely tapped – under the new circumstances, a word from Moriarty would persuade a judge of the proper political faith to allow that – but still seemed the only way. As soon as the police and the press withdrew, she left her house and called me from a member's place. Chances are, nobody listening in knows French. It should take a little time to get a recording translated, and we used every possible circumlocution. I don't think we let slip any hard-and-fast evidence that she was the person on the line. Still, she has undoubtedly compromised herself to a greater or lesser degree. It was a brave thing to do.'

'But also necessary,' Svoboda said. 'Our secret is in the worst danger it ever has been, no?'

'Mainly she wanted to give me and any other immortals I know an opportunity to get out from under, make ourselves invisible, if we want to.' Hanno lifted a clenched fist. 'By God, she has a free heart! I wish I could be as sure about her head. At the moment, she's for ending the masquerade, making a clean breast of everything.'

'Does she trust the government that much?' Svoboda wondered.

'It wouldn't be dangerous for her, I should think,' Wanderer said thoughtfully. 'Not at first, anyhow. Hard on us, maybe. Especially you, Hanno.'

The Phoenician laughed. 'I'd go hoarse, listing my crimes aloud. Just for openers, all those false identities of mine, complete with Social Security dog tags and annual tax returns, not to mention assorted licenses, birth and death certificates, passports – oh, I've been a desperate character, I have.'

'You might be let off easy, even pardoned,' Wanderer said. 'And the rest of us, for our petty offenses. We'd be such a sensation.' He grimaced. 'At worst, some years in jail wouldn't matter too greatly to us.' His tone belied the words. It recalled roofless heavens and boundless horizons.

'No, it would be hellishly dangerous,' Hanno declared. 'It might well become lethal, for us and a lot of bystanders. I couldn't explain why over the phone, what with the haste and the probable listeners and her poor French, but I did convince Macandal we must consider the possible consequences before we let our cat out of the bag – that a snap judgment would be completely irresponsible.'

Wanderer's voice went dry. 'From what you've told me about her, that was an argument she found hard to resist.'

'She knows from Aliyat I've been around a long time. Tentatively, she'll credit me with more knowledge of the world than she has. She'll disappear and lie low till we can better assess the situation.'

'How's she going to pull that off?'

'Oh, it is easy, if she has an organization loyal to her,' Svoboda said. 'I can imagine any number of ruses. For example, let a woman who resembles her come to the house. Inside, they exchange clothes, and Macandal walks out. After dark that should work. Her people will hide her until she can reach a refuge she surely prepared beforehand.'

'Hm, how shall we and she get in touch later, if we don't know each other's locations or aliases?' Wanderer asked.

'She must have told her comrade Aliyat what the possibilities are.'

'How can Aliyat tell us? In fact, why are we wasting air on this chatter, when she's a prisoner and the cops will shortly have the clues to her nature? Didn't Macandal point that out to you, Hanno?'

'No,' the other man said. 'It hadn't occurred to her. She was shocked, bewildered, harassed, grieved, exhausted. I'm amazed she could think straight at all. Since I wanted her to make her exit, I refrained from bringing the question up. Besides, the Aliyat matter is not entirely hopeless.'

'*Chto?*' Svoboda cried. 'What do you mean?'

'The truth won't come out overnight,' Hanno reminded them. 'Possibly it never would. I'm not certain that copies of prints from those obscure police files of decades ago ever got to Washington. If they did, or if the investigators get the idea of making a search, that'll take time. And then, if an identity is found – well, Thomas Jefferson, who was as enlightened a man as ever lived, once said he could more readily believe that some Yankee professors had lied than that stones fell from the sky. It would be scientifically more respectable to assume there'd been a mix-up in the records than that a human being could stay young for fifty or a hundred years.'

Svoboda scowled. 'Possession of her would not allow that assumption, I think. And she might decide that telling everything will be to her profit.'

'She might very well,' Hanno agreed, remembering. 'Oh, a thousand things could go wrong, from our viewpoint. Let's see if we can't take corrective action. For that purpose, and for more obvious reasons, we'll decamp tonight.'

'The gate is watched, you tell me,' Svoboda said glumly. 'How, I do not know. I have not noticed a parked car or men standing on that rural road.'

'Why should you? A battery-powered miniature TV camera in the brush opposite will serve. The road dead-ends at the lake, you may recall. Bound anywhere else, you head in the opposite direction and pass the Willows Lodge. No doubt two or three persons checked in a little while ago and spend more time in their cabin than is usual for vacationers.'

'You can glorify modern technology as much as you want,' Wanderer growled. 'Me, more and more I feel the walls closing in.'

'How shall we evade them?' Svoboda asked. Dread and despair had yielded to keenness.

Hanno grinned. 'Every fox has two holes to his burrow. Let's pack what we'll need. I keep plenty of cash on hand, together with traveler's checks, credit cards, assorted ID not made out to Tannahill. I'll hand the servants a plausible story, which'll contain a red herring. Tonight – A panel at the rear of the fence swings aside without touching off the alarm, if you know what to do. It gives on the woods, and the village is three miles beyond that. There's a man there, lives alone, grumpy old bachelor type, who likes my magazine except he complains it's too leftish. I always try to cultivate somebody, whenever I maintain a base for any span of time, somebody I can rely on to do me an occasional favor and not mention it to anyone else. He'll drive us to where we can get a bus or train. We'll probably be smart to switch conveyances en route, but we'll still be in New York tomorrow

14

The hospital building might well be a hundred years old, brick dark with grime, windows not lately washed. The modernization inside was minimal. This was for the poor, the indigent, the victims of accident and violence. Its neighbors were as drab. The traffic that rumbled and screeched about them was mostly commercial and industrial. The air was foul with its fumes.

A taxi drew up at the curb. Hanno passed the driver a twenty-dollar bill. 'Wait here,' he directed. 'We're fetching a friend. She'll be pretty weak, needs to get home right away.'

'I'll hafta circle the block if ya take too long,' the driver warned.

'Circle it fast, then, and park again whenever you see a chance. This is worth a nice tip.'

The driver looked dubious, understandable considering the institution. Svoboda ostentatiously jotted down his name and number. Hanno followed her out and closed the door. He carried a parcel, she an overnight bag. 'Remember, now, this will only work if we behave as though we owned the accounts receivable office,' he muttered.

'*You* remember I have been a sharpshooter and slipped through the Iron Curtain,' she answered haughtily.

'Uh, sorry, that was a stupid thing for me to say. I'm distracted. Ah, there he is.' Hanno inclined his head in the direction of Wanderer. Shabbily clad, hat pulled low, the Indian slouched along the sidewalk like one with nothing better to do.

Hanno and Svoboda entered a gloomy lobby. A uniformed guard cast them an incurious glance. Even these patients sometimes got visitors. Reconnoitering yesterday, they had ascertained that no police guard was on Rosa Donau. She had automatically been taken here and it was deemed unsafe to transfer her to a better hospital when the word came that money was available to pay for that. Therefore this place's security ought to suffice.

Hanno sought a men's room. It was unoccupied, but he entered a stall to be cautious. Opening his parcel, he unfolded a smock coat and donned it. He'd acquired it, plus a lot of other stuff, at a medical supply firm. It wasn't quite identical with what the orderlies wore, but should get by if nobody had cause to look closely. Outfits faded or stained were more the rule than the exception. He dropped the wrapping in a trash can and rejoined Svoboda. They took an elevator upward.

They had learned yesterday that Rosa Donau was on the seventh floor. The receptionist had told them she could only have very brief visits, and remarked on how many people came, anxiously inquiring.

Two women had been on hand when Hanno and Svoboda walked into the ward. They had brought flowers, which they could probably ill afford. Hanno smiled at them, went to the bedside, bent over the victim. She lay white, hollow-cheeked, shallowly breathing. He would not have recognized her had he not seen the pictures his detectives took for him. Indeed, without the hunch than this was she, he might well never have known her by those snapshots. It had been a long, long time.

He hoped that her Romaic Greek was no rustier than his. After all, he supposed, she'd mostly been in the Levant before coming to America. 'Aliyat, my friend and I believe we can smuggle you out. Do you want that? Otherwise you'll lose your liberty forever, you know. I have money. I can give you the freedom of the world. Do you want to escape?'

She lay mute for a moment that stretched, before she barely nodded.

'Well, do you think you can walk a short distance and make it look natural? A hundred meters, perhaps. We'll help you, but if you fall, we'll have to leave you and flee.'

A ghost of color tinged her skin. 'Yes,' she whispered, unthinkingly in English.

'Tomorrow afternoon, then. Make sure you have no callers. Tell these people you feel worse and need a few days undisturbed. Ask them to spread the word. Husband your strength.'

He straightened, to meet the stares of the women from Unity. 'I wasn't aware she's in this serious a condition,' he told them. 'Otherwise I'd have let her know beforehand my wife and I were coming.'

'You from out of town?' asked one.

'Yes. We hadn't seen her for quite a while, but we read about the, uh, incident, and since we're of her nationality and had business in New York anyway – Well, I am sorry. We'd better go, Olga. We'll see you later, Rosa, when you're more recovered. Take care.' He and Svoboda patted the limp hands. They left.

A walk around the seventh-floor halls, a quick peek into the ward as they went by, revealed no sign of a trap. If Aliyat didn't actually wish to leave, with the hazards and pains that meant, she could help herself by spilling the truth and ratting on Hanno. He had gambled on her distrust of authority being too ingrained, after her many centuries, or at least on her having the shrewdness to foresee that confession would close out every other choice.

This entire operation was a gamble. If it failed, and he and Svoboda could not make a getaway – He mustn't let worry dull his wits and sap his energy.

'Damn,' he said. 'No wheelchair. Let's try the next floor down.'

They got lucky there. Wheelchairs, gurneys, and the like commonly stood unattended in the corridors. He took what he wanted and pushed it briskly to the elevator. A nurse glanced at him, parted her lips, half shrugged and hurried onward. The staff was overworked, underpaid, and doubtless had considerable turnover on that account. Svoboda trailed him at a discreet distance, pretending to look for a room number.

Back on seven, they proceeded to Aliyat's ward. Speed was now the key to everything. Svoboda entered first. If a nurse or doctor was present, they'd have to continue prowling around, biding their chance. She stepped back to the doorway and beckoned. His heart bumped. He went in past her.

The dingy room held a double row of beds, most occupied. Some patients watched the televisions above either row, some dozed, some were vegetables, a few looked at the newcomer, but dully. None questioned him. Hanno hadn't expected they would. An environment like this was ghastly deadening. Aliyat too had fallen asleep. She blinked her eyes open when he touched her shoulder. Abruptly he did know her again, the ferret alertness that she had dissembled until too late for him, last time around.

He beamed. 'All right, Ms. Donau, let's go for those lab tests, shall we?' he said. She nodded and visibly braced herself. Oh, she knew this would hurt. He kept old sailor skills, such as carrying loads carefully, and while his body wasn't that of any Hercules, its wiriness had never flagged. He bent his knees, took hold, swung her from bed to chair. Her arms crept about his neck. He felt a brief, roguish flirt of fingers in his hair. He also heard the sharply indrawn breath.

Svoboda had kept aside, and continued to do so while he wheeled Aliyat to the elevator. She took it together with them. Yesterday he and she had found what they wanted on the second floor, minimizing the distance Aliyat must go on her feet. It was another gamble that the hydrotherapy bath would be vacant, but a fairly safe bet at this time of day. Hanno took Aliyat in, told her in a few words what came next, and left. Somebody else was walking by. Hanno went the opposite way, his expression preoccupied. Svoboda dawdled until she could slip in unobserved, carrying her overnight bag.

Again Hanno took shelter in a men's room and spent an agreed-on ten minutes by his watch, seated on a toilet and contemplating graffiti. They were uniformly vulgar and semi-literate. I should raise the tone of this joint, he decided. Anything to keep from fretting. He unclipped a pen, located a clear space, and printed carefully: '$x^n + y^n = z^n$ has no integral solution for all n greater than two. I have found a marvelous proof of this theorem, but there is not room in this stall to write it down.'

Time. He left his smock behind and returned to the bath. Svoboda was just emerging; splendid girl. Aliyat leaned on her, no longer in a hospital gown but a dress, stockings, shoes, a lightweight coat mat covered the bulges of bandages. Svoboda had kept the bag. Hanno joined them and lent his support. 'How're you doing?' he asked in English.

Air (and blood?) rattled. 'I'll make it,' Aliyat gasped, 'but – oh, shit – no, never mind.' Her weight pulled at him. She minced along, unevenly, now and then staggering. Sweat studded her face and reeked in his nostrils. He had seen corpses less blue-pale.

Nevertheless she moved. And it was as though she gained a bit of strength thereby, until you could almost say she walked. That's the wild card in *my* hand, Hanno thought. The vitality of the immortal. No normal human could do this so soon after such a wounding.

But she won't be able to, either, unless she draws on whatever wellsprings are her own.

In the downbound elevator, she sagged. Hanno and Svoboda upheld her. 'You must be firm and walk straight,' the Ukrainian said. 'It is only for a little way. Then you can rest. Then you will be free.'

Aliyat peeled lips back from teeth. 'There's ... a dance ... in the old dame ... yet.'

When they emerged in the lobby, she didn't exactly stride, but you'd have to look hard to notice how much help she needed. Hanno's eyes flickered back and forth. Where the hell – Yes, yonder sat the Indian, on the split and peeling plastic of a settee, thumbing through a decrepit magazine.

Wanderer saw them, lurched to his feet, reeled against a man passing by. 'Hey,' he shouted, 'why'n'chu look where ya going?' with an obscenity added for good measure.

'There's the front door,' Hanno murmured in Aliyat's ear. 'Hup, two, three, four.'

Wanderer's altercation loudened on his right. It caught everybody's attention. A couple of guards pushed toward him. Hanno hoped he wouldn't overdo it. The idea was to provide two or three minutes' distraction without getting arrested, merely expelled – Trouble with Wanderer, he's a gentleman by instinct, he doesn't have the talent for acting a belligerent drunk. He does have brains, however, and tact.

Into the open. Dusty though it was, sunlight momentarily dazzled. The taxi stood at the curb. Hermes, god of travelers, merchants, and thieves, thanks.

Hanno helped Aliyat in. She slumped bonelessly and struggled for breath. Svoboda took her other side. Hanno gave an address. The cab started off. As it wove its way through congestion and squawks, Aliyat's weight swayed to and fro. Svoboda felt beneath her coat, nodded pinch-lipped, took a towel from the bag and held it in place, more or less concealed. To blot up blood, Hanno knew; the injury was hemorrhaging.

'Say, that lady all right?' the driver asked. 'Looks to me like they shouldn't of let her go.'

'Schartz-Metterklume syndrome,' Hanno explained. 'She does need to get home and to bed as fast as you can make it.'

'Yeah,' Aliyat rasped. 'C'mon and see me tomorrow, big boy.'

The driver widened his mouth and rolled his eyes, but pushed on. At the destination, Hanno redeemed his promise of a lavish tip. It should buy silence, did pursuit guess that a taxi had been involved. Not that the story would help the police much, by that time.

'Around the corner,' Svoboda told Aliyat. 'Half a block.'

Red dripped onto the sidewalk. Nobody else seemed to notice, or if they did, they chose not to get involved. Hanno had counted on that.

A small moving van stood in a parking garage. Hanno had rented it yesterday, contracting to turn it in at Pocatello, Idaho. Its bulk screened from casual glances how her companions lifted Aliyat into the body of it. A foam mattress and bedding waited, together with what medical supplies one could readily buy. Hanno and Svoboda peeled her clothes off. They washed her, applied an antibiotic, dressed the wound anew, made her as comfortable as they could.

'I think she will recover,' Svoboda said.

'Damn straight I will,' Aliyat mumbled.

'Leave us,' Svoboda ordered Hanno. 'I will care for her.'

The Phoenician obeyed. She'd been a soldier, who knew first aid; she'd been a veterinarian, and humans aren't vastly unlike their kindred. He closed the tail doors on them and settled himself to wait in the cab. At least he could indulge in a pipe of tobacco now, and a slight case of the shakes.

Before long, Wanderer arrived. Hanno had rarely seen him this joyful. 'Whoopee ti-yi-yo,' he warbled.

'Maybe I better take the first stretch at the wheel,' Hanno said. The van growled to life. He paid the parking fee and set forth westward.

15

It was natural that Mr and Mrs Tu would arrange a picnic for their guests, the people they'd met in the cities, but the kids were disappointed that they weren't invited too. These seemed like real interesting folks, in spite of not saying much about themselves. First was convalescent Miss Adler, whom the Tus met in Pocatello and drove here; she was mending so fast that her trouble couldn't have been too bad. The rest had to stay at the hotel in town but spent their days on the ranch: Mr and Mrs Tazurin, Mr Langford, who admitted he was an Indian, and black Miss Edmonds, all different from each other and from everybody else.

Well, probably they wanted to be alone and talk about plans, like maybe for enlarging the house, making room for more fosterlings. They did act pretty solemn, nice enough but not like vacationers. Mostly they, including the Tus, strolled off by twos and threes, gone for hours.

On the brow of a hill that commanded a wide and beautiful view, Tu Shan had long since assembled a redwood table and benches. The party parked their cars nearby and got out. For a while they stood silent, looking. Halfway up the eastern sky, the sun made a few clouds as brilliant as the western snowpeaks. Between stretched a thousand greens, range, cropland, trees along the lazily shining river. A pair of hawks wheeled aloft, their wings edged with gold. A breeze mildened the air. It murmured and smelled of ripeness.

'Let's talk before we unload the eats,' Hanno proposed. That was unnecessary, having been understood, but it got things started. Humans were apt to put off making difficult decisions, and immortals especially so. 'I hope we can finish in time to relax and enjoy ourselves, but if need be we'll wrangle till sundown. That's the deadline, agreed?'

He sat down. Svoboda joined him on his right, Wanderer on the left. Opposite them were benched Tu Shan, Asagao, Aliyat, and she whose name among them remained Corinne Macandal. Yes, Hanno thought, in spite of having tried to get well acquainted and become a fellowship, we still unnoticingly divide up according to the partnerships we had.

None would have accepted a chairman, but one person had to take the initiative and he was the senior. 'Let me summarize the agenda,' he said. 'I can't tell you anything new or unobvious. However, maybe I can save us further repetition.

'The basic question is, shall we surrender to the government and reveal to the world what we are, or shall we continue our masquerade, using new masks?

'On the surface, there's no great hue and cry out for us. Rosa Donau was spirited from the hospital. Corinne Macandal dropped from sight. Likewise did Kenneth Tannahill and a couple of house guests, but that was elsewhere, and he often goes out of town, is away much more than he is at home. No sensation in the news, not even Rosa's disappearance. She's obscure, few people really care about the patients in that hospital, nobody has claimed she was kidnapped or otherwise met foul play, and in fact none of the persons I've named are charged with anything.

'I thought that must be too good to be true, and Corinne informs me it is. She's queried her connections – twice, was it? – from her hiding places. Ned Moriarty is still very interested. The FBI thinks the matter is worth looking into. Could possibly involve drugs or espionage or antics less spectacular but just as unlawful. Have you any later information, Corinne?'

Macandal shook her head. 'No,' she replied quietly, 'nor will I. Already I've put more strain on the honor of those men than I should have. I won't call them again.'

'I've pipelines of my own, from Seattle,' Hanno said, 'but using them gets dicier for every day that passes. Tannahill is associated with Tomek Enterprises. The FBI will at least be inquiring into that. They may decide there's nothing to it, that Tomek's friends have no idea why Tannahill vamoosed.

However, they certainly will not if they discover that those friends showed some awareness of the situation earlier. I'd rather not take that risk. We've plenty as is.'

He leaned forward, elbows on table. 'In short,' he finished, 'if we want to stay concealed, we'll have to do a total job of it. Abandon everything as fast as possible, permanently. Including this ranch. Tomek brought Shan and Asagao over and installed them here. Somebody will come around to ask some questions. He'll probably hear gossip about those visitors you had, so soon after the suspicious events. Once he gets descriptions of them, that's all she wrote.'

Aliyat's voice trembled a little. She could walk by now, within limits, and color was back in her face, but it would be a few weeks yet before her full recovery, in body or spirit. 'Then we can't go. We have to give up. Or else ... be poor again – homeless – no.'

Hanno smiled. 'Have you forgotten what I've told you, or don't you believe me?' he answered. 'I've squirreled money and other reserves away, around a large part of the world, for close to a hundred years. I have places to live, excellent cover stories, all details taken care of. Yes, periodically checked and updated. We can disperse or we can go live together, as we individually choose, but we'll be comfortable for at least the next fifty years, if this civilization lasts that long, and well prepared if it doesn't. Meanwhile we can be laying the foundations of fresh careers.'

'Are you sure?'

'I know considerable about this myself,' Wanderer said. 'I am sure. If you're afraid, Aliyat, why did you let us boost you out of that bed?'

Her eyes flickered. 'I was dazed, didn't know what to think, hardly could think. I had an idea of buying time.'

'That was my notion too,' Wanderer told the group. 'I kept my mouth shut, like her, but today we must be honest.'

Despite their comradeship, Hanno was jolted. 'Huh?' he exclaimed. 'You mean we should turn ourselves in? Why?'

The response was grave: 'If nothing else, I've heard Sam Giannotti on the subject. Once the world knows immortality is possible, they should be able to give it to everybody inside of – ten years? Twenty? Molecular biology's already far along. Have we the right to sit on the knowledge? How many millions or billions would we condemn to unnecessary death?'

Hanno sensed the undertone and pounced. 'You don't sound too convinced.'

Wanderer grimaced like a man in pain. 'I'm not. I had to spell the issue out, but – Could Earth survive?' He waved at the living land around them. 'How long before this would be under concrete, or polluted into an open sewer? Humans are already swamping in their own numbers. I wonder if it's possible to escape the big dieback, or the extinction. We could hasten that day a lot.'

'They'd practice birth control, when they didn't need children to carry on for them,' Macandal said.

'How many would?' Svoboda challenged. 'Nor could the serum reach everybody at once. I foresee riots, revolutions, terror.'

'Must it be that bad?' Tu Shan asked. 'People will know what to expect before it happens. They can prepare. I do not want to lose what we have here.'

'Nor forsake our children,' Asagao added.

'And what would become of the Unity?' Macandal put in. She turned to Aliyat. 'You know what it means to you. Think of the whole membership, your brothers and sisters.'

The Syrian woman bit her lip before responding, 'We've lost the Unity anyway, Corinne. If we came out in public, we couldn't be the same to its people. We wouldn't have time for them, either. And the whole world watching – No, the only way for the Unity to keep going, anything like what it was, is for us to disappear. If it's as strong as we hope, it'll find new leadership. If not, well, then it wasn't that great after all.'

'So you want to hide, now you know you'll be safe?'

'I didn't say that. Uh, I don't expect we'd have much in the way of legal problems. Even Hanno can probably pay fines, and make twice as much off lectures and a book and movie rights and endorsements and ... everything the biggest celebrities the world'll ever see, short of the Second Coming, everything we'll be offered.'

'Except peace.' Asagao's voice came troubled. 'No, I fear – Shan, my husband, I fear we would never again have freedom of the soul. Let us make provision for the children and then let us retire, retreat, and seek for tranquility and virtue.'

'I hate to lose this land,' Tu Shan protested.

'Aliyat's right, you'd be hounded off it regardless,' Hanno warned. 'Or taken into protective custody. You've lived sheltered lives, you two. You don't know how many murderous types are out there. Lunatics, fanatics, the insanely jealous, the little snots who'll kill just to get noticed at last. Until immortality was common, I suspect we'd still need a squad of bodyguards around the clock for decades, before we got taken for granted. No, let me show you some fresh countryside.'

He turned to Aliyat. 'That kind of existence may look glamorous to you, my dear,' he continued. 'Riches, high society, fame, fun. Maybe you wouldn't mind the dangers, the need for guards –' he chuckled – 'provided they're young, handsome, and virile, eh? But please think deeper. How much actual freedom would you have, how much real opportunity?'

'You spoke of finding meaning, purpose, in the Unity,' Svoboda said softly, to Aliyat and Macandal both. 'Can we not win to it together, we seven? Can we not work secretly for what is good, and do it better than in a glare of light and storm of noise?'

Aliyat's hand lay on the table. Macandal reached to take it in hers.

'Of course, if any of us wants to go out and reveal himself or herself, the rest of us have no way of preventing it,' Hanno said. 'We can only ask that you give us time to get well hidden. For my part, I intend to; and I and whoever goes with me will not leave behind any clues to our whereabouts. For one thing, I don't want to be around and visible when this country becomes the People's Republic of America.'

'I do not agree that is inevitable,' Macandal said. 'We may be past that stage of history.'

'Maybe. I'll keep my options open.'

'That would stick anybody who wanted to unmask with a problem,' Wanderer observed. 'You've tucked away evidence that you're an immortal, but how could we others prove we weren't lying or crazy?'

'I think we could provide enough indications that the authorities would be willing to wait and see,' Macandal said meditatively.

Hanno nodded. 'Also,' he admitted, 'Sam Giannotti whom I've told you about, he'd doubtless feel released from his vow of silence, and he's a respected man.'

'Might he talk if we all disappeared?' Svoboda wondered.

'No, in that case he'll have nothing to back so wild a story, and better sense than to spread it. He'll be heartbroken, poor decent fellow, but he'll plug on with the research. I'll try to arrange continued funding for the Rufus Lab, mainly for his sake.'

'Do you really mean to liquidate your companies?' Macandal asked. 'You would lose ... what? Hundreds of millions of dollars?'

'I have plenty hoarded, and I can make more,' Hanno assured her. 'The termination must be done as plausibly as is consistent with speed. Tomek will die and be cremated abroad, in accordance with his wishes. Robert Cauldwell – m-m, something similar had better happen to him, because unfortunately, he's left a potential trail. Joe Levine will get a job offer from an out-of-state firm ... Oh, I'll be busy for the rest of this year, but I do have standing preparations for a variety of emergencies, and I expect I can make things fade out in natural-looking ways. There'll be loose ends, inevitably; but then, there generally are in ordinary life, and the investigators will leave them dangling once it seems clear they wouldn't lead to anything much. Policemen don't lack for work, you know. Their lot is not a happy one.'

'But you could do so much with the money,' she begged. 'Yes, and with the power you, we, would have, the influence of our fame, in spite of any drawbacks. So much that cries out for doing.'

'Do you feel we are being selfish in wanting to stay hidden?' Svoboda queried.

'Well – Do you, then, want to?'

'Yes. And not for myself, or ourselves. I am afraid for the world.'

Wanderer nodded. Svoboda smiled at him, warmly though without mirth. 'You don't quite understand,' she said in his direction. 'You think of nature destroyed, the environment. But I think of humankind. I have seen revolutions, wars, breakdowns, ruin, for a thousand years. We Russians have learned to fear anarchy above all else. We would rather have tyranny than it. Hanno, you do wrong to look on people's republics, strong governments of every kind, as always evil. Freedom is perhaps better, but chaos is worse. If we let go our secret today, we let loose unforeseeable forces. Religion, politics, economics – yes, how shall a world of immortals order its economy? – a million contending dreams and dreads, for which men will war around the world. Can civilization itself endure that? Can the planet?'

'Muhammad came out of nowhere,' Aliyat whispered.

'And many another prophet, revolutionary, conqueror,' Svoboda said. 'The intentions can be noble. But who foresaw that the idea of democracy in France would bring the Reign of Terror, Napoleon, and a generation of war? Who foresaw that after Marx and Lenin would come Stalin and, yes, Hitler? The world volcano already smokes and shivers. Put this new thing in it that nobody ever thought of before, and I would *hope* for a tyranny that can prevent the final explosion; but I wonder if any such rule will be possible.'

'It won't be for lack of trying,' Hanno said. He had turned entirely grim. 'At the bare least, every corrupt politician and fat cat in the West, every totalitarian dictatorship abroad, every dirty little warlord who battens on backwardness, all will jump to screw down their power forever. Yes, death robs us of our loves and finally of ourselves. But death is also good riddance to bad rubbish. Do we dare change that? My friends, being ageless does not make us gods, and most certainly does not make us God.'

16

Nearly full, the moon frosted earth with light and dappled it with shadow. Air had gone still, but hour by hour a breath of autumn flowed down from the mountains. Somewhere an owl hooted, hunting. Windows glowed yellow in houses strewn across miles. They seemed almost as remote as the stars.

Hanno and Svoboda had driven from town, out onto the range, to walk alone. The wish was hers. 'Tomorrow evening what was ours begins coming to an end,' she had said. 'Can we steal a last few hours of peace? This country is very like the homeland I once had, wide and lonely.'

Their footfalls crunched on a dirt road. He broke a lengthy silence. 'You spoke of peace,' he said. Voices were small in the vastness. 'We'll have it again, dear. Yes, we've got a frantic time to go through first, and it'll hurt, but afterward – I believe the whole seven of us will be glad of the place we're going to.'

'I am sure it is lovely,' she replied, 'and we will be safely away from the world for as long as we need to be.'

'Not forever, remember. In fact, that wouldn't work. We're only gaining another mortal lifetime, the same as so often before. Then we'll have to start fresh under new masks.'

'I know. Until someday, perhaps soon, the scientists find immortality by themselves, and we may as well come forth.'

'Someday,' he said, more skeptically than enthusiastically.

'That is not what I think about, though,' Svoboda went on. 'Now we must think about us. We seven. It will not be easy. We are so different. And ... three men, four women.'

'We'll work out our arrangements.'

'For the rest of time? Nothing to change, ever?'

'Well –' She could hear the reluctance. 'Of course none of us can bind the rest. We'll each be free to leave, whenever we like. I do hope we'll stay in touch and ready to give help. Isn't freedom the whole of what we're trying to keep?'

'No, I do not feel that is enough,' she told him gravely. 'There must be more. I do not know what it is, not yet. But we must have something beyond survival to live for, or we shall not survive. The future will be too strange.'

'The future always was,' he answered from his three thousand years.

'What is coming, more strange than ever before.' She raised her eyes. Stars gleamed through the moon-glow, golden-red Arcturus, blue-white Altair, Polaris of the sailors, Vega where lately men had found spoor of planets. 'In Odysseus, Hamlet, Anna Karenina, we still see ourselves. But tomorrow, will they know those people, or us? Can we understand them, our children?'

She caught his left arm. He laid his right hand across hers, for whatever comfort that might give in the night.

They had talked of this already, a little. Once, while they rested for a day on their long journey from the east, she had guided him in trying to imagine what might happen ...

XIX

THULE

1

As it rose out of the darknesses that had severed it from Hanno, his machine self came back to him. Abruptly he was again down in the world that filled his human vision.

Clouds towered mountain-high. Their nether caverns were full of night and lightning. Their flanks billowed and streamed, streaked with strange tawnies and ochers, where winds beyond all hurricanes roared. Their thunderhead peaks caught sunlight, to blaze white against imperial blue.

Moment by moment the robot lifted, air thinned, linkage strengthened toward fullness. Hanno felt its haste in his bones, the jet thrust like blood and muscle. It burned, brawled, shouted into the storms that grabbed at it, spurned the monstrous gravity underneath. Heaven deepened to purple, to black and stars. Now he saw with eyes open to every color of light from radio to gamma. He tasted and smelled the changing chemistries until they thinned away and radiation sharpened. Sound likewise died; when the ion drive kindled, that was barely a thrum, less in his awareness than the flows of mathematics by which the robot guided itself to rendezvous with his ship.

Throughout, he was also a man looking forth, afloat in silence. At synchronous-orbit distance, he must turn his head a little if he would look from edge to edge of Jupiter. The king planet was at present half daylit. Intricacies wove along the frontiers of belts and zones. The effect was of pallid serenity. Deceptive – how well he knew. He had been there.

After a fashion. No worthwhile transmission could be made from the lower atmosphere. He would never experience yonder world-ocean, he would watch reconstructions and replays of what the robot had known through robotic senses, unless he ordered the data downloaded into his brain; and that would not be the exploration, but merely the borrowed memory of a machine.

People on Earth had wondered why he went to so much trouble and, yes, risk, for so small and scientifically valueless an accomplishment. He had refrained from arguing, simply replied that he wanted to do this. Having arranged suitable precautions, for a torchcraft mishandled could work more havoc than most ancient wars, the authorities let him. After all, he was the oldest man in existence. One must expect him to keep archaic urges.

They never heard him say, 'Trial run.'

The robot closed in. Hanno broke contact and uncoupled from the neuro-induction unit. Docking maneuvers would be both tedious and confusing to a human intellect. Masses moved readily enough, but the right phase-in was essential, lest the dance of electromagnetic fields around the ship be perturbed. Let it falter for one second, and the ambient radiation would end a life that began in the early Iron Age.

As always, for a span he felt stunned. The robot's input had been so much greater than anything unaided flesh and blood could ever perceive. Still more had been his partnership, slight though it was, with the computer. Bereft of it, he seemed witless.

The longing receded. He was again Hanno, a man with a man's unique part to play. Few on Earth understood that any longer. They thought they did, and in a way they were right, but they did not think like him.

He made his preparations. When the ship told him, 'All clear' he was ready. Obedient to his orders, it calculated the vectors of an optimum course for his next goal. Well aft of him, matter met antimatter and energy flamed. Weight came back. Jupiter drifted across the viewfield until the forward screen held only stars.

Under a one-gee boost, the time between planets was measured in days. He did not have the total freedom of them. Certain regions were lethal, even within his kind of shielding, such as the neighborhood of the sun. Certain were forbidden him, and rightly so. While he could pass near enough to the Web to admire its spidery vastness through his optical systems, a close approach could trouble some part of its functioning, garble the information it drank in from the universe. Subtlest, most enigmatic, was the scent of beings somewhere yonder in the galaxy.

Never mind. He was no passive passenger. Within the broad limits of law and its capability, the ship would do whatever he wanted. Recycling molecules in patterns tried and true or ingeniously new, it provided every necessity, most comforts, many luxuries. Almost the entire culture of the human race was in its databank, immediately available for his use or pleasure. That included minds for him to summon up when he desired to converse.

Living bodies, besides his own, he forewent. This *was* a trial run, the ship well-nigh minimal. He expected his tour of the Solar System would take a year or two, maybe three if he got really fascinated. That was hardly a blink of time.

Nevertheless, already impatience quivered in him.

2

From the height where it nestled, the shop overlooked the Great Valley of the Appalachians. Forest covered the land below, multitudinously green, a-ripple with wind. Slender spearshafts rose from among the trees, hundreds of meters tall, hundreds in number, each bearing a crown. Far down and across, made hazy by remoteness, the woods gave way to an immensity of lawns. There towers and lower buildings stood widely spaced. Iridescence played over their fantastical shapes.

Tu Shan knew the elven country for an illusion. He had seen the various, always precise forms of those trees close up. They lived not to leaf, flower, and fruit, but to grow materials that no natural plant ever made. The park held – not factories – a technocomplex where another kind of growth went on, atom by atom under the control of giant molecules, tended by machines and overseen by computer, wombs of engines and vessels and other things once made by hands wielding tools. The shafts were rectennas, receiving solar energy beamed as microwaves from collector stations on the moon. He spied it overhead, a wan crescent nearly lost in the blue, and remembered that 'overhead' was also an illusion.

Once men sought enlightenment, escape from the mirage that is the world. Today they held that the phantasm was all there was.

Tu Shan trudged down the knob of rock where the aircab had found a spot to let him out. The shop was a pleasant sight before him, a house in antique style, timber walls and shake roof. Several pines reared behind it. The wind brought their sun-warmed fragrance to him.

He knew it wasn't actually a shop. Bardon usually prepared his electronic displays here because this was where he lived more than anywhere else. However, Express Service took them to his customers, who were scattered across the globe.

He had seen the cab descend and waited on his porch. 'Well, howdy,' he called. 'Haven't heard from you in quite a spell.' After a pause, 'Goldurn, five years, I bet. Maybe more. Time sure flies, don't it?'

Tu Shan kept still until he reached the other man. He wanted to study him. Bardon had changed. He remained tall and lanky, but he had discarded shirt and trousers in favor of a fashionable scintillant gown; his hair was dressed into ram's-horn curves; when he smiled, his mouth glittered. Yes, he too had decided it was unattractive to regrow outworn teeth every century or so, and gotten the cells in his jaws modified to produce diamond.

His handshake was the same as before. 'What've you been up to, friend?' A trace of mountaineer drawl lingered. Perhaps he cultivated it. The past kept some small glamour.

Not respect. How could anyone revere old age when everyone was perpetually young?

'I tried farming,' Tu Shan said.

'What? … Hey, come in, come in, and we'll have a drink. Man, it is good to see you again.'

Tu Shan noticed how Bardon avoided noticing the box he carried.

Most furniture he recognized, but otherwise the interior of the house had become rather stark. It held no trace of wares, nor of a woman. That made for a sense of emptiness, when Anse and June Bardon had been together for as long as he had known them, but Tu Shan felt shy of inquiring. He took a chair. His host splashed whiskey into glasses – that, at least, was a constant – and settled down facing him.

'You farmed, you say?' Bardon asked. 'What do you mean?'

'I sought … independence.' Tu Shan groped for words. He despised self-pity. 'This modern world, I am not at home here. I spent all the basic share I had, together with my savings, and pledged the rest, to buy some hectares in Yunnan that nobody else wanted very much. And animals, and –'

Bardon stared. 'You went clear back to subsistence farmin'?'

Tu Shan smiled lopsidedly. 'Not quite. I knew that was impossible. I meant to trade what I did not eat for things I needed and could not make myself. I thought home-grown produce would have a novelty value. But no. It became a hard and bitter existence. And the world crowded in anyhow. At last they wanted my land for a recreation lodge. I did not ask what kind. I was glad, then, to sell for a tiny profit.'

Bardon shook his head. 'You were lucky. You should have talked with me first. I would've warned you. If your food fad caught on, nanotech would duplicate it exactly and undersell you. But chances were, it couldn't succeed in the first place. The computers dream up novelties of every kind faster than people can consume them, or even hear about them.'

'Well, I spent most of my life in a simpler world than yours,' Tu Shan sighed. 'I made my mistake, I have learned my lesson. Now I have made more things for you.' He gestured at the box, which rested on his lap. 'An elephant, a lotus pattern, and the Eight Immortals, carved in ivory.' Tank-grown ivory, but formed by hand, using traditional tools.

Bardon winced, tossed off a mouthful of whiskey, braced himself. 'I'm sorry. You should have stayed in touch. I closed down that business three years ago.'

Tu Shan sat mute.

'I don't think anybody else is handlin' stuff like this any more, either,' Bardon slogged ahead. 'The value is gone. Uh, it's not because they can grow perfect copies. Of course they can. The certification that it's an original in a historic style, that made the difference. Till people stopped carin'.'

He hurried on into the silence: 'They aren't oafs. We haven't turned into a race of featherheads, whatever you may be thinkin'. It's just that, well, after you've got a few such items, do you want to spend the rest of eternity acquirin' more? Especially when the computers keep generatin' whole new concepts of art.'

'I see,' Tu Shan said. The words fell dull. 'We, the Survivors, we have told and done everything that we had in us … Well, what do you do these days, Anse?'

'Different things,' Bardon answered, relieved. 'Like you and your friends should.'

'What are yours?'

'M-m, well, I'm lookin' around. Haven't found any promisin' line of work yet, but – oh, we've got our lives to develop, don't we? Me, I think I might go into Pioneer Land for a while.' Bardon brightened. 'You should try some thin' like that. An Asian networkin', maybe. You'd have a lot to contribute, with your background.'

Tu Shan shook his head. 'Thank you, no.'

'Really, you don't just lie around in an electronic dream. You give input to the network, to everybody else linked with you. You come out with memories the same as though you'd lived it in the flesh.'

Illusion twice over, Tu Shan thought.

'Are you scared you won't be earnin' anything meanwhile?' persisted Bardon. 'Don't worry. You told me you recovered your losses on the farm. Basic share will be plenty for you while you're in retreat. Why, you should come out refreshed, full of ideas for new enterprises.'

'You may,' Tu Shan mumbled. 'I would not.' He stared down at his hands where they lay on the box, his big useless hands.

3

Fiera, who had been Raphael, formed a slow smile. 'Oh, yes,' she purred. 'I do enjoy being a woman.'

'Will you always be?' asked Aliyat; and inwardly: Did he always want this, down underneath? Even when we were making love?

Half a cry: You were such a fine lover, Ray! Strong, sweet, knowing. Did you understand how it hurt when you told me you were going to get yourself remade?

The beautiful head shook. Tresses, naturally violet, rippled over shoulders. 'I think not. Long enough to explore it, however long that may be. Afterward – we'll see. By then they expect to have nonhuman modifications perfected.' Fiera stroked fingers down her flanks. 'Half otter, or dolphin, or snake – But that's for later, much later. I imagine first I'll be some kind of man again.'

'Some kind!' escaped Aliyat.

Fiera raised her brows. 'You are dismayed, are you not? Poor dear, is that why I've had no word or sign of you in all this time?'

'No, I, well –' Aliyat looked away from the image that seemed wholly solid. 'I was –' She forced herself to meet the golden gaze. 'I thought you didn't care about me any more.'

'But I told you I did. Believe me, I was sincere. I still care. Why else would I finally have taken the initiative?' Hands reached out. 'Aliyat, darling, come to me. Or let me come to you.'

'For what, … now?'

Fiera stiffened the least bit. Some warmth dropped from her tone. 'We'll find out, won't we? Don't tell me you're shocked. Or was I wrong? I thought you were by far the most open-minded of the Survivors.'

Aliyat swallowed. 'It isn't that. I'm not inhibited. It's only – No, it isn't "only." You've changed everything. Nothing could be what it was.'

'Certainly not. That's the whole idea.' Fiera laughed. 'Suppose you turn male. We should find that interesting. Not unique, but special. Piquant.'

'No!'

Fiera sat a minute silent. When she spoke, she had gone earnest. 'You're like the rest of your kind after all. Or perhaps worse. I gather most of them make some effort to cope. You, though, you … accept. Suddenly I realize that's what fooled me. You never railed against the world. You agreed it was bound to evolve onward. But under that surface, you've stayed what you were, a primitive, a leftover from the age of mortality.'

Aliyat's defiance guttered out. She slumped. The sensuousness of the seat reshaping itself as she did was lost on her. 'No doubt you're right.'

Fiera smiled anew, this time sweetly. 'You aren't condemned to that, you know. The whole organism is pliable, including the brain. You can have your psyche altered.'

'Long-drawn. Expensive. Actually, I couldn't afford a simple sex change.' Simple! flickered through Aliyat. I remember when they faked it with surgery and hormone shots. Today they cause organs, glands, muscles, bones, everything to grow into something else. If I became a genuine man, what would I *think* like?

'Haven't you understood modern economics yet? All goods and most services – all services a machine can give – are as abundant as the air we breathe. Or could be, if there were any reason. Share is simply the easiest means of, oh, keeping track, coordinating what people do. And, yes, allocating resources that are limited; land, for instance. If you genuinely need liberation from your misery, arrangements can be made. I'll help you make them.' Again the image extended its arms. 'Dearest, let me.'

Aliyat straightened. The tears that she swallowed burned in her throat. '"Dearest," you say. What do you mean by that?'

Taken aback, Fiera hesitated before replying slowly, 'I'm fond of you. I want your company available to me, I want your welfare.'

Aliyat nodded. 'What love amounts to these days. Affection because of enjoyment.'

Flora bit her lip. 'There you are, mired in the past. When the family was the unit for breeding, production, defense, and its members must needs find ways not to feel trapped. You can't imagine the modern range of emotions; you refuse to try.' She shrugged. 'Odd, considering the life you led then. But I suppose you nursed an unconscious longing for security – what passed for security in those nightmare societies.'

Aliyat recalled explaining to Raphael what a nightmare was.

'How selfish were your feelings about me?' Fiera demanded.

Anger cracked a whip. 'Don't flatter yourself,' Aliyat said. 'I'll admit I was infatuated, but I knew that'd end. I did hope it would turn into something that would last, not exclusive, no, but something real. All right, I've learned better.'

'I had that hope too!' Fiera cried.

She sank back into her own seat. Once more she fell silent, thoughtful. Aliyat's gaze went off in search of refuge. She occupied a single room on the fourth sublevel of the Fountains; technology would never synthesize space. It seldom felt cramped, when the walls formed facilities on command and otherwise provided any scenes she wanted. Earlier today, rather than a contemporary view, she had raised medieval Constantinople. Maybe that was due to a nostalgia she knew was unjustified, maybe it was an attempt at getting back self-esteem; she'd been a principal consultant to the developers of the simulacrum. Hagia Sophia soared above swarming, jostling humanity. Odors of smoke, sweat, dung, roasting food, tar, sea livened the air; it moved, a salt breeze off the Horn. When Fiera's visicall came, Aliyat had stopped the sound but kept the vision. She could virtually hear wheels, hoofs, feet, raucous voices, snatches of plangent music. Those ghosts were as alive as the ghost that confronted her.

Finally Fiera said, 'I believe I know what drew you to me – what held you, after the first casual attraction. I was interested in you. I didn't take you for granted. You eight were a sensation once you came into the open, but by now most people were born later than that. You're simply here, getting along on share or on what occasional special jobs somebody happens to want done. Fewer and fewer of those, aren't there? But I – to me you were a bit intriguing. I'm not sure why.'

Aliyat thought she heard her suppress whatever pain she had permitted before she went on: 'I'll be honest. I used you up. I found nothing further to discover. But then, I'd used myself up. I *had* to change. It was my escape from boredom and futility. Now we can find freshness in each other again, if you wish. Only for a while, though, a short while, until I've become used to perceiving you with a female mind and senses. Unless you change too. How, I can't tell you. At best, I can offer a suggestion or two. The choice must be yours.

'If you refuse, if you stay in your narrow existence with your fossil soul, you'll be more and more isolated, you'll find less and less meaning in anything, and at last you'll choose death because it is not that lonely.'

Aliyat drew the ancient air into her lungs. 'I kept going this long,' she said. 'I'm not about to give up.'

'I'm glad to hear that. I expected it of you. But think, my dear, think. Meanwhile, best I go.'

'Yes,' Aliyat said. The image vanished.

After some minutes Aliyat rose. She stalked the floor. It yielded slightly, deliciously to her feet. Byzantium surged around her. 'Blank that scene,' she snapped. Pastel blue succeeded it. 'Delivery Service.' A panel came into existence, ready to open an orifice.

What do I want? A happy pill? Chemistry tailored to me, harmless, instant cheerfulness, head quite clear, probably more clear than it is at this moment. In the bad old days we got drunk or smoked dope, abused our bodies and our brains. Now science has mapped how feelings work, and everybody is sane every hour of the twenty-four.

Everybody who decides to be.

Hanno, Wanderer, Shan, Patulcius, where are you? Or – never mind sex, that's an old-fashioned consolation, isn't it? – Corinne, Asagao, Svoboda – whatever you're calling yourselves, a name's become as changeable as a garment – where are you? Which of you can come to me, or I to you? We had our fellowship after we got together, we were the only immortals and the middle of each other's universe while time blew by outside like the wind, but since we came forth we've drifted apart, we meet by accident and seldom, we say hello and try to talk and feel relieved when it ends. Where are my brothers, my sisters, my loves?

4

While he flew, communications verified that Wanderer was the person he claimed to be and had a permit to visit the control reserve. His car landed as directed, in a parking lot outside town, and he emerged suitcase in hand. Many everyday things, such as clothes, were not spot-produced here. He had reached – not exactly a hermit community, not a settlement of eccentrics trying to re-create a past that never was – but a society that went its own way and held much of the world at arm's length.

The lot was near the water's edge. Weather Service maintained the original Pacific Northwest climate as closely as was feasible. Clouds hung heavy. Mist swirled on the bay, making vague the rocks that towered from the waves, mysterious, like a Chinese painting. The conifer forest stood mighty behind the village, its darkness hardly relieved by splashes of bracken. Yet this was all alive, in silver-gray, white, black, greens deep or bright and asparkle with remnant raindrops. Surf boomed and whispered. Seals barked hoarsely, gulls hovered and dipped and mewed. Breath went cool, moist, tangy through nostrils to blood.

A man waited. Clad in plain shirt and work pants, he was stocky and brown-skinned. Not many whites among his ancestors, Wanderer decided. What had they been, then? Makah, Quinault? No difference. Tribes were hardly even names any more.

'Hello, Mr Wanderer.' There was an anachronism for you. The man extended his hand. Wanderer took it, felt calluses and sturdiness. 'Welcome. I'm Charlie Davison.'

Wanderer had practiced old-time American English before he left Jalisco. 'Glad to meet you. I didn't expect this. Figured I'd get acquainted on my own.'

'Well, we talked it over in the Council and decided this was better. You're not just another jako.' That must be local slang for the few hundred outsiders a year allowed to experience the wilderness. It sounded mildly contemptuous. 'Nor a scientist or official agent, are you?'

'N-no.'

'Come on, I'll see you to the hotel, and later I'll sort of introduce you around.' They started off. Soon they were on an unpaved road where puddles glimmered. 'Because you're a Survivor.'

Wanderer's smile twitched rueful. 'I didn't want to advertise that right away.'

'We ran a routine check before agreeing you could come, same as we do for everybody. You eight may go pretty much unnoticed, but you sure were famous once. Your background popped right out of the scan. Word got around. I hate to say this, nothing personal, but you'll find some folks here who resent you.'

That was an ugly surprise. 'Really? Why?'

'You Survivors can have children whenever you like.'.

'I ... see.' Wanderer considered how to respond. Gravel scrunched underfoot. 'Jealousy isn't reasonable, though. We're freaks of nature. A crazy combination of genes, including several unlikely mutations, that doesn't breed true. Normal human beings who don't want to age have to undergo the process. Well, we can't then let them reproduce freely. Remember your history, population explosion, the Great Death, and that was before athanatics.'

'I know.' Davison sounded a bit miffed. 'Who doesn't?'

'Sorry, but I have met quite a few who don't. They think history's too depressing to study. I point out to them that they'll have their chance to be parents eventually. There are accidental losses to make up, and interplanetary colonies may yet be founded.'

'Yeah. The waiting list for children was several centuries long, last time I looked.'

'Uh-huh. But as for us Survivors, ever hear of a grandfather clause? By revealing ourselves, we opened up a treasure trove for scholars. Fair is fair. As a matter of fact, we hardly ever do become parents.' We hardly ever have partners who are eligible. And any offspring we have grew too soon alien.

'I understand all that,' Davison said. 'I don't object, myself. I'm only telling you we'd better be, uh, tactful. That's a reason why I met you.'

'I do appreciate it.' Wanderer attempted to drive his point home: 'You might remind those objectors to my status that they can beget kids every bit as lawfully, no limit.'

'Because they're willing to shrivel and die in a hundred years or less.'

'That's the bargain. They can drop out whenever they choose, get youth restored if they've lost it, join the immortals. There is simply that small, necessary price to pay.'

'Sure, sure, sure,' Davison snapped. 'Think we've never heard?' After half a dozen strides: 'My turn to say, "Sorry." I didn't mean to sound mad. To most of us, you'll be very welcome. What yarns you have to spin!'

'Nothing you can't play off the databank, I'm afraid,' Wanderer said. 'We were questioned and interviewed dry many years ago.'

Generations before you were born, Charlie, if your lineage is purely mortal. How old are you? Forty, fifty? I see white sown through your hair and crow's-feet at your eyes.

'Not the same,' Davison answered. 'Good Lord, I'm in company with a man who knew Sitting Bull!' Actually, Wanderer had not, but he let it pass. 'Hearing it from you in person means so much more. Don't you forget, our whole idea is to live naturally, like God intended.'

'That's why I've come.'

Davison's pace faltered. He stared. 'What? We supposed you were … interested, like the rest of our visitors.'

'I am. Of course. But more than that. I guess we'd better not mention this immediately. However, I think I might settle here, if people will have me.'

'You?' asked Davison in amazement.

'I go way back, you know. To the tribes, the brotherhoods, rites and beliefs and traditions, living by our wits and hands off the land and of the land. Oh, I'm not romantic about it. I remember the drawbacks too clearly, and would certainly not want to revive, say, the horse barbarians. But still, damn it, we had a oneness with our world such as doesn't exist now, except maybe among you.'

They were entering the village. Boats rocked at the wharf; men fished for the local market. Kitchen gardens and apple trees burgeoned behind neatly made wooden houses. Mere supplements, Wanderer must remind himself, like their handicrafts. The dwellers spend share and order stuff delivered, same as the rest of us. For added earnings, some of them take care of these woods and waters; or they attend to the tourists; or they do brainwork out of their homes, over the computer net. They haven't disowned the modern world.

He thrust away memories of what he had witnessed elsewhere around the planet, the deaths slow or swift, always anguished, that overtook obsolete communities and ways of life, the ghost towns, empty campsites, forsaken graves. Instead, he searched about him for the secret of this folk's endurance.

Those on the street were a mingled lot, every race of mankind, together in their faith, wish, and fear. A church, tallest of their buildings, lifted its steeple cloudward; the cross on top declared that life eternal was not of the flesh but of the soul. Children were the desire, the reward. When and where else had Wanderer last seen a small hand clutching mother's, a round face turned his way to marvel? Calm gray heads bore the sense of having staved off dehumanization.

They recognized the newcomer; word had indeed gotten about. None crowded close. Their greetings to Davison were self-conscious, and Wanderer felt the looks, heard the buzz at his back. Not that the atmosphere was hostile. Doubtless only a minority begrudged him his privilege, as nearly meaningless as it was. Most seemed as if they looked forward to knowing him, and were simply too polite to introduce themselves at once. (Or else, since they were few and close-knit, it had been agreed they wouldn't.) Adolescents instantly lost the sullenness that hung on them.

That last struck Wanderer first as peculiar, then as disturbing. He paid closer attention. The elderly were a bare handful. Drawn shades and neglected yards showed what houses stood vacant.

'Well, you begin by relaxing and enjoying yourself,' Davison advised. 'Take the tours. Meet the jakos. They're okay, we screen 'em pretty carefully. How about dinner at my place tomorrow? My wife's anxious to meet you too, the kids are starry-eyed, and we'll invite two-three other couples that I think you'll like.'

'You're awfully kind.'

'Oh, I'll benefit, and Martha, and –' The hotel was ahead, a rambling structure whose antiquarian verandah looked over the bay and the sea beyond. Davison slowed his gait and lowered his voice. 'Listen, we don't just want to hear stories from you. We want to ask about … details, the kind that don't get in the news or the databank, the kind we don't notice ourselves when we go outside, because we don't know what to watch for.'

The chill deepened in Wanderer. 'You mean you wish I'd explain how life there feels to me – to a person who didn't grow up in those ways?'

'Yes, that's it, if you please. I realize I'm asking a lot, but, well –'

456

'I'll try,' Wanderer said.

Unspoken: You're giving serious thought to moving away, Charlie, to renouncing this whole existence and creed and purpose.

I knew the enclave is shrinking, that its children usually leave soon after they reach legal adulthood, that recruits have become vanishingly scarce. I knew it's as doomed as the Shakers were in their day. But your middle-aged are also quitting, so quietly that the fact wasn't in what I studied about you. I'd hoped for a mortal lifetime or two of peace, of belonging. Set that aside, Wanderer.

Guests were clustered on the porch. They pointed and jabbered. He stopped and turned to see. Barely visible through the haze, three giant shapes slipped past the mouth of the bay.

'Whales,' Davison told him. 'They're multiplying fine. We spot more every year.'

'I know,' said Wanderer. 'Right whales, those. I remember when they were declared extinct.' I wept.

They were recreated in the laboratories, reintroduced to a nature that is completely managed. This is no wilderness other than in name. It's a control reserve, a standard of comparison for Ecological Service to use. No true wilderness is left, anywhere on Earth, unless in the human heart, and there too the intellect knows how to govern.

I shouldn't have come here. Now I'll have stay a week or so, for courtesy's sake, for the sake of this man and his kin; but I should have known better than to come.

I should be stronger than to let this hurt me so.

5

Nowhere was Yukiko ever alone with the stars.

Solitude she could have, yes. The powers and, mostly, the people were gracious to Survivors. She often thought that graciousness had become the common and principal virtue of humanity. It led to an impersonal kindliness. Unhindered room was the sole good in which the world was impoverished. Nevertheless, when she expressed her longing, this atoll became hers. Minuscule though it be, that was an Aladdin's gift.

Yet the stars were denied her.

A few blinked wan after dark, Sirius, Canopus, Alpha Centauri, sometimes others, together with Venus, Mars, Jupiter, Saturn. Their constellations lost in the nacreous luminance, she was rarely sure which she saw. Satellites twinkled swift across heaven. The moon shone mistily, and on its dark part she made out steady sparks, the light of technocomplexes and the Triple City. Aircraft went in firefly swarms. Occasionally a spacecraft passed, majestic meteor, and thunders rolled from horizon to horizon; but that was seldom, most operations being off Earth and robotic.

She had resigned herself to the loss. Weather control, atmosphere maintenance, massive energy transfers were necessary; they caused fluorescence; that was that. She could fill the walls and ceiling of her house with a starscape as grand as if she stood in an Arizona desert before Columbus, or she could visit a sensorium and know naked space. Still, ungratefully, when she was outdoors in this her refuge, she wished she didn't have to conjure the night sky out of memories.

The ocean murmured. Reflection sheened off much of it, where aquaculture did not blanket the waves. Brightnesses bobbed yonder, boats, ships, a bargetown plodding along. Surf made white unrest beyond the lagoon, which was a well of sky-glow. The noise felt hushed, less loud than coral gritting beneath her feet. Her lungs drank cool purity. Each day she wordlessly thanked untold gigabillions of microorganisms for keeping the planet clean. That humans – computers – had designed and produced them to do it made no difference; theirs was a wonderful karma.

She passed by her garden, dwarf trees, bamboo, stones, twining paths. A machine was noiselessly busy there. Newly returned from Australia, where she had found herself involved in one more fleeting affair, she hadn't thus far taken over that work again.

Well, she wasn't very gifted for it. If only Tu Shan – but he didn't like these surroundings.

Her house lay shadowy, a small and subtle blending of curves. Her worldlet, she was apt to think. It provided or had brought to her everything she needed and more. Self-repairing, it could do so for as long as the energy arrived. Now and then she wished it would make sense for her to take a dusting cloth in her hand.

And I was once a lady of the court, she thought. Wryness tugged her lips upward.

Dismiss those feelings. She had gone to sit by the sea and empty her mind, open her soul, until she felt ready to use her intelligence. Whatever harmony she had won to was fragile.

A wall opened for her. Light bloomed within. The room was furnished in ascetic ancient style. She knelt on a straw mat before the computer terminal and raised the electronic spirit.

A portion of that immense rationality identified her and spoke in suitable, musical language and phrases. 'What is your desire, my lady?'

No, not really suitable. Desire was the snare. She had even forsaken her old, old name of Morning Glory and become – once again, after a thousand years – Small Snow, as a sign to herself of renunciation. But that too had failed. 'I have meditated on what you told me about life and intelligence among the stars, and decided to learn as much of this as I am able. Teach me.'

'It is a matter complex and chaotic, my lady. As far as the exploratory robots have taken our knowledge, life is rare, and only three unmistakably sentient species are known, all technologically in an equivalent of the human paleolithic era. Three others are controversial. Their behavior may be elaborately instinctive, or it may arise in minds too unlike the Terrestrial to be recognizable as such. Whatever they are, these creatures too possess only simple implements. On the other hand, the Web has detected anomalous radiation sources at greater distances, which may mean high-energy civilizations analogous to ours. Depending on how the data are interpreted, they may number as many as seven hundred fifty-two. The nearest is at an estimated remove of four hundred seventy-five parsecs. Additionally, the Web is receiving signals that are almost certainly informational from twenty-three different sources, identified with bodies or regions that are astrophysically unusual. We doubt that these signals are directed at us especially. We do not know whether any transmitters are in direct contact with each other. There are indications that they use distinct codes. Data thus far are insufficient for more than the most tentative and fragmentary suggestions of possible meaning.'

'I know! Everybody does. You've told me already, and it was unnecessary then.'

Yukiko fought down irritation. The machine was godlike in its power, it could do a million years' worth of human reasoning in a day, but it had no right to patronize her ... It didn't intend to. It habitually repeated itself to humans because many of them needed that. She eased, let the emotion surge and die like a wave. Calm, she said, 'As I understand it, the messages are not about mathematics or physics.'

'They do not appear to be, and it seems implausible that civilizations would spend time and bandwidth exchanging knowledge that all must certainly possess. Perhaps they concern other sciences, such as biology. However, that implies that our understanding of physics is incomplete, that we have not by now delineated every possible kind of biochemistry in the universe. We have no evidence for such an assumption.'

'I know,' Yukiko repeated, but patiently. 'And I've heard the argument that it can't be politics or anything like that, when transmission times are in centuries. Do they compare histories, arts, philosophies?'

'Conceivably.'

'I believe that. It would make sense.' Unless organic life withers away. But won't machine minds also wonder about the ultimate? 'I want to master your ... analysis. I'm aware I can't make any contribution, nothing original.

Let me follow along, though. Give me the means to think about what you have learned and are learning.'

'That could be done, within limits,' said the gentle voice. 'It would require much time and effort on your part. Do you care to explain your reasons?'

Yukiko couldn't help it, her words trembled. 'They, those beings, they must be advanced far beyond us –'

'Not likely, my lady. To the best of present-day knowledge, and it appears seamless, nature sets bounds on technological possibilities; and we have determined what those bounds are.'

'I don't mean in engineering, I mean in, in understanding, enlightenment.' Inner peace was gone. Her pulse stammered. 'You don't see what I'm talking about. Would anybody nowadays, any human being?' Except Tu Shan and perhaps, if they tried, the rest of our fellowship. We hark back to when people felt these questions were real.

'Your purpose is clear,' said the electronics mildly. 'Your concept is not absurd. Quantum mechanics fails at such levels of complexity. Mathematically speaking, chaos sets in, and one must make empirical observations.'

'Yes, yes! We must learn the language and listen to them!'

Did she hear regret within the inexorability? The system could optimize its reactions for her. 'My lady, what information we have is totally inadequate. The mathematics leaves no doubt. Unless the character of what we receive changes in fundamental ways, we shall never be able to interpret it for any such subtleties. Be warned, if that is what interests you, studying the material will be an utter waste of your time.'

She had not dared lift hopes too high, but this smashed down upon her.

'Instead, wait,' counselled the system. 'Remember, our robotic explorers travel at virtual light speed. They should begin arriving at the nearer sources, to observe and interact, in about a millennium. Perhaps fifteen centuries after that, we, will begin to hear from them, and truly begin to learn. You are immortal, my lady. Wait.'

She smothered tears. I am not a saint. I cannot endure that long while existence has no meaning.

6

Suddenly, warningless, the rock gave way under Tersten's boots. For an instant he seemed frozen, arms flung wide, against an infinity of stars. Then he toppled from sight.

Svoboda, second in file, had time to thump her staff down and squeeze the firing button. Gas jetted white from vents as a piton shot into stone. The barrel locked onto the upper part of the shaft. She clung. The line slammed taut.

Even under lunar gravity, that force was brutal. Her soles skidded on a treacherously thin dust layer. Gripping the staff, she kept upright.

Violence ended. Silence pressed on the faint cosmic hiss in her earplugs. She had been yanked forward about two meters. The line continued upslope and over a verge formed when the ledge they had been following went to pieces. It should have been strained tight by Tersten's weight. She saw with horror that it drooped slack. Had it broken? No, it couldn't have.

'Tersten!' she cried. 'Are you all right?' The wavelength diffracted around the edge. If he hung there, it was only about a meter below. She got no response. The seething gibed.

She turned her head more than her body toward Mswati behind her. His beltflash cast a pool of undiffused light at his feet. Through a well-nigh invisible helmet it dazzled her, made him a shadow against the starlit gray of the mountainside. 'Come here,' she ordered. 'Carefully, carefully. Take hold of my staff.'

'Yes,' he acknowledged. Though she hadn't been leading the climb, she was the team captain. The expedition was her idea. Moreover, she was a Survivor. The others were in their twenties or thirties. Beneath all the informality and fellowship, they bore a certain awe of her.

'Stand by,' she said when he reached her. 'I'm going ahead to look. If more crumbles, I'll try to spring back, and may well fall off the ledge. Be prepared to brake me and haul me up.'

'No, I will go,' he protested. She dismissed that with a chopping gesture and set off on hands and knees.

It was a short crawl, but time stretched while she felt her way forward. On her right a cliff went nearly sheer into a nightful abyss. Flexible as skin, tough as armor, her space-suit wouldn't protect her against such a fall. Vision searched and probed. Sensors in the gloves told her more through her hands than they could have learned naked. At the back of her mind, it annoyed that she should be aware of sweat-smells and dry mouth. While the suit recycled air and water, at the moment she was overloading its thermostat and capacity for breaking down wastes.

The suface held. The ledge continued beyond a three-meter gap. She made out pockmarks near the break in it. So, she thought – she must not agonize over Tersten, not yet – once in the past a shotgun meteoroid shower had struck here. Probably radiation spalling then weakened the stone further, turning that section into an unforeseeable trap.

Well, everybody had said this undertaking was crazy. The first lunar circumambulation? To go clear around the moon on foot? *Why?* You'll endure toil and hardship and danger, for what? You won't carry out any observations a robot can't do better. You won't gain anything but a fleeting notoriety, largely for your foolishness. Nobody will ever repeat the stunt. There are gaudier thrills to be had in a sensorium, higher achievements among the computers.

'Because it is real,' was the best retort she found.

She came to the edge and put her head over. On the horizon a sliver of rising sun shone above a crater. It turned desolation into a jumble of light and dark. Her helmet saved her eyesight by immediately stopping the glare down to a dull gold. Elsewhere it stayed clear. Her heart thuttered. Tersten dangled beneath her, limp. She loudened radio reception and heard snoring breath.

'He's unconscious,' she reported to Mswati. Examining: 'I see what the trouble is. His line caught in a crack on this verge. Impact jammed it in tight.' She rose to her knees and tugged. 'I can't free it. Come.'

The young man joined her. She rose. 'We don't know how he's injured,' she said. 'We must be gentle. Secure the end of my line and lower me over the side. I'll clasp him and you haul us both in, me on the bottom to absorb any shocks and scrapes.'

That went well. Both were strong, and, complete with spacesuit and backpack full of intricate chemistries, a person weighed only some twenty kilos. While he was in her arms Tersten opened his eyes and moaned.

They laid him out on the ledge. Waiting till he could speak, Svoboda gazed west. The heights dropped down toward a level darkness that was Mare Crisium. Earth hung low, daylit part marbled white and blue, unutterably lovely. Memories of what it had once been struck like a knife. Damnation, why did that have to be the one solitary planet fit for humans?

Oh, the lunar cities and the inhabited satellites were pleasant, and unique diversions were available there. She was more at home in them than on Earth, actually – or, rather, was less an exile. Their people, such as these her comrades, sometimes thought and felt much as people used to think and feel. Though that too was changing. On which account you scarcely ever heard talk about terraforming Mars and Venus any longer. Now when it could be done, hardly anybody was interested.

Well, she and her seven kin had always known change. Merchant princes and brawling warriors were strangers to petty bourgeoisie and subservient peasants under the Tsars, who in turn were foreign to twentieth-century engineers and cosmonauts ... Yet they had all shared most of what they were with each other, and with her. How many still did?

Tersten brought her from her memories when he gasped, 'I'm awake,' and struggled to sit up. She knelt, urged caution, helped and supported him. 'Water,' he said. The suit swung a tube to his mouth and he drank greedily. 'A-a-ah, good.'

Concern furrowed Mswati's chocolate countenance. 'How are you?' he asked. 'What happened?'

'How should I know?' Clarity and a little vigor returned to Tersten's voice as he talked. 'Sore in the belly, sharp pains in my lower left chest, especially when I bend or take a deep breath. Earache, also.'

'Sounds like a cracked or broken rib, maybe two,' Svoboda said. Relief overwhelmed her. He could have been killed, suffered such brain damage that revivification would have been pointless. 'My guess is that a falling boulder hit you with more force than your suit could withstand. Hm, yes, see.' Her finger traced the semblance of a scar. The fabric had been ripped open, and promptly closed itself again. Within an hour it would be completely healed. 'Everything conspired against us, didn't it? We're not going to scale this mountain. No matter. It was hardly more than a whim of ours. Let's get you back down to camp.'

Tersten insisted he could walk, and managed a gait halfway between a step and a shuffle. 'We'll call for a vehicle to fetch you,' Mswati said. As if to confirm, a relay satellite flitted across the constellations. 'The rest of us can finish. It will be easier going from here than it was on farside.'

Tersten bridled. 'No, you don't! I'll not be cheated out of this.'

Svoboda smiled. 'Have no worries,' she reassured. 'I'm sure you'll just need a knitpatch or two injected, and they can return you to us in fifty hours or so. We'll wait where we are. Frankly, I wouldn't mind slacking off that long.' An inner glow: My kind of human is not altogether extinct.

Bleakness: How many years can you remain what you are, Tersten? You'll have no reason to.

Do I keep young in spirit, or merely immature? Has our history damned us, the Survivors, to linger retarded while our descendants evolve beyond our comprehension?

The plateau and camp came in view. Genia ran to meet the party. Someone must stay behind in case of trouble. She had gotten the shelter deployed. More a mothering organism than a tent, it spread beneath the radiation shields that curved like wings from the top of the freight carrier. 'Tersten, Tersten!' she called. 'I was terrified, listening in. If we'd lost you –' She reached them. All four embraced. For that moment, at least, under the stars, Svoboda was again among beloved friends.

7

'You see,' Patulcius strove to explain, 'what I have done is what the old Americans would have called "worked myself out of a job."'

The curator of Oxford, who for reasons unrevealed to him currently used the name Theta-Ennea, lifted her brows. She was comely in a gaunt fashion, but he never doubted that under the plumes growing from her otherwise bare scalp lay a formidable brain. 'The record indicates that you served well,' she said – or did she sing? 'However, why do you suppose you might find occupation here?'

Patulcius glanced from her, through the glass window of her almost as anachronistic office. Outside, wind chased sunlight and cloud shadows along High Street. Across it dreamed the beautiful buildings of Magdalen College. Three persons wandered by, looking, occasionally touching. He suspected they were young, though of course you couldn't tell. 'This isn't simply a museum,' he replied after a moment. 'People do live in the town. The preservation of things puts them in special relationships among themselves and to you. I imagine that makes a kind of community. My experience – They must have problems, nothing too serious but nevertheless problems, questions of conflicting rights, duties, wants. You must have mediational procedures. Procedures are my strong point.'

'Can you be more specific?' Theta-Ennea asked.

Patulcius turned his gaze back to her. 'I would first have to know the situation, the nature of the community, customs and expectations as well as rules and regulations,' he admitted. 'I can learn quickly and well.' He smiled. 'I did for two thousand years and more.'

'Ah, yes.' Theta-Ennea gave back the smile. 'Naturally, when you requested an interview, I tapped the databank about you. Fascinating. From Rome of the Caesars through the Byzantine and Ottoman Empires, the Turkish Republic, the Dynasts, and – Yes, a story as marvelous as it is long. That is why I invited you to come in person.' Ruefully: 'I too have an outmoded preference for concreteness and immediacy. Therefore I hold this position.' She sighed. 'It is not a sinecure. I confess I have not had time to assimilate everything about you.'

Patulcius manufactured a chuckle. 'Frankly, I'm glad of that. I didn't enjoy the burst of fame when we Survivors manifested ourselves. Gradually becoming obscure again was ... pleasant.'

Theta-Ennea leaned back behind her desk, which was of plain wood, possibly an antique, and bore nothing except a small omniterminal. 'If I recall rightly, you joined the other seven quite late.'

Patulcius nodded. 'After the bureaucratic structure finally and irreversibly collapsed around me. We'd kept in touch, of course, and they made me welcome, but I've never been, m-m, intimate with them.'

'Is that why you made more of an effort than they to become integrated with the modern world?'

Patulcius shrugged. 'Perhaps. I'm not given to self-analysis. Or perhaps I just happened to have an opportunity none of them did. My talent, such as it is, is for – no, "administration" claims too much. Operations maintenance; the humble but essential chores that keep the social machinery running. Or that used to.'

Theta-Ennea drooped her lids and regarded him closely before she said, 'You have done more than that in the past fifty or a hundred years.'

'Conditions were unique. For the first time in a long time, they were such that I was qualified to take a hand in coping. No credit to me. Historical happenstance. I am being honest with you. But I did gain experience.'

Again she pondered. 'Would you please explain? Give me your interpretation of those conditions.'

He blinked, surprised, and spoke hesitantly. 'I have nothing but banalities … Well, if you insist. The advanced countries – no, I should say the high-technology civilization – had gone so far, so fast. It and the societies that had not assimilated the revolution, they became like different species. It had to absorb them, the alternatives were all horrible, but the gap in ways of living, thinking, understanding, was huge. I was among the few who could … talk, function … more or less effectively on both sides of that gap. I gave what assistance I could to those poor people, developing suitable organization to get them through the transition – when *your* people no longer had an old-fashioned, paper-shuffling, purely human bureaucracy, and were not sure how to build one. That is what I did. I did not do it alone by any means,' he finished. 'My apologies for lecturing on the obvious.'

'It is not absolutely obvious,' Theta-Ennea said. 'You speak from a viewpoint that has no counterpart anywhere. I would like to hear much more. It should help me come nearer empathizing with those scores of generations who made this place what it was. Because I never quite could, you see. With all the curiosity and, yes, all the love in the world, I have never quite, been able to feel what they felt.'

She rested her arms on the desktop and went on compassionately, 'But you, Gnaeus Cornelius Patulcius, and the many other names you have borne – in spite of them, in spite of your recent engagements, you also have yet to understand. No, I have no job for you. You should have known as much. Since you did not, how can I explain?

'You assumed this must be a community in some sense, like those where you were, where the dwellers share certain interests and a certain sense of common identity. I have to tell you – this isn't simple, it isn't ever spelled out; hardly anybody realizes what is happening, just as hardly anybody in the time of Augustus or of Galileo realized what was happening – but I spend my life trying to fathom the currents of history –' Her laugh was forlorn. 'Pardon me, let me back up and start over.

'Except for a few moribund enclaves, community in a general sense has dissolved. We still use the word and go through some of the forms, but they are nearly as empty as a fertility rite or an election would be. Today we are purely individuals. Our loyalties, if "loyalty" has any meaning left, are to various and ever-varying configurations of personalities. Has this fact wholly escaped you?'

'Well, uh, well, no,' Patulcius floundered, 'but –'

'I can offer you nothing in the way of work,' Theta-Ennea finished. 'I doubt anyone anywhere can, any longer. However, if you care to stay a while in Oxford, we can talk. I think we might learn something from each other.'

For whatever help that may be to you afterward, she left unsaid.

8

The world abides. I am still I, bone, blood, and flesh, aware of the induction unit that enwraps me but also of walls and their views across the outside, silvery-hued turf, a fountain arcing in fractals, an enormous shell of diamond within which, I have heard, grows a new kind of comet-mining spacecraft, flashes in the sky as a weather control module implants energy, the allness exterior to me. So quiet is this room that I hear my breath go in and out, my pulse, the rustle of hair when my head moves on the couch. What happens to me is a waxing of interior cognizance until soon it is the outside that is the ghost.

I descend into myself. My whole past opens to my ranging. Again I am a slave, a fugitive, a servant, a leader, a companion; again I love and lose, bear and bury. I lie on a sunlit hillside with my man, the clover smell and buzz of bees are sweet to know, we watch a butterfly pass; it is gone, these five hundred years.

There are blurs, there are gaps. I am not sure whether lichen grew on yonder stone. Yes, quantum randomness gathers its tax – but slowly, and I can renew what matters, even as my body renews itself. A neuropeptide links to the receptor on a nerve cell …

Come. The thought is not mine. It becomes mine. I am conducted, I conduct myself, onward and inward.

Thus far went my training. Today I am ready for oneness.

I do not go into the network. Nothing moves but those fields, mathematical functions, that the world perceives as forces, particles, light, itself. In a sense the network enters me. Or it unfolds before me, as I before it.

My guide takes form. No shape walks beside me, no hand holds mine. Nonetheless I am conscious of the body, though it may lie halfway around the planet, in the way that I am conscious of my own. His person is tall, slender, blue-eyed. His personality is blithe and sensuous. *You were once Flora (I learn of you)*, he thinks to me. *Then I will be Faunus.* He would like us to meet afterward for purposes of exploration. That is the merest ripple through an intelligence born of a brain made flawless. He has the gift of sympathy too, that he may help a neophyte such as me begin to partake.

Timidly, then warily, then ardently I mesh the flow of my identity with his. Thereby I more and more know the entire linkage. I have studied an abstraction. Today I am in and of the reality. Currents go like billows, crest-ing, troughing, weaving new waves. From them spring figures many-patterned and crystalline as snowflakes, brilliancies that expand outward through multiple dimensions, shift, flicker, dance in eternal change; and this is the language and the music that speak to me. Afar, immanent, core, outermost, the great computer sustains the matrices of our beings, vivifies them, sends them on their orbits and summons them home. Yet it is at our behest. We are what happens, the oneness, the god.

We. Minds reach forth, touch, join. Here is Phyllis, my human teacher, who first accompanied me along the fringes. I have her self-image, small, dark, long-haired, though in dim wise because she is not thinking about her body. I recognize the gentleness, patience, toughness. Suddenly I can share her interest in tactile harmonics and microgravity laser polo. Her warmth embraces me.

And here is Nils. Even without image or name, I would know that laughter. We are good friends, we have sometimes been lovers. *Did you truly never want to be more than that, Nils? Do immortality and invulnerability breed fear of permanence?*

You belong to an age that is dead, my dear. You must free yourself of it. We will aid you.

How is it I feel cold, here where space is a fiction and time an inconstant? *No, this is not really you, Nils. I haven't sensed your thoughts before, but surely they would not float free of all feeling like these.*

You are right. I am not in the network. This is my double, the downloaded configuration of my mind. Whenever I rejoin it, I grow the richer by what it has known while I was away. (Increasingly I have found you dull and shallow. I had not the heart to tell you so, then, but now there is no more hiding.)

By his emotion I know that Faunus – glands, nerves, the whole animal heritage – is physically linked like me. *Be of good cheer, Flora. You have boundless choices. Evolve with us.*

Another mind comes to the forefront of me. It too is bodiless, but forever. A certain kindliness glows yet (because memories of loss and sorrow do, no longer felt yet still, in shadow fashion, understood?) to make it bid me *Behold.*

He was a physicist who dreamed of discoveries. Already the unification had been achieved, the grand equation written. Defiant, he cherished his hopes. He knew full well how unlikely it was that any law remained unknown, that any experiment would ever again give a result for which the synthesis could not account. Absolute proof of absolute knowledge is impossible, though. And if he never stumbled on some basic new phenomenon, the interplay of the quanta must keep casting forth surprises for him to quest through.

The computer system perfected itself. Nothing he had found with his subtlest and most powerful instrumentation was beyond its analysis. Everything he might find in his laboratories, it could predict beforehand, in ultimate detail. His science had reached the end of its search.

Idle hedonism repelled him. He set a device to shut down his body while it programmed the patterns that were his mind into the system.

Are you happy?

Your question is meaningless. I am occupied. I participate in operations, I am one with the accomplishments. Time is mine to do with as I will. For it may take an hour to plan Earth's weathers a year ahead, with the measures necessary to contain chaos; it may take a day to design an extension of the Web or compute the fate of a galaxy ten billion light-years hence on which it has accumulated sufficient data; but each bit of information processed is an event, and to me those hours are as a million years or more. Afterward I may descend to the pace of human thought and learn what went on while I was transfigured. On this I meditate. It is small but interesting. Grow into augmentation, Flora, and at last you will share splendor, promises the shade.

From Phyllis I understand that few desire such a destiny. They will stay organic, however mutable. Linkage is pleasure, enlightenment, challenge. Joined, we realize what we cannot realize singly, about each other and about the cosmos. We bring our revelations back and refashion them in our separate ways. New arts, skills, philosophies, joys, newnesses for which no old name exists, spring into being. Thus do we enlarge and fulfill ourselves.

Come. Try. Surrender what you are to find what you are.

I merge into Phyllis, Faunus, phantom Nils. We are a self that never was before. I am slave who won to freedom, teacher and sportswoman, photosculptor and sybarite, dilettante mathematician and serious athlete. We will need many unions to ease the conflicts and create a single creature –

A whirl, a wheeling, a measure in the dance. Others have been with us. I withdraw and merge again. I am servant who won to a sort of queenship, gilled inhabitant of the sea, professional imaginer, artificial personality designed by the whole in conjunction with the computer –

They fly together, they lose themselves, the hive mind blazes and thunders – No!

Let me out! – and I flee down endless echoful corridors. Fear howls at my heels. It is myself that pursues.

She was alone, save for the medical machine that watched over her. For a while she merely shuddered. The breath sawed in her throat. Her sweat stank.

Terror faded. The sense of unspeakable loss that followed went deeper and lasted longer. Only as that too drained from her did she gain the strength to weep.

I'm sorry, Phyllis, Faunus, Nils, everybody, she called into the empty room. You meant so well. I wanted to belong, I wanted to find meaning in this world of yours. I cannot. To me, becoming what I must become would be to destroy all I am, the whole of the centuries and the folk forgotten by everyone else and the comradeship in secret that formed me. I was born too soon for you. It is now too late for me. Can you understand, and forgive?

9

They met in reality. You cannot embrace an image. Fortune favored them. They were able to use a visitor house at Lake Mapourika control reserve, on the South Island of what Hanno to this day thought of as New Zealand.

The weather was as lovely as the setting. They gathered around a picnic table. He remembered another such board beneath another sky, long and long ago. Here a greensward sloped down to still waters in which forest and the white mountains behind stood mirrored. Woodland fragrances arose with the climbing of the sun. From high overhead drifted birdsong.

The eight matched the quietness of the morning. Yesterday passions had stormed and clamored. At the head of the table, Hanno said:

'I probably needn't speak. We seem to be pretty well agreed. Just the same, it's wise to talk this over calmly before making any final decision.

'We have no more home, anywhere on Earth. We've tried in our different ways to fit in, and people have tried to help us, but we finally face the fact that we can't and never shall. We're dinosaurs, left over in the age of the mammals.'

Aliyat shook her head. 'No, we're left-over humans,' she declared bitterly. 'The last alive.'

'I wouldn't say that,' Macandal replied. 'They are changing, more and faster than we can match, but I wouldn't take it on myself to define what is human.'

'Ironic,' Svoboda sighed. 'Should we have foreseen? A world where we could, at last, come forth would necessarily be a world altogether unlike any that ever was before.'

'Self-satisfied,' Wanderer said. 'Turned inward.'

'You're being unfair too,' Macandal told him. 'Tremendous things are going on. They simply aren't for us. The creativity, the discovery, has moved to – what? Inner space.'

'Perhaps,' Yukiko whispered. 'But what does it find there? Emptiness. Meaninglessness.'

'From your viewpoint,' Patulcius replied. 'I admit that I too am unhappy, for my own reasons. Still, when the Chinese stopped their seafaring under the Ming, they did not stop being artists.'

'But they sailed no more,' Tu Shan said. 'The robots tell us of countless new worlds among the stars; and nobody cares.'

'Earth is pretty special, as we should have expected all along,' Hanno reminded him needlessly. 'The nearest planet reported where humans *might* be able to live in natural surroundings is almost fifty light-years from here.

Why mount an enormous effort to send a handful of colonists that far, possibly to their doom, when everybody's doing well at home?'

'So they truly could live their – our own kind of lives again, on our own land,' Tu Shan said.

'A community,' Patulcius chimed in.

'If we failed, we could seek elsewhere.' Svoboda's voice rang. 'If nothing else, we would be human beings out yonder, doing and daring for ourselves.'

Her look challenged Hanno. The rest likewise turned toward him. Although until now he had barely hinted at his intentions, it was no great surprise when he spoke. Yet somehow the words came before them like a suddenly drawn sword.

'I think I can get us a ship.'

10

The conference was not a meeting of persons, nor even their images. That is, Hanno's representation went around the globe, and faces appeared shiftingly before his eyes; but this was mere supplement, a minute additional data input. Some of yonder minds were computer-linked, or in direct touch with each other, from time to time or all the time. Others were electronic. He thought of them not by names, though names were known to him, but by function; and the same function often spoke with differing voices. What he confronted, what enveloped him, were the ruling intellects of the world.

We've come a long way from you, Richelieu, he thought. I wish we hadn't.

'Yes, it is possible to build such a spacecraft,' said the Engineer. 'Indeed, preliminary designs were drawn up more than a century ago. They showed what the magnitude of the undertaking must be. That is a major reason why it was never done.'

'It can't be so far beyond the one I was flitting around the Solar System in,' Hanno protested. 'And the robotic vessels already push the speed of light.'

'You should have studied the subject more thoroughly before you broached your proposal.'

Hanno bit his lip. 'I tried.'

'It is transhumanly complex,' the Psychologist conceded. 'We ourselves are employing only a semitechnical summary.'

'The basic principles involved ought to be obvious,' the Engineer said. 'Robots have no need of life support, including the comforts necessary for human sanity, and they require minimal protection. For them, an interstellar carrier can be of very low mass, with small payload. Nevertheless, each represents a substantial investment, notably in antimatter.'

'"Investment" means resources diverted from other uses,' observed the Economist. 'Modern society is productive, rich, yes, but not infinitely so.

There are projects closer to home, that an increasing body of opinion maintains should be started.'

'The sheer size of the universe defeats us,' sighed the Astronomer. 'Consider. We have received the first beam-casts from robots that have gone about a hundred and fifty light-years. It will take longer before we hear from those few we have sent farther. The present sphere of communication contains an estimated forty thousand stars, much too many for us to have dispatched a vessel to each, the more so when the vast majority are dim red dwarfs or cold sub-dwarfs. The suns not too unlike Sol have generally proved disappointing. True, a flood of scientific discoveries already overwhelms the rate at which we can properly assimilate them; but the public finds little of it especially exciting, and nothing that could be considered a revolutionary revelation.'

'I know all that, of course I do –' Hanno began.

The Engineer interrupted him: 'You ask for a manned ship that can reach the same speeds. We grant you, no matter how long-lived you are, anything else makes little sense. Even for a handful of people, especially if they hope to found a colony, the hull must be spacious, correspondingly massive; and the mass of their necessities will exceed that by a large factor. Those necessities include laser and magnetohydrodynamic systems able to shield against radiation as well as to draw in sufficient interstellar gas for the reaction drive. The drive in turn will consume an amount of antimatter that will deplete our reserves here in the Solar System for years to come. It is not quickly or easily produced, you know.

'Moreover, the robot craft are standardized. A scaleup such as you have in mind demands complete, basic redesign. The preliminary work stored in the database indicates how much computer capability it will take – enough to significantly curtail operations elsewhere. Production, likewise, cannot use existing parts or facilities. Whole new plants, both nanotechnological and mechanical, and a whole new organization, must come into being. The time from startup to departure may well be as long as a decade, during which various elements of society will endure noticeable inconvenience.

'In short, you wish to impose a huge cost on mankind, in order to send a few individuals to a distant planet which, it seems, *may* be habitable for them.'

Yes, Hanno thought, the job will beggar the Pyramids. And after a while the Pharaohs stopped building pyramids. It was too expensive. Nobody wanted it any more.

Aloud, with a stiff smile: 'I am aware of everything you've told me, at least in a general way. I'm also aware that today's world can do the job without imposing hardship on anyone. Please don't poor-mouth me. You must see some merit in my idea, or we wouldn't be having this meeting.'

'You Survivors are unique,' murmured the Artist. 'To this day, you keep a certain appeal, and a certain special interest for those who care about whence we came.'

'And where we may be going!' Hanno exclaimed. 'I'm talking about the future, all humanity's. Earth and Sol won't last forever. We can make our *race* immortal.'

'Humankind will deal with geological problems when they arise,' the Astronomer said. 'They won't for several billion years.'

Hanno refrained from saying: I think anything that might be called human will be long extinct by then, here. Death, or transfiguration? I don't know. To me, it hardly matters which.

'Any idea of large-scale interstellar colonization is ludicrous,' declared the Economist.

'If it could be done,' said the Astronomer, 'it would have been done already, and we would know about it.'

Yes, I've heard the argument, over and over, from the twentieth century onward. If the Others exist, where are They? Why have Their exploring robots, at least, never visited Earth? We ourselves, we're interested enough to send follow-ups to those primitive sapients we've found. What little we've learned thus far has touched our thinking, our arts, our spirits in subtle ways – if nothing else, as much as Africa touched Europe when the white man opened it up. If only life and awareness weren't so seldom, so incidental or accidental. I think we'd be out there today, seeking, had the loneliness not reached in to freeze us.

Nevertheless, They exist!

'We must be patient,' the Astronomer went on. 'It seems clear that They are. In due course, robots will get there; or we may establish direct communication earlier.'

Across light-centuries. That long between question and answer.

'We don't know what They are like,' Hanno said. 'What the x many different Theys are like. You've read the written proposal I submitted. Haven't you? I went over each of the old arguments. They get down to simply this, that we do not know. What we do know is what we are capable of.'

'The limits of feasibility are contained within the limits of possibility,' declared the Economist.

'Yes, we have studied your report,' the Sociologist said. 'The reasons you give for mounting the enterprise are logically inadequate. True, some thousands of individuals believe they would like to go. They feel frustrated, bewildered, out of place, confined, or otherwise discontented. They dream of a fresh start on a fresh world. Most of them are immature and will outgrow it. Most of the rest are visionaries who would retreat, shocked, if offered the opportunity in reality. You are left with perhaps a few score, for whose emotional convenience you want the entire society to pay a high share-cost.'

'They're the ones that matter.'

'Do they, when they are so selfish that they will actually subject their descendants – for they will reproduce if they live – to the hazards and deprivations?'

Hanno's grin was stark. 'All parents have always made that kind of decision. It's in the nature of things. Would you deny your race the opportunities, discoveries, whole new ways of thinking and working and living, that *this* civilization forecloses?'

'Your point is not ill taken,' said the Psychologist. 'Still, you must agree that success is not guaranteed. On the contrary, you would take a rather wild gamble. It is not yet proven that any of the half-score planets thus far found which seem to have Earthlike environments and biochemistries, is not a long-range death trap.'

'We could look farther if need be. We've got the time. What we need is something worth doing with it.'

'You would indeed find marvels,' said the Artist. 'Perhaps you could understand them and convey them back to us in fashions that no robot is quite able to.'

Hanno nodded. 'I have a notion that intelligent life can only communicate fully with its own kind. Maybe I'm wrong, but how can we be certain before we've tried? We build our limitations and the limitations of our knowledge into our machines and their programs. Yes, they learn, adapt, modify themselves according to experience; the best of them think; but it's always along machine lines. What do we know about experiences they can't handle? Maybe scientific theory is complete, maybe not; but in any case it's a mighty big universe yonder. Much too big and full for us to predict. We need more than one breed of explorer.'

The Engineer frowned. 'So your petition maintains. Did you imagine its contentions are new? They have been brought up again and again, to be rejected as insufficient. The probability of success, and the value of any success that might be had, are too slight in relation to cost.'

Hanno noticed himself lean forward. It seemed a strange act in this disembodied conversation. 'I did not bring up my new argument,' he told them. 'I was hoping I wouldn't have to. But ... the situation has changed. You're dealing with us now, the Survivors. You said it, we are unique. We still have our special prestige, mystique, followings – nothing great, no, but we well know how to use such things. I in particular recall ways of raising holy hell with the powers that be. I got quite good at it, back in ancient times.

'Oh, yes, a gadfly. You can pretend to ignore us. If need be, you can destroy us. But that will cost you. We'll leave troublesome questions behind in many minds. They won't fade, because you've abolished death and databases don't forget. You've had your world running so smoothly for so long that you may

473

think the system is stable. It isn't. Nothing human ever was. Read your history.' The sweep and violence of it, the hidden reefs on which empires foundered with their pride and dreams and gods.

The Psychologist spoke in steely imperturbability: 'It is true that sociodynamics is, mathematically, chaotic.'

'I don't want to threaten you,' Hanno urged quickly. 'In fact, I'd fear the outcome too. It might be small, but it might be enormous. Instead –' he fashioned a laugh – 'malcontents traditionally were a favorite export of governments. And this will be something adventurous, romantic, in an age when adventure and romance are almost gone except for electronic shadow shows. People will enjoy it, support it … long enough for the ship to get under way. You'll find the kudos for yourselves quite useful in whatever else you want to do. Afterward –' He spread his palms. 'Who knows? Maybe a flat failure. But maybe an opening to everywhere.'

Silence thrummed.

The calm of the Administrator struck Hanno harder than any physical blow. 'We have anticipated this, too, from you. The factors have been weighed. The decision is positive. The ship shall be launched.'

Like that? In this single instant, victory?

Well, but the computers can have given it thousands of years' worth of human thinking time while I talked.

O Columbus!

'There are conditions,' tolled through his hearing. 'Suspended animation or no, the mass of fifty or more colonists, with supplies and equipment, is excessive, when the odds are so poor. You eight Survivors must go alone. Of course, you will have a complement of robots, up to. and including the intelligent and versatile but subservient, personalityless type, toward which you can develop no hostility. You will have such other materiel as appears called for. If your venture prospers, larger numbers may someday follow in slower carriers. We expect you will agree that this is reasonable.'

'Yes –' And the symbolism of it, uh-huh, shrewd. My God, I'll be glad to get out from under a system that calculates everything.

But I should not be ungrateful, should I? 'You're very generous. You always have been, to us. Thank you, thank you.'

'Thank society. You think in terms of kings, but personal power is obsolete.'

True, I suppose. As obsolete as the personal soul.

'Furthermore,' the Administrator continued, 'you shall not go to the planet suggested in your report. It does lie less than fifty light-years hence, but distance differences on that order of magnitude are comparatively unimportant when relativistic travel speeds are available. It is the best known of the terrestroid candidates, therefore the most promising for settlement. However, other considerations enter. You spoke of exploration. Very well, you shall explore.

'The sun and planet chosen for you lie in Pegasus, near the present limit of our communication sphere. You will recall that in that direction, beyond it, about fifteen hundred light-years hence, is the nearest of those radiation sources that may be high-energy civilizations.

'We do not know whether it is in fact any such thing; the anomalies are numerous. Nor do we know whether your presence can significantly advance the date at which we make contact. Probably not, since the robots en route to there have reported nothing but natural phenomena as far as they have gone. Going to that planet means you will face more unknowns, therefore more dangers, than otherwise – although we shall be receiving additional information about it while your ship is under construction. But, assigning the most plausible weights to the various uncertainties and imponderables, we have concluded that, on the whole, it is best that your expedition be toward the nearest neighbors comparable to ourselves that we may possibly have.'

It makes sense. I should have thought of it beforehand. But I'm only one man. We're only eight, only human, woundable flesh and sheddable blood.

'Do you and your associates accept these terms?'

'Yes.' Boundlessly yes.

11

Bid Earth farewell.

Something of her as once she was abides yet, an enclave, a reserve, a restoration, things small and alive in crannies, simple folk, archaisms, remembrance. Most people are gracious. They grant permission, they draw aside to create solitude or they come together in fellowship, they give whatever may be in their gift throughout these last few days.

Ocean roars, rises, rushes downward and up again. The waves are gray-green in a thousand hues and wrinkles along their backs, white-maned above the steep troughs. The boat surges to their swing and tramp, rigging sings, sails strain. Shrill and chill, the wind tastes of salt.

Wheat goldens toward harvest. It rustles whenever the air stirs, and ripples run across the leagues of it. Bees buzz in a clover meadow, from which the sun bakes sweetness. Some ways off, several cows rest, vividly red, by a chestnut tree whose crown snares light and scatters it back. A clod crumbles warm in the hand.

Candleglow turns faces as soft as the lilting music. Silver, porcelain, linen sheen with it. In tall goblets, champagne sends jewels aloft. It tickles the palate. Laughter runs around the table with the same lightness. The soup is leek-pungent, cream-rich. Fragrance from courses to come eddies about like a promise of merrymaking afterward until dawn.

The canyon wall lifts rusty red toward indigo heaven. Eons band it. Crags rear wind-whittled out of the down-slope; but today is so still that a raven's 'Gruk!' explodes through the heat. That blackness wings over pungency of sage and scrub juniper, which clutch at every roothold. The green is less sparse at the bottom, where a streamlet gleams and whispers.

Though pilgrims come no longer to the shrine, a latter-day kind of piety maintains it, and memories are many. Near its doorway an ancient cypress grips a ledge, limned in gnarled and silvery austerity. Thence vision descends the mountain, past a cliff cloven by a waterfall, over groves and terraces and the curve of a roof, into dawn mists filling the valley and on to blue heights beyond. Breath is cool. Suddenly a cuckoo calls.

A rainshower has ended. The birch forest sparkles with drops, on the blades that shiver overhead, on fern and moss beneath. Trunks rise girl-slim out of dappled shadows. Ahead, their whitenesses open on reeds, a lake, a deer that looks about startled and soars away. The mould is soft and wet underfoot. The odors are green.

Things and places may be had again in future, but as illusion, a ghost dance of electrons, photons, neurons. Here is the graspable reality. This picture on the wall came from a riverside stall long ago, that one was taken back when folk employed cameras. The table is nearly as old, its wood scarred by use, twice charred where a lighted cigar fell. The rest of the furniture is as comfortably shabby. The book has weight, its brown-spotted pages crackle between fingers, a name penned on the flyleaf is faded but unforgotten.

There are no more graveyards. Death is too rare, land too precious. The burial records of the humble seldom endured anyway. It is guesswork what sites to seek – in a city turned alien, in a remnant of countryside where grass and wild-flowers have taken back the plowland – and stand for a while, feeling not altogether alone, before saying very quietly, 'Goodbye now, and thank you.'

12

Fire raised the wind on which *Pytheas* fared outward. Sol dwindled aft, slowly at first under the low acceleration, but already, as the ship approached Jupiter, scarcely more than the brightest among the stars.

They filled the encompassing night with keen and steady radiances, white, silver-blue, amber-yellow, ruby-red. The Milky Way coursed heaven like a river of frost and light. Nebulae glowed in the death and birth of suns. Southward gleamed the Clouds of Magellan. Exquisite at its distance, a spiral, a sister galaxy, beckoned.

Hanno and Svoboda stood in the command center, looking at the optically enhanced sky. They often did. 'What are you thinking about?' he asked at last.

'Finality,' she answered low.

'What?'

'This maneuver ahead of us. Oh, yes, it's not absolutely irrevocable. We could still turn back – for quite some time to come, can't we? But what's soon going to happen, the course change, it's like – I don't know. Not birth or marriage or dying. Something as strange.'

He nodded. 'I believe I know what you mean, and I'm the hardheaded pragmatist. Wanderer certainly does. He mentioned to me that he and Corinne are planning a ceremony. Maybe we should all attend.'

She smiled. 'Rite of passage,' she murmured. 'I should have realized Wanderer would be the one who understands. I hope he can make a part for me.'

Hanno gave her a sharp glance. They had all paired off, informally and more or less tacitly, he with her, Wanderer with Macandal, Patulcius with Aliyat, Tu Shan and Yukiko renewing their alliance. Not that each man and each woman had never shared one another. It had been inevitable that they'd swap around occasionally, during the long time of their masquerade. But since, they had been more apart than together. How much emotional risk dared they take on this voyage? Fifteen years under way, with God knew what at the end –

Separations or no, after centuries a couple gained considerable mutual sensitivity. Svoboda's hand caught Hanno's. 'Not to worry,' she said in the American English that was their favorite dead language. 'I only have a solemnity in mind. We do need something to lift us out of ourselves. It's wrong to carry our pettinesses along to the stars.'

'We will, though,' he said. 'We can't help it. How do you escape being what you are?'

13

Screen fields warded particle radiation off as *Pytheas* slipped close by Jupiter. The planet laid its mighty gravitational hand upon the ship and swung it out of the ecliptic, northerly toward Pegasus. Inboard a drum thuttered, feet danced, a song called to the spirits.

When it was safely away, robots went outside. Flitting around the hull, they deployed the latticework of ramscoop and fire chamber. By this time, low boost under torch drive had built up a considerable speed. Interaction with the interstellar medium was becoming significant. By terrestrial standards it was a hard vacuum, averaging about one atom per cubic centimeter, overwhelmingly hydrogen. Yet a wide funnel traveling fast would gather a great deal. When the robots returned inside, *Pytheas* resembled a blunt torpedo caught in the net of a giant fisherman.

Its folk flashed their last laser beam to Earth, made then little speeches, received ceremonial good wishes. The ions and energies that were to surround them would blank out electromagnetic communications. Modulated neutrinos passed easily through, and *Pytheas* was equipped to receive them, but the beams it could cast dispersed too rapidly. That huge facility which was capable of sending an identifiable message hundreds or thousands of light-years was fixed in place, locked on remote targets that might eventually respond.

Now, through the net and beyond it, out to thousands of kilometers, the harvester fields came into being. Their forces meshed, intricate, powerful, precise, an ever-changing configuration molded by the controlling computers and what came to them through their sensors. New laser beams sprang from the ship's bows, swordlike, cleaving electron from nucleus. The fields seized on the plasma and swept it backward, well away from the hull; impact on metal would have released X-rays in swiftly lethal concentration. Aft to the fire chamber, which was itself a magnetohydrodynamic vortex, the gas went.

Another immaterial engine released a little of the antimatter it held suspended, ionized it, sped it into the maelstrom and the star gas. Particles met, annihilated, became energy, the ultimate conversion, nine times ten to the twentieth ergs per gram. That fury lit fusion reactions among other protons, and continued them. Behind the heavily shielded stern of *Pytheas*, a tiny sun blazed forth.

Powered by it, the fields hurled most of the plasma aft. Reaction drove the ship forward. Full weight came back to her crew, an Earth gravity of acceleration, nine hundred eighty centimeters per second added every second to velocity.

At that rising pace, in just less than a year the voyagers would transit half a light-year of distance, and their speed would be close to that of light.

14

Nothing natural could have steered the ship. It did itself, a set of systems joined in a unity as complex as a living organism, maintaining its motion and existence outwardly, its livable environment inwardly. Humans became passengers, occupying their time as best they might.

Living quarters were bleakly functional, eight individual staterooms, a gymnasium, a workshop, a galley, a dining saloon, a common room, certain auxiliaries such as bathrooms and a dream chamber. Making them pleasanter gave enjoyment to those whose talents lay in that direction. Yukiko urged that they begin with the common room. 'It is where we shall most be together,' she said. 'Not simply for ease and company. In trouble too, or communion, or awe.'

Hanno nodded. 'Our marketplace,' he agreed. 'And markets began with temples.'

'Well,' cautioned Tu Shan, 'we'd better plan things so the decorating doesn't interfere with the use.'

The three found themselves alone there one evening. The ship maintained Earth's immemorial cycle of day and night, the clock to whose beat life had arisen and evolved. It would gradually shift to the different rhythm of the destination world. Dinner was past and others had withdrawn to their rest or their recreations, none of which happened to be here. In the corridor beyond, twilight deepened toward darkness. Soon the widely spaced soft ganglights would turn on.

Tu Shan fixed a box to wall brackets he had forged in vine shapes. 'I thought you were going to carve decorations on that first,' Hanno remarked.

'I want to put soil in it now and begin raising flowers,' Tu Shan explained. 'Later I will make an ornamental railing and attach it.'

Yukiko gave him a smile. 'Yes, you do need flowers,' she agreed. 'Living things.' What grew beneath her own hands was a mural painting, a landscape of hills, village, bamboo, in the foreground a blossoming cherry bough.

'I will carve the railing in animal shapes.' He sighed. 'If only we could have animals aboard.' Their DNA patterns reposed in the databank. Someday, if all went well, there would be synthesis, growth tanks, release.

'Yes, I miss my ship's cats,' Hanno admitted. 'But a sailor got used to doing without most things. It made going ashore that much the happier.' His fingers plied rope, knot-work to hang at certain spots. Its Phoenician pattern would not clash with the Asian motif. He glanced at the mural. 'That's becoming lovely.'

Yukiko bowed in his direction. 'Thank you. A poor copy, I fear, of what I can remember from a building that perished centuries ago.' – before things were recorded, for presentation at will in total-sensory imaging.

'You should have done it on Earth.'

'Nobody seemed interested.'

'Or had you simply lost heart? Never mind. We'll beam it back from our planet. It's as special as anything we're likely to find there.' Its physical self would long since have gone down into the databank, its materials into the nanotech processors, converted to whatever was needed for the next project.

Aliyat had contended that the whole idea was foolish. No one wanted to spend fifteen years staring at a changeless picture. Why make it, to destroy and replace with something else, when projection panels could instantly create any of thousands of simulacra?

'I think before then, our friends will accept that this work was worth doing,' Hanno added.

'They kindly let me indulge in my pastime,' Yukiko said.

'No, I mean for its own sake. More than a pastime. We could invent plenty of mere amusements. We doubtless will. If necessary, we can just wait. A year goes by fast after you've had hundreds or thousands of them.'

'Unless much happens,' Tu Shan observed.

Hanno nodded. 'True. I don't pretend to understand what the physicists mean by time, but for people, it isn't so-and-so many measured units; it's events, experiences. A man who crowds his life and dies young has lived longer than one who got old sitting in tame sameness.'

'Perhaps the old man was finding his way toward wisdom,' Yukiko ventured. She lowered her brush. Her tone grew troubled. 'For me, that was never possible. My years of quietness always became, at last, a burden. It is the penalty of never aging. The body does not ease its hold on the spirit.'

'Nature meant us to die, get out of the way, leave whatever we gained to the new generations,' Tu Shan said heavily. 'Yet nature brought forth our kind. Are we monsters, freaks? Today everybody is like us. Should that be? Will it in the end cost the race its soul?'

Hanno kept busy with his ropework. 'I don't know,' he answered. 'I don't even know if your questions mean anything. We *are* unique, we Survivors. We were born into age and death. We grew up expecting them for ourselves. Then we endured them, over and over and over, in everybody we loved, till we found each other; and that didn't end the losing. The primitive world shaped us. Look at what we're making here. Maybe that's why it's us going to the stars. We're the oldest people alive, but maybe we're also the last of the children.'

15

A stateroom had space for little more than a seat, a dresser that doubled as a desk with terminal, and a bunk; but the bunk had width for two. Patulcius had stuck printouts of pictures onto his walls, scenes that existed no longer in their cities. The sonic playout gave a muted background of early twentieth-century jazz. That was the single kind of music on which he and Aliyat could agree. Later styles were too abstract for her, older Near Eastern tunes roused bad memories.

They lay side by side, sharing warmth and sweat. His passions were always rather quickly slaked, though; he liked to laze for a while afterward, daydreaming or talking, before he either fell asleep or went in search of refreshment.

Presently she stirred, kicked, sat up, hugged her knees, yawned. 'I wonder what's happening now at home,' she said.

'As I understand it, "now" means very little to us ... now,' he answered in his plodding fashion. 'It will mean less and less, the faster and farther we go.'

'Never mind. *Why* can't they stay in touch?'

'You know. Our drive screens out their beams.'

She glanced at him. He lay hands behind head, look upon the ceiling. 'Sure, but, uh, neutrinos.'

'Those facilities are tied up.'

'Yes,' she said bitterly. 'We weren't worth building new ones for. But aiming at some star a million light-years away –'

He smiled. 'Not that far. Not quite. Although a rather daunting distance, true.'

'Who cares? I mean, all they ever get is stuff they can't figure out. They don't think it's even meant for us, do they?'

'Yes and no. It's a reasonable guess that those are messages addressed "to whom it may concern." To anyone who may be listening. But why should the senders think enough like us that we can easily decipher their codes? Besides, they're almost certainly robots. Very possibly, what we detect are nothing but beacons, meant to attract more robots – like those we have sent toward them.'

She shivered a bit. 'Nothing really alive there?'

'Doubtful. Have you forgotten? Those are the strange places of the galaxy. Black holes, condensing nebulae, free matrices – is that the term I want? Modern cosmology baffles me too. But they're bound to be dangerous, generally lethal environments. At the same time, each is unique. Surely all starfaring civilizations will dispatch robots to investigate them. They are where everybody's machines will eventually meet. Therefore it makes sense that those already there will send messages they – or their builders – hope somebody new will catch. Those always were the likeliest places to find signs of intelligence, the best for us to focus our instruments on.'

'I know, I do know!' she snapped.

'As for why we have received nothing unambiguous from the mother civilizations –'

'Never mind! I wanted a breath of outside air, not a lecture!'

He did turn his face toward her. The heavy features drooped. 'I'm sorry, my dear,' he said. 'I find the subject fascinating.'

'I might, if I hadn't heard it all before, again and again. If something new could ever be said about it.'

'And if somebody new said it. Right?' he asked sadly. 'I bore you, don't I?'

She bit her lip. 'I'm out of sorts.'

He avoided remarking that she had not answered his question. However, his tone sharpened a bit. 'You knew you were leaving the social whirl behind.'

She jerked a nod. 'Of course,' she replied curtly. 'Do you suppose I didn't learn how to bide my time, already in Palmyra? But I don't have to like it.'

She swung her legs around, stood, reached for the robe she had hung on a hook. 'I'm not sleepy, either,' she said. 'I'm going to a dream box and get relaxed.' Unspoken was that evidently he had not eased her, though she had faked.

He sat up. 'You go too often,' he protested without force.

'That's my business.' She pulled the garment over her head, paused for a moment, met his eyes, glanced away again. 'Sorry, Gnaeus. I am being bitchy. Wish me a better mood tomorrow, will you?' She leaned down to ruffle the shag on his chest before she departed, barefoot as she had arrived. The deck surfacing was soft, springy, almost like turf.

The corridor reached empty, dimly lit at this hour. Ventilation gave a breeze and a susurrus. She rounded a corner and stopped. Wanderer did too.

'Why, hello, there,' Aliyat said in American English. 'Haven't seen much of you for a while.' She smiled. 'Where are you bound for?'

16

The closer *Pytheas* flew on the heels of light, the more alien it and the outside universe became to each other. One did not care to look long into the view-screens any more, if at all. The interior hull became like a set of caves, warm bright huddling places. Escape from their closeness lay in whatever work could be found or made; in sports, games, skills, reading, music, shows, trad-itional diversions; in the pseudo-lives of every sort that that computer engendered for those who linked with it.

The circumstances were by no means bad. Most of mankind throughout most of history would have considered them paradise. Still, as Hanno had once implied, it was as well that to immortals, a year could feel like quite a short span. And perhaps that was only true, or only true enough, of the Sur-vivors. Had any modern human lived sufficiently long? Would any ever learn how to tough out hard times, especially the hard times of the spirit? Was a subliminal doubt of it the underlying reason why none had hitherto ven-tured this faring?

Be that as it may, challenges became welcome.

Phaeacia – Hanno had suggested the name – was not Earth. The robot explorers reported an extraordinary degree of similarity: sun, orbit, mass, composition, spin, tectonics, satellite; countlessly many factors seemed necessary to beget life chemistry closely resembling the terrestrial. Such worlds were few indeed (though 'few,' given the size of the galaxy, might add up to hundreds). Yet nothing was identical and much, perhaps most, utterly foreign. The absence of anything sentient was merely the difference plainest to humans, and probably the least important.

Moreover, Phaeacia was less known than the goal Hanno had originally had in mind. It lay almost one hundred fifty light-years from Earth, near the edge of the communication sphere. Thus far a single mission had reached it and, when *Pytheas* left, a dozen years' worth of reports had been received. It was a *world*, as various and mysterious as ever Earth herself in her prehistory.

The robots were still investigating. *Pytheas* couldn't catch their messages while en route, but they would download their entire data-hoard when it arrived. Doubtless the astonishments that waited were enormous. The travelers might spend a year or more in orbit, assimilating, before they took their first boat to the surface.

Meanwhile, why not practice? To gain familiarity with the material was elementary prudence, incomplete and often wrong though it must be; hands-on experience was best gotten in advance, illusory though it must be.

The senses no longer knew the gymnasium. Overhead arched sky, virginally blue save for clouds that were like breaths off the snowpeaks at the horizon. The countryside round about lay verdant with blades that were not really grass; trees swayed to a lulling wind that smelled of their resin and the sun; wings swept that air, and afar a herd of beasts galloped, swift and graceful. Wanderer remembered Jackson Hole as once it had been. His heart cracked.

Mastering himself, he stooped to pluck a rock out of the spring bubbling at his feet. It glittered quartzlike. The heft of it was cold in his hand. Yes, he thought, I'd better brush up my geology.

'Cut some timber,' Tu Shan ordered the robots. He pointed. 'Over there. See if you can make planks.'

'So,' acknowledged the principal, and led its work gang off with their energy projectors, fluid reactants, and solid tools.

Wanderer swung his head toward his companion. The weight of the induction helmet reminded him that he wasn't in a dream box. He was supposedly training his entire organism; but he stood in a place that surely didn't exist as it was being presented to him. Well, he could believe that something not too unlike it did, on his new world. 'What're you doing?' he demanded.

'We'll need wood suitable for construction, wherever we decide to settle,' Tu Shan explained. 'We don't want to depend on the wretched synthesizers, do we? Wasn't that the point of leaving Earth?' He smiled, narrowed his eyes against the brilliance, dilated his nostrils, breathed deep. 'Yes, I like it here.'

'You won't farm this kind of site!' Wanderer cried.

Tu Shan stared at him. 'Why not?'

'There'll be plenty of others. This, it would be … wrong.'

Tu Shan scowled. 'How much of the planet do you want to keep for your private hunting preserve, forever?'

It shocked Wanderer: Have we carried the enmities of our forefathers through all these centuries and now through these light-years?

17

The nanoprocessors would take any material and transform it, atom by atom, into anything else for which they had a program. Out of their recycling came air, water, food. They could produce a complete, excellent meal, and often did according to individual choice. However, as a rule Macandal took just the basic ingredients and, aside from drink, made dinner for everybody. She was a gifted cook, enjoyed the work, and felt it was a service, something that lent her life some meaning. No pretense; machines lacked the personal touch that this archaic crew needed.

Certainly they did at a time of celebration. The ship's calendar held many feasts, holy days and national days that Earth had mostly forgotten, private anniversaries, special occasions upon the voyage. Each fulfilled year of it was among them. That was by inboard time, of course. The faster *Pytheas* flew, the shorter a span became in relation to the galactic wheel.

'It's getting kind of drunk out,' she remarked to Yukiko on the third of those evenings.

Having dined, folk had moved from the saloon to the spacious common room. Simulacrum panels had been raised, hiding the murals. They gave no scenes from home; it had been found that such were too likely to make an alcoholic party go somber. Patterns of light shifted and drifted, glowed and sparkled, through a violet-blue dusk. Nevertheless Hanno and Patulcius sat, goblets in hand, reminiscing about the twentieth century – the two widely sundered twentieth centuries that had been theirs. Wanderer and Svoboda revived the waltz, rotating embraced over the floor, earplugs giving Strauss to them alone; their eyes also excluded the world. Tu Shan and Aliyat danced, whooping and hand-clapping, to some livelier melody.

Kneeling as of old, Yukiko sipped at the bit of sake she was allowing herself. She smiled. 'It is good to see cheerfulness,' she said.

'Yes, I've felt tension in the air,' Macandal replied. 'Not that it's gone away.'

'– poor old Sam Giannotti, he tried so hard to get a little modern physics into my head,' Hanno related slurrily. 'Hell, I could barely manage a half-notion of what classical physics had been about. Made a song, I did, at last –'

Sweat darkened Tu Shan's tunic beneath the arms and sheened on Aliyat's bare shoulders and back.

'You should go join the fun,' Macandal said.

'Black bodies give off radiation,' sang Hanno off-key,
'And ought to continuously.
Black bodies give off radiation,
But do it by Planck's theory.

'*Bring back, bring back,*
Oh, bring back that old continuity!
Bring back, bring back,
Oh, bring back Clerk Maxwell to me.'

Yukiko smiled again. 'I am enjoying myself,' she said. 'But why don't you go? You were never a passive person, like me.'

'Ha, don't you kid me. In your peculiar ways, you're as active, as much a doer, as anybody I ever met.'

'*Though now we have Schrödinger functions,*
Dividing up h *by 2π*
That damn differential equation
Still has no solution for ψ.

'*Bring back, bring back –*'

Aliyat and Tu Shan laughed into each other's mouths. Wanderer and Svoboda circled as if through a dream.

'*Well, Heisenberg came to the rescue,*
Intending to make all secure.
What is the result of his efforts?
We are absolutely unsure.

'*Bring back, bring back –*'

Aliyat left her partner, approached, beckoned to Yukiko. Macandal stepped aside. The two whispered together.

'*Dirac spoke of energy levels,*
Both minus and plus. Oh, how droll!
And now, just because of his teaching,
We don't know our mass from a hole.

'*Bring back –*'

Aliyat returned to Tu Shan. They left the room arm in arm.

'She asked if you'd mind, didn't she?' Macandal inquired.

Yukiko nodded. 'I don't. I truly don't. She surely remembered that. But it was good of her to ask.'

Macandal sighed. 'His nature too, isn't it? I've wondered – I'm a trifle in my own cups – don't be offended, please, but I've wondered how much you really love him.'

'What is love? Among my people, most people, what counted was respect. Affection normally grew out of it.'

'Yeah.' Macandal's gaze followed the pair still on the floor.

Yukiko winced. 'Are you in pain, Corinne?'

'No, no. Nothing's going to happen with those two. Though, as you say, it shouldn't matter if anything did, should it?' Macandal made a laugh. 'Johnnie's a gentleman. He'll ask me for the next dance. I can wait.'

'Bring back, bring back,
Oh, bring back that old continuity –'

18

Stranger and ever stranger grew the cosmos that the ship beheld. Aberration of light sent star images crawling aside, while Doppler shift blued those forward and reddened those aft until many no longer shone at any wavelength the eye could perceive. In the ship's measure, the mass of the atoms that its fields scooped up increased with the rising velocity; distances that it was traversing shrank, as if space were flattening under the impact; time passed more quickly, less of it between one atomic pulsebeat and the next. *Pytheas* would never reach the haste of light, but the closer it sped, the more foreign to the rest of the universe it became.

Alone among the eight, Yukiko had taken to seeking communion yonder. She would settle in the navigation chamber, otherwise unused until journey's end drew nigh, and bid the screens give her the view. It was a huge and eerie grandeur, there around her shell of humming silence – blacknesses, ringfire, streams of radiance. Before the spirit could seek into it, the mind must. She studied the tensor equations as once she studied the sutras, she meditated upon the koans of science, and at last she began to feel her oneness with all that was, and in the vision find peace.

She did not let herself go wholly into it. Had she become able to, that would have been a desertion of comrades and dereliction of duty. She hoped she might help Tu Shan, and others if they wished, toward the serenity behind the awesomeness, once she herself had gone deeply enough. Not as a Boddhisatva, no, no, nor a guru, only as a friend who had something wonderful to share. It would help them so much, in the centuries to come.

They had need of every strength. Hardships and dangers counted for little, would often be gladdening, a gift of that reality which had slipped from their hands on Earth. The loneliness, though. Three hundred years between word and reply. How much more distanced might Earth become in three hundred more years?

Never before had the eight been this isolated for this long; and it would go on. Oh, it was scarcely worse than isolation had grown at home. (And if shiploads of settlers arrived, once Phaeacia was proven habitable – if it was; if they did – what would they really have in common with the Survivors?) But it worked on them more than they had foreseen. Forced in upon themselves, they discovered less than they perhaps had looked for.

Horizons and challenge should open them up again. Yet they might always be haunted by the understanding that they were not actually pioneers, mightily achieving what they had determined they would do. They were ... not quite outcasts ... failures, leftovers from a history that no longer mattered, sent on their way almost casually, as an act of indifferent kindness.

Their children, however; there was the future that Earth had lost. Yukiko ran a hand down her belly. Mother of nations! This body was not foredoomed in the way that women otherwise were, even today. The technology could keep you youthful, but it could not add one ovum to those with which you were born. (Well, doubtless it could, if people so desired, but of course they didn't.) Hers made new eggs as it made new teeth, during her entire unbounded life. (Don't scorn the machines. They'll save you from ever again having to watch your children grow old. They'll create the genetic variety that will allow four couples to people a planet.)

Yes, hope ranged yet. May it never go out of reach.

'Ship, what of the flight?' she called.

'Velocity point nine-six-four c,' sang the voice, 'mean ambient equivalent matter density one point zero four proton, all mission parameters within zero point three percent, navigating now by the Virgo cluster of galaxies and seven quasars near the limits of the observable universe.'

Stars across farness,
  Drift of dandelion seeds –
    What, springtime again?

19

After seven and a half of its own years, ten times as many celestial, *Pytheas* reached the halfway point of its journey. There was a brief spell of weightlessness as the vessel went on free trajectory, lasers and force-fields withdrawn except for what was required to shield the life within. Majestically, the hull turned around. Heavily armored, robots went out to reconfigure the generator net. When they were back inside, *Pytheas* unfurled snare and kindled engine. Fire reawakened. At one gravity of deceleration, the craft backed down toward its goal. Trumpet notes rang through the air.

Surely the travelers had special cause for festival. Macandal took three days preparing the banquet. She was in the galley, chopping and mixing, when Patulcius appeared. 'Hi,' she greeted him in English, which remained her language of choice. 'What can I do for you?'

He barely smiled. 'Or I for you. I think I have remembered what went into that appetizer I mentioned.'

'Hm?' She laid down her cleaver and brought finger to chin. 'Oh ... oh, yes. Tahini something. You made it sound good, but neither of us could recall what tahini was.'

'How much else has faded out of us?' he mumbled. Squaring his shoulders, he spoke briskly. 'I have brought the memory back, at least in part. It was a paste made from sesame meal. The dish I thought of combined it with garlic, lemon juice, cumin, and parsley.'

'Splendid. The nano can certainly make sesame, and here's a grinder, but I'll have to experiment, and you tell me how wide of the mark I am. It ought to go well with some other hors d'oeuvres I'm planning. We don't want anything too heavy before the main course.'

'What will that be, or is it still a secret?'

Macandal considered Patulcius. 'It is, but I'll let you in on it if you'll keep mum. Curried goose. A twenty-one-boy curry.'

'Delicious, I'm sure,' he said listlessly.

'Is that all you've got to say, you, our champion trencherman?'

He turned to go. She touched his arm. 'Wait,' she murmured. 'You're feeling absolutely rotten, aren't you? Can I help?'

He looked elsewhere. 'I doubt it. Unless –' He swallowed and grimaced. 'Never mind.'

'Come on, Gnaeus. We've been friends a long time.'

'Yes, you and I, we could somehow relax with each other better than – Okay!' he spat. 'Can you speak to Aliyat? No, surely not. Or if you do, what use?'

'I thought that was it,' said Macandal low. 'Her sleeping around. Well, I can't say I'm overjoyed when Johnnie spends a night with her, but it is something she needs. I've been thinking Hanno does wrong to ignore her passes at him.'

'Nymphomania.'

'No, not really. Grabbing out for love, assurance. And ... something to do. She spends too much time in the dream box as is.'

He struck fist in palm. 'But I am not something for her to do, am I?'

'Not any more? I suspected that too. Poor Gnaeus.' Macandal took his hand. 'Listen. I know her well, better than anybody else. I don't believe she wants to be unkind. If she avoids you, why, she feels – ashamed? No, more like being afraid of hurting you worse.' She paused. 'I'm going to take her aside and talk like a Dutch aunt.'

He flushed. 'Not on my account, please. I don't want pity.'

'No, but you deserve more consideration than you've gotten.'

'Sex isn't that big a thing, after all.'

'A sound philosophy,' Macandal said, 'but not too easy to put in practice when you aren't a saint and your body never grows older. How well I know. We can't have you racking yourself apart, Gnaeus. If I –' She drew breath, then smiled. 'We had some pretty good times in the past, you and I, didn't we? It was long ago, but I've not forgotten.'

He stared. A minute passed before he could stammer, 'You, you don't really m-mean that. It is sweet of you, but no, really, not necessary.'

Calm had come upon her. 'Don't think "mercy hump." I like you. Well, no hurry. Best we take our time and see how things develop. Lord knows we have plenty of time, and if we haven't learned a little patience by now, we might as well open the airlocks. I mean all of us aboard.'

After a moment: 'Too bad, isn't it, that this tremendous quest of ours hasn't made us worthy of itself. We're the same limited, foolish, mixed-up, ridiculous primitives we always were. Today's Earth people wouldn't have our problems. But it is we, not they, who've gone out here.'

Pytheas flew onward. Another three and a half years passed inside the hull before the universe broke through, like a storm wave crashing over the rail of a Grecian ship.

20

It came as suddenly, through the musical robotic voice: 'Attention! Attention! Instruments detect anomalous neutrino input. It appears to be coded.'

Hanno cried aloud, a seafaring oath not heard these past three millennia, and sprang from his bunk. 'Light,' he ordered. Illumination filled the room. It glowed amber in Svoboda's hair, the warmest color between the walls.

'From Earth?' she gasped, sitting straight. 'Did they build a transmitter?'

He shivered. 'I should think *Pytheas* would recognize –'

The answer interrupted him: 'The direction of origin is becoming clear, somewhat forward of us, broadcast rather than beamcast. Modulation is of pulse, amplitude, and spin. I am still engaged in observation and analysis, to determine the velocity of the source and compensate for Doppler shift and time dilation. At present the pattern appears mathematically simple.'

'Yeah, start by making us aware it's artificial.' Hanno's finger stabbed the intercom touchdisc. 'Has everybody heard? Meet in the saloon. I'll report to you there as soon as possible.' Needlessly – or was it? – he reached for his clothes. 'Want to come, Svoboda?'

Her grin was a hunter's. 'Try and stop me.'

Perhaps it was equally superfluous to seek the command room. It might even be unwise, to wait there amidst the terrible glory in the viewscreens. Too easily could that daunt the spirit and numb the mind. But sitting hand in hand, watching the numbers and graphic displays the ship generated for them, was like keeping a grip on a reality that otherwise would blow away into emptiness.

'Have you learned more?' Svoboda must ask.

'Give the computer a chance,' Hanno tried to laugh. 'It's only had a few minutes.'

'Every minute for us is – how much outside? An hour? How many millions of kilometers laid behind us?'

'I detect a similar source, much weaker but strengthening,' the ship told them. 'It is on the opposite side of our projected course.'

Hanno stared a while into distorted heaven before he said slowly, 'Yes, I think I understand. They know how we're headed, more or less, and have sent ... messengers ... to intercept us. However, of course they can't tell exactly – several different destinations may have looked possible to them, nor could they foresee factors like the boost we'd use – so they sent a number of messengers, pretty widely distributed, to lie radiating in the zone, or zones, we'd probably pass through.'

'They?' Svoboda asked.

'The Others. The aliens. Whoever and whatever they are. We've found a starfaring civilization at last. Or it's found us.'

Her own gaze went outward, gone rapt. 'They will rendezvous with us?'

He shook his head. 'Not quite, I think. Given all the uncertainties, and the distances, and the long, unpredictable time out here till we might arrive – they'd not dispatch living crews. Those must be low-mass, high-thrust robot craft, maybe made for this one purpose.'

She was silent half a minute. When she spoke, it sounded almost annoyed. 'How can you be so sure?'

'Why, it's obvious,' he answered, surprised. 'The radiation from our powerplant ran well ahead of us only during the first year, till we got close to light speed. That wouldn't give them nearly enough warning, if they set out to meet us when they picked it up. They can't live close by, or we'd have detected them from the Solar System.'

'Obvious, or smug?' she challenged. 'How much do we know? We have barely begun our first tiny venture into deep space. How long have they been exploring? Thousands of years? Millions? What have they discovered, what can they do?'

His smile twisted. 'I'm sorry. This is no moment to cast a shadow on.' He sighed. 'But I've met a great many dreams over the centuries, and most of them turned out to be no more than that. It's been quite some time since our physicists decided they'd found all the laws of nature, all the possibilities and impossibilities.' He lifted a hand. 'I realize that's a proposition that can never be proven. But the likelihood has come to seem very high, hasn't it? I'd love to learn the aliens own magic carpets flitting faster than light; but I don't expect to.'

Reluctantly, she nodded. 'At least, we must reason on the basis of what we do know. I suspect that's far less than you think, but – What shall we *do?*'

'Respond.'

'Of course! But how? I mean, we're slowing down, but we're still near light speed. By the time the, the machine, any of those machines up ahead receives our signal, won't we be past it? Won't its answer take … years to overtake us?'

He squeezed her hand. 'Smart girl. You always were.' To the ship: 'We want to establish contact as soon as may be. What do you advise?'

The answer jarred them both into bolt uprightness. 'That is contingent. The transmission has changed character. It has become considerably more complex.'

'You, you mean they know we're here? Where are they, anyway?'

'I am refining those figures as I obtain more parallax. The nearest source is approximately a light-year off our path, approximately twice that distance vectorially.'

'Baal! Then they *can* detect us instantly?'

'No. No, wait, Hanno.' Svoboda's words came a little unsteadily, but fast. 'That needn't be. Suppose the broadcast is automatic, a cycle. First a simple alert signal, then the message, then the alert signal again, over and over. The message alone – we might not have recognized it for what it is, supposed it was just some natural thing.'

'When I first acquired it,' *Pytheas* volunteered, 'I assumed it was a fluctuation in the background noise, conceivably of interest to astrophysicists but irrelevant to this mission. It was Dopplered and otherwise warped out of identifiability. The low-information transmission that succeeded it made clear that here is no random flux. It also provided unambiguous data by which the warp functions could be determined. I am now compensating for them and thus reconstructing the message proper.'

Hanno sagged back. 'How often have they done this,' he whispered, 'with how many others?'

'The reconstruction is not yet perfect, but it continually improves as additional data come in,' *Pytheas* went on. 'Since the cycle is short, in shipboard time, I should soon have good definition. The message itself must be fairly brief, with high redundancy, although I anticipate high resolution as well. This is a visual mapping.'

Darkness brimmed in a screen. Suddenly it was full of tiny light-points, uncountably numerous. Their blurriness dissipated, they sharpened, minute by minute. Colors appeared in them, and with that help eyes began to make out three-dimensional shapes, self-recurrent in infinite complexity.

'Prime numbers define a coordinate space,' said the ship. 'Digital impulses identify points within it, which in turn are members of fractal sets. Those functions should provide images, but the proper combinations must be found empirically. My mathematical component is running the search. When something intelligible emerges, that should give clues to obtaining further refinement and eventually extracting the entire content.'

'Well,' said Svoboda dazedly, 'if the computers on Earth could design *you* in a single year –'

Hanno at her side, she waited. The unrolling dance of curves and surfaces flowed together. A picture grew into being. It was of stars.

21

The six around the saloon table looked sharply around when the two entered. Coffee and remnants of food bespoke what hours had passed; more so did haggardness and tension. 'Well,' Patulcius snapped, 'about time!'

'Hush,' Macandal murmured. 'They've come as soon as they could.' Her glance added: An immortal ought to have more patience. But it has been hard, waiting.

Hanno and Svoboda benched themselves oppositely at the doorward end. 'You're right,' the Phoenician said. 'Getting a clear, complete message and deciding what it means took this long.'

'We do apologize, however,' Svoboda added. 'We should have given you … progress reports. We didn't think to, didn't realize how time was passing. There was never any, oh, revelation, any exact moment when we knew.' Weariness weighted her smile. 'I'm ravenous. What's available immediately?'

'You sit still, honey,' Macandal said, rising. 'I've got sandwiches already made. Figured this would be a long session.'

Aliyat's look followed her out, as if to ask: Has she, in our shared bewilderment, gone back to her Old South, or simply to her old caring?

'She'd better bring me some too, or you'll have a fight on your hands and halfway up your arms,' Hanno said to Svoboda. The jape rattled from nerves drawn wire-thin.

'All right,' Wanderer demanded, 'what is the news?'

'Corinne's entitled to hear from the start,' Svoboda replied.

His fingers clutched the table edge. The nails whitened. 'Yes. I'm sorry.'

She reached to stroke a hand. 'You merely forgot. We're beyond ourselves, every one of us.'

'Well, Corinne isn't fond of technical details,' Hanno said. 'I can start with those. And, uh, with apologies to those of you who aren't either. I'm no scientist myself, you know, so this will be short.'

Macandal returned while he was sketching the theory of the communication. Besides food on a tray, she bore a fresh pot of coffee and a bottle of brandy. 'Celebration,' she laughed. 'I hope!'

The fragrances were like blossoms in spring. 'Yes, yes,' Svoboda exulted. 'The discovery of the ages.'

'Theirs more than ours,' Hanno said. 'The aliens', I mean. But we have to decide what to do about it.'

Tu Shan leaned forward, elbows on table, heavy shoulders hunched. 'Well, what is the situation?' he asked levelly enough.

'We're receiving the same message, repeated and repeated,' Hanno told them while he ate and gulped. 'It's from two sources, one closer to our path than the other. Quite likely there are more that we haven't come in range of. If we continue on our present track, we may pick them up. The nearest is a couple of light-years from us. It appears to be on station relative to a line drawn between Sol and Phaeacia's sun, roughly the path we're following. *Pytheas* says that's easy to do; just keep yourself from orbiting away. As I was saying while you were out, Corinne, everything suggests that the aliens sent robots to sit broadcasting continuously. A little antimatter would provide ample power for centuries.'

'The message is pictorial,' Wanderer interjected.

'Well, graphic,' Hanno proceeded. 'You'll all see it later. Often, no doubt, trying to squeeze extra meaning out of it. I suspect you'll fail. No real images, just several … diagrams, maps, representations. Transmission to a ship traveling at Einsteinian speed, a changing speed at that, must be a tough problem, especially when the aliens can't know what our capabilities are for receiving and decoding – or how we think, or much of anything about us. Detailed pictures might be impossible for us to untangle. Evidently they composed the simplest, least ambiguous message that might serve. I would, in their place.'

'But what is their place?' Yukiko wondered.

Hanno chose to take her literally, 'I'm coming to that. What we got, first, was a lot of light-points in three-dimensional space. Then little bars appeared next to three of them. Then we got those three points in succession – it must be same ones – each by itself with the bar enlarged so we could see vertical lines on it. Then the view returned to the light-points in general, with a red line between two of those that are marked. Finally another line appeared, from about two-thirds along the first one, offside to the third marked light-point.

'That's all. Each exposure lasts about a minute. The sequence finishes and starts over. After sixteen cycles, it becomes a plain series of flashes, that could just as well be rendered by dots and dashes in sound waves. This goes on for the same total time, after which we return to the graphics. And so on, over and over.'

Hanno sat back. He grinned a bit. 'What do you make of it?'

'That isn't fair,' Patulcius complained.

'No, don't be a tease,' Aliyat agreed.

'Hold on.' Macandal's eyes shone darkly bright. 'It's worthwhile making us guess. Bring more minds to bear on the problem.'

'The ship's mind must already have solved it,' Patulcius said.

'Nevertheless – Lord, let's have a little fun. I think those light-points stand for stars, a map of this neighborhood in the galaxy. One of the three special ones has got to be Sol, the other Phaeacia Sun, and the third – where the aliens are!'

'Right.' Wanderer's tone quivered with an equal excitement. 'The bars, are they spectrograms?'

'Brilliant, you two,' Svoboda said happily.

Wanderer shook his head. 'Naw, it's pretty obvious, though I do look forward to actually seeing it. A sending from the Others –'

Hanno nodded. '*Pytheas* ran through the astronomy database and confirmed those identifications,' he related. 'The third was hardest, because the three-dimensional representation is on such a small scale. But by expanding the fractals as well as searching the records – Anyhow, it turns out to be a star on our port quarter, if I may speak two-dimensionally. About thirty degrees off our course and about three hundred fifty light-years from our present position. It's type G seven, not as bright as Sol but not too unlike.' He paused. 'It's still less unlike that star in Pegasus, the one we believe may be the home of the nearest high-tech civilization to us, more than a thousand light-years away.'

'Then they have come this far,' Yukiko said in awe.

'If they are from that civilization, if it is a civilization,' Svoboda reminded. 'We know nothing, nothing.'

'What powers have they, that they know about us?'

'We've tried to guess, we two,' Hanno said. He drew breath. 'Listen. Think. They – that third star – is about four hundred thirty light-years from Sol. That means it's within the radio sphere of Earth. For a while, starting in the twentieth century, Earth was the brightest radio object in the Solar System, outshining Sol in that band. That was interrupted, you remember, and afterward people developed communications that didn't clutter the spectrum so grossly; but the old wave front is still expanding. Even beyond Star Three, it's still detectable if you have instruments as good as ours, which the aliens certainly do.

'Very well. However they got to Star Three, they soon found that Sol had a brilliant radio companion. Nobody has spotted that at Pegasi, the Mother Star, assuming that is where the aliens originated. It's too distant; nothing from us will reach it for centuries. So the, uh, colonists or visitors at Three are on their own.

'Now take things from their viewpoint. In due course, Sol ought to be sending out ships too, if it hasn't already begun. It will be especially interested in contacting the nearest neighbor high-tech civilization it can identify, Mother Star's. The aliens could send robots to lie along the general path between those two. Our robots bound that way are smart and versatile. They would, at the least, beam word back to Earth. You recall they're equipped to do that from space, as we aren't, because they don't boost all the while; time touches them less than us. Unfortunately, I think, they must already have gone too far to acquire the signal – which indicates the aliens have not been at Three extremely long.

'There is another good possibility for the aliens. Sol folk should also be especially interested in stars like their own. Phaeacia Sun is that sort, and it lies in the same general, attractive direction as Mother Star. It's much the nearest to Sol that fits both requirements. So the aliens sent robots to lie along that path too. We've encountered those.'

Silence closed down, eyes dropped in thought or stared at walls, until Aliyat said, 'But robots went ahead of us to Phaeacia. Why haven't they reported anything about this?'

'Maybe the messenger craft hadn't gotten here when they passed by,' Patulcius said. 'We don't know when the messengers arrived.' He pondered. 'Except that it must have been less than – four hundred thirty years ago, did you say, Hanno? Otherwise the aliens could have had robots at Sol by now.'

'Maybe they do.' Aliyat shivered. 'We've been gone a long time.'

'I doubt it,' said Wanderer. 'That would be one hell of a coincidence.'

'They might not want to, for whatever reason,' Macandal pointed out. 'We're completely ignorant.'

'You're forgetting the nature of those robots at Phaeacia,' Svoboda said. 'They're not like the ones bound for Pegasi in the wake of messages beamed beforehand – great, intelligent, flexible machine minds intended to attempt conversation with other minds able to understand what they are. The Phaeacia robots were designed and programmed to go there and collect information on that specific planetary system. Almost monomaniacs. If they noticed these neutrino bursts en route, they paid no attention.' She smiled sardonically. 'Not their department.'

Yukiko nodded. 'Nobody can foresee everything,' she said. 'Nothing can.'

'But when we're surprised, we can investigate and learn.' Hanno's words rang. '*We* can.'

Their looks shot to him and struck fast, all but Svoboda's. The color mounted in her cheeks.

'What do you mean?' Tu Shan rumbled after several breaths.

'You know what,' Hanno replied. 'We'll change course and go to Star Three.'

'No!' Aliyat screamed. She half sprang to her feet, sank back down, and shuddered.

'Think,' Hanno urged. 'The diagram. That line between our course, this very point of our course, and Three. What is it but an invitation? They must be lonely too, and hopeful of hearing marvelous things.

Pytheas calculated it. If we change direction now, we can reach them in about a dozen years, ship's time. It's three hundred light-years more than we planned, but we are still at close to light speed and – A dozen little years, to meet the farers of the galaxy.'

'But we only had four to go!'

'Four years longer to our home.' Tu Shan knotted his fists on the tabletop. 'How far from it would you take us?'

Hanno hesitated. Svoboda answered: 'Between Three and Phaeacia Sun is about three hundred light-years. From a standing start, sixteen or seventeen ship years. We won't abandon our original purpose, only postpone it.'

'The hell you say,' Wanderer rapped. 'Whichever star we go to, we'll need more antimatter before we can take off for anywhere else. Building the production plant and then making the stuff, that's probably ten years by itself.'

'The aliens should have plenty on hand.'

'Should they? And will they share it, freely, just like that? How do you know? How can you tell what they want of us, anyway?'

'Wait, wait,' Macandal broke in. 'Let's not get paranoid. Whatever they are, it can't be monsters or, or bandits or anything evil. At their stage of civilization, that wouldn't make sense.'

'Now who's being cocksure?' Aliyat shrilled.

'What do we know about Star Three?' Yukiko asked.

Her quietness smoothed bristles down a little. Hanno shook his head. 'Not much, beyond its type and inferred age,' he admitted. 'Being normal, it's bound to have planets, but we have no information on them. Never been visited. My God, a sphere eight or nine hundred light-years across holds something like a hundred thousand stars.'

'But you say this one's not so bright as ours,' Macandal reminded him. 'Then the chances that it's got a planet where we could breathe are poor. Even with much better candidates –'

The table thudded beneath Tu Shan's smiting. 'That is what matters,' he said. 'After fifteen weary years, we were promised, we shall walk free on living ground. You would keep us locked in this hull for … eight years longer than that, and then at journey's end we still would be, for decades or centuries or forever. No.'

'But this chance, we cannot pass it by,' Svoboda protested.

Wanderer spoke crisply. 'We won't. Once we get to Phaeacia, we'll have the robots build us a proper transceiver and send a beam to Three, start conversation. Eventually we'll go there in person, those of us who care to. Or maybe the aliens will come to us.'

Hanno's countenance was stark. 'I told you, it's about three hundred light-years between Phaeacia and Three,' he said.

Wanderer shrugged. 'We have time ahead of us.'

'If Phaeacia doesn't kill us first. We were never guaranteed safety there, you know.'

'Earth should be getting in touch too, once we've informed them,' Macandal said.

Svoboda's tone lashed. 'Yes, by beam, and by robots that beam back. Who but us will ever go in person, and get to know the Others as they are?'

'It is true,' Yukiko said. 'Words and pictures alone, with centuries between, are good, but they are not enough. I think we here should understand that better than our fellow humans. We knew the dead of long ago as living bodies, minds, souls. To everyone else, what are they but relics and words?'

Svoboda regarded her. 'Then you want to set for Star Three?'

'Yes, oh, yes.'

Tu Shan's look upon her was stricken. 'Do you say that, Small Snow – Morning Glory?' He straightened. 'Well, it shall not be.'

'Absolutely not,' Patulcius vowed. 'We have our community to found.'

Aliyat caught his arm and leaned close against him. Her eyes defied Hanno. 'Our homes to make,' she said.

Macandal nodded. 'It's a hard decision, but ... we should go to Phaeacia first.'

'And last?' Hanno retorted. 'I tell you, if we let this chance escape us, we can very well never get it back. Do you want to change your mind, Peregrino?'

Wanderer sat expressionless for a while before he answered, 'It is a hard decision after all. The greatest, most important adventure in history, which we risk losing, against – what may be New Earth, a fresh start for *our* race. Which is better, the forest or the stars?' Again he was mute, brooding. Abruptly: 'Well, I said it before. The stars can wait.'

'Four against three,' Tu Shan reckoned, triumphant. 'We continue as we were.' Softening: 'I am sorry, friends.'

Hanno's voice, face, bearing went altogether bleak. 'I was afraid of this. Please think again.'

'I have had centuries to think,' Tu Shan said.

'To wish for the Earth of the past, you mean,' Yukiko told him, 'an Earth that never really was. No, you wouldn't deny humankind such a chance for knowledge, for coming closer to oneness with the universe. That would be nothing but selfish. You are not a selfish person, dear.'

He shook his head, ox-stubborn.

'Humankind has waited a long time for contact, and on the whole has not actually shown much interest,' Patulcius said. 'It can wait a while longer. Our first duty is to the children we shall have, and can have only on Phaeacia.'

'They can better wait than this can,' Svoboda argued. 'What we learn from the aliens, the help they give us, should make us the more secure when we do take our new home.'

'The opportunity may well be unique,' Hanno joined in. 'I repeat, the aliens at Three are likely few, and pretty newly arrived. Else the Web at Sol would have picked up trace of them, or spacecraft of theirs would have arrived there. Unless – But we simply don't know. Are they necessarily settled at Three? If we don't accept their invitation – and they have no way of telling whether we've gotten it – will they stay, or will they move on? And will they necessarily move on toward Sol?'

'Will they necessarily still be at Three when we come?' countered Macandal. 'If they are, will they necessarily be anything we can communicate with? No, it's a long, dangerous detour for the sake of something that may be grand but may just as well prove futile. Let's get on with our real business first.'

'As the computers and overlords on Earth planned for us,' Hanno gibed. He turned toward Wanderer. 'Wouldn't you, Peregrino, like for once to do something that wasn't planned, that broke through the whole damned scheme of the world today?'

The other man sighed. 'A tough call. Yes, I want to go to Three so bad I can taste it. And someday I hope to. But first and foremost, free life in a free nature –' Pleadingly: 'And I couldn't do it to Corinne and Aliyat. I just can't.'

'You're a knight,' Aliyat breathed.

Yukiko smiled sadly. 'Well, Hanno, Svoboda, we three are no worse off than we were yesterday, are we? Better, in fact, with a new dream before us.'

'For someday,' Svoboda mumbled. She lifted her head. 'I am not angry with you, my friends. I too am weary of machines and hungry for land. So be it.'

The tension began to ease. Smiles flickered.

'No,' said Hanno.

Attention stabbed at him. He rose. 'I am more sorry than you'll ever guess,' he stated. 'But I believe our need and our duty have changed. They are to go to Three. Till now, this venture was desperate. We pretended otherwise, but it was. Our chances looked about equal for perishing as miserably as the Norse did in Greenland, or settling into a sameness like the Polynesians in the Pacific.'

'You promoted it,' Patulcius virtually accused.

'Because I was desperate too. We all were. At least we'd be trying. We might, against the odds, eventually fill our planet with people who kept on looking and searching outward. What had we to lose? Well, this day we've discovered what. The universe.

'I am the captain. I am taking us to the Others.'

Tu Shan was first onto his own feet. 'You can't!' he bellowed.

'I can,' Hanno said. '*Pytheas* obeys me. I will order the course change at once. The sooner it's made, the sooner –'

'No, not against our will,' Wanderer interrupted.

'It would be wrong,' Yukiko pleaded.

Svoboda regarded Hanno with something akin to horror. 'You, you don't mean what you said,' she stammered.

'Don't you want me to do this?' he cast back.

Her jaw clenched. 'Not like that.'

'No, I suppose you wouldn't. Still, I am going to issue the order. You'll thank me afterward.'

'*Bozhe moi* –' She raised her voice. '*Pytheas*, you won't heed a single man, will you?'

'He is captain,' replied the ship. 'I must.'

'No matter what?' Patulcius shouted. 'Impossible!'

'Such is the programming.'

'You never told us,' Macandal whispered.

'I didn't expect the occasion would ever arise,' Hanno said, not quite firmly. 'I arranged it as a provision in case of emergency, best kept secret till then.'

'Jesus Christ!' Aliyat yelled. 'This is the emergency! You're making it yourself!'

'Yes,' Wanderer said. Sweat studded his skin. 'We didn't bargain for a dictator, and we're not going to knuckle under to any. We can't.' He looked upward, as if to find another face in the air. '*Pytheas*, it's become seven against one.'

'That is not a consideration,' the ship answered.

'It never was, at sea or anywhere men voyaged,' Hanno said. 'It couldn't be, if they were to make shore alive.'

'What if the captain is – is incapacitated?' Wanderer called. 'Insane?'

Did the ship take a few extra microseconds to scan its bio-psychological database and draw its conclusion? 'Derangement is impossible for any of you without the severest trauma,' it declared. 'That has not occurred.'

Tu Shan snarled. He started around the table. 'It can. A dead captain doesn't give orders.'

Svoboda moved to block him. 'Now you're the crazy one,' she groaned. He sought to push her aside. She resisted. 'Help me! A fight, no, we can't!'

Wanderer joined her. They gripped Tu Shan by the arms. He halted. The wind sobbed in and out of him.

'See what you nearly caused, Hanno.' Macandal spoke softly, though tears coursed down her cheeks. 'Your command would destroy us. You can't issue it.'

'Can and will.' The Phoenician stepped to the doorway, turned back toward them, stood alert but unmoving. His tone mildened. 'Once the decision's made, you won't go to pieces. I know you too well to believe you would. Nor will you try violence against me. You realize you can't spare one-eighth of our strength, one-fourth of the forefathers to come. And I am the one of us who's held command, not simply leadership but command, in ships and wars, trades and ventures beyond what was known, over and over for thousands of years. Without me, your survival on Phaeacia or anywhere else is more than doubtful.'

Gentler still: 'Oh, I'm no superman. All of you have your own special gifts, and we need them all. I'm as open as ever to your thoughts, advice – yes, your wishes. But someone has to take the final responsibility. Someone always had to. The captain.

'We've another dozen years ahead of us, with God knows what at the end. Don't make them any harder on yourselves than they must be.'

He left. The seven stood mute, half stupefied. At last Wanderer released Tu Shan, as Svoboda did, and said dully, 'He's right about that. We have no choice.'

'The course change process will commence in an hour,' Pytheas announced. 'In order to conserve fuel and minimize the undesired vector, it begins at that time with going free. Please make ready for a weightless period of approximately six hours.'

'That ... is ... it,' Aliyat choked.

Hanno returned. They knew he had sought the control room partly to look at its displays, as if that mattered, but mainly as a sign unto them. 'We'd better get busy,' he said. 'Here, I have printout copies of a checklist. Done is done. We're on our way.' He half smiled. 'Not everybody hates this.'

'Perhaps not,' Svoboda replied. '*Sobaka*. You dog. You total son of a bitch.' She took Wanderer by the hand.

22

And Christ appeared before Aliyat where she knelt. His radiance was not what she had imagined, brilliant as desert noonday; it filled the darkened hollowness of the church with a blue dusk and the last sunset gold. Almost, she thought she heard bells from a caravan returning home. Warmth glowed into the stones beneath and around her. Nor was his visage gaunt and stern. In the West (she had heard?) they showed him like this, a man who had tramped roads, shared wine and honeycomb, taken small children onto his lap. He smiled when he bent over her and with his white sleeve dried the tears off her face.

Straightening again, he said – oh, tenderly, 'Because you have kept your vigil, though the smoke of Hell blew about you, I have heard the prayer you dared not utter. For a time and a time, that which was lost shall be restored to you, and the latter end blessed more than the beginning.' He lifted both scarred hands on high. 'Blessed are they that mourn: for they shall be comforted.'

He was gone. Young Barikai sprang down from the bema and raised her into his arms. 'Beloved!' he jubilated before she stopped his mouth with hers.

Together they went out. Tadmor slumbered beneath a full moon, which frosted spires and dappled paving stones. A horse waited. Mane and tail were streams of moon-silver. Barikai swung into the saddle. He reached down. She answered his clasp by soaring up to settle against him.

Briefly, hoofs rang, then the horse leaped aloft and galloped the ways of air. Wind lulled. Stars gleamed soft, everywhere, around, in violet heaven. Aliyat's loosened hair blew backward to make a tent for her and Barikai. She was drunk with the odor of him, the strength that held her, the seeking lips. 'Where are we bound?' she asked.

'Home.' His laugh pealed. 'But not at once!'

They hastened onward, around the curve of the world into morning. His castle gleamed on its mountaintop. The horse came to rest in a courtyard of mosaics and flowers where a fountain danced. Aliyat gave them scant heed. Later she noticed that she had been unaware whether the servants who met their lord and lady had bodies.

They did provide feast, music, spectacle, when such was wanted. Otherwise Aliyat and Barikai kept to themselves, tireless until they fell embraced into a half-sleep from which they roused joyous.

That happiness grew calmer, love lingered more and more, so that at last it was a new bliss when he said, 'Now let us go home.'

Their horse brought them there at dawn. The household was just coming awake and nobody saw the arrival. Indeed, it was as if nothing had happened and they had never been away. Manu received her hug with some surprise, then much boyish dignity. Little Hairan took it for granted.

She savored ordinariness for the rest of the day and evening, minute by minute, each presence and place, task and talk, question and decision, everything that she owned and that owned her. When the final lamp guided her and Barikai to bed, she was ready for his words: 'I think best you sleep, truly sleep, this night and beyond.'

'Hold me until I do,' she asked of him.

He did, with kisses. 'Come not back too soon,' he said once, against her cheek. 'That would be unwise.'

'I know –' She drifted from him.

Opening her eyes after a time outside of time, she found she was crying. Maybe this had been a bad idea. Maybe she should not go back ever.

Come on, old girl, she thought. Stop this. You promised Corinne you'd help her with that tapestry she wants to make.

Uncoupling, she left the booth where she had lain but stood for a space more in the dream chamber, busy. Good habit, carrying a makeup kit in a purse. Sessions here did sometimes touch pretty near the bone. Well, she learned long ago how to cover the traces.

Svoboda was passing by in the corridor. 'Hello,' said Aliyat. She was about to move on when the other woman plucked her sleeve.

'A moment, if you please,' Svoboda requested.

'Uh, sure.' Aliyat glanced away.

Svoboda didn't take the hint. 'Don't resent this. I must say it. You should go in there less often.'

Anger quivered. 'Everybody else says it. Why not you? I know what I'm doing.'

'Well, I can't prescribe for you, but –'

'But you're afraid I'm curling up in a ball and someday I won't be able to uncurl.' Aliyat inhaled. Suddenly she felt like speaking. 'Listen, dear. You've been in situations in the past where you had to go away from yourself.'

Svoboda paled a bit. 'Yes.'

'I have a lot more than you. I know them pretty thoroughly, believe me. The dream box is a better escape than booze or dope or –' Aliyat grinned – 'closing my eyes and thinking of England.'

'But this isn't that kind of thing!'

'No, not exactly. Still – Listen. What happened today was that I got so furious that if I couldn't go conjure a private world, I'd've had to scream and smash things and generally throw a fit. What would that have done for crew morale?'

'What was the matter?'

'Hanno. What else? We met by chance and he buttonholed me and, oh, you can imagine. He repeated the same tired noises you just did, about me and the dream box. He tried to say, very roundabout – Never mind.'

Svoboda bared a brief smile. 'Let me guess. He implied you are a menace to relationships aboard ship.'

'Yeah. He'd like to pair off with me. Of course he would. Hasn't gotten laid for months now, has he? I suggested what he could do instead, and walked off. But I was volcano angry.'

'You were overreacting; you, of all people. Stress –'

'I s'pose.' Faintly surprised at how rage and loss alike had eased within her, Aliyat said, 'Look, I'm not addicted to dreams. Really I'm not. Everybody uses them once in a while. Why don't you share with me sometime? I'd like that. An interactive dream has more possibilities than letting the computer put into your head what it thinks you've demanded.'

Svoboda nodded. 'True. But –' She stopped.

'But you're afraid I might learn things about you you'd rather I didn't. That's it, right?' Aliyat shrugged. 'I'm not offended. Only, don't preach at me, okay?'

'Why did you resent Hanno's attempt?' Svoboda asked quickly. 'It was quite natural. You need not have cursed him for it.'

'After what he's done to us?' Counterattack: 'Do you still have a soft spot for him?'

Svoboda looked elsewhere. 'I shouldn't, I know. *On se veut –*'

'What?'

'Nothing, nothing. A stray memory.'

'About him.'

Svoboda met the challenge. Probably, Aliyat thought, she wants to be friendly toward me; feels she has to. 'Yes. Of no importance. Some lines we saw once. It was ... the late twentieth century, a few years after we – we seven had gone under cover, while Patulcius was still keeping his own camouflage. Hanno and I were traveling about incognito in France. We stayed one night at an old inn, yes, old already then, and in the guest book we found what somebody had written, long before. I was reminded now, that's all.'

'What was it?' Aliyat asked.

Again Svoboda looked past her. The wry words whispered forth as if of themselves.

'On se veut
On s'enlace
On s'en lasse
On s'en veut.'

Before Aliyat could respond, she nodded adieu and hurried on down the corridor.

23

Once more Yukiko was redecorating her room. Until she finished, it would be an uninhabitable clutter. Thus she spent most of her private hours in Tu Shan's, as well as sleeping there. In due course they would share hers while she worked on his. It was her proposal. He had assented without seeming to care. The brushstroke landscape and calligraphy she earlier put on his walls had over the years been seen until they were all but invisible. However, she had a feeling that he would never especially have noticed their disappearance.

Entering, she found him cross-legged on the bed, left hand supporting a picture screen, right hand busy with a light pencil. He drew something, considered it, made an alteration, studied it further. His big body seemed relaxed and the features bore no mark of a scowl.

'Why, what are you doing?' she asked.

He glanced up. 'I have an idea,' he said almost eagerly. 'It isn't clear to me yet, but sketching helps me think.'

She went around behind him and leaned over to see. His drawings were always delicate, a contrast to much of his work in stone or wood. This showed a man in traditional peasant garb, holding a spade. On a large rock beside him squatted a monkey, while a tiger stood below. Through the foreground flowed a stream wherein swam a carp.

'So you are finally going to try pictures?' she guessed.

He shook his head. 'No, no. You are far better at them than I will ever be. These are just thoughts about figures I mean to sculpture.' He gazed up at her. 'I think pictures may not help us much when we get to Tritos. Even on Earth, in old days, you remember how differently people in different times and countries would draw the same things. To the Alloi, any style of line, shade, color we might use may not make sense. Photographs may not. But a three-dimensional shape – no ghost in a computer; a solid thing they can handle – that should speak to them.'

Tritos, Alloi, he pronounced the names awkwardly; but one needed better words than 'Star Three' and 'Others,' and when Patulcius suggested these, the crew soon went along. Greek still bore its aura of science, learning, civilization. To three of those in the ship, it had been common speech for centuries. 'Metroaster' for 'Mother Star' had, though, been voted down, and 'Pegasi' was back in use. After all, nobody could say whether the Alloi at Tritos had come from there, or even whether it was sun to a sentient race.

Hanno sat mute through the discussion and merely nodded his acceptance. He spoke little these days, and others no more to him than was necessary.

'Yes, an excellent thought,' Yukiko said. 'What do you mean to show?'

'I am groping my way toward that,' Tu Shan replied. 'Your ideas will be welcome. Here, I think, might be a group – more creatures than these – arranged according to our degrees of kinship with the animals. That may lead the Alloi to show us something about their evolution, which ought to tell us things about them.'

'Excellent.' Yukiko trilled laughter. 'But how can you, now, keep up your pretense of being a simple-minded farmer and blacksmith?' She bent low, hugged him, laid her cheek on his. 'This makes me so happy. You were sullen and silent and, and I truly feared you were going back to that miserable, beastly way of living I found you in – how long ago!'

He stiffened. Harshness came into his voice. 'Why not? What else had our dear captain left us, before this came to me out of the dark? It will help fill a little of the emptiness ahead.'

She let go and slipped about to sit down on the bed in front of him. 'I wish you could be less bitter toward Hanno,' she said, troubled. 'You and the rest of them.'

'Have we no reason to?'

'Oh, he was high-handed, true. But has he not been punished enough for that? How dare we take for granted that what he's done is not for the best? It may prove to be what saves us.'

'Easy for you. You want to seek the Alloi.'

'But I don't want this hateful division between us. I dare not give him a friendly word myself, I'm afraid of making matters worse. It makes me wish we'd never received the message. Can't you see, dear, he is – like a righteous emperor of ancient times – taking on himself the heavy burden of leadership?'

Again Tu Shan shook his head, but violently. 'Nonsense. You are drawn to him – don't deny –'

Her tone went calm. 'To his spirit, yes. It isn't like mine, but it also seeks. And to his person, no doubt, but I've honestly not dwelt on that in my mind.' She closed hands upon his knee. 'You are the one I am with.'

It mildened him to a degree. Sternness remained. 'Well, stop imagining he's some kind of saint or sage. He's a scheming, knavish old sailor, who naturally wants to sail. This is his selfishness. He happens to have the power to force it on us.' He slapped the screen down onto the blanket, as if striking with a weapon. 'I am only trying to help us outlive the evil.'

She leaned close. Her smile trembled. 'That is enough to make me love you.'

24

Yet another Christmas drew nigh, in the ship's chronology. It was meaningless to ask whether it did on Earth just then – doubly meaningless, given the physics here and the forgottenness yonder. Hanno came upon Svoboda hanging ornaments in the common room. Evergreen boughs from the nanoprocessors were fresh and fragrant, bejeweled with berries of holly. They seemed as forlorn as the Danish carols from the speakers.

She saw him and tautened. He halted, not too close to her. 'Hello,' he proffered.

'How do you do,' she said.

He smiled. Her face stayed locked. 'What sort of party are you planning this year?' he asked.

She shrugged. 'No motif.'

'Oh, I'll keep out of the way, never fear.' Quickly: 'But we can't go on much longer like this. We'll lose skills, including the skills of teamwork. We must start having simulations and practicing in them again.'

'As the captain directs. I suppose, though, you're aware that Wanderer and I, at least, are doing so. We'll bring others in presently.'

Hanno made himself meet the blue gaze, and made it stay upon his. 'Yes, naturally I know. Good. For you two above all. A phantom wilderness is better than none, right?'

Svoboda bit her lip. 'We could have had the real thing.'

'You will, after we're through at Tritos. You wanted to go there first your-self. Why don't you look forward to it?'

'You know why. The cost to my comrades.' She closed a fist and clipped: 'Not that we can't cope. I outlived many bad husbands, dreary decades, tyrants, wars, everything men could wreak. I will outlive this too. *We* will.'

'Myself among you,' he said, and continued on his way.

It was to no particular goal. He often prowled, mostly at shipnight or through sections where nobody else had occasion to be. An immortal body needed little exercise to keep fit, but he worked regularly at his capabilities and developed new ones. He screened books and shows, listened to music, played with problems on the computers. Frequently, as in the past, when stimuli palled and thought flagged he disengaged his mind and let hours or days flow by, scarcely registering on him. That, however, was in its way as seductive, easily overdone as the dream chamber which he shunned. He could but hope that his crew rationed themselves on illusions.

Today impulse returned him to his stateroom. He sealed himself in, not that anyone would come calling, and settled down before his terminal. 'Acti-vate –' The command fell so flat across silence that he chopped it short. For a while he stared at the ceiling. His fingers drummed the desktop. 'Historical persons,' he said.

'Whom do you wish?' inquired the instrumentality.

Hanno's mouth writhed upward. 'You mean, *what* do I wish?'

What three-dimensional, full-color, changeably expressive, freely moving and speaking wraith? Siddhartha, Socrates, Hillel, Christ – Aeschylus, Vergil, Tu Fu, Firdousi, Shakespeare, Goethe, Mark Twain – Lucretius, Avicenna, Maimonides, Descartes, Pascal, Hume – Pericles, Alfred, Jefferson – Hatshepsut, Sappho, Murasaki, Rabi'a, Margrete I, Jeanne d'Arc, Elizabeth I, Sacajawea, Jane Austen, Florence Nightingale, Marie Curie, Isak Dinesen – yes, or if you liked, the great monsters and she-devils – Have your machine take everything history, archaeology, psychology knew of a person and that person's world, down to the last least scrap, with probabilities assigned to each uncertainty and conjecture; let it model, with subtle and powerful abstract manipulations, the individual whom this matrix could have pro-duced and who would have changed it in precisely those ways that were known; make it write the program, activate; and meet that human creature. The image of the body was a mere construct, as easily generated as any other; but while the program ran, the mind existed, sensed, thought, reacted, conscious of what it was but seldom troubled thereby, usually enthusiastic, interested, anxious to discourse.

'Old myths and nightmares have become real,' Svoboda said once, 'while old reality slips away from us. On Earth they now raise the dead, but are themselves only half alive.'

'That isn't strictly true, either side of it,' Hanno had replied. 'Take my advice from experience and don't call up anybody you ever actually knew. They're never quite right. Often they're grotesquely wrong.'

Unless memory failed after centuries. Or unless the past was as uncertain, as flickeringly quantum-variable, as everything else in the universe of physics.

Seated alone, Hanno winced, partly at recollection of a time when he sought advice from the electronic revenant of Cardinal Richelieu, partly at recalling how he and Svoboda had been together, then. 'I don't want any single companion,' he said to the machine. 'Nor a synthetic personality. Give me ... several ancient explorers. A meeting, a council – can you do that?'

'Certainly. It is a nonstandard interaction, requiring some creative preparation. One minute, please.' Sixty billion nanoseconds.

The first of the faces looking out was strong and serene. 'I don't quite know what to say,' Hanno began hesitantly, well-nigh timidly. 'You've been ... told about the situation here? Well, what do I need? What do you think I should do?'

'You should have taken more thought for your folk,' answered Fridtjof Nansen. The computer translated between them. 'But I understand it is too late to change course again. Be patient.'

'Endure,' said Ernest Shackleton. Ice gleamed in his beard. 'Never surrender.'

'Think of the others,' Nansen urged. 'Yes, you lead, and so you must; but think about how it feels to them.'

'Share your vision,' said Marc Aurel Stein. 'I died gladly because it was where I had wanted to go for sixty years. Help them want.'

'Ha, why are they sniveling?' roared Peter Freuchen. 'My God, what an adventure! Bring me back to see when you get there, lad!'

'Give me your guidance,' Hanno entreated. 'I've discovered I'm no Boethius, to console myself with philosophy. Maybe I have made a terrible mistake. Lend me your strength.'

'You'll only find strength in yourself, sir,' declared Henry Stanley. 'Not in spooks like us.'

'But you aren't! You're made out of what was real –'

'If something of what we did and were survives to this day, we should be proud, my friends,' said Nansen. 'Come, let us put it back into service. Let us try to find good counsel.'

Willem Barents shivered. 'For so strange a voyage, most likely to a lonely death? Commend your soul to God, Hanno. There is nothing else.'

'No, we owe them more than that,' said Nansen. 'They are human. As long as men and women fare outward, they will be human.'

25

Macandal sent her glance slowly from one to the next of the six who sat around the table in the saloon with her. 'I suppose you've guessed why I've asked you to come,' she said at length.

Most of them stayed unstirring. Svoboda grimaced. Wanderer, beside her, laid a hand on her thigh.

Macandal took a bottle and poured into a glass. The claret gurgled dusky rose; its pungency sweetened the air. She passed the bottle on. Glasses had been set out for everyone. 'Let's have a drink first,' she proposed.

Patulcius attempted a jest. 'Are you taking a leaf from the early Persians? Remember? When they had an important decision to make, they discussed it once while sober and once while drunk.'

'Not the worst idea ever,' Macandal said. 'Better than these modern drugs and neurostims.'

'If only because wine has tradition behind it,' Yukiko murmured. 'It means, it is more than its mere self.'

'How much tradition is left in the world?' Aliyat asked bitterly.

'We carry it,' Wanderer said. 'We are it.'

The bottle circulated. Macandal raised her goblet. 'To the voyage,' she toasted. After a moment: 'Yes, drink, all of you. What this meeting is about is restoring something good.'

'If it has not been wholly destroyed,' Tu Shan grated, but he joined the rest in the small, pregnant ceremony.

'Okay,' Macandal said. 'Now listen. Each of you knows I've been after him or her, arguing, wheedling, scolding, trying to wear down those walls of anger you've built around yourselves. Maybe some haven't noticed it was in fact each of you. Tonight's when we bring it out in the open.'

Svoboda spoke stiffly. 'What is there to talk about? Reconciliation with Hanno? We have no breach. Nobody has dreamed of mutiny. It's impossible. A change of course back to Phaeacia is impossible too; we haven't the anti-matter. We're making the best of things.'

'Honey, you know damn well we are not.' Steel toned beneath Macandal's mildness. 'Cold courtesy and mechanical obedience won't get us through whatever waits ahead. We need our fellowship back.'

'So you've told me, us, over and over.' Wanderer's voice was raw. 'You're right, of course. But we didn't break it. He did.'

Macandal regarded him for a quiet spell. 'You're really hurting, aren't you?'

'He was my best friend,' Wanderer said from behind his mask.

'He still is, Johnnie. It's you who've shut him out.'

'Well, he –' Speech trailed off.

Yukiko nodded. 'He has made approaches to you also, then,' she deduced. 'To everyone, I'm sure. Tactful, admitting he could be wrong –'

'He has not groveled,' Tu Shan conceded, 'but he has put down his pride.'

'Not insisting we are the ones mistaken,' Svoboda added, as if unwillingly.

'We may be, you know,' Yukiko argued. 'The choice had to be made, and only he could make it. At first you wanted this way yourself. Are you certain it was not just your own pride that turned you against him?'

'Why did *you* change your mind and join us?'

'For your sakes.'

Tu Shan sighed. 'Yukiko has worked on me,' he told the others. 'And Hanno, well, I have not forgotten what he did for us two in the past.'

'Ah, he has begun to make himself clear to you,' Patulcius observed. 'Me too, me too. I still don't agree with him, but the worst rancor has bled off. Who advised him how to speak with us?'

'He's had a long time alone for thinking,' Macandal said.

Aliyat shuddered. 'Too long. It's been too long.'

Svoboda's words fell sharp. 'I don't see how we can ever again be whole-hearted about him. But you are right, Corinne, we must rebuild … as much faith as we can.'

Heads nodded. It was no climax, it was the recognition of something fore-seen, so slow and grudging in its growth that the completion of it came as a kind of surprise.

Macandal need merely say, 'Grand. Oh, grand. Let's drink to that, and then relax and talk about old times. Tomorrow I'll cook a feast, and we'll throw a party and invite him and get drunk with him –' her laugh rang – 'in the finest Persian style!'

– Hours afterward, when she and Patulcius were in her room making ready for bed, he said, 'That was superbly handled, my dear. You should have gone into politics.'

'I did, once, sort of, you recall,' she answered with a slight smile.

'Hanno put you up to this, from the beginning, didn't he?'

'You're pretty shrewd yourself, Gnaeus.'

'And you coached him in how to behave – carefully, patiently, month after month – with each of us.'

'Well, I made suggestions. And he had help from … the ship. Advice. He never told me much about that. I think it was an experience too close to his heart.' She paused. 'He's always guarded his heart – too carefully; I guess because of the losses he suffered in all those thousands of years. But he's no fool either, where it comes to dealing with people.'

Patulcius looked at her a while. She had slipped off her gown and stood dark, supple before him. Her face against the wall, which was muraled with lilies, made him remember Egypt. 'You're a great woman,' he said low.

'You're not a bad guy.'

'Great for … accepting me,' he slogged on. 'I know it pained you when Wanderer went to Svoboda. I think it still pains you.'

'It's good for them. Maybe not ideal, but good; and we do need stable relationships.' Macandal flung her head back and laughed afresh. 'Hey, listen to me, talking like a twentieth-century social worker!' She swung her hips. 'C'mon over here, big boy.'

26

Clouds massed huge, blue-black over the high place. Lightning flared, thunder crashed. The fire before the altar leaped and cast sparks like stars down the wind. The acolytes led the sacrifice to the waiting priest. His knife glimmered. In the grove below, worshippers howled. Afar, the sea ran white and monsters rose from its depths.

'No!' Aliyat wailed. 'Stop! That's a child!'

'It is a beast, a lamb,' Wanderer called back against the noise; but he kept his glance elsewhere.

'It is both,' Hanno said to them. 'Be still.'

Knife flashed, limbs threshed, blood spurted and flowed dark over stone. The priest cast the body into the flames. Flesh sizzled on coals, fell away from bones, went up in fat smoke. Through the storm, terrible in their splendor, came the gods.

Pillar-tall, bull-broad, beard spilling down over the lion skin that clad him, eyes capturing the fire-gleam, Melqart snuffed deep. He licked his lips. 'It is done, it is well, it is life,' he boomed.

Wind tossed the hair of Ashtoreth, rain jeweled it, lightning-light sheened on breasts and belly. Her own nostrils drank. She clasped his gigantic organ as if it were a staff and raised her left hand into heaven. 'Bring forth the Resurrected!' she cried.

Baal-Adon leaned heavily on Adat, his beloved, his mourner, his avenger. He stumbled, still half blind after the murk of the underworld; he trembled, still half frozen from the grave. She guided him to the smoke of the offering. She took the bowl filled with its blood and gave him to drink. Warmth returned, beauty, wakefulness. He saw, he heard how men and women coupled in the grove and across the land in honor of his arising; and he turned to his consort.

More gods crowded about, Chushor out of the waves, Dagon out of the plowlands, Aliaan out of the springs and underground waters, Resheph out of the storm, and more and more. Clouds began to part. Distantly gleamed the twin pillars and pure lake before the home of El.

A sunbeam smote the eight who stood on the topheth near the betyl, invisible to priest and acolytes. The gods stared and stiffened. Melqart raised his club that had smitten the Sea, primordial Chaos, in the dawn of the world. 'Who dares betread the holy of holies?' he bellowed.

Hanno trod forward. 'Dread ones,' he said calmly, with respect but not abasing himself, looking straight into those eyes, 'we are eight from afar in space, time, and strangeness. We too command the powers of heaven, earth, and hell. But fain would we guest you a while and learn the wonders of your reigning. Behold, we bear gifts.' He signalled, and there appeared a treasure of golden ware, gems, precious woods, incense.

Melqart lowered his weapon and stared with a greed that awoke also in the features of Ashtoreth; but her regard was on the men.

27

One by one, they disengaged. That was a simple matter of removing induction helmets and feedback suits. The web of union between them and the guiding, creating computer had already vanished; the pseudo-experience was at an end. Nonetheless, after they had emerged from their booths into the commonplaceness of the dream chamber, it took them silent minutes to return altogether to themselves. Meanwhile they stood side by side, hand in hand, groping for comfort.

Eventually Patulcius mumbled, 'I thought I knew something about the ancient Near East. But that was the most damnable –'

'Horror and wonder,' Macandal said unevenly. 'Lust and love. Death and life. Was it really like that, Hanno?'

'I can't be sure,' the captain answered. 'The historical Tyre we visited seemed about right to me.' – in a full-sensory hallucination, where the computer drew on his memories and then let the seekers act and be acted on as they would have in a material world. 'Hard to tell, after so long. Besides, you know I'd tried to put it behind me, tried to grow away from what was bad in it. This, though, the Phoenician *conceptual* universe – No, I don't believe I ever thought in just that way, even when I was young and supposed I was mortal.'

'No matter authenticity,' Yukiko said. 'We want practice in dealing with aliens; and this was amply alien.'

'Too much.' Tu Shan's burly frame shivered. 'Come, dear. I want a time gentle and human, don't you?' She accompanied him out.

'What society shall we draw on next?' asked Svoboda. Her attention sought Wanderer. 'Those you knew must have been at least as foreign to the rest of us.'

'No doubt,' he replied rather grimly. 'In due course, yes, we will. But first a setting more ... rational. China, Russia?'

'We have plenty of time,' Patulcius said. 'Better we digest this before we think about anything else. *Kyrie eleison*, to have witnessed the gods at work!' He tugged at Macandal. 'I'm exhausted. A stiff drink, a long sleep, and several days' idleness.'

'Right.' Her smile was fainter than usual. They left.

Wanderer and Svoboda seemed aroused. Their gazes came aglow. She reddened. His breast rose and fell. They also departed.

Hanno took care not to watch. Aliyat had clasped his hand. Now she let go. He spoke dully. 'Well, how was it for you?'

'Terror and ecstasy and – a kind of homecoming,' she said, barely audible.

He nodded. 'Yes, even though you started life as a Christian, it wouldn't be totally foreign to you. In fact, I suspect the program used some memories of yours as input where mine weren't sufficient.'

'Weird enough, though.'

He stared beyond her. 'A dream within a dream,' he murmured, as if to himself.

'What do you mean?'

'Svoboda would understand. Once she and I imagined what kind of future it might be where we dared reveal what we were.' Hanno shook himself. 'Never mind. Goodnight.'

She caught his arm. 'No, wait.'

He stopped, lifted his brows, stood alert in a fashion weary and wary. Aliyat grasped his hand again. 'Take me along,' she said.

'Eh?'

'You're too lonely. And I am. Let's come back together, and stay.'

Deliberately, he said, 'Are you tired of subsisting on Svoboda's and Corinne's leavings?'

For a moment she lost color. She released him. Then she reddened and admitted, 'Yes. You and me, we're neither of us the other's first pick, are we? And you've never forgiven me for Constantinople, not really.'

'Why,' he said, taken aback, 'I've told you I have. Over and over I've told you. I hoped my actions proved –'

'Well, just don't let it make any difference that counts. What's the point of our living all these centuries if we haven't grown up even a little? Hanno, I'm offering you what nobody else in this ship will, yet. Maybe they never will. But we are getting back something of what we had. Between us, you and I could help that healing along.' She tossed her head. 'If you aren't game to try, to give in your turn, okay, goodnight and to hell with you.'

'No!' He seized her by the waist. 'Aliyat, of course I – I'm overwhelmed –'

'You're nothing of the sort, you calculating old scoundrel, and well I know it.' She came to him. The embrace went on.

Finally, flushed, disheveled, she said against his shoulder, 'Sure, I'm a rogue myself. Always will be, I guess. But – I learned more about you than I'd known, Hanno. It wasn't a dream while we were there, it was as real to us as – no, more real than these damned crowding walls. You stood up to the gods, outsmarted them, made them take us in, like nobody else alive could have. You *are* the skipper.'

She raised her face. Tears were on it, but a grin flashed malapert. 'They didn't wear me out. That's your job. And if we can't entirely trust each other, if the thing between us won't quite die away, why, doesn't that add a pinch of spice?'

28

Throughout the final months, as *Pytheas* backed ever more slowly down to destination, the universe again appeared familiar. Strange that a night crowded with unwinking brilliant stars, girded by the frost-road of the galaxy, where nebulae querned forth new suns and worlds while energies raged monstrous around those that had died and light that came from neighbor fire-wheels had left them before humanity was – should feel homelike. Waxing ahead, Tritos had barely more than half the brightness of Sol, a yellow hue that stirred memories of autumns on Earth. Yet it too was a hearth.

Instruments peered across narrowing distance. Ten planets orbited, five of them gas giants. The second inmost swung at somewhat less than one astronomical unit's radius. It possessed a satellite whose eccentric path indicated the primary mass was slightly over two and a third the terrestrial. Nevertheless that globe, though warmer on the average, was at reasonable temperatures, and its atmospheric spectrum revealed chemical disequilibria such as must be due to life.

Week by week, then day by day, excitement burned higher within the ship. There was no quenching it, and presently even Tu Shan and Patulcius stopped trying. They were committed; magnificent things might wait; and here was, for a while at least, an end of wayfaring.

The peace with Hanno that each had made on his or her own terms did not strengthen into the former fellowship. If anything, it thinned, stretched by a new guardedness. What might he want next, and how might someone else react? He had promised that eventually they would go on to Phaeacia; but when would that be, would it ever, could he then betray it? Nobody made accusations, or indeed brooded much on the matter. Conversation was generally free and easy, if not intimate, and he joined again in some recreations – but no more in shared dreams, once their training purpose had been served. He remained half the outsider, in whom none but Aliyat confided, and she little except for her body.

He did not attempt to change their attitudes. He knew better; and he knew, as well, how to pass lifetime after mortal lifetime among strangers to his spirit.

Tritos grew in sight.

Pytheas cast signals ahead, radio, laser, neutrino. Surely the Alloi had detected the ship from afar, roiling the dust and gas of space, braking with a flame out of the furnace engine. Receivers caught no flicker of response. 'Have they gone?' Macandal fretted. 'Have we come this whole way for nothing?'

'We're still many light-hours off,' Wanderer reminded her. The hunter's patience was upon him. 'Can't talk very readily. Not at all by electromagnetic waves, while our drive blazes in front of us. And … I would scan a newcomer first, before leaving my cover.'

She shook her head, half angrily. 'Forget the Stone Age, John. Anything like war or piracy between the stars isn't just obscene, it's absurd.'

'Can you be absolutely certain? Besides, we could be dangerous to them, or they to us, in ways neither party has managed to imagine.'

Tritos brightened. Without magnification, simply with the light stopped down, eyes beheld the disc, spots upon it, flares leaping aloft. Offside stood a bluish-white steady spark that was the second planet. Now spectroscopy gave details of land and water surfaces, air mostly nitrogen and oxygen. The travelers changed course to intercept. The name they bestowed was Xenogaia.

The hour came when *Pytheas* called, 'Attention! Attention! Coded signals detected.'

The eight crowded into the command room. That wasn't physically necessary. They could quite well have perceived and partaken from their separate quarters. It was merely impossible for them not to be side by side, breath mingling with breath.

The message employed the same basic system as had the robots – a dozen years ago ship's time, three and a half cosmic centuries – minus relativistic adjustments no longer required. It arrived by UHF radio, from somewhat aft, to avoid ionization that was no longer enormously strong but could still interfere. 'The source is a comparatively small object about a million kilometers distant,' *Pytheas* reported. 'It has presumably lain in orbit until we came this near. At present it is accelerating to match our vectors. Radiation is weak, indicating high efficiency.'

'A boat?' Hanno wondered. 'Has it a mother ship?'

Pytheas assembled the images transmitted. They sprang into vivid existence. First appeared a starscape, then an unmistakable Tritos (you could compare what was in a view-screen), then a dizzying zoom in on … forms, colors, a thing that swept lopsidedly around a larger. 'That must be Xenogaia,' Patulcius said into a thick silence. 'It must be where they stay.'

'I think they are preparing us for what comes next,' Yukiko said.

The representation vanished. A new form was there.

They could not, at once, properly see it. The contours, the mathematical dimensionality were too exotic, too far beyond any expectation. Thus had it been for Svoboda and Wanderer when first they glimpsed high mountains – snow-clouds, heaven gone wrinkled, or what? 'More art?' Tu Shan puzzled. 'They do not make pictures like any that humans ever did. I think they do not sense like us.'

'No,' Hanno said, 'this is likelier a straightforward hologram.' The hair stood up on his arms. 'Maybe they don't know how we see, either, but the reality is the same for all of us ... I hope.'

The image moved, a slow and careful pirouette revealing it from every angle. It reached out of the scene and brought back a lump of something soft, which it proceeded to mold into a series of geometrical solids, sphere, cube, cone, pyramid, interlinked rings. 'It's telling us it's intelligent,' Aliyat whispered. Blindly, she crossed herself.

Vision began to understand. If the image was life-size, the original stood about one hundred forty centimeters tall. Central was a stalk, a green that glittered and shimmered, supported on two thin limbs that were flexible or multiply jointed, ending in several bifurcated digits. At the top sprouted two similar arms. These forked, subdivided, sub-subdivided, dendritically, till the watchers were unable to count the last, spidery-delicate 'fingers.' From the sides spread a pair of – wings? membranes? – to a span that equaled the height. They looked as if made of nacre and diamond dust, but rippled like silk.

After a long time, Tu Shan muttered, 'If this is what they are, how shall we ever know them?'

'The way we knew the spirits, maybe,' Wanderer answered as softly. 'I remember kachina dances.'

'For God's sake,' Svoboda cried, 'what are we waiting for? Let's show them us!'

Hanno nodded. 'Of course.'

The spacecraft moved on together toward the living world.

29

So *Pytheas* came to harbor, took orbit about Xenogaia.

That required special care. There were other bodies to give a wide berth. Foremost was the moon. Scarred and ashen as Earth's, it had only a tenth the mass, but its path brought it inward to about a third the Lunar distance from its primary, then out again to three-fifths. Some cosmic accident must have caused that, more recent than the impacts that formed the planet.

A number of artificial satellites wheeled in their own courses. None resembled any in the Solar System. Boats, as Hanno dubbed them, came and went. His folk were unsure how many, for no two seemed alike; only slowly did they realize that form changed according to mission, and force-fields had more to do with it than crystal or fiber.

The Allosan mother ship (another human phrasing) orbited well beyond the moon. It appeared to be of fixed shape, a cylindroid almost ten kilometers in length and two in diameter, majestically rotating on its long axis, mother-of-pearl iridescent. Aft (?) was a complex of slender, curved members which might be the drive generator; it put Hanno in mind of interwoven vine patterns he had seen on Nordic runestones and in Irish Gospels. Forward (?) the hull flared and then came to a point, making Patulcius and Svoboda recall a minaret or a church spire. Yukiko wondered about its age. A million years did not seem unthinkable.

'They probably live aboard,' Wanderer opined. 'Uh, what weight does that spin provide?'

'Sixty-seven percent of standard terrestrial gravity,' the ship responded.

'Yeah, they look as if they come from that kind of environment. It means – let's see, you told us Xenogaian pull equals one point four times Earth's, so for them – no, no, let me show off,' Wanderer laughed. 'It's twice what they're used to. Can they take it?'

'We could, if we had to,' Macandal said. 'But the Altai do seem fragile.' She hesitated. 'Like crystal, or a bare tree iced over on a clear winter day. They are quite beautiful, once you learn how to look at them.'

'I think we shall have to,' declared Tu Shan harshly. 'I mean, bear an added forty kilos on each hundred.'

Their gazes followed his to that viewscreen in the common room which held an image of Xenogaia. They were passing the dayside, the planet nearly full. It was brighter than Earth, for it was more clouded. Whiteness swirled and billowed, thinly marbled with the blue of oceans, spotted with greenish-brown glimpses of land. Though the axis tilted a full thirty-one degrees, neither pole bore a cap; snow gleamed rarely on the tallest mountains.

Aliyat shivered. The motion loosened her hold on a table edge and sent her slowly off through the air. Hanno caught her. She clung to his hand. 'Go down there?' she asked. 'Must we?'

'You know we can't stay healthy in weightlessness,' he reminded her. 'We can for longer than mortals born, and we've got medications that help, but finally our muscles and bones will shrink too, and our immune systems fail.'

'Yes, yes, yes. But *yonder?*'

'We need a minimum weight. This ship isn't big enough to spin for that by itself. Too much radial variation, too much Coriolis force.'

She glared through tears. 'I am not an idiot. I have not forgotten. Nor have I f-f-forgotten the robots can fix that.'

'Yes, separate the payload and engine sections, hitch a long cable between, then spin them. The trouble is, that immobilizes *Pytheas* till it's reassembled. I think you'll all agree we'd better hang on to its capabilities, as well as the boats', at least till we know a lot more.'

'Shall we shelter on the first planet?' Tu Shan asked. 'A seared hell. The third isn't this large either, but a frozen, barren waste; and likewise every outer moon or asteroid.'

Svoboda looked still toward Xenogaia. 'Here is life,' she said. 'Forty percent additional weight won't harm us, given our innate hardiness. We will grow used to it.'

'We grew used to heavier burdens in the past,' Macandal observed quietly.

'But what I'm trying to say, if you'll let me,' Aliyat yelled, 'is, can't the Alloi do something for us?'

By this time considerable information exchange had taken place, diagrams, interior views of vessels, whatever the non-humans chose to offer and the humans thought to. It included sounds. From the Alloi, those were notes high and coldly sweet that might be speech or might be music or might be something incomprehensible. It seemed likely that they were going about establishing communication in systematic wise; but the naive newcomers had not yet fathomed the system. They dared hope that the first, most basic message had gotten through on both sides and was mutually honest: 'Our will is good, we want to be your friends.'

Hanno frowned. 'Do you imagine they can control gravitation? What about that, *Pytheas?*'

'They give no indication of any such technology,' answered the ship, 'and it is incompatible with known physics.'

'Uh-huh. If it did exist, if they could do it, I expect they'd have so many other powers they wouldn't bother with the kind of stuff we've met.' Hanno rubbed his chin. 'But they could build a spinnable orbital station to our specs.'

'A nice little artificial environment, for us to sit in and turn to lard, the way we were doing here?' exploded from Wanderer. 'No, by God! Not when we've got a world to walk on!'

Svoboda uttered a cheer. Tu Shan beamed. Patulcius nodded vigorously. 'Right,' said Macandal after a moment.

'That is provided we can survive there,' Yukiko pointed out. 'Chemistry, biology – it may be lethal to us.'

'Or maybe not,' Wanderer said. 'Let's get busy and find out.'

The ship and its robots commenced that task. In the beginning humans were hardly more than eager spectators. Instruments searched, sampled, analyzed; computers pondered. Boats entered atmosphere. After several sorties had provided knowledge of surface conditions, they landed. The intelligent machines that debarked transmitted back their findings. Then as the humans gained familiarity, they became increasingly a part of the team, first suggesting, later directing and deciding. They were not scientific specialists, nor need they be. The ship had ample information and logic power, the robots abundant skills. The travelers were the embodied curiosity, desire, will of the whole.

Hanno was barely peripheral. His concern was with the Alloi. Likewise did Yukiko's become. He longed most for what they might tell him about themselves and their farings among the stars; she thought of arts, philosophies, transcendence. Both had a gift for dealing with the foreign, an intuition that often overleaped jumbled, fragmentary data to reach a scheme that gave meaning. Thus had Newton, Planck, Einstein gone straight to insights that, inexplicably, proved to explain and predict. So had Darwin, de Vries, Oparin. And so, perhaps, had Gautama Buddha.

When explorers on Earth encountered peoples totally foreign to them – Europeans in America, for instance – the parties soon groped their way to understanding each other's languages. Nothing like that happened at Tritos. Here the sundering was not of culture and history, nor of species, phylum, kingdom. Two entire evolutions stood confronted. The beings not only did not think alike, they *could* not.

Compare just the human hand and its Allosan equivalent. The latter had less strength, although the grip was not negligible when all digits laid hold on something. It had vastly more sensitivity, especially in the fine outer branchlets: a lower threshold of perception and a wider, better coordinated field of it. The hairlike ultimate ends clung by molecular wringing, and the organism felt how they did. Thus the subjective world was tactilely richer than ours by orders of magnitude.

Was it optically poorer? Impossible to say, quite likely meaningless to ask. The Allosan 'wings' were partly regulators of body temperature, partly excretors of vaporous waste, mainly networks (?) of sensors. These included organs responsive to light, simpler than eyes but, in their numbers and diversity, perhaps capable of equal precision. Whether this was so or not depended on how the brain processed their input; and there did not seem to be any single structure corresponding to a brain.

Enough. It would probably take Hanno and Yukiko years to learn the anatomy; it would certainly take them longer to interpret it. For the moment, they understood – borrowing terrestrial concepts, grotesquely inappropriate – they were dealing not only with software unlike their own, but hardware. It was not to be expected that they would readily master its kind of language. Perhaps, beyond some kind of rudiments, they never would.

Presumably the Alloi had had earlier practice among aliens, and had developed various paradigms. The pair found themselves acquiring facility as they worked, not simply struggling to comprehend but making contributions to the effort. More and more, intent clarified. A primitive code took shape. Material contacts began, cautious to start with, bolder as confidence grew.

The fear was not of violence, or, for that matter – 'under these circumstances,' said Hanno, grinning – chicanery. It was of surprises that might lurk in a universe where life seemed to be incidental and intelligence accidental. What condition taken for granted by one race might harm the other? What innocuous or necessary microbes might elsewhere brew death?

Robots met in space. They traded samples that they took to shielded laboratories for study. (At any rate, it happened aboard *Pytheas*.) Nanotech and biotech gave quick responses. While the chemistries were similar, even to most amino acids, the deviations were such as to bar cross-infection. Yes, the specimens sent by the Alloi had things in them that probably corresponded somewhat to viruses; but the fundamental life-stuff resembled DNA no more than a file does a saw.

After repeated experiments of that general sort, robots paid visits to ships. The Allosan machines were graceful, multi-tentacular, a pleasure to watch swooping about. Within the Allosan vessel, the air was thin, dry, but humanly breathable. Temperatures went through cycles, as they did in *Pytheas*, the range being from cool to chilly. Light was tinged like that from Tritos, less bright than outside but adequate. Centrifugal weight was as predicted, two-thirds of a gee, also sufficient.

As for what else the great hull bore –

Work on Xenogaia proceeded more straightforwardly. Planetology was a mature discipline, a set of techniques, formulas, and computer models. This globe fitted the pattern. Meteorology and climatology were less exact; some predictions could never be made with certainty, for chaos inhered in the equations. However, the overall picture soon emerged.

A strong greenhouse effect overcompensated a high albedo; other things being equal, every clime was hotter than at the same latitude on Earth. Of course, things seldom were equal. Thus the tropics had their pleasant islands as well as their steaming continental swamps or blistering deserts. Axial tilt and rotation rate, once around in slightly more than twenty-one hours, made for powerful cyclonic wind patterns, but the heavy atmosphere and warm polar regions moderated weather almost everywhere. Though conditions were unstable compared to the terrestrial, subject to swifter and often unforeseeable change, dangerous storms were no commoner than on Earth before control. In composition the air was familiar: higher humidity, rather more carbon dioxide, several percent less oxygen. For humans, the latter was more than made up by the sea-level pressure, twice their standard. It was air they could safely inhale, and uncorrupted.

Life covered, filled, drenched the planet. Its chemistry was akin to the terrestrial and Allosan, with its own uniquenesses. Given considerations of energy, followed by the scores of cases robots had reported to Earth, that was expected. As always, the astonishments sprang from the details, the infinite versatility of protein and inventiveness of nature.

On the prosaic side, humans could eat most things, though probably few would taste very good, some would be poisonous, and none would provide complete nutrition. Probably they would be safe from every predator microbe and virus; mutation might eventually change that, but modern biomedicine should handily cope. For the Survivors, with their peculiar immune and regenerative systems, the hazard would almost be nonexistent. They could grow terrestrial crops if they chose, and then animals to feed on the grass and grain.

This was not virgin Earth given back to them. It was not Phaeacia of their dreams. Yet here they could make a home.

Here they would have neighbors.

'– and he's been so lonely,' Macandal said to Patulcius. 'She and Hanno – no, no monkey business between them. Might be better if there were. It's just that they're both wrapped up in their research till it's as if nothing and nobody else quite exists for them. Aliyat's complained to me. I can't do much for her, but I've gotten an idea about Tu Shan.'

She singled out others and gave them the same thought, privately, in words she deemed suited to each. Nobody objected. On the chosen evening, after she had done the poor best that could be done to produce a feast in weightlessness, she called for a vote, and Tu Shan received his surprise.

A spaceboat descended. Assisted by two robots, because initial problems with gravity were unavoidable after this long in orbit, he stepped forth, the first human being on Xenogaia. He had left off his shoes. The soil lay warm and moist. Its odors enriched his breath. He wept.

Shortly afterward, Hanno and Yukiko returned from the Allosan ship. The visit had been their first. The six aboard *Pytheas* gathered around them in the common room. All floated watchful as pikes in a lake. A mural, enlarged from '*Falaise à Varengeville*' – sea, sky, cliff, its shadow on the water, brush golden with sunlight – seemed more remote in time and space than Monet himself.

'No, I cannot tell you what we saw,' Yukiko said, almost like one who speaks in sleep. 'We haven't the words, not even for the images they've sent here. But … somehow, that interior is alive.'

'Not just dead metal and electronic trickery,' Hanno added. He was altogether awake, ablaze. 'Oh, they've much to teach us! And I do believe we'll have news for them, once we've found how to tell it. But it seems they can't come to us in person. We don't know why, what's wrong with our environment, but I think that if they were able to, they would.'

'Then they doubtless have the same handicap on the planet,' Wanderer said slowly. 'We can do what their machines never can. They must be glad we came.'

'They are, they are,' Yukiko exulted. 'They sang to us –'

'They want us to come live with them!' Hanno cried.

A kind of gasp went around the room. 'Are you sure?' Svoboda's question was half demand.

'Yes, I am. We've achieved some communication, and it's a simple message, after all.' The words tumbled from Hanno. 'How better can we get to really know each other and work together? They showed us the section we can have. It's plenty big and we're free to bring over whatever we want, make whatever we like. The weight's enough to keep us fit. The air, the general conditions are no worse than in mountains we remember. We'll get used to that; and we can set up cozy retreats. Besides, we'll spend a lot of time in space, exploring, discovering, maybe building –'

'No,' said Wanderer.

The single sound was a hammerfall. Silence echoed behind it. Eyes sought eyes. One by one, faces stiffened.

'I'm sorry,' Wanderer went on. 'This is marvelous. I'm tempted. But we've sailed too many years with the Flying Dutchman. Now there's a world for us, and we're going to take it.'

'Wait, wait,' Yukiko protested. 'Of course we mean to study Xenogaia. Mainly it, in fact. It, the sapients, they must be why the Alloi have lingered. We'll establish bases, work out of them –'

Tu Shan shook his heavy head. 'We will build homes,' he answered.

'It is decided,' Patulcius said. 'We will cooperate with the Alloi when we have seen to our needs. I daresay we can investigate the planet better, living on it, than in a series of … of junkets. Be that as it may –' he smiled coldly – '*je suis, je reste.*'

'Hold on,' Hanno argued. 'You talk as though you mean to stay on permanently. You know that was never the idea. Xenogaia may be habitable, but it's far from what we had in mind. Eventually we'll take on fresh antimatter. I think the Alloi have a production facility near the sun, but in any case, they'll help us. We'll go to Phaeacia as we intended.'

'When?' challenged Macandal.

'When we're finished here.'

'How long will that take? Decades, at least. Centuries, possibly. You two will enjoy them. And the rest of us, sure, we'll be fascinated, we'll help whenever we can. But meanwhile and mainly, we have our own lives and rights. And our children's.'

'If in the end we leave,' Svoboda said low, 'it will not be the first home any of us forsook; and first we will have had a home.'

Hanno captured her gaze. 'You wanted to explore,' he recalled.

'And I shall, in a living land. Also … we need every pair of hands. I cannot desert my comrades.'

'You're outvoted,' Aliyat said, 'and this time you can't do anything about it.' She reached to stroke fingers over Hanno's cheek. Her smile quivered. 'There are seas down there for you to sail on.'

'Since when were you a bold pioneer?' he taunted.

She flushed. 'Yes, I'm a city girl, but I can learn. Do you suppose I liked lolling useless? I thought better of you. Well, in the past I crossed deserts, mountains, oceans, I survived in alleys, through wars and plagues and famines. Go to hell.'

'No, please, we must not quarrel,' Yukiko pleaded.

'Right,' Wanderer agreed. 'We'll take our time, think, talk this over like friends.'

Hanno straightened, so that he floated upright before the cliff and the sky. 'If you want,' he said bleakly. 'But I can tell you now, in the teeth of your old tribal hope for a consensus, we won't reach any. You're bound and determined to strike roots on the planet. And I, I will not throw away this opportunity the Alloi have offered. I cannot. Instead of fighting, let's plan how we can make the best of what's to be.'

Tu Shan's countenance twisted. 'Yukiko?' he croaked.

She flew to his arms. He held her close. What she gulped forth was, 'Forgive me.'

30

'I think you should go,' Macandal said. 'It seems to be something you'd understand best among us.'

'No, really,' Aliyat began, 'you've always –'

Macandal smiled. 'You've gotten too shy, honey. Think back. Way back, like to New York.'

Still Aliyat hesitated. She wasn't simply unsure whether she could deal with the Ithagenē in what was clearly a critical situation. As a matter of fact, she had gotten more grasp of their language and ways – in some aspects, at least – than anybody else. (Had her earlier life made her quick to catch nuances?) But Tu Shan could ill spare her help, nursing the fields through this season of a drought year; and in spare moments, she was collating the mass of data and writing up the significant experiences that Wanderer and Svoboda sent back from their exploration of the northern woodlands. 'I'd have to stay in touch with you anyway,' she said.

'Well, that's wise,' the other woman replied, 'but you'll be on the spot and the only one really qualified to make decisions. I'll support you. We all will.'

She was not the boss at Hestia, nobody was, yet it had tacitly come to pass that her word carried the most weight in the councils of the six. More lay behind that than finding the advice was sound. Wanderer had remarked once, 'I think we, with our science and high technology, four and a third light-centuries from Earth, are discovering old truths again: spirit, mana, call it what you will. Maybe, even, God.'

'Besides,' Macandal continued, 'I've got my hands full.' She always did, her own work, what she shared with Patulcius, what belonged to the community; and at three years, Joseph was several handsful by himself. Her laugh rolled. 'Also my belly.' Their second. Pregnancy was not disabling, bodies had hardened to Xenogaian weight, but you had better be careful. 'Don't worry, we'll pitch in to see your man through; and maybe you won't be gone long.' Soberly: 'Take what time you need, though. This means a great deal to them. It might mean everything to us.'

Therefore Aliyat packed her gear and rations, and departed.

Coming out of her house in the morning, she stopped for a minute and looked. Not yet was the scene too familiar to see. The sky reached milky, an overcast riven in places to reveal the wan blue beyond. Nowhere beneath were the clouds that should have brought rain. Air hung still and hot, full of sulfury smells. The stream that ran from the eastern hills through the settlement had become little more than a trickle; she barely heard it fall over the verge nearby and tumble to the river. Down in the estuary, banks and bars shone wider than erstwhile at low tide.

Regardless, Hestia abided. The three homes and several auxiliary buildings stood foursquare, solidly timbered. Russet native turf between them had withered, but watering preserved the shade trees and the beds of roses, hollyhocks, violets along walls. A kilometer northward, robots were busy around the farmstead and in the fields; the meadow and its cows made a fantastic vividness of green and red. Farther off, the spaceboat reared above the aircraft hangar, into heaven, like a watchtower over the whole small realm. From this height Aliyat spied a brighter gleam on the eastern horizon, the Amethyst Sea.

We'll survive, she knew. At worst, the synthesizers will have to feed us and our livestock till the drought breaks, and next year we'll have to start over. Oh, I hope not. We've worked so hard – machines too few – and hoped so much. An enlarged base, surplus, the future, the children – All right, I have been selfish, not wanting to be bothered with any of my own, but isn't Hestia glad that I'm free today?

Elsewhere Minoa reached as of old. South, across the river, forest crowns bore a thousand hues, ocher, brown, greenish bronze, dulled by dryness. The same growth bordered the cleared land on the north; then, westerly on this side, hills climbed. Above their ridges lifted a white blur, Mount Pytheas wrapped in its mists.

Human names. Throat and tongue could form the language of the dwellers after a fashion, understandably if they paid close attention, but soon grew hoarse. The concepts behind that speech were more difficult.

Aliyat turned to kiss Tu Shan goodbye. His body was hard, his arms strong. Already at this hour he smelled of sweat, soil, maleness. 'Be careful,' he said anxiously.

'You be,' she retorted. Xenogaia surely harbored more surprises and treacheries than had struck thus far. He'd been injured oftenest. He was a darling, but drove himself overly hard.

He shook his head. 'I fear for you. From what I have heard, this is a sacred matter. Can we tell how they will act?'

'They're not stupid. They won't expect me to know their mysteries. Remember, they *asked* if somebody would come and –' And what? It wasn't clear. Help, counsel, judge? 'They haven't lost their awe of us.'

Had they not? What did a creature not of Earth, no kin whatsoever, feel? The natives had certainly been hospitable. They readily gave this piece of ground, had indeed offered a site closer to their city; but the humans feared possible ecological problems. There had been abundant exchange of objects as well as ideas, useful as well as interesting or beautiful. But did this prove more than that the Ithagen? – another Greek word – had their share of common sense and, one supposed, curiosity?

'I've got to go. Keep well.' Aliyat walked off, as fast as was safe under a backpack. She'd developed muscles like a judo black belter's, which gave a terrifically sexy figure and gait, but bones remained all too breakable.

Someday we'll leave. Phaeacia waits, promising us to be like Earth. Does she lie? How much will we miss this world of toils and triumphs?

Four Ithagenē waited at the head of the path. They wore mesh mail and their hook-halberds gleamed sharp. They were an honor guard; or so she thought of them. Deferential, they divided to precede and follow her down the switchbacks across the fjord wall to the river. At the floating dock, the envoy was already in the vessel that brought them. Long, gracefully curved at prow and stern, it little resembled the two human-made boats tied nearby. No more did it have rowers, though, and the yards were bare of sails. A motor, such as the fabricator robots had lately accumulated the resources to make, was an imperial gift. Supplies of fuel renewed it ongoingly.

The humans often wondered what they were doing to this civilization, for good or ill – ultimately, to this world.

Aliyat recognized S'saa. That was as closely as she could render the name. She did her best with a phrase that they guessed, in Hestia, was half formal greeting, half prayer. Lo responded in kind. ('Lo, le, la.' What else could you say when sexes were three, none corresponding quite to male or female or neuter, and the language lacked genders?) She and her escort boarded, a crew member cast off, another took the rudder, the motor purred, they bore upstream.

'May you now tell me what you want?' Aliyat asked.

'The matter is too grave for uttering elsewhere than in the Halidom,' S'saa answered. 'We shall sing of it.'

The notes keened forth to set an emotional tone, prepare both body and mind. Aliyat heard distress, anger, fear, bewilderment, resolution. Surely much escaped her, but in the past year or two she had finally begun to comprehend, yes, feel such music, as she had failed to do with many kinds on Earth. Wanderer and Macandal were experimenting with adaptations of it, composing songs of quiet, eerie power.

You wouldn't have thought of these beings as artists. Barrel torsos, some one hundred fifty centimeters tall on four stumpy limbs, covered with big scales or flaps, brown and leathery, that could individually lift to show a soft pink undersurface for fluid intake, excretion, sensing; no head to speak of, a bulge on top where a mouth underlay one scale and four retractable eyestalks protruded; four tentacles below, each terminating in four digits, that could be stiffened at will by turgor. But how repulsive did a body look that was scaleless as a flayed corpse? The humans took care always to be fully clothed among Xenogaians.

Rapidly driven, the boat passed several galleys bound the same way, then numbers of lesser craft 'fishing' or freighting. None were going downstream; the tide had begun to flow, and although the moon was fairly distant today, the bore up the river would be considerable. At ebb the argosies would set forth. This was a seafaring nation (?) whose folk hunted great aquatic beasts and harvested great weed fields, traded around the coasts and among the islands, occasionally fought pirates or barbarians or whatever their enemies were. As tactfully as possible, the six at Hestia refused to give any military aid. They didn't know the rights or wrongs, they only knew that this appeared to be the most advanced civilization on the planet but someday they'd want to start getting acquainted with more. Of course, doubtless their local friends had found uses both warlike and peaceful for what they acquired from them.

A pair of hours slipped by. On the south side, forest gave way to orchards and croplands. Foliage drooped sere. On the north, while hills heightened in the background, bluffs declined to gentle slopes. Towers came into hazy view, grew clearer, loomed sheer above masts crowded along the wharfs; and Aliyat went ashore into Xenoknossos.

Warded by stream and fleet, the city had no need of outer walls. Along wide, clean streets, colonnades and façades rose intricately sculptured. Glass flashed in color patterns of contrasting simplicity. The effect was not busy but harmonious, airy, like trees and vines in wind or kelp in currents undersea, strange to behold on a world that dragged so heavily. The raucous turbulence of human crowds was absent. Dwellers moved deliberately; even the looks and remarks that followed Aliyat were decorous. It was their voices that danced, twittered, strove, joined together – their voices and the sounds of instruments from places where they took their pleasure.

Not all was thus. Climbing a hill, she saw down to a camp outside the city, a wretched huddle of makeshift shelters. The beings within stood ominously bunched. Armed guards were posted about. Chill touched her. This must, somehow, be the reason she was called.

On the hilltop fountained the building she knew as the Halidom. Its stone had weathered pale amber. Nothing like its interwoven, many-branched vaults and arches, spiral windows and calyx eaves, was ever on Earth. Imagination yonder had never ranged in those directions. When the images arrived, architecture, together with music and poesy and much else, might well have a rebirth, if anybody still cared about such things.

S'saa accompanied her inside. A chamber vast and dim opened before them. The mighty of Xenoknossos had gathered, expectant, in a half circle before a dais. Thereon were those three, one of each sex, who reigned or presided or led. Hearing tell of them, Hanno had from space proposed dubbing them the Triad, but later those at Hestia thought a better word might be the Triune.

She approached.

That night she radioed back from the apartment lent her. She camped in it, really, as ill suited as the furnishings were; but it served. A window was unshuttered to warm darkness, the booming of a breeze. The small horned moon tinted clouds and cast ghostly shimmers on the river. Fires burned sullen among the squatters in the field.

Exhaustion flattened her voice, though her mind had seldom felt more awake. 'We've been at it all day,' she said. 'Not that the trouble is complicated in itself, but it involves beliefs, traditions, prejudices, everything that's so knitted into a person – Think of a pagan Celt and a pious Muslim trying to explain, to justify, the status and rights of women to each other.'

'The Ithagenē did have the wisdom to ask for an outside opinion,' Patulcius remarked. 'How many human societies ever did?'

'Well, this is unprecedented,' Wanderer answered from the outback. 'We never had any real aliens among us on Earth. Maybe in future we'll benefit – Go on, Aliyat.'

'It's how they breed,' copulating in fresh water, which must be still if conception was to result; a certain concentration of certain dissolved organic materials was essential. That set no more of a handicap, on a world where most regions were normally wet, than loss of the ability to synthesize vitamin C in the body had done for her species. 'You remember, the city people use that lake in the hills behind town.' Holy Lake became the human name, for it seemed lovemaking was a religious rite in this society. 'Well, throughout the hinterlands, most others have dried up to the point where they're useless. The habitants have gotten together and demand access to Holy Lake till the drought's over. It's badly shrunken too, but enough is left for everybody if triples ration their turns.' Aliyat's laugh clanked. 'How that would go over with our race! But of course the Ithagenē don't think of it the way we do. What has the Xenoknossians up in arms is the thought of … outsiders profaning their particular mystery, the presence of their, their tutelary spirit or god or whatever it is. The Triune told the countryfolk to go home and wait out the bad times. They shouldn't breed anyway till the rains come again. But you know about the sacred Year-Births –'

'Yes,' Tu Shan said. 'Besides, they live primitively, infant mortality is always high, they feel they must be fecund whatever happens.'

'The realm, this whole section of Minoa, is close to civil war,' Aliyat told them. 'There've been killings. Now the, uh, tribes have jointly sent two or three thousand here, who insist that soon, come what may, they'll go to the lake. Nothing can stop them, short of a massacre. Nobody wants that, but to give in could tear things apart almost as terribly.'

Macandal whistled low. 'And we had no idea. If only they'd come to us sooner.'

'I don't suppose it occurred to them before they got desperate,' Patulcius guessed. 'If we don't find a solution fast, I suspect it will be too late.'

'That's why you went, Aliyat.' Macandal's tone wavered. 'I gathered, from S'saa's hints, that it concerned this kind of thing, and you, with your experience – Don't misunderstand!'

'No offense,' Aliyat said. 'I did, I hope, slowly get a feel for what's going on, and a notion. It may be worthless.'

'Tell us,' Svoboda begged.

If you could use human words for Ithagenean emotions and make sense, Aliyat thought, then the assembly next morning was appalled. 'No!' exclaimed the le of the Triune. 'This is impossible!'

'Not so, Foreseers,' she maintained. 'It can be quickly and easily done. Behold.' She unfolded a sheet of paper. Copied thereon, a transmission from Hestia to a machine she had carried along, was an enlarged aerial photograph of Holy Lake and its vicinity. The Ithagenē didn't object to overflights, though none had ever accepted an invitation to ride. (Did some instinct forbid, was it a prohibition, or what?) She pointed. 'The lake lies as in a bowl, fed by rain' and runoff. Here, a short way below, is a hollow. Let us clear it of trees and brush, then dig a channel through the hill above. Some of the life-giving water will drain out to fill it, while enough will remain for you after the channel is closed again. There, out of sight of your people, the countryfolk can engender according to their own customs. For you this would be a huge undertaking, but you know of our machines and explosives. We will do it for you.' Hissings and rustlings filled the gloom. S'saa must explain to Aliyat, patching out the native language with what human speech Io commanded: 'Although they are reluctant, they would agree, lest worse befall. However, they fear the habitants will refuse, will take the proposal as a deadly threat. Knowing Kth and Hru'ngg, the leaders, I think this is true. For a life-site is not any pond; it is hallowed by ancient use, by the life it has given in the past. To triple elsewhere would be to set the world awry. The rains might never return, or the violators might never have another birth.'

Dismay struck whetted. 'You don't believe that!'

'Not we who are here, no. But those are simple upcountry folk. And it is true that not all bodies of water grant the blessing. Many do not, though surely they were tried at some time.'

'That is because – oh – oh, Christ, what's the use?'

'Water flows from your eyes. Do you invoke?'

'No, I – You have no word. Yes, I invoke the dead, and the loss, and – Wait! Wait!'

'You leap, you raise your arms, you utter noises.'

'I, I have a new thought. Maybe this will serve. I must ask the council. Then I must … must doubtless go to the habitants and … learn if it feels right to them.' Aliyat turned around to face the Triune.

For days heaven had been almost clear, an iron-hard blue, clouds nowhere but in the west. Heat lightning sometimes flickered yonder, and thunder muttered into windlessness. Now sunset reddened those reaches. Its beams struck through gaps and down valleys until they splashed the new tarn as if with human blood. Trees bulked black against it. More and more, the Ithagenē gathered in their hundreds became masses of shadow, a wall around the water. Their singing beat like a heart.

Out of them trod the Eldritch Ones, three couples, for it was known that that was their nature. On their right walked the Foreseers of the City, lanterns aloft on poles to cast many-patterned light; on their left, torches flared and smoked among the Sower Chieftains. These halted at the marge. The six went onward.

Aliyat felt drowned turf crisp beneath her feet. The water lapped around her ankles, knees, loins. Warmth from the day remained in it, but a coolness was rising from below, a pledge to years unborn. 'Here's where we stop,' she said. 'The bottom slopes fast. Farther on, we'd soon be over our heads.' She couldn't fight back a giggle. 'That'd make it hard to go about this dignified, wouldn't it?'

'I am not sure what we should do,' Tu Shan confessed.

'Nothing much. We have our clothes on, after all. They don't know how we make babies anyway. But we must take our time and –' A sudden odd shyness: 'And get them to see we love each other.'

His arms enfolded her. She pressed herself close. Their mouths met. Vague in the twilight, she glimpsed Patulcius and Macandal, Wanderer and Svoboda. The hymn from the shore reached into her.

A necking party in a pool, she thought crazily. Ridiculous. Absurd as real lovemaking, as everything human, everything alive. We've sailed from those stars blinking forth overhead, to stage a Stone Age fertility rite.

But it was working. It consecrated the mere, it kindled the magic. In peace would Minoa await the resurrection of the land.

'Tu Shan,' she whispered, straining against him, 'when we get home, I want your child.'

31

'Joyful is the word that has come to us,' related the Alios whom the humans thought of as Lightfall. 'Share it. From rendezvous has it fared, the closest rendezvous, 147 light-years yonder.' Many-branched fingers marked off a part of the sky, then closed on a point within. Made by a shape that looked so frail, limned against naked space as revealed in a transparency of the ship, the gesture became doubly strong.

The direction was well away from Sol, but not toward Pegasi. The Alloi had roved widely from the world that mothered their race.

'Rendezvous,' said Yukiko, perforce aloud and in a language of Earth. She was understood, as she understood what was communicated to her. However, difficulties and failures of comprehension were still many. That was inevitable, when minds could not translate directly what senses perceived, but must pass it through a metalanguage worked out in the course of years. 'I do not quite identify your reference.'

'Starfarers have established stations, orbital about chosen suns, to which they report their discoveries and experiences,' Quicksilver explained. 'These pass the information on to the rest. So do nodes of knowledge grow, and the beams between them form nets that piece by piece knit together.'

Hanno nodded. He had been aware of this; his explorations with Alloi companions had taken him near the vast gossamer web they had made to circle Tritos, while Yukiko was searching into their arts, philosophies, dreams. 'There's a primitive version in the Solar System,' he reminded her. 'Or was, when we left. After they start receiving our 'casts, they can upgrade it and join the community.'

'If they care to.' She looked out to where stars drowned in the icy cataract of their own numbers, and away again, with a slight shudder. What she and he had learned here gave scant hope of that.

Hanno was less daunted. 'What is this news?' he asked avidly.

'A ship came to the rendezvous,' Lightfall told. 'All do thus from time to time, that they may take in the fresh data; for the stations cannot well broadcast continuously to those who may be anywhere, at any velocity. Such of our report on this system as had arrived by then determined the crew on proceeding next to Tritos. We have encountered them before; it is clear to us that the Xenoga-ians hold special interest and promise for them. May we have an image?'

'Provided,' agreed Star Wing, and activated a projector. A hulking form sprang forth. Hanno's immediate thought was of a rhinoceros. Granted, the resemblance was faint and fanciful, like comparing a man to a caterpillar. The body was of minor interest in any case, except insofar as it was the mat-rix of mind, of spirit.

'Y-yes,' he ventured, 'they're from a big planet too, aren't they? I daresay they see just enough cultural similarity here to themselves that they may reap a harvest of ideas from the differences.'

Yukiko's eyes shone. 'When will they come?'

'Their message is that they wished to spend a few years at the rendezvous first, studying and thinking about the data,' Lightfall imparted. 'That is usual, to take advantage of facilities that no vessel can accommodate. Doubtless they are on their way at this moment. Since they are accustomed to high accelerations, they should arrive just a few months later than their announce-ment that they have set forth.'

'Several years yet, then.' Yukiko smiled. 'Time to prepare a festive reception.'

'Do they travel by the same doctrine as you?' Hanno inquired.

'Yes,' Lightfall answered, 'which we recommend you also adopt.'

'I'm thinking about it. We'd need some basic modifications in our ship, you know.'

'More in your thoughts.'

'Touché!' Hanno laughed. 'Conceded, we are impatient parvenus.'

The Alloi did not boost continuously between stars. They got close to light speed, then went on free trajectory, using centrifugal weight. The saving in antimatter allowed huge hulls, with everything that that implied. The price was that time dilation became less. A journey that might have been accom-plished in ten shipboard years would take perhaps twice as long; and the farther you went, the larger the factor grew. All voyagers were ageless, but none escaped from time.

The practice accounted for observers at Sol never having picked up sign of starcraft. Enormous though the energies were, radiation was only at begin-ning and end of a passage, a candle-flicker; and starcraft were very few.

'Perhaps you do yourself an injustice,' suggested Volant. 'Perhaps your hastiness will fill a need we older spacegoing races did not know we had. You may go beyond this tiny segment of the galaxy that we have reached, from end to end of it, in less than a million cosmic years. You may be those who weave it together.'

Yukiko's hands fluttered. 'No, no. You honor us far beyond what we deserve.'

'Let us abide the future,' flowed from Star Wing: the patience of ancientness. These beings had left Pegasi fifteen thousand years ago; no individual lifetime of theirs was shorter than half of that. They knew of explorations that had been going on, in other directions, a hundred times as long.

'Well, this is ... wonderful,' Hanno said. Glancing at Yukiko: 'Maybe you can find words, dear. I'm dumbstruck.'

She caught his hand. 'You brought us here. You.'

They had become able to sense when Alloi turned grave. 'Friends,' Lightfall told them, 'you must make certain decisions among yourselves. Soon after the – (?) – arrive, we will leave.' Through shock and suddenly racketing pulse, they gathered: 'You may remain if you desire. They will be rapturous at meeting new members of the fellowship. You can help them, and they help you, to know Xenogaia and its awarenesses, quite likely even more than you and we have helped each other. Everything that we have built in this system shall stay for your use.'

'But, but you go away?' Yukiko stammered. 'Why?'

Stalky limbs traced symbols. Membranes quivered; opalescences ran over them. The declaration was calm, inexorable, and maybe, maybe regretful. 'We have spent more than four centuries at Tritos. I believe you realize that was partly because of what we had detected from Sol: our hope, which was fulfilled, that we could call travelers from there to us. Meanwhile we explored these planets and above all the diverse life-ways, histories, achievements, horrors, glories of the sentients on Xenogaia. It was effort richly rewarded, as we foreknew it would be. Another whole concept of the universe opened for us. Something of what we learned has entered our inwardness.

'And yet you humans, in your decade and a half, have gathered more than we imagined was there. It happens your home world, your evolution, more closely resembles theirs. Nature has better prepared you to comprehend them.

'For our part, we found ourselves drawn to you as never to them. You too are the kind of beings who reach for the stars.

'We could stay here till this sun begins to die, and not discover all that there is to discover; for it is so much, and always changing. Life is a rare thing, sapience more seldom yet. Why, then, will we not linger?

'It is that we hope for more than we have gained here; and we know that if we seek long enough, we shall find it.'

Hanno had nothing but merchant words. 'I see. You've gone past the point of diminishing returns. Your best strategy is to start fresh.'

As it seemed mother civilizations did not, could not.

'Will you go on to Sol?' Yukiko asked unsteadily.

'Someday, perhaps,' Star Wing conveyed.

'Likelier not,' Quicksilver asserted. 'I think that what you have revealed to us will suffice – for they have been evolving onward.'

'Let Sol and Pegasi communicate,' Volant scoffed.

'No, you are too impetuous, and too thoughtless of our friends,' Lightfall admonished. 'We have years ahead of us in which to consider.' To the humans: 'You too, with your kindred down on the planet, you must take thought. Do you wish to commence at once?'

Hanno and Yukiko traded a look. Mutely, she nodded. After a moment, he did likewise. They bowed, one of many motions that had gradually acquired eloquence, and went from the coralline room.

A passageway took them along the great curve of the ship. Past the part of it that was alive stretched, today, a simulated vista of ruddy hills, lean crags, fronds rippling around a frozen pool, beneath a violet-blue sky where rings arched like undying rainbows – a world the Alloi had once come upon and found beautiful, for it was much as their mother world was before the machines. They had left colonists.

Beyond lay a room of exercise equipment made for the humans. It could be spun through a hollow ring around the hull to provide higher weight. Thus did they maintain a physical condition that allowed them to visit the planet without being too badly handicapped in relation to those who lived there.

Farther on was their home section, Yukiko's little garden, a post upholding the model of a caravel that Hanno had once constructed, the compartment that housed them. Air inside it remained thin and dry, but it was warm and to their eyes the lighting was pure white.

The three rooms held their possessions, a few carried from Earth, more that were remembrances of their years here, but there was no clutter. He kept his sailor's tidiness, she her basic austerity. Opposite the electronic complex a calligraphic scroll hung above a low table where a bowl of water contained a single shapely stone.

They removed their outer garments. 'Shall I make tea?' she proposed.

'Do, if you like.' His face drew taut. 'I want to call planetside now.'

'Well, it is tremendous news, but we shall have to talk about it over and over –'

'In person. We're going down and stay a while, you and I.'

'That will be very welcome,' she sighed.

'Yes, I admit I'll enjoy some unfaked shirtsleeve outdoors, a sea, a salt wind.'

'And our comrades, not images but real flesh again. How the children must have grown.'

He missed the wistfulness, and not until later did he recall how ardently she entered into the life around her when they touched down. The occasions had been infrequent and brief. You must live with the Alloi, work side by side with them, share hardships and dangers as well as victories and celebrations, if you would reach an understanding of them and of what they had won on their endless voyage. To him the sacrifices were small.

'Never mind how many years we may have to make ready,' he said. 'We'd better begin straightaway.'

She smiled. 'You mean that you cannot sit still for a cup of tea.'

Ignoring the gentle gibe, he settled before the complex and ordered a beam to Hestia. The ship was at present above the opposite hemisphere, but the Alloi had long since orbited relay satellites. The screen came alight. 'Summoning,' said the artificial voice. A minute passed, and another. 'Summoning.'

Yukiko brought up an outside view. The planet shone blue-veined white. Lightnings threaded the darkened edge. She smote hands together. 'We forgot!' she cried. 'It's night where they are.'

'Damn,' said Hanno without remorse.

Svoboda's likeness entered the screen, three-dimensional, as if she herself stood behind a shut window. Her hair was tousled. A robe hastily thrown on gaped over milk-heavy breasts. 'What's wrong?' she exclaimed.

'No emergency,' Hanno replied. 'News. I'll tell you, you tell whoever else got roused, and then go back to sleep if you can.'

She bridled. 'It couldn't wait?'

'Listen.' He made his announcement in short, clanging words. 'We need to begin studying what information the Alloi can give us about these other beings, as soon as they've assembled it. Before then we need to confer. Yukiko and I – Expect our boat, m-m, shortly after sunrise ... What's the matter?'

'What is the hurry?' Svoboda's response crackled. 'Aren't you aware this is harvest season? We'll be working ourselves sweatless, people and robots both, for the next several days. We already are. I heard the summons only because I'd just fallen asleep after the baby kept me awake for hours. Now you want us to sweep and garnish quarters for you and meet in instant council.'

'Don't you *care*? Why in hell's name did you sign on?'

'We're sorry,' Yukiko interjected. 'We were so excited, everything else dropped from our minds. Pardon us.'

The other woman fleered. 'Is he sorry?'

'Hold on,' Hanno said. 'I made a mistake. But this that's happening –'

Svoboda cut him off. 'Yes, it's important. But so is your arrogance. The main thing you're forgetting is that you, sitting up there in the sky, are not God Almighty.'

'Please,' Yukiko begged.

Hanno spoke coldly. 'I am the captain. I'll have respect from you.'

Svoboda shook her head. A blond lock tossed on her temple. 'That has changed. Nobody is indispensable any longer. We'll accept whatever leader we may need, if we judge that person will serve us well.' She paused. 'Somebody will call tomorrow, when we've conferred, and make proper arrangements.' With a smile: 'Yukiko, this isn't your fault. Everybody knows that. Goodnight.' The screen blanked.

Hanno sat staring into it.

Yukiko went to stand behind him, a hand on his shoulder. 'Don't take this hard,' she said. 'She was simply short on sleep, therefore short on temper. After she has rested, she will shrug it off.'

He shook his head. 'No, it goes deeper than that. I hadn't realized – we've been away too much – down underneath, they carry their resentment yet.'

'No. I swear not. No more. You did bring them, us to something far more wonderful and meaningful than we had dared hope for. It is true, you are not vitally necessary now. Your captaincy is not unquestioned. And you did act thoughtlessly. But the wound is nothing, it will heal by morning.'

'Some things never heal.' He rose. 'Well, no use brooding.' A crooked grin. 'What about that cup of tea?'

She regarded him in silence before she said, most quietly, 'You two can still hurt one another, can you not?'

His voice went brusque. 'How often do you miss Tu Shan?' He drew her to him. 'Regardless, these have been good years for me. Thank you.'

She laid her cheek against his breast. 'And for me.'

He forced a chuckle. 'I repeat, what became of the tea?'

32

First light grayed the east, made dull silver of the stream. Heights westward hulked black and haze dimmed a sinking huge moon. The waterfall rushed loud down its cliff into the river, which clucked and purled. Coolness blew, laden with silty odors.

Hanno and Wanderer stood on the dock. Their tongues felt awkward. 'Well,' said Wanderer, 'have fun.'

'You too,' Hanno replied. 'Uh, how long did you say you'd be gone?'

'Don't know for sure. Three, four days. But you come home this evening, hear me?'

'Of course. We Phoenicians never spent a night at sea if we could help it.'

Wanderer's shadowed countenance darkened further. 'I wish you wouldn't go at all. Especially alone.'

'I heard you before. You're going alone yourself, and not even taking a communicator along.'

'That's different. I know those woods. But none of us really know the waters. We've just puttered around a little in our boats or taken passage with natives, and that was to study the crew, not the seamanship.'

'Look, Peregrino, I know perfectly well the conditions aren't identical with Earth. I've tried them out, remember? Please remember, too, that I was sailing, in flimsier vessels than I like thinking about, two thousand years before you were born. Always the second law of the sea is "Take care."'

'What's the first?'

'"It's in the bilge!"'

They laughed together a bit. 'Okay, okay,' Wanderer said. 'So we both need to go walkabout, in our different ways. I suspect the same's true for Corinne. She didn't really have to confer with the Triune at this exact time.' He left unspoken: Escape, relief, slack off the tension that has built up in us through these past days of wrangling. Shall we abide here, shall we accompany the Alloi when they leave, or what? Seek within ourselves for our true desires. We have years yet in which to decide, but the divisions between us have festered longer than that, ranker than we knew.

'Thanks for your help,' said Hanno.

'*De nada, amigo.*' They shook hands. It was the heartiest clasp Hanno had ever felt, or given, in Hestia. He couldn't ask outright, but he believed Wanderer had altogether forgiven him. Well, whatever rift had occurred was not over something fundamental to the man's life, as for some others; and from Wanderer's viewpoint, events had fairly well vindicated his old friend. At these latest conclaves of the eight, they had argued side by side.

It wasn't the same with Macandal, Patulcius, Aliyat, Tu Shan, Svoboda – Svoboda – Oh, she was perfectly gracious; after all, in principle she too favored exploring. But by tacit agreement, she and Yukiko stayed abed when their men got up to carry the gear down to the boat.

Wanderer turned. His stride whispered over the dock, his tall form strode up the path and disappeared in remnant darknesses. Hanno boarded. Quickly he uncovered and unfurled the mainsail, took the jib from its bag, raised them, cleated the sheets, cast off. The fabric stood ghost-white athwart strengthening dawn, slatted, caught wind and filled. *Ariadne* listed over and slipped downstream.

She was a sweet little craft, a six-meter sloop that on Earth would once have been an ocean racer (who there went sailing any more?), built at odd moments by Tu Shan with robot help according to plans in the database. Mainly, he had wanted to make something beautiful as well as purposeful. It turned out that nobody found time to use her much, finally not at all. The Ithagenē were intrigued, but the layout was wrong for them. Hanno patted the deck beside the cockpit. 'Poor girl,' he said. 'Did you cry sometimes at night, lying always alone? We'll take a real run today, we will.' Surprised, he noticed he had spoken in Punic. When had he last?

The estuary broadened. Unhindered, the land breeze blew harder. He had it, the current, and the tide to bear him. Ebb should end just about when he reached the sea; slack water for the transition was desirable. Waves, rips, every kind of turbulence went faster, more forcefully, less foreseeably on Xenogaia, under its gravity, than on Earth.

The sun rose ahead, blurred and reddened by overcast, not so far to starboard as it would have been on Earth at this latitude and time of year. Though the planet rotated somewhat faster, the axial tilt promised him a long, long summer day. Cloud banks towered murky in the south. He hoped they wouldn't move northward and rain on him. The wettest season had passed, but you never knew. Xenogaian meteorology was still largely guess-work. The parameters were unfamiliar; the humans and their computers had too much else, too much more interesting, to consider. Also, it seemed the weather was highly unstable. Chaos, in the physics sense of the word, took over early in any sequence.

Well, this was a sturdy, forgiving boat; he and Wanderer had carried down an outboard for her; if he got in bad trouble, he could call, and an aircraft would come take him off. He scowled at the thought.

Think about pleasanter things, then. Faring out again among the stars – No, that cut too near. That was what divided the. house of the Survivors against itself.

You couldn't blame those who wanted to stay. They'd toiled, suffered, wrought mightily; this had become home for them, it was the cosmos for their children. As for those who wanted to quest, why, Minoa with its multi-tudinous realms was only one continent on an entire world. For those who would liefest dwell near nonhumans, a whole new race of them was coming. What more dared you wish?

Dismiss it for now. Lose yourself in this day.

The sea opened before *Ariadne*, gunmetal whitecaps, surge and brawl, wind abruptly southeast and stiff. She leaped, leaned, ran happily lee rail under. It throbbed in deck and tiller. The wind sang. Spindrift blew salt kisses. Hanno closed his jacket and drew up its hood against the chill. Fingers brushed the gas cartridge that would at need inflate it. Tricky sailing, and his muscles not yet fully retrained to bear his weight. He couldn't have single-handed were it not for the servos and computer. At that, he must pay constant heed. Good. So did he wish it to be.

A native ship was inbound, beating across the wind, a bravery of sails. She must have lain out, waiting for the tide to turn. Now she would ride the flow upstream, doubtless to Xenoknossos. Probably she would have to take shel-ter in one of the bays the Ithagenē had dug along the banks, while the bore went rumbling by. It would be especially dangerous today; the moon was both full and close.

Northward, some five kilometers off the mainland, water churned and jumped white, black forms reared up – the Forbidden Ground, a nasty patch of rocks and shoals. A current from the south swept strongly around it. Hanno trimmed his sails. He wanted to be well clear before the incoming tide reinforced that rush.

Tacking, he made for the nearest of three islands that lay dim in the eastern distance. He would scarcely get that far before midafternoon, when prudence dictated he turn back, but it was something to steer by.

A goal, he thought. A harbor I won't make. Odysseus, setting forth from ashy Troy for Ithaca, lured by the Lotus Eaters, bereaved by the Cyclops, at strife with winds and wild men, seduced by an enchantress who took away humanity, descending to the dead, raiding the fields of the sun, passing through the gate of destruction, made captive by her who loved him, cast ashore at Phaeacia – but Odysseus came home at last.

How many ports had he, Hanno, failed to make in his millennia? All?

Tritos climbed to a breach in the overcast. Light flamed. He sailed on the Amethyst Sea, and it was strewn with diamond dust and the manes of the waves blew white. It was as lovely and wild as a woman.

Tanithel, her black hair garlanded with anemones, who whispered her wish that she had not had to sacrifice her virginity in the temple before she came to him; Adoniah, who read the stars from her tower above Tyre – twice he cast anchor, the lights of home glimmered through dusk, and then ebb tide bore that country off and he lay again on empty waters. Afterward – Merab, Althea, Nirouphar, Cordelia, Brangwyn, Thorgerd, Maria, Jehanne, Margaret, Natalia, O Ashtoreth, the dear ghosts were beyond counting or remembering, but had they ever been much more than ghosts, belonging as they did to death? To men he felt closer, they could not bear the same thing off with them – Baalram, Thuti, Umlele, Pytheas, Ezra, rough old Rufus, yes, that hurt, somewhere inside himself Hanno had forever mourned Rufus.

Stop sniveling!

The wind skirled louder. *Ariadne* heeled sharply. The sun disappeared behind gray, beneath which wrack began to fly. Cloud masses bulked mountainous, drawing closer. Lightning sprang about in their blue-black caverns. The islands were lost in scud-haze, the mainland aft lay low and vague. 'What time is it?' Hanno asked. He whistled when the computer told him. His body had sailed for him while his mind drifted awash in the past, longer than he knew.

He'd grown hungry too without noticing, but would be rash to trust the helm to the machinery even to duck below and fix a sandwich. 'Give me Hestia,' he ordered the communicator.

'Summoning.'

'Hello, hello, is anybody there? Hanno calling.'

Wind tore Yukiko's voice from the speaker, seas trampled its tatters underfoot. He barely heard: '– frightened for you … satellite report … weather moving faster and faster … please –'

'Yes, certainly, I'll return. Don't worry. This boat can take a knockdown and right herself. I'll be back for supper,' If I catch the tide right. Got to keep well offshore till I can run straight down the slot. Well, the motor has plenty of kilowatts. Better that to claw off with than men rowing till their hearts burst.

He didn't want to use it unless and until he must. He needed a fight, wits and nerve as well as sinews against the wolf-gods. Coming around was a long and tough maneuver. Once a wave smashed clear across the deck. *Ariadne* shuddered, but still her mast swayed on high, an uplifted lance. Gallant girl. Like Svoboda – like all of them, Yukiko, Corinne, Aliyat, all of them Survivors in ways their men had never had to be.

He did let the servos keep the tiller while he shortened sail. A sheet escaped his grasp and slashed his wrist before he captured and cleated it. Spume washed the blood off. The world had gone dark, driving gray, save for the lightning flashes southward. Water swung to and fro in the cockpit till the pump flung it overside. He remembered bailing Pytheas' ship during a Baltic storm. As he took the helm back, a song abruptly lilted through his head. 'Oh, hand me down my walking cane –' Where had it come from? English language, old, old, nineteenth or early twentieth century, impudent, a pulsing, railroad kind of tune.

'– *Oh, Mama, come go my bail,*
Get me out of this God damn jail.
All my sins are taken away.'

Railroad, the West, a world that had seemed boundless but lost its horizons and itself in a blink of centuries and was one with Troy. Then some looked starward and dreamed of New America. The upshot ... machines, eight human beings, immensities as impassable and unanswering as death.

'*Oh, hell is deep and hell is wide,*
Oh, hell is deep and hell is wide,
Oh, hell is deep and hell is wide,
Ain't got no bottom, ain't got no side.
All my sins are taken away.'

Hanno showed the wind his teeth. Odysseus went there and won back. If the stars held no New America, they offered what was infinitely more.

The noise rammed him. It was a monstrous rush and boom, pierced by a risen screech. To port the cloud wall had vanished behind a whiteness that overran waves and kilometers.

'Strike sail!' he bawled. That was not merely a gale, that was a line squall come from behind sight and bound for him. Weather on Xenogaia heeded no law of Grecian Aeolus. Wind speeds were commonly low, but when they did go high, they bore twice the weight of violent air. His left hand took the switch that lowered the outboard. Point bows into seas and hold them fast!

The fist smote. Rain flayed and blinded. Waves topped the rails. *Ariadne* climbed, swayed amidst cataracting foam, plunged into troughs. Hanno clung.

Something snatched him.

He was down in roaring black. He whirled and tumbled. At the middle of it rested a cold steadiness, his mind. I'm overboard, he knew. Inflate the jacket. Don't breathe water or you're done.

He broke surface, gasped air full of rain and salt foam, threshed limbs against heaviness that tore. The hood swelled into a pillowlike collar, upbearing his head as the rest of the garment floated his body. He squinted about. Where was the boat? No sign of her. He didn't think she'd gone under, not that staunch little lady, but wind and waves must have borne her from him, maybe not very far as yet – far enough, though, when he could see only the billows savaging him.

What had happened? His brain cleared, shook off shock, became a computer programmed to calculate survival. Wind might have caught the unfurled loose mainsail, swung the hull around, shoved it so low that a broaching sea swept him out. Well, if he kept alert, he'd drift free till rescue came. That should be soon after this flaw of weather had passed. Yukiko was probably trying right now to call him. An aircraft – Those carried aboard *Pytheas* were designed for Phaeacia. They flew on Xenogaia, but it was rather precarious; given conditions at all unusual, you needed a human pilot as well as the machine. Maybe the Hestia folk should have ordered modifications, but the job was big, they had so much else on hand, they could stay aground when in doubt.

Pilots. Wanderer's the best, I think that's generally agreed. He's out of touch today. Otherwise Svoboda; and she's got her kid to think about. The colony is tiny, a beachhead on a shore not made for our kind. She has no right to risk herself needlessly. Of course, she will take off the moment it looks practical, which should be when this gust is over. High winds aren't an unacceptable hazard in themselves, if they're reasonably steady.

The trick will be to stay alive till then. Exposure is the enemy. This water isn't too cold, it's a warm current from the south. However, a few degrees below skin temperature will suck the heat out in time. I remember – But that was on another voyage, and besides, the men are dead. I also know some ancient Asian ways of controlling blood flow; at dire need, I can call up my ultimate reserves, while they last.

Swim. Save your strength, but do not let yourself be rolled about and smothered. Find the rhythms. Who was it, what goddess, who lived at the bottom of the sea and spread her nets for sailormen? Oh, yes, Ran of the Norse. Shall we dance, my lady Ran?

Wind screamed, seas crashed. How long had this gone on? No telling. A minute could amount to an hour, reverse time dilation, the cosmos flying away from a man. He'd been mistaken about the blow. It wasn't any quick squall. Though rain had thinned, the wind raved wilder. Unforeseen, unforeseeable, as ignorant as men and, yes, their smug machines still were. The universe held as many surprises as it did stars. No, more. That was its glory. But someday one of them was bound to kill you.

Thunder ahead. Hanno rose onto a crest. He saw black teeth, the rocks and skerries, the Forbidden Ground. Water seethed, geysered, exploded. The current had swept him to this. Flashingly, he hoped *Ariadne* remained free, for her people to recover. He readied himself.

It was hard to do. A sense of warmth in hands and feet crept treacherously toward his breast. He knew that consciousness was dimming; he couldn't tell which lights had by now gone out.

A comber took him along.

He smashed into the white.

White … He lay on stone. Weed wrapped him, yellow-brown ropes. Waves roiled and roared under a low, flying sky. Oftener and oftener, water rushed over the roughness beneath him. He would inhale it, choke, cough, reach for air.

He scarcely noticed. Cold, pain, struggle were of the world, the storm. Impersonal, he watched them, like a man drowsy at- his hearthside watching flames. The rising tide would claim him, but he would not be here. He would be – where? What? He didn't know. It didn't matter.

So this is how it ends. Not too bad a way for an old sailor-man. I do wish I could lie remembering. But memory slips from me, wishing does, being does. Farewell, farewell, you ghosts. Fare always well.

A whickering whine through wind and surf, a shadow, a shape, a jolt that awakens awareness.

You fool! he raged dimly. Go back! You could lose your life!

The aircraft bucked and rocked, fell, climbed, did battle. From its teardrop snaked a line. The cord passed half a meter above Hanno. His hand tried to reach and grab it, but couldn't. It whirled on past. Again. Again.

It withdrew. The engine overhead snarled louder. The line descended afresh. A loop was at the end, for the feet of a clinging man.

Tu Shan hit the reef. He took the impact in his muscles, got his foothold, stood while a surge ran ankle-deep around him. With his left hand he kept hold of the line; and he advanced step by gripping step.

The strongest among us, thought Hanno bewilderedly. But I've been all this time with his woman.

Tu Shan's right arm went under his shoulders, raised him, held him fast. The aircraft winched the line in. They swung like a bell clapper. '*Proclaim Liberty throughout the world –*'

They were aboard. Svoboda gained altitude and made for shore. Tu Shan laid Hanno out in the aisle, which shivered and banged. He examined him with rough skill. 'Slight concussion, I think,' he growled. 'Maybe a broken rib or two. Mainly a bad chill, uh, hypothermia. He'll live.'

He administered initial treatment. Blood quickened. Svoboda brought the aircraft slanting down. 'How did you know?' Hanno mumbled.

'Yukiko called the Alloi,' Svoboda said from the controls. Rain dashed across the viewscreen before her. 'They couldn't enter atmosphere themselves. Even their robots have trouble in bad weather. But they sent a spaceboat on low trajectory. Its detectors registered an infrared anomaly in the rocks. That was where you might well be.'

'You shouldn't have, you shouldn't –'

She made a near-vertical descent. Contact jarred the machine. She snapped off her harness and came to kneel beside him. 'Did you think we'd want to be without you?' she asked. 'Did we ever?'

33

Seldom was a day this brilliant. Sunlight spilled from a sky in which clouds were blue-shadowed white, like enormous snowbanks. It gleamed off wings cruising aloft; glimpses of river and sea shone molten. The eight seated around a plank table were thinly clad. From the top of their knoll vision ranged between Hestia, at its distance a toybox, westward to where Mount Pytheas rose pure beyond the hills.

Twice before have we met this way, in open air, remembered Hanno. Do we have some unknown need? Yes, the reasons are practical, be undistracted, leave the children in care of the robots for these few hours, and hope that fresh surroundings will freshen our thinking. But do our souls believe that when we most want wisdom, we must seek it from earth and heaven?

They are not ours, even now. This close-knit turf that is not grass, yonder squat trees and serpentine bushes, somber hues of everything that grows, sharp fragrances, the very taste of spring water, none came from the womb of Gaia. Nor can any of it ever truly become hers, nor should it.

The looks upon him were expectant. He cleared his throat and sat straighter. The motion hurt, his injuries were not yet entirely healed, but he ignored that. 'I won't ask for a vote today,' he said. 'We have years ahead before we must commit ourselves. But my news may change some minds.'

Unless that had already happened. Certainly it had done so as regarded him. He didn't know whether his near death had been necessary to snuff out the last rancor. Maybe that would have faded away in time; but maybe it would have smoldered on and on, eating hearts hollow. No matter. The fellowship was whole again. Little had been spoken outright; everything had been felt. He had an intuition, moreover, that in typical irrational human fashion, this was in turn catalyzing another oneness.

We'll see, he thought. All of us.

'As you know,' he went on, 'Yukiko and I have been communicating a lot with the Alloi these past few days. They've reached a decision of their own.'

He raised a hand against anxiety. 'Nothing radical, except in what it can mean for the long haul. They will stay on till the new ship arrives, and for several years afterward. There'll be an unforeknowably great deal of information to exchange and, well, rapport to build and enjoy. In due course, though, the Alloi are going elsewhere.

'What's new is – if we, at that time, leave for Phaeacia, they will come with us.'

He and his partner smiled into the amazement, savored it. 'In God's name, why?' exclaimed Patulcius. 'What have they to gain there?'

'Knowledge, to start with,' Hanno answered. 'A whole different set of planets.'

'But planetary systems are common enough,' Wanderer said. 'I thought that what interests them most is intelligent life.'

'True,' Yukiko told them. 'At Phaeacia, that will be us; and for us, they will be.'

'They want to know us better,' Hanno said. 'They see tremendous potential in our race. Far more than in the Ithagenē, much though they've gotten from them in the way of scientific discovery and artistic inspiration. We are spacefarers too. The odds are, the Ithagenē never will be, none of them; at best, in the remote future.'

'But the Alloi need only stay here, and they can observe both races, and interact with that other set of travelers to boot,' Patulcius argued.

Yukiko shook her head. 'They do not expect we can or will remain. Certainly our numbers could only grow slowly, and never become large, on Xenogaia; and therefore what we, humans in space, were able to do, or at last cared to do, would be hopelessly limited.'

'You six – no, we eight have been like the English Puritans on Earth,' Hanno said. 'Looking for a home, they meant to settle in Virginia, but weather drove them north and they ended in New England. It wasn't what they'd hoped for, but they made the best of it, and that's how the Yankees came to be. Suppose New England had been all there ever was for them. Think of such a country, stagnant, poor, narrow and narrow-minded. Da you want that for yourselves and your children?'

'The Yankees put down strong roots,' Tu Shan responded. 'They did have America beyond.'

'We have nothing like that,' Macandal said. 'Xenogaia belongs to its people. We have no right to anything but this little patch they gave us. If we took more, God ought to strike us down.'

Wanderer nodded.

'So you have often said, dear,' Patulcius demurred, 'and I have tried to point out that as a practical matter –'

'Yes, we have our investment here,' Svoboda interrupted, 'sweat and tears and dreams. It will hurt to scrap that. But I always believed, myself, that someday we must.' Her voice clanged. 'And now we've been given this opportunity!'

'That's it,' Hanno chimed in. 'Phaeacia has no natives for us to harm. It seems to be almost a reborn Earth. *Seems.* Maybe it's a death trap. We can't know till we've tried. We understood the risk of failure, extinction. Well, with the Alloi at our backs, that won't happen. United, we can overcome anything. You see, they want us to live, to flourish. They want humans among the stars.'

'Why us?' asked Macandal. 'I realize – our psyches, our special talents, we and they doing more, becoming more, than either could alone, like a good marriage – but if they'd like human company, why not go on to Earth?'

'Have you forgotten why?' retorted Hanno grimly.

Her eyes widened. Fingers touched lips. 'How can they be sure?'

'They aren't, not absolutely; but from what we've described, they can guess with pretty high probability. Earth is going the selfsame way Pegasi did, and the rest that they know about. Oh, we'll swap messages with it, no doubt. But it's too far off' – a galactically minuscule four and a third light-centuries – 'to make the voyage appear worthwhile. The Alloi would rather help us get established, come really to know us, and finally plan ventures together.'

Tu Shan gazed upward. 'Phaeacia,' he breathed. 'Like Earth. Not truly, but ... green leaves, rich soil, clear skies.' He closed his eyes against the sun and let its warmth lave his face. 'Most nights we will see stars.'

Patulcius shifted about on the bench. 'This does put quite a different complexion on matters,' he admitted. As much eagerness as his heavy features ever showed danced across them. 'The survival of more than simply us. Of humanity, true humanity.'

It blazed from Wanderer: 'Not just a settlement or nation. A base, a frontier camp. We can be patient, we and the Alloi. We can make the planet ours, raise generations of young, till we're many and strong. But then we'll go to space again.'

'Those of you who wish,' said Tu Shan.

Macandal's tone shook. 'To learn and grow. To keep life alive.'

Aliyat spoke through sudden, brief tears. 'Yes, take the universe back from the damned machines.'

'Where are they?'

The story is that Enrico Fermi first raised the question in the twentieth century, when scientists first dared wonder publicly about such things. If other thinking beings than us existed – how strange and sad if none did, in the entire vastness and diversity of creation – why had we on Earth found no trace or track of them? There we were, on the verge of making our own star-ward leap. Had nobody gone before us?

Perhaps it was impractical or impossible for flesh and blood. It certainly was not for machines we knew in principle how to make. They could be our explorers, sending home their findings. Reaching far planets, they could build more like themselves, instilling the same imperative: Discover. (No menace to life in their proliferation; at any given sun, a few tons of raw material from some barren asteroid or moon would suffice.) Under conservative assumptions, calculation showed that such robots would spread from end to end of the galaxy in about a million years. That was the merest eyeblink of cosmic time. Why, a million years ago our ancestors were approaching full humanness. Had no race anywhere even that much of a head start? All it would take was one.

Still easier to send were signals. We tried. We listened. Silence, until we thought to try in certain new directions; then, enigma.

Guesses teemed. The Others were transmitting, but not by means that we yet knew. They had come here, but in the prehistoric past. They were here, but concealed. They destroyed themselves, as we feared we might, before they could send or go. They had no high-technological civilizations among them; ours was unique. They did not exist; we were indeed alone ...

Fermi went to his grave, time blew onward through its night, humankind entered upon a new path of evolution. The answer to his question was less found than it was created, by what the children of Earth themselves did; and it proved to be twofold.

Dispatch your robots. They go forth to marvels and magnificences. Every star is a sun, every planet a world, multifarious, astounding, its secrets not exhaustible in less than many decades. When it bears life, they are inexhaustible forever, because life is not only infinite in its variousness, it never remains the same, it is forever changing. When it is intelligent, this rises to a whole new dimensionality, a different order of being.

The farther your emissaries range, the faster grows the realm of the unknown. Double the radius, and you roughly octuple the number of stars to ransack. You also double the time of faring and the time for a signal to cross between ship and home.

Ten or twelve years from departure to arrival, ten years more to receive the first recounting, are reasonable. Fifty years are not unreasonable. But a hundred or two hundred or five hundred years either way? Suns and planets have fallen into classes; they no longer hold revelations. If you know the basic parameters, you can compute their properties. It is pointless to lengthen your list of them.

Life forms are something else. Yet if you desire to study these, you have a sufficiency on worlds already attained. Indeed, you have overwhelmingly much. Your information-processing capabilities, that part of them devoted to this endeavor, grow saturated.

The data include data on sapient beings. Those are rare, but they do occur and are fascinating beyond measure. Nevertheless, when the time lag grows much greater than lifetimes of theirs, and moreover your field scientists are machines, how can you truly come to know them? (Those that have been found are primitive and mortal. Science and high technology result from chains of unlikely historical accidents.) Wiser to hold your attention on those near enough that you can to some limited extent follow what the robots do and observe.

There is no precise limit. There is simply a radius, on the order of a light-century or two, beyond which it is unprofitable to search farther. Having foreseen this, you have never built self-multiplying von Neumann machines.

Exceptions exist. When your instruments detect the radiations that suggest a civilization at some star, you will send your beams and perhaps your robots; but the span until anything can come of that, if anything does, is multimillennial. At the end, will your race still care?

Other exceptions are cosmic, astrophysical – extraordinary stars, clouds where stars are coming to birth, recent supernovae, black holes in peculiar circumstances, the monstrosities at the core of the galaxy, and comparable rarities. You will dispatch your observers that far (thirty thousand light-years from Sol to galactic center) and wait.

All of the few starfaring civilizations will do likewise. Therefore all that have reached these goals will beamcast from them, in hopes of making contact. They will wait.

All have become entities that can wait.

Here is the second half of the solution to the riddle.

It is not sentient organic life that the robots seek to summon. It is other robots.

Machines do not conquer their mother worlds. They gently, gradually absorb their creators into their systems, at the wish of those beings, whose overmatching physical and intellectual superiors they have become. Then in the course of time, more and more they direct their attention from mere life, toward problems and undertakings they find worthy of themselves.

When the original thinking animals live on, as happens occasionally, it is because they too have turned their concerns elsewhere, inward, searching for joys and fulfillments or possibly imaginary enlightenments toward which no machine can aid them, realms quite outside the universe of the stars.

'No,' said Svoboda, 'we do wrong if we feel hostile. Postbiotic evolution is nevertheless evolution, reality finding newness in itself.' She colored and laughed. 'Oh, but that sounds pretentious! I only meant that the advanced, independent robots are no threat to us. We'll continue keeping robots of our own, we have to, but for purposes of our own. We'll do what the postbiotics not only don't care to do any more, they never really could. That's to deal with life of our kind, the old kind, not by peering and listening, centuries between question and answer, but by being there ourselves, sharing, yes, loving. And so we'll come to understand what we can't now imagine.'

'Those of you who choose to be seekers.' Patulcius' remark fell doubly dry after her torrenting enthusiasm. 'Like Tu Shan, I shall cultivate my garden. I daresay most of our descendants will so prefer.'

'No doubt,' Hanno said. 'That's fine. They'll be our reserve. Peregrino's right; some will always want more than that.'

'The Phaeacians won't settle down into rustic innocence,' Macandal predicted. 'They can't. If they aren't to go the way of Earth – and that would make their whole effort meaningless, wouldn't it? – they'll have to find some new path for themselves. They'll have to evolve too.'

'And those of us in space will, along our own lines,' Wanderer added. 'Not in body, in genes; I aim to be around for a mighty long spell. In our minds, our spirits.'

Yukiko smiled. 'The stars and their worlds for our teachers.' Earnestly: 'But let us remember what a hard school that will be. Today we count for nothing. Every crew of starfarers the Alloi have any knowledge of – and they are less than a dozen – are like us, leftovers, malcontents, atavisms, outcasts.'

'I know. I don't admit we count for nothing, though. We *are*.'

'Yes. And if we are wise, if we can humble ourselves enough to hear what the lowliest of living beings have to tell us, at last we will meet the postbiotics as equals. In a million years? I don't know. But when we are ready, it will be as you said, we will have become something other than what we are now.'

Hanno nodded. 'I wonder if, at the end, we and our allies won't be more than the equals of the machines.'

His comrades regarded him, a little puzzled. 'I've been playing with an idea,' he explained. 'It seems to have worked this way on Earth, and what we've seen here and heard from the Alloi suggests it may be a general principle. Most steps in evolution haven't been triumphal advances. No, the failures of the earlier stages made them, the desperate ones – in Yukiko's words, the atavisms and outcasts.

'Why should a fish doing well in the water struggle onto the land? It was those that couldn't compete that did it, because they had to go somewhere else or die. And the ancestors of the reptiles were forced out of the amphibians' swamps, the birds forced into the air, and mammals forced to find niches where the dinosaurs weren't, and certain apes forced out of the trees, and – and we Phoenicians held only a thin strip of territory, so we took to the sea, and hardly anybody went to America or Australia who was comfortable at home in Europe –

'Well, we'll see. We'll see. A million years, you guessed, Yukiko.' He laughed. 'Shall we make a date? One million years from this day, we'll all meet again and remember.'

'First we must survive,' said Patulcius.

'Surviving is what we're good at,' replied Wanderer.

Macandal sighed. 'So far. Let's not wax overconfident. No guarantees. Never were, never will be. A million years are a lot of days and nights to get through. Can we?'

'We shall try,' said Tu Shan.

'Together,' vowed Svoboda.

'Then we'd better learn,' said Aliyat, 'better than before, how to share.'

34

The ships departed, *Pytheas* and friend. For a while, some months, until speeds grew too high, word went between them, imagery, love; rites celebrated the mysteries of community and communion; for everywhere around them thronged suns.

'When I consider thy heavens, the work of thy fingers, the moon and the stars, which thou hast ordained; What is man, that thou art mindful of him?'

Hanno and Svoboda stood in the darkened command center, looking out. Through clasped hands they felt each other's nearness and warmth. 'Is this why we were born?' she whispered.

'We'll make it be,' he promised.

CHRONOLOGY

Except for the first, all dates are Anno Domini. Each is the year in which its chapter begins. Occasionally the narrative thereafter moves forward or backward in time.

GLOSSARY

Chinese names are transcribed according to the Wade-Giles system. This probably remains somewhat more familiar to Anglophone readers than Pinyin or Yale, and is no more inaccurate a rendition of ancient or regional pronunciations.

Armorica:	Brittany.
Berytus:	Beirut.
Bravellir:	Probably near modern Norrköping, Sweden.
Britannia:	England and Wales.
Burdigala:	Bordeaux.
Ch'ang-an:	Near modern Sian (Pinyin 'Xian').
Constantinople:	Istanbul.
Damasek:	Damascus.
Dumnonia:	Cornwall and Devon.
Duranius:	The River Dordogne.
Emesa:	Horns.
Falernia:	An area in the region of Naples, anciently noted for its wines.
Gadeira:	Cadiz (Latin 'Gades,' Semitic 'Agadir').
Gallia:	Gaul, France with parts of Belgium, Germany, and Switzerland.
Gardhariki:	Western Russia.
Garumna:	The River Garonne.
Gautland:	Southern Sweden, apparently between Scania and Lake Vänern.
Heian-kyo:	Kyoto.
Hleidhra:	Lejre, in Denmark.
Khalep:	Aleppo.
Kiyiv:	Kiev.
Lakota:	Dakota (Sioux).
Lugdunensis:	A province in Gaul, comprising most of northern and a fair portion of central France.
Lugdunum:	Lyons.
Makkah:	Mecca.

Massalia:	Marseilles (Latin 'Massilia').
Medinat Rasul Allah:	Medina.
Nidharos:	Trondheim, in Norway.
Pariki:	Pawnee.
Peking:	Beijing.
Poitou:	Former French province, now divided into the departments of La Vendée, Deux-Sèvres, and Vienne.
Pretania:	Britain, including Scotland.
Sor:	Tyre.
Stalingrad:	Volgograd.
Syria:	A province of the Roman (later the East Roman or Byzantine) Empire, approximately the same as the modern country.
Tadmor:	Palmyra, in Syria.
Tartessos:	Southwestern Iberia (conjectural).
Thule:	Southern Norway (conjectural).
Tripolis:	Tripoli, in Lebanon, also known anciently as 'Tarabulus.'
Wendland:	A region bordering on the southern Baltic shores.
Wichita mountains:	In southwestern Oklahoma.
Yathrib:	Original name of Medina.

THE GUARDIANS OF TIME

CONTENTS

TIME PATROL

1

MEN WANTED – *21-40, pref. single, mil. or tech. exp., good physique, for high-pay work with foreign travel. Engineering Studies Co., 305 E. 45, 9-12 & 2-6.*

'The work is, you understand, somewhat unusual,' said Mr Gordon. 'And confidential. I trust you can keep a secret?'

'Normally,' said Manse Everard. 'Depends on what the secret is, of course.'

Mr Gordon smiled. It was a curious smile, a closed curve of his lips which was not quite like any Everard had seen before. He spoke easy colloquial General American, and wore an undistinguished business suit, but there was a foreignness over him which was more than dark complexion, beardless cheeks, and the incongruity of Mongolian eyes above a thin Caucasian nose. It was hard to place.

'We're not spies, if that's what you're thinking,' he said.

Everard grinned. 'Sorry. Please don't think I've gone as hysterical as the rest of the country. I've never had access to confidential data anyway. But your ad mentioned overseas operations, and the way things are – I'd like to keep my passport, you understand.'

He was a big man, with blocky shoulders and a slightly battered face under crew-cut brown hair. His papers lay before him: Army discharge, the record of work in several places as a mechanical engineer. Mr Gordon had seemed barely to glance at them.

The office was ordinary, a desk and a couple of chairs, a filing cabinet, and a door leading off in the rear. A window opened on the banging traffic of New York, six stories down.

'Independent spirit,' said the man behind the desk. 'I like that. So many of them come cringing in, as if they'd be grateful for a kick. Of course, with your background you aren't desperate yet. You can still get work, even in … ah, I believe the current term is a rolling readjustment.'

'I was interested,' said Everard. 'I've worked abroad, as you can see, and would like to travel again. But frankly, I still don't have the faintest idea what your outfit does.'

'We do a good many things,' said Mr Gordon. 'Let me see ... you've been in combat. France and Germany.' Everard blinked; his papers had included a record of medals, but he'd have sworn the man hadn't had time to read them. 'Um ... would you mind grasping those knobs on the arms of your chair? Thank you. Now, how do you react to physical danger?'

Everard bristled. 'Look here –'

Mr Gordon's eyes flicked to an instrument on his desk: it was merely a box with an indicator needle and a couple of dials. 'Never mind. What are your views on internationalism?'

'Say, now –'

'Communism? Fascism? Women? Your personal ambitions? ... That's all. You don't have to answer.'

'What the devil is this, anyway?' snapped Everard.

'A bit of psychological testing. Forget it. I've no interest in your opinions except as they reflect basic emotional orientation.' Mr Gordon leaned back, making a bridge of his fingers. 'Very promising so far. Now, here's the setup. We're doing work which is, as I've told you, highly confidential. We ... ah ... we're planning to spring a surprise on our competitors.' He chuckled. 'Go ahead and report me to the FBI if you wish. We've already been investigated and have a clean bill of health. You'll find that we really do carry on world-wide financial and engineering operations. But there's another aspect of the job, and that's the one we want men for. I'll pay you one hundred dollars to go in the back room and take a set of tests. It'll last about three hours. If you don't pass, that's the end of it. If you do, we'll sign you on, tell you the facts, and start you training. Are you game?'

Everard hesitated. He had a feeling of being rushed. There was more to this enterprise than an office and one bland stranger. Still ...

Decision. 'I'll sign on *after* you've told me what it's all about.'

'As you wish,' shrugged Mr Gordon. 'Suit yourself. The tests will say whether you're going to or not, you know. We use some very advanced techniques.'

That, at least, was entirely true. Everard knew a little something about modern psychology: encephalographs, association tests, the Minnesota profile. He did not recognize any of the hooded machines that hummed and blinked around him. The questions which the assistant – a white-skinned, completely hairless man of indeterminate age, with a heavy accent and no facial expression – fired at him seemed irrelevant to anything. And what was the metal cap he was supposed to wear on his head? Into what did the wires from it lead?

He stole glances at the meter faces, but the letters and numerals were like nothing he had seen before. Not English, French, Russian, Greek, Chinese, anything belonging to 1954 AD. Perhaps he was already beginning to realize the truth, even then.

A curious self-knowledge grew in him as the tests proceeded. Manson Emmert Everard, age 30, onetime lieutenant in the US Army Engineers; design and production experience in America, Sweden, Arabia; still a bachelor, though with increasingly wistful thoughts about his married friends; no current girl, no close ties of any kind; a bit of a bibliophile; a dogged poker player; fondness for sailboats and horses and rifles; a camper and fisherman on his vacations. He had known it all, of course, but only as isolated shards of fact. It was peculiar, this sudden sensing of himself as an integrated organism, this realization that each characteristic was a single inevitable facet of an over-all pattern.

He came out exhausted and wringing wet. Mr Gordon offered him a cigarette and swept eyes rapidly over a series of coded sheets which the assistant gave him. Now and then he muttered a phrase: ' ... Zeth-20 cortical ... undifferentiated evaluation here ... psychic reaction to antitoxin ... weakness in central coordination ...' He had slipped into an accent, a lilt and a treatment of vowels which were like nothing Everard had heard in a long experience of the ways in which the English language can be mangled.

It was half an hour before he looked up again. Everard was getting restless, a faint anger stirring at this cavalier treatment, but interest kept him sitting quietly. Mr Gordon flashed improbably white teeth in a broad, satisfied grin. 'Ah. At last. Do you know, I've had to reject twenty-four candidates already? But you'll do. You'll definitely do.'

'Do for what?' Everard leaned forward, conscious of his pulse picking up.

'The Patrol. You're going to be a kind of policeman.'

'Yeh? Where?'

'Everywhere. And everywhen. Brace yourself, this is going to be a shock.

'You see, our company, while legitimate enough, is only a front and a source of funds. Our real business is patrolling time.'

2

The Academy was in the American West. It was also in the Oligocene period, a warm age of forests and grasslands when man's ratty ancestors scuttled away from the tread of giant mammals. It had been built a thousand years ago; it would be maintained for half a million – long enough to graduate as many as the Time Patrol would require – and then be carefully demolished so that no trace would remain. Later the glaciers would come, and there would be men, and in the year 19352 AD (the 7841st year of the Morennian Triumph), these men would find a way to travel through time and return to the Oligocene to establish the Academy.

It was a complex of long, low buildings, smooth curves and shifting colors, spreading over a greensward between enormous ancient trees. Beyond it, hills and woods rolled off to a great brown river, and at night you could sometimes hear the bellowing of titanotheres or the distant squall of a sabertooth.

Everard stepped out of the time shuttle – a big, featureless metal box – with a dryness in his throat. It felt like his first day in the Army, twelve years ago – or fifteen to twenty million years in the future, if you preferred – lonely and helpless, and wishing desperately for some honorable way to go home. It was a small comfort to see the other shuttles, discharging a total of fifty-odd young men and women. The recruits moved slowly together, forming an awkward clump. They didn't speak at first, but stood staring at each other. Everard recognized a Hoover collar and a bowler; the styles of dress and hairdo moved up through 1954 and on. Where was she from, the girl with the iridiscent, close-fitting culottes and the green lipstick and the fantastically waved yellow hair? No … when?

A man of about twenty-five happened to stand beside him: obviously British, from the threadbare tweeds and the long, thin face. He seemed to be hiding a truculent bitterness under his mannered exterior. 'Hello,' said Everard. 'Might as well get acquainted.' He gave his name and origin.

'Charles Whitcomb, London, 1947,' said the other shyly. 'I was just demobbed – RAF – and this looked like a good chance. Now I wonder.'

'It may be,' said Everard, thinking of the salary. Fifteen thousand a year to start with! How did they figure years, though? Must be in terms of one's actual duration-sense.

A man strolled in their direction. He was a slender young fellow in a skin-tight gray uniform with a deep-blue cloak which seemed to twinkle, as if it had stars sewn in. His face was pleasant, smiling, and he spoke genially with a neutral accent: 'Hello, there! Welcome to the Academy. I take it you all know English?' Everard noticed a man in the shabby remnants of a German uniform, and a Hindu, and others who were probably from several foreign countries.

'We'll use English, then, till you've all learned Temporal.' The man lounged easily, hands on his hips. 'My name is Dard Kelm. I was born in – let me see – 9573 Christian reckoning, but I've made a specialty of your period. Which, by the way, extends from 1850 to 2000, though you're all from some in-between years. I'm your official wailing wall, if something goes wrong.

'This place is run along different lines from what you've probably been expecting. We don't turn out men en masse, so the elaborate discipline of a classroom or an army is not required. Each of you will have individual as well as general instruction. We don't need to punish failure in studies, because the preliminary tests have guaranteed there won't be any and made the chance of failure on the job small. Each of you has a high maturity rating in terms of your particular cultures. However, the variation in aptitudes means that if we're to develop each individual to the fullest, there must be personal guidance.

'There's little formality here beyond normal courtesy. You'll have chances for recreation as well as study. We never expect more of you than you can give. I might add that the hunting and fishing are still pretty good even in this neighborhood, and if you fly just a few hundred miles they're fantastic.

'Now, if there aren't any questions, please follow me and I'll get you settled.'

Dard Kelm demonstrated the gadgets in a typical room. They were the sort you would have expected by, say, 2000 AD: unobtrusive furniture readily adjusted to a perfect fit, refresher cabinets, screens which could draw on a huge library of recorded sight and sound for entertainment. Nothing too advanced, as yet. Each cadet had his own room in the 'dormitory' building; meals were in a central refectory, but arrangements could be made for private parties. Everard felt the tension easing within him.

A welcoming banquet was held. The courses were familiar but the silent machines which rolled up to serve them were not. There was wine, beer, an ample supply of tobacco. Maybe something had been slipped into the food, for Everard felt as euphoric as the others. He ended up beating out boogie on a piano while half a dozen people made the air hideous with attempts at song.

Only Charles Whitcomb held back. Sipping a moody glass over in a corner by himself, Dard Kelm was tactful and did not try to force him into joining.

Everard decided he was going to like it. But the work and the organization and the purpose were still shadows.

'Time travel was discovered at a period when the Chorite Heresiarchy was breaking up,' said Kelm, in the lecture hall. 'You'll study the details later; for now, take my word that it was a turbulent age, when commercial and genetic rivalry was a tooth-and-claw matter between giant combines; anything went, and the various governments were pawns in a galactic game. The time effect was the by-product of a search for a means of instantaneous transportation, which some of you will realize requires infinitely discontinuous functions for its mathematical description ... as does travel into the past. I won't go into the theory of it – you'll get some of that in the physics classes – but merely state that it involves the concept of infinite-valued relationships in a continuum of 4N dimensions, where N is the total number of particles in the universe.

'Naturally, the group which discovered this, the Nine, were aware of the possibilities. Not only commercial – trading, mining, and other enterprises you can readily imagine – but the chance of striking a death-blow at their enemies. You see, time is variable; the past can be changed –'

'Question!' It was the girl from 1972, Elizabeth Gray, who was a rising young physicist in her own period.

'Yes?' said Kelm politely.

'I think you're describing a logically impossible situation. I'll grant the possibility of time travel, seeing that we're here, but an event cannot both *have* happened and *not* happened. That's self-contradictory.'

'Only if you insist on a logic which is not Aleph-sub-Aleph-valued,' said Kelm. 'What happens is like this: suppose I went back in time and prevented your father from meeting your mother. You would never have been born. That portion of universal history would read differently; it would always have been different, though I would retain memory of the "original" state of affairs.'

'Well, how about doing the same to yourself?' asked Elizabeth. 'Would you cease existing?'

'No, because I would belong to the section of history prior to my own intervention. Let's apply it to you. If you went back to, I would guess, 1946, and worked to prevent your parents' marriage in 1947, you would still have existed in that year; you would not go out of existence just because you had influenced events. The same would apply even if you had only been in 1946 one microsecond before shooting the man who would otherwise have become your father.'

'But then I'd exist without – without an origin!' she protested. 'I'd have life, and memories, and ... everything ... though *nothing* had produced them.'

Kelm shrugged. 'What of it? You insist that the causal law, or strictly speaking the conservation-of-energy law, involve only continuous functions. Actually, discontinuity is entirely possible.'

He laughed and leaned on the lectern. 'Of course, there are impossibilities,' he said. 'You could not be your own mother, for instance, because of sheer genetics. If you went back and married your former father, the children would be different, none of them you, because each would have only half your chromosomes.'

Clearing his throat: 'Let's not stray from the subject. You'll learn the details in other classes. I'm only giving you a general background. To continue: the Nine saw the possibility of going back in time and preventing their enemies from ever having gotten started, even from ever being born. But then the Danellians appeared.'

For the first time, his casual, half-humorous air dropped, and he stood there as a man in the presence of the unknowable. He spoke quietly: 'The Danellians are part of the future – our future, more than a million years ahead of me. Man has evolved into something ... impossible to describe. You'll probably never meet a Danellian. If you ever should, it will be ... rather a shock. They aren't malignant – nor benevolent – they are as far beyond anything we can know or feel as we are beyond those insectivores who are going to be our ancestors. It isn't good to meet that sort of thing face to face.

'They were simply concerned with protecting their own existence. Time travel was old when they emerged, there had been uncountable opportunities for the foolish and the greedy and the mad to go back and turn history inside out. They did not wish to forbid the travel – it was part of the complex which had led to them – but they had to regulate it. The Nine were prevented from carrying out their schemes. And the Patrol was set up to police the time lanes.

'Your work will be mostly within your own eras, unless you graduate to unattached status. You will live, on the whole, ordinary lives, family and friends as usual; the secret part of those lives will have the satisfactions of good pay, protection, occasional vacations in some very interesting places, supremely worthwhile work. But you will always be on call. Sometimes you will help time travelers who have gotten into difficulties, one way or another. Sometimes you will work on missions, the apprehension of would-be political or military or economic conquistadors. Sometimes the Patrol will accept damage as done, and work instead to set up counteracting influences in later periods which will swing history back to the desired track.

'I wish all of you luck.'

The first part of instruction was physical and psychological. Everard had never realized how his own life had crippled him, in body and mind; he was only half the man he could be. It came hard, but in the end it was a joy to feel the utterly controlled power of muscles, the emotions which had grown deeper for being disciplined, the swiftness and precision of conscious thought.

Somewhere along the line he was thoroughly conditioned against revealing anything about the Patrol, even hinting at its existence, to any unauthorized person. It was simply impossible for him to do so, under any influence; as impossible as jumping to the moon. He also learned the ins and outs of his twentieth-century public *persona*.

Temporal, the artificial language with which Patrolmen from all ages could communicate without being understood by strangers, was a miracle of logically organized expressiveness.

He thought he knew something about combat, but he had to learn the tricks and the weapons of fifty thousand years, all the way from a Bronze Age rapier to a cyclic blast which could annihilate a continent. Returned to his own era, he would be given a limited arsenal, but he might be called into other periods and overt anachronism was rarely permissible.

There was the study of history, science, arts and philosophies, fine details of dialect and mannerism. These last were only for the 1850–1975 period;

if he had occasion to go elsewhere he would pick up special instruction from a hypnotic conditioner. It was such machines that made it possible to complete his training in three months.

He learned the organization of the Patrol. Up 'ahead' lay the mystery which was Danellian civilization, but there was little direct contact with it. The Patrol was set up in semimilitary fashion, with ranks, though without special formalities. History was divided into milieus, with a head office located in a major city for a selected twenty-year period (disguised by some ostensible activity such as commerce) and various branch offices. For his time, there were three milieus: the Western world, headquarters in London; Russia, in Moscow; Asia, in Peiping; each in the easygoing years 1890–1910, when concealment was less difficult than in later decades, when there were smaller offices such as Gordon's. An ordinary attached agent lived as usual in his own time, often with an authentic job. Communication between years was by tiny robot shuttles or by courier, with automatic shunts to keep such messages from piling up at one instant.

The entire organization was so vast that he could not really appreciate the fact. He had entered something new and exciting, that was all he truly grasped with all layers of consciousness … as yet.

He found his instructors friendly, ready to gab. The grizzled veteran who taught him to handle spaceships had fought in the Martian war of 3890. 'You boys catch on fairly quick,' he said. 'It's hell, though, teaching pre-industrial people. We've quit even trying to give them more than the rudiments. Had a Roman here once – Caesar's time – fairly bright boy, too, but he never got it through his head that a machine can't be treated like a horse. As for the Babylonians, time travel just wasn't in their world-picture. We had to give them a battle-of-the-gods routine.'

'What routine are you giving us?' asked Whitcomb.

The spaceman regarded him narrowly. 'The truth,' he said at last. 'As much of it as you can take.'

'How did you get into this job?'

'Oh … I was shot up off Jupiter. Not much left of me. They picked me up, built me a new body – since none of my people were alive, and I was presumed dead, there didn't seem much point in going back home. No fun living under the Guidance Corps. So I took this position here. Good company, easy living, and furloughs in a lot of eras.' The spaceman grinned. 'Wait till you've been to the decadent stage of the Third Matriarchy! You don't know what fun is.'

Everard said nothing. He was too captured by the spectacle of Earth, rolling enormous against the stars.

He made friends with his fellow cadets. They were a congenial bunch – naturally, with the same type being picked for Patrollers, bold and intelligent minds. There were a couple of romances. No *Portrait of Jenny* stuff; marriage was entirely possible, with the couple picking some year in which to set up housekeeping. He himself liked the girls, but kept his head.

Oddly, it was the silent and morose Whitcomb with whom he struck up the closest friendship. There was something appealing about the Englishman; he was so cultured, such a thoroughly good fellow, and still somehow lost.

They were out riding one day, on horses whose remote ancestors scampered before their gigantic descendants. Everard had a rifle, in the hope of bagging a shovel-tusker he had seen. Both wore Academy uniform, light grays which were cool and silky under the hot yellow sun.

'I wonder we're allowed to hunt,' remarked the American. 'Suppose I shoot a sabertooth – in Asia, I suppose – which was originally slated to eat one of those prehuman insectivores. Won't that change the whole future?'

'No,' said Whitcomb. He had progressed faster in studying the theory of time travel. 'You see, it's rather as if the continuum were a mesh of tough rubber bands. It isn't easy to distort it; the tendency is always for it to snap back to its, uh, "former" shape. One individual insectivore doesn't matter, it's the total genetic pool of their species which led to man.

'Likewise, if I killed a sheep in the Middle Ages, I wouldn't wipe out all its later descendants, maybe all the sheep there were by 1940. Rather, those would still be there, unchanged down to their very genes in spite of a different ancestry, because over so long a period of time all the sheep, or men, are descendants of *all* the earlier sheep or men. Compensation don't you see; somewhere along the line, some other ancestor supplies the genes you thought you had eliminated.

'In the same way ... oh, suppose I went back and prevented Booth from killing Lincoln. Unless I took very elaborate precautions, it would probably happen that someone else did the shooting and Booth got blamed anyway.

'That resilience of time is the reason travel is permitted at all. If you want to change things, you have to go about it just right and work very hard, usually.'

His mouth twisted. 'Indoctrination! We're told again and again that if *we* interfere, there's going to be punishment for us. I'm not allowed to go back and shoot that ruddy bastard Hitler in his cradle. I'm supposed to let him grow up as he did, and start the war, and kill my girl.'

Everard rode quietly for a while. The only noise was the squeak of saddle leather and the rustle of long grass. 'Oh,' he said at last. 'I'm sorry. Want to talk about it?'

'Yes. I do. But there isn't much. She was in the WAAF – Mary Nelson – we were going to get married after the war. She was in London in '44. November seventeenth, I'll never forget that date. The V-bombs got her. She'd gone over to a neighbor's house in Streatham – was on furlough you see, staying with her mother. That house was blown up; her own home wasn't scratched.'

Whitcomb's cheeks were bloodless. He stared emptily before him. 'It's going to be jolly hard not to ... not to go back, just a few years, and see her at the very least. Only see her again ... No! I don't dare.'

Everard laid a hand on the man's shoulder, awkwardly, and they rode on in silence.

The class moved ahead, each at his own pace, but there was enough compensation so that all graduated together: a brief ceremony followed by a huge party and many maudlin arrangements for later reunions. Then each went back to the same year he had come from: the same hour.

Everard accepted Gordon's congratulations, got a list of contemporary agents (several of them holding jobs in places like military intelligence), and returned to his apartment. Later he might find work arranged for him in some sensitive listening post, but his present assignment – for income-tax purposes, 'special consultant to Engineering Studies Co' – was only to read a dozen papers a day for the indications of time travel he had been taught to spot, and hold himself ready for a call.

As it happened, he made his own first job.

3

It was a peculiar feeling to read the headlines and know, more or less, what was coming next. It took the edge off, but added a sadness, for this was a tragic era. He could sympathize with Whitcomb's desire to go back and change history.

Only, of course, one man was too limited. He could not change it for the better, except by some freak; most likely he would bungle everything. Go back and kill Hitler and the Japanese and Soviet leaders – maybe someone shrewder would take their place. Maybe atomic energy would lie fallow, and the glorious flowering of the Venusian Renaissance never happen. The devil we know ...

He looked out of his window. Lights flamed against a hectic sky; the street crawled with automobiles and a hurrying, faceless crowd; he could not see the towers of Manhattan from here, but he knew they reared arrogant toward the clouds. And it was all one swirl on a river that swept from the peaceful prehuman landscape where he had been to the unimaginable Danellian future. How many billions and trillions of human creatures lived, laughed, wept, worked, hoped, and died in its currents!

Well ... He sighed, stoked his pipe, and turned back. A long walk had not made him less restless; his mind and body were impatient for something to do. But it was late and ... He went over to the bookshelf, picked out a volume more or less at random, and started to read. It was a collection of Victorian and Edwardian stories.

A passing reference struck him. Something about a tragedy at Addleton and the singular contents of an ancient British barrow. Nothing more. Hm. Time travel? He smiled to himself.

Still ...

No, he thought. *This is crazy.*

It wouldn't do any harm to check up, though. The incident was mentioned as occurring in the year 1894, in England. He could get out back files of the London *Times*. Nothing else to do ... Probably that was why he was stuck with his dull newspaper assignment: so that his mind, grown nervous from boredom, would prowl into every conceivable corner.

He was on the steps of the public library as it opened.

The account was there, dated 25 June 1894, and several days following. Addleton was a village in Kent, distinguished chiefly by a Jacobean estate belonging to Lord Wyndham and a barrow of unknown age. The nobleman, an enthusiastic amateur archeologist, had been excavating it, together with one James Rotherhithe, an expert from the British Museum who happened to be a relative. Lord Wyndham had uncovered a rather meager burial chamber: a few artifacts nearly rusted and rotted away, bones of men and horses. There was also a chest in surprisingly good condition, containing ingots of an unknown metal presumed to be a lead or silver alloy. He fell deathly ill, with symptoms of a peculiarly lethal poisoning; Rotherhithe, who had barely looked into the casket, was not affected, and circumstantial evidence suggested that he had slipped the nobleman a dose of some obscure Asiatic concoction. Scotland Yard arrested the man when Lord Wyndham died, on the twenty-fifth. Rotherhithe's family engaged the services of a well-known private detective, who was able to show, by most ingenious reasoning, followed by tests on animals, that the accused was innocent and that a 'deadly emanation' from the chest was responsible. Box and contents had been thrown into the English Channel. Congratulations all around. Fadeout to happy ending.

Everard sat quietly in the long, hushed room. The story didn't tell enough. But it was highly suggestive, to say the least.

Then why hadn't the Victorian office of the Patrol investigated? Or had they? Probably. They wouldn't advertise their results, of course.

Still, he'd better send a memorandum.

Returning to his apartment, he took one of the little message shuttles given him, laid a report in it, and set the control studs for the London office, 25 June 1894. When he pushed the final button the box vanished with a small whoosh of air rushing in where it had been.

It returned in a few minutes. Everard opened it and took out a sheet of foolscap covered with neat typing – yes, the typewriter had been invented by then, of course. He scanned it with the swiftness he had learned.

'Dear Sir:

'In reply to yrs of 6 September 1954, beg to acknowledge receipt and would commend your diligence. The affair has only just begun at this end, and we are much occupied at present with preventing assassination of Her Majesty, as well as with the Balkan Question, the deplorable opium trade with China, &c. While we can, of course, settle current business and then return to this, it is well to avoid *curiosa* such as being in two places at once, which might be noticed. Would therefore much appreciate it if you and some qualified British agent would come to our assistance. Unless we hear otherwise, we shall expect you at 14-B, Old Osborne Road, on 26 June 1894, at 12 midnight. Believe me, Sir, yr humble & obt svt,

J. Mainwethering'

There followed a note of the spatio-temporal coordinates, incongruous under all that floridness.

Everard called up Gordon, got an okay, and arranged to pick up a time hopper at the 'company's' warehouse. Then he shot a note to Charlie Whitcomb in 1947, got a one-word reply – 'Surely' – and went off to get his machine.

It was reminiscent of a motorcycle without wheels or handlebars. There were two saddles and an antigravity propulsion unit. Everard set the dials for Whitcomb's era, touched the main button, and found himself in another warehouse.

London, 1947. He sat for a moment, reflecting that at this instant he himself, seven years younger, was attending college back in the States. Then Whitcomb shouldered past the watchman and took his hand. 'Good to see you again, old chap,' he said. His haggard face lit up in the curiously charming smile which Everard had come to know. 'And so Victoria, eh?'

'Reckon so. Jump on.' Everard reset. This time he would emerge in an office. A very private inner office.

It blinked into existence around him. There was an unexpectedly heavy effect to the oak furniture, the thick carpet, the flaring gas mantles. Electric lights were available, but Dalhousie & Roberts was a solid, conservative import house. Mainwethering himself got out of a chair and came to greet them: a large and pompous man with bushy side whiskers and a monocle. But he had also an air of strength, and an Oxford accent so cultivated that Everard could hardly understand it.

'Good evening, gentlemen. Pleasant journey, I trust? Oh, yes ... sorry ... you gentlemen are new to the business, eh, what? Always a bit disconcerting at first. I remember how shocked I was on a visit to the twenty-first century. Not British at all ... Only a *res naturae*, though, only another facet of an always surprising universe, eh? You must excuse my lack of hospitality, but we really are frightfully busy. Fanatic German up in 1917 learned the time-travel secret from an unwary anthropologist, stole a machine, has come to London to assassinate Her Majesty. We're having the devil's own time finding him.'

'Will you?' asked Whitcomb.

'Oh, yes. But deuced hard work, gentlemen, especially when we must operate secretly. I'd like to engage a private inquiry agent, but the only worthwhile one is entirely too clever. He operates on the principle that when one has eliminated the impossible, whatever remains, however improbable, must be the truth. And time trafficking may not be too improbable for him.'

'I'll bet he's the same man who's working on the Addleton case, or will be tomorrow,' said Everard. 'That isn't important; we know he'll prove Rotherhithe's innocence. What matters is the strong probability that there's been hanky-panky going on back in ancient British times.'

'Saxon, you mean,' corrected Whitcomb, who had checked on the data himself. 'Good many people confuse British and Saxons.'

'Almost as many as confuse Saxons and Jutes,' said Mainwethering blandly. 'Kent was invaded from Jutland, I understand ... Ah. Hm. Clothes here, gentlemen. And funds. And papers, all prepared for you. I sometimes think you field agents don't appreciate how much work we have to do in the offices for even the smallest operation. Haw! Pardon. Have you a plan of campaign?'

'Yes.' Everard began stripping off his twentieth-century garments. 'I think so. We both know enough about the Victorian era to get by. I'll have to remain American, though ... yes, I see you put that in my papers.'

Mainwethering looked mournful. 'If the barrow incident has gotten into a famous piece of literature as you say, we will be getting a hundred memoranda about it. Yours happened to come first. Two others have arrived since, from 1923 and 1960. Dear me, how I wish I were allowed a robot secretary!'

Everard struggled with the awkward suit. It fitted him well enough, his measurements were on file in this office, but he hadn't appreciated the relative comfort of his own fashions before. Damn that waistcoat! 'Look here,' he said, 'this business may be quite harmless. In fact, since we're here now, it must have *been* harmless. Eh?'

'As of now,' said Mainwethering. 'But consider. You two gentlemen go back to Jutish times and find the marauder. But you fail. Perhaps he shoots you before you can shoot him; perhaps he waylays those we send after you. Then he goes on to establish an industrial revolution or whatever he's after. History changes. You, being back there before the change-point, still exist ... if only as cadavers ... but we up here have never been. This conversation never took place. As Horace puts it –'

'Never mind!' laughed Whitcomb. 'We'll investigate the barrow first, in this year, then pop back here and decide what's next.' He bent over and began transferring equipment from a twentieth-century suitcase to a Gladstonian monstrosity of flowered cloth. A couple of guns, some physical and chemical apparatus which his own age had not invented, a tiny radio with which to call up the office in case of trouble.

Mainwethering consulted his Bradshaw. 'You can get the 8:23 out of Charing Cross tomorrow morning,' he said. 'Allow half an hour to get from here to the station.'

'Okay.' Everard and Whitcomb remounted their hopper and vanished. Mainwethering sighed, yawned, left instructions with his clerk, and went home. At 7:45 a.m. the clerk was there when the hopper materialized.

4

This was the first moment that the reality of time travel struck home to Everard. He had known it with the top of his mind, been duly impressed, but it was, for his emotions, merely exotic. Now, clopping through a London he did not know in a hansom cab (not a tourist-trap anachronism, but a working machine, dusty and battered), smelling an air which held more smoke than a twentieth-century city but no gasoline fumes, seeing the crowds which milled past – gentlemen in bowlers and top hats, sooty navvies, long-skirted women, and not actors but real, talking, perspiring, laughing and somber human beings off on real business – it hit him with full force that he was *here*. At this moment his mother had not been born, his grandparents were young couples just getting settled to harness, Grover Cleveland was President of the United States and Victoria was Queen of England, Kipling was writing and the last Indian uprisings in America yet to come … It was like a blow on the head.

Whitcomb took it more calmly, but his eyes were never still as he watched this day of England's glory. 'I begin to understand,' he murmured. 'They never have agreed whether this was a period of unnatural, stuffy convention and thinly veneered brutality, or the last flower of Western civilization before it started going to seed. Just seeing these people makes me realize; it was everything they have said about it, good and bad, because it wasn't a simple thing happening to everyone, but millions of individual lives.'

'Sure,' said Everard. 'That must be true of every age.'

The train was almost familiar, not very different from the carriages of British railways anno 1954, which gave Whitcomb occasion for sardonic remarks about inviolable traditions. In a couple of hours it let them off at a sleepy village station among carefully tended flower gardens, where they engaged a buggy to drive them to the Wyndham estate.

A polite constable admitted them after a few questions. They were passing themselves off as archeologists, Everard from America and Whitcomb from Australia, who had been quite anxious to meet Lord Wyndham and were shocked by his tragic end. Mainwethering, who seemed to have tentacles everywhere, had supplied them with letters of introduction from a well-known authority at the British Museum. The inspector from Scotland Yard agreed to let them look at the barrow – 'the case is solved, gentlemen, there are no more clues, even if my colleague does not agree, hah, hah!' The private agent smiled sourly and watched them with a narrow eye as they approached the mound; he was tall, thin, hawk-faced, and accompanied by a burly, mustached fellow with a limp who seemed a kind of amanuensis.

The barrow was long and high, covered with grass save where a raw scar showed excavation to the funeral chamber. This had been lined with rough-hewn timbers but had long ago collapsed; fragments of what had been wood still lay on the dirt. 'The newspapers mentioned something about a metal casket,' said Everard. 'I wonder if we might have a look at it too?'

The inspector nodded agreeably and led them off to an outbuilding where the major finds were laid forth on a table. Except for the box, they were only fragments of corroded metal and crumbled bone.

'Hm,' said Whitcomb. His gaze was thoughtful on the sleek, bare face of the small chest. It shimmered bluely, some time-proof alloy yet to be discovered. 'Most unusual. Not primitive at all. You'd almost think it had been machined, eh?'

Everard approached it warily. He had a pretty good idea of what was inside, and all the caution about such matters natural to a citizen of the *soi-disant* Atomic Age. Pulling a counter out of his bag, he aimed it at the box. Its needle wavered, not much but ...

'Interesting item there,' said the inspector. 'May I ask what it is?'

'An experimental electroscope,' lied Everard. Carefully, he threw back the lid and held the counter above the box.

God! There was enough radioactivity inside to kill a man in a day! He had just a glimpse of heavy, dull-shining ingots before he slammed the lid down again. 'Be careful with that stuff,' he said shakily. Praise heaven, whoever carried that devil's load had come from an age when they knew how to block off radiation!

The private detective had come up behind them, noiselessly. A hunter's look grew on his keen face. 'So you recognized the contents, sir?' he asked quietly.

'Yes. I think so.' Everard remembered that Becquerel would not discover radioactivity for almost two years; even X rays were still more than a year in the future. He had to be cautious. 'That is ... in Indian territory I've heard stories about an ore like this which is poisonous –'

'*Most* interesting.' The detective began to stuff a big-bowled pipe. 'Like mercury vapor, what?'

'So Rotherhithe placed that box in the grave, did he?' muttered the inspector.

'Don't be ridiculous!' snapped the detective. 'I have three lines of conclusive proof that Rotherhithe is entirely innocent. What puzzled me was the actual cause of his lordship's death. But if, as this gentleman says, there happened to be a deadly poison buried in that mound … to discourage grave-robbers? I wonder, though, how the old Saxons came by an American mineral. Perhaps there is something to these theories about early Phoenician voyages across the Atlantic. I have done a little research on a notion of mine that there are Chaldean elements in the Cymric language, and this seems to bear me out.'

Everard felt guilty about what he was doing to the science of archeology. Oh, well, this box was going to be dumped in the Channel and forgotten. He and Whitcomb made an excuse to leave as soon as possible.

On the way back to London, when they were safely alone in their compartment, the Englishman took out a moldering fragment of wood. 'Slipped this into my pocket at the barrow,' he said. 'It'll help us date the thing. Hand me that radiocarbon counter, will you?' He popped the wood into the device, turned some knobs, and read off the answer. 'One thousand, four hundred and thirty years, plus or minus about ten. The mound went up around … um … 464 AD, then, when the Jutes were just getting established in Kent.'

'If those ingots are still that hellish after so long,' murmured Everard, 'I wonder what they were like originally? Hard to see how you could have that much activity with such a long half-life, but then, up in the future they can do things with the atom my period hasn't dreamed of.'

Turning in their report to Mainwethering, they spent a day sight-seeing while he sent messages across time and activated the great machine of the Patrol. Everard was interested in Victorian London, almost captivated in spite of the grime and poverty. Whitcomb got a faraway look in his eyes. 'I'd liked to have lived here,' he said.

'Yeah? With their medicine and dentistry?'

'And no bombs falling.' Whitcomb's answer held a defiance.

Mainwethering had arrangements made when they returned to his office. Puffing a cigar, he strode up and down, pudgy hands clasped behind his tailcoat, and rattled off the story.

'Metal been identified with high probability. Isotopic fuel from around the thirtieth century. Checkup reveals that a merchant from the Ing Empire was visiting year 2987 to barter his raw materials for their synthrope, secret of which had been lost in the Interregnum. Naturally, he took precautions, tried to pass himself off as a trader from the Saturnian System, but nevertheless disappeared. So did his time shuttle. Presumably someone in 2987 found out what he was and murdered him for his machine. Patrol notified, but no trace of machine. Finally recovered from fifth-century England by two Patrolmen named, haw! Everard and Whitcomb.'

'If we've already succeeded, why bother?' grinned the American.

Mainwethering looked shocked. 'But my dear fellow! You have not already succeeded. The job is yet to do, in terms of your and my duration-sense. And please do not take success for granted merely because history records it. Time is not rigid; man has free will. If you fail, history will change and will not ever have recorded your success; I will not have told you about it. That is undoubtedly what happened, if I may use the term "happened," in the few cases where the Patrol has a record of failure. Those cases are still being worked on, and if success is achieved at last, history will be changed and there will "always" have been success. *Tempus non nascitur, fit,* if I may indulge in a slight parody.'

'All right, all right, I was only joking,' said Everard. 'Let's get going. *Tempus fugit.*' He added an extra 'g' with malice aforethought, and Mainwethering winced.

It turned out that even the Patrol knew little about the dark period when the Romans had left Britain, the Romano-British civilization was crumbling, and the British were moving in. It had never seemed an important one. The office at London, 1000 AD, sent up what material it had, together with suits of clothes that would get by. Everard and Whitcomb spent an hour unconscious under the hypnotic educators, to emerge with fluency in Latin and in several Saxon and Jutish dialects, and with a fair knowledge of the mores.

The clothes were awkward: trousers, shirts, and coats of rough wool, leather cloaks, an interminable collection of thongs and laces. Long flaxen wigs covered modern haircuts; a clean shave would pass unnoticed, even in the fifth century. Whitcomb carried an ax, Everard a sword, both made to measure of high-carbon steel, but put more reliance on the little twenty-sixth-century sonic stun guns stuck under their coats. Armor had not been included, but the time hopper had a pair of motorcycle crash helmets in one saddlebag: these would not attract much attention in an age of homemade equipment, and were a good deal stronger and more comfortable than the real thing. They also stowed away a picnic lunch and some earthenware jugs full of good Victorian ale.

'Excellent.' Mainwethering pulled a watch out of his pocket and consulted it. 'I shall expect you back here at … shall we say four o'clock? I will have some armed guards on hand, in case you have a prisoner along, and we can go out to tea afterward.' He shook their hands. 'Good hunting!'

Everard swung onto the time hopper, set the controls for 464 AD at Addleton Barrow, a summer midnight, and threw the switch.

5

There was a full moon. Under it, the land lay big and lonely, with a darkness of forest blocking out the horizon. Somewhere a wolf howled. The mound was there yet; they had come late.

Rising on the antigravity unit, they peered across a dense, shadowy wood.

A thorp lay about a mile from the barrow, one hall of hewn timber and a cluster of smaller buildings around a courtyard. In the drenching moonlight, it was very quiet.

'Cultivated fields,' observed Whitcomb. His voice was hushed in the stillness. 'The Jutes and Saxons were mostly yeomen, you know, who came here looking for land. Imagine the Britons were pretty well cleared out of this area some years ago.'

'We've got to find out about that burial,' said Everard. 'Shall we go back and locate the moment the grave was made? No, it might be safer to inquire now, at a later date when whatever excitement there was has died down. Say tomorrow morning.'

Whitcomb nodded, and Everard brought the hopper down into the concealment of a thicket and jumped up five hours. The sun was blinding in the northeast, dew glistened on the long grass, and the birds were making an unholy racket. Dismounting, the agents sent the hopper shooting up at fantastic velocity, to hover ten miles above-ground and come to them when called on a midget radio built into their helmets.

They approached the thorp openly, whacking off the savage-looking dogs which came snarling at them with the flat of sword and ax. Entering the courtyard, they found it unpaved but richly carpeted with mud and manure. A couple of naked, tow-headed children gaped at them from a hut of earth and wattles. A girl who was sitting outside milking a scrubby little cow let out a small shriek; a thick-built, low-browed farmhand swilling the pigs grabbed for a spear. Wrinkling his nose, Everard wished that some of the 'Noble Nordic' enthusiasts of his century could visit this one.

A gray-bearded man with an ax in his hand appeared in the hall entrance. Like everyone else of this period, he was several inches shorter than the twentieth-century average. He studied them warily before wishing them good morning.

Everard smiled politely. 'I hight Uffa Hundingsson, and my brother is Knubbi,' he said. 'We are merchants from Jutland, come hither to trade at Canterbury.' (He gave it the present name, Cant-wara-byrig.) 'Wandering from the place where our ship is beached, we lost our way, and after fumbling about all night found your home.'

'I hight Wulfnoth, son of Aelfred,' said the yeoman. 'Enter and break your fast with us.'

The hall was big and dim and smoky, full of a chattering crowd: Wulfnoth's children, their spouses and children, dependent carls and *their* wives and children and grandchildren. Breakfast consisted of great wooden trenchers of half-cooked pork, washed down by horns of thin sour beer. It was not hard to get a conversation going; these people were as gossipy as isolated yokels anywhere. The trouble was with inventing plausible accounts of what was going on in Jutland. Once or twice Wulfnoth, who was no fool, caught them in some mistake, but Everard said firmly: 'You have heard a falsehood. News takes strange forms when it crosses the sea.' He was surprised to learn how much contact there still was with the old countries. But the talk of weather and crops was not very different from the kind he knew in the twentieth century Middle West.

Only later was he able to slip in a question about the barrow. Wulfnoth frowned, and his plump, toothless wife hastily made a protective sign toward a rude wooden idol. 'It is not good to speak of such things,' muttered the Jute. 'I would the wizard had not been buried on my land. But he was close to my father, who died last year and would hear of naught else.'

'Wizard?' Whitcomb pricked up his ears. 'What tale is this?'

'Well, you may as well know,' grumbled Wulfnoth. 'He was a stranger hight Stane, who appeared in Canterbury some six years ago. He must have been from far away, for he spoke not the English or British tongues, but King Hengist guested him and eftsoons he learned. He gave the king strange but goodly gifts, and was a crafty redesman, on whom the king came more and more to lean. None dared cross him, for he had a wand which threw thunderbolts and had been seen to cleave rocks and once, in battle with the Britons, burn men down. There are those who thought he was Woden, but that cannot be since he died.'

'Ah, so.' Everard felt a tingle of eagerness. 'And what did he whilst yet he lived?'

'Oh ... he gave the king wise redes, as I have said. It was his thought that we of Kent should cease thrusting back the Britons and calling in ever more of our kinsmen from the old country; rather, we should make peace with the natives. He thought that with our strength and their Roman learning, we could together shape a mighty realm. He may have been right, though I for one see little use in all these books and baths, to say naught of that weird cross-god they have ... Well, anyhow, he was slain by unknowns three years ago, and buried here with sacrifices and such of his possessions as his foes had not reaved. We give him an offering twice a year, and I must say his ghost has not made trouble for us. But still am I somewhat uneasy about it.'

'Three years, eh?' breathed Whitcomb. 'I see ...'

It took a good hour to break away, and Wulfnoth insisted on sending a boy along to guide them to the river. Everard, who didn't feel like walking that far, grinned and called down the hopper. As he and Whitcomb mounted it, he said gravely to the bulging-eyed lad: 'Know that thou hast guested Woden and Thunor, who will hereafter guard thy folk from harm.' Then he jumped three years back in time.

'Now comes the rough part,' he said, peering out of the thicket at the nighted thorp. The mound was not there now, the wizard Stane was still alive.

'It's easy enough to put on a magic show for a kid, but we've got to extract this character from the middle of a big, tough town where he's the king's right-hand man. *And* he has a blast-ray.'

'Apparently we succeeded – or will succeed,' said Whitcomb.

'Nope. It's not irrevocable, you know. If we fail, Wulfnoth will be telling us a different story three years from now, probably that Stane is there – he may kill us twice! And England, pulled out of the Dark Ages into a neoclassical culture, won't evolve into anything you'd recognize by 1894 ... I wonder what Stane's game is.'

He lifted the hopper and sent it through the sky toward Canterbury. A night wind whistled darkly past his face. Presently the town loomed near, and he grounded in a copse. The moon was white on the half-ruined Roman walls of ancient Durovernum, dappled black on the newer earth and wood of the Jutish repairs. Nobody would get in after sunset.

Again the hopper brought them to daytime – near noon – and was sent skyward. His breakfast, two hours ago and three years in the future, felt soggy as Everard led the way onto a crumbling Roman road and toward the city. There was a goodly traffic, mostly farmers driving creaky oxcarts of produce in to market. A pair of vicious-looking guards halted them at the gate and demanded their business. This time they were the agents of a trader on Thanet who had sent them to interview various artisans here. The hoodlums looked surly till Whitcomb slipped them a couple of Roman coins; then the spears went down and they were waved past.

The city brawled and bustled around them, though again it was the ripe smell which impressed Everard most. Among the jostling Jutes, he spotted an occasional Romano-Briton, disdainfully picking a way through the muck and pulling his shabby tunic clear of contact with these savages. It would have been funny if it weren't pathetic.

There was an extraordinarily dirty inn filling the moss-grown ruins of what had been a rich man's town house. Everard and Whitcomb found that their money was of high value here where trade was principally in kind. By standing a few rounds of drinks, they got all the information they wanted. King Hengist's hall was near the middle of town ... not really a hall, an old building which had been deplorably prettied up under the direction of that outlander Stane ... not that our good and doughty king is any pantywaist, don't get me wrong, stranger ... why, only last month ... oh, yes, Stane! He lived in the house right next to it. Strange fellow, some said he was a god ... he certainly had an eye for the girls ... Yes, they said he was behind all this peace-talk with the Britons. More and more of those slickers coming in every day, it's getting so an honest man can't let a little blood without ... Of course, Stane is very wise, I wouldn't say anything against him, understand, after all, he can throw lightning ...

'So what do we do?' asked Whitcomb, back in their own room. 'Go on in and arrest him?'

'No, I doubt if that's possible,' said Everard cautiously. 'I've got a sort of a plan, but it depends on guessing what he really intends. Let's see if we can't get an audience.' As he got off the straw tick which served for a bed, he was scratching. 'Damn! What this period needs isn't literacy but flea powder!'

The house had been carefully renovated, its white, porticoed facade almost painfully clean against the grubbiness around it. Two guards lounged on the stairs, snapping to alertness as the agents approached. Everard fed them money and a story about being a visitor who had news that would surely interest the great wizard. 'Tell him, "Man from tomorrow." 'Tis a password. Got it?'

'It makes not sense,' complained the guard.

'Passwords need not make sense,' said Everard with hauteur.

The Jute clanked off, shaking his head dolefully. All these newfangled notions!

'Are you sure this is wise?' asked Whitcomb. 'He'll be on the alert now, you know.'

'I also know a VIP isn't going to waste time on just any stranger. This business is urgent, man! So far, he hasn't accomplished anything permanent, not even enough to become a lasting legend. But if Hengist should make a genuine union with the Britons ...'

The guard returned, grunted something, and led them up the stairs and across the peristyle. Beyond was the atrium, a good-sized room where modern bearskin rugs jarred with chipped marble and faded mosaics. A man stood waiting before a rude wooden couch. As they entered, he raised his hand, and Everard saw the slim barrel of a thirtieth-century blast-ray.

'Keep your hands in sight and well away from your sides,' said the man gently, 'Otherwise I shall belike have to smite you with a thunderbolt.'

Whitcomb sucked in a sharp, dismayed breath, but Everard had been rather expecting this. Even so, there was a cold knot in his stomach.

The wizard Stane was a small man, dressed in a fine embroidered tunic which must have come from some British villa. His body was lithe, his head large, with a face of rather engaging ugliness under a shock of black hair. A grin of tension bent his lips.

'Search them, Eadgar,' he ordered. 'Take out aught they may bear in their clothing.'

The Jute's frisking was clumsy, but he found the stunners and tossed them to the floor. 'Thou mayst go,' said Stane.

'Is there no danger from them, my lord?' asked the soldier.

Stane grinned wider. 'With this in my hand? Nay, go.' Eadgar shambled out. *At least we still have sword and ax*, thought Everard. *But they're not much use with that thing looking at us.*

'So you come from tomorrow,' murmured Stane. A sudden film of sweat glistened on his forehead. 'I wondered about that. Speak you the later English tongue?'

Whitcomb opened his mouth, but Everard, improvising with his life at wager, beat him to the draw. 'What tongue mean you?'

'Thus-wise.' Stane broke into an English which had a peculiar accent but was recognizable to twentieth-century ears: 'Ih want know where an' when y're from, what y'r 'tentions air, an' all else. Gimme d' facts 'r Ih'll burn y' doon.'

Everard shook his head. 'Nay,' he answered in Jutish. 'I understand you not.' Whitcomb threw him a glance and then subsided, ready to follow the American's lead. Everard's mind raced; under the brassiness of desperation, he knew that death waited for his first mistake. 'In our day we talked thus ...' And he reeled off a paragraph of Mexican-Spanish chatter, garbling it as much as he dared.

'So ... a Latin tongue!' Stane's eyes glittered. The blaster shook in his hand. '*When* be you from?'

'The twentieth century after Christ, and our land hight Lyonesse. It lies across the western ocean –'

'America!' It was a gasp. 'Was it ever called America?'

'No. I wot not what you speak of.'

Stane shuddered uncontrollably. Mastering himself: 'Know you the Roman tongue?'

Everard nodded.

Stane laughed nervously. 'Then let us speak that. If you know how sick I am of this local hog-language ...' His Latin was a little broken, obviously he had picked it up in this century, but fluent enough. He waved the blaster. 'Pardon my discourtesy. But I have to be careful.'

'Naturally,' said Everard. 'Ah ... my name is Mencius, and my friend is Iuvenalis. We came from the future, as you have guessed; we are historians, and time travel has just been invented.'

'Properly speaking, I am Rozher Schtein, from the year 2987. Have you ... heard of me?'

'Who else?' said Everard. 'We came back looking for this mysterious Stane who seemed to be one of the crucial figures of history. We suspected he might have been a time traveler, *peregrinator temporis*, that is. Now we know.'

'Three years,' Schtein began pacing feverishly, the blaster swinging in his hand; but he was too far off for a sudden leap. 'Three years I have been here. If you knew how often I have lain awake, wondering if I would succeed ... Tell me, is your world united?'

'The world and the planets,' said Everard. 'They have been for a long time.'

Inwardly, he shivered. His life hung on his ability to guess what Schtein's plans were.

'And you are a free people?'

'We are. That is to say, the Emperor presides, but the Senate makes the laws and it is elected by the people.'

There was an almost holy look on the gnomish face, transfiguring it. 'As I dreamed,' whispered Schtein. 'Thank you.'

'So you came back from your period to … create history?'

'No,' said Schtein. 'To change it.'

Words tumbled out of him, as if he had wished to speak and dared not for many years: 'I was a historian too. By chance I met a man who claimed to be a merchant from the Saturnian moons, but since I had lived there once, I saw through the fraud. Investigating, I learned the truth. He was a time traveler from the very far future.

'You must understand, the age I lived in was a terrible one, and as a psychographic historian I realized that the war, poverty, and tyranny which cursed us were not due to any innate evil in man, but to simple cause and effect. Machine technology had risen in a world divided against itself, and war grew to be an ever larger and more destructive enterprise. There had been periods of peace, even fairly long ones; but the disease was too deep-rooted, conflict was a part of our very civilization. My family had been wiped out in a Venusian raid, I had nothing to lose. I took the time machine after … disposing … of its owner.

'The great mistake, I thought, had been made back in the Dark Ages. Rome had united a vast empire in peace, and out of peace justice can always arise. But Rome exhausted herself in the effort, and was now falling apart. The barbarians coming in were vigorous, they could do much, but they were quickly corrupted.

'But here is England. It has been isolated from the rotting fabric of Roman society. The Germanics are entering, filthy oafs but strong and willing to learn. In my history, they simply wiped out British civilization and then, being intellectually helpless, were swallowed up by the new – and evil – civilization called Western. I want to see something better happen.

'It hasn't been easy. You would be surprised how hard it is to survive in a different age until you know your way around, even if you have modern weapons and interesting gifts for the king. But I have Hengist's respect now, and increasingly more of the confidence of the Britons. I can unite the two peoples in a mutual war on the Picts. England will be one kingdom, with Saxon strength and Roman learning, powerful enough to stand off all invaders. Christianity is inevitable, of course, but I will see to it that it is the right kind of Christianity, one which will educate and civilize men without shackling their minds.

'Eventually England will be in a position to start taking over on the Continent. Finally, one world. I will stay here long enough to get the anti-Pictish union started, then vanish with a promise to return later. If I reappear at, say, fifty-year intervals for the next several centuries, I will be a legend, a god, who can make sure they stay on the right track.'

'I have read much about St Stanius,' said Everard slowly.

'And I won!' cried Schtein. 'I gave peace to the world.' Tears were on his cheeks.

Everard moved closer. Schtein pointed the blast-ray at his belly, not yet quite trusting him. Everard circled casually, and Schtein swiveled to keep him covered. But the man was too agitated by the seeming proof of his own success to remember Whitcomb. Everard threw a look over his shoulder at the Englishman.

Whitcomb hurled his ax. Everard dove for the floor. Schtein screamed, and the blast-ray sizzled. The ax had cloven his shoulder. Whitcomb sprang, getting a grip on his gun hand. Schtein howled, struggling to force the blaster around. Everard jumped up to help. There was a moment of confusion.

Then the blaster went off again and Schtein was suddenly a dead weight in their arms. Blood drenched their coats from the hideous opening in his chest.

The two guards came running in. Everard snatched his stunner off the floor and thumbed the ratchet up to full intensity. A flung spear grazed his arm. He fired twice, and the burly forms crashed. They'd be out for hours.

Crouching a moment, Everard listened. A feminine scream sounded from the inner chambers, but no one was entering at the door. 'I guess we've carried it off,' he panted.

'Yes.' Whitcomb looked dully at the corpse sprawled before him. It seemed pathetically small.

'I didn't mean for him to die,' said Everard. 'But time is ... tough. It was written, I suppose.'

'Better this way than a Patrol court and the exile planet,' said Whitcomb.

'Technically, at least, he was a thief and a murderer,' said Everard. 'But it was a great dream he had.'

'And we upset it.'

'History might have upset it. Probably would have. One man just isn't powerful enough, or wise enough. I think most human misery is due to well-meaning fanatics like him.'

'So we just fold our hands and take what comes.'

'Think of all your friends, up in 1947. They'd never even have existed.'

Whitcomb took off his cloak and tried to wipe the blood from his clothes.

'Let's get going,' said Everard. He trotted through the rear portal. A frightened concubine watched him with large eyes.

He had to blast the lock off an inner door. The room beyond held an Ing-model time shuttle, a few boxes with weapons and supplies, some books.

Everard loaded it all into the machine except the fuel chest. That had to be left, so that up in the future he would learn of this and come back to stop the man who would be God.

'Suppose you take this to the warehouse in 1894,' he said. 'I'll ride our hopper back and meet you at the office.'

Whitcomb gave him a long stare. The man's face was drawn. Even as Everard watched him, it stiffened with resolution.

'All right, old chap,' said the Englishman. He smiled, almost wistfully, and clasped Everard's hand. 'So long. Good luck.'

Everard stared after him as he entered the great steel cylinder. That was an odd thing to say, when they'd be having tea up in 1894 in a couple of hours.

Worry nagged him as he went out of the building and mingled with the crowd. Charlie was a peculiar cuss. Well ...

No one interfered with him as he left the city and entered the thicket beyond. He called the time hopper back down and, in spite of the need for haste lest someone come to see what kind of bird had landed, cracked a jug of ale. He needed it badly. Then he took a last look at Old England and jumped up to 1894.

Mainwethering and his guards were there as promised. The officer looked alarmed at the sight of one man arriving with blood clotting across his garments, but Everard gave him a reassuring report.

It took a while to wash up, change clothes, and deliver a full account to the secretary. By then, Whitcomb should have arrived in a hansom, but there was no sign of him. Mainwethering called the warehouse on the radio, and turned back with a frown. 'He hasn't come yet,' he said. 'Could something have gone wrong?'

'Hardly. Those machines are foolproof.' Everard gnawed his lip. 'I don't know what the matter is. Maybe he misunderstood and went up to 1947 instead.'

An exchange of notes revealed that Whitcomb had not reported in at that end either. Everard and Mainwethering went out for their tea. There was still no trace of Whitcomb when they got back.

'I had best inform the field agency,' said Mainwethering. 'Eh, what? They should be able to find him.'

'No. Wait.' Everard stood for a moment, thinking. The idea had been germinating in him for some time. It was dreadful.

'Have you a notion?'

'Yes. Sort of.' Everard began shucking his Victorian suit. His hands trembled. 'Get my twentieth-century clothes, will you? I may be able to find him by myself.'

'The Patrol will want a preliminary report of your idea and intentions,' reminded Mainwethering.

'To hell with the Patrol,' said Everard.

6

London, 1944. The early winter night had fallen, and a thin cold wind blew down streets which were gulfs of darkness. Somewhere came the *crump* of an explosion, and a fire was burning, great red banners flapping above the roofs.

Everard left his hopper on the sidewalk – nobody was out when the V-bombs were falling – and groped slowly through the murk. November seventeenth; his trained memory had called up the date for him. Mary Nelson had died this day.

He found a public phone booth on the corner and looked in the directory. There were a lot of Nelsons, but only one Mary listed for the Streatham area. That would be the mother, of course. He had to guess that the daughter would have the same first name. Nor did he know the time at which the bomb had struck, but there were ways to learn that.

Fire and thunder roared at him as he came out. He flung himself on his belly while glass whistled where he had been. 17 November 1944. The younger Manse Everard, lieutenant in the United States Army Engineers, was somewhere across the Channel, near the German guns. He couldn't recall exactly where, just then, and did not stop to make the effort. It didn't matter. He knew he was going to survive *that* danger.

The new blaze was a-dance behind him as he ran for his machine. He jumped aboard and took off into the air. High above London, he saw only a vast darkness spotted with flame. *Walpurgisnacht*, and all hell let loose on earth!

He remembered Streatham well, a dreary stretch of brick inhabited by little clerks and greengrocers and mechanics, the very petite bourgeoisie who had stood up and fought the power which conquered Europe to a standstill. There had been a girl living there, back in 1943 … Eventually she married someone else.

Skimming low, he tried to find the address. A volcano erupted not far off. His mount staggered in the air, he almost lost his seat. Hurrying toward the place, he saw a house tumbled and smashed and flaming. It was only three blocks from the Nelson home. He was too late.

No! He checked the time – just 10:30 – and jumped back two hours. It was still night, but the slain house stood solid in the gloom. For a second he wanted to warn those inside. But no. All over the world, people were dying. He was not Schtein, to take history on his shoulders.

He grinned wryly, dismounted, and walked through the gate. He was not a damned Danellian either. He knocked on the door, and it opened. A middle-aged woman looked at him through the murk, and he realized it was odd to see an American in civilian clothes here.

'Excuse me,' he said. 'Do you know Miss Mary Nelson?'

'Why, yes.' Hesitation. 'She lives nearby. She's coming over soon. Are you a friend?'

Everard nodded. 'She sent me here with a message for you, Mrs ... ah ...'

'Enderby.'

'Oh, yes, Mrs Enderby. I'm terribly forgetful. Look, Miss Nelson wanted me to say she's very sorry but she can't come. However, she wants you and your entire family over at 10:30.'

'All of us, sir? But the children –'

'By all means, the children too. Every one of you. She has a very special surprise arranged, something she can only show you then. All of you have to be there.'

'Well ... all right, sir, if she says so.'

'All of you at 10:30, without fail. I'll see you then, Mrs Enderby.' Everard nodded and walked back to the street.

He had done what he could. Next was the Nelson house. He rode his hopper three blocks down, parked it in the gloom of an alley, and walked up to the house. He was guilty too now, as guilty as Schtein. He wondered what the exile planet was like.

There was no sign of the Ing shuttle, and it was too big to conceal. So Charlie hadn't arrived yet. He'd have to play by ear till then.

As he knocked on the door, he wondered what his saving of the Enderby family would mean. Those children would grow up, have children of their own: quite insignificant middle-class Englishmen, no doubt, but somewhere in the centuries to come an important man would be born or fail to be born. Of course, time was not very inflexible. Except in rare cases, the precise ancestry didn't matter, only the broad pool of human genes and human society did. Still, this might be one of those rare cases.

A young woman opened the door for him. She was a pretty little girl, not spectacular but nice looking in her trim uniform. 'Miss Nelson?'

'Yes?'

'My name is Everard. I'm a friend of Charlie Whitcomb. May I come in? I have a rather surprising bit of news for you.'

'I was about to go out,' she said apologetically.

'No, you weren't.' Wrong line; she was stiffening with indignation. 'Sorry. Please, may I explain?'

She led him into a drab and cluttered parlor. 'Won't you sit down, Mr Everard? Please don't talk too loudly. The family are all asleep. They get up early.'

Everard made himself comfortable. Mary perched on the edge of the sofa, watching him with large eyes. He wondered if Wulfnoth and Eadgar were among her ancestors. Yes ... undoubtedly they were, after all these centuries. Maybe Schtein was too.

'Are you in the Air Force?' she asked. 'Is that how you met Charlie?'

'No. I'm in Intelligence, which is the reason for this mufti. May I ask when you last saw him?'

'Oh, weeks ago. He's stationed in France just now. I hope this war will soon be over. So silly of them to keep on when they must know they're finished, isn't it?' She cocked her head curiously. 'But what is this news you have?'

'I'll come to it in a moment.' He began to ramble as much as he dared, talking of conditions across the Channel. It was strange to sit conversing with a ghost. And his conditioning prevented him from telling the truth. He wanted to, but when he tried his tongue froze up on him.

' ... and what it costs to get a bottle of red-ink ordinaire –'

'Please,' she interrupted impatiently. 'Would you mind coming to the point? I do have an engagement for tonight.'

'Oh, sorry. Very sorry, I'm sure. You see, it's this way –'

A knock at the door saved him. 'Excuse me,' she murmured, and went out past the blackout drapes to open it. Everard padded after her.

She stepped back with a small shriek. 'Charlie!'

Whitcomb pressed her to him, heedless of the blood still wet on his Jutish clothes. Everard came into the hall. The Englishman stared with a kind of horror. 'You ...'

He snatched for his stunner, but Everard's was already out. 'Don't be a fool,' said the American. 'I'm your friend. I want to help you. What crazy scheme did you have, anyway?'

'I ... keep her here ... keep her from going to –'

'And do you think *they* haven't got means of spotting you?' Everard slipped into Temporal, the only possible language in Mary's frightened presence. 'When I left Mainwethering, he was getting damn suspicious. Unless we do this right, every unit of the Patrol is going to be alerted. The error will be rectified, probably by killing her. You'll go to exile.'

'I ...' Whitcomb gulped. His face was a mask of fear. 'You ... would you let her go ahead and die?'

'No. But this has to be done more carefully.'

'We'll escape ... find some period away from everything ... go back to the dinosaur age, if we must.'

Mary slipped free of him. Her mouth was pulled open, ready to scream. 'Shut up!' said Everard to her. 'Your life is in danger, and we're trying to save you. If you don't trust me, trust Charlie.'

Turning back to the man, he went on in Temporal: 'Look, fellow, there isn't any place or any time you can hide in. Mary Nelson died tonight. That's history. She wasn't around in 1947. That's history. I've already got myself in Dutch: the family she was going to visit will be out of their home when the

582

bomb hits it. If you try to run away with her, you'll be found. It's pure luck that a Patrol unit hasn't already arrived.'

Whitcomb fought for steadiness. 'Suppose I jump up to 1948 with her. How do you know she hasn't suddenly reappeared in 1948? Maybe that's history too.'

'Man, you *can't*. Try it. Go on, tell her you're going to hop her four years into the future.'

Whitcomb groaned. 'A giveaway – and I'm conditioned –'

'Yeh. You have barely enough latitude to appear this way before her, but talking to her, you'll have to lie out of it because you can't help yourself. Anyway, how would you explain her? If she stays Mary Nelson, she's a deserter from the WAAF If she takes another name, where's her birth certificate, her school record, her ration book, any of those bits of paper these twentieth-century governments worship so devoutly? It's hopeless, son.'

'Then what can we do?'

'Face the Patrol and slug it out. Wait here a minute.' There was a cold calm over Everard, no time to be afraid or to wonder at his own behavior.

Returning to the street, he located his hopper and set it to emerge five years in the future, at high noon in Piccadilly Circus. He slapped down the main switch, saw the machine vanish, and went back inside. Mary was in Whitcomb's arms, shuddering and weeping. The poor, damned babes in the woods!

'Okay.' Everard led them back to the parlor and sat down with his gun ready. 'Now we wait some more.'

It didn't take long. A hopper appeared, with two men in Patrol gray aboard. There were weapons in their hands. Everard cut them down with a low-powered stun beam. 'Help me tie 'em up, Charlie,' he said.

Mary huddled voiceless in a corner.

When the men awoke, Everard stood over them with a bleak smile. 'What are we charged with, boys?' he asked in Temporal.

'I think you know,' said one of the prisoners calmly. 'The main office had us trace you. Checking up next week, we found that you had evacuated a family scheduled to be bombed. Whitcomb's record suggested you had then come here, to help him save this woman who was supposed to die tonight. Better let us go or it will be the worse for you.'

'I have not changed history,' said Everard.

'The Danellians are still up there, aren't they?'

'Yes, of course, but –'

'How did you know the Enderby family was supposed to die?'

'Their house was struck, and they said they had only left it because –'

'Ah, but the point is they did leave it. That's written. Now it's you who wants to change the past.'

'But this woman here –'

'Are you sure there wasn't a Mary Nelson who, let us say, settled in London in 1850 and died of old age about 1900?'

The lean face grinned. 'You're trying hard, aren't you? It won't work. You can't fight the entire Patrol.'

'Can't I, though? I can leave you here to be found by the Enderbys. I've set my hopper to emerge in public at an instant known only to myself. What's that going to do to history?'

'The Patrol will take corrective measures … as you did back in the fifth century.'

'Perhaps! I can make it a lot easier for them, though, if they'll hear my appeal. I want a Danellian.'

'*What?*'

'You heard me,' said Everard. 'If necessary, I'll mount that hopper of yours and ride a million years up. I'll point out to them personally how much simpler it'll be if they give us a break.'

That will not be necessary.

Everard spun around with a gasp. The stunner fell from his hand.

He could not look at the shape which blazed before his eyes. There was a dry sobbing in his throat as he backed away.

Your appeal has been considered, said the soundless voice. *It was known and weighed ages before you were born. But you were still a necessary link in the chain of time. If you had failed tonight, there would not be mercy.*

To us, it was a matter of record that one Charles and Mary Whitcomb lived in Victoria's England. It was also a matter of record that Mary Nelson died with the family she was visiting in 1944, and that Charles Whitcomb had lived a bachelor and finally been killed on active duty with the Patrol. The discrepancy was noted, and as even the smallest paradox is a dangerous weakness in the spacetime fabric, it had to be rectified by eliminating one or the other fact from ever having existed. You have decided which it will be.

Everard knew, somewhere in his shaking brain, that the Patrolmen were suddenly free. He knew that his hopper had been … was being … would be snatched invisibly away the instant it materialized. He knew that history now read: WAAF Mary Nelson missing, presumed killed by bomb near the home of the Enderby family, who had all been at her house when their own was destroyed; Charles Whitcomb disappearing in 1947, presumed accidentally drowned. He knew that Mary was given the truth, conditioned against ever revealing it, and sent back with Charlie to 1850. He knew they would make their middle-class way through life, never feeling quite at home in Victoria's reign, that Charlie would often have wistful thoughts of what he had been in the Patrol … and then turn to his wife and children and decide it had not been such a great sacrifice after all.

That much he knew, and then the Danellian was gone. As the whirling darkness in his head subsided and he looked with clearing eyes at the two Patrolmen, he did not know what his own destiny was.

'Come on,' said the first man. 'Let's get out of here before somebody wakes up. We'll give you a lift back to your year. 1954, isn't it?'

'And then what?' asked Everard.

The Patrolman shrugged. Under his casual manner lay the shock which had seized him in the Danellian's presence. 'Report to your sector chief. You've shown yourself obviously unfit for steady work.'

'So ... just cashiered, huh?'

'You needn't be so dramatic. Did you think this case was the only one of its kind in a million years of Patrol work? There's a regular procedure for it.

'You'll want more training, of course. Your type of personality goes best with Unattached status – any age, any place, wherever and whenever you may be needed. I think you'll like it.'

Everard climbed weakly aboard the hopper. And when he got off again, a decade had passed.

BRAVE TO BE A KING

1

On an evening in mid-twentieth century New York, Manse Everard had changed into a threadbare lounging outfit and was mixing himself a drink. The doorbell interrupted. He swore at it. A tiring several days lay behind him and he wanted no other company than the lost narratives of Dr Watson.

Well, maybe this character could be gotten rid of. He slippered across his apartment and opened the door, his expression mutinous. 'Hello,' he said coldly.

And then, all at once, it was as if he were aboard some early spaceship which had just entered free fall; he stood weightless and helpless in a blaze of stars.

'Oh,' he said. 'I didn't know ... Come in.'

Cynthia Denison paused a moment, looking past him to the bar. He had hung two crossed spears and a horse-plumed helmet from the Achaean Bronze Age over it. They were dark and shining and incredibly beautiful. She tried to speak with steadiness, but failed. 'Could I have a drink, Manse? Right away?'

'Of course.' He clamped his mouth shut and helped her off with her coat. She closed the door and sat down on a Swedish modern couch as clean and functional as the Homeric weapons. Her hands fumbled with her purse, getting out cigarettes. For a time she did not look at him, nor he at her.

'Do you still drink Irish on the rocks?' he asked. His words seemed to come from far away, and his body was awkward among bottles and glasses, forgetting how the Time Patrol had trained it.

'Yes,' she said. 'So you do remember.' Her lighter snapped, unexpectedly loud in the room.

'It's been just a few months,' he said, for lack of other phrases.

'Entropic time. Regular, untampered-with, twenty-four-hours-to-the-day time.' She blew a cloud of smoke and stared at it. 'Not much more than that for me. I've been in now almost continuously since my, my wedding. Just eight and a half months of my personal, biological, lifeline time since Keith and I ... But how long has it been for you, Manse? How many years have you rung up, in how many different epochs, since you were Keith's best man?'

She had always had a rather high and thin voice. It was the only flaw he had ever found in her, unless you counted her being so small – barely five feet. So she could never put much expression into her tones. But he could hear that she was staving off a scream.

He gave her a drink. 'Down the hatch,' he said. 'All of it.' She obeyed, strangling a little. He got her a refill and completed his own Scotch and soda. Then he drew up a chair and took pipe and tobacco from the depths of his moth-eaten smoking jacket. His hands still shook, but so faintly he didn't think she would notice. It had been wise of her not to blurt whatever news she carried; they both needed a chance to get back their control.

Now he even dared to look straight at her. She hadn't changed. Her figure was almost perfect in a delicate way, as the black dress emphasized. Sunlight-colored hair fell to her shoulders; the eyes were blue and enormous, under arched brows, in a tip-tilted face with the lips always just a little parted. She hadn't enough makeup for him to tell for sure if she had cried lately. But she looked very near to it.

Everard became busy filling his pipe. 'Okay, Cyn,' he said. 'Want to tell me?'

She shivered. Finally she got out: 'Keith. He's disappeared.'

'Huh?' Everard sat up straight. 'On a mission?'

'Yes. Where else? Ancient Iran. He went back there and never returned. That was a week ago.' She set her glass down-on the couch arm and twisted her fingers together. 'The Patrol searched, of course. I just heard the results today. They can't find him. They can't even find out what happened to him.'

'Judas,' whispered Everard.

'Keith always … always thought of you as his best friend,' she said frantically. 'You wouldn't believe how often he spoke of you. Honestly, Manse, I know we've neglected you, but you never seemed to be in and …'

'Of course,' he said. 'How childish do you think I am? I was busy. And after all, you two were newly married.'

After I introduced you, that night beneath Mauna Loa and the moon. The Time Patrol doesn't bother with snobbishness. A youngster like Cynthia Cunningham, a mere clerk fresh out of the Academy and Attached to her own century, is quite free to see a ranking veterah … like myself, for instance … as often as they both wish, off duty. There is no reason why he should not use his skill at disguise to take her waltzing in Strauss' Vienna or to the theater in Shakespeare's London – as well as exploring funny little bars in Tom Lehrer's New York or playing tag in the sun and surf of Hawaii a thousand years before the canoe men arrived. And a fellow member of the Patrol is equally free to join them both. And later to marry her. Sure.

Everard got his pipe going. When his face was screened with smoke, he said: 'Begin at the beginning. I've been out of touch with you for – two or three years of my own lifeline time – so I'm not certain precisely what Keith was working on.'

'That long?' she asked wonderingly. 'You never even spent your furloughs in this decade? We did want you to come visit us.'

'Quit apologizing!' he snapped. 'I could have dropped in if I'd wished.' The elfin face looked as if he had slapped it. He backed up, appalled. 'I'm sorry. Naturally I wanted to. But as I said ... we Unattached agents are so damned busy, hopping around in all space-time like fleas on a griddle ... Oh, hell,' he tried to smile, 'you know me, Cyn, tactless, but it doesn't mean anything. I originated a chimaera legend all by myself, back in Classic Greece. I was known as the *dilaiopod*, a curious monster with two left feet, both in its mouth.'

She returned a dutiful quirk of lips and picked up her cigarette from the ashtray. 'I'm still just a clerk in Engineering Studies,' she said. 'But it puts me in close contact with all the other offices in this entire milieu, including headquarters. So I know exactly what's been done about Keith ... and it isn't enough! They're just abandoning him! Manse, if you won't help him Keith is dead!'

She stopped, shakily. To give them both a little more time, Everard reviewed the career of Keith Denison.

Born Cambridge, Mass, 1927, to a moderately wealthy family. PhD in archeology with a distinguished thesis at the age of twenty-three, after having also taken a collegiate boxing championship and crossed the Atlantic in a thirty-foot ketch. Drafted in 1950, served in Korea with a bravery which would have earned him some fame in a more popular war. Yet you had to know him quite a while before you learned any of this. He spoke, with a gift of dry humor, about impersonal things, until there was work to be done. Then, without needless fuss, he did it. *Sure*, thought Everard, *the best man got the girl. Keith could've made Unattached easily, if he'd cared to. But he had roots here that I didn't. More stable, I guess.*

Discharged and at loose ends in 1952, Denison was contacted by a Patrol agent and recruited. He had accepted the fact of time travel more readily than most. His mind was supple and, after all, he was an archeologist. Once trained, he found a happy coincidence of his own interests and the needs of the Patrol; he became a Specialist, East Indo-European Protohistory, and in many ways a more important man than Everard.

For the Unattached officer might rove up and down the time lanes, rescuing the distressed and arresting the lawbreaker and keeping the fabric of human destiny secure. But how could he tell what he was doing without a record? Ages before the first hieroglyphics there had been wars and wanderings, discoveries and achievements, whose consequences reached through all the continuum. The Patrol had to know them. Charting their course was a job for the Specialist ratings.

Besides all of which, Keith was a friend of mine.

Everard took the pipe from his mouth. 'Okay, Cynthia,' he said. 'Tell me what did happen.'

2

The little voice was almost dry now, so rigidly had she harnessed herself. 'He was tracing the migrations of the different Aryan clans. They're very obscure, you know. You have to start at a point when the history is known for certain, and work backward. So on this last job, Keith was going to Iran in the year 558 BC. That was near the close of the Median period, he said. He'd make inquiries among the people, learn their own traditions, and then afterward check back at a still earlier point, and so on … But you must know all about this, Manse. You helped him once, before we met. He often spoke about that.'

'Oh, I just went along in case of trouble,' shrugged Everard. 'He was studying the prehistoric trek of a certain band from the Don over the Hindu Kush. We told their chief we were passing hunters, claimed hospitality, and accompanied the wagon train for a few weeks. It was fun.'

He remembered steppes and enormous skies, a windy gallop after antelope and a feast by campfires and a certain girl whose hair had held the bittersweet of woodsmoke. For a while he wished he could have lived and died as one of those tribesmen.

'Keith went back alone this time,' continued Cynthia. 'They're always so shorthanded in his branch, in the entire Patrol, I suppose. So many thousands of years to watch and so few man-life-times to do it with. He'd gone alone before. I was always afraid to let him, but he said … dressed as a wandering shepherd with nothing worth stealing … he'd be safer in the Iranian highlands than crossing Broadway. Only this time he wasn't!'

'I take it, then,' said Everard quickly, 'he left – a week ago, did you say? – intending to get his information, report it to the clearinghouse of his specialty, and come back to the same day here as he'd left you.' *Because only a blind buckethead would let more of your lifespan pass without being there himself.* 'But he didn't.'

'Yes.' She lit another cigarette from the butt of the first. 'I got worried right away. I asked the boss about it. He obliged me by querying himself a week ahead – today – and got the answer that Keith had not returned. The information clearing-house said he never came to them. So we checked with Records in milieu headquarters. Their answer was … was … Keith never did come back and no trace of him was ever found.'

Everard nodded with great care. 'Then, of course, the search was ordered which MHQ has a record of.'

Mutable time made for a lot of paradoxes, he reflected for the thousandth occasion.

In the case of a missing man, you were not required to search for him just because a record somewhere said you had done so. But how else would you stand a chance of finding him? You *might* possibly go back and thereby change events so that you did find him after all – in which case the report you filed would 'always' have recorded your success, and you alone would know the 'former' truth.

It could get very messed up. No wonder the Patrol was fussy, even about small changes which would not affect the main pattern.

'Our office notified the boys in the Old Iranian milieu, who sent a party to investigate the spot,' foretold Everard. 'They only knew the approximate site at which Keith had intended to materialize, didn't they? I mean, since he couldn't know exactly where he'd be able to hide the scooter, he didn't file precise coordinates.' Cynthia nodded. 'But what I don't understand is, why didn't they find the machine afterward? Whatever happened to Keith, the scooter would still be somewhere around, in some cave or whatever. The Patrol has detectors. They should have been able to track down the scooter, at least, and then work backwards from it to locate Keith.'

She drew on her cigarette with a violence that caved in her cheeks. 'They tried,' she said. 'But I'm told it's a wild, rugged country, hard to search. Nothing turned up. They couldn't find a trace. They might have, if they'd looked very, very hard – made a mile-by-mile, hour-by-hour search. But they didn't dare. You see, that particular milieu is critical. Mr Gordon showed me the analysis. I couldn't follow all those symbols, but he said it was a very dangerous century to tamper with.'

Everard closed one large hand on the bowl of his pipe. Its warmth was somehow comforting. Critical eras gave him the willies.

'I see,' he said. 'They couldn't search as thoroughly as they wanted, because it might disturb too many of the local yokels, which might make them act differently when the big crisis came. Uh-huh. But how about making inquiries in disguise, among the people?'

'Several Patrol experts did. They tried that for weeks, Persian time. And the natives never even gave them a hint. Those tribes are so wild and suspicious ... maybe they feared our agents were spies from the Median king, I understand they didn't like his rule ... No. The Patrol couldn't find a trace. And anyhow, there's no reason to think the pattern was affected. They believe Keith was murdered and his scooter vanished somehow. And what difference –' Cynthia sprang to her feet. Suddenly she yelled – 'What difference does one more skeleton in one more gully make?'

Everard rose too, she came into his arms and he let her have it out. For himself, he had never thought it would be this bad. He had stopped remembering her, except maybe ten times a day, but now she came to him and the forgetting would have to be done all over again.

'Can't they go back locally?' she pleaded. 'Can't somebody hop back a week from now, just to tell him not to go, is that so much to ask? What kind of monsters made that law against it?'

'Ordinary men did,' said Everard. 'If we once started doubling back to tinker with our personal pasts, we'd soon get so tangled up that none of us would exist.'

'But in a million years or more – there must be exceptions!'

Everard didn't answer. He knew that there were. He knew also that Keith Denison's case wouldn't be one of them. The Patrol was not staffed by saints, but its people dared not corrupt their own law for their own ends. You took your losses like any other corps, and raised a glass to the memory of your dead, and you did not travel back to look upon them again while they had lived.

Presently Cynthia left him, returned to her drink and tossed it down. The yellow locks swirled past her face as she did. 'I'm sorry,' she said. She got out a handkerchief and wiped her eyes. 'I didn't mean to bawl.'

'It's okay.'

She stared at the floor. 'You could try to help Keith. The regular agents have given up, but you could try.'

It was an appeal from which he had no recourse. 'I could,' he told her. 'I might not succeed. The existing records show that, if I tried, I failed. And any alteration of space-time is frowned on, even a trivial one like this.'

'It isn't trivial to Keith,' she said.

'You know, Cyn,' he murmured, 'you're one of the few women that ever lived who'd have phrased it that way. Most would have said, It isn't trivial to me.'

Her eyes captured his, and for a moment she stood very quiet. Then, whispering:

'I'm sorry, Manse. I didn't realize … I thought, what with all the time that's gone past for you, you would have –'

'What are you talking about?' he defended himself.

'Can't the Patrol psychs do anything for you?' she asked. Her head drooped again. 'I mean, if they can condition us so we just simply can't tell anyone unauthorized that time travel exists … I should think it would also be possible to, to condition a person out of –'

'Skip it,' said Everard roughly.

He gnawed his pipestem a while. 'Okay,' he said at last. 'I've an idea or two of my own that may not have been tried. If Keith can be rescued in any way, you'll get him back before tomorrow noon.'

'Could you time-hop me up to that moment, Manse?' She was beginning to tremble.

'I could,' he said, 'but I won't. One way or another, you'll need to be rested tomorrow. I'll take you home now and see that you swallow a sleepy pill. And then I'll come back here and think about the situation.' He twisted his mouth into a sort of grin. 'Cut out that shimmy, huh? I told you I had to think.'

'Manse ...' Her hands closed about his.

He knew a sudden hope for which he cursed himself.

3

In the fall of the year 542 BC, a solitary man came down out of the mountains and into the valley of the Kur. He rode a handsome chestnut gelding, bigger even than most cavalry horses, which might elsewhere have been an invitation to bandits; but the Great King had given so much law to his dominions that it was said a virgin with a sack of gold could walk unmolested across all Persia. It was one reason Manse Everard had chosen to hop to this date, sixteen years after Keith Denison's destination.

Another motive was to arrive long after any excitement which the time traveler had conceivably produced in 558 had died away. Whatever the truth about Keith's fate, it might be more approachable from the rear; at least, straightforward methods had failed.

Finally, according to the Achaemenid Milieu office, autumn 542 happened to be the first season of relative tranquility since the disappearance. The years 558–553 had been tense ones when the Persian king of Anshan, Kuru-sh (he whom the future knew as Koresh and Cyrus), was more and more at odds with his Median overlord Astyages. Then came three years when Cyrus revolted, civil war racked the empire, and the Persians finally overcame their northerly neighbors. But Cyrus was scarcely victorious before he must face counteruprisings, as well as Turanian incursions; he spent four years putting down that trouble and extending his rule eastward. This alarmed his fellow monarchs: Babylon, Egypt, Lydia, and Sparta formed a coalition to destroy him, with King Croesus of Lydia leading an invasion in 546. The Lydians were broken and annexed, but they revolted and had to be broken all over again; the troublesome Greek colonies of Ionia, Caria, and Lycia must be settled with; and while his generals did all this in the west, Cyrus himself must war in the east, forcing back the savage horsemen who would otherwise burn his cities.

Now there was a breathing spell. Cilicia would yield without a fight, seeing that Persia's other conquests were governed with a humanity and a tolerance of local custom such as the world had not known before. Cyrus would leave the eastern marches to his nobles, and devote himself to consolidating what he had won. Not until 539 would the war with Babylon be taken up again and Mesopotamia acquired. And then Cyrus would have another time of peace, until the wild men grew too strong beyond the Aral Sea and the King rode forth against them to his death.

Manse Everard entered Pasargadae as if into a springtime of hope.

Not that any actual era lends itself to such flowery metaphors. He jogged through miles where peasants bent with sickles, loading creaky unpainted oxcarts, and dust smoked off the stubble fields into his eyes. Ragged children sucked their thumbs outside windowless mud huts and stared at him. A chicken squawked back and forth on the highway until the galloping royal messenger who had alarmed it was past and the chicken dead. A squad of lancers trotting by were costumed picturesquely enough, baggy pants and scaly armor, spiked or plumed helmets, gaily striped cloaks; but they were also dusty, sweaty, and swapping foul jokes. Behind adobe walls the aristocrats possessed large houses with very beautiful gardens, but an economy like this would not support many such estates. Pasargadae was 90 percent an Oriental town of twisted slimy streets between faceless hovels, greasy headcloths and dingy robes, screaming merchants in the bazaars, beggars displaying their sores, traders leading strings of battered camels and overloaded donkeys, dogs raiding offal heaps, tavern music like a cat in a washing machine, men who windmilled their arms and screamed curses – what ever started this yarn about the inscrutable East?

'Alms, lord. Alms, for the love of Light! Alms, and Mithras will smile upon you! ...'

'Behold, sir! By my father's beard I swear that never was there finer work from a more skilled hand than this bridle which I offer to you, most fortunate of men, for the ridiculous sum of ...'

'This way, master, this way, only four houses down to the finest sarai in all Persia – no, in all the world. Our pallets are stuffed with swan's down, my father serves wine fit for a Devi, my mother cooks a pilau whose fame has spread to the ends of the earth, and my sisters are three moons of delight available for a mere ...'

Everard ignored the childish runners who clamored at his sides. One of them tugged his ankle, he swore and kicked and the boy grinned without shame. The man hoped to avoid staying at an inn; the Persians were cleaner than most folk in this age, but there would still be insect life.

He tried not to feel defenseless. Ordinarily a Patrolman could have an ace in the hole: say, a thirtieth-century stun pistol beneath his coat and a midget radio to call the hidden space-time anti-gravity scooter to him. But not when he might be frisked. Everard wore a Greek outfit; tunic and sandals and long wool cloak, sword at waist, helmet and shield hung at the horse's crupper, and that was it; only the steel was anachronistic. He could turn to no local branch office if he got into trouble, for this relatively poor and turbulent transition epoch attracted no Temporal commerce; the nearest Patrol unit was milieu HQ in Persepolis, a generation futureward.

The streets widened as he pushed on, bazaars thinned out and houses grew larger. At last he emerged in a square enclosed by four mansions. He could see pruned trees above their outer walls. Guards, lean lightly armed youths, squatted beneath on their heels because standing at attention had not yet been invented. But they rose, nocking wary arrows, as Everard approached. He might simply have crossed the plaza, but he veered and hailed a fellow who looked like a captain.

'Greetings, sir, may the sun fall bright upon you.' The Persian which he had learned in an hour under hypno flowed readily off his tongue. 'I seek hospitality from some great man who may care to hear my poor tales of foreign travel.'

'May your days be many,' said the guard. Everard remembered that he must not offer baksheesh: these Persians of Cyrus's own clans were a proud hardy folk, hunters, herdsmen, and warriors. All spoke with the dignified politeness common to their type throughout history. 'I serve Croesus the Lydian, servant of the Great King. He will not refuse his roof to –'

'Meander from Athens,' supplied Everard. It was an alias which would explain his large bones, light complexion, and short hair. He had, though, been forced to stick a realistic Van Dyke effect on his chin. Herodotus was not the first Greek globetrotter, so an Athenian would not be inconveniently outre. At the same time, half a century before Marathon, Europeans were still uncommon enough here to excite interest.

A slave was called, who got hold of the majordomo, who sent another slave, who invited the stranger through the gate. The garden beyond was as cool and green as hoped; there was no fear that anything would be stolen from his baggage in this household; the food and drink should be good; and Croesus himself would certainly interview the guest at length. *We're playing in luck, lad*, Everard assured himself, and accepted a hot bath, fragrant oils, fresh clothing, dates and wine brought to his austerely furnished room, a couch and a pleasant view. He only missed a cigar.

Of attainable things, that is.

To be sure, if Keith had unamendably died ...

'Hell and purple frogs,' muttered Everard. 'Cut that out, will you?'

4

After sunset it grew chilly. Lamps were lit with much ceremony, fire being sacred, and braziers were blown up. A slave prostrated himself to announce that dinner was served. Everard accompanied him down a long hall where vigorous murals showed the Sun and the Bull of Mithras, past a couple of spearmen, and into a small chamber brightly lit, sweet with incense and lavish with carpeting. Two couches were drawn up in the Hellenic manner at a table covered with un-Hellenic dishes of silver and gold; slave waiters hovered in the background and Chinese-sounding music twanged from an inner door.

Croesus of Lydia nodded graciously. He had been handsome once, with regular features, but seemed to have aged a lot in the few years since his wealth and power were proverbial. Grizzled of beard and with long hair, he was dressed in a Grecian chlamys but wore rouge in the Persian manner. 'Rejoice, Meander of Athens,' he said in Greek, and lifted his face.

Everard kissed his cheek as indicated. It was nice of Croesus thus to imply that Meander's rank was but little inferior to his own, even if Croesus had been eating garlic. 'Rejoice, master. I thank you for your kindness.'

'This solitary meal was not to demean you,' said the ex-king. 'I only thought ...' He hesitated. 'I have always considered myself near kin to the Greeks, and we could talk seriously –'

'My lord honors me beyond my worth.' They went through various rituals and finally got to the food. Everard spun out a prepared yarn about his travels; now and then Croesus would ask a disconcertingly sharp question, but a Patrolman soon learned how to evade that kind.

'Indeed times are changing, you are fortunate in coming at the very dawn of a new age,' said Croesus. 'Never has the world known a more glorious King than,' etc., etc., doubtless for the benefit of any retainers who doubled as royal spies. Though it happened to be true.

'The very gods have favored our King,' went on Croesus. 'Had I known how they sheltered him – for truth, I mean, not for the mere fable which I believed it was – I should never have dared oppose myself to him. For it cannot be doubted, he is a Chosen One.'

Everard maintained his Greek character by watering the wine and wishing he had picked some less temperature nationality. 'What is that tale, my lord?' he asked. 'I knew only that the Great King was the son of Cambyses, who held this province as a vassal of Median Astyages. Is there more?'

Croesus leaned forward. In the uncertain light, his eyes held a curious bright look, a Dionysian blend of terror and enthusiasm which Everard's age had long forgotten. 'Hear, and bring the account to your countrymen,' he said. 'Astyages wed his daughter Mandane to Cambyses, for he knew that the Persians were restless under his own heavy yoke and he wished to tie their leaders to his house. But Cambyses became ill and weak. If he died and his infant son Cyrus succeeded in Anshan, there would be a troublesome regency of Persian nobles not bound to Astyages. Dreams also warned the Median king that Cyrus would be the death of his dominion.

'Thereafter Astyages ordered his kinsman, the King's Eye Aurvagaush [Croesus rendered the name Harpagus, as he Hellenized all local names], to do away with the prince. Harpagus took the child despite Queen Mandane's protests; Cambyses lay too sick to help her, nor could Persia in any case revolt without preparation. But Harpagus could not bring himself to the deed. He exchanged the prince for the stillborn child of a herdsman in the mountains, whom he swore to secrecy. The dead baby was wrapped in royal clothes and left on a hillside; presently officials of the Median court were summoned to witness that it had been exposed, and buried it. Our lord Cyrus grew up as a herdsman.

'Cambyses lived for twenty years more without begetting other sons, not strong enough in his own person to avenge the first-born. But at last he was plainly dying, with no successor whom the Persians would feel obliged to obey. Again Astyages feared trouble. At this time Cyrus came forth, his identity being made known through various signs. Astyages, regretting what had gone before, welcomed him and confirmed him as Cambyses' heir.

'Cyrus remained a vassal for five years, but found the tyranny of the Medes ever more odious. Harpagus in Ecbatana had also a dreadful thing to avenge: as punishment for his disobedience in the matter of Cyrus, Astyages made Harpagus eat his own son. So Harpagus conspired with certain Median nobles. They chose Cyrus as their leader, Persia revolted, and after three years of war Cyrus made himself the master of the two peoples. Since then, of course, he has added many others. When ever did the gods show their will more plainly?'

Everard lay quiet on the couch for a little. He heard autumn leaves rustle dryly in the garden, under a cold wind.

'This is true, and no fanciful gossip?' he asked.

'I have confirmed it often enough since I joined the Persian court. The King himself has vouched for it to me, as well as Harpagus and others who were directly concerned.'

The Lydian could not be lying if he cited his ruler's testimony: the upper-class Persians were fanatics about truthfulness. And yet Everard had heard nothing so incredible in all his Patrol career. For it was the story which Herodotus recorded – with a few modifications to be found in the *Shah Nameh* – and anybody could spot that as a typical hero myth. Essentially the same yarn had been told about Moses, Romulus, Sigurd, a hundred great men. There was no reason to believe it held any fact, no reason to doubt that Cyrus had been raised in a perfectly normal manner at his father's house, had succeeded by plain right of birth and revolted for the usual reasons.

Only, this tall tale was sworn to by eyewitnesses!

There was a mystery here. It brought Everard back to his purpose. After appropriate marveling remarks, he led the conversation until he could say: 'I have heard rumors that sixteen years ago a stranger entered Pasargadae, clad as a poor shepherd but in truth a mage who did miracles. He may have died here. Does my gracious host know anything of it?'

He waited then, tensed. He was playing a hunch, that Keith Denison had not been murdered by some hillbilly, fallen off a cliff and broken his neck, or come to grief in any such way. Because in that case, the scooter should still have been around when the Patrol searched. They might have gridded the area too loosely to find Denison himself, but how could their detectors miss a time hopper?

So, Everard thought, something more complicated had happened. And if Keith survived at all, he would have come down here to civilization.

'Sixteen years ago?' Croesus tugged his beard. 'I was not here then. And surely in any case the land would have been full of portents, for that was when Cyrus left the mountains and took his rightful crown of Anshan. No, Meander, I know nothing of it.'

'I have been anxious to find this person,' said Everard, 'because an oracle,' etc., etc.

'You can inquire among the servants and townspeople,' suggested Croesus. 'I will ask at court on your behalf. You will stay here awhile, will you not? Perhaps the King himself will wish to see you; he is always interested in foreigners.'

The conversation broke up soon after. Croesus explained with a rather sour smile that the Persians believed in early to bed, early to rise, and he must be at the royal palace by dawn. A slave conducted Everard back to his room, where he found a good-looking girl waiting with an expectant smile. He hesitated a moment, remembering a time twenty-four hundred years hence. But – the hell with that. A man had to take whatever the gods offered him, and they were a miserly lot.

5

It was not long after sunrise when a troop reined up in the plaza and shouted for Meander the Athenian. Everard left his breakfast to go out and stare up a gray stallion into the hard, hairy hawk-face of a captain of those guards called the Immortals. The men made a backdrop of restless horses, cloaks and plumes blowing, metal jingling and leather squeaking, the young sun ablaze on polished mail.

'You are summoned by the Chiliarch,' rapped the officer. The title he actually used was Persian: commander of the guard and grand vizier of the empire.

Everard stood for a moment, weighing the situation. His muscles tightened. This was not a very cordial invitation. But he could scarcely plead a previous engagement.

'I hear and obey,' he said. 'Let me but fetch a small gift from my baggage, in token of the honor paid me.'

'The Chiliarch said you were to come at once. Here is a horse.'

An archer sentry offered cupped hands, but Everard pulled himself into the saddle without help, a trick it was useful to know in eras before stirrups were introduced. The captain nodded a harsh approval, whirled his mount, and led at a gallop off the plaza and up a wide avenue lined with sphinxes and the homes of the great. This was not as heavily trafficked as the bazaar streets, but there were enough riders, chariots, litters, and pedestrians scrambling out of the way. The Immortals stopped for no man. They roared through palace gates flung open before them. Gravel spurted under hoofs, they tore around a lawn where fountains sparkled, and clanged to a stop outside the west wing.

The palace, gaudily painted brick, stood on a wide platform with several lesser buildings. The captain himself sprang down, gestured curtly, and strode up a marble staircase. Everard followed, hemmed in by warriors who had taken the light battle axes from their saddlebows for his benefit. The party went among household slaves, robed and turbaned and flat on their faces, through a red and yellow colonnade, down a mosaic hall whose beauty Everard was in no mood to appreciate, and so past a squad of guards into a room where slender columns upheld a peacock dome and the fragrance of late-blooming roses entered through arched windows.

There the Immortals made obeisance. *What's good enough for them is good enough for you, son*, thought Everard, and kissed the Persian carpet. The man on the couch nodded. 'Rise and attend,' he said. 'Fetch a cushion for the Greek.' The soldiers took their stance by him. A Nubian bustled forth with a pillow, which he laid on the floor beneath his master's seat. Everard sat down on it, cross-legged. His mouth felt dry.

The Chiliarch, whom he remembered Croesus identifying as Harpagus, leaned forward. Against the tiger skin on the couch and the gorgeous red robe on his own gaunt frame, the Mede showed as an aging man, his shoulder-length hair the color of iron and his dark craggy-nosed face sunken into a mesh of wrinkles. But shrewd eyes considered the newcomer.

'Well,' he said, his Persian having the rough accent of a North Iranian, 'so you are the man from Athens. The noble Croesus spoke of your advent this morning and mentioned some inquiries you were making. Since the safety of the state may be involved, I would know just what it is you seek.' He stroked his beard with a jewel-flashing hand and smiled frostily. 'It may even be, if your search is harmless, that I can help it.'

He had been careful not to employ the usual formulas of greeting, to offer refreshment, or otherwise give Meander the quasi-sacred status of guest. This was an interrogation. 'Lord, what is it you wish to know?' asked Everard. He could well imagine, and it was a troublous anticipation.

'You sought a mage in shepherd guise, who entered Pasargadae sixteen summers ago and did miracles.' The voice was ugly with tension. 'Why is this and what more have you heard of such matters? Do not pause to invent a lie – speak!'

'Great lord,' said Everard, 'the oracle at Delphi told me I should mend my fortunes if I learned the fate of a herdsman who entered the Persian capital in, er, the third year of the first tyranny of Pisistratus. More than that I have never known. My lord is aware how dark are the oracular sayings.'

'Hm, hm.' Fear touched the lean countenance and Harpagus drew the sign of the cross, which was a Mithraic sun-symbol. Then, roughly: 'What have you discovered so far?'

'Nothing, great lord. No one could tell –'

'You lie!' snarled Harpagus. 'All Greeks are liars. Have a care, for you touch on unholy matters. Who else have you spoken to?'

Everard saw a nervous tic lift the Chiliarch's mouth. His own stomach was a cold jump in him. He had stumbled on something which Harpagus had thought safely buried, something so big that the risk of a clash with Croesus, who was duty bound to protect a guest, became nothing. And the most reliable gag ever invented was a snickersnee … after rack and pincers had extracted precisely what the stranger knew … *But what the blue hell do I know?*

'None, my lord,' he husked. 'None but the oracle, and the Sun God whose voice the oracle is, and who sent me here, has heard of this before last night.'

Harpagus sucked in a sharp breath, taken aback by the invocation. But then, almost visibly squaring his shoulders: 'We have only your word, the word of a Greek, that you were told by an oracle – that you did not spy out state secrets. Or even if the God did indeed send you here, it may as well have been to destroy you for your sins. We shall ask further about this.' He nodded at the captain. 'Take him below. In the King's name.'

The King!

It blazed upon Everard. He jumped to his feet. 'Yes, the King!' he shouted. 'The God told me … there would be a sign … and then I should bear his word to the Persian King!'

'Seize him!' yelled Harpagus.

The guardsmen whirled to obey. Everard sprang back, yelling for King Cyrus as loudly as he could. Let them arrest him. Word would be carried to the throne and … Two men hemmed him against the wall, their axes raised. Others pressed behind them. Over their helmets, he saw Harpagus leap up on the couch.

'Take him out and behead him!' ordered the Mede.

'My lord,' protested the captain, 'he called upon the King.'

'To cast a spell! I know him now, the son of Zohak and agent of Ahriman! Kill him!'

'No, wait,' cried Everard, 'wait, can you not see, it is this traitor who would keep me from telling the King … Let go, you sod!'

A hand closed on his right arm. He had been prepared to sit a few hours in jail, till the big boss heard of the affair and bailed him out, but matters were a bit more urgent after all. He threw a left hook which ended in a squelching of nose. The guardsman staggered back. Everard plucked the ax from his hand, spun about, and parried the blow of the warrior on his left.

The Immortals attacked. Everard's ax clanged against metal, darted in and smashed a knuckle. He outreached most of these people. But he hadn't a cellophane snowball's chance in hell of standing them off. A blow whistled toward his head. He ducked behind a column; chips flew. An opening – he stiff-armed one man, hopped over the clashing mailclad form as it fell, and got onto open floor under the dome. Harpagus scuttled up, drawing a saber from beneath his robe; the old bastard was brave enough. Everard twirled to meet him, so that the Chiliarch was between him and the guards. Ax and sword rattled together. Everard tried to close in … a clinch would keep the Persians from throwing their weapons at him, but they were circling to get at his rear. Judas, this might be the end of one more Patrolman …

'Halt! Fall on your faces! The King comes!'

Three times it was blared. The guardsmen froze in their tracks, stared at the gigantic scarlet-robed person who stood bellowing in the doorway, and hit the rug. Harpagus dropped his sword. Everard almost brained him; then, remembering, and hearing the hurried tramp of warriors in the hall, let go his own weapon. For a moment he and the Chiliarch panted into each other's faces.

'So … he got word … and came … at once,' gasped Everard.

The Mede crouched like a cat and hissed back: 'Have a care, then! I will be watching you. If you poison his mind there will be poison for you, or a dagger …'

'The King! The King!' bellowed the herald.

Everard joined Harpagus on the floor.

A band of Immortals trotted into the room and made an alley to the couch. A chamberlain dashed to throw a special tapestry over it. Then Cyrus himself entered, robe billowing around long muscular strides. A few courtiers followed, leathery men privileged to bear arms in the royal presence, and a slave MC wringing his hands in their wake at not having been given time to spread a carpet or summon musicians.

The King's voice rang through the silence: 'What is this? Where is the stranger who called on me?'

Everard risked a peek. Cyrus was tall, broad of shoulder and slim of body, older-looking than Croesus' account suggested – he was forty-seven years old, Everard knew with a shudder – but kept supple by sixteen years of war and the chase. He had a narrow dark countenance with hazel eyes, a sword scar on the left cheekbone, a straight nose and full lips. His black hair, faintly grizzled, was brushed back and his beard trimmed more closely than was Persian custom. He was dressed as plainly as his status allowed.

'Where is the stranger whom the slave ran to tell me of?'

'I am he, Great King,' said Evarard.

'Arise. Declare your name.'

Everard stood up and murmured: 'Hi, Keith.'

6

Vines rioted about a marble pergola. They almost hid the archers who ringed it. Keith Denison slumped on a bench, stared at leaf shadows dappled onto the floor, and said wryly, 'At least we can keep our talk private. The English language hasn't been invented yet.'

After a moment he continued, with a rusty accent: 'Sometimes I've thought that was the hardest thing to take about this situation, never having a minute to myself. The best I can do is throw everybody out of the room I'm in; but they stick around just beyond the door, under the windows, guarding, listening. I hope their dear loyal souls fry.'

'Privacy hasn't been invented yet either,' Everard reminded him. 'And VIP's like you never did have much, in all history.'

Denison raised a tired visage. 'I keep wanting to ask how Cynthia is,' he said, 'but of course for her it has been – will be – not so long. A week, perhaps. Did you by any chance bring some cigarettes?'

'Left 'em in the scooter,' said Everard. 'I figured I'd have trouble enough without explaining that away. I never expected to find you running this whole shebang.'

'I didn't myself.' Denison shrugged. 'It was the damnedest fantastic thing. The time paradoxes –'

'So what did happen?'

Denison rubbed his eyes and sighed. 'I got myself caught in the local gears. You know, sometimes everything that went before seems unreal to me, like a dream. Were there ever such things as Christendom, contrapuntal music, or the Bill of Rights? Not to mention all the people I knew. You yourself don't belong here, Manse, I keep expecting to wake up ... Well, let me think back.

'Do you know what the situation was? The Medes and the Persians are pretty near kin, racially and culturally, but the Medes were top dog then, and they'd picked up a lot of habits from the Assyrians which didn't sit so well in the Persian viewpoint. We're ranchers and freehold farmers, mostly, and of course it isn't right that we should be vassals –' Denison blinked. 'Hey, there I go again! What do I mean "we"? Anyhow, Persia was restless. King Astyages of Media had ordered the murder of little Prince Cyrus twenty years before, but now he regretted it, because Cyrus's father was dying and the dispute over succession could touch off a civil war.

'Well, I appeared in the mountains. I had to scout a little bit in both space and time – hopping through a few days and several miles – to find a good hiding place for my scooter. That's why the Patrol couldn't locate it afterward ... part of the reason. You see, I did finally park it in a cave and set out on foot, but right away I came to grief. A Median army was bound through that region to discourage the Persians from making trouble. One of their scouts saw me emerge, checked my back trail – first thing I knew, I'd been seized and their officer was grilling me about what that gadget was I had in the cave. His men took me for a magician of some kind and were in considerable awe, but more afraid of showing fear than they were of me. Naturally, the word ran like a brushfire through the ranks and across the countryside. Soon all the area knew that a stranger had appeared under remarkable circumstances.

'Their general was Harpagus himself, as smart and tough-minded a devil as the world has ever seen. He thought I could be used. He ordered me to make my brazen horse perform, but I wasn't allowed to mount it. However, I did get a chance to kick it into time-drive. That's why the search party didn't find the thing. It was only a few hours in this century, then it probably went clear back to the Beginning.'

'Good work,' said Everard.

'Oh, I knew the orders forbidding that degree of anachronism.' Denison's lips twisted. 'But I also expected the Patrol to rescue me. If I'd known they wouldn't, I'm not so sure I'd have stayed a good self-sacrificing Patrolman. I might have hung on to my scooter, and played Harpagus' game till a chance came to escape on my own.'

Everard looked at him a moment, somberly. Keith had changed, he thought: not just in age, but the years among aliens had marked him more deeply then he knew. 'If you risked altering the future,' he said, 'you risked Cynthia's existence.'

'Yes. Yes, true. I remember thinking of that ... at the time ... How long ago it seems!'

Denison leaned forward, elbows on knees, staring into the pergola screen. His words continued, flat. 'Harpagus spit rivets, of course. I thought for a while he was going to kill me. I was carried off, trussed up like butcher's meat. But as I told you, there were already rumors about me, which were losing nothing in repetition. Harpagus saw a still better chance. He gave me a choice, string along with him or have my throat cut. What else could I do? It wasn't even a matter of hazarding an alteration; I soon saw I was playing a role which history had *already* written.

'You see, Harpagus bribed a herdsman to support his tale, and produced me as Cyrus, son of Cambyses.'

Everard nodded, unsurprised. 'What's in it for him?' he asked.

'At the time, he only wanted to bolster the Median rule. A king in Anshan under his thumb would have to be loyal to Astyages, and thereby help keep all the Persians in line. I was rushed along, too bewildered to do more than follow his lead, still hoping minute by minute for a Patrol hopper to appear and get me out of the mess. The truth fetish of all these Iranian aristocrats helped us a lot – few of them suspected I perjured myself in swearing I was Cyrus, though I imagine Astyages quietly ignored the discrepancies. And he put Harpagus in his place by punishing him in an especially gruesome way for not having done away with Cyrus as ordered – even if Cyrus turned out to be useful now – and of course the double irony was that Harpagus really had followed orders, two decades before!

'As for me, in the course of five years I got more and more sickened by Astyages myself. Now, looking back, I see he wasn't really such a hound from hell, just a typical Oriental monarch of the ancient world, but that's kind of hard to appreciate when you're forced to watch a man being racked.

'So Harpagus, wanting revenge, engineered a revolt, and I accepted the leadership of it which he offered me.' Denison grinned crookedly. 'After all, I was Cyrus the Great, with a destiny to play out. We had a rough time at first, the Medes clobbered us again and again, but you know, Manse, I found myself enjoying it. Not like that wretched twentieth-century business of sitting in a foxhole wondering if the enemy barrage will ever let up. Oh, war is miserable enough here, especially if you're a buck private when disease breaks out, as it always does. But when you fight, by God, you fight, with your own hands! And I even found a talent for that sort of thing. We've pulled some gorgeous stunts.' Everard watched life flow back into him: 'Like the time the Lydian cavalry had us outnumbered. We sent our baggage camels in the van, with the infantry behind and horse last. Croesus' nags got a whiff of the camels and stampeded. For all I know, they're running yet. We mopped him up!'

He jarred to silence, stared awhile into Everard's eyes, and bit his lip. 'Sorry. I keep forgetting. Now and then I remember I was not a killer at home – after a battle, when I see the dead scattered around, and worst of all the wounded. But I couldn't help it, Manse! I've had to fight! First there was the revolt. If I hadn't played along with Harpagus, how long do you think I'd have lasted, personally? And then there's been the realm itself. I didn't ask the Lydians to invade us, or the eastern barbarians. Have you ever seen a town sacked by Turanians, Manse? It's them or us, and when *we* conquer somebody we don't march them off in chains, they keep their own lands and customs and ... For Mithras' sake, Manse, could I do anything else?'

Everard sat listening to the garden rustle under a breeze. At last: 'No. I understand. I hope it hasn't been too lonesome.'

'I got used to it,' said Denison carefully. 'Harpagus is an acquired taste, but interesting. Croesus turned out to be a very decent fellow. Kobad the Mage has some original thoughts, and he's the only man alive who dares beat me at chess. And there's the feasting, and hunting, and women …' He gave the other a defiant look. 'Yeah. What else would you have me do?'

'Nothing,' said Everard. 'Sixteen years is a long time.'

'Cassandane, my chief wife, is worth a lot of the trouble I've had. Though Cynthia – God in heaven, Manse!' Denison stood up and laid hands on Everard's shoulders. The fingers closed with bruising strength; they had held ax, bow, and bridle for a decade and a half. The King of the Persians shouted aloud:

'How are you going to get me out of here?'

7

Everard rose too, walked to the floor's edge and stared through lacy stone-work, thumbs hooked in his belt and head lowered.

'I don't see how,' he answered.

Denison smote a fist into one palm. 'I've been afraid of that. Year by year I've grown more afraid that if the Patrol ever finds me it'll … You've got to help.'

'I tell you, I can't!' Everard's voice cracked. He did not turn around. 'Think it over. You must have done so already. You're not some lousy little barbarian chief whose career won't make a lot of difference a hundred years from now. You're Cyrus, the founder of the Persian Empire, a key figure in a key milieu. If Cyrus goes, so does the whole future! There won't have been any twenti-eth-century with Cynthia in it.'

'Are you certain?' pleaded the man at his back.

'I boned up on the facts before hopping here,' said Everard through clenched jaws. 'Stop kidding yourself. We're prejudiced against the Persians because at one time they were the enemies of Greece, and we happen to get some of the more conspicuous features of our own culture from Hellenic sources. But the Persians are at least as important!

'You've watched it happen. Sure, they're pretty brutal by your standards: the whole era is, including the Greeks. And they're not democratic, but you can't blame them for not making a European invention outside their whole mental horizon. What counts is this:

'Persia was the first conquering power which made an effort to respect and conciliate the people it took over; which obeyed its own laws; which pacified enough territory to open steady contact with the Far East; which created a viable world-religion, Zoroastrianism, not limited to any one race or locality. Maybe you don't know how much Christian belief and ritual is of Mithraic origin, but believe me, it's plenty. Not to mention Judaism, which you, Cyrus the Great, are personally going to rescue. Remember? You'll take over Baby-lon and allow those Jews who've kept their identity to return home; without you, they'd be swallowed up and lost in the general ruck as the ten other tribes already have been.

'Even when it gets decadent, the Persian Empire will be a matrix for civilization. What were most of Alexander's conquests but just taking over Persian territory? And that spread Hellenism through the known world! And there'll be Persian successor states: Pontus, Parthia, the Persia of Firduzi and Omar and Hafiz, the Iran we know and the Iran of a future beyond the twentieth-century ...'

Everard turned on his heel. 'If you quit,' he said, 'I can imagine them still building ziggurats and reading entrails – and running through the woods up in Europe, with America undiscovered – three thousand years from now!'

Denison sagged. 'Yeah,' he answered. 'I thought so.'

He paced awhile, hands behind his back. The dark face looked older each minute. 'Thirteen more years,' he murmured, almost to himself. 'In thirteen years I'll fall in battle against the nomads. I don't know exactly how. One way or another, circumstances will force me to it. Why not? They're forced me into everything else I've done, willy-nilly ... in spite of everything I can do to train him, I know my own son Cambyses will turn out to be a sadistic incompetent and it will take Darius to save the empire – God!' He covered his face with a flowing sleeve. 'Excuse me. I do despise self-pity, but I can't help this.'

Everard sat down, avoiding the sight. He heard how the breath rattled in Denison's lungs.

Finally the King poured wine into two chalices, joined Everard on the bench and said in a dry tone: 'Sorry. I'm okay now. And I haven't given up yet.'

'I can refer your problem to headquarters,' said Everard with a touch of sarcasm.

Denison echoed it: 'Thanks, little chum. I remember their attitude well enough. We're expendable. They'll interdict the entire lifetime of Cyrus to visitors, just so I won't be tempted, and send me a nice message. They will point out that I'm the absolute monarch of a civilized people, with palaces, slaves, vintages, chefs, entertainers, concubines, and hunting grounds at my disposal in unlimited quantities, so what am I complaining about? No, Manse, this is something you and I will have to work out between us.'

Everard clenched his fists till he felt the nails bite into the palms. 'You're putting me in a hell of a spot, Keith,' he said.

'I'm only asking you to think on the problem – and Ahriman damn you, you will!' Again the fingers closed on his flesh, and the conqueror of the East snapped forth a command. The old Keith would never have taken that tone, thought Everard, anger flickering up; and he thought:

If you don't come home, and Cynthia is told that you never will ... She could come back and join you, one more foreign girl in the King's harem won't affect history. But if I reported to headquarters before seeing her, reported the problem as insoluble, which it doubtless is in fact ... why, then the reign of Cyrus would be interdicted and she could not join you.

'I've been over this ground before, with myself,' said Denison more calmly. 'I know the implications as well as you do. But look, I can show you the cave where my machine rested for those few hours. You could go back to the moment I appeared there and warn me.'

'No,' said Everard. 'That's out. Two reasons. First, the regulation against that sort of thing, which is a sensible one. They might make an exception under different circumstances, but there's a second reason too: you are Cyrus. They're not going to wipe out an entire future for one man's sake.'

Would I do it for one woman's? I'm not sure. I hope not ... Cynthia wouldn't have to know the facts. It would be kinder if she didn't. I could use my Unattached authority to keep the truth secret from lower echelons and tell her nothing except that Keith had irrevocably died under circumstances which forced us to shut off this period to time traffic. She'd grieve awhile, of course, but she's too healthy to mourn forever ... Sure, it's a lousy trick. But wouldn't it be kinder in the long run than letting her come back here, to servile status, and share her man with at least the dozen princesses that politics forces him to be married to? Wouldn't it be better for her to make a clean break and a fresh start, among her own people?

'Uh-huh,' said Denison. 'I mentioned that idea only to dispose of it. But there must be some other way. Look, Manse, sixteen years ago a situation existed from which everything else has followed, not through human caprice but through the sheer logic of events. Suppose I had not showed up? Mightn't Harpagus have found a different pseudo-Cyrus? The exact identity of the King doesn't matter. Another Cyrus would have acted differently from me in a million day-to-day details. Naturally. But if he wasn't a hopeless moron or maniac, if he was a reasonably able and decent person – give me credit for being that much – then his career wuld have been the same as mine in all the important ways, the ways that got into the history books. You know that as well as I do. Except at the crucial points, time always reverts to its own shape. The small differences damp out in days or years, negative feedback. It's only at key instants that a positive feedback can be set up and the effects multiply with passing time instead of disappearing. You know that!'

'Sure,' said Everard. 'But judging from your own account, your appearance in the cave *was* crucial. It was that which put the idea in Harpagus' head. Without it, well, I can imagine a decadent Median Empire falling apart, maybe falling prey to Lydia, or to the Turanians, because the Persians wouldn't have had the kind of royal divine-right-by-birth leadership they needed ... No. I wouldn't come near that moment in the cave without authorization from anyone less than a Danellian.'

Denison looked at him over a raised chalice, lowered it and kept on looking. His face congealed into a stranger's. He said at last, very softly:

'You don't want me to come back, do you?'

Everard leaped off the bench. He dropped his own cup, it rang on the floor and wine ran from it like blood.

'Shut up!' he yelled.

Dennison nodded. 'I am the King,' he said. 'If I raise my finger, those guards will hack you in pieces.'

'That's a hell of a way to get my help,' growled Everard.

Denison's body jerked. He sat motionless for a while, before he got out: 'I'm sorry. You don't realize what a shock ... Oh, yes, yes, it hasn't been a bad life. It's had more color in it than most, and this business of being quasi-divine grows on you. I suppose that's why I'll take the field beyond the Jaxartes, thirteen years from now: because I can't do anything else, with all those young lion eyes on me. Hell, I may even think it was worth it.'

His expression writhed smilewards. 'Some of my girls have been absolute knockouts. And there's always Cassandane. I made her my chief wife because in a dark way she reminds me of Cynthia. I think. It's hard to tell, after all this time. The twentieth century isn't real to me. And there's more actual satisfaction in a good horse than a sports car ... and I know my work here is valuable, which isn't a knowledge granted to many ... Yeh. I'm sorry I barked at you. I know you'd help if you dared. Since you don't, and I don't blame you, you needn't regret it for my sake.'

'Cut that out!' groaned Everard.

It felt as if there were gears in his brain, spinning against emptiness. Overhead he saw a painted roof, where a youth killed a bull, and the Bull was the Sun and the Man. Beyond columns and vines trod guards in dragon skin mailcoats, their bows strung, their faces like carved wood. The harem wing of the palace could be glimpsed, where a hundred or a thousand young women counted themselves fortunate to await the King's occasional pleasure. Beyond the city walls lay harvest fields where peasants readied sacrifice to an Earth Mother who was old in this land when the Aryans came, and that was in a dark predawn past. High over the walls floated the mountains, haunted by wolf, lion, boar and demon. It was too alien a place. Everard had thought himself hardened to otherness, but now he wanted suddenly to run and hide, up to his own century and his own people and a forgetting.

He said in a careful voice, 'Let me consult a few associates. We can check the whole period in detail. There might be some kind of switch point where ... I'm not competent to handle this alone, Keith. Let me go back upstairs and get some advice. If we work out anything we'll return to ... this very night.'

'Where's your scooter?' asked Denison.

Everard waved a hand. 'Up in the hills.'

Denison stroked his beard. 'You aren't telling me more than that, eh? Well, it's wise. I'm not sure I'd trust myself, if I knew where a time machine could be gotten.'

'I don't mean that!' shouted Everard.

'Oh, never mind. Let's not fight about it.' Denison sighed. 'Sure, go on home and see what you can do. Want an escort?'

'Better not. It isn't necessary, is it?'

'No. We've made this area safer than Central Park.'

'That isn't saying much.' Everard held out his hand. 'Just get me back my horse. I'd hate to lose him: special Patrol animal, trained to time hop.' His gaze closed with the other man's. 'I'll return. In person. Whatever the decision is.'

'Sure, Manse,' said Denison.

They walked out together, to go through the various formalities of notifying guardsmen and gatekeepers. Denison indicated a palace bedchamber where he said he would be every night for a week, as a rendezvous. And then at last Everard kissed the King's feet, and when the royal presence had departed he got aboard his horse and jogged slowly out through the palace gates.

He felt empty inside. There was really nothing to be done; and he promised to come back himself and pass that sentence upon the King.

8

Late that day he was in the hills, where cedars gloomed above cold, brawling brooks and the side road onto which he had turned became a rutted upward track. Though arid enough, the Iran of this age still had a few such forests. The horse plodded beneath him, worn down. He should find some herdsman's house and request lodging, simply to spare the creature. But no, there would be a full moon, he could walk if he must and reach the scooter before sunrise. He didn't think he could sleep.

A place of long sere grass and ripe berries did invite him to rest, though. He had food in the saddlebags, a wineskin, and a stomach unfilled since dawn. He clucked encouragingly to the horse and turned.

Something caught his eye. Far down the road, level sunlight glowed off a dust cloud. It grew bigger even as he watched. Several riders, he guessed, coming in one devil of a hurry. King's messengers? But why, into this section? Uneasiness tickled his nerves. He put on his helmet cap, buckled the helmet itself above, hung shield on arm and loosened the short sword in its sheath. Doubtless the party would just hurrah on past him, but …

Now he could see that there were eight men. They had good horseflesh beneath them, and the rearmost led a string of remounts. Nevertheless the animals were pretty jaded; sweat had made streaks down their dusty flanks and manes were plastered to necks. It must have been a long gallop. The riders were decently clad in the usual full white pants, shirt, boots, cloak, and tall brimless hat: not courtiers or professional soldiers, but not bandits either. They were armed with sabers, bows, and lariats.

Suddenly Everard recognized the greybeard at their head. It exploded in him: Harpagus!

And through whirling haze he could also see – even for ancient Iranians, the followers were a tough-looking crew.

'Oh-oh,' said Everard, half aloud. 'School's out.'

His mind clicked over. There wasn't time to be afraid, only to think. Harpagus had no other obvious motive for hightailing into the hills than to catch the Greek Meander. Surely, in a court riddled with spies and blabbermouths, Harpagus would have learned within an hour that the King spoke to the stranger as an equal in some unknown tongue and let him go back northward. It would take the Chiliarch a while longer to manufacture some excuse for leaving the palace, round up his personal bully boys, and give chase. Why? Because 'Cyrus' had once appeared in these uplands, riding some device which Harpagus had coveted. No fool, the Mede must never have been satisfied with the evasive yarn Keith had handed him. It would seem reasonable that one day another mage from the King's home country must appear; and this time Harpagus would not let the engine go from him so easily.

Everard paused no longer. They were only a hundred yards away. He could see the Chiliarch's eyes glitter beneath shaggy brows. He spurred his horse, off the road and across the meadow.

'Stop!' yelled a remembered voice behind him. 'Stop, Greek!'

Everard got an exhausted trot out of his mount. The cedars threw long shadows across him.

'Stop or we shoot! … halt! … shoot, then! Not to kill! Get the steed!'

At the forest edge, Everard slipped from his saddle. He heard an angry whirr and a score of thumps. The horse screamed. Everard cast a glance behind; the poor beast was on its knees. By God, somebody would pay for this! But he was one man and they were eight. He hurried under the trees. A shaft smote a trunk by his left shoulder, burying itself.

He ran, crouched, zigzag in a chilly sweet-smelling twilight. Now and then a low branch whipped across his face. He could have used more underbrush, there were some Algonquian stunts for a hunted man to try, but at least the soft floor was noiseless under his sandals. The Persians were lost to sight. Almost instinctively, they had tried to ride after him. Cracking and crashing and loud obscenities ripped the air to show how well that had worked.

They'd come on foot in a minute. He cocked his head. A faint rush of water … He moved in its direction, up a steep boulder-strewn slope. His hunters were not helpless urbanites, he thought. At least some of them were sure to be mountaineers, with eyes to read the dimmest signs of his passage. He had to break the trail; then he could hole up until Harpagus must return to court duties. The breath grew harsh in his throat. Behind him voices snapped forth, a note of decision, but he couldn't make out what was said. Too far. And the blood pounded so loudly in his ears.

If Harpagus had fired on the King's guest, then Harpagus surely did not intend that that guest should ever report it to the King. Capture, torture till he revealed where the machine lay and how to operate it, and a final mercy of cold steel were the program. *Judas*, thought Everard through the clamor in his veins, *I've mucked this operation up till it's a manual of how not to be a Patrolman. And the first item is, don't think so hard about a certain girl who isn't yours that you neglect elementary precautions.*

He came out on the edge of a high, wet bank. A brook roiled valleyward below him. They'd see he had come this far, but it would be a tossup which way he splashed in the streambed … which should it be, anyhow? … the mud was cold and slippery on his skin as he scrambled down. Better go upstream. That would bring him closer to his scooter, and Harpagus might assume it more likely he'd try to double back to the King.

Stones bruised his feet and the water numbed them. The trees made a wall above either bank, so that he was roofed by a narrow strip of sky whose blue deepened momentarily. High up there floated an eagle. The air grew colder. But he had one piece of luck: the brook twisted like a snake in delirium and he had quickly slipped and stumbled his way from sight of his entry point. *I'll go on a mile or so*, he thought, *and maybe there'll be an overhanging branch I can grab so I won't leave an outgoing trail.* Slow minutes passed.

So I get to the scooter, he thought, *and go upstairs and ask my chiefs for help. I know damn well they aren't going to give me any. Why not sacrifice one man to insure their own existence and everything they care about? Therefore Keith is stuck here, with thirteen years to go till the barbarians cut him down. But Cynthia will still be young in thirteen years, and after so long a nightmare of exile and knowing her man's time to die, she'd be cut off, an alien in an interdicted era, alone in the frightened court of mad Cambyses II … No, I've got to keep the truth from her, keep her at home, thinking Keith is dead. He'd want it that way himself. And after a year or two she'd be happy again; I could teach her to be happy.*

He had stopped noticing how the rocks smashed at his thinly shod feet, how his body pitched and staggered or how noisy the water was. But then he came around a bend and saw the Persians.

There were two of them, wading downstream. Evidently his capture meant enough to overcome their religious prejudice against defiling a river. Two more walked above, threading between the trees on either bank. One of the latter was Harpagus. Their long swords hissed from the scabbards.

'Stop!' called the Chiliarch. 'Halt, Greek! Yield!'

Everard stood death-still. The water purled about his ankles. The pair who splashed to meet him were unreal down here in a well of shadow, their dark faces blotted out so that he saw only white clothes and a shimmer along saber blades. It hit him in the belly: the pursuers had seen his trail down into the brook. So they split up, half in each direction, running faster on solid ground than he could move in the bed. Having gone beyond his possible range, they started working their way back, more slowly when they were bound to the stream's course but quite certain of their quarry.

'Take him alive,' reminded Harpagus. 'Hamstring him if you must, but take him alive.'

Everard snarled and turned toward that bank. 'Okay, buster, you asked for it,' he said in English. The two men in the water yelled and began to run. One tripped and went on his face. The man opposite tobogganed down the slope on his backside.

The mud was slippery. Everard chopped the lower edge of his shield into it and toiled up. Harpagus moved coolly to await him. As he came near, the old noble's blade whirred, striking from above. Everard rolled his head and caught the blow on his helmet, which bonged. The edge slid down a cheek-piece and cut his right shoulder, but not badly. He felt only a sting and then was too busy to feel anything.

He didn't expect to win out. But he would make them kill him, and pay for the privilege.

He came onto grass and raised his shield just in time to protect his eyes. Harpagus probed for the knees. Everard beat that aside with his own short sword. The Median saber whistled. But at close quarters a lightly armed Asian hadn't a chance against the hoplite, as history was to prove a couple of generations hence. *By God*, thought Everard, *if only I had cuirass and greaves, I might be able to take all four of 'em!* He used his big shield with skill, put it in front of every blow and thrust, and always worked near to get beneath the longer blade and into Harpagus' defenseless guts.

The Chiliarch grinned tautly through tangled gray whiskers and skipped away. A play for time, of course. It succeeded. The other three men climbed the bank, shouted and rushed. It was a disorderly attack. Superb fighters as individuals, the Persians had never developed the mass discipline of Europe, on which they would break themselves at Marathon and Gaugamela. But four against unarmored one was impossible odds. Everard got his back to a tree bole. The first man came in recklessly, sword clashing on the Greek shield. Everard's blade darted from behind the bronze oblong. There was a soft, somehow heavy resistance. He knew that feeling from other days, pulled his weapon out and stepped quickly aside. The Persian sat down, spilling out his life. He groaned once, saw he was a dead man, and raised his face toward the sky.

His mates were already at Everard, one to a side. Overhanging boughs made lassos useless; they would have to do battle. The Patrolman held off the lefthand blade with his shield. That exposed his right ribs, but since his opponents were ordered not to kill he could afford it. The righthand man slashed at Everard's ankles. Everard sprang in the air and the sword hissed under his feet. The lefthand attacked stabbed low. Everard sensed a dull shock and saw steel in his calf. He jerked free. A sunset ray came between bunched needles and touched the blood, making it an impossibly brilliant red. Everard felt that leg buckle under him.

'So, so,' cried Harpagus, hovering ten feet away. 'Chop him!'

Everard growled above his shield rim: 'A task your jackal leader has no courage to attempt for himself, after I drove him back with his tail between his legs!'

It was calculated. The attack on him stopped a bare instant. He reeled forward. 'If you Persians must be the dogs of a Mede,' he croaked, 'can you not choose a Mede who is a man, rather than this creature which betrayed its king and now runs from a single Greek?'

Even this far west and this long ago, an Oriental could not lose face in such a manner. Not that Harpagus had ever been a coward; Everard knew how unfair his taunts were. But the Chiliarch spat a curse and dashed at him. Everard had a moment's glimpse of eyes wild in a sunken hooknosed face. He lumbered lopsidedly forward. The two Persians hesitated for a second more. That was long enough for Everard and Harpagus to meet. The Median saber rose and fell, bounced off Greek helmet and shield, snaked sideways for another leg cut. A loose white tunic flapped before Everard's gaze. He hunched shoulders and drove his sword in.

He withdrew it with the cruel professional twist which assures a mortal wound, pivoted on his right heel, and caught a blow on his shield. For a minute he and one Persian traded fury. At the edge of an eye, he saw the other circling about to get behind him. Well, he thought in a remote way, he had killed the one man dangerous to Cynthia ...

'Hold! Halt!'

The call was a weak flutter in the air, less loud than the mountain stream, but the warriors stepped back and lowered their blades. Even the dying Persian took his eyes from heaven.

Harpagus struggled to sit up, in a puddle of his own blood. His skin was turned gray. 'No ... hold,' he whispered. 'Wait. There is a purpose here. Mithras would not have struck me down unless ...'

He beckoned, a somehow lordly gesture. Everard dropped his sword, limped over and knelt by Harpagus. The Mede sank back into his arms.

'You are from the King's homeland,' he rasped in the bloody beard. 'Do not deny that. But know ... Aurvagaush the son of Khshayavarsha ... is no traitor.' The thin form stiffened itself, imperious, as if ordering death to wait upon its pleasure. 'I knew there were powers – of heaven, of hell, I know not which to this day – powers behind the King's advent. I used them, I used him, not for myself, but because I had sworn loyalty to my own king, Astyages, and he needed a ... a Cyrus ... lest the realm be torn asunder. Afterward, by his cruelty, Astyages forfeited my oath. But I was still a Mede. I saw in Cyrus the only hope – the best hope – of Media. For he has been a good king to us also – we are honored in his domains second only to the Persians ... Do you understand, you from the King's home?' Dim eyes rolled about, trying to see into Everard's but without enough control. 'I wanted to capture you – to force your engine and its use from you, and then to kill you ... yes ... but not for my own gain. It was for the realm's. I feared you would take the King home, as I know he has longed to go. And what would become of us? Be merciful, as you too must hope for mercy.'

'I shall,' said Everard. 'The King will remain.'

'It is well,' sighed Harpagus. 'I believe you speak the truth ... I dare not believe otherwise ... Then I have atoned?' he asked in a thin anxious voice. 'For the murder I did at my old King's behest – that I laid a helpless infant upon the mountainside and watched him die – have I atoned, King's countryman? For it was that prince's death ... which brought the land close to ruin ... but I found another Cyrus! I saved us! Have I atoned?'

'You have,' said Everard, and wondered how much absolution it lay in his power to give.

Harpagus closed his eyes. 'Then leave me,' he said, like the fading echo of a command.

Everard laid him upon the earth and hobbled away. The two Persians knelt by their master, performing certain rites. The third man returned to his own contemplations. Everard sat down under a tree, tore a strip from his cloak and bandaged his hurts. The leg cut would need attention. Somehow he must get to the scooter. That wouldn't be fun, but he could manage it and then a Patrol doctor could repair him in a few hours with a medical science future to his home era. He'd go to some branch office in an obscure milieu, because there'd be too many questions in the twentieth century.

And he couldn't afford that. If his superiors knew what he planned, they would probably forbid it.

The answer had come to him not as a blinding revelation, but as a tired consciousness of knowledge which he might well have had subconsciously for a long time. He leaned back, getting his breath. The other four Persians arrived and were told what had happened. All of them ignored Everard, except for glances where terror struggled with pride and made furtive signs against evil. They lifted their dead chief and their dying companion and bore them into the forest. Darkness thickened. Somewhere an owl hooted.

9

The great King sat up in bed. There had been a noise beyond the curtains.

Cassandane, the Queen, stirred invisibly. One slim hand touched his face. 'What is it, sun of my heaven?' she asked.

'I do not know.' He fumbled for the sword which lay always beneath his pillow. 'Nothing.'

Her palm slipped down over his breast. 'No, it is much,' she whispered, suddenly shaken. 'Your heart goes like a war drum.'

'Stay there.' He trod out past the drapes.

Moonlight streamed from a deep-purple sky, through an arched window to the floor. It glanced almost blindingly off a bronze mirror. The air was cold upon bare skin.

A thing of dark metal, whose rider gripped two handlebars and touched tiny controls on a panel, drifted like another shadow. It landed on the carpet without a sound and the rider got off. He was a burly man in Grecian tunic and helmet. 'Keith,' he breathed.

'Manse!' Denison stepped into the moonlight. 'You came!'

'Tell me more,' snorted Everard sarcastically. 'Think anybody will hear us? I don't believe I was noticed. Materialized directly over the roof and floated slowly down on antigrav.'

'There are guards just outside the door,' said Denison, 'but they won't come in unless I strike that gong, or yell.'

'Good. Put on some clothes.'

Denison dropped his sword. He stood rigid for an instant, then it blazed from him: 'You've got a way out?'

'Maybe. Maybe.' Everard looked away from the other man, drummed fingers on his machine's control panel. 'Look, Keith,' he said at last, 'I've an idea which might or might not work. I'll need your help to carry it out. If it does work, you can go home. The front office will accept a *fait accompli* and wink at any broken regulations. But if it fails, you'll have to come back to this very night and live out your life as Cyrus. Can you do that?'

Denison shivered with more than chill. Very low: 'I think so.'

'I'm stronger than you are,' said Everard roughly, 'and I'll have the only weapons. If necessary, I'll shanghai you back here. Please don't make me.'

Denison drew a long breath. 'I won't.'

'Then let's hope the Norns cooperate. Come on, get dressed. I'll explain as we go. Kiss this year goodbye, and trust it isn't, "So long" – because if my notion pans out, neither you nor anyone else will ever see it again.'

Denison, who had half turned to the garments thrown in a corner for a slave to replace before dawn, stopped. 'What?' he said.

'We're going to try rewriting history,' said Everard. 'Or maybe to restore the history which was there in the first place. I don't know. Come on, hop to it!'

'But –'

'Quick, man, quick! D'you realize I came back to the same day as I left you, that at this moment I'm crawling through the mountains with one leg stabbed open, just to save you that extra time? Get moving!'

Decision closed upon Denison. His face was in darkness, but he spoke very low and clear: 'I've got one personal goodbye to say.'

'What?'

'Cassandane. She's been my wife here for, God, for fourteen years! She's borne me three children, and nursed me through two fevers and a hundred fits of despair, and once when the Medes were at our gates she led the women of Pasargadae out to rally us and we won ... Give me five minutes, Manse.'

'All right, all right. Though it'll take more than that to send a eunuch to her room and –'

'She's here.'

Denison vanished behind the bed curtains.

Everard stood for a moment as if struck. *You expected me to come tonight,* he thought, *and you hoped I'd be able to take you back to Cynthia. So you sent for Cassandane.*

And then, when his fingertips had begun to hurt from the tightness of his grip on the sword hilt: *Oh, shut up, Everard, you smug self-righteous whelp.*

Presently Denison came back. He did not speak as he put on his clothes and mounted the rear seat on the scooter. Everard spacehopped, an instant-aneous jump; the room vanished and moonlight flooded the hills far below. A cold gust searched around the men in the sky.

'Now for Ecbatana.' Everard turned on his dashlight and adjusted controls according to notes scribbled on the pilot pad.

'Ec – Oh, you mean Hagmatan? The old Median capital?' Denison sounded astonished. 'But it's only a summer residence now.'

'I mean Ecbatana thirty-six years ago,' said Everard.

'Huh?'

'Look, all the scientific historians in the future are convinced that the story of Cyrus's childhood as told by Herodotus and the Persians is pure fable. Well, maybe they were right all along. Maybe your experiences here have been only one of those little quirks in space-time which the Patrol tries to eliminate.'

'I see,' said Denison slowly.

'You were at Astyages' court pretty often when you were his vassal, I suppose. Okay, you guide me. We want the old guy himself, preferably alone at night.'

'Sixteen years was a long time,' said Denison.

'Hm?'

'If you're going to change the past anyway, why use me at this point? Come get me when I'd been Cyrus only one year, long enough to be familiar with Ecbatana but –'

'Sorry, no. I don't dare. We're steering close enough to the wind as is. Lord knows what a secondary loop in the world lines could lead to. Even if we got away with it, the Patrol would send us both to the exile planet for taking that kind of chance.'

'Well … yes. I see your point.'

'Also,' said Everard, 'you're not a suicidal type. Would you actually want the you of this instant never to have existed? Think for a minute precisely what that implies.'

He completed his settings. The man behind him suddered. 'Mithras!' said Denison. 'You're right. Let's not talk more about it.'

'Here goes, then.' Everard threw the main switch.

He hung over a walled city on an unfamiliar plain. Though this was also a moonlit night, the city was only a black huddle to his eyes. He reached into the saddlebags. 'Here,' he said. 'Let's put on these costumes. I had the boys in the Middle Mohenjodaro office fix 'em up to my specs. Their situation is such that they often need this type of disguise for themselves.'

Air whistled darkly as the hopper slanted earthward. Denison reached an arm past Everard to point. 'That's the palace. The royal bedchamber is over on the east side …'

It was a heavier, less graceful building than its Persian successor in Pasargadae. Everard glimpsed a pair of winged bulls, white in an autumnal garden, left over from the Assyrians. He saw that the windows before him were too narrow for entrance, swore, and aimed at the nearest doorway. A pair of mounted sentries looked up, saw what was coming, and shrieked. Their horses reared, throwing them. Everard's machine splintered the door. One more miracle wasn't going to affect history, especially when such things were believed in as devoutly as vitamin pills at home, and possibly with more reason. Lamps guided him down a corridor where slaves and guards squalled their terror. At the royal bedroom he drew his sword and knocked with the pommel. 'Take over, Keith,' he said. 'You know the Median version of Aryan.'

'Open, Astyages!' roared Denison. 'Open to the messengers of Ahuramazda!'

Somewhat to Everard's surprise, the man within obeyed. Astyages was as brave as most of his people. But when the king – a thickset, hard-faced person in early middle age – saw two beings, luminously robed, halos around their heads and fountaining wings of light on their backs, seated on an iron throne in midair, he fell prostrate.

Everard heard Denison thunder in the best tent-meeting style, using a dialect he could not follow:

'O infamous vessel of iniquity, heaven's anger is upon you! Do you believe that your least thought, though it skulk in the darkness which begot it, was ever hidden from the Day's Eye? Do you believe that almighty Ahuramazda would permit a deed so foul as you plot …'

Everard didn't listen. He strayed into his own thoughts: Harpagus was probably somewhere in this very city, full of his youth and unridden as yet by guilt. Now he would never bear that burden. He would never lay a child upon the mountain and lean on his spear as it cried and shivered and finally became still. He would revolt in the future, for his own reasons, and become the Chiliarch of Cyrus, but he would not die in his enemy's arms in a haunted forest; and a certain Persian, whose name Everard did not know, would also be spared a Greek sword and a slow falling into emptiness.

Yet the memory of two men whom I killed is printed on my brain cells; there is a thin white scar on my leg; Keith Denison is forty-seven years old and has learned to think like a king.

' … Know, Astyages, that this child Cyrus is favored of heaven. And heaven is merciful: you have been warned that if you stain your soul with his innocent blood, the sin can never be washed away. Leave Cyrus to grow up in Anshan, or burn forever with Ahriman! Mithras has spoken!'

Astyages groveled, beating his head on the floor.

'Let's go,' said Denison in English.

Everard hopped to Persian hills, thirty-six years futureward. Moonlight fell upon cedars near a road and a stream. It was cold, and a wolf howled.

He landed the scooter, got off and began to remove his costume. Denison's bearded face came out of the mask, with strangeness written upon it. 'I wonder,' he said. His voice was nearly lost in the silence under the mountains. 'I wonder if we didn't throw too much of a scare into Astyages. History does record that he gave Cyrus a three-year fight when the Persians revolted.'

'We can always go back to the outbreak of the war and provide a vision encouraging him to resist,' said Everard, struggling to be matter-of-fact; for there were ghosts around him. 'But I don't believe that'll be necessary. He'll keep hands off the prince, but when a vassal rebels, well, he'll be mad enough to discount what by then will seem like a dream. Also, his own nobles, Median vested interests, would hardly allow him to give in. But let's check up. Doesn't the King lead a procession at the winter solstice festival?'

'Yeah. Let's go. Quickly.'

And the sunlight burned around them, high above Pasargadae. They left their machine hidden and walked down on foot, two travelers among many streaming in to celebrate the Birthday of Mithras. On the way, they inquired what had happened, explaining that they had been long abroad. The answers satisfied them, even in small details which Denison's memories recorded but the chronicles hadn't mentioned.

At last they stood under a frosty-blue sky, among thousands of people, and salaamed when Cyrus the Great King rode past with his chief courtiers Kobad, Croesus, and Harpagus, and the pride and pomp and priesthood of Persia followed.

'He's younger than I was,' whispered Denison. 'He would be, I guess. And a little smaller ... different face entirely, isn't it? ... but he'll do.'

'Want to stay for the fun?' asked Everard.

Denison drew his cloak around him. The air was bitter. 'No,' he said. 'Let's go back. It's been a long time. Even if it never happened.'

'Uh-huh.' Everard seemed more grim than a victorious rescuer should be. 'It never happened.'

10

Keith Denison left the elevator of a building in New York. He was vaguely surprised that he had not remembered what it looked like. He couldn't even recall his apartment number, but had to check with the directory. Details, details. He tried to stop trembling.

Cynthia opened the door as he reached it. 'Keith,' she said, almost wonderingly.

He could find no other words than: 'Manse warned you about me, didn't he? He said he would.'

'Yes. It doesn't matter. I didn't realize your looks would have changed that much. But it doesn't matter. Oh, my darling!'

She drew him inside, closed the door and crept into his arms.

He looked around the place. He had forgotten how cramped it was. And he had never liked her taste in decoration, though he had yielded to her.

The habit of giving in to a woman, even of asking her opinion, was one he'd have to learn all over again. It wouldn't be easy.

She raised a wet face for his kiss. Was *that* how she looked? But he didn't remember – he didn't. After all that time, he had only remembered she was little and blond. He had lived with her a few months; Cassandane had called him her morning star and given him three children and waited to do his will for fourteen years.

'Oh, Keith, welcome home,' said the high small voice.

Home! he thought. *God!*

GIBRALTAR FALLS

The Time Patrol base would only remain for the hundred-odd years of inflow. During that while, few people other than scientists and maintenance crew would stay there for long at a stretch. Thus it was small, a lodge and a couple of service buildings, nearly lost in the land.

Five and a half million years before he was born, Tom Nomura found that southern end of Iberia still more steep than he remembered it. Hills climbed sharply northward until they became low mountains walling the sky, riven by canyons where shadows lay blue. It was dry country, rained on violently but briefly in winter, its streams shrunken to runnels or nothing as its grass burnt yellow in summer. Trees and shrubs grew far apart, thorn, mimosa, acacia, pine, aloe; around the waterholes palm, fern, orchid.

Withal, it was rich in life. Hawks and vultures were always at hover in cloudless heaven. Grazing herds mingled their millions together; among their scores of kinds of zebra-striped ponies, primitive rhinoceros, okapi-like ancestors of the giraffe, sometimes mastodon – thinly red-haired, hugely tusked – or peculiar elephants. Among the predators and scavengers were sabertooths, early forms of the big cats, hyenas, and scuttering ground apes which occasionally walked on their hind legs. Antheaps lifted six feet into the air. Marmots whistled.

It smelled of hay, scorch, baked dung and warm flesh. When wind awoke, it boomed, pushed, threw dust and heat into the face. Often the earth resounded to hoofbeats, birds clamored or beasts trumpeted. At night a sudden chill struck down, and the stars were so many that one didn't much notice the alienness of their constellations.

Thus had things been until lately. And as yet there was no great change. But now had begun a hundred years of thunder. When that was done, nothing would ever be the same again.

Manse Everard regarded Tom Nomura and Feliz a Rach for a squinting moment before he smiled and said, 'No, thanks, I'll just poke around here today. You go have fun.'

Did an eyelid of the big, bent-nosed, slightly grizzled man droop a little in Nomura's direction? The latter couldn't be sure. They were from the same milieu, indeed the same country. That Everard had been recruited in New York, 1954 AD, and Nomura in San Francisco, 1972, ought to make scant difference. The upheavals of that generation were bubble pops against what had happened before and what would happen after. However, Nomura was fresh out of the Academy, a bare twenty-five years of lifespan behind him. Everard hadn't told how much time his own farings through the world's duration added up to; and given the longevity treatment the Patrol offered its people, it was impossible to guess. Nomura suspected the Unattached agent had seen enough existence to have become more foreign to him than Feliz – who was born two millenniums past either of them.

'Very well, let's start,' she said. Curt though it was, Nomura thought her voice made music of the Temporal language.

They stepped from the veranda and walked across the yard. A couple of other corpsmen hailed them, with a pleasure directed at her. Nomura agreed. She was young and tall, the curve-nosed strength of her features softened by large green eyes, large mobile mouth, hair that shone auburn in spite of being hacked off at the ears. The usual gray coverall and stout boots could not hide her figure or the suppleness of her stride. Nomura knew he himself wasn't bad-looking – a stocky but limber frame, high-cheeked regular features, tawny skin – but she made him feel drab.

Also inside, he thought. *How does a new-minted Patrolman – not even slated for police duty, a mere naturalist – how does he tell an aristocrat of the First Matriarchy that he's fallen in love with her?*

The rumbling which always filled the air, these miles from the cataracts, sounded to him like a chorus. Was it imagination, or did he really sense an endless shudder through the ground, up into his bones?

Feliz opened a shed. Several hoppers stood inside, vaguely resembling wheelless two-seater motorcycles, propelled by antigravity and capable of leaping across several thousand years. (They and their present riders had been transported hither in heavy-duty shuttles.) Hers was loaded with recording gear. He had failed to convince her it was overburdened and knew she'd never forgive him if he finked on her. His invitation to Everard – the ranking officer in hand, though here-now simply on vacation – to join them today had been made in a vague hope that the latter would see that load and order her to let her assistant carry part of it.

She sprang to the saddle. 'Come on!' she said. 'The morning's getting old.'

He mounted his vehicle and touched controls. Both glided outside and aloft. At eagle height, they leveled off and bore south, where the River Ocean poured into the Middle of the World.

Banks of upflung mist always edged that horizon, argent smoking off into azure. As one drew near afoot, they loomed topplingly overhead. Further on, the universe swirled gray, shaken by the roar, bitter on human lips, while water flowed off rock and gouged through mud. So thick was the cold salt fog that it was unsafe to breathé for more than a few minutes.

From well above, the sight was yet more awesome. There one could see the end of a geological epoch. For a million and a half years the Mediterranean basin had lain a desert. Now the Gates of Hercules stood open and the Atlantic was coming through.

The wind of his passage around him, Nomura peered west across unrestful, many-hued and intricately foam-streaked immensity. He could see the currents run, sucked toward the new-made gap between Europe and Africa. There they clashed together and recoiled, a white and green chaos whose violence toned from earth to heaven and back, crumbled cliffs, overwhelmed valleys, blanketed the shore in spume for miles inland. From them came a stream, snow-colored in its fury, with flashes of livid emerald, to stand in an eight-mile wall between the continents and bellow. Spray roiled aloft, dimming the torrent after torrent, wherein the sea crashed onward.

Rainbows wheeled through the clouds it made. This far aloft, the noise was no more than a monstrous millstone grinding. Nomura could clearly hear Feliz's voice out of his receiver, as she stopped her vehicle and lifted an arm. 'Hold. I want a few more takes before we go on.'

'Haven't you enough?' he asked.

Her words softened. 'How can we get enough of a miracle?'

His heart jumped. *She's not a she-soldier, born to lord it over a ruck of underlings. In spite of her early life and ways, she isn't. She feels the dread, the beauty, yes, the sense of God at work –*

A wry grin at himself: *She'd better!*

After all, her task was to make a full-sensory record of the whole thing, from its beginning until that day when a hundred years hence, the basin was full and the sea lapped calm where Odysseus would sail. It would take months of her lifespan. (*And mine, please, mine.*) Everybody in the corps wanted to experience this stupendousness; the hope of adventure was practically required for recruitment. But it wasn't feasible for many to come so far downstairs, crowding into so narrow a time-slot. Most would have to do it vicariously. Their chiefs would not have picked someone who was not a considerable artist, to live it on their behalf and pass it on to them.

Nomura remembered his astonishment when he was assigned to assist her. Short-handed as it was, could the Patrol afford artists?

Well, after he answered a cryptic advertisement and took several puzzling tests and learned about intertemporal traffic, he had wondered if police and rescue work were possible and been told that, usually, they were. He could see the need for administrative and clerical personnel, resident agents, historiorgraphers, anthropologists, and, yes, natural scientists like himself. In the weeks they had been working together, Feliz convinced him that a few artists were at least as vital. Man does not live by bread alone, nor guns, paperwork, theses, naked practicalities.

She re-stowed her apparatus. 'Come,' she ordered. As she flashed eastward ahead of him, her hair caught a sunbeam and shone as if molten. He trudged mute in her wake.

The Mediterranean floor lay ten thousand feet below sea level. The inflow took most of that drop within a fifty-mile strait. Its volume amounted to ten thousand cubic miles a year, a hundred Victoria Falls or a thousand Niagaras.

Thus the statistics. The reality was a roar of white water, spray-shrouded, earth-sundering, mountain-shaking. Men could see, hear, feel, smell, taste the thing; they could not imagine it.

When the channel widened, the flow grew smoother, until it ran green and black. Then mists diminished and islands appeared, like ships which cast up huge bow waves; and life could again grow or go clear to the shore. Yet most of those islands would be eroded away before the century was out, and much of that life would perish in weather turned strange. For this event would move the planet from its Miocene to its Pliocene epoch.

And as he flitted onward, Nomura did not hear less noise, but more. Though the stream itself was quieter here, it moved toward a bass clamor which grew and grew till heaven was one brazen bell. He recognized a headland whose worndown remnant would someday bear the name Gibraltar. Not far beyond, a cataract twenty miles wide made almost half the total plunge.

With terrifying ease, the waters slipped over that brink. They were glass-green against the darkling cliffs and umber grass of the continents. Light flamed off their heights. At their bottom another cloud bank rolled white in ever-ending winds. Beyond reached a blue sheet, a lake whence rivers hewed canyons, out and out across the alkaline sparkle, dust devils and mirage shimmers of the furnace land which they would make into a sea.

It boomed, it brawled, it querned.

Again Feliz poised her flyer. Nomura drew alongside. They were high; the air whittered chilly around them.

'Today,' she told him, 'I want to try for an impression of the sheer size. I'll move in close to the top, recording as I go, and then down.'

'Not too close,' he warned.

She bridled. 'I'll judge that.'

'Uh, I … I'm not trying to boss you or anything.' *I'd better not. I, a plebe and a male.* 'As a favor, please –' Nomura flinched at his own clumsy speech. ' – be careful, will you? I mean, you're important to me.'

Her smile burst upon him. She leaned hard against her safety harness to catch his hand. 'Thank you, Tom.' After a moment, turned grave: 'Men like you make me understand what is wrong in the age I come from.'

622

She had often spoken kindly to him: most times, in fact. Had she been a strident militant, no amount of comeliness would have kept him awake nights. He wondered if perhaps he had begun loving her when first he noticed how conscientiously she strove to regard him as her equal. It was not easy for her, she being almost as new in the Patrol as he – no easier than it was for men from other areas to believe, down inside where it counted, that she had the same capabilities they did and that it was right she use herself to the full.

She couldn't stay solemn. 'Come on!' she shouted. 'Hurry! That straight dropoff won't last another twenty years!'

Her machine darted. He slapped down the face screen of his helmet and plunged after, bearing the tapes and power cells and other auxiliary items. *Be careful*, he pleaded, *oh, be careful, my darling*.

She had gotten well ahead. He saw her like a comet, a dragonfly, everything vivid and swift, limned athwart yonder mile-high precipice of sea. The noise grew in him till there was nothing else, his skull was full of its doomsday.

Yards from the waters, she rode her hopper chasmward. Her head was buried in a dial-studded box, her hands at work on its settings; she steered with her knees. Salt spray began to fog Nomura's screen. He activated the self-cleaner.

Turbulence clawed at him; his carrier lurched. His eardrums, guarded against sound but not changing pressure, stabbed with pain.

He had come quite near Feliz when her vehicle went crazy. He saw it spin, saw it strike the green immensity, saw it and her engulfed. He could not hear himself scream through the thunder.

He rammed the speech switch, swooped after her. Was it blind instinct which sent him whirling away again, inches before the torrent grabbed him too? She was gone from sight. There was only the water wall, clouds below and unpitying blue calm above, the noise that took him in its jaws to shake him apart, the cold, the damp, the salt on his mouth that tasted like tears.

He fled for help.

Noonday glowered outside. The land looked bleached, lay moveless and lifeless except for a carrion bird. The distant falls alone had voice.

A knock on the door of his room brought Nomura off the bed, onto his feet. Through an immediately rackety pulse he croaked, 'Come in. Do.'

Everard entered. In spite of air conditioning, sweat spotted his garments. He gnawed a fireless pipe and his shoulders slumped.

'What's the word?' Nomura begged of him.

'As I feared. Nothing. She never returned home.'

Nomura sank into a chair and stared before him. 'You're certain?'

Everard sat down on the bed, which creaked beneath his weight. 'Yeah.

The message capsule just arrived. In answer to my inquiry, et cetera, Agent Feliz a Rach has not reported back to her home milieu base from the Gibraltar assignment, and they have no further record of her.'

'Not in *any* era?'

'The way agents move around in time and space, nobody keeps dossiers, except maybe the Danellians.'

'Ask them!'

'Do you imagine they'd reply?' Everard snapped – they, the supermen of the remote future who were the founders and ultimate masters of the Patrol. One big fist clenched on his knee. 'And don't tell me we ordinary mortals could keep closer tabs if we wanted to. Have you checked your personal future, son? We don't want to, and that's that.'

The roughness left him. He shifted the pipe about in his grip and said most gently, 'If we live long enough, we outlive those we've cared for. The common fate of man; nothing unique to our corps. But I'm sorry you had to strike it so young.'

'Never mind me!' Nomura exclaimed. 'What of her?'

'Yes ... I've been thinking about your account. My guess is, the airflow patterns are worse than tricky around that fall. What should've been expected, no doubt. Overloaded, her hopper was less controllable than usual. An air pocket, a flaw, whatever it was, something like that grabbed her without warning and tossed her into the stream.'

Nomura's fingers writhed against each other. 'And I was supposed to look after her.'

Everard shook his head. 'Don't punish yourself worse. You were simply her assistant. She should have been more careful.'

'But – God damn it, we can rescue her still, and you won't allow us to?' Nomura half screamed.

'Stop,' Everard warned. 'Stop right there.'

Never say it: that several Patrolmen could ride backward in time, lay hold on her with tractor beams and haul her free of the abyss. Or that I could tell her and my earlier self to beware. It did not happen, therefore it will not happen.

It must *not happen.*

For the past becomes in fact mutable, as soon as we on our machines have transformed it into our present. And if ever a mortal takes himself that power, where can the changing end? We start by saving a glad girl; we go on to save Lincoln, but somebody else tries to save the Confederate States – No, none less than God can be trusted with time. The Patrol exists to guard what is real. Its men may no more violate that faith than they may violate their own mothers.

'I'm sorry,' Nomura mumbled.

'It's okay, Tom.'

'No, I ... I thought ... when I saw her vanish, my first thought was that we could make up a party, ride back to that very instant and snatch her clear –'

'A natural thought in a new man. Old habits of the mind die hard. The fact is, we did not. It'd scarcely have been authorized anyway. Too dangerous. We can ill afford to lose more. Certainly we can't when the record shows that our rescue attempt would be foredoomed if we made it.'

'Is there no way to get around that?'

Everard sighed. 'I can't think of any. Make your peace with fate, Tom.' He hesitated. 'Can I ... can we do anything for you?'

'No.' It came harsh out of Nomura's throat. 'Except leave me be for a while.'

'Sure.' Everard rose. 'You weren't the only person who thought a lot of her,' he reminded, and left.

When the door had closed behind him, the sound of the falls seemed to wax, grinding, grinding. Nomura stared at emptiness. The sun passed its apex and began to slide very slowly toward night.

I should have gone after her myself, at once.

And risked my life.

Why not follow her into death, then?

No. That's senseless. Two deaths do not make a life. I couldn't have saved her. I didn't have the equipment or – The sane thing was to fetch help.

Only the help was denied – whether by man or by fate hardly matters, does it? – and so she went down. The stream hurled her into the gulf, she had a moment's terror before it smashed the awareness out of her, then at the bottom it crushed her, plucked her apart, strewed the pieces of her bones across the floor of a sea that I, a youngster, will sail upon one holiday, unknowing that there is a Time Patrol or ever was a Feliz. Oh, God, I want my dust down with hers, five and a half million years from this hour!

A remote cannonade went through the air, a tremor through earth and floor. An undercut bank must have crumbled into the torrent. It was the kind of scene she would have loved to capture.

'Would have?' Nomura yelled and surged from the chair. The ground still vibrated beneath him. 'She will!'

He ought to have consulted Everard, but feared – perhaps mistakenly, in his grief and his inexperience – that he would be refused permission and sent upstairs at once.

He ought to have rested for several days, but feared that his manner would betray him. A stimulant pill must serve in place of nature.

He ought to have checked out a tractor unit, not smuggled it into the locker on his vehicle.

When he took the hopper forth, a Patrolman who saw asked where he was bound. 'For a ride,' Nomura answered. The other nodded sympathetically.

He might not suspect that a love had been lost, but the loss of a comrade was bad enough. Nomura was careful to get well over the northern horizon before he swung toward the seafall.

Right and left, it reached further than he could see. Here, more than halfway down that cliff of green glass, the very curve of the planet hid its ends from him. Then as he entered the spume clouds, whiteness enfolded him, roiling and stinging.

His face shield stayed clear, but vision was ragged, upward along immensity. The helmet warded his hearing but could not stave off the storm which rattled his teeth and heart and skeleton. Winds whirled and smote, the carrier staggered, he must fight for every inch of control.

And to find the exact second –

Back and forth he leaped across time, reset the verniers, reflicked the main switch, glimpsed himself vague in the mists, and peered through them toward heaven: over and over, until abruptly he was *then*.

Twin gleams far above … He saw the one strike and go under, go down, while the other darted around until soon it ran away. Its rider had not seen him, where he lurked in the chill salt mists. His presence was not on any damned record.

He darted forward. Yet patience was upon him. He could cruise for a long piece of lifespan if need be, seeking the trice which would be his. The fear of death, even the knowing that she might be dead when he found her, were like half-remembered dreams. The elemental powers had taken him. He was a will that flew.

He hovered within a yard of the water. Gusts tried to cast him into its grip, as they had done to her. He was ready for them, danced free, returned to peer – returned through time as well as space, so that a score of him searched along the fall in that span of seconds when Feliz might be alive.

He paid his other selves no heed. They were merely stages he had gone through or must still go through.

THERE!

The dim dark shape tumbled past him, beneath the flood, on its way to destruction. He spun a control. A tractor beam locked onto the other machine. His reeled and went after it, unable to pull such a mass free of such a might.

The tide nearly had him when help came. Two vehicles, three, four, all straining together, they hauled Feliz's loose. She sagged horribly limp in her saddle harness. He didn't go to her at once. First he went back those few blinks in time, and back, and back, to be her rescuer and his own.

When finally they were alone among fogs and furies, she freed and in his arms, he would have burnt a hole through the sky to get shore where he could care for her. But she stirred, her eyes blinked open, after a minute she smiled at him. Then he wept.

Beside them, the ocean roared onward.

The sunset to which Nomura had leaped ahead was not on anybody's record either. It turned the land golden. The falls must be afire with it. Their song resounded beneath the evening star.

Feliz propped pillows against headboard, sat straighter in the bed where she was resting, and told Everard: 'If you lay charges against him, that he broke regulations or whatever male stupidity you are thinking of, I'll also quit your bloody Patrol.'

'Oh, no.' The big man lifted a palm as if to fend off attack. 'Please. You misunderstand. I only meant to say, we're in a slightly awkward position.'

'How?' Nomura demanded, from the chair in which he sat and held Feliz' hand. 'I wasn't under any orders not to attempt this, was I? All right, agents are supposed to safeguard their own lives if possible, as being valuable to the corps. Well, doesn't it follow that the salvaging of a life is worthwhile too?'

'Yes. Sure.' Everard paced the floor. It thudded beneath his boots, above the drumbeat of the flood. 'Nobody quarrels with success, even in a much tighter organization than ours. In fact, Tom, the initiative you showed today makes your future prospects look good, believe me.' A grin went lopsided around his pipestem. 'As for an old soldier like myself, it'll be forgiven that I was too ready to give up.' A flick of somberness: 'I've seen so many lost beyond hope.'

He stopped in his treading, confronted them both, and stated: 'But we cannot have loose ends. The fact is, her unit does not list Feliz a Rach as returning, ever.'

Their clasps tightened on each other.

Everard gave him and her a smile – haunted, nevertheless a smile – before he continued: 'Don't get scared, though. Tom, earlier you wondered why we, we ordinary humans at least, don't keep closer track of our people. Now do you see the reason?

'Feliz a Rach never checked back into her original base. She may have visited her former home, of course, but we don't ask officially what agents do on their furloughs.' He drew breath. 'As for the rest of her career, if she should want to transfer to a different headquarters and adopt a different name, why, any officer of sufficient rank could approve that. Me, for example.

'We operate loose in the Patrol. We dare not do otherwise.'

Nomura understood, and shivered.

Feliz recalled him to the ordinary world. 'But who might I become?' she wondered.

He pounced on the cue. 'Well,' he said, half in laughter and half in thunder, 'how about Mrs Thomas Nomura?'

THE ONLY GAME IN TOWN

1

John Sandoval did not belong to his name. Nor did it seem right that he should stand in slacks and aloha shirt before an apartment window opening on midtwentieth-century Manhattan. Everard was used to anachronism, but the dark hooked face confronting him always seemed to want warpaint, a horse, and a gun sighted on some pale thief.

'Okay,' he said. 'The Chinese discovered America. Interesting, but why does the fact need my services?'

'I wish to hell I knew,' Sandoval answered.

His rangy form turned about on the polar-bear rug, which Bjarni Herjulf-sson had once given to Everard, until he was staring outward. Towers were sharp against a clear sky; the noise of traffic was muted by height. His hands clasped and unclasped behind his back.

'I was ordered to co-opt an Unattached agent, go back with him and take whatever measures seemed indicated,' he went on after a while. 'I knew you best, so ...' His voice trailed off.

'But shouldn't you get an Indian like yourself?' asked Everard. 'I'd seem rather out of place in thirteenth-century America.'

'So much the better. Make it impressive, mysterious ... It won't be too tough a job, really.'

'Of course not,' said Everard. 'Whatever the job actually is.'

He took pipe and tobacco pouch from his disreputable smoking jacket and stuffed the bowl in quick, nervous jabs. One of the hardest lessons he had had to learn, when first recruited into the Time Patrol, was that every important task does not require a vast organization. That was the characteristic twentieth-century approach; but earlier cultures, like Athenian Hellas and Kamakura Japan – and later civilizations too, here and there in history – had concentrated on the development of individual excellence. A single graduate of the Patrol Academy (equipped, to be sure, with tools and weapons of the future) could be the equivalent of a brigade.

But it was a matter of necessity as well as aesthetics. There were all too few people to watch over all too many thousands of years.

'I get the impression,' said Everard slowly, 'that this is not a simple rectification of extratemporal interference.'

'Right,' said Sandoval in a harsh voice. 'When I reported what I'd found, the Yuan milieu office made a thorough investigation. No time travelers are involved. Kublai Khan thought this up entirely by himself. He may have been inspired by Marco Polo's accounts of Venetian and Arab sea voyages, but it was legitimate history, even if Marco's book doesn't mention anything of the sort.'

'The Chinese had quite a nautical tradition of their own,' said Everard. 'Oh, it's all very natural. So how do we come in?'

He got his pipe lit and drew hard on it. Sandoval still hadn't spoken, so he asked, 'How did you happen to find this expedition? It wasn't in Navajo country, was it?'

'Hell, I'm not confined to studying my own tribe,' Sandoval answered. 'Too few Amerinds in the Patrol as is, and it's a nuisance disguising other breeds. I've been working on Athabascan migrations generally.' Like Keith Denison, he was an ethnic Specialist, tracing the history of peoples who never wrote their own so that the Patrol could know exactly what the events were that it safeguarded.

'I was working along the eastern slope of the Cascades, near Crater Lake,' he went on. 'That's Lutuami country, but I had reason to believe an Athabascan tribe I'd lost track of had passed that way. The natives spoke of mysterious strangers coming from the north. I went to have a look, and there the expedition was, Mongols with horses. I checked their back trail and found their camp at the mouth of the Chehalis River, where a few more Mongols were helping the Chinese sailors guard the ships. I hopped back upstairs like a bat out of Los Angeles and reported.'

Everard sat down and stared at the other man. 'How through an investigation did get made at the Chinese end?' he said. 'Are you absolutely certain there was no extratemporal interference? It could be one of those unplanned blunders, you know, whose consequences aren't obvious for decades.'

'I thought of that too, when I got my assignment,' Sandoval nodded. 'I even went directly to Yuan milieu HQ in Khan Baligh – Cambaluc, or Peking to you. They told me they'd checked it clear back to Genghis's lifetime, and spatially as far as Indonesia. And it was all perfectly okay, like the Norse and their Vinland. It simply didn't happen to have gotten the same publicity. As far as the Chinese court knew, an expedition had been sent out and had never returned, and Kublai decided it wasn't worthwhile to send another. The record of it lay in the Imperial archives, but was destroyed during the Ming revolt which expelled the Mongols. Historiography forgot the incident.'

Still Everard brooded. Normally he liked his work, but there was something abnormal about this occasion.

'Obviously,' he said, 'the expedition met a disaster. We'd like to know what. But why do you need an Unattached agent to spy on them?'

Sandoval turned from the window. It crossed Everard's mind again, fleetingly, how little the Navajo belonged here. He was born in 1930, had fought in Korea and gone through college on the G.I. bill before the Patrol contacted him, but somehow he never quite fitted the twentieth century.

Well, do any of us? Could any man with real roots stand knowing what will eventually happen to his own people?

'But I'm not supposed to spy!' Sandoval exclaimed. 'When I'd reported, my orders came straight back from Danellian headquarters. No explanation, no excuses, the naked command: to arrange that disaster. To revise history myself!'

2

Anno Domini One Thousand Two Hundred Eighty:

The writ of Kublai Khan ran over degrees of latitude and longitude; he dreamed of world empire, and his court honored any guest who brought fresh knowledge or new philosophy. A young Venetian merchant named Marco Polo had become a particular favorite. But not all peoples desired a Mongol overlord. Revolutionary secret societies germinated throughout those several conquered realms lumped together as Cathay. Japan, with the Hojo family an able power behind the throne, had already repelled one invasion. Nor were the Mongols unified, save in theory. The Russian princes had become tax collectors for the Golden Horde; the Il-Khan Abaka sat in Baghdad.

Elsewhere, a shadowy Abbasid Caliphate had refuge in Cairo; Delhi was under the Slave Dynasty; Nicholas III was Pope; Guelphs and Ghibbelines were ripping up Italy; Rudolf of Habsburg was German Emperor, Philip the Bold was King of France, Edward Longshanks ruled England. Contemporaries included Dante Alighieri, Joannes Duns Scotus, Roger Bacon, and Thomas the Rhymer.

And in North America, Manse Everard and John Sandoval reined their horses to stare down a long hill.

'The date I first saw them is last week,' said the Navajo. 'They've come quite a ways since. At this rate, they'll be in Mexico in a couple of months, even allowing for some rugged country ahead.'

'By Mongol standards,' Everard told him, 'they're proceeding leisurely.'

He raised his binoculars. Around him, the land burned green with April. Even the highest and oldest beeches fluttered gay young leaves. Pines roared in the wind, which blew down off the mountains cold and swift and smelling of melted snow, through a sky where birds were homebound in such flocks that they could darken the sun. The peaks of the Cascade range seemed to float in the west, blue-white, distant, and holy. Eastward the foothills tumbled in clumps of forest and meadow to a valley, and so at last, beyond the horizon, to prairies thunderous under buffalo herds.

Everard focused on the expedition. It wound through the open areas, more or less following a small river. Some seventy men rode shaggy, dun-colored, short-legged, long-headed Asian horses. They led pack animals and remounts. He identified a few native guides, as much by their awkward seat in the saddle as by their physiognomy and clothing. But the newcomers held his attention most.

'A lot of pregnant mares toting packs,' he remarked, half to himself. 'I suppose they took as many horses in the ships as they could, letting them out to exercise and graze wherever they made a stop. Now they're breeding more as they go along. That kind of pony is tough enough to survive such treatment.'

'The detachment at the ships is also raising horses,' Sandoval informed him. 'I saw that much.'

'What else do you know about this bunch?'

'No more than I've told you, which is little more than you've now seen. And that record which lay for a while in Kublai's archives. But you recall, it barely notes that four ships under the command of the Noyon Toktai and the scholar Li Tai-Tsung were dispatched to explore the islands beyond Japan.'

Everard nodded absently. No sense in sitting here and rehashing what they'd already gone over a hundred times. It was only a way of postponing action.

Sandoval cleared his throat. 'I'm still dubious about both of us going down there,' he said. 'Why don't you stay in reserve, in case they get nasty?'

'Hero complex, huh?' said Everard. 'No, we're better off together. I don't expect trouble anyhow. Not yet. Those boys are much too intelligent to antagonize anyone gratuitously. They've stayed on good terms with the Indians, haven't they? And we'll be a far more unknown quantity … I wouldn't mind a drink beforehand, though.'

'Yeh. And afterward, too!'

Each dipped in his saddlebag, took out a half-gallon canteen and hoisted it. The Scotch was pungent in Everard's throat, heartening in his veins. He clucked to his horse and both Patrolmen rode down the slope.

A whistling cut the air. They had been seen. He maintained a steady pace toward the head of the Mongol line. A pair of outriders closed in on either flank, arrows nocked to their short powerful bows, but did not interfere.

I suppose we look harmless, Everard thought. Like Sandoval, he wore twentieth-century outdoor clothes: hunting jacket to break the wind, hat to keep off the rain. His own outfit was a good deal less elegant than the Navajo's Abercrombie & Fitch special. They both bore daggers for show, Mauser machine pistols and thirtieth-century stun-beam projectors for business.

The troop reined in, so disciplined that it was almost like one man halting. Everard scanned them closely as he neared. He had gotten a pretty complete electronic education in an hour or so before departure – language, history, technology, manners, morals – of Mongols and Chinese and even the local Indians. But he had never before seen these people close up.

They weren't spectacular: stocky, bowlegged, with thin beards and flat, broad faces that shone greased in the sunlight. They were all well equipped, wearing boots and trousers, laminated leather cuirasses with lacquer ornamentation, conical steel helmets that might have a spike or plume on top. Their weapons were curved sword, knife, lance, compound bow. One man near the head of the line bore a standard of gold-braided yak tails. They watched the Patrolmen approach, their narrow dark eyes impassive.

The chief was readily identified. He rode in the van, and a tattered silken cloak blew from his shoulders. He was rather larger and even more hard-faced than his average trooper, with a reddish beard and almost Roman nose. The Indian guide beside him gaped and huddled back; but Toktai Noyon held his place, measuring Everard with a steady carnivore look.

'Greeting,' he called, when the newcomers were in earshot. 'What spirit brings you?' He spoke the Lutuami dialect, which was later to become the Klamath language, with an atrocious accent.

Everard replied in flawless, barking Mongolian:'Greeting to you, Toktai son of Batu. The Tengri willing, we come in peace.'

It was an effective touch. Everard glimpsed Mongols reaching for lucky charms or making signs against the evil eye. But the man mounted at Toktai's left was quick to recover a schooled self-possession. 'Ah,' he said, 'so men of the Western lands have also reached this country. We did not know that.'

Everard looked at him. He was taller than any Mongol, his skin almost white, his features and hands delicate. Though dressed much like the others, he was unarmed. He seemed older than the Noyon, perhaps fifty. Everard bowed in the saddle and switched to North Chinese: 'Honored Li Tai-Tsung, it grieves this insignificant person to contradict your eminence, but we belong to the great realm further south.'

'We have heard rumors,' said the scholar. He couldn't quite suppress excitement. 'Even this far north, tales have been borne of a rich and splendid country. We are seeking it that we may bring your Khan the greeting of the Kha Khan, Kublai son of Tuli, son of Genghis; the earth lies at his feet.'

'We know of the Kha Khan,' said Everard, 'as we know of the Caliph, the Pope, the Emperor, and all lesser monarchs.' He had to pick his way with care, not openly insulting Cathay's ruler but still subtly putting him in his place. 'Little is known in return of us, for our master does not seek the outside world, nor encourage it to seek him. Permit me to introduce my unworthy self. I am called Everard and am not, as my appearance would suggest, a Russian or Westerner. I belong to the border guardians.'

Let them figure out what that meant.

'You didn't come with much company,' snapped Toktai.

'More was not required,' said Everard in his smoothest voice.

'And you are far from home,' put in Li.

'No farther than you would be, honorable sirs, in the Kirghiz marches.'

Toktai clapped a hand to his sword hilt. His eyes were chill and wary. 'Come,' he said. 'Be welcome as ambassadors, then. Let's make camp and hear the word of your king.'

3

The sun, low above the western peaks, turned their snowcaps tarnished silver. Shadows lengthened down in the valley, the forest darkened, but the open meadow seemed to glow all the brighter. The underlying quiet made almost a sounding board for such noises as existed: rapid swirl and cluck of the river, ring of an ax, horses cropping in long grass. Woodsmoke tinged the air.

The Mongols were obviously taken aback at their visitors and this early halt. They kept wooden faces, but their eyes would stray to Everard and Sandoval and they would mutter formulas of their various religions – chiefly pagan, but some Buddhist, Moslem, or Nestorian prayers. It did not impair the efficiency with which they set up camp, posted guard, cared for the animals, prepared to cook supper. But Everard judged they were more quiet than usual. The patterns impressed on his brain by the educator called Mongols talkative and cheerful as a rule.

He sat cross-legged on a tent floor. Sandoval, Toktai, and Li completed the circle. Rugs lay under them, and a brazier kept a pot of tea hot. It was the only tent pitched, probably the only one available, taken along for use on ceremonial occasions like this. Toktai poured *kumiss* with his own hands and offered it to Everard, who slurped as loudly as etiquette demanded and passed it on. He had drunk worse things than fermented mare's milk, but was glad that everyone switched to tea after the ritual.

The Mongol chief spoke. He couldn't keep his tone smooth, as his Chinese amanuensis did. There was an instinctive bristling: what foreigner dares approach the Kha Khan's man, save on his belly? But the words remained courteous: 'Now let our guests declare the business of their king. First, would you name him for us?'

'His name may not be spoken,' said Everard. 'Of his realm you have heard only the palest rumors. You may judge his power, Noyon, by the fact that he needed only us two to come this far, and that we needed only one mount apiece.'

Toktai grunted. 'Those are handsome animals you ride, though I wonder how well they'd do on the steppes. Did it take you long to get here?'

'No more than a day, Noyon. We have means.' Everard reached in his jacket and brought out a couple of small gift-wrapped parcels. 'Our lord bade us present the Cathayan leaders with these tokens of regard.'

While the paper was being removed, Sandoval leaned over and hissed in English: 'Dig their expressions, Manse. We goofed a bit.'

'How?'

'That flashy cellophane and stuff impresses a barbarian like Toktai. But notice Li. His civilization was doing calligraphy when the ancestors of Bonwit Teller were painting themselves blue. His opinion of our taste has just nosedived.'

Everard shrugged imperceptibly. 'Well, he's right, isn't he?'

Their colloquy had not escaped the others. Toktai gave them a hard stare, but returned to his present, a flashlight, which had to be demonstrated and exclaimed over. He was a little afraid of it at first, even mumbled a charm; then he remembered that a Mongol wasn't allowed to be afraid of anything except thunder, mastered himself, and was soon as delighted as a child. The best bet for a Confucian scholar like Li seemed to be a book, the *Family of Man* collection, whose diversity and alien pictorial technique might impress him. He was effusive in his thanks, but Everard doubted if he was overwhelmed. A Patrolman soon learned that sophistication exists at any level of technology.

Gifts must be made in return: a fine Chinese sword and a bundle of sea-otter pelts from the coast. It was quite some time before the conversation could turn back to business. Then Sandoval managed to get the other party's account first.

'Since you know so much,' Toktai began, 'you must also know that our invasion of Japan failed several years ago.'

'The will of heaven was otherwise,' said Li, with courtier blandness.

'Horse apples!' growled Toktai. 'The stupidity of men was otherwise, you mean. We were too few, too ignorant, and we'd come too far in seas too rough. And what of it? We'll return there one day.'

Everard knew rather sadly that they would, and that a storm would destroy the fleet and drown who knows how many young men. But he let Toktai continue:

'The Kha Khan realized we must learn more about the islands. Perhaps we should try to establish a base somewhere north of Hokkaido. Then, too, we have long heard rumors about lands farther west. Fishermen are blown off course now and then, and have glimpses; traders from Siberia speak of a strait and a country beyond. The Kha Khan got four ships with Chinese crews and told me to take a hundred Mongol warriors and see what I could discover.'

Everard nodded, unsurprised. The Chinese had been sailing junks for hundreds of years, some holding up to a thousand passengers. True, these craft weren't as seaworthy as they would become in later centuries under

Portuguese influence, and their owners had never been much attracted by any ocean, let alone the cold northern waters. But still, there were some Chinese navigators who would have picked up tricks of the trade from stray Koreans and Formosans, if not from their own fathers. They must have a little familiarity with the Kuriles, at least.

'We followed two chains of islands, one after another,' said Toktai. 'They were bleak enough, but we could stop here and there, let the horses out, and learn something from the natives. Though the Tengri know it's hard to do that last, when you may have to interpret through six languages! We did find out that there are two mainlands, Siberia and another, which come so close together up north that a man might cross in a skin boat, or walk across the ice in winter sometimes. Finally we came to the new mainland. A big country; forests, much game and seals. Too rainy, though. Our ships seemed to want to continue, so we followed the coast, more or less.'

Everard visualized a map. If you go first along the Kuriles and then the Aleutians, you are never far from land. Fortunate to avoid the shipwreck which had been a distinct possibility, the shallow-draft junks had been able to find anchorage even at those rocky islands. Also, the current urged them along, and they were very nearly on a great-circle course. Toktai had discovered Alaska before he quite knew what had happened. Since the country grew ever more hospitable as he coasted south, he passed up Puget Sound and proceeded clear to the Chehalis River. Maybe the Indians had warned him the Columbia mouth, further on, was dangerous – and, more recently, had helped his horsemen cross the great stream on rafts.

'We set up camp when the war was waning,' said the Mongol. 'The tribes thereabouts are backward, but friendly. They gave us all the food, women, and help we could ask for. In return, our sailors taught them some tricks of fishing and boatbuilding. We wintered there, learned some of the languages, and made trips inland. Everywhere were tales of huge forests and plains where herds of wild cattle blacken the earth. We saw enough to know the stories were true. I've never been in so rich a land.' His eyes gleamed tigerishly. 'And so few dwellers, who don't even know the use of iron.'

'Noyon,' murmured Li warningly. He nodded his head very slightly toward the Patrolmen. Toktai clamped his mouth shut.

Li turned to Everard and said, 'There were also rumors of a golden realm far to the south. We felt it our duty to investigate this, as well as explore the country in between. We had not looked for the honor of being met by your eminent selves.'

'The honor is all ours,' Everard purred. Then, putting on his gravest face: 'My lord of the Golden Empire, who may not be named, has sent us in a spirit of friendship. It would grieve him to see you meet disaster. We come to warn you.'

'What?' Toktai sat up straight. One sinewy hand snatched for the sword which, politely, he wasn't wearing. 'What in the hells is this?'

'In the hells indeed, Noyon. Pleasant though this country seems, it lies under a curse. Tell him, my brother.'

Sandoval, who had a better speaking voice, took over. His yarn had been concocted with an eye to exploiting that superstition which still lingered in the half-civilized Mongols, without generating too much Chinese skepticism. There were really two great southern kingdoms, he explained. Their own lay far away; its rival was somewhat north and east of it, with a citadel on the plains. Both states possessed immense powers, call them sorcery or subtle engineering, as you wished. The northerly empire, Badguys, considered all this territory as its own and would not tolerate a foreign expedition. Its scouts were certain to discover the Mongols before long, and would annihilate them with thunderbolts. The benevolent southern land of Goodguys could offer no protection, could only send emissaries warning the Mongols to turn home again.

'Why have the natives not spoken of these overlords?' asked Li shrewdly.

'Has every little tribesman in the jungles of Burma heard about the Kha Khan?' responded Sandoval.

'I am a stranger and ignorant,' said Li. 'Forgive me if I do not understand your talk of irresistible weapons.'

Which is the politest way I've ever been called a liar, thought Everard. Aloud: 'I can offer a small demonstration, if the Noyon has an animal that may be killed.'

Toktai considered. His visage might have been scarred stone, but sweat filmed it. He clapped his hands and barked orders to the guard who looked in. Thereafter they made small talk against a silence that thickened.

A warrior appeared after some endless part of an hour. He said that a couple of horsemen had lassoed a deer. Would it serve the Noyon's purpose? It would. Toktai led the way out, shouldering through a thick and buzzing swarm of men. Everard followed, wishing this weren't needful. He slipped the rifle stock onto his Mauser. 'Care to do the job?' he asked Sandoval.

'Christ, no.'

The deer, a doe, had been forced back to camp. She trembled by the river, the horsehair ropes about her neck. The sun, just touching the western peaks, turned her to bronze. There was a blind sort of gentleness in her look at Everard. He waved back the men around her and took aim. The first slug killed her, but he kept the gun chattering till her carcass was gruesome.

When he lowered his weapon, the air felt somehow rigid. He looked across all the thick bandy-legged bodies, the flat, grimly controlled faces; he could smell them with unnatural sharpness, a clean odor of sweat and horses and smoke. He felt himself as nonhuman as they must see him.

'That is the least of the arms used here,' he said. 'A soul so torn from the body would not find its way home.'

He turned on his heel. Sandoval followed him. Their horses had been staked out, the gear piled close by. They saddled, unspeaking, mounted and rode off into the forest.

4

The fire blazed up in a gust of wind. Sparingly laid by a woodsman, in that moment it barely brought the two out of shadow – a glimpse of brow, nose, and cheekbones, a gleam of eyes. It sank down again to red and blue sputtering above white coals, and darkness took the men.

Everard wasn't sorry. He fumbled his pipe in his hands, bit hard on it and drank smoke, but found little comfort. When he spoke, the vast soughing of trees, high up in the night, almost buried his voice, and he did not regret that either.

Nearby were their sleeping bags, their horses, the scooter – antigravity sled cum space-time hopper – which had brought them. Otherwise the land was empty; mile upon mile, human fires like their own were as small and lonely as stars in the universe. Somewhere a wolf howled.

'I suppose,' Everard said, 'every cop feels like a bastard occasionally. You've just been an observer so far, Jack. Active assignments, such as I get, are often hard to accept.'

'Yeh.' Sandoval had been even more quiet than his friend. He had scarcely stirred since supper.

'And now this. Whatever you have to do to cancel a temporal interference, you can at least think you're restoring the original line of development.' Everard fumed on his pipe. 'Don't remind me that "original" is meaningless in this context. It's a consoling word.'

'Uh-huh.'

'But when our bosses, our dead Danellian supermen, tell *us* to interfere … We know Toktai's people never came back to Cathay. Why should you or I have to take a hand? If they ran into hostile Indians or something and were wiped-out, I wouldn't mind. At least, no more than I mind any similar incident in that Goddamned slaughterhouse they call human history.'

'We don't have to kill them, you know. Just make them turn back. Your demonstration this afternoon may be enough.'

'Yeah. Turn back … and what? Probably perish at sea. They won't have an easy trip home – storm, fog, contrary currents, rocks – in those primitive ships meant mostly for rivers. And we'll have set them on that trip at precisely that time! If we didn't interfere, they'd start home later, the circumstances of the voyage would be different … Why should we take the guilt?'

'They could even make it home,' murmured Sandoval.

'What?' Everard started.

'The way Toktai was talking. I'm sure he plans to go back on a horse, not on those ships. As he's guessed, Bering Strait is easy to cross; the Aleuts do it all the time. Manse, I'm afraid it isn't enough simply to spare them.'

'But they aren't going to get home! We know that!'

'Suppose they do make it.' Sandoval began to talk a bit louder and much faster. The night wind roared around his words. 'Let's play with ideas awhile. Suppose Toktai pushes on southeastward. It's hard to see what could stop him. His men can live off the country, even the deserts, far more handily than Coronado of any of those boys. He hasn't terribly far to go before he reaches a high-grade neolithic people, the agricultural Pueblo tribes. That will encourage him all the more. He'll be in Mexico before August. Mexico's just as dazzling now as it was – will be – in Cortez's day. And even more tempting: the Aztecs and Toltecs are still settling who's to be master, with any number of other tribes hanging around ready to help a newcomer against both. The Spanish guns made, will make, no real difference, as you'll recall if you've read Diaz. The Mongols are as superior, man for man, as any Spaniard ... Not that I imagine Toktai would wade right in. He'd doubtless be very polite, spend the winter, learn everything he could. Next year he'd go back north, proceed home, and report to Kublai that some of the richest, most gold-stuffed territory on earth was wide open for conquest!'

'How about the other Indians?' put in Everard. 'I'm vague on them.'

'The Mayan New Empire is at its height. A tough nut to crack, but a correspondingly rewarding one. I should think, once the Mongols got established in Mexico, there'd be no stopping them. Peru has an even higher culture at this moment, and much less organization than Pizarro faced; the Quechua-Aymar, the so-called Inca race, are still only one power down there among several.

'And then, the land! Can you visualize what a Mongol tribe would make of the Great Plains?'

'I can't see them emigrating in hordes,' said Everard. There was that about Sandoval's voice which made him uneasy and defensive. 'Too much Siberia and Alaska in the way.'

'Worse obstacles have been overcome. I don't mean they'd pour in all at once. It might take them a few centuries to start mass immigration, as it will take the Europeans. I can imagine a string of clans and tribes being established in the course of some years, all down western North America. Mexico and Yucatan get gobbled up – or, more likely, become khanates. The herding tribes move eastward as their own population grows and as new immigrants arrive. Remember, the Yuan dynasty is due to be overthrown in less than a century. That'll put additional pressure on the Mongols in Asia to go else-where. And Chinese will come here too, to farm and to share in the gold.'

'I should think, if you don't mind my saying so,' Everard broke in softly, 'that you of all people wouldn't want to hasten the conquest of America.'

'It'd be a different conquest,' said Sandoval. 'I don't care about the Aztecs; if you study them, you'll agree that Cortez did Mexico a favor. It'd be rough on other, more harmless tribes too – for a while. And yet, the Mongols aren't such devils. Are they? A Western background prejudices us. We forget how much torture and massacre the Europeans were enjoying at the same time.

'The Mongols are quite a bit like the old Romans, really. Same practice of depopulating areas that resist, but respecting the rights of those who make submission. Same armed protection and competent government. Same unimaginative, uncreative national character; but the same vague awe and envy of true civilization. The *Pax Mongolica*, right now, unites a bigger area, and brings more different peoples into stimulating contact, than that piddling Roman Empire ever imagined.

'As for the Indians – remember, the Mongols are herdsmen. There won't be anything like the unsolvable conflict between hunter and farmer that made the white man destroy the Indian. The Mongol hasn't got race prejudices, either. And after a little fighting, the average Navajo, Cherokee, Seminole, Algonquin, Chippewa, Dakota, will be glad to submit and become allied. Why not? He'll get horses, sheep, cattle, textiles, metallurgy. He'll outnumber the invaders, and be on much more nearly equal terms with them than with white farmers and machine-age industry. And there'll be the Chinese, I repeat, leavening the whole mixture, teaching civilization and sharpening wits ...

'Good God, Manse! When Columbus gets here, he'll find his Grand Cham all right! The Sachem Khan of the strongest nation on earth!'

Sandoval stopped. Everard listened to the gallows creak of branches in the wind. He looked into the night for a long while before he said, 'It could be. Of course, we'd have to stay in this century till the crucial point was past. Our own world wouldn't exist. Wouldn't ever have existed.'

'It wasn't such a hell of a good world anyway,' said Sandoval, as if in dream.

'You might think about your ... oh ... parents. They'd never have been born either.'

'They lived in a tumbledown hogan. I saw my father crying once, because he couldn't buy shoes for us in winter. My mother died of T.B.'

Everard sat unstirring. It was Sandoval who shook himself and jumped to his feet with a rattling kind of laugh. 'What have I been mumbling? It was just a yarn, Manse. Let's turn in. Shall I take first watch?'

Everard agreed, but lay long awake.

5

The scooter had jumped two days futureward and now hovered invisibly far above to the naked eye. Around it, the air was thin and sharply cold. Everard shivered as he adjusted the electronic telescope. Even at full magnification, the caravan was little more than specks toiling across green immensity. But no one else in the Western Hemisphere could have been riding horses.

He twisted in the saddle to face his companion. 'So now what?'

Sandoval's broad countenance was unreadable. 'Well, if our demonstration didn't work –'

'It sure as hell didn't! I swear they're moving south twice as fast as before. Why?'

'I'd have to know all of them a lot better than I do, as individuals, to give you a real answer, Manse. But essentially it must be that we challenged their courage. A warlike culture, nerve and hardihood its only absolute virtues ... what choice have they got but to go on? If they retreated before a mere threat, they'd never be able to live with themselves.'

'But Mongols aren't idiots! They didn't conquer everybody in sight by bull strength, but by jolly well understanding military principles better. Toktai should retreat, report to the Emperor what he saw, and organize a bigger expedition.'

'The men at the ships can do that,' Sandoval reminded. 'Now that I think about it, I see how grossly we underestimated Toktai. He must have set a date, presumably next year, for the ships to try and go home if he doesn't return. When he finds something interesting along the way, like us, he can dispatch an Indian with a letter to the base camp.'

Everard nodded. It occurred to him that he had been rushed into this job, all the way down the line, with never a pause to plan it as he should have done. Hence this botch. But how much blame must fall on the subconscious reluctance of John Sandoval? After a minute Everard said: 'They may even have smelled something fishy about us. The Mongols were always good at psychological warfare.'

'Could be. But what's our next move?'

Swoop down from above, fire a few blasts from the forty-first-century energy gun mounted in this timecycle, and that's the end ... No, by God, they can send me to the exile planet before I'll do any such thing. There are decent limits.

'We'll rig up a more impressive demonstration,' said Everard.

'And if it flops too?'

'Shut up! Give it a chance!'

'I was just wondering.' The wind harried under Sandoval's words. 'Why not cancel the expedition instead? Go back in time a couple of years and persuade Kublai Khan it isn't worthwhile sending explorers eastward. Then all this would never have happened.'

'You know Patrol regs forbid us to make historical changes.'

'What do you call this we're doing?'

'Something specifically ordered by supreme HQ Perhaps to correct some interference elsewhere, elsewhen. How should I know? I'm only a step on the evolutionary ladder. They have abilities a million years hence that I can't even guess at.'

'Father knows best,' murmured Sandoval.

Everard set his jaws. 'The fact remains,' he said, 'the court of Kublai, the most powerful man on earth, is more important and crucial than anything here in America. No, you rang me in on this miserable job, and now I'll pull rank on you if I must. Our orders are to make these people give up their exploration. What happens afterward is none of our business. So they don't make it home. We won't be the proximate cause, any more than you're a murderer if you invite a man to dinner and he has a fatal accident on the way.'

'Stop quacking and let's get to work,' rapped Sandoval.

Everard sent the scooter gliding forward. 'See that hill?' he pointed after a while. 'It's on Toktai's line of march, but I think he'll camp a few miles short of it tonight, down in that little meadow by the stream. The hill will be in his plain view, though. Let's set up shop on it.'

'And make fireworks? It'll have to be pretty fancy. Those Cathayans know about gunpowder. They even have military rockets.'

'Small ones. I know. But when I assembled my gear for this trip, I packed away some fairly versatile gadgetry, in case my first attempt failed.'

The hill bore a sparse crown of pine trees. Everard landed the scooter among them and began to unload boxes from its sizeable baggage compartments. Sandoval helped, wordless. The horses, Patrol trained, stepped calmly off the framework stalls which had borne them and started grazing along the slope.

After a while the Indian broke his silence. 'This isn't my line of work. What are you rigging?'

Everard patted the small machine he had half assembled. 'It's adapted from a weather-control system used in the Cold Centuries era upstairs. A potential distributor. It can make some of the damnedest lightning you ever saw, with thunder to match.'

'Mmm … the great Mongol weakness.' Suddenly Sandoval grinned. 'You win. We might as well relax and enjoy this.'

'Fix us a supper, will you, while I put the gimmick together? No fire, naturally. We don't want any mundane smoke … Oh, yes, I also have a mirage projector. If you'll change clothes and put on a hood or something at the appropriate moment, so you can't be recognized, I'll paint a mile-high picture of you, half as ugly as life.'

'How about a P.A. system? Navajo chants can be fairly alarming, if you don't know it's just a *yeibichai* or whatever.'

'Coming up!'

The day waned. It grew murky under the pines; the air was chill and pungent. At last Everard devoured a sandwich and watched through his binoculars as the Mongol vanguard checked that campsite he had predicted. Others came riding in with their day's catch of game and went to work cooking. The main body showed up at sundown, posted itself efficiently, and ate. Toktai was indeed pushing hard, using every daylight moment. As darkness closed down, Everard glimpsed outposts mounted and with strung bows. He could not keep up his own spirits, however hard he tried. He was bucking men who had shaken the earth.

Early stars glittered above snowpeaks. It was time to begin work.

'Got our horses tethered, Jack? They might panic. I'm fairly sure the Mongol horses will! Okay, here goes.' Everard flipped a main switch and squatted by the dimly lit control dials of his apparatus.

First there was the palest blue flicker between earth and sky. Then the lightnings began, tongue after forked tongue leaping, trees smashed at a blow, the mountainsides rocking under their noise. Everard threw out ball lightning, spheres of flame which whirled and curvetted, trailing sparks, shooting across to the camp and exploding above it till the sky seemed white hot.

Deafened and half blinded, he managed to project a sheet of fluorescing ionization. Like northern lights the great banners curled, bloody red and bone white, hissing under the repeated thunder cracks. Sandoval trod forth. He had stripped to his pants, daubed clay on his body in archaic patterns; his face was not veiled after all, but smeared with earth and twisted into something Everard would not have known. The machine scanned him and altered its output. That which stood forth against the aurora was taller than a mountain. It moved in a shuffling dance, from horizon to horizon and back to the sky, and it wailed and barked in a falsetto louder than thunder.

Everard crouched beneath the lurid light, his fingers stiff on the control board. He knew a primitive fear of his own; the dance woke things in him that he had forgotten.

Judas priest! If this doesn't make them quit …

His mind returned to him. He even looked at his watch. Half an hour … give them another fifteen minutes, in which the display tapered off … They'd surely stay in camp till dawn rather than blunder wildly out in the dark, they had that much discipline. So keep everything under wraps for several hours more, then administer the last stroke to their nerves by a single electric bolt smiting a tree right next to them … Everard waved Sandoval back. The Indian sat down, panting harder than his exertions seemed to warrant.

When the noise was gone, Everard said, 'Nice show, Jack.' His voice sounded tinny and strange in his ears.

'I hadn't done anything like that for years,' muttered Sandoval. He struck a match, startling noise in the quietness. The brief flame showed his lips gone thin. Then he shook out the match and only his cigarette-end glowed.

'Nobody I knew, on the reservation, took that stuff seriously,' he went on after a moment. 'A few of the older men wanted us boys to learn it to keep the custom alive, to remind us we were still a people. But mostly our idea was to pick up some change by dancing for tourists.'

There was a longer pause. Everard doused the projector completely. In the murk that followed, Sandoval's cigarette waxed and waned, a tiny red Algol.

'Tourists!' he said at last.

After more minutes: 'Tonight I was dancing for a purpose. It meant something. I never felt that way before.'

Everard was silent.

Until one of the horses, which had plunged at its halter's end during the performance and was still nervous, whinnied.

Everard looked up. Night met his eyes. 'Did you hear anything, Jack?'

The flashlight beam speared him.

For an instant he stared blinded at it. Then he sprang erect, cursing and snatching for his stun pistol. A shadow ran from behind one of the trees. It struck him in the ribs. He lurched back. The beam gun flew to his hand. He shot at random.

The flashlight swept about once more. Everard glimpsed Sandoval. The Navajo had not donned his weapons again. Unarmed, he dodged the sweep of a Mongol blade. The swordsman ran after him. Sandoval reverted to Patrol judo. He went to one knee. Clumsy afoot, the Mongol slashed, missed, and ran straight into a shoulder block to the belly. Sandoval rose with the blow. The heel of his hand jolted upward to the Mongol's chin. The helmeted head snapped back. Sandoval chopped a hand at the Adam's apple, yanked the sword from its owner's grasp, turned and parried a cut from behind.

A voice yammered above the Mongol yipping, giving orders. Everard backed away. He had knocked one attacker out with a bolt from his pistol. There were others between him and the scooter. He circled to face them. A lariat curled around his shoulders. It tightened with one expert heave. He went over. Four men piled on him. He saw half a dozen lance butts crack down on Sandoval's head, then there wasn't time for anything but fighting. Twice he got to his feet, but his gun was gone by now, the Mauser was plucked from its holster – the little men were pretty good at *yawara*-style combat themselves. They dragged him down and hit him with fists, boots, dagger pommels. He never quite lost consciousness, but he finally stopped caring.

6

Toktai struck camp before dawn. The first sun saw his troop wind between scattered copses on a broad valley floor. The land was turning flat and arid, the mountains to the right farther away, fewer snowpeaks visible and those ghostly in a pale sky.

The hardy small Mongol horses trotted ahead – plop of hoofs, squeak and jingle of harness. Looking back, Everard saw the line as a compact mass; lances rose and fell, pennants and plumes and cloaks fluttered beneath, and under that were the helmets, with a brown slit-eyed face and a grotesquely painted cuirass visible here and there. No one spoke, and he couldn't read any of those expressions.

His brain felt sandy. They had left his hands free, but lashed his ankles to the stirrups, and the cord chafed. They had also stripped him naked – sensible precaution, who knew what instruments might be sewn into his garments? – and the Mongol garb given him in exchange was ludicrously small. The seams had had to be slit before he could even get the tunic on.

The projector and the scooter lay back at the hill. Toktai would not take any risks with those things of power. He had had to roar down several of his own frightened warriors before they would even agree to bring the strange horses, with saddle and bedroll, riderless among the pack mares.

Hoofs thudded rapidly. One of the bowmen flanking Everard grunted and moved his pony a little aside. Li Tai-Tsung rode close.

The Patrolman gave him a dull stare. 'Well?' he said.

'I fear your friend will not waken again,' answered the Chinese. 'I made him a little more comfortable.'

But lying strapped on an improvised litter between two ponies, unconscious ... Yes, concussion, when they clubbed him last night. A Patrol hospital could put him to rights soon enough. But the nearest Patrol office is in Cambaluc, and I can't see Toktai letting me go back to the scooter and use its radio. John Sandoval is going to die here, six hundred and fifty years before he was born.

Everard looked into cool brown eyes, interested, not unsympathetic, but alien to him. It was no use, he knew; arguments which were logical in his culture were gibberish today; but one had to try. 'Can you, at least, not make Toktai understand what ruin he is going to bring on himself, on his whole people, by this?'

Li stroked his fork beard. 'It is plain to see, honored sir, your nation has arts unknown to us,' he said. 'But what of it? The barbarians –' He gave Everard's Mongol guards a quick glance, but evidently they didn't understand the Sung Chinese he used – 'took many kingdoms superior to them in every way but fighting skill. Now already we know that you, ah, amended the truth when you spoke of a hostile empire near these lands. Why should your king try to frighten us away with a falsehood, did he not have reason to fear us?'

Everard spoke with care: 'Our glorious emperor dislikes bloodshed. But if you force him to strike you down –'

'Please.' Li looked pained. He waved one slender hand, as if brushing off an insect. 'Say what you will to Toktai, and I shall not interfere. It would not sadden me to return home; I came only under Imperial orders. But let us two, speaking confidentially, not insult each other's intelligence. Do you not see, eminent lord, that there is no possible harm with which you can threaten these men? Death they despise; even the most lingering torture must kill them in time; even the most-disgraceful mutilation can be made as naught by a man willing to bite through his tongue and die. Toktai sees eternal shame if he turns back at this stage of events, and a good chance of eternal glory and uncountable wealth if he continues.'

Everard sighed. His own humiliating capture had indeed been the turning point. The Mongols had been very near bolting at the thunder show. Many had groveled and wailed (and from now on would be all the more aggressive, to erase that memory). Toktai charged the source as much in horror as defiance; a few men and horses had been able to come along. Li himself was partly responsible: scholar, skeptic, familiar with sleight-of-hand and pyrotechnic displays, the Chinese had helped hearten Toktai to attack before one of those thunderbolts did strike home.

The truth of the matter is, son, we misjudged these people. We should have taken along a Specialist, who'd have an intuitive feeling for the nuances of this culture. But no, we assumed a brainful of facts would be enough. Now what? A Patrol relief expedition may show up eventually, but Jack will be dead in another day or two ... Everard looked at the stony warrior face on his left. *Quite probably I'll be also. They're still on edge. They'd sooner scrag me than not.*

And even if he should (unlikely chance!) survive to be hauled out of this mess by another Patrol band – it would be tough to face his comrades. An Unattached agent, with all the special privileges of his rank, was expected to handle situations without extra help. Without leading valuable men to their deaths.

'So I advise you most sincerely not to attempt any more deceptions.'

'What?' Everard turned back to Li.

'You do understand, do you not,' said the Chinese, 'that our native guides did flee? That you are now taking their place? But we expect to meet other tribes before long, establish communication ...'

Everard nodded a throbbing head. The sunlight pierced his eyes. He was not astonished at the ready Mongol progress through scores of separate language areas. If you aren't fussy about grammar, a few hours suffice to pick up the small number of basic words and gestures; thereafter you can take days or weeks actually learning to speak with your hired escort.

'... and obtain guides from stage to stage, as we did before,' continued Li. 'Any misdirection you may have given will soon be apparent. Toktai will punish it in most uncivilized ways. On the other hand, faithful service will be rewarded. You may hope in time to rise high in the provincial court, after the conquest.'

Everard sat unmoving. The casual boast was like an explosion in his mind.

He had been assuming the Patrol would send another force. Obviously *something* was going to prevent Toktai's return. But was it so obvious? Why had this interference been ordered at all, if there were not – in some paradoxical way his twentieth-century logic couldn't grasp – an uncertainty, a shakiness in the continuum right at this point?

Judas in hell! Perhaps the Mongol expedition was going to succeed! Perhaps all the future of an American Khanate which Sandoval had not quite dared dream of ... was the real future.

There are quirks and discontinuities in space-time. The world lines can double back and bite themselves off, so that things and events appear causelessly, meaningless flutters soon lost and forgotten. Such as Manse Everard, marooned in the past with a dead John Sandoval, after coming from a future that never existed as the agent of a Time Patrol which never was.

7

At sundown their unmerciful pace had brought the expedition into sagebrush and greasewood country. The hills were steep and brown; dust smoked under hoofs; silvery-green bushes grew sparse, sweetening the air when bruised but offering little else.

Everard helped lay Sandoval on the ground. The Navajo's eyes were closed, his face sunken and hot. Sometimes he tossed and muttered a bit. Everard squeezed water from a wetted cloth past the cracked lips, but could do nothing more.

The Mongols established themselves more gaily than of late. They had overcome two great sorcerers and suffered no further attack, and the implications were growing upon them. They went about their chores chattering to each other, and after a frugal meal they broke out the leather bags of *kumiss*.

Everard remained with Sandoval, near the middle of camp. Two guards had been posted on him, who sat with strung bows a few yards away but didn't talk. Now and then one of them would get up to tend the small fire. Presently silence fell on their comrades too. Even this leathery host was tired; men rolled up and went to sleep, the outposts rode their rounds drowsy-eyed, other watch-fires burned to embers while stars kindled overhead, a coyote yelped across miles. Everard covered Sandoval against the gathering cold; his own low flames showed rime frost on sage leaves. He huddled into a cloak and wished his captors would at least give him back his pipe.

A football crunched dry soil. Everard's guards snatched arrows for their bows. Toktai moved into the light, his head bare above a mantle. The guards bent low and moved back into shadow.

Toktai halted. Everard looked up and then down again. The Noyon stared a while at Sandoval. Finally, almost gently, he said: 'I do not think your friend will live to next sunset.'

Everard grunted.

'Have you any medicines which might help?' asked Toktai. 'There are some queer things in your saddlebags.'

'I have a remedy against infection, and another against pain,' said Everard mechanically. 'But for a cracked skull, he must be taken to skillful physicians.'

Toktai sat down and held his hands to the fire. 'I'm sorry we have no surgeons along.'

'You could let us go,' said Everard without hope. 'My chariot, back at the last camp, could get him to help in time.'

'Now you know I can't do that!' Toktai chuckled. His pity for the dying man flickered out. 'After all, Eburar, you started the trouble.'

Since it was true, the Patrolman made no retort.

'I don't hold it against you,' went on Toktai. 'In fact, I'm still anxious to be friends. If I weren't I'd stop for a few days and wring all you know out of you.'

Everard flared up. 'You could try!'

'And succeed, I think, with a man who has to carry medicine against pain.' Toktai's grin was wolfish. 'However, you may be useful as a hostage or something. And I do like your nerve. I'll even tell you an idea I have. I think maybe you don't belong to this rich southland at all. I think you're an adventurer, one of a little band of shamans. You have the southern king in your power, or hope to, and don't want strangers interfering.' Toktai spat into the fire. 'There are old stories about that sort of thing, and finally a hero overthrew the wizard. Why not me?'

Everard sighed. 'You will learn why not, Noyon.' He wondered how correct that was.

'Oh, now.' Toktai clapped him on the back. 'Can't you tell me even a little? There's no blood feud between us. Let's be friends.'

Everard jerked a thumb at Sandoval.

'It's a shame, that,' said Toktai, 'but he would keep on resisting an officer of the Kha Khan. Come, let's have a drink together, Eburar. I'll send a man for a bag.'

The Patrolman made a face. 'That's no way to pacify me!'

'Oh, your people don't like *kumiss?* I'm afraid it's all we have. We drank up our wine long ago.'

'You could let me have my whisky.' Everard looked at Sandoval again, and out into night, and felt the cold creep inward. 'God, but I could use that!'

'Eh?'

'A drink of our own. We had some in our saddlebags.'

'Well ...' Toktai hesitated. 'Very well. Come along and we'll fetch it.'

The guards followed their chief and their prisoner, through the brush and the sleeping warriors, up to a pile of assorted gear also under guard. One of the latter sentries ignited a stick in his fire to give Everard some light. The Patrolman's back muscles tensed – arrows were aimed at him now, drawn to the barb – but he squatted and went through his own stuff, careful not to move fast. When he had both canteens of Scotch, he returned to his own place.

Toktai sat down across the fire. He watched Everard pour a shot into the canteen cap and toss it off. 'Smells odd,' he said.

'Try.' The Patrolman handed over the canteen.

It was an impulse of sheer loneliness. Toktai wasn't such a bad sort. Not in his own terms. And when you sit by your dying partner, you'd bouse with the devil himself, just to keep from thinking. The Mongol sniffed dubiously, looked back at Everard, paused, and then raised the bottle to his lips with a bravura gesture.

'*Whoo-oo-oo!*'

Everard scrambled to catch the flask before too much was spilled. Toktai gasped and spat. One guardsman nocked an arrow, the other sprang to lay a hard hand on Everard's shoulder. A sword gleaming high. 'It's not poison!' the Patrolman exclaimed. 'It's only too strong for him. See, I'll drink some more myself.'

Toktai waved the guards back and glared from watery eyes. 'What do you make that of?' he choked. 'Dragon's blood?'

'Barley.' Everard didn't feel like explaining distillation. He poured himself another slug. 'Go ahead, drink your mare's milk.'

Toktai smacked his lips. 'It does warm you up, doesn't it? Like pepper.' He reached out a grimy hand. 'Give me some more.'

Everard sat still for a few seconds. 'Well?' growled Toktai.

The Patrolman shook his head. 'I told you, it's too strong for Mongols.'

'What? See here, you whey-faced son of a Turk –'

'On your head be it, then. I warn you fairly, with your men here as witnesses, you will be sick tomorrow.'

Toktai guzzled heartily, belched, and passed the canteen back. 'Nonsense. I simply wasn't prepared for it, the first time. Drink up!'

Everard took his time. Toktai grew impatient. 'Hurry along there. No, give me the other flask.'

'Very well. You are the chief. But I beg you, don't try to match me draught for draught. You can't do it.'

'What do you mean, I can't do it? Why, I've drunk twenty men senseless in Karakorum. None of your gutless Chinks, either: they were all Mongols.' Toktai poured down a couple of ounces more.

Everard sipped with care. But he hardly felt the effect anyway, save as a burning along his gullet. He was too tightly strung. Suddenly he was glimpsing what might be a way out.

'Here, it's a cold night,' he said, and offered his canteen to the nearest guardsman. 'You lads have one to keep you warm.'

Toktai looked up, a trifle muzzily. 'Good stuff, this,' he objected. 'Too good for …' He remembered himself and snapped his words off short. Cruel and absolute the Mongol Empire might be, but officers shared equally with the humblest of their men.

The warrior grabbed the jug, giving his chief a resentful look, and slanted it to his mouth. 'Easy, there,' said Everard. 'It's heady.'

'Nothin's heady to me.' Toktai poured a further dose into himself. 'Sober as a bonze.' He wagged his finger. 'That's the trouble bein' a Mongol. You're so hardy you can't get drunk.'

'Are you bragging or complaining?' said Everard. The first warrior fanned his tongue, resumed a stance of alertness, and passed the bottle to his companion. Toktai hoisted the other canteen again.

'Ahhh!' He stared, owlish. 'That was fine. Well, better get to sleep now. Give him back his liquor, men.'

Everard's throat tightened. But he managed to leer. 'Yes, thanks, I'll want some more,' he said. 'I'm glad you realize you can't take it.'

'Wha' d'you mean?' Toktai glared at him. 'No such thing as too much. Not for a Mongol!' He glugged afresh. The first guardsman received the other flask and took a hasty snort before it should be too late.

Everard sucked in a shaken breath. It might work out after all. It might.

Toktai was used to carousing. There was no doubt that he or his men could handle *kumiss*, wine, ale, mead, *kvass*, that thin beer miscalled rice wine – any beverage of this era. They'd know when they'd had enough, say goodnight, and walk a straight line to their bedrolls. The trouble was, no substance merely fermented can get over about 24 proof – the process is stopped by its waste product – and most of what they brewed in the thirteenth century ran well under 5 per cent alcohol, with a high foodstuff content to boot.

Scotch whisky is in quite a different class. If you try to drink that like beer, or even like wine, you are in trouble. Your judgment will be gone before you've noticed its absence, and consciousness follows soon after.

Everard reached for the canteen held by one of the guards. 'Give me that!' he said. 'You'll drink it all up!'

The warrior grinned and took another long gulp, before passing it on to his fellow. Everard stood up and made an undignified scrabble for it. A guard poked him in the stomach. He went over on his backside. The Mongols bawled laughter, leaning on each other. So good a joke called for another drink.

When Toktai folded, Everard alone noticed. The Noyon slid from a cross-legged to a recumbent position. The fire sputtered up long enough to show a silly smile on his face. Everard squatted wire-tense.

The end of one sentry came a few minutes later. He reeled, went on all fours, and began to jettison his dinner. The other one turned, blinking, fumbling after a sword. 'Wha's mattuh?' he groaned. 'Wha' yuh done? Poison?'

Everard moved.

He had hopped over the fire and fallen on Toktai before the last guard realized it. The Mongol stumbled forward, crying out. Everard found Toktai's sword. It flashed from the scabbard as he bounded up. The warrior got his own blade aloft. Everard didn't like to kill a nearly helpless man. He stepped close, knocked the other weapon aside, and his fist clopped. The Mongol sank to his knees, retched, and slept.

Everard bounded away. Men stirred in the dark, calling. He heard hoofs drum, one of the mounted sentries racing to investigate. Somebody took a brand from an almost extinct fire and whirled it till it flared. Everard went flat on his belly.

A warrior pelted by, not seeing him in the brush. He glided toward deeper darknesses. A yell behind him, a machine-gun volley of curses, told that someone had found the Noyon.

Everard stood up and began to run.

The horses had been hobbled and turned out under guard as usual. They were a dark mass on the plain, which lay gray-white beneath a sky crowded with sharp stars. Everard saw one of the Mongol watchers gallop to meet him. A voice barked: 'What's happening?'

He pitched his answer high. 'Attack on camp!' It was only to gain time, lest the horseman recognize him and fire an arrow. He crouched, visible as a hunched and cloaked shape. The Mongol reined in with a spurt of dust. Everard sprang.

He got hold of the pony's bridle before he was recognized. Then the sentry yelled and drew sword. He hewed downward. But Everard was on the left side. The blow from above came awkwardly, easily parried. Everard chopped in return and felt his edge go into meat. The horse reared in alarm. Its rider fell from the saddle. He rolled over and staggered up again, bellowing. Everard already had one foot in a pan-shaped stirrup. The Mongol limped toward him, blood running black in that light from a wounded leg. Everard mounted and laid the flat of his own blade on the horse's crupper.

He got going toward the herd. Another rider pounded to intercept him. Everard ducked. An arrow buzzed where he had been. The stolen pony plunged, fighting its unfamiliar burden. Everard needed a minute to get it under control again. The archer might have taken him then, by coming up and going at it hand to hand. But habit sent the man past at a gallop, shooting. He missed in the dimness. Before he could turn, Everard was out of night view.

The Patrolman uncoiled a lariat at the saddlebow and broke into the skittish herd. He roped the nearest animal, which accepted it with blessed meekness. Leaning over, he slashed the hobbles with his sword and rode off, leading the remount. They came out the other side of the herd and started north.

A *stern chase is a long chase*, Everard told himself inappropriately. *But they're bound to overhaul me if I don't lose 'em. Let's see, if I remember my geography, the lava beds lie north-west of here.*

He cast a glance behind. No one pursued yet. They'd need a while to organize themselves. However …

Thin lightnings winked from above. The cloven air boomed behind them. He felt a chill, deeper than the night cold. But he eased his pace. There was no more reason for hurry. That must be Manse Everard –

– who had returned to the Patrol vehicle and ridden it south in space and backward in time to this same instant.

That was cutting it fine, he thought. Patrol doctrine frowned on helping oneself thus. Too much danger of a close causal loop, or of tangling past and future.

But in this case, I'll get away with it. No reprimands, even. Because it's to rescue Jack Sandoval, not myself. I've already gotten free. I could shake pursuit in the mountains, which I know and the Mongols don't. The time-hopping is only to save my friend's life.

Besides, (an upsurging bitterness) *what's this whole mission been, except the future doubling back to create its own past? Without us, the Mongols might have well taken over America, and then there'd never have been any us.*

The sky was enormous, crystalline black; you rarely saw that many stars. The Great Bear flashed above hoar earth; hoofbeats rang through silence. Everard had not felt so alone before now.

'And what am I doing back there?' he asked aloud.

The answer came to him, and he eased a little, fell into the rhythm of his horses and started eating miles. He wanted to get this over with. But what he must do turned out to be less bad than he had feared.

Toktai and Li Tai-Tsung never came home. But that was not because they perished at sea or in the forests. It was because a sorcerer rode down from heaven and killed all their horses with thunderbolts, and smashed and burned their ships in the river mouth. No Chinese sailor would venture onto those tricky seas in whatever clumsy vessel could be built here; no Mongol would think it possible to go home on foot. Indeed, it probably wasn't. The expedition would stay, marry into the Indians, live out their days. Chinook, Tlingit, Nootka, all the potlatch tribes, with their big seagoing canoes, lodges and copperworking, furs and cloths and haughtiness … well, a Mongol Noyon, even a Confucian scholar might live less happily and usefully than in creating such a life for such a race.

Everard nodded to himself. So much for that. What was harder to take than the thwarting of Toktai's bloodthirsty ambitions was the truth about his own corps; which was his own family and nation and reason for living. The distant supermen turned out to be not quite such idealists after all. They weren't merely safeguarding a perhaps divinely ordained history which led to them. Here and there they, too, meddled, to create their own past … Don't ask if there ever was any 'original' scheme of things. Keep your mind shut. Regard the rutted road mankind had to travel, and tell yourself that if it could be better in places, in other places it could be worse.

'It may be a crooked game,' said Everard, 'but it's the only one in town.'

His voice came so loud, in that huge rime-white land, that he didn't speak any more. He clucked at his horse and rode a little faster northward.

DELENDA EST

1

The hunting is good in Europe twenty thousand years ago, and the winter sports are unexcelled anywhen. So the Time Patrol, always solicitous for its highly trained personnel, maintains a lodge in the Pleistocene Pyrenees.

Manse Everard stood on a glassed-in verandah and looked across ice-blue distances toward the northern slopes where the mountains fell off into woodland, marsh, and tundra. His big body was clad in loose green trousers and tunic of twenty-third-century insulsynth, boots handmade by a nineteenth-century French-Canadian; he smoked a foul old briar of indeterminate origin. There was a vague restlessness about him, and he ignored the noise from within, where half a dozen agents were drinking and talking and playing the piano.

A Cro-Magnon guide went by across the snow-covered yard, a tall handsome fellow dressed rather like an Eskimo (why had romance never credited paleolithic man with enough sense to wear jacket, pants, and footgear in a glacial period?), his face painted, one of the steel knives which had hired him at his belt. The Patrol could act quite freely, this far back in time; there was no danger of upsetting the past, for the metal would rust away and the strangers be forgotten in a few centuries. The main nuisance was that female agents from the more libertine periods upstairs were always having affairs with the native hunters.

Piet van Sarawak (Dutch-Indonesian-Venusian, early twenty-fourth AD), a slim, dark young man whose looks and technique gave the guides some stiff competition, joined Everard. They stood for a moment in companionable silence. He was also Unattached, on call to help out in any milieu, and had worked with the American before. They had taken their vacation together.

He spoke first, in Temporal. 'I hear they've spotted a few mammoths near Toulouse.' The city would not be built for a long while yet, but habit was powerful.

'I've bagged one,' said Everard impatiently. 'I've also been skiing and mountain-climbing and watched the native dances.'

Van Sarawak nodded, took out a cigarette, and puffed it into lighting. The bones stood out in his lean brown face as he sucked the smoke inward. 'A pleasant loafing spell, this,' he agreed, 'but after a bit the outdoor life begins to pall.'

There were still two weeks left of their furlough. In theory, since he could return almost to the moment of departure, an agent could take indefinite vacations; but actually he was supposed to devote a certain percentage of his probable lifetime to the job. (They never told you when you were scheduled to die, and you had better sense than to try finding out for yourself. It wouldn't have been certain anyhow, time being mutable. One perquisite of an agent's office was the Danellian longevity treatment.)

'What I would enjoy,' continued Van Sarawak, 'is some bright lights, music, girls who've never heard of time travel –'

'Done!' said Everard.

'Augustan Rome?' asked the other eagerly. 'I've never been there. I could get a hypno on language and customs here.'

Everard shook his head. 'It's overrated. Unless we want to go 'way upstairs, the most glorious decadence available is right in my own milieu. New York, say ... If you know the right phone numbers, and I do.'

Van Sarawak chuckled. 'I know a few places in my own sector,' he replied, 'but by and large, a pioneer society has little use for the finer arts of amusement. Very good, let's be off to New York, in – when?'

'Make it 1960. That was the last time I was there, in my public *persona*, before coming here-now.'

They grinned at each other and went off to pack. Everard had foresightedly brought along some midtwentieth garments in his friend's size.

Throwing clothes and razor into a small suitcase, the American wondered if he could keep up with Van Sarawak. He had never been a high-powered roisterer, and wouldn't have known how to buckle a swash anywhere in spacetime. A good book, a bull session, a case of beer – that was about his speed. But even the soberest men must kick over the traces occasionally.

Or a little more than that, if he was an Unattached agent of the Time Patrol; if his job with the Engineering Studies Company was only a blind for his wanderings and warrings through all history; if he had seen that history rewritten in minor things – not by God, which would have been endurable, but by mortal and fallible men – for even the Danellians were somewhat less than God; if he was forever haunted by the possibility of a major change, such that he and his entire world would never have existed at all ... Everard's battered, homely face screwed into a grimace. He ran a hand through his stiff brown hair, as if to brush the idea away. Useless to think about. Language and logic broke down in the face of the paradox. Better to relax at such moments as he could.

He picked up the suitcase and went to join Piet Van Sarawak.

Their little two-place antigravity scooter waited on its skids in the garage. You wouldn't believe, to look at it, that the controls could be set for any place on Earth and any moment of time. But an airplane is wonderful too, or a ship, or a fire.

Aupres de ma blonde
Qu'il fait bon, fait bon, fait bon,
Aupres de ma blonde
Qu'il fait bon dormir!

Van Sarawak sang it aloud, his breath steaming from him in the frosty air as he hopped onto the rear saddle. He'd picked up the song once when accompanying the army of Louis XIV. Everard laughed. 'Down, boy!'

'Oh, come, now,' warbled the younger man. 'It is a beautiful continuum, a gay and gorgeous cosmos. Hurry up this machine.'

Everard was not so sure; he had seen enough human misery in all the ages. You got casehardened after a while, but down underneath, when a peasant stared at you with sick brutalized eyes, or a soldier screamed with a pike through him, or a city went up in radioactive flame, something wept. He could understand the fanatics who had tried to change events. It was only that their work was so unlikely to make anything better ...

He set the controls for the Engineering Studies warehouse, a good confidential place to emerge. Thereafter they'd go to his apartment, and then the fun could start.

'I trust you've said goodbye to all your lady friends here,' Everard remarked.

'Oh, most gallantly, I assure you. Come along there. You're as slow as molasses on Pluto. For your information, this vehicle does not have to be rowed home.'

Everard shrugged and threw the main switch. The garage blinked out of sight.

2

For a moment, shock held them unstirring.

The scene registered in bits and pieces. They had materialized a few inches above ground level – the scooter was designed never to come out inside a solid object – and since that was unexpected, they hit the pavement with a teeth-rattling bump. They were in some kind of square. Nearby a fountain jetted, its stone basin carved with intertwining vines. Around the plaza, streets led off between squarish buildings six to ten stories high, of brick or concrete, wildly painted and ornamented. There were automobiles, big clumsy-looking things of no recognizable type, and a crowd of people.

'Jumping gods!' Everard glared at the meters. The scooter had landed them in lower Manhattan, 23 October 1960, at 11:30 a.m. and the spatial coordinates of the warehouse. But there was a blustery wind throwing dust and soot in his face, the smell of chimneys, and ...

Van Sarawak's sonic stunner jumped into his fist. The crowd was milling away from them, shouting in some babble they couldn't understand. It was a mixed lot: tall, fair roundheads, with a great deal of red hair; a number of Amerinds; half-breeds in all combinations. The men wore loose colorful blouses, tartan kilts, a sort of Scotch bonnet, shoes and knee-length stockings. Their hair was long and many favored drooping mustaches. The women had full skirts reaching to the ankles and tresses coiled under hooded cloaks. Both sexes went in for massive bracelets and necklaces.

'What happened?' whispered the Venusian. 'Where are we?'

Everard sat rigid. His mind clicked over, whirling through all the eras he had known or read about. Industrial culture – those looked like steam cars, but why the sharp prows and figurehead? – coal-burning – postnuclear Reconstruction? No, they hadn't worn kilts then, and they had spoken English …

It didn't fit. There was no such milieu recorded.

'We're getting out of here!'

His hands were on the controls when the large man jumped him. They went over on the pavement in a rage of fists and feet. Van Sarawak fired and sent someone else down unconscious; then he was seized from behind. The mob piled on top of them both, and things became hazy.

Everard had a confused impression of men in shining coppery breastplates and helmets, who shoved a billy-swinging way through the riot. He was fished out and supported in his grogginess while handcuffs were snapped on his wrists. Then he and Van Sarawak were searched and hustled off to a big enclosed vehicle. The Black Maria is much the same in all times.

He didn't come back to full consciousness until they were in a damp and chilly cell with an iron-barred door.

'Name of a flame!' The Venusian slumped on a wooden cot and put his face in his hands.

Everard stood at the door, looking out. All he could see was a narrow concrete hall and the cell across it. The map of Ireland stared cheerfully through those bars and called something unintelligible.

'What's going on?' Van Sarawak's slim body shuddered.

'I don't know,' said Everard very slowly. 'I just don't know. That machine was supposed to be foolproof, but maybe we're bigger fools than they allowed for.'

'There's no such place as this,' said Van Sarawak desperately. 'A dream?' He pinched himself and managed a rueful smile. His lip was cut and swelling, and he had the start of a gorgeous shiner. 'Logically, my friend, a pinch is no test of reality, but it has a certain reassuring effect.'

'I wish it didn't,' said Everard.

He grabbed the bars so hard they rattled. 'Could the controls have been askew, in spite of everything? Is there any city, anywhen on Earth – because

I'm damned sure this is Earth, at least – any city, however obscure, which was ever like this?'

'Not to my knowledge.'

Everard hung onto his sanity and rallied all the mental training the Patrol had ever given him. That included total recall; and he had studied history, even the history of ages he had never seen, with a thoroughness that should have earned him several Ph.D's.

'No,' he said at last. 'Kilted brachycephalic whites, mixed up with Indians and using steam-driven automobiles, haven't happened.'

'Coordinator Stantel V,' said Van Sarawak faintly. 'In the thirty-eighth century. The Great Experimenter – colonies reproducing past societies –'

'Not any like this,' said Everard.

The truth was growing in him, and he would have traded his soul for things to be otherwise. It took all the strength he had to keep from screaming and bashing his brains out against the wall.

'We'll have to see,' he said in a flat tone.

A policeman (Everard assumed they were in the hands of the law) brought them a meal and tried to talk to them. Van Sarawak said the language sounded Celtic, but he couldn't make out more than a few words. The meal wasn't bad.

Toward evening, they were led off to a washroom and got cleaned up under official guns. Everard studied the weapons: eight-shot revolvers and long-barreled rifles. There were gas lights, whose brackets repeated the motif of wreathing vines and snakes. The facilities and firearms, as well as the smell, suggested a technology roughly equivalent to the earlier nineteenth century.

On the way back he spied a couple of signs on the walls. The script was obviously Semitic, but though Van Sarawak had some knowledge of Hebrew through dealing with the Israeli colonies on Venus, he couldn't read it.

Locked in again, they saw the other prisoners led off to do their own washing: a surprisingly merry crowd of bums, toughs, and drunks. 'Seems we get special treatment,' remarked Van Sarawak.

'Hardly astonishing,' said Everard. 'What would you do with total strangers who appeared out of nowhere and used unheard-of-weapons?'

Van Sarawak's face turned to him with an unwonted grimness. 'Are you thinking what I'm thinking?' he asked.

'Probably.'

The Venusian's mouth twisted, and horror rode his voice: 'Another time line. Somebody *has* managed to change history.'

Everard nodded.

They spent an unhappy night. It would have been a boon to sleep, but the other cells were too noisy. Discipline seemed to be lax here. Also, there were bedbugs.

After a bleary breakfast, Everard and Van Sarawak were allowed to wash again and shave with safety razors not unlike the familiar type. Then a ten-man guard marched them into an office and planted itself around the walls.

They sat down before a desk and waited. The furniture was as disquietingly half-homelike, half-alien, as everything else. It was some time before the big wheels showed up. There were two: a white-haired, ruddy-cheeked man in cuirass and green tunic, presumably the chief of police, and a lean, hard-faced half-breed, gray-haired but black-mustached, wearing a blue tunic, a tam o'shanter, and on his left breast a golden bull's head which seemed an insigne of rank. He would have had a certain aquiline dignity had it not been for the thin hairy legs beneath his kilt. He was followed by two younger men, armed and uniformed much like himself, who took up their places behind him as he sat down.

Everard leaned over and whispered: 'The military, I'll bet. We seem to be of interest.'

Van Sarawak nodded sickly.

The police chief cleared his throat with conscious importance and said something to the – general? The latter answered impatiently, and addressed himself to the prisoners. He barked his words out with a clarity that helped Everard get the phonemes, but with a manner that was not exactly reassuring.

Somewhere along the line, communication would have to be established. Everard pointed to himself. 'Manse Everard,' he said. Van Sarawak followed the lead and introduced himself similarly.

The general started and went into a huddle with the chief. Turning back, he snapped, '*Yrn Cimberland?*'

'*Gothland? Svea? Nairoin Teutonach?*'

'Those names – if they are names – they sound Germanic, don't they?' muttered Van Sarawak.

'So do our names, come to think of it,' answered Everard tautly. 'Maybe they think we're Germans.' To the general: '*Sprechen sie Deutsch?*' Blankness rewarded him. '*Taler ni svensk? Niederlands? Dönsk tunga? Parlez-vous francais?* Goddamit, *habla usted espanol?*'

The police chief cleared his throat again and pointed to himself. 'Cadwallader Mac Barca,' he said. The general hight Cynyth ap Ceorn. Or so, at least, Everard's Anglo-Saxon mind interpreted the noises picked up by his ears.

'Celtic, all right,' he said. Sweat prickled under his arms. 'But just to make sure ...' He pointed inquiringly at a few other men, being rewarded with monickers like Hamilcar ap Angus, Asshur yr Cathlan, and Finn O'Carthia. 'No ... there's a distinct Semitic element here too. That fits in with their alphabet.'

Van Sarawak wet his lips. 'Try classical languages,' he urged harshly. 'Maybe we can find out where this history went insane.'

'*Loquerisne latine?*' That drew a blank. 'Ἑλλευίζεις?'

General ap Ceorn jerked, blew out his mustache, and narrowed his eyes. *'Hellenach?'* he demanded. *'Yrn Parthia?'*

Everard shook his head. 'They've at least heard of Greek,' he said slowly. He tried a few more words, but no one knew the tongue.

Ap Ceorn growled something to one of his men, who bowed and went out. There was a long silence.

Everard found himself losing personal fear. He was in a bad spot, yes, and might not live very long; but whatever happened to him was ludicrously unimportant compared to what had been done to the entire world.

God in Heaven! To the universe!

He couldn't grasp it. Sharp in his mind rose the land he knew, broad plains and tall mountains and prideful cities. There was the grave image of his father, and yet he remembered being a small child and lifted up skyward while his father laughed beneath him. And his mother ... they had a good life together, those two.

There had been a girl he knew in college, the sweetest little wench a man could ever have been privileged to walk in the rain with; and Bernie Aaronson, the nights of beer and smoke and talk; Phil Brackney, who had picked him out of the mud in France when machine guns were raking a ruined field; Charlie and Mary Whitcomb, high tea and a low cannel fire in Victoria's London: Keith and Cynthia Denison in their chrome-plated eyrie above New York; Jack Sandoval among tawny Arizona crags; a dog he had once had; the austere cantos of Dante and the ringing thunder of Shakespeare; the glory which was York Minster and the Golden Gate Bridge – Christ, a man's life, and the lives of who knew how many billions of human creatures, toiling and enduring and laughing and going down into dust to make room for their sons ... It had never been.

He shook his head, dazed with grief, and sat devoid of real understanding.

The soldier came back with a map and spread it out on the desk. Ap Ceorn gestured curtly, and Everard and Van Sarawak bent over it.

Yes, Earth, a Mercator projection, through eidetic memory showed that the mapping was rather crude. The continents and islands were there in bright colors, but the nations were something else.

'Can you read those names, Van?'

'I can make a guess, on the basis of the Hebraic alphabet,' said the Venusian. He began to read out the words. Ap Ceorn grunted and corrected him.

North America down to about Colombia was Ynys yr Afallon, seemingly one country divided into states. South America was a big realm, Huy Braseal, and some smaller countries whose names looked Indian. Australasia, Indonesia, Borneo, Burma, eastern India, and a good deal of the Pacific belonged to Hinduraj. Afghanistan and the rest of India were Punjab. Han included China, Korea, Japan, and eastern Siberia. Littorn owned the rest of Russia and reached well into Europe. The British Isles were Brittys, France and the

Low Countries were Gallis, the Iberian peninsula was Celtan. Central Europe and the Balkans were divided into many small nations, some of which had Hunnish-looking names. Switzerland and Austria made up Helveti; Italy was Cimberland; the Scandinavian peninsula was split down the middle, Svea in the north and Gothland in the south. North Africa looked like a confederacy, reaching from Senegal to Suez and nearly to the equator under the name of Carthagalann; the southern part of the continent was partitioned among minor sovereignties, many of which had purely African titles. The Near East held Parthia and Arabia.

Van Sarawak looked up. He had tears in his eyes.

Ap Ceorn snarled a question and waved his finger about. He wanted to know where they were from.

Everard shrugged and pointed skyward. The one thing he could not admit was the truth. He and Van Sarawak had agreed to claim they were from another planet, since this world hardly had space travel.

Ap Ceorn spoke to the chief, who nodded and replied. The prisoners were returned to their cell.

3

'And now what?' Van Sarawak slumped on his cot and stared at the floor.

'We play along,' said Everard grayly. 'We do anything to get at our scooter and escape. Once we're free, we can take stock.'

'But what happened?'

'I don't know, I tell you! Offhand, it looks as if something upset the Graeco-Romans and the Celts took over, but I couldn't say what it was.' Everard prowled the room. A bitter determination was growing in him.

'Remember your basic theory,' he said. 'Events are the result of a complex. There are no single causes. That's why it's so hard to change history. If I went back to, say, the Middle Ages, and shot one of F.D.R.'s Dutch forebears, he'd still be born in the late nineteenth century – because he and his genes resulted from the entire world of his ancestors, and there'd have been compensation. But every so often, a really key event does occur. Some one happening is a nexus of so many world lines that its outcome is decisive for the whole future.

'Somehow, for some reason, somebody has ripped up one of those events, back in the past.'

'No more Hesperus City,' mumbled Van Sarawak. 'No more sitting by the canals in the blue twilight, no more Aphrodite vintages, no more – did you know I had a sister on Venus?'

'Shut up!' Everard almost shouted it. 'I know. To hell with that. What counts is what we can do.

'Look,' he went on after a moment, 'the Patrol and the Danellians are wiped out. (Don't ask me why they weren't "always" wiped out; why this is the first time we came back from the far past to find a changed future. I don't understand the mutable-time paradoxes. We just did, that's all.) But anyhow, such of the Patrol offices and resorts as antedate the switchpoint won't have been affected. There must be a few hundred agents we can rally.'

'If we can get back to them.'

'We can then find that key event and stop whatever interference there was with it. We've got to!'

'A pleasant thought. But ...'

Feet tramped outside. A key clicked in the lock. The prisoners backed away. Then, all at once, Van Sarawak was bowing and beaming and spilling gallantries. Even Everard had to gape.

The girl who entered in front of three soldiers was a knockout. She was tall, with a sweep of rusty-red hair past her shoulders to the slim waist; her eyes were green and alight, her face came from all the Irish colleens who had ever lived; the long white dress was snug around a figure meant to stand on the walls of Troy. Everard noticed vaguely that this time-line used cosmetics, but she had small need of them. He paid no attention to the gold and amber of her jewelry, or to the guns behind her.

She smiled, a little timidly, and spoke: 'Can you understand me? It was thought you might know Greek.'

Her language was classical rather than modern. Everard, who had once had a job in Alexandrine times, could follow it through her accent if he paid close heed – which was inevitable anyway.

'Indeed I do,' he replied, his words stumbling over each other in their haste to get out.

'What are you snakkering?' demanded Van Sarawak.

'Ancient Greek,' said Everard.

'It would be,' mourned the Venusian. His despair seemed to have vanished, and his eyes bugged.

Everard introduce himself and his companion. The girl said her name was Deirdre Mac Morn. 'Oh, no,' groaned Van Sarawak. 'This is too much. Manse, teach me Greek. Fast.'

'Shut up,' said Everard. 'This is serious business.'

'Well, but can't I have some of the business?'

Everard ignored him and invited the girl to sit down. He joined her on a cot, while the other Patrolman hovered unhappily by. The guards kept their weapons ready.

'Is Greek still a living language?' asked Everard.

'Only in Parthia, and there it is most corrupt,' said Deirdre. 'I am a classical scholar, among other things. *Saorann* ap Ceorn is my uncle, so he asked me to see if I could talk with you. Not many in Afallon know the Attic tongue.'

'Well –' Everard suppressed a silly grin – 'I am most grateful to your uncle.'

Her eyes rested gravely on him. 'Where are you from? And how does it happen that you speak only Greek, of all known languages?'

'I speak Latin too.'

'Latin?' She frowned in thought. 'Oh, the Roman speech, was it not? I am afraid you will find no one who knows much about it.'

'Greek will do,' said Everard firmly.

'But you have not told me whence you came,' she insisted.

Everard shrugged. 'We've not been treated very politely,' he hinted.

'I'm sorry.' It seemed genuine. 'But our people are so excitable. Especially now, with the international situation what it is. And when you two appeared out of thin air ...'

Everard introduced himself and his companion. That had an unpleasantly familiar ring. 'What do you mean?' he inquired.

'Surely you know. With Huy Braseal and Hinduraj about to go to war, and all of us wondering what will happen ... It is not easy to be a small power.'

'A small power? But I saw a map. Afallon looked big enough to me.'

'We wore ourselves out two hundred years ago, in the great war with Littorn. Now none of our confederated states can agree on a single policy.' Deirdre looked directly into his eyes. 'What is this ignorance of yours?'

Everard swallowed and said, 'We're from another world.'

'What?'

'Yes. A planet (no, that means "wanderer") ... an orb encircling Sirius. That's our name for a certain star.'

'But – what do you mean? A world attendant on a star? I cannot understand you.'

'Don't you know? A star is a sun like ...'

Deirdre shrank back and made a sign with her finger. 'The Great Baal aid us,' she whispered. 'Either you are mad or ... The stars are mounted in a crystal sphere.'

Oh, no!

'What of the wandering stars you can see?' asked Everard slowly. 'Mars and Venus and –'

'I know not those names. If you mean Moloch, Ashtoreth, and the rest, of course they are worlds like ours, attendant on the sun like our own. One holds the spirits of the dead, one is the home of witches, one ...'

All this and steam cars too. Everard smiled shakily. 'If you'll not believe me, then what do you think I am?'

Deirdre regarded him with large eyes. 'I think you must be sorcerers,' she said.

There was no answer to that. Everard asked a few weak questions, but learned little more than that this city was Catuvellaunan, a trading and manufacturing center. Deirdre estimated its population at two million, and that of all Afallon at fifty million, but wasn't sure. They didn't take censuses here.

The Patrolmen's fate was equally undetermined. Their scooter and other possessions had been sequestrated by the military, but no one dared monkey with the stuff, and treatment of the owners was being hotly debated. Everard got the impression that all government, including the leadership of the armed forces, was rather a sloppy process of individualistic wrangling. Afallon itself was the loosest of confederacies, built out of former nations – Brittic colonies and Indians who had adopted European culture – all jealous of their rights. The old Mayan Empire, destroyed in a war with Texas (Tehannach) and annexed, had not forgotten its time of glory, and sent the most rambunctious delegates of all to the Council of Suffetes.

The Mayans wanted to make an alliance with Huy Braseal, perhaps out of friendship for fellow Indians. The West Coast states, fearful of Hinduraj, were toadies of the Southeast Asian empire. The Middle West (of course) was isolationist; the Eastern States were torn every which way, but inclined to follow the lead of Brittys.

When he gathered that slavery existed here, though not on racial lines, Everard wondered briefly and wildly if the time changers might not have been Dixiecrats.

Enough! He had his own neck, and Van's, to think about. 'We are from Sirius,' he declared loftily. 'Your ideas about the stars are mistaken. We came as peaceful explorers, and if we are molested, there will be others of our kind to take vengeance.'

Deirdre looked so unhappy that he felt conscience-striken. 'Will they spare the children?' she begged. 'The children had nothing to do with it.' Everard could imagine the vision in her head, small crying captives led off to the slave markets of a world of witches.

'There need be no trouble at all if we are released and our property returned,' he said.

'I shall speak to my uncle,' she promised, 'but even if I can sway him, he is only one man on the Council. The thought of what your weapons could mean if we had them has driven men mad.'

She rose. Everard clasped both her hands – they lay warm and soft in his – and smiled crookedly at her. 'Buck up, kid,' he said in English. She shivered, pulled free of him, and made the hex sign again.

'Well,' demanded Van Sarawak when they were alone, 'what did you find out?' After being told, he stroked his chin and murmured. 'That was one glorious little collection of sinusoids. There could be worse worlds than this.'

'Or better,' said Everard roughly. 'They don't have atomic bombs, but neither do they have penicillin, I'll bet. Our job is not to play God.'

'No. No, I suppose not.' The Venusian sighed.

4

They spent a restless day. Night had fallen when lanterns glimmered in the corridor and a military guard unlocked the cell. The prisoners were led silently to a rear exit where two automobiles waited; they were put into one, and the whole troop drove off.

Catuvellaunan did not have outdoor lighting, and there wasn't much night traffic. Somehow that made the sprawling city unreal in the dark. Everard paid attention to the mechanics of his car. Steam-powered, as he had guessed, burning powdered coal; rubber-tired wheels; a sleek body with a sharp nose and serpent figurehead; the whole simple to operate and honestly built, but not too well designed. Apparently this world had gradually developed a rule-of-thumb engineering, but no systematic science worth talking about.

They crossed a clumsy iron bridge to Long Island, here also a residential section for the well-to-do. Despite the dimness of oil-lamp headlights, their speed was high. Twice they came near having an accident: no traffic signals, and seemingly no drivers who did not hold caution in contempt.

Government and traffic ... hm. It all looked French, somehow, ignoring those rare interludes, when France got a Henry of Navarre or a Charles de Gaulle. And even in Everard's own twentieth century, France was largely Celtic. He was no respector of windy theories about inborn racial traits, but there was something to be said for traditions so ancient as to be unconscious and ineradicable. A Western world in which the Celts had become dominant, the Germanic peoples reduced to a few small outposts ... Yes, look at the Ireland of home; or recall how tribal politics had queered Vercingetorix's revolt ... But what about Littorn? Wait a minute! In *his* early Middle Ages, Lithuania had been a powerful state; it had held off Germans, Poles, and Russians alike for a long time, and hadn't even taken Christianity till the fifteenth century. Without German competition, Lithuania might very well have advanced eastward ...

In spite of the Celtic political instability, this was a world of large states, fewer separate nations than Everard's. That argued an older society. If his own Western civilization had developed out of the decaying Roman Empire about, say, 600 AD, the Celts in this world must have taken over earlier than that.

Everard was beginning to realize what had happened to Rome, but reserved his conclusions for the time being.

The cars drew up before an ornamental gate set in a long stone wall. The drivers talked with two armed guards wearing the livery of a private estate and the thin steel collars of slaves. The gate was opened and the cars went along a graveled driveway between lawns and trees. At the far end, almost on the beach, stood a house. Everard and Van Sarawak were gestured out and led toward it.

It was a rambling wooden structure. Gas lamps on the porch showed it painted in gaudy stripes; the gables and beam-ends were carved into dragon heads. Close by he heard the sea, and there was enough light from a sinking crescent moon for Everard to make out a ship standing in close: presumably a freighter, with a tall smokestack and a figurehead.

The windows glowed yellow. A slave butler admitted the party. The interior was paneled in dark wood, also carved, the floors thickly carpeted. At the end of the hall was a living room with overstuffed furniture, several paintings in a stiff conventionalized style, and a merry blaze in an enormous stone fireplace.

Saorann ap Ceorn sat in one chair, Deirdre in another. She laid aside a book as they entered and rose, smiling. The officer puffed a cigar and glowered. Some words were swapped, and the guards disappeared. The butler fetched in wine on a tray, and Deirdre invited the Patrolmen to sit down.

Everard sipped from his glass – the wine was an excellent Burgundy – and asked bluntly, 'Why are we here?'

Deirdre dazzled him with a smile. 'Surely you find it more pleasant than the jail.'

'Of course. As well as more ornamental. But I still want to know. Are we being released?'

'You are ...' She hunted for a diplomatic answer, but there seemed to be too much frankness in her. 'You are welcome here, but may not leave the estate. We hope you can be persuaded to help us. You would be richly rewarded.'

'Help? How?'

'By showing our artisans and Druids how to make more weapons and magical carts like your own.'

Everard sighed. It was no use trying to explain. They didn't have the tools to make the tools to make what was needed, but how could he get that across to a folk who believed in witchcraft?

'Is this your uncle's home?' he asked.

'No, my own,' said Deirdre. 'I am the only child of my parents, who were wealthy nobles. They died last year.'

Ap Ceorn clipped out several words. Deirdre translated with a worried frown: 'The tale of your advent is known to all Catuvellaunan by now; and that includes the foreign spies. We hope you can remain hidden from them here.'

Everard, remembering the pranks Axis and Allies had played in little neutral nations like Portugal, shivered. Men made desperate by approaching war would not likely be as courteous as the Afallonians.

'What is this conflict going to be about?' he inquired

'The control of the Icenian Ocean, of course. In particular, certain rich islands we call Ynys yr Lyonnach.' Deirdre got up in a single flowing movement and pointed out Hawaii on a globe. 'You see,' she went on earnestly, 'as I told you, Littorn and the western alliance – including us – wore each other out fighting. The great powers today, expanding, quarreling, are Huy Braseal and Hinduraj. Their conflict sucks in the lesser nations, for the clash is not only between ambitions, but between systems: the monarchy of Hinduraj against the sun-worshipping theocracy of Huy Braseal.'

'What is your religion, if I may ask?'

Deirdre blinked. The question seemed almost meaningless to her. 'The more educated people think that there is a Great Baal who made all the lesser gods,' she answered at last, slowly. 'But naturally, we maintain the ancient cults, and pay respect to the more powerful foreign gods too, such as Littorn's Perkunas and Czernebog, Wotan Ammon of Cimberland, Brahma, the Sun ... Best not to chance their anger.'

'I see.'

Ap Ceorn offered cigars and matches. Van Sarawak inhaled and said querulously, 'Damn it, this would have to be a time line where they don't speak any language I know.' He brightened. 'But I'm pretty quick to learn, even without hypno. I'll get Deirdre to teach me.'

'You and me both,' said Everard in haste. 'But listen, Van.' He reported what he had learned.

'Hm.' The younger man rubbed his chin. 'Not so good, eh? Of course, if they'd just let us aboard our scooter, we could make an easy getaway. Why not play along with them?'

'They're not such fools,' answered Everard. 'They may believe in magic, but not in undiluted altruism.'

'Funny they should be so backward intellectually, and still have combustion engines.'

'No. It's quite understandable. That's why I asked about their religion. It's always been purely pagan; even Judaism seems to have disappeared, and Buddhism hasn't been very influential. As Whitehead pointed out, the medieval idea of one almighty God was important to the growth of science, by inculcating the notion of lawfulness in nature. And Lewis Mumford added that the early monasteries were probably responsible for the mechanical clock – a very basic invention – because of having regular hours for prayer. Clocks seem to have come late in this world.' Everard smiled wryly, a shield against the sadness within. 'Odd to talk like this. Whitehead and Mumford never lived.'

'Nevertheless –'

'Just a minute,' Everard turned to Deirdre. 'When was Afallon discovered?'

'By white men? In the year 4827.'

'Um ... when does your reckoning start from?'

Deirdre seemed immune to further startlement. 'The creation of the world. At least, the date some philosophers have given. That is 5964 years ago.'

Which agreed with Bishop Ussher's famous 4004 BC, perhaps by sheer coincidence – but still, there was definitely a Semitic element in this culture. The creation story in Genesis was of Babylonian origin too.

'And when was steam *(pneuma)* first used to drive engines?' he asked.

'About a thousand years ago. The great Druid Boroihme O'Fiona –'

'Never mind.' Everard smoked his cigar and mulled his thoughts for a while before looking back at Van Sarawak.

'I'm beginning to get the picture,' he said. 'The Gauls were anything but the barbarians most people think. They'd learned a lot from Phoenician traders and Greek colonists, as well as from the Etruscans in cisalpine Gaul. A very energetic and enterprising race. The Romans, on the other hand, were a stolid lot, with few intellectual interests. There was little technological progress in our world till the Dark Ages, when the Empire had been swept out of the way.

'In *this* history, the Romans vanished early. So, I'm pretty sure, did the Jews. My guess is, without the balance-of-power effect of Rome, the Syrians did suppress the Maccabees; it was a near thing even in our history. Judaism disappeared and therefore Christianity never came into existence. But anyhow, with Rome removed, the Gauls got the supremacy. They started exploring, building better ships, discovering America in the ninth century. But they weren't so far ahead of the Indians that those couldn't catch up ... could even be stimulated to build empires of their own, like Huy Braseal today. In the eleventh century, the Celts began tinkering with steam engines. They seem to have gotten gunpowder too, maybe from China, and to have made several other inventions. But it's all been cut-and-try, with no basis of real science.'

Van Sarawak nodded. 'I suppose you're right. But what did happen to Rome?'

'I don't know. Yet. But our key point is back there somewhere.'

Everard returned his attention to Deirdre. 'This may surprise you,' he said smoothly. 'Our people visited this world about 2500 years ago. That's why I speak Greek but don't know what has occurred since. I would like to find out from you; I take it you're quite a scholar.'

She flushed and lowered long dark lashes such as few redheads possess. 'I will be glad to help as much as I can.' With a sudden appeal: 'But will you help us in return?'

'I don't know,' said Everard heavily. 'I'd like to. But I don't know if we can.' *Because after all, my job is to condemn you and your entire world to death.*

5

When Everard was shown to his room, he discovered that local hospitality was more than generous. He was too tired and depressed to take advantage of it … but at least, he thought on the edge of sleep, Van's slave girl wouldn't be disappointed.

They got up early here. From his upstairs window, Everard saw guards pacing the beach, but they didn't detract from the morning's freshness. He came down with Van Sarawak to breakfast, where bacon and eggs, toast and coffee added the last touch of dream. Ap Ceorn had gone back to town to confer, said Deirdre; she herself had put wistfulness aside and chattered gaily of trivia. Everard learned that she belonged to an amateur dramatic group which sometimes gave Classical Greek plays in the original: hence her fluency. She liked to ride, hunt, sail, swim – 'And shall we?' she asked.

'Huh?'

'Swim, of course?' Deirdre sprang from her chair on the lawn, where they had been sitting under flame-colored leaves, and whirled innocently out of her clothes. Everard thought he heard a dull clunk as Van Sarawak's jaw hit the ground.

'Come!' she laughed. 'Last one in is a Sassenach!'

She was already tumbling in the gray surf when Everard and Van Sarawak shuddered their way down to the beach. The Venusian groaned. 'I come from a warm planet. My ancestors were Indonesians. Tropical birds.'

'There were some Dutchmen too, weren't there?' grinned Everard.

'They had the sense to move to Indonesia.'

'All right, stay ashore.'

'Hell! If she can do it, I can!' Van Sarawak put a toe in the water and groaned again.

Everard summoned up all the control he had ever learned and ran in. Deirdre threw water at him. He plunged, got hold of a slender leg, and pulled her under. They frolicked about for several minutes before running back to the house for a hot shower. Van Sarawak followed in a blue haze.

'Speak about Tantalus,' he mumbled. 'The most beautiful girl in the whole continuum, and I can't talk to her and she's half polar bear.'

Toweled dry and dressed in the local garb by slaves, Everard returned to stand before the living-room fire. 'What pattern is this?' he asked, pointing to the tartan of his kilt.

Deirdre lifted her ruddy head. 'My own clan's,' she answered. 'An honored guest is always taken as a clan member during his stay, even if a blood feud is going on.' She smiled shyly. 'And there is none between us, Manslach.'

It cast him back into bleakness. He remembered what his purpose was.

'I'd like to ask you about history,' he said. 'It is a special interest of mine.'

She nodded, adjusted a gold fillet on her hair, and got a book from a crowded shelf. 'This is the best world history, I think. I can look up any details you might wish to know.'

And tell me what I must do to destroy you.

Everard sat down with her on a couch. The butler wheeled in lunch. He ate moodily, untasting.

To follow up his hunch – 'Did Rome and Carthage ever fight a war?'

'Yes. Two, in fact. They were allied at first, against Epirus, but fell out. Rome won the first war and tried to restrict Carthaginian enterprise.' Her clean profile bent over the pages, like a studious child. 'The second war broke out 23 years later, and lasted … hm … 11 years all told, though the last three were only a mopping up after Hannibal had taken and burned Rome.'

Ah-hah! Somehow, Everard did not feel happy at his success.

The Second Punic War (they called it the Roman War here – or, rather, some crucial incident thereof – was the turning point. But partly out of curiosity, partly because he feared to tip his hand, Everard did not at once try to identify the deviation. He'd first have to get straight in his mind what had actually happened, anyway. (No … what had not happened. The reality was here, warm and breathing beside him; he was the ghost.)

'So what came next?' he asked tonelessly.

'The Carthaginian empire came to include Hispania, southern Gaul, and the toe of Italy,' she said. 'The rest of Italy was impotent and chaotic, after the Roman confederacy had been broken up. But the Carthaginian government was too venal to remain strong. Hannibal himself was assassinated by men who thought his honesty stood in their way. Meanwhile, Syria and Parthia fought for the eastern Mediterranean, with Parthia winning and thus coming under still greater Hellenic influence than before.

'About a hundred years after the Roman Wars, some Germanic tribes overran Italy.' (That would be the Cimbri, with their allies the Teutones and Ambrones, whom Marius had stopped in Everard's world.) 'Their destructive path through Gaul had set the Celts moving too, eventually into Hispania and North Africa as Carthage declined. And from Carthage the Gauls learned much.

'A long period of wars followed, during which Parthia waned and the Celtic states grew. The Huns broke the Germans in middle Europe, but were in turn defeated by Parthia; so the Gauls moved in and the only Germans left were in Italy and Hyperborea.' (That must be the Scandinavian peninsula.) 'As ships improved, trade grew up with the Far East, both from Arabia and directly around Africa.' (In Everard's history, Julius Caesar had been astonished to find the Veneti building better vessels than any in the Mediterranean.) 'The Celtanians discovered southern Afallon, which they thought was an island – hence the "Ynys" – but they were thrown out by the Mayans. The Brittic colonies further north did survive, though, and eventually won their independence.

'Meanwhile Littorn was growing apace. It swallowed up most of Europe for a while. The western end of the continent only regained its freedom as part of the peace settlement after the Hundred Years' War I've told you about. The Asian countries have shaken off their exhausted European masters and modernized themselves, while the Western nations have declined in their turn.' Deirdre looked up from the book, which she had been skimming as she talked. 'But this is only the barest outline, Manslach. Shall I go on?'

Everard shook his head. 'No, thanks.' After a moment: 'You are very honest about the situation of your own country.'

Deirdre said roughly, 'Most of us won't admit it, but I think it best to look truth in the eyes.'

With a surge of eagerness: 'But tell me of your own world. This is a marvel past belief.'

Everard sighed, switched off his conscience, and began lying.

The raid took place that afternoon.

Van Sarawak had recovered his poise and was busily learning the Afallonian language from Deirdre. They walked through the garden hand in hand, stopping to name objects and act out verbs. Everard followed, wondering vaguely if he was a third wheel or not, most of him bent to the problem of how to get at the scooter.

Bright sunlight spilled from a pale cloudless sky. A maple was a shout of scarlet, a drift of yellow leaves scudded across the grass. An elderly slave was raking the yard in a leisurely fashion, a young-looking guard of Indian race lounged with his rifle slung on one shoulder, a pair of wolfhounds dozed under a hedge. It was a peaceful scene; hard to believe that men prepared murder beyond these walls.

But man was man, in any history. This culture might not have the ruthless will and sophisticated cruelty of Western civilization; in fact, in some ways it looked strangely innocent. Still, that wasn't for lack of trying. And in this world, a genuine science might never emerge, man might endlessly repeat the cycle of war, empire, collapse, and war. In Everard's future, the race had finally broken out of it.

For what? He could not honestly say that this continuum was worse or better than his own. It was different, that was all. And didn't these people have as much right to their existence as – as his own, who were damned to nullity if he failed?

He knotted his fists. The issue was too big. No man should have to decide something like this.

At the showdown, he knew, no abstract sense of duty would compel him, but the little things and the little folk he remembered.

They rounded the house and Deirdre pointed to the sea. 'Awarlann,' she said. Her loose hair burned in the wind.

'Now does that mean "ocean" or "Atlantic" or "water"?' laughed Van Sarawak. 'Let's go see.' He led her toward the beach.

Everard trailed. A kind of steam launch, long and fast, was skipping over the waves, a mile or two offshore. Gulls trailed it in a snowstorm of wings. He thought that if he'd been in charge, a Navy ship would have been on picket out there.

Did he even have to decide anything? There were other Patrolmen in the pre-Roman past. They'd return to their respective eras and ...

Everard stiffened. A chill ran down his back and congealed in his belly.

They'd return, and see what had happened, and try to correct the trouble. If any of them succeeded, this world would blink out of spacetime, and he would go with it.

Deirdre paused. Everard, standing in a sweat, hardly noticed what she was staring at, till she cried out and pointed. Then he joined her and squinted across the sea.

The launch was standing in close, its high stack fuming smoke and sparks, the gilt snake figurehead agleam. He could see the forms of men aboard, and something white, with wings ... It rose from the poopdeck and trailed at the end of a rope, mounting. A glider! Celtic aeronautics had gotten that far, at least.

'Pretty,' said Van Sarawak. 'I suppose they have balloons too.'

The glider cast its tow and swooped inward. One of the guards on the beach shouted. The rest pelted from behind the house. Sunlight flashed off their guns. The launch headed straight for the shore. The glider landed, plowing a furrow in the beach.

An officer yelled and waved the Patrolmen back. Everard had a glimpse of Deirdre's face, white and uncomprehending. Then a turret on the glider swiveled – a detached part of his mind guessed it was manually operated – and a light cannon spoke.

Everard hit the dirt. Van Sarawak followed, dragging the girl with him. Grapeshot plowed hideously through the Afallonian soldiers.

There followed a spiteful crack of guns. Men sprang from the aircraft, dark-faced men in turbans and sarongs. *Hinduraj!* thought Everard. They traded shots with the surviving guards, who rallied about their captain.

The officer roared and led a charge. Everard looked up from the sand to see him almost upon the glider's crew. Van Sarawak leaped to his feet. Everard rolled over, caught him by the ankle, and pulled him down before he could join the fight.

'Let me go!' The Venusian writhed, sobbing. The dead and wounded left by the cannon sprawled nightmare red. The racket of battle seemed to fill the sky.

'No, you bloody fool! It's us they're after, and that wild Irishman's done the worst thing he could have –' A fresh outburst yanked Everard's attention elsewhere.

The launch, shallow-draft and screw-propelled, had run up into the shallows and was retching armed men. Too late the Afallonians realized that they had discharged their weapons and were now being attacked from the rear.

'Come on!' Everard hauled Deirdre and Van Sarawak to their feet. 'We've got to get out of here – get to the neighbors ...'

A detachment from the boat saw him and veered. He felt rather than heard the flat smack of a bullet into soil, as he reached the lawn. Slaves screamed hysterically inside the house. The two wolfhounds attacked the invaders and were gunned down.

Crouched, zigzag, that was the way: over the wall and out onto the road! Everard might have made it, but Deirdre stumbled and fell. Van Sarawak halted to guard her. Everard stopped also, and then it was too late. They were covered.

The leader of the dark men snapped something at the girl. She sat up, giving him a defiant answer. He laughed shortly and jerked his thumb at the launch.

'What do they want?' asked Everard in Greek.

'You.' She looked at him with horror. 'You two –' The officer spoke again. 'And me to translate ... No!'

She twisted in the hands that had closed on her arms, got partly free and clawed at a face. Everard's fist traveled in a short arc that ended in a squashing of nose. It was too good to last. A clubbed rifle descended on his head, and he was only dimly aware of being frogmarched off to the launch.

6

The crew left the glider behind, shoved their boat into deeper water, and revved it up. They left all the guardsmen slain or disabled, but took their own casualties along.

Everard sat on a bench on the plunging deck and stared with slowly clearing eyes as the shoreline dwindled. Deirdre wept on Van Sarawak's shoulder, and the Venusian tried to console her. A chill noisy wind flung spindrift in their faces.

When two white men emerged from the deck-house, Everard's mind was jarred back into motion. Not Asians after all. Europeans! And now when he looked closely, he saw the rest of the crew also had Caucasian features. The brown complexions were merely grease paint.

He stood up and regarded his new owners warily. One was a portly, middle-aged man of average height, in a red silk blouse and baggy white trousers and a sort of astrakhan hat; he was clean-shaven and his dark hair was twisted into a queue. The other was somewhat younger, a shaggy blond giant in a tunic sewn with copper links, legginged breeches, a leather cloak, and a purely ornamental horned helmet. Both wore revolvers at their belts and were treated deferentially by the sailors.

'What the devil?' Everard looked around once more. They were already out of sight of land, and bending north. The hull quivered with the haste of the engine, spray sheeted when the bows bit a wave.

The older man spoke first in Afallonian. Everard shrugged. Then the bearded Nordic tried, first in a completely unrecognizable dialect but afterward: *'Taelan thu Cimbric?'*

Everard, who knew several Germanic languages, took a chance, while Van Sarawak pricked up his Dutch ears. Deirdre huddled back, wide-eyed, too bewildered to move.

'Ja,' said Everard, *'ein wenig.'* When Goldilocks looked uncertain, he amended it: 'A little.'

'Ah, aen litt. Gode!' The big man rubbed his hands. *'Ik hait Boierik Wulfilasson ok main gefreond heer erran Boleslav Arkonsky.'*

It was no language Everard had ever heard of – couldn't even be the original Cimbric, after all these centuries – but the Patrolman could follow it reasonably well. The trouble came in speaking; he couldn't predict how it had evolved.

'What the hell erran thu maching, anyway?' he blustered. 'Ik bin aen man auf Sirius – the stern Sirius, mit planeten ok all. Set uns gebach or willen be der Teufel to pay!'

Boierik Wulfilasson looked pained and suggested that the discussion be continued inside, with the young lady for interpreter. He led the way back into the deckhouse, which turned out to include a small but comfortably furnished saloon. The door remained open, with an armed guard looking in and more on call.

Boleslav Arkonsky said something in Afallonian to Deirdre. She nodded, and he gave her a glass of wine. It seemed to steady her, but she spoke to Everard in a thin voice.

'We've been captured, Manslach. Their spies found out where you were kept. Another group is supposed to steal your traveling machine. They know where that is, too.'

'So I imagined,' replied Everard. 'But who in Baal's name are they?'

Boierik guffawed at the question and expounded lengthily his own cleverness. The idea was to make the Suffetes of Afallon think Hinduraj was responsible. Actually, the secret alliance of Littorn and Cimberland had built up quite an effective spy service. They were now bound for the Littornian embassy's summer retreat on Ynys Llangollen (Nantucket), where the wizards would be induced to explain their spells and a surprise prepared for the great powers.

'And if we don't do this?'

Deirdre translated Arkonsky's answer word for word: 'I regret the consequences to you. We are civilized men, and will pay well in gold and honor for your free cooperation. If that is withheld, we will get your forced cooperation. The existence of our countries is at stake.'

Everard looked closely at them. Boierik seemed embarrassed and unhappy, the boastful glee evaporated from him. Boleslav Arkonsky drummed on the tabletop, his lips compressed but a certain appeal in his eyes. *Don't make us do this. We have to live with ourselves.*

They were probably husbands and fathers, they must enjoy a mug of beer and a friendly game of dice as well as the next man, maybe Boierik bred horses in Italy and Arkonsky was a rose fancier on the Baltic shores. But none of this would do their captives a bit of good, when the almighty Nation locked horns with its kin.

Everard paused to admire the sheer artistry of this operation, and then began wondering what to do. The launch was fast, but would need something like twenty hours to reach Nantucket, as he remembered the trip. There was that much time, at least.

'We are weary,' he said in English. 'May we not rest awhile?'

'Ja deedly,' said Boierik with a clumsy graciousness. *'Ok wir skallen gode gefreonds bin, ni?'*

Sunset smoldered in the west. Deirdre and Van Sarawak stood at the rail, looking across a gray waste of waters. Three crewmen, their makeup and costumes removed, poised alert and weaponed on the poop; a man steered by compass; Boierik and Everard paced the quarterdeck. All wore heavy clothes against the wind.

Everard was getting some proficiency in the Cimbrian language; his tongue still limped, but he could make himself understood. Mostly, though, he let Boierik do the talking.

'So you are from the stars? These matters I do not understand. I am a simple man. Had I my way, I would manage my Tuscan estate in peace and let the world rave as it will. But we of the Folk have our obligations.' The Teutonics seemed to have replaced the Latins altogether in Italy, as the English had done the Britons in Everard's world.

'I know how you feel,' said the Patrolman. 'Strange that so many should fight when so few want to.'

'Oh, but this is necessary.' A near whine. 'Carthagalann stole Egypt, our rightful possession.'

'Italia irredenta,' murmured Everard.

'Hunh?'

'Never mind. So you Cimbri are allied with Littorn, and hope to grab off Europe and Africa while the big powers are fighting in the East.'

'Not at all!' said Boierik indignantly. ' We are merely asserting our rightful and historic territorial claims. Why, the king himself said ...' And so on and so on.

Everard braced himself against the roll of the deck. 'Seems to me you treat us wizards rather hard,' he remarked. 'Beware lest we get really angered at you.'

'All of us are protected against curses and shapings.'

'Well –'

'I wish you would help us freely. I will be happy to demonstrate to you the justice of our cause, if you have a few hours to spare.'

Everard shook his head, walked off and stopped by Deirdre. Her face was a blur in the thickening dusk, but he caught a forlorn fury in her voice: 'I hope you told him what to do with his plans, Manslach.'

'No,' said Everard heavily. 'We are going to help them.'

She stood as if struck.

'What are you saying, Manse?' asked Van Sarawak. Everard told him.

'No!' said the Venusian.

'Yes,' said Everard.

'By God, no! I'll –'

Everard grabbed his arm and said coldly: 'Be quiet. I know what I'm doing. We can't take sides in this world; we're against everybody, and you'd better realize it. The only thing to do is play along with these fellows for a while. And don't tell that to Deirdre.'

Van Sarawak bent his head and stood for a moment, thinking. 'All right,' he said dully.

7

The Littornian resort was on the southern shore of Nantucket, near a fishing village but walled off from it. The embassy had built in the style of its homeland: long, timber houses with roofs arched like a cat's back, a main hall and its outbuildings enclosing a flagged courtyard. Everard finished a night's sleep and a breakfast which Deirdre's eyes had made miserable by standing on deck as they came in to the private pier. Another, bigger launch was already there, and the grounds swarmed with hard-looking men. Arkonsky's excitement flared up as he said in Afallonian: 'I see the magic engine has been brought. We can go right to work.'

When Boierik interpreted, Everard felt his heart slam.

The guests, as the Cimbrian insisted on calling them, were led into an out-size room where Arkonsky bowed the knee to an idol with four faces, that Svantevit which the Danes had chopped up for firewood in the other history. A fire burned on the hearth against the autumn chill, and guards were posted around the walls. Everard had eyes only for the scooter, where it stood gleaming on the door.

'I hear the fight was hard in Catuvellaunan to gain this thing,' remarked Boierik. 'Many were killed; but our gang got away without being followed.'

He touched a handlebar gingerly. 'And this wain can truly appear anywhere its rider wishes, out of thin air?'

'Yes,' said Everard.

Deirdre gave him a look of scorn such as he had rarely known. She stood haughtily away from him and Van Sarawak.

Arkonsky spoke to her; something he wanted translated. She spat at his feet. Boierik sighed and gave the word to Everard:

'We wish the engine demonstrated. You and I will go for a ride on it. I warn you, I will have a revolver at your back. You will tell me in advance everything you mean to do, and if aught untoward happens, I will shoot. Your friends will remain here as hostages, also to be shot on the first suspicion. But I'm sure,' he added, 'that we will all be good friends.'

Everard nodded. Tautness thrummed in him; his palms felt cold and wet. 'First I must say a spell,' he answered.

His eyes flickered. One glance memorized the spatial reading of the position meters and the time reading of the clock on the scooter. Another look showed Van Sarawak seated on a bench, under Arkonsky's drawn pistol and the rifles of the guards. Deirdre sat down too, stiffly, as far from him as she could get. Everard made a close estimate of the bench's position relative to the scooter's, lifted his arms, and chanted in Temporal:

'Van, I'm going to try to pull you out of here. Stay exactly where you are now, repeat, exactly. I'll pick you up on the fly. If all goes well, that'll happen about one minute after I blink off with our hairy comrade.'

The Venusian sat wooden-faced, but a thin beading of sweat sprang out on his forehead.

'Very good,' said Everard in his pidgin Cimbric. 'Mount on the rear saddle, Boierik, and we'll put this magic horse through her paces.'

The blond man nodded and obeyed. As Everard took the front seat, he felt a gun muzzle held shakily against his back. 'Tell Arkonsky we'll be back in half an hour,' he instructed. They had approximately the same time units here as in his world, both descended from the Babylonian. When that had been taken care of, Everard said.

'The first thing we will do is appear in midair over the ocean and hover.'

'F-f-fine,' said Boierik. He didn't sound very convinced.

Everard set the space controls for ten miles east and a thousand feet up, and threw the main switch.

They sat like witches astride a broom, looking down on greenish-gray immensity and the distant blur which was land. The wind was high, it caught at them and Everard gripped tight with his knees. He heard Boierik's oath and smiled stiffly.

'Well,' he asked, 'how do you like this?'

'Why … it's wonderful.' As he grew accustomed to the idea, the Cimbrian gathered enthusiasm. 'Balloons are as nothing beside it. With machines like this, we can soar above enemy cities and rain fire down on them.'

Somehow, that made Everard feel better about what he was going to do.

'Now we will fly ahead,' he announced, and sent the scooter gliding through the air. Boierik whooped exultantly. 'And now we will make the instantaneous jump to your homeland.'

Everard threw the maneuver switch. The scooter looped the loop and dropped at a three-gee acceleration.

Forewarned, the Patrolman could still barely hang on. He never knew whether the curve or the dive had thrown Boierik. He only got a moment's glimpse of the man, plunging down through windy spaces to the sea, and wished he hadn't.

For a little while, then, Everard hung above the waves. His first reaction was a shudder. Suppose Boierik had had time to shoot? His second was a thick guilt. Both he dismissed, and concentrated on the problem of rescuing Van Sarawak.

He set the space verniers for one foot in front of the prisoners' bench, the time unit for one minute after he had departed. His right hand he kept by the controls – he'd have to work fast – and his left free.

Hang on to your hats, fellahs. Here we go again.

The machine flashed into existence almost in front of Van Sarawak. Everard clutched the Venusian's tunic and hauled him close, inside the spatiotemporal drive field, even as his right hand spun the time dial back and snapped down the main switch.

A bullet caromed off metal. Everard had a moment's glimpse of Arkonsky shouting. And then it was all gone and they were on a grassy hill sloping down to the beach. It was two thousand years ago.

He collapsed shivering over the handlebars.

A cry brought him back to awareness. He twisted around to look at Van Sarawak where the Venusian sprawled on the hillside. One arm was still around Deirdre's waist.

The wind lulled, and the sea rolled in to a broad white strand, and clouds walked high in heaven.

'Can't say I blame you, Van.' Everard paced before the scooter and looked at the ground. 'But it does complicate matters.'

'What was I supposed to do?' the other man asked on a raw note. 'Leave her there for those bastards to kill – or to be snuffed out with her entire universe?'

'Remember, we're conditioned. Without authorization, we couldn't tell her the truth even if we wanted to. And I, for one, don't want to.'

Everard glanced at the girl. She stood breathing heavily, but with a dawn in her eyes. The wind ruffled her hair and the long thin dress.

She shook her head, as if to clear it of nightmare, ran over and clasped their hands. 'Forgive me, Manslach,' she breathed. 'I should have known you'd not betray us.'

She kissed them both. Van Sarawak responded as eagerly as expected, but Everard couldn't bring himself to. He would have remembered Judas.

'Where are we?' she continued. 'It looks almost like Llangollen, but no dwellers. Have you taken us to the Happy Isles?' She spun on one foot and danced among summer flowers. 'Can we rest here a while before returning home?'

Everard drew a long breath. 'I've bad news for you, Deirdre,' he said.

She grew silent. He saw her gather herself.

'We can't go back.'

She waited mutely.

'The ... the spells I had to use, to save our lives – I had no choice. But those spells debar us from returning home.'

'There is no hope?' He could barely hear her.

His eyes stung. 'No,' he said.

She turned and walked away. Van Sarawak moved to follow her, but thought better of it and sat down beside Everard. 'What'd you tell her?' he asked.

Everard repeated his words. 'It seems the best compromise,' he finished. 'I can't send her back to what's waiting for this world.'

'No.' Van Sarawak sat quiet for a while, staring across the sea. Then: 'What year is this? About the time of Christ? Then we're still upstairs of the turning point.'

'Yeh. And we still have to find out what it was.'

'Let's go back to some Patrol office in the farther past. We can recruit help there.'

'Maybe.' Everard lay down in the grass and regarded the sky. Reaction overwhelmed him. 'I think I can locate the key event right here, though, with Deirdre's help. Wake me when she comes back.'

She returned dry-eyed, though one could see she had wept. When Everard asked if she would assist in his own mission, she nodded, 'Of course. My life is yours who saved it.'

After getting you into the mess in the first place. Everard said carefully: 'All I want from you is some information. Do you know about ... about putting people to sleep, a sleep in which they may believe anything they're told?'

She nodded doubtfully. 'I've seen medical Druids do that.'

'It won't harm you. I only wish to make you sleep so you can remember everything you know, things you believe forgotten. It won't take long.'

Her trustfulness was hard for him to endure. Using Patrol techniques, he put her in a hypnotic state of total recall and dredged out all she had ever heard or read about the Second Punic War. That added up to enough for his purposes.

Roman interference with Carthaginian enterprise south of the Ebro, in direct violation of treaty, had been the final roweling. In 219 BC Hannibal Barca, governor of Carthaginian Spain, laid siege to Saguntum. After eight months he took it, and thus provoked his long-planned war with Rome. At the beginning of May, 218, he crossed the Pyrenees with 90,000 infantry, 12,000 cavalry, and 37 elephants, marched through Gaul, and went over the Alps. His losses en route were gruesome: only 20,000 foot and 6,000 horse reached Italy late in the year. Nevertheless, near the Ticinus River he met and broke a superior Roman force. In the course of the following year, he fought several bloodily victorious battles and advanced into Apulia and Campania.

The Apulians, Lucanians, Bruttians, and Samnites went over to his side. Quintus Fabius Maximus fought a grim guerrilla war, which laid Italy waste and decided nothing. But meanwhile Hasdrubal Barca was organizing Spain, and in 211 he arrived with reinforcements. In 210 Hannibal took and burned Rome, and by 207 the last cities of the confederacy had surrendered to him.

'That's it,' said Everard. He stroked the coppery mane of the girl lying beside him. 'Go to sleep now. Sleep well and wake up glad of heart.'

'What'd she tell you?' asked Van Sarawak.

'A lot of detail,' said Everard. The whole story had required more than an hour. 'The important thing is this: her knowledge of those times is good, but she never mentioned the Scipios.'

'The who's?'

'Publius Cornelius Scipio commanded the Roman army at Ticinus. He was beaten there all right, in our world. But later he had the intelligence to turn westward and gnaw away the Carthaginian base in Spain. It ended with Hannibal being effectively cut off in Italy, and what little Iberian help could be sent him was annihilated. Scipio's son of the same name also held a high command, and was the man who finally whipped Hannibal at Zama; that's Scipio Africanus the Elder.

'Father and son were by far the best leaders Rome had. But Deirdre never heard of them.'

'So ...' Van Sarawak stared eastward across the sea, where Gauls and Cimbri and Parthians were ramping through the shattered Classical world. 'What happened to them in this time line?'

'My own total recall tells me that both the Scipios were at Ticinus, and very nearly killed. The son saved his father's life during the retreat, which I imagine was more like a stampede. One gets you ten that in *this* history the Scipios died there.'

'Somebody must have knocked them off,' said Van Sarawak. His voice tightened. 'Some time traveler. It could only have been that.'

'Well, it seems probable, anyhow. We'll see.' Everard looked away from Deirdre's slumbrous face. 'We'll see.'

8

At the Pleistocene resort – half an hour after having left it for New York – the Patrolmen put the girl in charge of a sympathetic Greek-speaking matron and summoned their colleagues. Then the message capsules began jumping through space-time.

All offices prior to 218 BC – the closest was Alexandria, 250-230 – were 'still' there, with 200 or so agents altogether. Written contact with the future was confirmed to be impossible, and a few short jaunts upstairs clinched the proof. A worried conference met at the Academy, back in the Oligocene Period. Unattached agents ranked those with steady assignments, but not each other; on the basis of his own experience, Everard found himself the chairman of a committee of top-bracket officers.

That was a frustrating job. These men and women had leaped centuries and wielded the weapons of gods. But they were still human, with all the ingrained orneriness of their race.

Everyone agreed that the damage would have to be repaired. But there was fear for those agents who had gone ahead into time before being warned, as Everard himself had done. If they weren't back when history was re-altered, they would never be seen again. Everard deputized parties to attempt rescue, but doubted there'd be much success. He warned them sternly to return within a day, local time, or face the consequences.

A man from the Scientific Renaissance had another point to make. Granted, the survivors' plain duty was to restore the 'original' time track. But they had a duty to knowledge as well. Here was a unique chance to study a whole new phase of humankind. Several years' anthropological work should be done before – Everard slapped him down with difficulty. There weren't so many Patrolmen left that they could take the risk.

Study groups had to determine the exact moment and circumstances of the change. The wrangling over methods went on interminably. Everard glared out the window, into the prehuman night, and wondered if the saber-tooths weren't doing a better job after all than their simian successors.

When he had finally gotten his various gangs dispatched, he broke out a bottle and got drunk with Van Sarawak.

Reconvening next day, the steering committee heard from its deputies, who had run up a total of years in the future. A dozen Patrolmen had been rescued from more or less ignominious situations; another score would simply have to be written off. The spy group's report was more interesting. It seemed that two Helvetian mercenaries had joined Hannibal in the Alps and won his confidence. After the war, they had risen to high positions in Carthage. Under the names of Phrontes and Himilco, they had practically run the government, engineered Hannibal's murder, and set new records for luxurious living. One of the Patrolmen had seen their homes and the men themselves. 'A lot of improvements that hadn't been thought of in Classical times. The fellows looked to me like Neldorians, 205th millennium.'

Everard nodded. That was an age of bandits who had 'already' given the Patrol a lot of work. 'I think we've settled the matter,' he said. 'It makes no difference whether they were with Hannibal before Ticinus or not. We'd have hell's own time arresting them in the Alps without such a fuss that we'd change the future ourselves. What counts is that they seem to have rubbed out the Scipios, and that's the point we'll have to strike at.'

A nineteenth-century Britisher, competent but with elements of Colonel Blimp, unrolled a map and discoursed on his aerial observations of the battle. He'd used an infra-red telescope to look through low clouds. 'And here the Romans stood –'

'I know,' said Everard. 'A thin red line. The moment when they took flight is the critical one, but the confusion then also gives us our chance. Okay, we'll want to surround the battlefield unobtrusively, but I don't think we can get away with more than two agents actually on the scene. The baddies are going to be alert, you know, looking for possible counter-interference. The Alexandria office can supply Van and me with costumes.'

'I say,' exclaimed the Englishman, 'I thought I'd have the privilege.'

'No. Sorry.' Everard smiled with one corner of his mouth. 'No privilege, anyway. Just risking your neck, in order to negate a world full of people like yourself.'

'But dash it all –'

Everard rose. 'I've got to go,' he said flatly. 'I don't know why, but I've got to.'

Van Sarawak nodded.

They left their scooter in a clump of trees and started across the field.

Around the horizon and up in the sky waited a hundred armed Patrolmen, but that was small consolation here among spears and arrows. Lowering clouds hurried before a cold whistling wind, there was a spatter of rain; sunny Italy was enjoying its late fall.

The cuirass was heavy on Everard's shoulders as he trotted across blood-slippery mud. He had helmet, greaves, a Roman shield on his left arm and a sword at his waist; but his right hand gripped a stunner. Van Sarawak loped behind, similarly equipped, eyes shifting under the windruffled officer's plume.

Trumpets howled and drums stuttered. It was all but lost among the yells of men and tramp of feet, screaming, riderless horses and whining arrows. Only a few captains and scouts were still mounted; as often before stirrups were invented, what started to be a cavalry battle had become entirely a fight on foot after the lancers fell off their mounts. The Carthaginians were pressing in, hammering edged metal against the buckling Roman lines. Here and there the struggle was already breaking up into small knots, where men cursed and cut at strangers.

The combat had passed over this area already. Death lay around Everard. He hurried behind the Roman force, toward the distant gleam of the eagles. Across helmets and corpses, he made out a banner that fluttered triumphant red and purple. And there, looming monstrous against the gray sky, lifting their trunks and bawling, came a squad of elephants.

War was always the same: not a neat affair of lines across maps, nor a hallooing gallantry, but men who gasped and sweated and bled in bewilderment.

A slight, dark-faced youth squirmed nearby, trying feebly to pull out the javelin which had pierced his stomach. He was a slinger from Carthage, but the burly Italian peasant who sat next to him, staring without belief at the stump of an arm, paid no attention.

A flight of crows hovered overhead, riding the wind and waiting.

'This way,' muttered Everard. 'Hurry up, for God's sake! That line's going to break any minute.'

The breath was raw in his throat as he jogged toward the standards of the Republic. It came to him that he'd always rather wished Hannibal had won. There was something repellent about the frigid, unimaginative greed of Rome. And here he was, trying to save the city. Well-a-day, life was often an odd business.

It was some consolation that Scipio Africanus was one of the few decent men left after the war.

Screaming and clangor lifted, and the Italians reeled back. Everard saw something like a wave smashed against a rock. But it was the rock which advanced, crying out and stabbing, stabbing.

He began to run. A legionary went past, howling his panic. A grizzled Roman veteran spat on the ground, braced his feet, and stood where he was till they cut him down. Hannibal's elephants squealed and blundered about. The ranks of Carthage held firm, advancing to an inhuman pulse of drums.

Up ahead, now! Everard saw men on horseback, Roman officers. They held the eagles aloft and shouted, but nobody could hear them above the din.

A small group of legionaries trotted past. Their leader hailed the Patrolmen: 'Over here! We'll give 'em a fight, by the belly of Venus!'

Everard shook his head and continued. The Roman snarled and sprang at him. 'Come here, you cowardly ...' A stun beam cut off his words. He crashed into the muck. His men shuddered, someone wailed, and the party broke into flight.

The Carthaginians were very near, shield to shield and swords running red. Everard could see a scar livid on the cheek of one man, the great hook nose of another. A hurled spear clanged off his helmet. He lowered his head and ran.

A combat loomed before him. He tried to go around, and tripped on a gashed corpse. A Roman stumbled over him in turn. Van Sarawak cursed and dragged him clear. A sword furrowed the Venusian's arm.

Beyond, Scipio's men were surrounded and battling without hope. Everard halted, sucked air into starved lungs, and looked into the thin rain. Armor gleamed wetly as a troop of Roman horsemen galloped closer, with mud up to their mounts' noses. That must be the son, Scipio Africanus to be, hastening to rescue his father. The hoofbeats made thunder in the earth.

'Over there!'

Van Sarawak cried out and pointed. Everard crouched where he was, rain dripping off his helmet and down his face. From another direction, a Carthaginian party was riding toward the battle around the eagles. And at their head were two men with the height and craggy features of Neldor. They wore G.I. armor, but each of them held a slim-barreled gun.

'This way!' Everard spun on his heel and dashed toward them. The leather in his cuirass creaked as he ran.

The Patrolmen were close to the Carthaginians before they were seen. Then a horseman called the warning. Two crazy Romans! Everard saw how he grinned in his beard. One of the Neldorians raised his blast rifle.

Everard flopped on his stomach. The vicious blue-white beam sizzled where he had been. He snapped a shot, and one of the African horses went over in a roar of metal. Van Sarawak stood his ground and fired steadily. Two, three, four – and there went a Neldorian, down in the mud!

Men hewed at each other around the Scipios. The Neldorians' escort yelled with terror. They must have had the blaster demonstrated beforehand, but these invisible blows were something else. They bolted. The second of the bandits got his horse under control and turned to follow.

'Take care of the one you potted, Van,' gasped Everard. 'Drag him off the battlefield – we'll want to question –' He himself scrambled to his feet and made for a riderless horse. He was in the saddle and after the Neldorian before he was fully aware of it.

Behind him, Publius Cornelius Scipio and his son fought clear and joined their retreating army.

Everard fled through chaos: He urged speed from his mount, but was content to pursue. Once they had gotten out of sight, a scooter could swoop down and make short work of his quarry.

The same thought must have occurred to the time rover. He reined in and took aim. Everard saw the blinding flash and felt his cheek sting with a near miss. He set his pistol to wide beam and rode in shooting.

Another fire-bolt took his horse full in the breast. The animal toppled and Everard went out of the saddle. Trained reflexes softened the fall. He bounced to his feet and lurched toward his enemy. The stunner was gone, fallen into the mud, no time to look for it. Never mind, it could be salvaged later, if he lived. The widened beam had found its mark; it wasn't strong enough at such dilution to knock a man out, but the Neldorian had dropped his blaster and the horse stood swaying with closed eyes.

Rain beat in Everard's face. He slogged up to the mount. The Neldorian jumped to earth and drew a sword. Everard's own blade rasped forth.

'As you will,' he said in Latin. 'One of us will not leave this field.'

10

The moon rose over mountains and turned the snow to a sudden wan glitter. Far in the north, a glacier threw back the light, and a wolf howled. The Cro-Magnons chanted in their cave, the noise drifted faintly through to the verandah.

Deirdre stood in darkness, looking out. Moonlight dappled her face and caught a gleam of tears. She started as Everard and Van Sarawak came up behind her.

'Are you back so soon?' she asked. 'You only came here and left me this morning.'

'It didn't take long,' said Van Sarawak. He had gotten a hypno in Attic Greek.

'I hope –' She tried to smile – 'I hope you have finished your task and can rest from your labors.'

'Yes,' said Everard, 'we finished it.'

They stood side by side for a while, looking out on a world of winter.

'Is it true what you said, that I can never go home?' Deirdre spoke gently.

'I'm afraid so. The spells ...' Everard swapped a glance with Van Sarawak.

They had official permission to tell the girl as much as they wished and take her wherever they thought she could live best. Van Sarawak maintained that would be Venus in his century, and Everard was too tired to argue.

Deirdre drew a long breath. 'So be it,' she said. 'I'll not waste of life lamenting. But the Baal grant that they have it well, my people at home.'

'I'm sure they will,' said Everard.

Suddenly he could do no more. He only wanted to sleep. Let Van Sarawak say what had to be said, and reap whatever rewards there might be.

He nodded at his companion. 'I'm turning in,' he declared. 'Carry on, Van.'

The Venusian took the girl's arm. Everard went slowly back to his room.

If you've enjoyed these books and would
like to read more, you'll find literally thousands
of classic Science Fiction & Fantasy titles
through the **SF Gateway**

*

*For the new home of
Science Fiction & Fantasy . . .*

*

*For the most comprehensive collection
of classic SF on the internet . . .*

*

Visit the SF Gateway

www.sfgateway.com

Poul Anderson (1926–2001)

Poul William Anderson was born in Pennsylvania to Scandinavian parents. His family lived for a time in Denmark but moved back to the United States after the outbreak of the Second World War. They settled in Minnesota, where Anderson received a degree in physics from the University of Minnesota.

Anderson began writing while still an undergraduate and published his first story in 1947. He was active throughout the second half of the twentieth century, producing such classic works as the Dominic Flandry books and *The High Crusade*, and winning multiple Hugo and Nebula awards. He has served as President of Science Fiction and Fantasy Writers of America and was a founding member of the Society for Creative Anachronism. In 1998 he was named an SFWA Grand Master. He collaborated regularly with wife, Karen, and their daughter is married to noted SF writer Greg Bear. Poul Anderson died in July 2001.